THE ODYSSEY

A VERSE TRANSLATION
BACKGROUNDS
CRITICISM

SECOND EDITION

D0112108

A NORTON CRITICAL EDITION

Homer

THE ODYSSEY

A VERSE TRANSLATION
BACKGROUNDS
CRITICISM

SECOND EDITION

Translated and Edited by
ALBERT COOK

BROWN UNIVERSITY

W · W · NORTON & COMPANY · *New York* · *London*

This title is printed on permanent paper containing
30 percent post-consumer waste recycled fiber.

The text of this book is composed in Electra, with display in Bernhard. Composition and manufacturing by the Maple-Vail Book Group.

Library of Congress Cataloging-in-Publication Data
Homer.
[Odyssey. English]
The Odyssey : a new verse translation, backgrounds, the Odyssey in
antiquity, criticism / Homer ; translated and edited by Albert Cook.
—2nd ed.
p.   cm.—(A Norton critical edition)
Includes bibliographical references.
1. Odysseus (Greek mythology)—Poetry.   2. Epic poetry, Greek—
Translations into English.   3. Epic poetry, Greek—History and
criticism.   4. Odysseus (Greek mythology) in literature.   5. Homer.
Odyssey.   I. Cook, Albert Spaulding.   II. Title.
PA4025.A5C57   1993
883'.01—dc20   92-39868

ISBN 0-393-96405-1 (paper)

W. W. Norton & Company, Inc., 500 Fifth Avenue, New York, N.Y. 10110
www.wwnorton.com
W. W. Norton & Company Ltd., Castle House, 75/76 Wells Street, London W1T 3QT

1 2 3 4 5 6 7 8 9 0

Contents

Foreword

I hope this collection will help the student to see many sides of the *Odyssey*; that is its purpose.

In light of that purpose, two features of the translation itself should be emphasized: first, that it tries to render the poem not only literally, but line by line, so that almost always the expressions in a given line of Greek are those in the corresponding English line. Second, it is, I believe, wholly faithful to the formulaic character of the poem that so many commentators today have stressed. The poem is built of hundreds of repeated lines, groups of lines, and half lines. In this translation those many repetitions are faithfully and exactly retained in all cases.

In Backgrounds, various kinds of information are provided—on the language of the poem, the lands and peoples it discusses, its poetic conventions, and the kind of society it depicts. Also in Backgrounds, The Odyssey in Antiquity presents commentary from Pindar to "Eustathius." The brief selections under "Scholia" and "Eustathius" offer very small samples of the kind of comment a Byzantine bishop and various anonymous scholars in ancient and medieval times thought that the poem called for. Their quirky concerns stand in striking contrast to the passing homage paid in the Criticism section by Racine, Goethe, and Ezra Pound, and also to the deliberate and sensitive meditations on the poem by the modern commentators with which this collection concludes.

Preface on the Translation

To hear and re-create the sound and sense of the original is always the task of the translator, whether of the impressionist or of the literalist camp. Except when the sense of the original is tied up in lost or unsurfaceable data (the jokes of Aristophanes), or when the sound is so elaborately structured as to be wholly inimitable (*The Divine Comedy*, or possibly any case of regular rhyme), there is no reason why the literalist cannot aspire to as full a re-creation as the impressionist—and therefore to a fuller one, since literalists have the advantage of confining themselves to bringing over as much of the designative sense as possible. Of course they too miss by a considerable margin; and of course any translator faces the problem of catching the flow of overtones and sequences of sense—and of sound.

For both sound and sense, the Homeric line is a unit, and this literal translation seeks as its major goal to preserve that crucial unit in its integrity while trying to catch something of Homer's flow. A line with a syllabic base (almost always in the range of twelve to seventeen syllables) is one possible option for an equivalent to the Homeric hexameter.

For sense, the heavily formulaic character of Homer recommends that one render words, lines, and phrases as nearly identically as possible. This conviction suggests that one should not opt for a variety in translating *kalos* ("fine," "beautiful," "lovely," "pretty," "fair," and so on) but choose one and stick to it most of the time. I chose "lovely." The English words "ocean" and "sea" must do duty for more than two Homeric words; and the translator is forced, if he or she would utilize both, to overlook the fact that the proper name "Ocean" in Homer designates something special. Distinguishing *Okeanos* by a slightly Anglicized proper name "Oceanos"[1] and rendering *pontos* as "ocean" seems

1. My middle-of-the-road position on spelling Greek names results in a mixture between Latin norm for English and true Greek transliteration. In this way I have tried to combine the familiarity of the Latin usage with the Hellenic flavor of a Greekish new-spelling. Hitting between *Oceanus*, or merely *Ocean*, on the Latin side, and *Okeanos* on the Greek, I have produced *Oceanos*, a case I am less happy with than I am with *Telemachos* for the young man who has been known for centuries in English as *Telemachus*. But I believe the principle of combination (producing usually a Latin-like base and a Greek-like termination) is fairly consistent.

preferable to calling it "sea" along with *hals* and *thalassa*, or to picking a metaphoric archaism like "the deep."

For *demos*, there are implications of a geographical "region," one sufficiently more restricted than a French *pays* for us to render the word "district." Sometimes the area is primarily meant, and "land" is the closest term; and sometimes the inhabitants, the "people," are primarily indicated. In this case I have settled for "district" as a normative use, and the other three when their emphases seemed the primary ones. English convention could be ignored in some cases. If *glaukopis* probably means "bright-eyed," [2] we can ignore the English translation of rendering it "gray-eyed." And the same with the more hallowed "wine-dark," a rendering based on a specious phenomenological inference. There is no color word in the Greek.

The choices are not always easy of course. An obscure attribution of Hermes, *Argeiphontes*, presents three choices: "slayer of Argos," "the one who appears swiftly," or the opaque expression itself, *Argeiphontes*. On the hunch that the expression would not have sounded opaque to the normal reader of Homer in antiquity, I have followed the inclination of much contemporary opinion toward the first rendering.

Or again, in simple grammar, we get *theos*, masculine, "god," and *thea*, feminine, "goddess." What do we do with *theos*, with or (more usually) without feminine adjective when it is applied to a goddess? The distinction between *thea* and *theos*, confined almost exclusively to Homer, is an elusive one not to be accounted for wholly by metrical convenience. Unless translators are prepared to identify *thea* and *theos* as "goddess," they are forced to strengthen the common-gender tinge of "god" and use that one word for the one word *theos*, masculine or feminine. "God" does sound a little odd when applied to a female immortal; *theos* is rare enough in the feminine to have struck an ancient reader as comparably odd.

The literalist provides the reader, or at least the student, with the comfortable assurance that for the vast designative tapestry of the original a pink thread may sometimes do duty for a red one, or a blurred one for a blurred one—but never a blue one for a red one, and never a polychrome burst for a single color of the original. Impressionists, on the other hand, for all the rationales they can muster, can never free themselves of the charge leveled by T. S. Eliot at Gilbert Murray (who translates rather more literally than most of the impressionists of recent decades): "So here are two striking phrases which we owe to Mr. Murray; it is he who has sapped our soul and shattered the cup of all life for Euripides. . . . Professor Murray has simply interposed between Euripides and ourselves a barrier more impenetrable than the Greek language."

2. Manu Leumann, *Homerische Wörter* (Basel, 1950) 148–52.

Any rendering builds a wall. One can only hope to build a translucent one. We always need masonry, but also bricks that are translucent to begin with.

ALBERT COOK

The Text of
THE ODYSSEY

I

Homer:

Tell me, Muse, about the man of many turns, who many
Ways wandered when he had sacked Troy's holy citadel;
He saw the cities of many men, and he knew their thought;   → understand people
On the ocean he suffered many pains within his heart,
Striving for his life and his companions' return.   5
But he did not save his companions, though he wanted to:
They lost their own lives because of their recklessness.
The fools, they devoured the cattle of Hyperion,
The Sun, and he took away the day of their return.
Begin the tale somewhere for us also, goddess, daughter of Zeus.[1]   10
Then all the others, as many as escaped sheer destruction,
Were at home, having fled both the war and the sea.
Yet he alone, longing for his wife and for a return,
Was held back in a hollowed cave by the queenly nymph Calypso,[2]
The divine goddess, who was eager for him to be her husband.   15
But when in the circling seasons the year came around,
The gods spun the thread for him to return to his home,
To Ithaca; and he did not escape struggle there either,
Even among his dear ones. All the gods pitied him,
Except Poseidon,[3] who contended unremittingly   20
With godlike Odysseus, till the man reached his own land.
But the god had gone to the far-off Ethiopians—
The Ethiopians, remotest of men, divided asunder,
Some where Hyperion sets, and some where he rises.
He was taking part in the sacrifice of bulls and rams,   25
And enjoyed being present at a feast there. The others
Were gathered together in the halls of Olympian Zeus.
The father of men and gods began to speak among them.
In his heart he was remembering excellent Aigisthos[4]
Whom Agamemnon's son, far-famed Orestes,[5] had slain.   30
Thinking of that man, he made his speech to the immortals:
"Well now, how indeed mortal men do blame the gods!
They say it is from us evils come, yet they themselves
By their own recklessness have pains beyond their lot.
So this Aigisthos married beyond his lot the lawful   35

1. I.e., the muse of epic poetry. Zeus, the son of Cronos, was king of the gods and specifically
the god of the sky and of weather.
2. Daughter of Atlas.
3. Son of Cronos and brother of Zeus; god of the sea, especially hostile toward Odysseus.
4. Cousin of Agamemnon and lover of Clytemnestra; after Agamemnon's murder he became
king of Mycenae.
5. Agamemnon was leader of the Greeks at Troy and was killed by Clytemnestra on his return
home; Orestes killed Clytemnestra and Aigisthos to avenge his father's murder.

Wife of the son of Atreus, and killed him on his return;
Knowing he would be destroyed, since we told him beforehand:
We had sent sharp-eyed Hermes, the slayer of Argos,[6]
To tell him not to kill the man and not to woo his wife,
Or payment would come through Orestes, descendant of Atreus,   40
As soon as he came of age and longed for his own land.
So Hermes told him; but, though of good mind himself, he did not
Change Aigisthos' mind. And now he has paid for it all."
Then the bright-eyed goddess Athene[7] answered him:
"Our father, son of Cronos,[8] highest of all rulers,   45
As for that man, he surely lies in a fitting death.
May anyone else also perish who would do such deeds.
But the heart within me is torn over skillful Odysseus,
The hard-fated man, who long suffers griefs far from his dear ones
On a flood-circled island where the navel of the sea is.   50
The island is wooded, a goddess there has her dwelling,
The daughter of destruction-minded Atlas,[9] who knows
The depths of the whole sea, and holds up by himself
The enormous pillars that hold apart earth and heaven.
His daughter has kept back the wretched and grieving man,   55
And perpetually, with tender and wheedling speeches,
She charms him to forget Ithaca. Odysseus, however,
Wanting to catch sight even of smoke leaping up
From his land, is longing to die. But your own heart
Does not turn toward it, Olympian one. Did Odysseus   60
Not please you in broad Troy by the ships of the Argives
When he made sacrifice? Why, then, are you so angry at him, Zeus?"
In answer to her, cloud-gathering Zeus spoke out:
"My child, what sort of word has got past the bar of your teeth?
How could I at any time forget godlike Odysseus,   65
Who stands out among mortals for thought, and for the sacrifices
He has given the immortal gods who possess broad heaven?
But Poseidon, who holds up the earth, remains obstinately
Enraged about the Cyclops whom he blinded in the eye,
Godlike Polyphemos, who possesses the greatest strength   70
Of all the Cyclopes.[1] The nymph Thoosa gave him birth,
The daughter of Phorcys,[2] ruler over the barren sea,
In hollow caves, after she had lain with Poseidon.
For that, to be sure, earth-shaking Poseidon has not
Killed Odysseus but does make him wander far from his homeland.   75
Well, come now, let all of us here carefully devise

6. Hermes was son of Zeus, messenger of the gods, and guide of the dead. The obscure compound *Argeiphontes* could also mean "appear rapidly" or "appear brightly."
7. Goddess of reason and the arts and special patron of Odysseus.
8. One of the older gods; the father of Zeus, Poseidon, Hera, Hades.
9. The supporter of the pillars of heaven.
1. A lawless race of giants met by Odysseus.
2. A lesser sea divinity.

His return, so he may arrive; and Poseidon will slacken
His rage, for counter to all the immortals he cannot
Carry on strife alone against the will of the gods."
Then the bright-eyed goddess Athene answered him: 80
"Our father, son of Cronos, highest of all rulers,
If this course is now really dear to the blessed gods,
That many-minded Odysseus return to his own home,
Then let us urge on the runner Hermes, slayer of Argos,
To the island of Ogygia,³ in order that with all speed   85
He may tell the fair-braided nymph an unerring plan
For the return of stout-hearted Odysseus, so he may go back.
And I myself will go to Ithaca, so that I the better
May urge his son on and place a strength in his mind
To call the long-haired Achaians⁴ into an assembly   90
And to speak out to all the suitors, who are always slaying
His throngs of sheep, and his shamble-footed, crumple-horned cattle.
I shall send him on to Sparta, and also to sandy Pylos,
To learn of his dear father's return, if he may hear somehow,
And so a noble renown among men may belong to him."   95
When she had said this, she bound under her feet the lovely sandals,
The ambrosial golden ones that bear her either over water
Or over the limitless land swift as blasts of the wind.
She grasped the valiant spear, pointed with sharp bronze,
Ponderous, big, and stout, with which she daunts the ranks of men, 100
Of heroes at whom she is angry, the daughter of a mighty father,
She went down in a rush from the summits of Olympos and stood
In the district of Ithaca before Odysseus' gates
At the courtyard threshold. In her fist she held the bronze spear,
Likening herself to a stranger, the Taphian leader Mentes.   105
She came upon the bold suitors. They at the moment
Were delighting their hearts with a diceboard before the doors,
Seated on the skins of oxen they had killed themselves.
Heralds attended on them, and capable servants also;
Some of these were mixing wine and water in bowls,   110
Others were cleaning off the tables with porous sponges,
And setting them, and dividing up the meat in many pieces.
Godlike Telemachos was by far the first to see her,
For he sat among the suitors, crushed in his own heart,
Seeing his noble father in his mind, if from somewhere   115
He would come and make those suitors scatter through the halls,
So that he himself might have honor and command his own goods.
Thinking this over while seated with the suitors, he sighted Athene.
He went straight to the gate, and he resented in his heart
That the stranger stood so long at the door. Standing near her   120

3. The legendary island home of Calypso.
4. A collective appellation of the Greeks besieging Troy.

He took her right hand and received the bronze spear;
Speaking out to her, he uttered wingèd words:
"Greetings, stranger, you shall be welcomed among us. And when
You have eaten dinner, you will tell what it is you need."
When he had said that, he led on, and Pallas[5] Athene followed.   125
And when they had got inside of the lofty house,
He stood the spear he was carrying against the long pillar
Inside the well-polished spearcase, where many other
Spears of stout-hearted Odysseus were also standing.
He led her on and seated her in an armchair, spreading linen be-
     neath,   130
Lovely and skillfully wrought. A stool was under her feet.
He placed a broidered seat alongside, apart from the others,
The suitors, lest the stranger might be disturbed at the uproar
When mingling with the insolent, and lose appetite for dinner,
And so he might ask her of the father who had gone away.   135
A handmaid poured water from a pitcher she was carrying,
A lovely golden one, over into a silver basin,
For washing the hands; she set up a polished table alongside.
A respected housekeeper served bread she was carrying,
Laying out many dishes, gracious with the provisions.   140
A carver lifted up and set out trenchers of meats
Of all sorts, and set out gold goblets alongside for them.
A herald served them attentively, pouring out the wine.
The bold suitors came in. And then they themselves
Sat down one after another in seats and in armchairs.   145
Heralds were pouring water for them over their hands.
And serving maids were heaping bread up on trays.
Young men were filling bowls up to the brim for drinking,
They stretched forth their hands to the food that was spread out ready.
But when the suitors had taken their fill of food and drink,   150
Other matters came to their minds for attention:
Singing and dancing, which are the graces of a banquet.
Into Phemios'[6] hands a herald placed a lyre
Of supreme beauty; he sang for the suitors under compulsion.
Playing his instrument, he struck up a lovely song.   155
Telemachos, however, addressed bright-eyed Athene,
Holding his head close so that the others might not hear:
"Dear stranger, will you resent it if I say something?
These men are concerned with this, the lyre and singing,
At their ease, since they devour scot-free another man's living,   160
A man whose white bones somewhere are rotting in the rain,
Lying on a shore, or a wave tumbles them in the sea.
If they ever see that man returning to Ithaca,

5. An epithet of Athene.
6. Son of Terpis ("Pleasure") and bard at Odysseus' palace.

They will all pray to be nimbler on their feet
Rather than to be richer in clothing and in gold.   165
As it is, an evil fate has killed him, surely; there is
No comfort for us even if some one of the men on earth
Says he will come. The day of his return is lost.
But come now, tell me this, and explain truthfully:
What men are you from? Where are your city and parents?   170
On what sort of ship did you come? How did the sailors
Bring you to Ithaca? What men did they claim to be?
For I do not think you could have got here at all on foot.
Tell me this exactly, so that I may well know
Whether you come on a first visit or are a friend   175
Of my father's, since many other men come to our home,
And since he was himself well acquainted among men."
Then the bright-eyed goddess Athene addressed him:
"All right, then, I will tell you this quite truthfully.
I declare I am Mentes, son of skillful Anchialos,   180
And I rule over the Taphians, who are fond of rowing.
Just now I have come this way by ship, with companions,
Sailing on the wine-faced sea to men of alien tongue,
To Temese for bronze, and I carry glittering iron.
My vessel stands here by the fields far off from the city,   185
In the harbor of Reithron, below wooded Neion.
We declare we are guest friends of one another through our fathers
Originally; if you will, go and ask Laertes,[7]
The old warrior, who they say no longer comes
To the city, but suffers griefs off by himself on his field,   190
With an old servant woman, who serves him food and drink
Whenever a weariness overcomes his limbs
As he creeps along the knoll of the vine-bearing garden.
But I have come now because they said the man really was in the
     district,
Your father. But him have the gods hindered on his journey.   195
The godly Odysseus has not yet died on the earth,
But he is still alive somewhere, held back on the broad ocean
On a flood-circled island, and troublesome men hold him,
Savages, who somehow keep him back against his will.
Well, I will now tell you a prophecy, how the immortals   200
Cast it in my heart, and how I think it will end,
Though I am not a prophet, and have no clear skill with birds.[8]
Not much longer now, surely, will he be away
From his dear fatherland; not even if iron bands hold him.
He will devise how to return, since he has many resources.   205
But come now, tell me this, and explain it truthfully,

7. Father of Odysseus and former king of Ithaca.
8. An augur would make divinations based on the behavior of birds, as in book 2, lines 146–60, and elsewhere.

If, big as you are, you are really the son of Odysseus himself.
You resemble him strangely in your head and your fine eyes,
Since we had contact quite often with one another
Before he embarked for Troy, where the other noblest   210
Men of the Argives were headed in their hollow ships.
Since then I have not seen Odysseus, nor has he seen me."
Then the sound-minded Telemachos answered her:
"All right, stranger, I shall speak quite truthfully.
My mother calls me the son of the man. But I myself   215
Do not know. No one has ever been certain of his father.
Ah, would that I were the fortunate son of some man
Whom old age came upon with all his possessions!
As it is, he has been the most ill-fated of mortal men,
The man they say I was born of, since you ask me this."   220
And then the bright-eyed goddess Athene addressed him:
"The gods have not set it down that your race hereafter
Be nameless, since Penelope bore such a man as you.
But come, tell me this, and explain it truthfully,
What feast, what gathering is this? What is your need here?   225
A banquet or a marriage? The guests have brought no share to it.
How overweening they seem to be, how presumptuous
To be feasting in the hall! A man with any sense
Who came on these shameful things would be angry to see them."
Then the sound-minded Telemachos answered her: 230
"Stranger, since you ask me this and inquire about it,
This house was once supposed to be wealthy and blameless,
So long as that very man was still here in the district.
Now the gods have wished otherwise and decreed misfortune;
They have made that person vanish more completely than all   235
Men. No, I would not grieve this way if he had died,
If with his companions he had gone under in the land of the Trojans,
Or in the arms of his friends, after he had wound up the war.
Then all the Achaians would have made him a funeral mound,
And he would have won great glory for his son, too, hereafter;   240
As it is, the storm winds have snatched him off without glory.
He is gone, vanished and unperceived, and has left me
Pains and laments. Yet I no longer moan and grieve for that man
Only, since the gods have fashioned other evil cares for me.
All of the noblemen who rule over the islands,   245
Dulichion and Samê and also wooded Zakynthos,
And all those who are masters in craggy Ithaca,
Are paying court to my mother and wearing down my home.
She neither refuses the hateful marriage nor can she
Make an end of it. But they are wasting my home away   250
As they devour it. Soon they will tear me to pieces myself."
Pallas Athene was greatly disturbed and spoke out to him:
"Ah well, you do need Odysseus who is gone away

Very much indeed, to lay hand to these shameless suitors.
Would that he came now to the outer doors of the house   255
And stood there with a helmet and a shield and two spears,
And were the sort of man he was when I first saw him
In our very own home drinking and taking his pleasure,
As he went from Ephyre, leaving Ilos the son of Mermeros.
Odysseus had traveled there upon a rapid ship   260
Seeking after a man-killing drug, so that he might
Smear bronze-tipped arrows with it, but the man did not
Give it, since he dreaded the ever-living gods.
But my father gave it to him; he loved him terribly.
As that sort of man might Odysseus contend with the suitors!   265
They would all be swift in their doom and bitter in marriage.
Well, all these matters lie in the laps of the gods,
Whether he will return and pay them off or not,
In his own halls. So I bid you to consider
In what way you may drive the suitors out of the hall.   270
Come now, pay attention and take note of my words:
Tomorrow call the Achaian warriors to assembly;
Make a declaration to all. Let the gods witness it.
Order the suitors to disperse to their own affairs.
And your mother, if her spirit urges her to marry,   275
Let her go back to the hall of her father who is great in power.
They will prepare a wedding and set in array
The many gifts that ought to go with a dear daughter.
For yourself, I strongly advise you, if you will listen,
To fit out the ship that is best with twenty oarsmen   280
And go in search of your father who has been gone so long,
On the chance some mortal may tell you of him, or you hear from Zeus
The voice that best of all brings report to men.
First go to Pylos and question the godly Nestor.[9]
From there go on to Sparta and blond Menelaos,[1]   285
Who has come back the last of the bronze-clad Achaians.
If you do hear your father is alive and will return,
Though worn down, you might bear out yet another year.
But if you hear that he is dead and exists no more,
Return home then to your own dear fatherland,   290
Heap up a monument for him, and perform the many
Rites that are fitting, and give your mother to a husband.
When you have accomplished all this and brought it to pass,
Then you may consider in your heart and in your mind
How you may slaughter the suitors in your halls,   295
Either by cunning or openly. There is really no need
To indulge in childishness. You are not that age.

9. The aged king of Pylos and chief adviser for the Greeks at Troy.
1. Brother of Agamemnon and husband of Helen; co-commander of the Greeks at Troy.

Or have you not heard how much glory godly Orestes seized
Among all men when he killed his father's murderer,
The cunning Aigisthos, who killed his renowned father?   300
You too, my dear friend, since I see you are handsome and great;
Be brave, so that a man born in the future would praise you.
Well, by now I should be going down to my swift ship
And the companions who are impatiently awaiting me.
Be concerned yourself. Pay attention to my words."   305
Then the sound-minded Telemachos answered her:
"Stranger, you have spoken these friendly words wisely
Like a father to his son, and I shall never forget them.
Come now, wait a while, though you are eager for the journey,
So that once you are bathed, delighted in your own heart,   310
You may board your ship rejoicing in spirit, with a gift,
An honorable and lovely one that will be a keepsake
From me, of the kind that fond guest friends give each other."
Then the bright-eyed goddess Athene answered him:
"Do not hold me back now, longing as I am for the journey.   315
Whatever gift your own heart bids to you give me,
Give it to me to carry home when I return again.
And pick a lovely one. It will be worth the exchange to you."
Having spoken so, bright-eyed Athene went off.
She flew upward like a bird. Into his spirit   320
She had put strength and courage. She put him in mind
Of his father more than before. When he thought it over,
He was amazed in his spirit; he thought she was a god.
And at once the godlike mortal went toward the suitors.
A renowned singer was singing to them. They were sitting   325
In silence listening. He sang of the baleful return
Of the Achaians from Troy that Pallas Athene laid on them.
The daughter of Icarios, prudent Penelope,
From her upper chamber hearkened to the divine song.
She descended the lofty stairway from her dwelling,   330
Not alone, but two servants followed along with her.
And when the godly woman had come to the suitors,
She stood by the pillar of the stoutly fashioned roof,
Holding the glistening headbands before her cheeks.
A devoted servant maid stood near her on either side.   335
Then, weeping, she addressed the godlike singer:
"Phemios, you know many other ravishments for mortals,
The deeds of men and of gods that singers glorify.
Sing one of these as you sit among them. And let the men
Drink wine in silence. But stop singing this baleful song   340
Which forever wears away my own heart in my breast,
Since an unforgettable grief affects me heavily.
I long for a person so dear, remembering always
That man whose glory is wide through Greece and middle Argos."

Then the sound-minded Telemachos answered her: 345
"Mother, for what reason do you begrudge the trusty singer's
Giving pleasure with whatever his thought rouses in him? Singers
Are not guilty; I suppose Zeus is guilty, who gives
To bread-earning men, to each one as he wishes.
It is no wrong for this man to sing about the evil fate   350
Of the Danaans.[2] Men acclaim that song the most
Which has come round newest of all to those who hear it.
Let your mind and spirit resign you to listening.
Odysseus is not alone to have lost his day of return
In Troy. Many other mortals perished there also.   355
Well, come into the house, and apply yourself to work,
To the loom and the distaff, and give orders to your servants
To set at the work. This talk will concern all the men,
But me especially. For the power in the house is mine."
She was amazed at him, and back into the house she went.   360
The sound-minded speech of her son she took to heart.
She entered the upper chamber with her serving women,
And then wept for Odysseus, her dear husband, until
Bright-eyed Athene cast sweet sleep upon her eyelids.
The suitors were making a din through the shadowy halls.   365
They all gave voice to the prayer of lying in her bed.
Sound-minded Telemachos began speaking to them:
"Suitors of my mother, with your excessive insolence,
Let us now take our pleasure and dine. And let there be
No noise, since it is lovely to listen to a singer   370
Of the kind this one is, who resembles the gods in his voice.
And at dawn tomorrow let us all go and take our seats
In council, so that I may tell you something outright;
Get out of the halls and partake of other dinners,
Eating your own goods, visiting each other's homes.   375
And if it seems better and preferable to you
To consume one man's livelihood scot-free,
Waste on. But I shall call on the eternal gods for help,
So that Zeus may grant there to be acts of retribution,
And then scot-free within this house you may die."   380
So he said, and they all set their teeth on their lips
And wondered at Telemachos that he spoke so courageously.
Antinoos,[3] the son of Eupeithes, addressed him first:
"Well, Telemachos, the gods themselves must be teaching you
To be presumptuous and speak courageously.   385
May the son of Cronos over sea-circled Ithaca
Not make you king, your paternal right by birth."
Sound-minded Telemachos addressed him in answer:

2. The Greeks (Achaians) collectively; seen as descendants of a mythical king, Danaos.
3. The ringleader and most insolent of Penelope's suitors.

"Antinoos, even if you are offended at what I say,
Still I would wish this very thing done if Zeus were to give it.   390
Would you call this the worst thing to happen among men?
It would not be bad at all to be king. There comes at once
An opulent home for the man, and he is himself more honored.
Yes, there are also other kings of the Achaians,
Many in sea-circled Ithaca, young ones and old ones.   395
And one of them shall have this, since godly Odysseus is dead.
But as for me, I shall be lord over our household,
And over the servants whom godly Odysseus won for me."
Eurymachos, son of Polybos, addressed him in answer:
"Telemachos, all this lies in the laps of the gods,   400
Who of the Achaians shall rule in sea-circled Ithaca.
May you have your own possessions and be lord in your own home.
May a man never come, while Ithaca is inhabited,
Who would tear your possessions away from you by force.
But I want to ask you, my brave man, about this stranger.   405
Where did the man come from, and what country did he claim
To be from? Where are his birthplace and his father's land?
Does he bring some message that your father is coming home?
Or did he come here seeking some personal need of his own?
He started up so, and went at once, nor did he wait   410
For us to find him out. Yet his face did not look like a coward's."
Then sound-minded Telemachos addressed him in answer:
"Eurymachos, surely my father's return has been lost.
I put no trust in a message, wherever it comes from,
And I give no heed to any divination my mother   415
Might ask of a diviner, calling him to the hall.
The stranger is a guest friend of my father's from Taphos.
He declares he is Mentes, son of skillful Anchialos,
And he rules over the Taphians, who are fond of rowing."
So Telemachos said, but in his mind knew the immortal god.   420
The men turned then to dancing and delightful song
And took their pleasure, and waited for evening to come.
As they took their pleasure black evening came upon them.
Then they went away, each to his own home to sleep.
But Telemachos, where his bedroom was, built aloft   425
In the very lovely courtyard in a place with a view all around,
Went to bed pondering many things in his mind.
Eurycleia went in with him and carried the flaming torches,
The devoted daughter of Ops, Peisenor's son.
Laertes bought her once as one of his possessions   430
When she was still in her first youth; he gave twenty cattle for her,
And honored her the same as the devoted wife in the halls.
But he had never lain with her, for he feared his wife's wrath.
Going with him, she carried the flaming torches. She loved him
Most of all the servants, and had tended him as a child.   435

She opened up the doors of the stoutly fashioned bedroom.
He sat down on the bed and took off his soft tunic
And put it in the hands of the shrewd-minded old woman.
She folded up the tunic, put it in smooth order
And hung it on a peg beside the jointed bed.   440
Then she went out of the bedroom, drew the door shut with a ring
Of silver, and drew the bolt full length by its thong.
There all night long, wrapped up in the sheepskin,
He pondered in his mind the course that Athene had shown.

II

And when the early-born, rosy-fingered dawn appeared,
The dear son of Odysseus rose up out of his bed,
Put on his clothes, and set the sharp sword round his shoulder,
Bound the lovely sandals beneath his shining feet
And went on out of the bedroom, like a god to look at.   5
At once he ordered the heralds with their piercing voices
To summon the long-haired Achaians to an assembly.
The heralds made summons, and they gathered together quickly.
And when they were gathered and had come together
He went to the assembly and held his bronze spear in his fist—   10
Not alone, but the swift-footed dogs went along with him.
Moreover, Athene shed a divine grace around him.
The people all marveled at him as he was coming up.
He sat down in his father's seat, and the old men gave way.
Then the hero Aigyptios began to speak among them,   15
A man bent with age who knew numberless things.
He too had a dear son, who went with godlike Odysseus
In the hollow ships to Ilion [1] that abounds in horses,
The spearman Antiphos. But the savage Cyclops killed him
In his hollowed cave, and prepared him as his final meal.   20
Three other sons he had; one fell in with the suitors,
Eurynomos; and two stayed always on their father's lands.
But still he remembered the other one, in grief and sorrow.
For him he wept as he spoke and addressed the assembly:
"Listen to me now, Ithacans, in what I say.   25
Our assembly has not once met or sat in session
From the time godly Odysseus went off in the hollow ships.
And now who has called it together? And to which of the young men
Or of those who are older, has there come so great a need?
Has he heard some message about an army coming on   30
That he might plainly tell us, since he was the first to hear it?
Does he declare and announce some other public matter?

1. Another name for Troy.

Noble he seems to me, well favored. For him may Zeus
Bring about whatever good thing he desires in his mind."
So he said, and Odysseus' dear son was glad for his statement.   35
Nor did he stay seated longer but he felt a desire to speak.
He stood up in the midst of the assembly. The herald Peisenor,
Who was full of sound advice, put the scepter in his hand.
Then he began to speak, first addressing the old man:
"Old sir, this man is not far, you yourself shall soon know it,   40
He who gathered the people: it is I. The pain comes most to me.
I heard no message about an army coming on
That I might plainly tell you, since I was the first to hear it;
I declare and announce no other public matter
But my own need, that an evil has befallen my home,   45
And a double one: I lost my noble father, who ruled as king
Over all of you here once, and was mild as a father.
And now there is a much greater evil too, that will soon
Fully tear my whole house apart and destroy all my living.
Suitors are assailing my mother against her will,   50
The dear sons of the men who are the noblest in this place.
They shudder to make a trip to the house of her father
Icarios, so he might set his daughter's dowry himself,
And give her to the man she wants, him who pleases her most.
But they cluster to our house day after day.   55
Slaughtering oxen and sheep and fat goats,
They carry on their revels and drink the sparkling wine
Wantonly. Many things are wasted. And there is no man
Of the kind Odysseus was, to ward off harm from the house.
Nor are we at all the kind to ward it off. Even hereafter   60
We shall be pitiable and not have acquired strength.
I would ward it off myself, if I had the power.
Unendurable deeds have been done; in no pretty way
Has my house been destroyed. Be indignant yourselves!
Be ashamed toward the other men of our neighborhood   65
Who live around us. Fear, too, the wrath of the gods,
Lest, aghast at all the evil deeds, they work some change.
I beseech you, both by Olympian Zeus, and by Themis,[2]
Who disbands and also convokes the assemblies of men,
Leave off, my friends; and let me wear away alone   70
In my woeful grief, unless my noble father Odysseus
Was ever hostile to the well-greaved[3] Achaians and did them harm;
For this you pay me back, are hostile and do me harm
By urging these men on. It would be better for me
If you were to devour my property and my herd yourselves;   75
If you were to eat them, there might be some recompense.

2. Goddess of Just Order.
3. A greave is a stiff protector worn on the lower leg.

In that case we should carry the story around the town,
Demanding back our goods, till they were all given back.
As it is, you are heaping incurable pains on my heart."
So he spoke, in anger. He threw the scepter down on the ground,   80
Bursting out in tears. And pity gripped all the people.
Then all the others there were silent. No one could bear
To reply to Telemachos with severe words;
Antinoos alone addressed him in reply:
"High-talking Telemachos, unchecked in your anger, what is this   85
You say to shame us? You would like to fix blame on us!
The Achaian suitors are not guilty toward you.
No, it is your dear mother, who knows advantages well.
It is the third year already, and will soon be a fourth,
Since she has slighted the spirit in the Achaians' hearts.   90
She gives hope to all, and she promises every man,
Sending out messages. But her thought wishes otherwise.
And she has devised in her mind this other deceit.
She set a great loom in the halls and on it she wove
A large and delicate fabric. She told us at once: 95
'Young men, my suitors, since godly Odysseus is dead,
Wait, though you are eager for this marriage of mine, till I finish
This robe, so that the yarn will not waste in vain,
The burial sheet of warrior Laertes for the time
The ruinous fate of long-sorrowful death seizes him,   100
Lest one of the Achaian women in the district blame me
If he who had won so much lie without covering!'
So she said, and the bold heart was persuaded within us,
Then every day she kept weaving on the great loom.
And in the nights she undid it when she had the torches set up.   105
So three years she has fooled the Achaians and persuaded them.
But when the fourth year came and the seasons came on,
Right then one of the women, who perceived it clearly, told it,
And we happened upon her undoing the shining fabric.
So she has finished it, though unwilling and under duress.   110
The suitors answer you this way in order that for yourself
You may know it in your heart; that all the Achaians may know it.
Send your mother away; command her to marry
Whatever man her father bids and who pleases her.
But if she incites the sons of the Achaians much longer,   115
Attending in her heart to the gifts Athene gave her
Beyond others, skill at beautiful tasks, a noble mind,
And wiles, such as we have heard of none of the women
Of old, the fair-braided Achaians who existed before,
Tyro and Alcmene and Mycene of the lovely crown[4]—   120

---

4. Tyro, bride of Poseidon, grandmother of Nestor and Jason; Alcmene, mother of Heracles;
   Mycene, daughter of the river Inachos and patroness of Mycenae.

No one of them had ideas the like of Penelope's.
Yet in this she has not had a propitious idea,
Because truly they will devour your living and your possessions
As long as she keeps this purpose that the gods
Have now placed in her heart. For herself she makes great renown,   125
But for you, the longing for a plentiful livelihood.
We are not going first to our lands or anywhere else
Till she marries whichever of the Achaians she wishes."
Then sound-minded Telemachos addressed him in answer:
"Antinoos, in no way can I force her who bore and raised me   130
Out of the house against her will, while elsewhere on earth
My father is alive or dead. It would be a bad thing to pay
Icarios a large fine if I sent my mother off on my own.
From her father I should then suffer ills, and a god would give
Others, when my mother had invoked the dread Erinyes,[5]   135
As she went away from the house. The resentment of men
Would be upon me. So I shall never utter such a word.
And if your own spirit can feel the resentment,
Get out of the halls, partake of other dinners,
Eating your own goods, visiting each others' homes.   140
But if this seems better and preferable to you,
To use up one man's livelihood scot-free,
Waste on. But I shall call on the eternal gods for help,
So that Zeus may grant there to be acts of retribution,
And then scot-free within this house you may die."   145
So Telemachos spoke, and broad-seeing Zeus sent him
Two eagles from above from the crest of the mountain flying.
They for a time flew down along with the blasts of the wind,
Stretching their wings out close to one another.
But when they came to the midst of the many-voiced assembly,   150
Then they whirled about and beat their wings rapidly.
They went to the heads of all and destruction was in their look,
As they tore each other's cheeks and throats on both sides with their
   claws.
Then they sped off on the right, past the men's homes and city.
They were amazed at the birds when they saw them with their own
   eyes.   155
They turned over in their hearts what was going to happen.
Then the old warrior Halitherses addressed them,
The son of Mastor. He alone excelled those of his age
For knowing about birds and explaining the auspices.
Well disposed toward them, he spoke out and addressed them: 160
"Listen to me now, Ithacans, in what I say.
I declare this especially to make it known to the suitors.
A great trouble for them is gathering force. Odysseus

---

5. Goddesses who fulfill curses and avenge crimes.

Will not long be far from his dear ones. In fact already, perhaps,
He is nearby, breeding murder and fate for these men,   165
All of them. And it will also be ill for many of the rest
Of us who inhabit sunny Ithaca. Yet far beforehand
Let us consider how we may stop them. Let the men
Stop themselves. And surely this is better for them.
Not as a novice do I prophesy, but as one who knows,   170
And I say everything has come to pass for that man,
As I explained to him when the Argives went off
To Ilion, and with them went many-minded Odysseus.
I said he would suffer many ills, lose all his friends,
And then unknown to all in the twentieth year   175
He would get home. Now all these things are indeed coming to pass."
Eurymachos, son of Polybos, addressed him in answer:
"Old man, go on now and prophesy to your children,
Go on home, lest they suffer some ill afterward.
I am much better at prophesying about this than you.   180
And there are many birds that wander beneath the beams
Of the sun, and not all are in accord with fate. Odysseus
Has perished far off, and would that you too had perished
Along with him. You would not say so much in augury,
Nor would you so incite the angered Telemachos,   185
Expecting a gift for your house, if he provide one.
I will tell you this right out. And it will come to pass:
If, when you know so many ancient matters, you prevail
Over a younger man, and with your speeches urge him to rage;
First, this will be very tormenting to the man himself,   190
And he will be able to do absolutely nothing about it.
But on you, old man, we shall set a charge you will grieve
In your heart to pay off. It will be a hard pain for you.
I shall advise Telemachos myself in the presence of all:
Let him bid his mother go back to her father's house.   195
They will work out a marriage and array many bridal gifts,
As many as should go along with a dear daughter.
Before then I do not think the sons of the Achaians will cease
From the wearisome suit, since we fear no one anyway—
No, not Telemachos, however full of speeches he is,   200
And we do not give heed, old man, to the augury you tell,
Which is unfulfilled; and you are still the more hated.
Moreover, the goods shall be vilely eaten, and their equal
Shall never exist,[6] so long as she herself puts the Achaians off
About her marriage. But we are waiting day after day   205
And compete over her excellence, and we do not go
Among the other women it is fit for each of us to marry."
Then sound-minded Telemachos addressed him in answer,

---

6. Obscure in Greek. It means, probably, that there will be no equal recompense for them.

"Eurymachos, and all the rest of you noble suitors,
I will not implore you about this or speak out any more.   210
Already the gods know this, and all the Achaians.
But come, give me a fast ship and twenty companions
Who can complete a journey with me, thither and back.
I am going to Sparta and also to sandy Pylos
To learn of the return of my father, who is gone so long,   215
On the chance some mortal may tell of him, or I hear from Zeus
The voice that most of all brings report to men.
If I do hear my father is living and will return,
Then, though worn down, I could bear out yet another year.
But if I hear that he is dead and exists no more,   220
I will then return to my own dear fatherland,
Heap up a monument for him and perform the many
Rites that are fitting, and give my mother to a husband."
When he had said just this, he sat down. There stood up among them
Mentor, who was a companion of excellent Odysseus;   225
When he went on the ships he turned over his whole home to him,
To obey the old man[7] and steadfastly to protect all.
Well disposed to them, he spoke out and addressed them:
"Listen to me now, Ithacans, in what I say.
Let no scepter-bearing king be deliberately   230
Kind and mild any longer, or keep his mind on the right,
But may he be perpetually harsh and act unjustly,
Since there is no one who remembers the godly Odysseus
Of the people he ruled; and he was mild as a father.
No, I do not make objection about the bold suitors   235
That they do violent deeds, with evil weaving of thought,
For they stake their own heads when they devour violently
The home of Odysseus, who, they say, will return no more.
But now I blame the rest of the people, for the way you all
Sit in silence, that you do not address these few suitors   240
With speeches, and restrain them, being yourselves so many."
Leocritos, son of Euenor, addressed him in answer:
"Stubborn Mentor, crazed in your mind, what is this you say
Urging them to put us down? But it is disastrous
To fight over a banquet, and with men greater in number.   245
Yes, even if Ithacan Odysseus himself were to come
Upon the noble suitors banqueting in his house
And plan in his heart to drive them out of the hall,
His wife, though she longed for it much, would not rejoice
At his coming, but he would meet his wretched fate right there,   250
If he fought against many. You have not spoken properly.
But come, let the people disperse, each one to his tasks;
Mentor and Halitherses will hasten the man on his way.

---

7. Probably Laertes, though some take it as meaning that the household shall obey Mentor.

They have been his father's companions from the beginning.
And yet I believe he will stay a long time in Ithaca   255
And listen for the news, but will never complete this journey."
So he spoke, and he dismissed the assembly quickly.
And they did disperse, each one to his own dwelling.
But the suitors went into the dwelling of godly Odysseus.
Telemachos went off apart to the sands of the sea,   260
Washed his hands in gray salt water, and prayed to Athene:
"Hear me, you who yesterday came as a god to our house
And bade me to go in a ship onto the murky sea
To learn of the return of my father who is gone so long,
But the Achaians delay over all these things,   265
And the wickedly presumptuous suitors most of all."
So he spoke in prayer. Athene came close to him,
Likening herself to Mentor in form and in voice.
And speaking out to him, she uttered wingèd words:
"Telemachos, hereafter you will not be a coward or senseless.   270
If there is really instilled in you the good might of your father
And you are as he was to achieve both word and deed,
Then the journey will not be fruitless or unachieved.
But if you are not the offspring of him and Penelope,
Then I have no hope that you will achieve what you wish.   275
Few indeed are the sons who are equal to their fathers;
Most are worse, but few are better than their fathers.
But since you will not be a coward hereafter or senseless,
And the shrewdness of Odysseus has not quite forsaken you,
There is hope in that case you will bring these deeds to pass.   280
Therefore let the plan and the thought of the suitors go,
Mad as they are, since they are neither thoughtful nor just.
They do not know at all about the death and black fate
That is really near them, to destroy them all on a single day.
The journey you desire will not be distant for long.   285
Since I am for you the companion I was for your father,
I will get a fast ship ready for you and come with you myself.
But go on back to your house and talk with the suitors,
Lay up provisions and fit everything in containers;
Wine in jugs, and barley, the marrow of men,   290
In close-sewn skins. And I myself will soon gather
Willing companions around the district. There are
Many ships in sea-circled Ithaca, new and old.
I myself will look them over and see which is best for you.
We will soon get it ready and send it on the broad ocean."   295
So spoke Athene, the daughter of Zeus. Telemachos
Did not tarry long when he heard the voice of the god.
He went on to his home, troubled in his own heart,
And he did indeed find the bold suitors in the halls,
Flaying goats and singeing fat hogs in the courtyard.   300

Antinoos with a laugh went straight to Telemachos,
Took his hand, and spoke right out directly to him:
"High-talking Telemachos, unchecked in your anger,
Give heed in your breast to no other evil word or deed,
But do eat for my sake, and drink, just as before.   305
The Achaians will accomplish for you all these things,
A ship and chosen rowers, so you may get swiftly
To hallowed Pylos for word about your illustrious father."
Then sound-minded Telemachos addressed him in answer:
"Antinoos, there is no way I could dine in silence   310
With you, insolent men, and enjoy myself securely.
Or is it not enough, you suitors, that beforehand you wasted
Many noble possessions of mine while I was still a child?
And now that I am big and learn about the story,
Hearing it from others, and the spirit does wax within me,   315
I shall try some way to fling evil fates upon you,
Either by going to Pylos or here in this very district.
I am going, and the journey I speak of will not be fruitless—
As a passenger, for I have the disposal of neither
Ship nor rowers; that, I suppose, is the way it seemed better to you."   320
He spoke and drew his hand from Antinoos' hand
Lightly. The suitors busied themselves through the house with dinner.
They spoke in mockery and made abusive speeches,
And this is what one of the overbearing young men would say:
"Well, Telemachos is devising slaughter for us.   325
He will bring some defenders either from sandy Pylos
Or even from Sparta, since he wants to so terribly,
Or else he wishes to go to Ephyre, the fertile land,
In order that he may get a life-killing drug there,
Put it in a bowl, and do away with us all."   330
And then another of the overbearing young men would say
"Who knows but that he too, going in the hollow ship
Far from his dear ones, will die wandering like Odysseus?
That way he would increase our labor even more!
For we would divide up all the possessions; the house, moreover,   335
We would give to his mother to have, and to whoever weds her."
So they spoke. He entered his father's high-roofed chamber,
A broad one, where gold and bronze lay piled up,
Clothing in coffers and abundance of fragrant oil,
And in it were large jars of aged, sweet-tasting wine   340
Standing, which contained an unmixed godly drink,
Set in a row beside the wall, if ever Odysseus
Should homeward return, though he had suffered many pains.
Bolt-fitted planks were upon it, stoutly fashioned,
Double doors, and a housekeeper by night and by day   345
Held it, who guarded all in her resourcefulness of mind,
Eurycleia, daughter of Ops, Peisenor's son.

Then Telemachos spoke to her and called her to the chamber:
"Good mother, come draw wine off for me into jars with handles,
Sweet wine, except for the most savory that you keep,   350
Thinking of that ill-fated man, in case he comes from somewhere,
Zeus-born Odysseus, and wards off destiny and death.
Fill up twelve of them, and fit them all with lids,
And pour barley for me into well-stitched leather bags.
Let there be twenty measures of mill-crushed barley flakes.   355
Keep this to yourself. Let it all be readied together.
I shall take it away in the evening myself at the time
When my mother enters the upper room and thinks of rest.
I am going to Sparta and also to sandy Pylos
To learn of my dear father's return, if I may hear somehow."   360
So he spoke, and his dear nurse Eurycleia cried out,
And while she was sobbing she uttered wingèd words:
"How, dear child, does this thought come to be in your mind?
And where do you wish to go upon the broad earth,
Being a belovèd only child? Zeus-born Odysseus has died   365
Far from his fatherland in a country of strangers.
From the moment you are gone they will devise evils against you,
How by deceit you may die. Then they will divide all this themselves.
No, remain here among your own. There is no need
For you to wander and suffer ills on the barren ocean."   370
Then sound-minded Telemachos addressed her in answer:
"Take cheer, nurse; this plan is not without a god.
But swear you will tell nothing of this to my dear mother
Before the eleventh or the twelfth day has come,
Unless she misses me and hears that I am gone off,   375
So that she might not weep and injure her lovely skin."
So he spoke; and the old woman swore by the gods she would not,
A great oath; and then when she swore and completed the oath,
Right away she drew off wine for him in the jars with handles
And poured barley for him into well-stitched leather bags.   380
Telemachos went to the house and joined the suitors.
Then the bright-eyed goddess Athene had another thought.
Likening herself to Telemachos, she went all through the city.
She stood beside each mortal man and she uttered a speech
And bade them to gather at evening by the swift ship.   385
And then she asked Noemon, glorious son of Phronios,
For his swift ship. And he granted it graciously.
The sun went down and all the ways were shadowed.
Then she had the swift ship dragged to the sea. And in it
She put all the tackle that well-timbered ships carry.   390
She moored it at the verge of the bay. His noble companions
Were gathered together. The goddess urged each one on.
Then the bright-eyed goddess Athene had another thought.
And she went on to the halls of godlike Odysseus.

There she diffused sweet slumber down on the suitors,   395
And confused them as they drank. The goblets fell from their hands.
They rose up to go sleep through the city. And not long
Did they sit, when once slumber fell on their eyelids.
Then the bright-eyed goddess Athene spoke to Telemachos,
Calling him out of the well-situated halls,   400
Likening herself to Mentor in form and in voice:
"Telemachos, already your well-greaved companions
Are seated at the oars awaiting your urging.
Let us go, so that we may not long delay from the journey."
So did Pallas Athene speak, and she led on   405
Speedily. He went along in the god's footsteps.
But when they had got down to the ship and the sea,
They found the long-haired companions there on the sand.
And Telemachos addressed them in his holy might:
"Over here, friends. Let us load on provisions. Already   410
All are gathered in the chamber. My mother has not found out,
Nor the other serving maids. One alone has heard the tale."
So he spoke, and led them, and they went along with him.
When they had brought everything to the well-timbered ship,
They stowed it away as Odysseus' dear son ordered them.   415
Telemachos then boarded the ship, but Athene went first
And sat down in the stern of the ship. Close beside her
Telemachos sat. They let the stern cables loose,
And themselves boarded and sat down at the oarlocks.
Bright-eyed Athene sent them a driving breeze,   420
A driving West Wind roaring on the wine-faced sea.
Telemachos, as he urged his companions on, told them
To grasp the tackle. And they hearkened to his urging.
They stood a fir-wood mast in the hollow mast-block;
They raised it up, and with forestays they made it fast.   425
Then they hauled up the white sails with well-plaited oxhide ropes.
A wind swelled the midsail, and the purple wave
About the stem sounded loud as the ship went on.
She ran into the wave, accomplishing her course.
When they had tied down the tackle on the swift black ship,   430
They set up mixing bowls filled to the brim with wine,
And poured libations to the deathless, ever-living gods,
And of all especially to the bright-eyed daughter of Zeus.
All night the ship pierced her course, and at morning too.

III

The sun rose up, leaving the beautiful water,
Into the bronze-covered heaven, to shine for immortals
And also for mortal men upon the grain-giving earth.

They came to Pylos, the well-established city
Of Neleus.[1] On the sands of the sea those men were sacrificing   5
Bulls all of black to the earth-shaker with blue locks.
There were nine groups, and in each one five hundred men
Were sitting. And for each group they put forward nine bulls.
While these were eating the entrails and burning the thighs to the god,
The others sailed straight in, furling into place the sails   10
Of the balanced ship; they pulled her up, and got out themselves.
Telemachos got out of the ship, and Athene went ahead.
The bright-eyed goddess Athene addressed him first:
"Telemachos, there is no longer the least need for you to be modest,
For just this did you sail on the ocean to learn about your father,   15
Where the earth has hidden him and what fate he has met.
But come now, go straight to Nestor, breaker of horses.
We will see what advice he has hidden in his breast.
Entreat him yourself to speak unerringly.
He will not speak falsely. For he is very sound of mind."   20
Then sound-minded Telemachos addressed her in answer:
"Mentor, how then shall I go? How shall I approach him?
For in quick responses I have no experience.
Modesty becomes a young man addressing an elder."
Then the bright-eyed goddess Athene spoke to him: 25
"Telemachos, some thoughts you will have in your mind,
And a god will suggest others. For I do not think
You were born and raised without the favor of the gods."
So did Pallas Athene speak, and she led the way
Speedily. He went along in the god's footsteps.   30
They came to the conclave and sessions of the men of Pylos,
Where Nestor sat with his sons, and about him companions
Prepared a feast, roasting some meat and skewering the rest.
When these men saw the strangers, they all came over in a body
And hailed them with gestures and asked them to sit down.   35
First Peisistratos, Nestor's son, came near,
Took the hands of both men and sat them down at the feast
In soft fleeces upon the sands of the salt sea,
Beside his brother Thrasymedes and his father.
He gave them shares of the entrails and poured out wine   40
In a golden goblet. Pledging her, he addressed
Pallas Athene, daughter of aegis-bearing[2] Zeus.
"Say a prayer now, stranger, to Lord Poseidon,
Whose feast you have come upon in arriving hither.
But when you have poured a libation and prayed, which is fitting,   45
Then give this man also a cup of honey-sweet wine
To pour a libation, since I believe he too says prayers

1. Founder of Pylos; son of Poseidon and father of Nestor.
2. The aegis was a weapon, or later a breastplate, carried only by Zeus and Athene.

To the immortals. All men have need of the gods.
But he is younger, and equal in age to myself.
Therefore I will first give you the gold cup of libation."   50
When he had said this, he put the cup of sweet wine in her hand.
Athene was pleased at the sound-minded, judicious man
Because he had given her first the gold cup of libation.
At once she said many things in prayer to Lord Poseidon:
"Listen, Poseidon, you who hold up the earth. Bear no grudge   55
Against us as we are praying to bring these deeds to pass.
First of all, grant renown to Nestor and his sons.
And then give the others, all the men of Pylos together,
A pleasing recompense for their illustrious hecatomb.[3]
Grant that Telemachos and I may go back, when we have done   60
That which we came here in the swift black ship to do."
So she prayed then. But she herself brought it all to pass.
She gave Telemachos the lovely two-handled cup.
The dear son of Odysseus prayed in the same way.
When the others had roasted the outer pieces of meat and unskewered
    them,   65
They divided the portions and dined on the hearty feast.
But when they had taken their fill of food and drink,
Nestor, the Gerenian horseman, began speaking to them:
"Now is the best time to inquire, and to ask
Strangers who they are, after they have enjoyed food.   70
Strangers, who are you? Whence have you sailed the watery ways?
For some sort of gain, or do you wander at hazard
The way pirates do who wander over the sea,
Risking their lives, bearing evil to foreigners?"
Then sound-minded Telemachos addressed him in answer,   75
Taking courage, for Athene herself had put in his mind
Courage to ask him about the father who had gone away,
And so that a noble renown among men might belong to him:
"Nestor, son of Neleus, great pride of the Achaians,
You ask where we are from. And I will inform you.   80
We have come from Ithaca, which is under Mount Neion.
It is a private affair, not a public one, that I speak of.
I seek widespread report of my father, if somehow I may hear,
Of the stout-hearted, godly Odysseus, who once, they say,
Sacked the city of the Trojans, fighting at your side.   85
Of all the other men who waged war on the Trojans,
We have heard where each one perished by a woeful death.
But the son of Cronos made that man's death not to be heard of.
No one is able to say clearly just where he perished,
Whether on the mainland he went under to hostile men   90

3. Sacrifice of a hundred oxen.

Or on the open sea in Amphitrite's[4] waves.
So I now embrace your knees to ask if you are willing
To tell about that man's woeful death, if you saw it
With your own eyes, perhaps, or heard the tale from another
Wanderer. For excessive sorrow did his mother bear him!   95
Sweeten nothing out of pity or respect for me,
But tell me straight out how you encountered the sight.
I beseech you, if ever my father noble Odysseus
Promised you any word or deed and carried it out
In the Trojans' land, where you Achaians suffered troubles;   100
Recall that for me now and tell me unerringly."
Then Nestor, the Gerenian horseman, answered him:
"Ah friend, since you have reminded me of the woe we suffered
In that land, we sons of the Achaians, unchecked in our anger;
How much, both in the ships upon the murky sea,   105
Wandering for booty wherever Achilles led,
And how much, too, we fought around the great city
Of Lord Priam![5] There at that time all the best were slain!
There lies warlike Ajax, there lies Achilles,[6]
There Patroclos,[7] a counselor equal in weight to the gods: 110
There lies my dear son, at once mighty and excellent,
Antilochos, outstanding as a runner and as a fighter.
Many other ills we endured besides these. Who
Of mortal men could ever recount all of them?
Not if you stayed five years, no, not six, could you ask   115
To the end of the ills the godly Achaians endured there.
Before that you would tire and return to your fatherland.
Nine years we busied ourselves weaving ills for them
By all sorts of wiles. The son of Cronos barely brought it to pass.
And no one there ever wanted to be compared to him openly   120
For craftiness, since godly Odysseus far surpassed
In all sorts of wiles—your father, if it is true
You are that man's offspring. Awe holds me to look upon you.
Yes, indeed, your speech is like his. You would not think
A man so young could speak in such a likely way.   125
There the whole time I myself and godly Odysseus
Never once spoke diversely in assembly or in council,
But holding one spirit in mind and in prudent counsel,
We advised the Argives how it should come out by far the best.
And when we had sacked the lofty city of Priam   130
And gone off in the ships, and a god had scattered the Achaians,
Then Zeus plotted out in his mind a woeful return

4. Amphitrite is a sea goddess, here identified with the sea itself.
5. The aged king of Troy killed by the Greeks.
6. Ajax was son of Telamon, second to Achilles in prowess; Achilles, captain of the Myrmidons
   and the greatest hero of the Greeks at Troy.
7. The closest friend of Achilles; his death inspired Achilles to return to battle.

For the Argives, since they were not all prudent or just.
Therefore many of them encountered an evil fate
Because of the destructive wrath of the bright-eyed daughter   135
Of a strong father, who set strife on the two sons of Atreus.
The two of them called all the Achaians to a council,
Rashly, in no orderly way, at the sun's setting,
And the sons of the Achaians came, weighed down with wine.
They told the story of why they had gathered the people.   140
Then Menelaos commanded all the Achaians
To take thought of a return on the broad back of the sea.
But that did not please Agamemnon at all, for he wanted
To hold back the people and to offer sacred hecatombs
So as to appease the dreadful rage of Athene.   145
The fool, he did not know she was not to be persuaded.
The mind of the ever-living gods is not quickly turned.
And so they stood there and replied to each other
With harsh speeches. And the well-greaved Achaians rose up
With a wondrous noise. The plan pleased them diversely.   150
We spent the night turning over harsh thoughts in our minds
Against one another. For Zeus was shaping an evil woe.
At dawn some of us dragged the ships to the bright salt water;
We put our possessions and the deep-girdled women in.
But half of the people held back, staying on behind   155
With Atreus' son Agamemnon, shepherd of the people.
The other half embarked and went on. Swiftly indeed
They sailed, and a god smoothed out the great-gulfed ocean.
When we came to Tenedos we sacrificed to the gods,
Wanting to go home. But Zeus intended no return yet,   160
Cruel, as he stirred up evil strife for the second time.
Some turned their bobbing ships around and went their way,
Those about skillful devious-minded Lord Odysseus;
And they again favored Agamemnon, son of Atreus.
But I, with the massed ships that were following me,   165
Kept fleeing, since I knew the god was intending evil.
The warlike son of Tydeus fled and aroused his companions.
Blond Menelaos came along with us later on.
He found us in Lesbos thinking over the long voyage,
Whether we should take our way above rugged Chios   170
By the island of Psyra, keeping that on our left,
Or should go below Chios along by windy Mimas.
We besought the god to make a portent appear, and he did
Show us one and ordered us to cleave the middle sea
To Euboia, so we might soonest flee from under misfortune.   175
A sharp breeze rose up and blew. Our ships swiftly
Ran over the fish-laden courses. During the night
They put in at Geraistos. We dedicated the thighs
Of many bulls to Poseidon, when we had measured the great sea.

It was the fourth day when the companions of Diomede,[8]   180
Tydeus' horse-taming son, moored their balanced ships in Argos.
As for me, I held toward Pylos. Never did the breeze
Lull, from the very first time the god set it on to blow.
So I arrived, dear child, with no news. I know nothing
About them, which Achaians were saved, and which perished.   185
As much as I could learn sitting in my own halls,
You shall find out, as is right. I will not conceal it from you.
They say the spear-wielding Myrmidons[9] came safely,
Whose leader was the famous son of great-hearted Achilles,
And safely came Philoctetes, Poeas' glorious son.   190
Idomeneus[1] led all his companions to Crete,
Who escaped from the war. The ocean deprived him of none.
You have heard about the son of Atreus, though you live far away—
How he arrived, how Aigisthos plotted his woeful death.
Ah, but that man did pay for it terribly.   195
And how good it is for a man to leave behind when he dies
A son, since that son avenged his father's murderer,
The cunning Aigisthos, who killed his renowned father!
You too, my dear friend, since I see you are handsome and great;
Be brave, so that a man born in the future would praise you."   200
Then sound-minded Telemachos addressed him in answer:
"Nestor, son of Neleus, great glory of the Achaians,
Yes, that man avenged himself well. And the Achaians
Will bring him wide renown and a song for men to come.
Would that the gods might invest me with so great a power,   205
To take vengeance on the suitors for their painful transgression,
Men who in their pride devise reckless deeds against me.
But the gods have not spun the thread of so great a bliss
For my father and me. Now it must be endured, all the same."
Nestor, the Gerenian horseman, then answered him: 210
"Dear friend, since you have mentioned this and spoken of it to me,
They do say that there are many suitors for your mother
Who are devising evils in your halls against your will.
Tell me, are you willingly subjected? Or do the people
Despise you in the district, yielding to the voice of a god?   215
Who knows if he may come some day and punish their violence,
Either himself alone or all the Achaians together?
For if only the bright-eyed Athene did wish to favor you → IRONY
The way she cared once for glorious Odysseus,
In the Trojans' land where we Achaians suffered troubles—   220
I never saw the gods so openly showing favor
The way Pallas Athene stood openly by that man—
If she did wish to favor you and care in her heart that way,

8. Ruler of Argos; a major Greek hero at Troy.
9. Followers of Achilles.
1. The grandson of Minos and king in Crete.

Then some of those men would surely forget the marriage."
Then sound-minded Telemachos addressed him in answer: 225
"Old man, I think this word will never be fulfilled.
You have said a great deal. Wonder holds me. Not for my hope
Would this happen, not even if the gods wished it to."
Then the bright-eyed goddess Athene spoke to him:
"Telemachos, what sort of word has got past the bar of your teeth?   230
A god may easily if he wish save a man, even from afar.
I should rather myself be distressed with many pains
And travel homeward to see the day of my return
Than to arrive and perish at my hearth, as Agamemnon
Was killed by the guile of Aigisthos and his own wife.   235
Yet not even the gods can ward off from a man they love
The death that is common to all at whatever time
The ruinous fate of long-sorrowful death seizes him."
Then sound-minded Telemachos addressed her in answer:
"Mentor, let us speak of this no more, though we care for him.   240
There is no longer a real return for that man. Already
The immortal gods have devised for him death and black fate.
But now I want to ask and inquire about another story
From Nestor, since he knows justice and prudence beyond others.
For they say he has three times ruled the generations of men.   245
Like an immortal he strikes me to look upon.
O Nestor, son of Neleus, do utter the truth:
How did Atreus' son, broad-ruling Agamemnon, die?
Where was Menelaos? What sort of destruction did cunning
Aigisthos plot for him, when he killed a far better man?   250
Or was it not in Achaian Argos, but did he wander
Somewhere else among men, and the other took courage and mur-
   dered?"
Then Nestor, the Gerenian horseman, answered him,
"All right, my child, I shall tell you all of the truth.
Surely you may think for yourself how this would have happened   255
If Atreus' son, blond Menelaos, arriving from Troy,
Had come upon Aigisthos still alive in the halls.
They would not have spread a heap of earth over him when he died.
But the dogs and also the birds would have devoured him
As he lay on a plain far from the city. And none   260
Of the Achaian women would have wept, for he devised a huge deed.
While we stayed there bringing many combats to an end,
He, secure in a nook of horse-nourishing Argos,
Enchanted Agamemnon's wife with many words.
Actually, she at first rejected the sorry act,   265
Godly Clytemnestra, since she practiced good sense.
And there was a singer with her, too, whom the son of Atreus
When he went off to Troy had strongly ordered to guard his wife.
But when the fate of the gods bound her to be overcome,

Then Aigisthos brought the singer to a desert island   270
And left the man to become a prey and a spoil for birds.
And a willing man led to his house a willing woman.
He burned many thighs on the holy altars of the gods
And set up many ornaments of woven work and gold,
Having achieved a huge deed he had never hoped in his heart.   275
Now we sailed on together as he went from Troy,
The son of Atreus and I, knowing each what pleased the other.
When we reached holy Sunion, headland of Athens,
There Phoebos Apollo[2] slew the pilot of Menelaos,
Visiting him with his soothing shafts while the man   280
Was holding in his hands the rudder of the coursing ship,
Phrontis, Onetor's son, who surpassed the tribes of men
In piloting a ship wherever the storm winds rushed.
So he was held back there, though pressing on for the journey,
Till he should bury his companion and perform due rites.   285
But when he had gone again upon the wine-faced sea
In the hollow ships and, as he sped along, had reached
Maleia, the sheer mountain, broad-seeing Zeus devised
A hateful journey and poured on a blast of shrill winds
And monstrous swollen waves as big as mountains.   290
He separated the ships there and brought some of them near Crete
Where the Cydonians dwelt by the streams of the Iardanos.
A certain smooth rock stands there sheer to the sea
At the extreme point of Gortyn in the murky ocean,
Where the south wind pushes a great wave up against the left peak   295
To Phaistos and a small stone holds back a great wave.
Some ships did get there, and the men barely escaped destruction,
But the waves shattered the ships upon the reefs.
Yet the wind and the water carried and brought five
Of the dark blue-prowed ships right on up to Egypt.   300
So he gathered there a great deal of provisions and gold
And wandered with his ships among men of alien tongue.
Meanwhile Aigisthos plotted these woeful things at home.
For seven years he ruled Mycenae,[3] the rich in gold
When he had killed Atreus' son, and the people were subdued under
    him.   305
In the eighth year, an evil for him, godly Orestes
Came back from Athens and killed his father's murderer,
The cunning Aigisthos, who had killed his renowned father.
When he had killed him, he gave the Argives a funeral feast
Both for his hateful mother and for cowardly Aigisthos.   310
That day Menelaos, good at the war cry, came to him bringing
Many possessions, as great a burden as his ships could bear.

2. Son of Zeus and brother of Artemis; the god of sun and light.
3. The chief city of bronze-age Greece and residence of Agamemnon.

As for you, too, my friend, do not wander long from your home
And leave behind in your home the possessions and the men
Presumptuous as they are, lest they divide and devour   315
All your possessions, and you have gone on a fruitless journey.
But I exhort you and urge you to proceed on
To Menelaos. For he has come recently from elsewhere,
From men from whom no one would expect in his heart
To return, whom storm winds had once led astray   320
Into a sea so great that not even the birds
Could get through in a year, it is so great and dire.
But go on now with your ship and your companions.
If you wish to go by land, a chariot and horses are here;
My own sons are here also, who will be your guides   325
To godly Lacedemon, where blond Menelaos lives.
Beseech him yourself that he may speak unerringly.
He will not speak falsely. For he is very sound of mind."
So he said. The sun went down and darkness came on.
Then the bright-eyed goddess Athene spoke to them.   330
"Old sir, indeed you have told all this properly.
Come now, cut up tongues for offering and mix wine,
So when we have poured a libation to Poseidon and the other
Immortals, we may think of sleep. It is the hour for it.
Light is already gone under the dusk. Nor does it seem right 335
To sit a long time at the gods' feast, but to go on."
So spoke Zeus's daughter, and they hearkened to her voice.
Heralds poured out water for them over their hands.
Young men were filling bowls up to the brim with drink;
And served round to all, putting the first drops in the cups. 340
They cast the tongues on the fire and did libation standing.
But when they had poured libation and drunk as much
As the spirit moved, Athene and godlike Telemachos
Both then wanted to go on to the hollow ship.
Nestor restrained them and addressed them with a speech: 345
"May Zeus and the other immortal gods prevent
Your going away from my house to the swift ship
As from someone wholly without raiment, or destitute,
Who does not have coverlets and many rugs in his house
Either for himself or for his guests to sleep in softly.   350
But there are coverlets and lovely rugs at my disposal.
Not indeed will the dear son of this man Odysseus
Lie down on his ship's deck so long as I am alive
And so long as children are left to me in the halls
To entertain guests, whoever comes to my house."   355
Then the bright-eyed goddess Athene answered him:
"Dear old sir, you have said this well: It does seem right
That Telemachos obey you, as it is much better thus.
But now he will go along with you here, so he may sleep

In your halls. I myself will go to the black ship   360
So I may cheer our companions and tell them the details.
I declare I am the only older man among them,
The others follow along in friendship, younger men,
All the same age as great-hearted Telemachos.
There may I lay myself down in the hollow black ship   365
Right now. But at dawn to the great-hearted Kaucones
I am going, where a debt is owed me, not a recent one,
Or a small one. And since this man has come to your house,
Send him off with a chariot and your son. Give him the horses
That are nimblest at running and the best in strength."   370
When she had said this, bright-eyed Athene went off,
Likening herself to a sea eagle. Wonder seized all the Achaians.
The old man was amazed when he saw it with his eyes,
He took Telemachos' hand and spoke right out directly:
"My friend, I do not suppose you would be craven and cowardly   375
If the gods so accompany a young man like you as guides.
This is no other of those who holds the halls of Olympos
Than the daughter of Zeus, the glorious Tritogeneia.[4]
Among the Argives she honored your noble father too.
Come, mistress, be gracious and grant me a noble renown   380
For myself and my children and my respected wife.
I shall sacrifice to you a yearling heifer of broad brow,
Untamed, that a man has never led under the yoke.
I will sacrifice her, and deck her horns with gold."
So he spoke in prayer, and Pallas Athene heard him.   385
Nestor, the Gerenian horseman, led them on,
His sons and his sons-in-law, to his beautiful home;
But when they arrived at the famous home of the ruler,
They sat down one after another in seats and in armchairs.
As they came, the old man mixed up for them a bowl   390
Of wine, sweet to drink, that in the eleventh year
The serving maid had opened and untied the seal string from.
The old man mixed it in a bowl. As he poured libation
He prayed much to Athene, daughter of aegis-bearing Zeus.
But when they had poured libation and drunk their fill,   395
They went to lie down to sleep, each in his own house.
But there Nestor, the Gerenian horseman, bedded down
Telemachos, the dear son of godly Odysseus,
In the jointed bed under the resounding portico.
Beside him was Peisistratos of the good ash spear, chief of men,   400
Who of the children in his halls was still unmarried.
But he himself slept in a nook of the lofty house,
And his lady wife prepared him a bed and a resting place.
And when the early-born, rosy-fingered dawn appeared,

---

4. A name of Athene referring obscurely to her birth.

Nestor, the Gerenian horseman, rose up out of his bed.   405
He went out and sat himself down on the polished stones
That belonged to him out in front of his lofty portals,
White ones, glistening with oil. Upon them of old
Neleus used to sit, an adviser equal in weight to the gods,
But already he had succumbed to his fate and gone to Hades.[5]   410
Then Gerenian Nestor, bulwark of the Achaians, sat there,
Bearing the scepter. His sons were gathered round in a group
As they came from their bedrooms, Echephron and Stratios,
Perseus and Aretos and the godlike Thrasymedes.
And then sixth among them came the hero Peisistratos.   415
They led godly Telemachos in and sat him at their side.
The Gerenian horseman Nestor began to speak among them:
"Dear children, fulfill my wish very speedily,
So that first of the gods I may propitiate Athene,
Who came in clear form to the lavish feast of the god.   420
Come now, let one man go to the plain for an heifer,
So it come with all speed, and the herd of the oxen drive her.
Let one of you, going to great-hearted Telemachos'
Black ship, lead all his companions, and leave just two.
Let one of them summon the goldsmith Laerkes to come   425
Hither, so he may gild the heifer's horns round with gold,
And all you others stay here in a group. Tell the maids
Within to prepare a feast through the famous halls.
Bring seats and logs for the place, and shining water."
So he said, and they all got busy. The heifer came   430
From the plain, and there came from the swift, balanced ship
The companions of great-hearted Telemachos. The smith came
Carrying bronze implements in his hands, the tools of the trade,
An anvil and a hammer and well-made fire tongs
With which he worked gold. And Athene came to take part   435
In the sacrifice. The old charioteer Nestor gave gold,
And then the other gilded it round and decked the heifer's horns,
So that the goddess would be pleased to see the decoration.
Stratios and godly Echephron led the heifer by the horns.
Aretos came from the chamber carrying water for washing   440
In a flower-chased vessel. He held barley grains in a basket
In his other hand. And Thrasymedes, the steady in battle,
Stood by, holding in his hand a sharp ax to strike the heifer.
Perseus held the blood-bowl. The old charioteer Nestor led off
By washing his hands and sprinkling barley. As he started,   445
He prayed much to Athene, throwing hairs of its head in the fire.
And when they had prayed and tossed the barley offering on,
At once Nestor's son, high-spirited Thrasymedes,
Stood close and struck it. The ax slit the tendons

5. That is, to the ruler of the underworld. In Homer, Hades is a person, not a place.

Of the neck. The heifer's strength was loosed; the women shrieked,   450
His daughters and daughter-in-law and the respected wife
Of Nestor, Eurydice, eldest of Clymenos' daughters.
At that point they lifted it up from the wide-traveled earth
And held it. Peisistratos, chief of the men, cut its throat.
When black blood flowed from it and the spirit left the bones,   455
They quickly dismembered it and at once cut up
The whole thighs duly and covered them over with fat,
Making a double fold, and put the raw meat thereon.
The old man burned it on split wood. He poured sparkling wine
Over that. The young men beside him held the five-pronged forks   460
In their hands. When the thighs were burned and they had eaten of the
    entrails,
They cut up the rest in small pieces and pierced it on spits,
And they roasted it, holding the sharp-pointed spits in their hands.
Meanwhile, the lovely Polykaste, youngest daughter
Of Nestor, the son of Neleus, washed Telemachos.   465
And when she had washed him and anointed him richly with oil,
She put a lovely mantle on him and a tunic.
And he left the bathtub in body like the immortals;
He went and sat down by Nestor, shepherd of the people.
When they had roasted the outer flesh and pulled it off,   470
They sat feasting. Noble men did watchful service
Pouring out the wine into the golden goblets.
But when they had taken their fill of food and drink,
Nestor, the Gerenian horseman, began speaking to them:
"Come my sons, bring the lovely-haired horses, and yoke them up   475
To the chariot for Telemachos, so he may speed on his way."
So he said, and they listened to him right away and obeyed.
Nimbly they yoked swift horses to the chariot,
And the woman who kept them put in food and wine
And cooked meat, such as kings eat who are nourished by Zeus.   480
Telemachos got into the beautiful chariot.
Nestor's son, Peisistratos, chief of the men, along with him
Got into the chariot and took the reins in his hands.
He whipped to start up. Not against their will the pair flew
To the plain, and they left the sheer citadel of Pylos.   485
All day they shook the yoke, holding it up on either side.
The sun went down and all the ways were shadowed.
They arrived at Pherai and to the home of Diocles,
Son of Ortilochos, whom Alpheus[6] sired as his son.
There they slept the night, and he gave them the fare of a guest.   490
But when the early-born, rosy-fingered dawn appeared,
They yoked up the horses and mounted the inlaid chariot.
And they drove out of the forecourt and the resounding portico.

6. A river god.

He whipped to start up. Not against their will the pair flew.
They reached the wheat-bearing plain. From then on they strove   495
To finish their journey. So the swift horses bore onward.
The sun went down and all the ways were shadowed.

IV

They came to hollow Lacedemon, full of ravines,
And drove on to the halls of glorious Menelaos.
They found him holding a wedding feast with his many clansmen
For a son and an excellent daughter in his own house.
He was sending the girl to the son of rank-breaking Achilles.   5
He had betrothed her first in Troy and had nodded
For her to be given; the gods were fulfilling the marriage.
He was then sending her off with horses and chariots
To the famous city of the Myrmidons, whom the man ruled,
And he was bringing the daughter of Alektor from Sparta for his son,   10
The dearly beloved, valiant Megapenthes, born to him
From a slave girl; the gods no longer granted childbirth to Helen
When she had once given birth to her charming daughter
Hermione, who had the form of golden Aphrodite.
So they banqueted under the great high-roofed hall,   15
The neighbors and clansmen of glorious Menelaos,
Enjoying themselves. Among them a divine singer sang
And played on the lyre. And a pair of tumblers about them
Started off at the song and whirled about in their midst.
Then the two of them stood in the gateway of the house,   20
The hero Telemachos and the illustrious son of Nestor,
They and their horses. The lord Eteoneus came forth
And saw them, the capable servant of glorious Menelaos.
He went through the halls to tell the shepherd of the people,
And he stood close to him and uttered wingèd words;   25
"Menelaos, nourished by Zeus, some strangers are here,
Two men, and they resemble the race·of mighty Zeus.
Tell me, shall we unharness their swift horses for them
Or send them to reach another who will befriend them?"
Greatly disturbed, blond Menelaos spoke to him: 30
"Eteoneus, son of Boethoüs, you were never a fool
Before. But now you mouth foolishness like a child.
We ourselves, indeed, ate many guest offerings
Of other men as we came here, if only in the future
Zeus were ever to make woe cease. But unhitch the horses   35
Of the strangers. Go bring them forward to be entertained."
So he said, and the man passed quickly through the hall and called
Other capable servants to follow along with him.
They unhitched the sweating horses from under the yoke

And they haltered them in the mangers for horses.   40
They threw in emmer grains, and they mixed white barley in,
And leaned the chariot against the resplendent walls.
Then they led the men to the godly house. When they saw
The hall of the Zeus-nourished king, they wondered at it.
There was a gleam like that of the sun or of the moon   45
Beneath the high-roofed hall of glorious Menelaos.
But when they had taken their joy of looking with their eyes,
They went out and got washed in the well-polished bathtubs.
And when the maidservants had washed them and rubbed them with
    oil,
They put woolen cloaks around them and also tunics,   50
And they sat on armchairs beside Menelaos, son of Atreus.
A handmaid poured water from a pitcher she was carrying,
A lovely golden one, over into a silver basin,
For washing the hands. She set up a polished table alongside.
A respected housekeeper served bread she was carrying,   55
Laying out many dishes, gracious with the provisions.
A carver lifted up and set out trenchers of meats
Of all sorts, and set out gold goblets alongside for them.
Making a sign to the two men, blond Menelaos addressed them:
"Take some of the food and enjoy yourselves; and when   60
You have partaken of dinner, we shall ask what men
You may be. The race of your parents is not lost in you;
But you are of the race of men who are scepter-bearing kings,
Nourished by Zeus, since mean men would not produce sons like these."
So he spoke, and he took in his hands and set before them   65
The fat roast ox-back he had been given as an honor himself.
They stretched forth their hands to the food that was spread out ready.
But when they had taken their fill of food and drink,
Then Telemachos spoke out to the son of Nestor,
Holding his head close so that the others might not hear: 70
"Son of Nestor, you who have delighted my heart,
Notice the flash of bronze through the echoing halls,
Of gold and of amber, of silver and of ivory;
The court of Olympian Zeus must be like this inside,
So many wonders are here. Awe holds me when I look at them."   75
Blond Menelaos was aware of him as he spoke.
He addressed his voice to them and uttered wingèd words:
"Dear children, surely no mortal may contend with Zeus.
Immortal are his dwelling and his possessions.
But of men few if any could contend with me   80
In possessions. Yes, I suffered much and wandered much
When I brought them in the ships and arrived in the eighth year.
I wandered to Cyprus, to Phoenicia, and to the Egyptians;
I reached the Ethiopians, the Sidonians, and the Erembi,
And Libya, where the lambs are born sprouting horns at once.   85

The sheep give birth three times within a complete year.
No lord there, and also no shepherd, is at all lacking
In cheese and in meats, and not in sweet milk either;
But the flocks always furnish abundant milk for suckling.
I wandered thereabouts getting a great livelihood   90
While another man killed my brother unawares,
Secretly, through the cunning of his accursèd wife.
So it is not in delight that I rule over these possessions.
You will have heard about this from your fathers, whoever
They may be, since I suffered much, and ruined a home,   95
A good habitation, containing many noble things.
Would I might dwell in my halls with just a third share
Of those things, and the men were safe who perished then
In broad Troy, far away from horse-nourishing Argos!
But nevertheless I frequently sit in our halls   100
Mourning and grieving over all of them; sometimes
I please my mind with lamentation and sometimes
I cease from it. For quick is the glut of cold lamentation.
I do not, though I am grieved, mourn for them all so much
As I do for one man, who makes food and sleep hateful to me   105
When I think of him, since none of the Achaians suffered as much
As Odysseus suffered and bore. For him there were destined
To be troubles, and for me a perpetually ceaseless grief
Over him, since he has long been gone, and we do not know
If he lives or is dead. I suppose they are mourning him now,   110
The old Laertes and constant Penelope,
And Telemachos, whom he left as a newborn child in his house."
So he spoke, and roused in him a longing to mourn his father.
A tear fell on the ground from his eyelids as he heard of his father,
And he held the purple mantle up before his eyes   115
With both of his hands. Menelaos perceived him
And turned it over in his mind and in his heart
Whether he should allow him to mention his father himself
Or should first inquire and test him in the details.
While he pondered these matters in his mind and in his heart,   120
Helen[1] came out of the high-roofed fragrant bedroom,
She who resembled Artemis[2] of the golden shafts.
Adreste went with her and set up a well-made couch for her,
And Alcippé carried in a rug of soft wool.
Phylo carried a silver basket that Alcandré   125
Had given her, the wife of Polybos, who dwelt
In Egyptian Thebes, where the most goods are stored in the houses.
He gave two bathtubs of silver to Menelaos
And a pair of cauldrons and ten talents of gold.

---

1. Wife of Menelaos; carried off by Paris to Troy.
2. Daughter of Zeus and sister of Apollo.

His wife on her own presented the loveliest gifts to Helen;   130
She gave her a gold distaff, a basket with wheels underneath
Made of silver, and the rims of it were finished with gold.
The servant Phylo brought it in and set it out before her,
Stuffed with artfully arranged thread, and on it
There lay a distaff holding dark violet wool.   135
She sat in the chair; a footstool was beneath for her feet.
Right away she asked her husband in words for the details:
"Menelaos, nourished by Zeus, do we know who these people
Who have come to our home claim to be among men?
Shall I dissemble or speak the truth? My heart bids me to.   140
I think I have never yet seen anyone so like him,
A man or a woman; wonder holds me as I see this man,
For the way he looks like great-hearted Odysseus' son
Telemachos, whom he left as a newborn child in his house.
He did so when you Achaians, because of my bitch-faced self,   145
Went up under Troy intending a strenuous war."
And blond Menelaos addressed her in answer:
"My wife, I also now think it is just as you suppose.
His feet are the same as that man's, his hands are the same,
And the glances of his eyes, and his head, and the hair upon it.   150
Yes, just now I was remembering about Odysseus
And telling how much that man suffered in his grief
For my sake, and he shed quick tears from under his eyebrows,
Holding up the purple mantle in front of his eyes."
Peisistratos, son of Nestor, addressed him in answer: 155
"Son of Atreus, Zeus-nourished Menelaos, chief of the people,
This is really the son of the man, as you say.
But he is prudent; and in his heart he is ashamed
To come so the first time and make a show of bold talk
Before you, in whose voice we both delight as in a god's.   160
Now, the Gerenian horseman Nestor sent me out
To go along with him as a guide. He longed to see you,
So that you might provide him with something, a word or a deed.
The son of a father who is gone away has many pains
Within his halls, if there be no other helpers for him,   165
As now for Telemachos he is gone away, and there are
No others in the district who might ward off misery."
And blond Menelaos addressed him in answer:
"Well now, he comes to my house as the son of a man indeed
Very dear to me, one who suffered many trials for my sake,   170
And I thought when he came I would befriend him above all
Of the Argives, if broad-seeing Olympian Zeus had granted
A return for us both in our swift ships over the sea.
I would have settled him in a city in Argos and made a house,
Bringing him from Ithaca with his goods and his son   175
And all of his people, when I had sacked one city

Of those settled nearby that are ruled over by me.
When they were here we would often have mingled. Nothing else
Could have parted us two in our friendship and delight,
At least till the black cloud of death had veiled us about.   180
But the god himself must somehow have been jealous
To have made that wretched man alone fail to return."
So he said, and roused desire for lamentation in them all.
The Argive Helen wept, she who was born of Zeus,
And Telemachos wept, and Menelaos too, son of Atreus;   185
Nor did the son of Nestor keep his eyes without tears,
For in his heart he remembered excellent Antilochos,
Whom the glorious son of the brilliant Dawn had slain.
As he called that man to mind, he uttered wingèd words:
"Son of Atreus, old Nestor used to declare you to be   190
Sound-minded above mortals when we in his halls
Called you to mind and asked one another about you,
And now, if it may be, listen to me; I for my part
Do not enjoy mourning at dinner. And besides,
The early-born dawn will be here. I do not at all blame   195
Weeping for any mortal who dies and meets his fate.
This indeed is the sole honor for sorrowful mortals,
To cut the hair for them and let a tear fall from our cheeks.
Yes, my brother is dead, too, by no means the worst
Of the Argives. You probably knew him; I for my part   200
Never met him or saw him. They say Antilochos
Was better than others in fighting and in speed of running."
Then blond Menelaos addressed him in answer:
"My friend, you have said as much as a sound-minded man
Would say and perform, even one who was born before you.   205
You are the son of a great father, to speak so sound-mindedly.
Easily known is the seed of a man for whom the son of Cronos
Weaves the thread of wealth when he marries and when he is born,
Such as he has now steadily given Nestor all his days;
So the man himself may grow sleekly old in his halls,   210
And his sons may be wise and may excel with spears;
But let us cease the lamentation that was made before,
And let us once more think about dinner; let them pour
Water on our hands. There will be stories after dawn
For Telemachos and me to talk out with one another."   215
So he said, and Asphalion poured water over their hands,
The capable servant of glorious Menelaos.
And they stretched forth their hands to the food that was spread out
    ready.
Then Helen, who was born of Zeus, had another thought.
Right away she dropped a drug in the wine they were drinking,   220
A soothing pain-killer, that made one forget all his ills,
And whoever swallowed it down when it was mixed in the bowl

Would not shed a tear down his cheeks the whole day long,
Not if his mother and his father were both to die,
Not if right in front of him his brother or his dear son   225
Were slaughtered with a sword, and he see it with his own eyes.
Drugs of such devices did the daughter of Zeus have,
Good ones, which Polydamna gave her, wife of Thon,
From Egypt, where the grain-giving earth bears the most drugs,
Many of them good in mixture, and many harmful;   230
And each man is a physician, knowledgeable beyond
All men. For they are truly of the race of Paieon.[3]
But when she had put it in and called for wine to be poured,
She answered with a speech and spoke out once again:
"Zeus-nourished Menelaos, son of Atreus, and you men too,   235
Who are children of noble men—well, Zeus as a god gives
Good and evil now to one man and now to another;
For he can do all things. But come, sit and dine now in the hall,
And enjoy the tales. I shall tell an appropriate one.
Now I shall not be able to tell or enumerate all   240
Of the many trials there were for stout-hearted Odysseus;
But what a deed this one was the mighty man did and dared
In the land of the Trojans where you Achaians suffered troubles
When he had submitted himself to disfiguring blows,
He threw a poor covering over his shoulders, and in the likeness   245
Of a servant he entered the enemy's broad-streeted city.
He likened himself in his concealment to another mortal,
To a beggar, he who by the Achaians' ships was nothing like that.
In that guise he entered the city of the Trojans. They all
Overlooked him. I alone recognized him as he was.   250
And I questioned him. He eluded me cunningly.
But when I was washing him and rubbing him with oil,
And had put garments on him and sworn a mighty oath
That I would not reveal Odysseus to the Trojans before
He should make his way back to the huts and the swift ships,   255
Then he told me the entire purpose of the Achaians.
Many of the Trojans he killed with the long-edged sword,
And went back to the Argives, and brought much information;
Then the other Trojan women lamented loudly. My heart, though,
Rejoiced, since already the heart within me was turned   260
To go back home, and I bemoaned the madness Aphrodite
Gave me when she led me there far from my own fatherland,
Abandoning my daughter, my bedchamber, and my husband,
Who was lacking in nothing, either of mind or of form."
The blond Menelaos addressed her in answer: 265
"Yes, indeed, my wife, you have said all this properly.
Already I have learned the purpose and the thought of many

3. A legendary physician of the gods; later, Apollo.

Men, of heroes, and I have traveled to many lands,
But never yet did I see with my own eyes such a man
As stout-minded Odysseus was, in his own heart,   270
Nor such a deed as that mighty man did and dared
In the polished horse, where all the noblest of us Argives
Sat inside bearing murder and destiny for the Trojans;
And then you came there. Some god must have beckoned you,
One of those who wished to bring glory to the Trojans;   275
Yes, and Deiphobos,[4] like a god, followed you as you went.
Three times you walked round the hollow decoy, handling it,
And called out the best of the Danaans, naming them by name,
Making your voice like that of the wives of all the Argives.
I and the son of Tydeus and godlike Odysseus,   280
As we sat in their midst, heard you as you shouted.
And the two of us were eager to make a start,
Either to get outside or to reply at once from within.
But Odysseus held us back and restrained us, though we wanted to.
Then all the other sons of the Achaians were silent   285
And Antilochos alone wished to give you answer
With a speech. But Odysseus steadily pressed the man's mouth
With his powerful hands, and he saved all the Achaians.
He held him until Pallas Athene led you away."
Then sound-minded Telemachos addressed him in answer: 290
"Menelaos, Zeus-nourished son of Atreus, chief of the people,
The more painful it is! This did not ward off his sad death
Nor would have, if the heart had been of iron within him.
But come, send us off to bed, so that right away
We may take the pleasure of lying down under sweet sleep."   295
So he said, and Argive Helen called to the serving maids
To put bedsteads down in the colonnade and to throw on
Lovely purple rugs, and to spread blankets above them,
And to put down woolen mantles on top of all that.
They went out of the hall bearing each a torch in her hand   300
And covered the bedsteads. And a herald led the strangers out.
So they went to sleep right there in the forecourt of the house,
The hero Telemachos and the illustrious son of Nestor.
The son of Atreus slept in a nook of the lofty house,
And by him lay Helen of the long gown, a goddess among women.   305
And when the early-born, rosy-fingered dawn appeared,
Menelaos, good at the war cry, rose up out of his bed,
Put on his clothes, set the sharp sword round his shoulder,
Bound the lovely sandals beneath his shining feet,
And went on out of the bedroom like a god to look at.   310
He sat by Telemachos, and spoke out to him directly:
"Hero Telemachos, what need brought you hither

4. Son of Priam and Hecuba; a prominent Trojan warrior.

To godly Lacedemon, upon the broad back of the sea,
A public one or your own? Tell me this unerringly."
Sound-minded Telemachos addressed him in answer: 315
"Menelaos, Zeus-nourished son of Atreus, chief of the people,
I came to see if you might tell me some news of my father.
My house is being eaten up, my fertile lands are ruined,
My home is full of enemy men who perpetually slay
My throngs of sheep and my shamble-footed, crumple-horned
    cattle,   320
Suitors of my mother, who possess presumptuous pride.
So now I embrace your knees to ask if you are willing
To tell me about that man's woeful death, if you saw it
With your own eyes, perhaps, or heard the tale from another
Wanderer. For excessive sorrow did his mother bear him!   325
Sweeten nothing out of pity or respect for me,
But tell me straight out how you encountered the sight,
I beseech you, if ever my father, noble Odysseus,
Promised you any word or deed and carried it out
In the Trojan's land where you Achaians suffered troubles,   330
Remember that for me now, and tell me unerringly."
Greatly disturbed, blond Menelaos spoke to him:
"Well now, they who are themselves without courage
Have wished to lie down in the bed of a stouthearted man!
As when a deer in the thicket of a mighty lion   335
Has put her newborn milk-sucking fawn to sleep,
And goes questing over the spurs and the grassy gorges
For grazing, and just then he comes into his own lair
And upon the two of them brings a wretched fate;
So upon these men will Odysseus bring a wretched fate.   340
Father Zeus and Athene and Apollo, I wish
He might be as he once was in well-established Lesbos,
When he stood up and wrestled in a fight with Philomelides,
Threw him down mightily, and all the Achaians rejoiced—
As that sort of man might Odysseus contend with the suitors.   345
They would all be swift in their doom and bitter in marriage.
As for what you ask and beseech me about, I myself
Will say nothing at all off the point, nor will I deceive.
But what the unerring old man of the sea told me,
Not a word of that shall I hide from you or conceal.   350
The gods were still holding me in Egypt, though I was striving
To return here, as I had not sacrificed full hecatombs for them.
The gods have always wished their injunctions to be kept in mind.
Well, there is a certain island in the much-surging ocean,
Over before the Nile, and they call it Pharos,   355
Just so far away as a hollow ship in a day
Could reach it, with a shrill breeze blowing on behind.
There is a well-sheltered harbor in it, from which men launch

Balanced ships on the ocean, when they have drawn black water on
    board.
There the gods held me twenty days. No breezes ever   360
Came blowing upon the sea, the ones that become
Escorts for ships over the broad back of the sea.
And all the food would have been spent, and the men's strength,
If one of the gods had not felt sorry for me and pitied me,
The daughter of mighty Proteus, old man of the sea,   365
Eidothëe; her heart I aroused especially,
When she met me walking alone apart from my companions,
For they were always roaming around the island fishing
With bent fishhooks, and hunger wore on their stomachs.
She stood close to me, spoke, and uttered a speech: 370
'Are you a fool, stranger? Are you too slack of mind?
Do you willingly let go and enjoy suffering pain?
So long a time are you held back on the island and cannot
Find a way out, and the heart dwindles in your companions.'
So she said, and I addressed her in answer: 375
'I shall tell you right out, whatever goddess you are,
That I do not hold back at all willingly, but I must have
Trespassed against the immortals who possess broad heaven.
But you tell me now yourself—the gods know all—
Which of the immortals constrains and binds me from my way;   380
And tell about my return, how I may go on the fish-laden ocean?'
So I said; she, the divine goddess, answered at once:
'All right, stranger, I shall speak out truthfully.
A certain unerring old man of the sea comes here,
The immortal Egyptian, Proteus, who knows   385
The depths of the whole sea, a subject to Poseidon.
They say he is my own father and sired me.
If somehow you could hide in an ambush and catch him
He will tell you your course and the measures of your way,
About a return, how you may go on the fish-laden ocean,   390
And he may tell you, too, if you wish, you who are nourished by Zeus,
Whatever good and evil has been done in your halls
While you have been gone on the long and burdensome journey.'
So did she speak, and I addressed her in answer:
'Show me now yourself the ambush for the divine old man,   395
Lest somehow he see me or learn of me first and escape,
As it is hard for a god to be subdued by a mortal man.'
So I said, and she, the divine goddess, answered at once:
'All right, I shall speak straight out to you truthfully.
At the time when the sun strides the middle of heaven,   400
Then the unerring old man of the sea comes from the sea
Under the blowing West Wind, hidden in a black ripple;
And when he gets out he sleeps down inside the hollow caves.
Around him the foot-swimming seals of the lovely sea's daughter

Sleep in a flock, when they have risen out of the hoary sea,   405
Exhaling a bitter smell of the sea that has many depths;
There I will lead you myself when the dawn appears
And will lay you down in due order. Make a good choice
Of three companions who are your best in the well-timbered ships,
And I shall tell you all the cunning of this old man.   410
At first he will number the seals and go over them,
But when he has counted them by fives and looked at them all,
He will lie in their midst like a shepherd amid flocks of sheep.
And when you first see him lying down to rest,
At that very moment give heed to your strength and might.   415
Hold him struggling there, though he be violent to escape.
He will try it by becoming all the many creatures
That move on the earth; and then water, and divinely kindled fire.
But hold him firmly yourselves and constrain him the more.
When at last he questions you with a speech as himself   420
And is the way he was when you saw him resting,
Then, hero, hold back your strength and release the old man,
And ask him which one of the gods oppresses you,
And about a return, how you may go on the fish-laden ocean.'
When she had said this, she vanished into the ocean's surging
    waves.   425
But I went to the ships where they were standing on the sands.
The heart within me brooded about much as I went.
But when I arrived at the ship and at the sea,
And had prepared dinner, and ambrosial night came on,
Then did we lie down to sleep by the surf of the sea.   430
And when the early-born, rosy-fingered dawn appeared,
I went on along the strand of the wide-pathed sea,
Supplicating the gods very much. And I brought along
Three companions whom I most trusted for every course.
Meanwhile she had gone down under the broad bosom of the sea   435
And she took four skins of the seals out of the ocean;
All of them were new-flayed. And she planned a trick on her father.
When she had scooped out beds in the sands of the sea,
She sat waiting. We came up very close to her.
She bedded us down in a row and threw a skin over each;   440
There the ambush would have been most dreadful. The dire smell
Of the sea-nourished seals oppressed us dreadfully,
For who would lie down to sleep with a monster of the sea?
But she saved us herself and thought up a great remedy;
She brought and put under each one's nostrils, ambrosia   445
That has a sweet aroma, and it destroyed the smell of seal,
And we waited with enduring heart the whole morning.
The seals came up in a flock from the sea. Then in a row
They lay down to sleep along the surf of the sea.
At full light the old man came from the sea and found his seals   450

Well nourished; he went over them all and counted their number,
And us he numbered first among the seals, nor did it occur
To his heart that there was a trick. Then he lay down himself.
But we rushed on him with a shout and threw our hands
Around him. The old man did not forget his wily skill.   455
First of all he became a lion with a mighty beard,
And then a serpent, and a panther, and a great boar.
Then he became watery water, and a lofty-leaved tree.
But we held on firmly with an enduring heart,
And when the old man of cunning skill was exhausted,   460
He spoke out to me and questioned me with a speech:
'Which of the gods, son of Atreus, has devised plots for you
That you catch me in ambush against my will? What do you need?'
So he spoke, and I for my part addressed him in answer:
'You know, old man—why do you say this and put me off?—   465
How long I am held back on this island and can find
No way out, and the heart is dwindling within me.
But you yourself tell me now—the gods know all—
Which of the immortals constrains me and binds me from my way,
And my return, how I may go on the fish-laden ocean?'   470
So I said, and right away he addressed me in answer:
'Surely before embarking you ought to have made fair sacrifices
To Zeus and the other gods, so that you may very soon
Reach your fatherland, sailing on the wine-faced sea.
For it will not be your lot to see your friends and to reach   475
Your well-established home and your own fatherland
Until you come once again to the waters of the Nile,
The Zeus-fallen [5] river, and there perform sacred hecatombs
To the immortal gods who possess broad heaven.
Then the gods will give you the journey you desire.'   480
So he said, but my own heart was shattered within me,
Because he ordered me back onto the murky ocean,
To go to the Nile, a long and burdensome journey.
Yet this is what I answered, addressing him with a speech:
'So shall I perform it, old man, just as you direct me.   485
But come now, tell me this, and speak out truthfully:
Did all the Achaians arrive safe and sound with their ships,
Those whom Nestor and I left when we went from Troy,
Or did any of them perish on his ship by a harsh death?
Or in the arms of his friends, after he had wound up the war?'   490
So I said, and he straightway addressed me in answer:
'Son of Atreus, why do you ask me all this? There is no need
For you to know it or learn my thoughts. And I say that you
Will not long be tearless when you have found it all out.
Many of them were overcome, and many are left.   495

5. This probably means "rain-fed," since it is "Zeus" who "rains" in ancient Greece.

But two leaders alone of the bronze-clad Achaians
Died on the return. As for the battle, you were there yourself.
A single man, perhaps still alive, is held back on the broad ocean.
Ajax[6] was overcome in the midst of his long-oared ships.
Poseidon at first brought him up close to Gyrai,   500
The great headlands, and rescued him out of the sea.
And he would have escaped his fate, though hated by Athene,
If he had not thrown out a bold word and lost his senses.
He said he had escaped the sea's great-gulf against the god's will,
And Poseidon heard him as he uttered his great boast;   505
Straightway then he took his trident in his muscular hands,
Struck the headland of Gyrai, and split some of it off;
One part stayed on the spot; the fragment fell in the ocean,
The one Ajax was perched on when he lost his senses,
And it carried him down to the boundless wave-breaking ocean.   510
So he perished there, when he had drunk the salty water.
Your brother, though, escaped the fates and eluded them
In his hollow ships. And the queenly Hera[7] saved him.
But just at the time when he was set to arrive at the sheer
Mountain of Malea, a tempest snatched him up   515
And carried him heavily groaning on the fish-laden ocean,
To the verge of the land where the halls of Thyestes were
Beforehand, but now Thyestes' son Aigisthos lived there.
And when from that place, too, a safe return appeared,
The gods turned the breeze back again and sent him homeward.   520
Rejoicing, he set foot on the soil of his fatherland,
And he kept kissing the fatherland as he touched it. Many warm tears
Poured from his eyes when in gladness he saw his land.
But a watchman saw him from a watch point, whom cunning
Aigisthos had led and stationed there, and promised a reward,   525
Two talents of gold, and he watched there for a year
Lest the man should slip by him and recall his impetuous might.
He went through the halls to tell the shepherd of the people.
Right away Aigisthos thought up a crafty design.
He picked out the twenty best men in the district and set   530
An ambush, and bid them make dinner on the other side.
And he went to call Agamemnon, shepherd of the people,
With horses and chariot, planning his horrid plans.
He led him in unaware of his destruction,
And after feasting him, slew him, as one kills an ox at the crib.   535
None of the comrades was left who followed the son of Atreus,
And none of Aigisthos' but they were killed in the halls.'
So he said, but my own heart was shattered within me.
And I wept as I sat on the sand, and wished in my heart

6. This is the "second" Ajax, son of Oileus, not the better-known son of Telamon.
7. Queen of the gods; wife and sister of Zeus.

Not to live any longer and see the light of the sun.   540
But when I had enough of weeping and groveling,
Then the unerring old man of the sea addressed me:
'Son of Atreus, do not weep any more so persistently
And so long, since we shall find no result from that,
But try to arrive as soon as you can at your fatherland.   545
You may find the man alive, or Orestes will have gone ahead
And killed him, and you may come upon his funeral.'
So he said, and the heart within me and the bold spirit
Were warmed again in my breast, even though I was grieved.
And speaking out to him, I uttered wingèd words: 550
'These men I know of. But tell me about the third man,
The one who was held back upon the broad sea, still alive,
Or he is dead. Though I am grieved, I want to hear of him.'
So I said, and right away he addressed me in answer:
'That is the son of Laertes, whose home is in Ithaca,   555
I saw him on an island shedding a swelling tear
In the halls of the nymph Calypso, who by compulsion
Is holding him back, and he cannot reach his fatherland,
For he has no ships there with oars, and no companions
Who might convey him over the broad back of the sea.   560
And for you it is not decreed, Zeus-nourished Menelaos,
In horse-pasturing Argos to die and to meet your fate.
But the immortals will send you to the Elysian plain
And the end of the earth, where blond Rhadamanthys[8] is,
And where the easiest living exists for men.   565
No snow is there, not much winter, and never rain,
But instead clearly blowing breezes of the West Wind
Does Oceanos[9] always send on to put a fresh breath in men,
Because you have Helen and are for them a son-in-law of Zeus.'
When he had said this, he went down under the wave-breaking
    ocean.   570
But I went to the ships with my godlike companions,
And the heart within me was troubled as I went.
But when we arrived at the ships and at the sea
And had prepared a dinner and ambrosial night came on,
Then did we lie down to sleep by the surf of the sea.   575
And when the early-born, rosy-fingered dawn appeared,
First of all we dragged our ships to the godly sea
And set up masts and sails upon the balanced ships,
Then we ourselves boarded and sat down at the oarlocks.
Seated in a row, we beat the hoary sea with our oars.   580
Back at the Egyptian Nile, the Zeus-fallen river,
I beached the ships and sacrificed complete hecatombs.

8. A judge over the dead.
9. The mythical ocean encircling the earth.

When I had calmed down the wrath of the ever-living gods
I set up a mound for Agamemnon so his fame would be unquenched.
When I completed this, I left. The immortals gave me   585
A breeze, and they sent me quickly to my dear fatherland—
But come, stay on for the time being here in my halls,
Until the eleventh day comes, and also the twelfth.
Then I will send you off well; I will give you glorious gifts,
Three horses and a well-polished chariot. And then   590
I will give you a lovely libation cup, so you may pour
To the immortal gods, remembering me all your days."
Then sound-minded Telemachos addressed him in answer:
"Son of Atreus, do not hold me back here a long time.
I myself would surely stay sitting here with you   595
For a year, and no longing for home or parents would take me;
So terribly pleased am I to be listening to your words
And stories. Already my companions in hollowed Pylos
Are worrying, and you have held me back here for some time.
As for the gift you would give me, let it be a keepsake.   600
I will not bring horses to Ithaca, but I shall leave them here
As an adornment for yourself. You rule a broad plain
And in it there is much clover and galingale,
Wheat in it, and emmer grain, and broad-growing white barley.
In Ithaca there are no broad courses or any meadow;   605
It has pasture for goats and is pleasanter than a horse pasture.
But none of the islands that lie by the sea has good meadows
Or a place for driving horses, and Ithaca surpasses them all."
So he said, and Menalaos, good at the war cry, smiled.
He caressed him with one hand, and spoke out to him directly: 610
"You are of good blood, dear child, to judge by what you say,
And so I will exchange these for you, since I can.
Of the gifts that lie stored as keepsakes in my house,
I shall give you the one that is loveliest and of highest worth.
I shall give you a well-fashioned mixing bowl. It is all   615
Of silver, and its rim is finished round with gold,
The work of Hephaistos. The hero Phaidimos gave it,
King of the Sidonians, when his house took me in
As I had returned that far. I would like to give it to you."
And so they said such things to one another,   620
While the dinner guests went to the halls of the godly king.
They drove in sheep and brought in wine that is good for men,
And their wives with beautiful shawls sent them bread.
So they were busying themselves about dinner in the halls.
Meanwhile the suitors out in front of the hall of Odysseus   625
Were amusing themselves by throwing weights and javelins
On the leveled terrace, as before, in their insolence.
Antinoos sat by, and the godlike Eurymachos,
Leaders of the suitors, who for excellence were far the best.

Noemon, the son of Phronios, came close to them   630
And addressed Antinoos, questioning him with a speech:
"Antinoos, do we or do we not know in our minds
When Telemachos is coming back from sandy Pylos?
He has gone off in my ship. A need for it has arisen
To cross over to Elis of the broad dancing-place   635
Where I have twelve brood mares, and suckling mules, tough workers,
That are untrained; one of these I would drive and tame."
So he said. They were amazed at heart. They did not think
He had gone to Nelean Pylos, but was somewhere there
Around in the fields with the sheep or with the swineherd.   640
Then Antinoos, son of Eupeithes, addressed him:
"Tell me unerringly when he went away and what
Young men went with him. Were they the chosen of Ithaca
Or his own slaves and hirelings? He could have done this too.
Tell me this exactly, so that I may know it well,   645
Did he take the black ship by force from you against your will,
Or did you give it willingly when he begged you with a speech?"
Noemon, son of Phronios, addressed him in answer:
"I gave it to him willingly. What would another man do
When a man of such a kind had cares in his heart   650
And requested it? It would be hard to refuse the gift.
The young men who are best in the district, next to us,
Went with him. And I noticed Mentor boarding as leader,
Or a god who in every way resembled him.
And I wonder at this; I saw godlike Mentor here   655
Yesterday morning. Yet he was gone then in the ship to Pylos."
When he had said this, he went off to the halls of his father.
And in both of them the bold spirit was amazed.
They sat the suitors down together and stopped their contests.
Antinoos, son of Eupeithes, spoke out to them,   660
Troubled. For his heart, black all round, was greatly filled
With rage. And his eyes resembled a shining fire:
"Well now, this voyage is a great deed carried out very boldly
By Telemachos. We thought he would not carry it out.
In spite of us all, he went off, the young child, just like that,   665
When he had dragged down the ship and chosen the best in the district.
He will begin to be a trouble even more. Yet may Zeus
Destroy his power before he gains the measure of manhood.
But come now, give me a swift ship and twenty companions,
So that I may lie in ambush and watch for him as he comes   670
In the channel between Ithaca and rugged Samos,
That this voyage for his father may be a grievous one."
So he said, and they all spoke out and assented.
They stood up at once then and went to the house of Odysseus,
Nor was Penelope for a long time unaware   675
Of the plots that the suitors were pondering in their hearts:

Medon, the herald, told her, who had listened to their plans
When he was outside the courtyard; they were weaving their deceit within.
He went through the halls to announce it to Penelope,
And Penelope addressed him as he stepped down on the threshold: 680
"Herald, why did the noble suitors send you out?
To bid the maidservants of the godly Odysseus
To cease from their labors and fix a dinner for them?
May they never go wooing or come together elsewhere;
May they dine here now for the last and final time.   685
You who often gather and consume a large living,
The wealth of skilled Telemachos, did you not hear
From your fathers long ago, when you were children,
The sort of man Odysseus was among your parents?
He never performed or said anything unjust   690
In the district—this is the way of godly kings,
Who might despise one mortal and love another—
But he never acted recklessly against any man.
Now your own hearts and your disgraceful deeds
Are clear. There are no thanks afterward for deeds well done."   695
Then Medon, sound-minded in knowledge, addressed her:
"Well, my queen, may this be your greatest misfortune.
But the suitors are devising another one greater by far
And more disastrous. May the son of Cronos not bring it to pass!
They are eager to murder Telemachos with the sharp sword   700
As he comes homeward. He went off to hear of his father
To divine Pylos, and also to godly Lacedemon."
So he said; right there her knees and her own heart went slack.
Speechlessness seized her for a long time. Her two eyes
Were filled with tears, and her resonant voice was held back.   705
She answered him at last with a speech and addressed him:
"Herald, why did my son go away? There was no need
At all to embark in the swift-faring ships, that are
Horses of the sea for men and cross over much water.
Was it so that not even his name might be left among men?"   710
Then Medon, sound-minded in knowledge, answered her:
"I do not know whether some god incited him
Or his own spirit roused him to go to Pylos to learn
If his father will return or has met his fate."
When he had said this, he went into the house of Odysseus.   715
But heartbreaking anguish poured over her. No longer
Could she bear sitting on a chair, and many were in the house.
But she sat down on the threshold of the richly adorned bedroom,
Lamenting piteously, and the serving maids moaned about her,
All the many that were in the halls, young and old.   720
When she had moaned heavily, Penelope spoke out to them:
"Hear me, my friends. For Olympian Zeus has given me pain
Beyond all the women who were born and raised in my time;

Beforehand I lost a noble lion-hearted husband,
Who excelled in all the virtues among the Danaans,   725
A noble man whose glory is wide through Greece and middle Argos.
And now storms have snatched away my beloved son
Unnoticed from the halls; nor did I hear of his rushing off.
Cruel ones—why did each of you at least not put it in her mind
To wake me out of bed, when you clearly knew in your heart   730
The time he was going down to the hollow black ship?
If I had found out he was considering the voyage,
Then, though eager for voyage, he would surely have stayed here,
Or else he would have left me in the halls a dead woman.
But let someone speedily call the old man Dolios,   735
My servant, whom my father gave me before I came here,
Who tends my garden with its many trees; so he shall right away
Sit down beside Laertes and explain all this to him;
If somehow that man may weave some plan in his mind
And may go out and complain to the people about these men   740
Who wish to destroy his stock and that of godly Odysseus."
Then the beloved nurse Eurycleia addressed her:
"Dear bride, you may slay me with the pitiless sword,
Or leave me in the house. I will not hide the story from you.
I knew all this. I provided all that he ordered,   745
Bread and sweet wine. He put me under a great oath
Not to tell you until either the twelfth day should come,
Or you should miss him yourself and hear of his rushing off,
So you might not weep and injure your lovely skin.
But do take a bath and put clean clothes on your skin.   750
Then ascend to the upper chamber with the serving women
And pray to Athene, daughter of aegis-bearing Zeus,
For she can save him in that case, even from death.
Do not trouble the troubled old man. I do not think
The offspring of Arkesios' son is entirely hated   755
By the blessed gods; there may yet be someone to own
The high-roofed dwelling and the rich fields far away."
So she said, and soothed the other's weeping: she held her eyes from
     weeping.
She did take a bath and put clean clothes on her skin,
Ascended to the upper chamber with the serving women,   760
Put barley for sprinkling in a basket, and prayed to Athene.
"Hear me, unwearying child of aegis-bearing Zeus,
If ever in his halls Odysseus of many devices
Burned the fat thighs of an ox or a sheep for you,
Remember them now for me and save my dear son.   765
Ward the suitors off in their evil presumption."
She wailed as she said this. And the goddess heard her prayer.
The suitors were making a din through the shadowy halls,
And this is what one of the overbearing young men would say:

"Yes, indeed, the much-wooed queen is planning a wedding   770
For us, and does not know that murder is prepared for her son."
So one would say, and they did not know how it was prepared.
And Antinoos spoke out to them and addressed them:
"You fools, keep away from all insolent speeches
Entirely, lest someone announce them inside as well.   775
But come, let us stand up, and accomplish in silence
The very plan that suited the minds of all of us."
When he had said this, he selected the twenty men that were best
And they went on down to the swift ship and the strand of the sea.
First of all they dragged the ship into a depth of salt water,   780
Then set up a mast and sails upon the black ship.
They fitted the oars into the straps made of leather
All in order—and then stretched out the white sails.
Proud-spirited servants carried equipment on for them.
High in flowing water they moored her, and got out themselves.   785
There they took dinner and waited for evening to come.
The prudent Penelope there in her upper chamber
Lay without eating, not partaking of food or drink,
Pondering whether her excellent son might escape death,
Or would go under to the presumptuous suitors.   790
As much as a lion deliberates in a crowd of men,
Fearing when they draw the stealthy circle about him;
So much did she ponder, and balmy sleep came upon her.
She sank back, and slept, and her limbs were all slackened.
Then the bright-eyed goddess Athene had another thought.   795
She made an image and likened it in form to a woman,
To Iphthime, daughter of great-hearted Icarios
That Eumelos, whose house of dwelling was in Pherai, married.
She sent her to the halls of the godly Odysseus,
So that she could make the grieving and wailing Penelope   800
Cease from her tearful wailing and lamentation.
She went into the bedroom by the thong of the bolt,
Stood over her head, and addressed a speech to her:
"Are you asleep, Penelope, sorrowing in your own heart?
No, the gods who live without care do not allow you   805
To mourn or to grieve, since your son is still set
To return. For he is in no way sinful before the gods."
And then the prudent Penelope answered her,
Slumbering very sweetly within the gates of dreams:
"My kinswoman, why have you come here? Never before   810
Did you visit, since the halls you dwell in are far, far away.
Do you bid me to desist from sorrow and from pains,
The many that beset me in my mind and in my heart?
Beforehand I lost a noble, lion-hearted husband,
A noble man whose glory is wide through Greece and middle
  Argos.   815

Who excelled in all the virtues among the Danaans,
And now my dear son has gone off in a hollow ship,
A foolish child who has no good knowledge of toils or of councils,
And I am more grieved about him than about the other.
I tremble for him and fear lest he suffer something   820
In the land of those he has gone to, or on the ocean,
For there are many hostile men who contrive against him,
Wanting to kill him before he reaches his fatherland."
The shadowy image answered and addressed her:
"Take courage; do not fear excessively in your mind.   825
Such is she who goes as his guide, she whom other men
Have prayed to stand by them, and she has the power,
Pallas Athene. She takes pity on your lamenting
And has sent me forth now to say these things to you."
Then the prudent Penelope spoke forth to her: 830
"If indeed you are a god, and have heard the voice of a god,
Come tell me also about that sorrowful man,
Whether he still lives somehow and sees the light of the sun,
Or has already died and is in the halls of Hades."
The shadowy image answered her and addressed her: 835
"About that man I shall not tell you in full detail
Whether he is dead or alive. It is bad to utter windy things."
When it had said this, it slipped through the bolt of the doorpost
Into the blasts of the wind. The daughter of Icarios
Rose up out of sleep. And her own heart was gladdened,   840
So clear had the dream rushed upon her in the gloom of the night.
The suitors had boarded and were sailing on the watery ways,
Devising in their minds sheer murder for Telemachos.
There is a rocky island in the middle of the sea,
Halfway between Ithaca and rugged Samos,   845
Asteris, not large. Its harbors have coves for ships,
On both sides. There the Achaians lay waiting in ambush.

V

Dawn, out of her bed, from beside the noble Tithonos, [1]
Rose up to bring light to immortals and to mortals.
The gods took their seats in assembly. And in their midst
Was high-thundering Zeus, who has the greatest might.
Athene spoke to them, reminding them of the many cares   5
Of Odysseus. His being in the nymph's home concerned her.
"Father Zeus, and you other blessed; ever-living gods,
Let no scepter-bearing king be deliberately
Kind and mild any longer, or keep his mind on the right,

1. The mortal husband of Dawn, granted immortality but not perpetual youth.

But may he be perpetually harsh and act unjustly;   10
Since there is no one who remembers the godly Odysseus
Of the people he ruled; and he was mild as a father.
He is staying on an island suffering strong pains
In the halls of the nymph Calypso, who by compulsion
Is holding him back, and he cannot reach his fatherland,   15
For he has no ships there with oars and no companions
Who might convey him over the broad back of the sea.
And now they are striving to kill his beloved son
As he comes homeward. He went off to hear of his father,
To divine Pylos, and also to godly Lacedemon."   20
And cloud-gathering Zeus addressed her in answer:
"My child, what sort of word has got past the bar of your teeth?
Why did you not think out this idea by yourself,
That Odysseus might indeed take vengeance on them when he came?
Guide Telemachos yourself, skillfully; you can do it,   25
So that he may arrive unscathed at his fatherland,
And so the suitors may go in their ship back where they came from."
He said that, and addressed in turn his dear son Hermes:
"Hermes—for in other matters you are my messenger—
Tell the nymph of the fair braids my unerring plan,   30
A return for stout-hearted Odysseus, how he may go back
Without an escort of gods or one of mortal men.
Yes, and he, on a strongly-bound raft, suffering troubles,
Will arrive at rich-loamed Scheria on the twentieth day,
To the land of the Phaeacians, who are close kin to the gods,   35
And they will honor him most heartily as a god.
They will send him in a ship to his dear fatherland
When they have given him bronze and gold and sufficient clothing,
Much more than Odysseus would ever have taken from Troy
If he had come safe and sound and got his share of the booty.   40
And so it is his lot to see his dear ones and arrive
At his high-roofed home and his own fatherland."
So he said, and the runner, slayer of Argos, did not disobey.
At once, then, he bound beneath his feet the lovely sandals,
The ambrosial golden ones that carry him over water   45
Or the limitless land, swift as the blasts of the wind.
And he took the wand with which he entrances the eyes
Of those men he wishes, and wakes up others who are sleeping.
The strong god, slayer of Argos, flew on with that in his hands.
He passed Pieria, and fell from the air on the ocean,   50
Then he hastened upon the wave as a sea gull does
That over the terrible gulfs of the barren sea
Dips its rapid wings, while catching fish, in the brine.
Like one of these, Hermes bore himself over many waves.
But when he arrived at the island that was far away,   55
He stepped from the violetlike ocean onto the dry land,

And went on till he came to the great cave wherein the nymph
Of the fair braids was dwelling. He came upon her within.
On the hearth a big fire was burning, and the smell from afar
Of cedar and easy-split citron was exhaled through the island   60
As it blazed. She within, singing in a lovely voice,
Moved to and fro at the loom and wove with a gold shuttle.
Wood was growing in abundance around the cave,
Alder and black poplar and fine-scented cypress,
Where the birds with their long wings went to sleep,   65
Horned owls and hawks and, with their long tongues,
Salt water crows, who are busy with things of the sea.
And right on the spot round the hollow cave had been drawn
A trained vine in bloom that was blossoming with clusters.
Four springs one after another flowed with white water   70
All close together; one turned one way, one another.
All around soft meadows of violet and wild parsley
Were blooming. And even an immortal who might come there
Would wonder to look and be delighted in his mind.
As he stood there, the Runner, the slayer of Argos, wondered,   75
But when he had wondered in his heart at it all,
He went right away into the broad cave. As she faced him,
Calypso, the divine goddess, did not fail to know him by sight,
For the gods never fail to know one another,
The immortals, not even one who lives in a far-off home.   80
And he did not come upon the great-hearted Odysseus within;
The man was weeping, seated on the beach where he had been before,
Shattering his heart with tears and laments and groans.
He was looking out on the barren sea, shedding tears.
But Calypso, the divine goddess, questioned Hermes,   85
When she had seated him upon a bright, glistening chair.
"Hermes of the golden wand, my respected friend,
Why have you come to me? You have not come often before.
Say what you have in mind. My spirit bids me to do it
If I am able to do it and if it can be done;   90
But follow me, so I may entertain you as a guest."
When she had said this, the goddess set a table alongside
Full of ambrosia, and she mixed up ruddy nectar.
Then the Runner, the slayer of Argos, ate and drank.
When he had dined and satisfied his heart with food,   95
He spoke out and addressed her in answer with a speech:
"You, a goddess, ask me, a god, why I come. And I
Will tell you the story unerringly, since you ask me.
Zeus ordered me to come here against my own will.
Who would willingly cross so much indescribable   100
Salt water? There is no city of mortals nearby
Who offer sacrifices and choice hecatombs to the gods.
But in no way is it possible for another god

To slip by or frustrate the purpose of aegis-bearing Zeus.
He says you have with you the wretchedest man of all   105
Those men who were fighting around the city of Priam
For nine years; and in the tenth year sacked the city
And went home. But on the return they sinned against Athene,
Who roused up against them an ill wind and great waves.
Then all the others, his noble companions, perished.   110
But the wind and the water carried and brought him here.
Zeus now orders you to send him off as fast as you can.
For it is not right he should waste here far from his dear ones.
No, his fate is still to see his dear ones and come
To his high-roofed home and his own fatherland."   115
So he said, and Calypso, the divine goddess, went cold;
And she spoke out to him and uttered wingèd words:
"You are cruel, you gods, jealous above all others,
Who begrudge it to goddesses when they sleep with men
Openly, if one wants to make a man her dear husband.   120
So when the rosy-fingered Dawn chose Orion,
You gods, who live at ease, begrudged him to her
Till the chaste golden-throned Artemis in Ortygia
Came upon him and slew him with her soothing shafts.
And so when fair-braided Demeter yielded in her heart   125
To Iasion,[2] and lay with him in love and in bed
In a thrice-plowed fallow, it did not take Zeus long
To find out; he slew him, hurling a dazzling thunderbolt.
So now you gods begrudge a mortal man's being with me.
I myself saved him as he was bestriding his keel   130
All alone, when Zeus with a dazzling thunderbolt
Crushed his swift ship, and sank it in the middle of the wine-faced sea.
Then all the others, his noble companions, perished.
But the wind and the water carried and brought him here.
I have loved him and nourished him and I have declared to him   135
I would make him immortal and ageless all his days.
But in no way is it possible for another god
To slip by or frustrate the purpose of aegis-bearing Zeus.
Let him go, if that god commands him and drives him
Out on the barren ocean. I myself will send him nowhere,   140
For I have no ships here with oars, and no companions
Who might convey him over the broad back of the sea.
But I shall advise him graciously, and shall conceal nothing,
So that he may arrive unscathed at his fatherland."
And then the Runner, the slayer of Argos, spoke to her: 145
"Send him off this way now, and respect the wrath of Zeus,
So that afterward he will not be enraged and hold it against you."

2. Probably an early cult figure, an agricultural god who may have been united with Demeter,
the grain goddess, in a primitive rite on a plowed field (as suggested in these lines).

When he had said this, the strong slayer of Argos departed,
And the queenly nymph went to great-hearted Odysseus,
Since she had indeed given ear to the message of Zeus.   150
She found him seated on the shore. His eyes never
Were dry of tears, but his sweet life was flowing away
As he mourned for a return, since the nymph no longer pleased him.
But he slept the nights with her by necessity
In the hollow cave, an unwilling man with a willing woman.   155
During the days, sitting up on the rocks and on the beaches,
Shattering his heart with tears and laments and groans,
He kept looking over the barren ocean, shedding tears.
The divine goddess stood close to him and addressed him:
"Ill-fated man, do not mourn here longer beside me, do not let   160
Your life waste away, for I shall now graciously send you off.
But come, cut long pieces of wood and fit them with a bronze ax
For a wide raft. And fashion half-decks upon it
High up, so that it may bear you over the murky sea.
And in it I shall put food and water and ruddy wine   165
That are satisfying and will check your hunger.
I shall dress you in clothes and send a breeze behind you,
So that you may arrive unscathed at your fatherland,
If the gods are willing, who possess broad heaven,
Who are more powerful than I at planning and achieving."   170
So she said, and godly Odysseus, who had borne much, went cold,
And he spoke out to her and uttered wingèd words:
"You devise this, goddess, for some other reason, not to get me there,
And you bid me to traverse in a raft the great gulf of the sea,
Terrible and disastrous, which not even balanced ships,   175
In their swift course, may cross, exulting in the breeze of Zeus.
I would not for my part board the raft against your will
Unless you will put up with swearing me a great oath, goddess,
That you will not plot some other bad trouble against me."
So he said, and the divine goddess Calypso smiled,   180
She caressed him with one hand, and spoke out to him directly:
"Ah, you are a real rogue, skilled in tricks that are not futile,
To have conceived and uttered a speech of this sort.
May the earth and broad heaven above witness this oath,
And the flowing water of Styx,[3] which is the greatest   185
And most dreadful oath there is for the blessed gods:
I will not plot any other bad trouble against you,
But I am thinking and considering the very things
I would plan for myself should an equal need come upon me.
Yes, and this is my fitting intention. The heart   190
In my breast is not of iron, but a pitying one."
When she had said this, the divine goddess led the way

---

3. River of the Underworld by which the gods swore oaths.

Nimbly. And he went along in the footsteps of the god.
The god and the man arrived at the hollow cave
And he sat down there on the chair out of which Hermes   195
Had risen up. The nymph set out every sort of dish
To eat and drink, of the kind that mortal men eat.
She herself sat down facing the godly Odysseus,
And handmaids placed ambrosia before her and nectar.
They stretched forth their hands to the food that was spread out
    ready,   200
And when they had taken their pleasure of eating and drinking
Calypso, the divine goddess, began a speech to him:
"Zeus-born son of Laertes, much-contriving Odysseus,
Do you really want to go home to your dear fatherland
Right at once, now? Well, even so, luck be with you!   205
If you knew in your mind how many sorrows it is
Your fate to fulfill before reaching your fatherland,
Then you would stay right here with me and keep this home
And you would be immortal, even though you would desire
To see your wife, whom you long for always every day.   210
I declare I am not a bit inferior to that woman
In form or in shape, since it is not at all seemly
For mortals to contend with immortals in looks and in form."
Odysseus of many devices addressed her in answer:
"Lady goddess, be not angry at me this way. I myself know   215
All this, that beside you the prudent Penelope
Seen face to face is less striking in form and size.
For she is a mortal and you are immortal and ageless.
Yet even so I am wishing and longing all my days
To go home and to see the day of my return.   220
And if one of the gods wrecks me on the wine-faced sea,
I shall bear it in my breast, with a long-grieving heart.
For I have suffered much already and endured much,
On the waves and in war; and let this be added to those."
So he said, and the sun went down, and darkness came on.   225
The two of them went into a nook of the hollow cave
And took pleasure of love, abiding with one another.
And when the early-born, rosy-fingered dawn appeared,
Then Odysseus at once put on his cloak and his tunic,
And the nymph herself put on a great shining mantle   230
Finely made and pleasing, and a lovely gold sash
Around her waist, and a veil upon her head above.
Then she took thought about sending great-hearted Odysseus away;
She gave him a great ax fitted to the palms,
A bronze one, sharpened at both ends; upon it there was   235
A beautiful olive wood handle, well fitted in place.
Then she gave him a well-polished adz and led the way
To the verge of the island where tall trees were growing,

Alder and poplar, and fir that was tall to the heavens,
Dry for a long time, well seasoned, that would float lightly for him.   240
And when she had shown him where the tall trees were growing,
Calypso, the divine goddess, went back to her home.
But he cut beams, and the work went quickly for him.
He felled twenty in all and hewed them with the bronze ax,
Planed them skillfully, and set a straight line upon them.   245
Meanwhile, the divine goddess Calypso brought along augers,
And he then bored them all and fitted them to one another.
Then he made it fast with pegs and with fastenings;
And just the way a man who is a well-skilled craftsman
Rounds off the hull of a broad ship for carrying freight,   250
The same measure did Odysseus make for his own broad raft.
He made it by setting deck planks on and fitting them
To the close-set ribs. And he finished it off with long gunwales.
Then he made a mast and a yardarm fitted to it.
He made a rudder, too, so that he might steer straight.   255
And he plaited it all through with wicker osiers
To be a bulwark against the wave. And he set much wood upon it.
Meanwhile the divine goddess brought along a piece of cloth
For making sails, and he fashioned those well too.
Upon it he tied braces and halyards and tackle and sheets,   260
And with levers he dragged it down to the godly sea.
It was the fourth day, and he had finished everything.
On the fifth day the divine Calypso sent him from the island
After she had clothed him in fragrant garments and bathed him.
The goddess put on board for him a skin of dark wine,   265
And another, a big one of water, and food, too,
In a bag. And she put many satisfying morsels in for him.
And then she sent on a soothing and gentle breeze.
Delighted at the breeze, godly Odysseus stretched his sails
And he steered on with the rudder skillfully   270
As he sat. Nor did sleep fall upon his eyelids
While he watched the Pleiades and late-setting Boötes,
And the Bear, which they call, too, by the name of the Wagon,
Which turns in one place and also points at Orion,
And alone has no share in the washings of Oceanos.   275
The divine goddess Calypso bade him to keep that star
Upon his left hand, as he fared over the sea.
He sailed seventeen days, faring on the sea,
And on the eighteenth there appeared the shadowy mountains
Of the land of the Phaeacians where it was nearest him.   280
It seemed to be just like a shield on the murky sea.
But the earth-shaking ruler, coming back from the Ethiopians,
Saw him from afar, from the mountains of the Solumoi;
He was seen sailing the ocean. The god in his heart
Got very angry. He shook his head and addressed his spirit: 285

"Well, the gods have now made quite a different plan
About Odysseus, while I was with the Ethiopians;
He is near the Phaeacians' land, where it is his lot
To escape the great bound of woe which has come upon him.
And I think I will still drive him into quite enough evil."   290
When he had said this, he gathered clouds and troubled the ocean,
Grasping the trident in his hands. He stirred up whole storms
Of all the winds and covered earth and ocean alike
With clouds. And night rose up from the heavens.
The East Wind fell down, and the South Wind and the hard-blowing
    West Wind,   295
And the North Wind that makes clear skies, rolling a great wave.
Then Odysseus' knees and his own heart went slack;
He was distressed, and he spoke to his own great-hearted spirit:
"Ah, wretched as I am, what will happen at last to me now?
I fear that the goddess spoke all unerringly   300
When she said I would have a fill of pains on the ocean
Before reaching my fatherland. It has all come to pass,
With such large clouds has Zeus crowned heaven about
And has disturbed the ocean; and storms are rushing on
Of all the winds. Now my sheer destruction is sure.   305
Thrice and four times blessed are the Danaans who perished
In broad Troy then, doing the pleasure of the sons of Atreus.
Would that I myself had died and had met my fate
On that day when numbers of the Trojans did hurl
Bronze-tipped spears at me over the dead son of Peleus: 310
I would have gotten my rites; the Achaians would have spread my glory.
But now I am fated to get caught in a miserable death."
A great wave dashed on him as he said that, pushing
Fearfully from its peak, and it spun the raft about.
He himself fell far from the raft. The rudder   315
Shot out of his hands. A fearful storm of intermingled
Winds came up and broke the mast in the middle.
The sail and the yardarm fell into the ocean.
It put him under the water a long time, and he could not
Quickly rise up from the rush of the great wave,   320
For the clothes weighed him down that divine Calypso gave him.
At last he did come up, and spat out of his mouth
The bitter brine that flowed plenteously off his head.
Nor did he forget the raft, though he was wearied.
But as he rushed into the waves he caught hold of it   325
And sat in the middle, shunning the end of death.
A great wave carried it here and there along the current.
As when the North Wind at harvest time carries thistles
Over the plain, but they hold close to one another,
So the winds carried it here and there over the sea.   330
Sometimes the South Wind threw it to the North Wind to carry

And sometimes the East Wind yielded it to the South Wind for pursuit.
But Cadmos' daughter saw him, Ino [4] of the lovely ankles,
Leucothea, who earlier had a mortal voice
And now in the sea swells gets honor from the gods.   335
She took pity on Odysseus as he was driven about in his pains.
Like a shearwater she rose in flight from the sea,
Perched on the raft, and addressed a speech to him:
"Ill-fated man, why is the earth-shaker Poseidon
So strikingly angry that he spawns you these many ills?   340
He will not wear you down, however he may desire it.
But do as follows: you do not seem foolish to me:
Take off these clothes and leave the raft for the winds
To carry; and swim with your hands, and strive for reaching
The Phaeacians' land, where it is your fate to escape.   345
And here now, stretch this veil out across your chest.
It is immortal. Have no fear of suffering or dying,
But when you have touched the mainland with your hands,
Untie it again and throw it into the wine-faced sea,
Far from the mainland, and turn yourself the other way."   350
When she had said this, the goddess gave him the veil.
She plunged back herself into the surging waves of the ocean
Like a shearwater. And a black wave covered her.
Godly Odysseus, who had borne much, meditated;
And he spoke, grieving, to his own great-hearted spirit: 355
"Alas for me, I fear one of the immortals is weaving
A snare for me, to have bade me get off the raft;
I shall not yet obey her, since I saw with my own eyes
The land far off where she said was a refuge for me.
But this I shall do, and it seems to be best to me.   360
So long as the beams are fitted to their fastenings,
I will stay here and hold out while I suffer pain.
But when a wave does shake my raft into pieces,
I shall swim, since there is nothing better to think of."
While he pondered these things in his mind and in his heart,   365
Earth-shaker Poseidon stirred up a great wave,
A terrible disastrous one, overarching; it dashed him.
As when a blustering wind shakes up a heap
Of dry husks, and scatters them in all directions,
So it scattered the raft's long beams. And Odysseus   370
Bestrode one spar as if he were riding a horse.
He took off the clothes that divine Calypso gave him,
And he stretched the veil right away beneath his chest.
He fell headlong down in the sea, spreading out his hands
And striving to swim. The lord who disturbs the earth saw him;   375

4. She leaped into the sea to save her son, and was made a goddess; her father, Cadmos, was
   founder of Thebes.

He shook his head and spoke out to his own spirit;
"So wander now on the ocean, after suffering many ills,
Until you may mingle with men who are nourished by Zeus.
Yet I do not expect you will find fault with your misfortune."
When he had said this, he whipped up his lovely-maned horses [5]   380
And arrived at Aigai, where his renowned dwelling is.
But Athene, daughter of Zeus, had another thought.
She bound up the courses of all the other winds
And bade them die down and all go to sleep.
She stirred up a rapid North Wind and broke waves before it   385
Till Zeus-born Odysseus could mingle with the Phaeacians,
Who love rowing, when he had warded off destinies and death.
Then for two nights and two days upon the thick wave
He wandered, and his heart many times saw destruction ahead.
But when fair-braided Dawn finished the third day,   390
Then at that point the wind died down and there was
A windless calm, and he sighted land nearby,
Scanning sharply, as he raised himself from the great wave.
As when it appears delightful to sons if their father
Lives, who lies in sickness and undergoes strong pains,   395
Long wasting away, and some dread god has assailed him,
Whom now the gods have delightfully freed from misfortune;
So delightful did land and forest appear to Odysseus.
Vigorously he swam to set foot on the mainland.
But when he was as far off as a shout may carry,   400
And had heard against the reefs the noise of the sea—
For the great wave was dashing upon the dry mainland.
Fearfully spraying, it covered all with saltwater foam;
For there were indeed no secure harbors for ships, or channels,
But headlands there were, jutting out, and reefs and cliffs;   405
Then Odysseus' knees and his own heart went slack,
And, grieving, he addressed his own great-hearted spirit:
"Alas, that Zeus has granted me to see unhoped-for land
And I have come to the end of cleaving this gulf,
And no way of escape appears from the hoary sea.   410
But offshore there are sharp reefs, and the wave about them
Moans as it surges, and the rock runs on up smooth.
The sea is deep close in, and there is no way
To stand with both feet and to escape misfortune,
For a great wave perhaps may snatch me as I am getting out   415
And hurl me on rough rock, and my trying would be in vain.
But if I can swim along still further and can find
Spits of land jutting out and harbors of the sea,
Then I fear that a storm will seize me back again
And bear me heavily groaning onto the fish-laden ocean,   420

5. Poseidon is fabled to ride a horse chariot through the waves.

Or some god may drive a great monster on me from the sea,
Of the kind that in numbers the renowned Amphitrite[6] feeds;
For I know how angry the renowned earth-shaker is at me."
He pondered these matters in his mind and in his heart
Till a great wave bore him up on the rugged shore.   425
There his skin would all have been stripped off and his bones broken
If the bright-eyed goddess Athene had not put a thought in his mind;
He caught at the rock with both hands as he dashed upon it,
And held onto it moaning, till a great wave came along.
And he avoided it so, but it struck him again with its backwash,   430
And dashed on him and threw him far into the ocean.
As when an octopus is pulled out of its den,
Numerous pebbles are caught in its suckers,
So against the rocks the skin from his stout hands
Was stripped off. And the great wave covered him over.   435
Then surely wretched Odysseus would have died in excess of fate
If bright-eyed Athene had not given him presence of mind.
Getting up out of the wave that spewed on the mainland,
He swam along it outside, looking for land, if he might happen
On spits of land jutting out and harbors of the sea.   440
But when as he swam on he came up to the mouth
Of a fair-flowing river, there the best place seemed to him to be.
It was bare of rocks, and it had a shelter from the wind.
He perceived it flowing and prayed to it in his heart.
"Hear me Lord,[7] whoever you are; I approach you with many   445
Prayers, fleeing the rebukes of Poseidon out of the ocean.
A man should be respected even by the immortal gods
When anyone approaches, wandering, as now I,
Who have suffered much, approach your knees and your flowing.
Have pity, Lord. I declare I am a suppliant to you."   450
So he said. At once the river stopped flowing and held the wave.
It made a calm in front of him and rescued him
At the issue of the river. Then he bent both his knees
And his stout hands. For his own heart was downed by salt water.
All his skin was swollen, and much seawater oozed   455
From his mouth and his nostrils. Breathless and voiceless
He lay with slight strength, and dread fatigue came upon him.
But when he caught his breath and the spirit in his mind
Awakened, he unbound the god's veil from himself
And he let it go into the sea-mingling river.   460
A great wave bore it back down the stream. Ino quickly
Took it in her own hands. He slipped out of the river,
Lay down on a rush bed, and kissed the grain-giving earth.
Then, grieving, he spoke to his own great-hearted spirit:

6. A goddess of the sea.
7. The rivers are gods in Homer.

"Ah, what do I suffer; what will happen to me at last?   465
If I watch through the troublesome night beside the river,
I fear that the evil frost and gentle dew together
May subdue my winded spirit in its slight strength,
For a cold breeze blows from the river just before dawn.
But if I ascend the slope to the shadowy wood   470
And go to sleep in the thick bushes; even if fatigue
And cold let go of me and sweet sleep does come upon me,
I fear I may become a spoil and a prey to wild beasts."
So, as he thought, this seemed to him to be better.
He went on into the wood; he found it near the water   475
In the clearing around, and came upon two bushes growing
From the same place, one of wild olive, one of tame.
Nor did the moist force of the blowing winds breathe through them,
And the shining sun never struck them with its beams,
Nor did rain ever reach through to them, so thick   480
Did they grow over and under each other. Odysseus
Went in beneath them. He quickly gathered a broad bed
With his own hands. Leaf-shedding had been quite plentiful,
Enough to give shelter for two or three men
In the winter season, even if it were especially hard.   485
Godly Odysseus, who had borne much, rejoiced to see it.
He lay down in the middle, heaping the fallen leaves over him,
As a man may cover a torch with black embers
At the edge of a field, where no neighors may be by,
And save the fire's seed, so he need not light it from elsewhere.   490
So Odysseus covered himself with leaves. Athene
Shed sleep on his eyes, so it might release him quite soon
From toilsome fatigue, and she covered his eyelids over.

VI

And so godly Odysseus, who had suffered much, slept there,
Worn out with fatigue and sleepiness. Yet Athene
Went on to the district and city of the Phaeacians,
Who at one time dwelt in Hyperia of the broad dancing-place,
Close to the Cyclopes, presumptuous men   5
Who used to injure them, and were more powerful in strength.
Then godlike Nausithoos[1] rose up and led them off
And settled them in Scheria, far from bread-earning men.
He set a wall around the city, built houses,
Made temples to the gods, and divided up the fields.   10
But already he had succumbed to his fate and gone to Hades.
Alcinoos ruled at the time, who had his thoughts from the gods.

---

1. The colonizer of Scheria; son of Poseidon.

The bright-eyed goddess Athene went to his home,
Devising a return for great-hearted Odysseus.
She entered the highly wrought bedroom where there was sleeping   15
A girl like the immortals in shape and in form,
Nausicaa,[2] daughter of great-hearted Alcinoos,
And beside her two servants, who had beauty from the Graces,
On either side of the door posts. The bright doors were shut.
She rushed to the girl's bed like a blast of the wind,   20
Stood over her head and spoke a word to her,
Likening herself to the daughter of Dymas, famous for ships,
Who was the girl's own age and delighted her heart.
In the likeness of her, bright-eyed Athene spoke out:
"Nausicaa, how did your mother have such a careless child?   25
Your shining garments are lying uncared for,
And your wedding is near, when you yourself will need
Lovely clothes to put on, and to give to the men who will lead you;
Through them does a noble reputation arise
Among men, and a father and queenly mother rejoice.   30
But let us go washing as soon as dawn appears.
I will follow as a helper so you may array yourself
Very soon, since you will not be a maiden much longer.
Already in the land the best men of all the Phaeacians,
Where your own family is too, are wooing you.   35
But come, and urge your illustrious father at dawn
To harness up mules and a wagon to carry you
And the girdles and the gowns and the shining mantles.
It is much better for you to go that way yourself
Than by foot. For the place of washing is far from the city."   40
When she had said this, the bright-eyed Athene went off
To Olympos, where they say the gods' seat is forever
Secure. It is not shaken with winds and is never wet
With rain, nor does snow fall there, but a cloudless clarity
Spreads far upon it, and a white gleam runs over it.   45
In that place the blessed gods enjoy themselves day after day.
The bright-eyed one went off there when she had prompted the girl.
And right away the fair-throned Dawn came and awakened
The fair-gowned Nausicaa. At once she wondered at her dream,
And went through the halls to announce it to her parents,   50
Her dear father and mother. She found them within.
Her mother sat at the hearth with her serving women
Turning sea purple yarn on the distaff. She came on her father
At the door as he was going with his illustrious kings
To council, where the noble Phaeacians were summoning him.   55
She stood very close to her dear father and addressed him:
"Papa dear, won't you have a chariot harnessed for me,

2. Daughter of Alcinoos and Arete.

A high one with good wheels, so I may take the splendid clothes
And wash them at the river, the ones I have lying dirty?
Yes, and it is fitting for you to be with the chief men   60
And hold council, wearing clothes on your skin that are clean.
And five dear sons have been born to you in the halls,
Two of them are married; three are blooming youths
Who are always wanting to wear freshly washed garments
To go dancing; all these cares are on my mind."   65
So she said. But she was ashamed to speak of lusty marriage
To her dear father. He saw all, and replied with a word:
"I do not begrudge you mules or anything else, child—
Come, the servants will harness you a chariot,
A high one, with good wheels, fitted with a hood."   70
When he had said this, he ordered the servants, and they obeyed.
Outside they set up a well-running wagon for mules.
They brought up mules and yoked them to the chariot.
The girl brought the shining garments from the bedroom
And she put them upon the well-polished chariot.   75
Her mother put all sorts of satisfying food
In a chest, and put in dainties, and poured wine
In a goatskin bag. Her daughter got up on the chariot.
And she gave her moist olive oil in a golden flask
So she and her serving women might anoint themselves.   80
And she took hold of the whip and the glistening reins
And whipped them to go; there was clatter of the two mules.
They drew it strenuously and bore the clothes and the girl,
Not alone: along with her other serving women went also.
And when they came to the beautiful stream of the river   85
Where there were plentiful places to wash and much
Lovely water flowed forth to clean what had got very dirty,
There they unharnessed the mules from the chariot
And shooed them out along the eddying river
To graze on honey-sweet field-grass. From the chariot   90
They took the clothes in their hands, carried them to the black water,
And trod them in pits, swiftly vying with one another.
But when they had washed and cleaned all the dirty clothes,
They spread them in a row on the strand where especially
The ocean washed pebbles up along the shore.   95
They bathed and anointed themselves richly with olive oil.
Then they had their dinner along the banks of the river
And waited for the clothes to dry in the gleam of the sun.
When she herself and the serving maids had enjoyed the food,
They played with a ball, having taken off their shawls.   100
White-armed Nausicaa began the sport with them.
Just as arrow-shooting Artemis goes along mountains,
Along the lofty Taygetos or Erimanthos,
Delighting in the boars and in the swift deer;

And field-haunting nymphs, daughters of aegis-bearing Zeus,　105
Play with her, and Leto[3] rejoices in her mind;
She holds her head and her forehead higher than all
And is easily outstanding, but all are lovely:
So the unwed girl stood out among her serving maids.
But when she was ready to go back home again　110
And had hitched up the mules and folded the lovely clothes,
Then the bright-eyed goddess Athene had another thought:
Odysseus would wake up, he would see the fair-faced girl,
And she would conduct him to the city of the Phaeacians.
Then the princess threw the ball to a serving maid;　115
She missed the maid and shot it into a deep eddy.
They gave a long shout. And godly Odysseus woke up.
He sat there and deliberated in his mind and heart:
"Ah me, to what land of mortals have I come this time?
Are these men proud and savage and without justice,　120
Or are they friendly to strangers and have a god-fearing mind?
How the sound of girls' voices has surrounded me,
Of nymphs, who hold the lofty peaks of mountains,
And the sources of rivers and the grassy meadows!
Or am I somewhere near men who are of clear speech?　125
Well, come, I shall make a trial myself and see."
When he had said this, godly Odysseus came from under the bushes.
From the thick wood he broke off in his stout hand a branch
With leaves, that it might cover the skin round a man's loins,
And he went like a mountain-bred lion, who, relying　130
On his strength, goes rained on and blown on, but his eyes within
Are burning, and he chases after oxen or sheep
Or after the wild deer, and his belly bids him
To try for sheep and to go into their thick fold—
So was Odysseus about to mingle with the fair-braided girls,　135
Although he was naked. For need had come upon him.
Frightfully begrimed with brine did he appear to them.
One ran one way, one another, on the jutting shores.
The daughter of Alcinoos alone stayed; Athene
Had put courage in her mind and taken fear from her limbs.　140
She stood in one place, facing him. Odysseus wondered
Whether he should grasp the fair-faced girl's knees in prayer
Or supplicate her where he was at a distance, with soothing words,
To show him the city and also to give him clothes.
As he thought it over, it seemed better to him　145
To supplicate her at a distance with soothing words,
Lest if he grasped her knees the girl's mind be angered.
Right at once he made a soothing and wily speech:

3. Mother of Apollo and Artemis.

"I am at your knees, mistress. Are you some god or a mortal?
If you are one of the gods who possess broad heaven,   150
I myself would liken you in look and size and form
Most closely to Artemis, the daughter of great Zeus.
And if you are one of the mortals who dwells on the land,
Three times blessed are your father and your queenly mother,
And three times blessed your kinsmen. Surely their hearts   155
Must be warmed forever with happiness on your account,
Beholding so fine a flower stepping into the dance.
Blessed above all others within his heart is the man
Who, laden down with bride-gifts, may lead you home.
Never before have I seen with my eyes such a person,   160
Either man or woman. Awe holds me as I look.
On Delos [4] once by the altar of Apollo I caught sight
Of such a one, the sapling of a date palm coming up.
For I went there also, and a large company followed me
On that journey whereon evil cares lay in store for me.   165
When I saw that, I was stunned in spirit a long time, lady,
Since such a shaft never rose from the ground; the same way
That I wonder at you, and am stunned, and dreadfully fear
To touch your knees. And a difficult sorrow comes on me.
Yesterday, on the twentieth day, I fled the wine-faced ocean.   170
All during that time did the waves and rapid storms carry me
From the island of Ogygia. Now a god has cast me here
To suffer some evil in this place. I do not think
It will stop, but the gods will perform many things yet first.
Do have pity, mistress. As one who has endured many evils   175
I come to you first. I know not one of the others,
Of the men who possess this city and this land.
Point the town out to me. Give me a rag to throw on,
If perhaps when you come here you had some wrapper for the clothing.
May the gods grant you as much as you wish in your mind.   180
May they provide you a husband and also a home,
And noble sympathy. Nothing is better or higher than that,
When a man and wife have a home who are sympathetic
In their thoughts. It gives many pains to their enemies
And joys to their friends. And they know it best themselves."   185
Then white-armed Nausicaa spoke to him in answer:
"Stranger, since you seem like a man neither evil nor senseless,
And Olympian Zeus himself controls prosperity for men,
For the noble and the evil, as he wishes for each,
So perhaps he gave you this, and still you have to bear it.   190
And now, since you have come to our city and our land,
You will not want for clothing, or for anything else

4. A small island sacred to Apollo.

That befits a long-suffering suppliant who encounters us.
I will show you the town and tell you the name of the people.
The Phaeacians possess this city and this land.   195
I am the daughter of great-hearted Alcinoos,
On whom the strength and might of the Phaeacians depend."
So she said, and she called out to her fair-braided servants,
"Come here to me, servants. Where do you flee when you see a man?
Surely you don't think him to be one of our enemies?   200
There is no man so vigorous and no mortal born
Who would come to the land of the Phaeacian men
Bringing hostility. For they are very dear to the gods.
And we dwell far away in the much-surging ocean,
The remotest of men. And no other mortal has congress with us.   205
Now this man, a wretched wanderer, has come here,
Whom we must look after, for all strangers and beggars
Are in the care of Zeus, and a gift, even small, is friendly.
Come, maidens, give food and drink to the stranger.
Wash him in the river where there is shelter against the wind."   210
So she said, and they stood and urged one another,
And they took Odysseus down to a shelter, as Nausicaa,
Daughter of great-hearted Alcinoos, had ordered.
They put down a mantle and a tunic and clothes for him,
And gave him liquid olive oil in a golden flask,   215
And bade him to wash himself in the streams of the river.
Then godly Odysseus addressed the servant maids:
"Maidens, stand off where you are, so that I myself
May wash the brine from my shoulders and with olive oil
May anoint me all over. Oil has been long from my skin;   220
I do not want to wash in front of you. I am ashamed
To come out naked in the midst of fair-braided girls."
So he said, and they went apart and spoke to the girl.
But Odysseus in the river washed off of his skin
The brine that he had on his back and his broad shoulders,   225
And he wiped from his head the scurf of barren salt water.
When he had fully washed and had rubbed himself richly,
He put on the clothes that the unwed girl had provided,
And Athene, she who was born from Zeus, made him
Bigger to look at and stouter, and on his head   230
Made his hair flow in curls, like the hyacinth flower.
As when some man overlays gold upon silver,
A skilled man whom Hephaistos[5] and Pallas Athene have taught
Art of all kinds, and he turns out graceful handiwork;
So she poured grace upon his head and his shoulders.   235
Then he sat off apart, when he had gone along the beach of the sea,

5. Son of Zeus and husband of Aphrodite; god of fire and the forge.

Gleaming with beauty and graces. And the girl marveled.
And then she spoke out to her fair-braided serving maids:
"Listen to me, white-armed servants, in what I say.
Not against the will of all the gods who hold Olympos   240
Does this man mix with the Phaeacians, who are equal to gods.
Beforehand he appeared to me to be unseemly,
And now he seems like the gods who possess broad heaven.
Would that a man of this sort might be called my husband
And be dwelling here, and it might please him to stay   245
In this place. But, maidens, give the stranger food and drink."
So she said, and they listened closely and obeyed her.
They set out before Odysseus food and drink.
Godly Odysseus, who had suffered much, ate and drank
Greedily, for he had been a long time without eating.   250
But white-armed Nausicaa had another thought.
She folded up the clothes, put them on the lovely chariot,
Harnessed the stout-hooved mules, got in herself,
And urged Odysseus on, speaking out to him directly:
"Rise up now, stranger, to go to the city, so I may   255
Convey you to my skillful father's home, where I think
You may get to know all the noblest of the Phaeacians.
Well, this is what you should do—you do not seem to me to be foolish.
As long as we are passing the fields and the farms of men,
Come speedily along with the serving maids behind the mules   260
And the chariot. And I myself shall lead the way.
But when we walk into the city—about it there is a high
Tower wall, and there is a lovely harbor on either side of the city
And a narrow entrance, and bobbing ships from the voyage
Are pulled in there—it is a slip for one and all.   265
There is the assembly place, round a fine temple to Poseidon,
Fashioned from deep-bedded stones that have been quarried.
And there they take care of the tackle of the black ships,
Cables and sails, and they sharpen oars off to a point.
For the Phaeacians the bow and the quiver are of no concern,   270
But sails and the oars of ships and the balanced ships;
Delighting in these, they traverse the hoary sea.
I shun an unseemly repute among them, lest one
Rebuke me hereafter. For there are presumptuous men in the district,
And this is what some meaner one, if he met us, might say: 275
'Who is this great and handsome stranger that follows
Nausicaa? Where did she find him? He will be her husband.
She must have brought him off his own ship wandering
From distant men, since there are not any near at hand;
Or else some much-invoked god has come at her prayer,   280
Descending from the sky and will have her all her days.
Better so, if she went herself and found a husband

From elsewhere. For she despises these men in the district,
The Phaeacians, though many men who are noble woo her.'
So they will say. And these reproaches will come against me.   285
I myself would blame anyone else who should do such things,
Who against the will of her dear ones, a father and mother still alive,
Should mingle with men before coming to open marriage.
Stranger, understand quickly what I say, so you may
Very soon get an escort and a return from my father.   290
Near the road you will find a shining grove of Athene,
One of poplars; a spring flows in it, a meadow is about it.
There is my father's preserve and his fruitful vineyard,
The same distance from the city that a shout would carry.
Sit there a while and wait till the time that we   295
Come to the town and arrive at the house of my father.
But when you consider that we have arrived at the house,
Then go to the city of the Phaeacians and ask
For the house of my father, great-hearted Alcinoos.
It is easy to recognize; even a foolish child   300
Could lead you. There is none of the Phaeacians' houses
Made to resemble the home of Alcinoos,
Who is a hero. But when the house and courtyard enclose you,
Go very swiftly through the hall until you reach
My mother. She sits at the hearth in the fire's gleam,   305
And turns sea purple yarn on the distaff, a wonder to see,
Propped against a pillar. And serving maids sit behind her.
And there the chair of my father is propped up against hers,
Where, seated like an immortal, he drinks his wine.
Pass him by and throw your hands around the knees   310
Of my mother, so you may speedily rejoice and see
The day of your return, even if you are from very far away.
And if that woman thinks kindly of you in her heart,
Then there is hope for you of seeing your dear ones and reaching
Your well-established home and your own fatherland."   315
When she had said this, she lashed with her shiny whip
At the mules, and they quickly left the streams of the river.
They ran along well and nimbly bent their legs.
She managed the reins so that the servants and Odysseus
Might follow on foot. And she skillfully applied the lash.   320
The sun went down and they came to the famous grove
Sacred to Athene, and there godly Odysseus sat down.
Then at once he prayed to the daughter of great Zeus:
"Hear me, unwearied one, child of aegis-bearing Zeus,
Hear me now, since you did not hear me before   325
When I was smitten and the famous earth-shaker smote me.
Grant that I come to the Phaeacians as a pitied man and a friend."
So he said in prayer; and Pallas Athene heard him,
But she did not yet appear to him face to face. For she feared

Her father's brother. He was contending vehemently   330
With godlike Odysseus till the man reached his own land.

VII

And so godly Odysseus, who had suffered much, prayed there
While the strength of the two mules bore the girl toward the town.
And when she had arrived at her father's famous house
She halted them in the gateway, and her brothers were standing
About her like immortals; they unhitched the mules   5
From the chariot and carried the clothing on inside.
She herself went to her bedroom. An old woman of Apeire
Was kindling a fire for her, the chambermaid Eurymedousa,
Whom once the bobbing ships took away from Apeire,
And they chose her as a prize for Alcinoos because he ruled   10
All the Phaeacians. The people obeyed him like a god.
She waited on white-armed Nausicaa in the halls,
And kindled the fire for her, and set out her dinner within.
And then Odysseus got up to go to the city. Athene,
With kind thoughts for Odysseus, shed a thick mist about him,   15
Lest some great-hearted Phaeacian should confront him,
Taunt him with a speech, and ask him who he might be.
But when he was ready to enter the charming city,
Then the bright-eyed goddess Athene confronted him.
Likenening herself to a virginal young girl with a pitcher,   20
She stood in front of him, and godly Odysseus asked:
"My child, would you lead me to the home of Alcinoos,
The man who is the ruler over these people?
For I have come here as a long-suffering stranger
From afar, from a distant land; so I know no one   25
Of the men who possess this city and its fields."
Then the bright-eyed goddess Athene addressed him:
"Yes, father stranger, I will show you the home
You ask of, since it lies close to my blameless father's.
But come very silently and I shall lead the way.   30
Do not catch any man's eye or question anyone.
Those here do not easily endure strange men,
And they do not befriend or welcome one coming from elsewhere.
Putting their confidence in the swift and speedy ships,
They traverse the great gulf, since the earth-shaker gave it to them, 35
And their ships are as swift as any wing or thought."
When she had said this, Pallas Athene conducted him
Speedily; he went along in the footsteps of the goddess.
But the Phaeacians, famous for ships, did not perceive him
As he went through the town among them, for fair-braided Athene,   40
The dreadful goddess, did not allow it; she shed

A divine fog about him, with kind thoughts in her heart.
Odysseus wondered at the harbors and the balanced ships,
The meeting places of the heroes themselves, and the walls,
Long and lofty, fitted with stakes, a wonder to behold.   45
When they came to the illustrious house of the king,
The bright-eyed goddess Athene began to speak among them:
"Father stranger, this is the house that you requested me
To point out to you. You will find kings nourished by Zeus
Eating dinner there. Go in and do not be frightened   50
In your heart. A man who is bold in all his deeds
Thrives better, even when he comes from somewhere else.
You will first come upon the mistress in the halls.
Arete [1] is the name she is called, and her ancestors
Are the same ones who begot King Alcinoos.   55
First Nausithoos was born of earth-shaker Poseidon
And of Periboea, the best for her form, among women,
The youngest daughter of great-hearted Eurymedon,
Who ruled as king over the high-spirited Giants.
But he destroyed his reckless people, and was himself destroyed.   60
Then Poseidon lay with the girl and fathered a son,
Great-spirited Nausithoos, who ruled the Phaeacians.
Nausithoos begat Rhexenor and Alcinoos.
Apollo of the silver bow slew the first while still sonless
And a bridegroom in the hall: he left one sole daughter,   65
Arete. And her did Alcinoos make his wife.
He honored her as no other woman on earth is honored,
Of all women who now have a household under men.
So she was highly honored in heart, and she still is,
By her beloved children and by Alcinoos himself   70
And by the people who look on her as on a god
And welcome her with speeches as she goes through the town.
Nor is she herself at all lacking in any noble thought.
She dissolves disputes for those of whom she thinks well, even for men.
And if that woman has kind thoughts for you in her heart,   75
There is hope for you of seeing your dear ones and reaching
Your lofty-roofed house and your own fatherland."
When she had said this, bright-eyed Athene went away
Over the barren ocean, and left charming Scheria;
She arrived at Marathon, and at Athens with its broad streets,   80
And entered the stout house of Erechtheus. Meanwhile Odysseus
Went to the famous house of Alcinoos. His heart
Pondered much as he stood there before reaching the bronze threshold.
There was a gleam like that of the sun or of the moon
Beneath the high-roofed hall of great-hearted Alcinoos.   85
Bronze walls were run round it on every side to the corner

---

1. Queen of the Phaeacians; wife of Alcinoos and mother of Nausicaa.

From the threshold, and there was a frieze of dark blue about it.
Golden portals shut up the stout home within,
And silver door posts were set upon the bronze threshold,
And a silver lintel above, and a golden handle.   90
And on either side there were gold and silver dogs
That Hephaistos with his skillful faculties had formed
To watch over the house of great-hearted Alcinoos;
They were immortal, and ageless for all their days.
Inside, armchairs had been propped round the wall here and there   95
To the corner from the threshold in unbroken line. And cloths
Were strewn there, fine and well-woven, the work of women.
And there the leaders of the Phaeacians were seated
When they ate and drank. They possessed unfailing abundance.
And there were golden youths on well-built pedestals   100
That stood there holding in their hands flaming torches
Illuminating the nights for the diners through the halls.
And there were fifty serving maids through the hall, women
Who grind up in a mill grain of an apple hue,
And who do weaving on looms and turn the distaff   105
Seated, the way the leaves of the tall poplar turn;
And from the close-woven linen the moist oil drops off.
As the Phaeacians are knowing beyond all other men
To drive a swift ship in the ocean, so their women
Are skilled in weaving. Athene has endowed them highly   110
With skill in beautiful tasks and with noble minds.
Outside the courtyard is a great garden before the portals,
One of four measures. A fence runs round it on both sides.
And in that place tall blossoming trees are growing.
Pears, and pomegranates, apple trees with shining fruit,   115
And sweet fig trees and blossoming olive trees.
Of these the fruit never perishes and never leaves off
In winter or summertime, all the year round. But always
A blowing West Wind makes some grow and ripens others.
Pear matures upon pear, apple upon apple,   120
Grape cluster on grape cluster, and fig on fig,
And there is rooted a vineyard that bears much fruit,
One part of which, light-parched in a level place,
Dries in the sun, and others they harvest at vintage.
Still others they tread. First there are the unripe grapes   125
Shedding flowers, and others are darkening underneath.
Well-ordered vegetable beds in the last row there
Grow things of all kinds and shine green in unceasing abundance.
And in it are two springs: one through the whole garden
Is dispersed, and the other rises by the courtyard threshold   130
Before the lofty house, whence the townspeople draw water.
Such were the gods' glorious gifts to Alcinoos' house.
As he stood there, godly Odysseus, who had endured much, marveled.

And when he had marveled in his heart at everything,
He went speedily over the threshold into the hall.   135
He found the leaders and counselors of the Phaeacians pouring
Libations to the far-sighted god, the slayer of Argos.
They poured him the last cup whenever they remembered sleep.
But godly Odysseus, who had endured much, went through the hall,
Clad in the large mist that Athene had shed about him,   140
Until he reached Arete and King Alcinoos.
Odysseus threw his hands about the knees of Arete,
And then the divine mist poured away from him.
They grew silent through the hall when they saw the man
And wondered to behold him. Odysseus pleaded with her: 145
"Arete, daughter of Phrexenor, who was equal to a god,
I, who have suffered much, fall at your knees and your husband's
And all those dining here: may the gods grant them to live
With blessings; and may each one turn his possessions over
To his children in his halls, and any prize the people have given.   150
But call up an escort for me to reach my fatherland
Soon, as I have long suffered woes apart from my dear ones."
When he had said this, he sat down on the hearth in the ashes
By the fire. And they all became silent in stillness.
After a pause the old hero Echeneus spoke out,   155
A man who was oldest by birth of the Phaeacian men,
Who excelled in speaking and knew many ancient things.
In good will he spoke out to them and addressed them:
"Alcinoos, this does not seem to be very good,
To let a stranger sit on the ground by the hearth in the ashes.   160
Those here are holding back and waiting for your word.
Come now, have the stranger stand up, and sit him down
In a chair studded with silver; give your herald bidding
To mix up more wine so we may pour a libation
To bolt-hurling Zeus, who protects pious suppliants.   165
Let a housekeeper give the stranger dinner from what is within."
When Alcinoos in his sacred strength had heard this,
He took the hand of skillful, various-minded Odysseus,
Raised him from the hearth, and seated him on a shining chair.
He had his son stand up, the manly Laodamas,   170
Who sat nearest to him and whom he loved especially.
And a handmaid poured water from a pitcher she was carrying,
A lovely golden one, over into a silver basin,
For washing the hands; she set up a polished table alongside.
A respected servant served bread she was carrying,   175
Laying out many dishes, gracious with the provisions.
Godly Odysseus, who had suffered much, ate and drank,
Then Alcinoos in his might spoke out to the herald:
"Pontonoos, mix up a bowl and serve out the wine
To all through the hall so we may pour a libation   180

To bolt-hurling Zeus, who protects pious suppliants."
So he said, and Pontonoos mixed the mind-honeying wine
And distributed the first drops into the cups of all.
When they had poured and drunk as much as the spirit wished,
Alcinoos spoke out to them and addressed them: 185
"Hear me, leaders and counselors of the Phaeacians,
So I may say what the spirit in my breast bids me to.
Now that you have dined, go home and go to bed,
And at dawn when we have beckoned more of the elders,
Let us welcome the stranger in the halls and offer   190
Fine sacrifices to the gods; then let us take thought
For a convoy, so this stranger without pain or distress
Under our convoy may arrive at his fatherland,
And speedily rejoice, even if he is from very far away.
May he undergo no evil or suffering in mid-passage   195
Before coming upon his land; but then he will suffer
Whatever his fate and the grave Spinners[2] have spun for him
With his birth thread at the time when his mother bore him.
And if he has come down as one of the immortals from heaven,
Then it is something else that the gods are contriving in this.   200
Always before have the gods appeared to us plainly
Whenever we have offered the famous hecatombs,
And they dined along with us seated where we are;
Even if some wayfarer meets them when he is alone
They conceal it not at all, since we are close to them,   205
As are the Cyclopes and the wild tribes of the Giants."
Odysseus of many devices spoke to him in answer:
"Alcinoos, concern yourself with something else. As for me,
I am not like the immortals who possess broad heaven,
Either in body or form, but am like mortal men.   210
Whomever you may know among men who have borne
The most woe, I would equal myself to them in griefs,
And indeed I myself might tell of still further ills
Of the great number I have endured at the will of the gods.
But permit me to eat dinner, burdened as I am with cares,   215
For there is nothing at all more shameless than the hateful belly
Which bids a man to remember it by compulsion,
Even one who is much worn down and has sorrow in his mind,
As I now have sorrow in my mind. It perpetually
Bids me to eat and drink and makes me forget   220
All I have undergone, and commands me to fill up.
But arouse yourselves at the appearance of dawn
And bring me, wretched as I am, to my fatherland.
Indeed I have suffered much. May my life abandon me

2. Often identified with the three Fates—Clotho, Lachesis, and Atropos—who have in charge
the "thread" of a man's life.

Once I have seen my goods, my servants, and my great high house." 225
So he said, and they all assented and gave orders
To guide the stranger off, since he had spoken properly.
When they had poured and drunk as much as the spirit wished,
They went on off to sleep, each one to his own house.
But godly Odysseus was left behind in the hall.   230
And with him Arete and Alcinoos, godly in form,
Were sitting. Servants put the dishes of the meal in order.
Arete of the white arms began to speak among them.
She recognized the mantle, tunic, and clothes when she saw them,
Lovely ones, that she made herself with her serving women.   235
And she spoke out to him and uttered wingèd words:
"Stranger, I should first like to ask you a question myself:
Who are you? What men are you from? Who gave you these clothes?
Did you not say you got here wandering on the ocean?"
Odysseus of many wiles addressed her in answer: 240
"It is difficult, queen, to speak out in full detail
About troubles, when the celestial gods have given me so many.
But this I will tell you that you ask and question me of.
A certain island, Ogygia, lies far off in the sea,
Where the daughter of Atlas dwells, wily Calypso   245
Of the fair braids, a dread goddess. With her no one
Has intercourse, either of gods or of mortal men.
But some god led me to her hearth, wretched as I am,
All alone, when Zeus with a dazzling thunderbolt
Crushed my swift ship, and sank it in the middle of the wine-faced
     sea.   250
Then all the others, my noble companions, perished,
But I alone took in my hands the keel of the bobbing ship
And was carried nine days. And on the tenth black night
The gods brought me near the island Ogygia, where Calypso
Of the fair braids dwells, dread goddess. She took me in   255
And kindly befriended me, nourished me, and said
She would make me immortal and ageless all my days,
But she did not persuade the heart within my breast.
I waited there steadily seven years. And always I moistened
With my tears the ambrosial clothes that Calypso gave me.   260
But when the eighth year in its cycle came around,
Then she urged me and bid me to go away,
Because of a message from Zeus, or else her mind had changed:
She sent me on a strongly-bound raft, gave me much
Bread and sweet wine, clothed me in ambrosial garments,   265
And then she sent on a soothing and gentle breeze.
Seventeen days, faring upon the ocean, I sailed,
And on the eighteenth there appeared the shadowy mountains
Of your land. And my own heart was delighted in me,
Ill-fated as I was. And yet I was to have still more to do   270

With the great distress earth-shaker Poseidon raised against me.
He stirred up winds and hindered me from the voyage
And he raised an indescribable sea so the wave did not
Allow me, heavily groaning, to be borne on the raft.
Then a tempest scattered it, and I myself   275
Cleft this gulf as I swam on through, until the wind
And water carried me and brought me near your land.
Then the wave as I tried to get out would have driven me on land,
Throwing me against great rocks and a joyless place,
But I withdrew and swam the other way until I came   280
To the river, where the best place seemed to me to be,
Smooth of rocks, and where there was shelter from the wind.
I fell out struggling for life, and ambrosial night
Came on. Back away from the Zeus-fallen river
I stepped out and went to sleep in the bushes and heaped   285
Leaves about me. A god poured down boundless sleep.
There in the leaves, wearied in my own heart I slept
All the night long, and till dawn and the middle day,
And the sun declined, and then sweet sleep let me free.
Then I noticed your daughter's serving maids playing   290
On the strand. She herself was among them, like the goddesses.
I begged her, and she did not fail of such noble intent,
As one would not expect a young person he encountered
To demonstrate. For the very young are always thoughtless.
She gave me sufficient food and sparkling wine   295
And had me washed in the river and gave me these clothes.
This is the truth I have told you, though I am distressed."
Then Alcinoos spoke out and answered him:
"Stranger, of this at least my daughter did not properly
Take thought, in that she did not lead you to our house,   300
With her serving women. For you besought her first."
Odysseus of many wiles addressed him in answer:
"Do not, hero, reproach your blameless daughter for my sake.
She bade me to follow along with the serving women,
But I did not want to, as I was afraid and ashamed   305
Lest somehow your heart be offended at seeing me.
Very suspicious are we tribes of men on the earth."
Then Alcinoos spoke out and answered him:
"Stranger, my own heart in my breast is not such
As to rage easily. Everything proper is best.   310
Would that by father Zeus, Athene, and Apollo,
Being such as you are, and of a mind like my own,
You might have my daughter and be called my son-in-law,
And stay here. I would give you a home and property
If you willingly stayed. No Phaeacian would hold you back   315
Against your will. May that not be pleasing to father Zeus.
I appoint your convoy for a day, so you may know it well,

That is, tomorrow. Then you may lie overcome in sleep.
And they will row on a calm sea until you arrive
At fatherland, home, and whatever is dear to you,   320
Even if it is very much farther off than Euboea,
Which those of our people say to be farthest off
Who saw it when they brought blond Rhadamanthys
To go and see Tityos, the son of Gaia.
They went there and accomplished it without difficulty   325
On the same day, and completed the voyage back home.
You too shall know in your own mind how much the best
Our ships and our youths are who toss up the sea with their oars."
So he said, and godly Odysseus, who had borne much, rejoiced.
He said a prayer then, and spoke right out directly: 330
"Father Zeus, may Alcinoos bring to pass all
That he has said; may his fame be unquenchable
On the grain-giving earth; may I reach my fatherland."
So they addressed such speeches to one another.
And white-armed Arete bade her serving women   335
To put bedsteads down in the colonnade, and to throw on
Lovely purple rugs, and to spread blankets above them
And to put down woolen mantles on top of all that.
They went from the hall with torches in their hands.
And when they had spread down the thick bed busily,   340
They stood beside Odysseus and urged him with speeches:
"Come rise up, stranger, the bed is made for you."
So they said. It seemed welcome to him to lie down.
So godly Odysseus, who had endured much, slept there
In the jointed bed under the resounding portico.   345
Alcinoos slept in a nook of the lofty house;
His lady wife beside him prepared a bed and a resting place.

VIII

And when the early-born, rosy-fingered dawn appeared,
Alcinoos rose up out of bed in his sacred strength.
And Odysseus, the Zeus-born sacker of cities, rose up.
Alcinoos in his sacred strength led them to the assembly place
Of the Phaeacians, which was made for them beside the ships.   5
When they got there they sat down on the polished stones
Close together. Pallas Athene went on through the town,
Likening herself to a herald of skillful Alcinoos,
Devising a return for the great-hearted Odysseus.
And she said something to each man, standing beside him: 10
"Come hither, leaders and counselors of the Phaeacians;
Go to the assembly, so you may learn about the stranger
Who has recently come to skillful Alcinoos' house,

Having wandered the ocean, like the immortals in form."
When she had said this, she aroused the strength and the heart of
    each.   15
Speedily the assembly and its seats filled up with men
As they gathered. And many marveled to behold
The skillful son of Laertes. On his behalf Athene
Shed a divine grace over his head and his shoulders,
And she made him loftier and stouter to behold,   20
So that he might become cherished by all the Phaeacians,
And fearful, and respected, and might carry out many
Of the contests in which the Phaeacians tested Odysseus.
But when they were gathered and had come together,
Alcinoos spoke out to them and addressed them: 25
"Hear me, leaders and counselors of the Phaeacians,
That I may say what the spirit in my breast bids me to.
This stranger—I know not who he is—reached my house,
From the men of the dawn or of the evening,[1] wandering.
He urges a convoy and beseeches that it be assured,   30
And let us ourselves, as before, speed on a convoy,
For never did anyone else who came to my halls
Wait here and long lament for the sake of a convoy.
Come then, let us drag a black ship on its first voyage
To the godly sea, and let two and fifty young men   35
Be picked through the land of those who are far the best up to now.
And when you have fastened the oars well in the oarlocks,
All of you get out of it. Then come to my house and partake
Of a hasty meal. I shall make good provision for all.
This I command the young men. And as for you others,   40
You scepter-bearing kings, come to my lovely home,
So that we may entertain the stranger in the halls.
Let no one refuse. Summon the godlike singer
Demodocos.[2] The gods have granted him to please beyond others
With whatever kind of song his spirit urges him to sing."   45
When he had said this, he led on, and the scepter-bearing kings
Followed along. A herald brought in the godly singer.
The two and fifty young men were selected
And went, as he bade them, to the strand of the barren sea.
But when they got down to the ship and to the sea   50
They dragged the black ship into a depth of salt water
And set up a mast and sails upon the black ship.
Then they fitted the oars into the straps made of leather
All in order and then stretched out the white sails.
Then they anchored her high in flowing water, and then   55
They entered the great house of skillful Alcinoos.

1. That is, of east and west.
2. The blind bard of the Phaeacians.

The porticoes and courts and rooms were filled with the men
As they gathered. There were many, both old and young.
And among them Alcinoos sacrificed twelve sheep,
Eight shining-tusked sows and two shamble-footed heifers.   60
They flayed them and prepared them and made a delightful banquet.
Then a herald came near, leading the trusty singer
Whom the Muse loved dearly and gave both good and ill.
She blinded him in the eyes but gave him a sweet song.
Pontonoos set out a silver-studded armchair for him   65
In the midst of the banqueters, propping it on a tall pillar.
The herald hung his clear-toned lyre from a peg
There above his head and showed him how to take it
In his hands. He put a basket and lovely table alongside
And a cup of wine for when the spirit should bid him to drink.   70
They stretched forth their hands to the food that was spread out ready,
And when they had taken their fill of food and drink
The Muse bade the singer to sing famous deeds of men
From the lay whose fame had by then reached broad heaven,
The quarrel of Odysseus and Achilles, son of Peleus,   75
How once they wrangled at an abundant feast of the gods
With terrible words, but the lord of men, Agamemnon,
Was pleased in his mind that the best Achaians were wrangling.
For so Phoebos Apollo had told him by an oracle
In divine Pytho[3] where he had gone over the stone threshold   80
Seeking an oracle. For then the beginning of trouble was rolling
On the Trojans and Danaans through the plans of great Zeus.
This did the far-famed singer sing. But Odysseus
Took his great purple mantle in his stout hands,
Pulled it over his head, and concealed his handsome face;   85
He was ashamed before the Phaeacians for shedding tears under his eye-
    brows.
And whenever the godlike singer paused in his singing,
He lifted the mantle over his head and wiped the tears,
Took a two-handled cup, and poured libation to the gods.
But whenever he started again and the Phaeacian nobles   90
Urged him on to sing, since they were pleased with his stories,
Odysseus again covered his head over and moaned.
Now, as he shed tears, he escaped the notice of all the others.
But Alcinoos alone took note of him and perceived him,
While seated near him, and heard him as he deeply groaned.   95
At once he addressed the Phaeacians, who are fond of rowing:
"Listen, leaders and counselors of the Phaeacians,
Now we have sated our spirits with a well-shared feast
And the lyre, the consort of an abundant banquet;
Now let us go out and make trial in all sorts   100

3. The oracle of Apollo at Delphi.

Of contests, so that the stranger may tell his friends
When he returns home how much we surpass others
In boxing and wrestling, in jumping and also in running."
When he had said this, he led, and they followed along.
The herald hung the clear-toned lyre up on its peg,   105
Took Demodocos' hand, and led him from the hall.
He led him along the same path that the other
Phaeacian nobles took to gaze upon the contests.
They went to the assembly, and a large crowd followed along,
Myriads. And many young noblemen stood up.   110
Acroneus rose up, Ocyalos and Elatreus,[4]
Nauteus and Prymneus and Anchialos and Eretmeus,
Ponteus and Proireus, Thoon and Anabesineus,
And Amphialos, son of Polyneus, son of Tecton,
And Euryalos too, the equal of man-slaying Ares,[5]   115
Naubolos' son, who was best in form and in body
Of all the Phaeacians, after excellent Laodamas.
And the three sons of excellent Alcinoos stood up,
Laodamas and Halios and godlike Clytoneus.
And first they made a trial at a running race.   120
And their running was strained from the turning post on, and all
Flew speedily together, raising dust on the plain.
The best of them at running was excellent Clytoneus.
By as much as the range of two mules in a fallow field
He ran ahead and reached the crowd, and they were left behind.   125
Then they made a trial of painful wrestling.
And in that Euryalos surpassed all the best.
In jumping, Amphialos was most outstanding of all.
And Elatreus was by far the best of all with the weight.
In boxing it was Laodamas, Alcinoos' good son.   130
And when they had all delighted their minds with the contests,
Laodamas, the son of Alcinoos, addressed them:
"Come, friends, let us ask the stranger if there is any contest
That he knows and is skilled in. He is not bad in form,
In his thighs and in his calves and both hands above them,   135
And his neck is stout, and his strength great, nor does he lack
His prime; but he is broken down by many evils.
I think for my part there is nothing worse than the sea
To shatter a man, even though he be very strong."
Then Euryalos answered him and addressed him: 140
"Laodamas, indeed you have said this properly.
Go challenge him now yourself and say what you said."
And when the good son of Alcinoos heard that,
He went and stood in the middle and addressed Odysseus:

4. These are all names formed on marine terms: Ship-top, Swift-sea, Rower, and so on.
5. Son of Zeus; the god of war.

"Father stranger, come here too, and try the contests,   145
If you have ever learned any—you seem to know about contests.
Yes, there is no greater glory for a man as long as he lives
Than what he achieves by his feet or by his hands.
Come now, have a try; scatter the cares from your heart.
Your journey is not far off, and already the ship   150
Is drawn down for you, and the companions are ready."
Odysseus of many wiles addressed him in answer:
"Laodamas, why do you taunt me in calling me to this?
Troubles are more in my mind than contests are.
As a man who has endured much before and suffered much,   155
I am now sitting in your assembly, seeking
A return, beseeching your king and all the people."
Euryalos answered and rebuked him to his face:
"No, stranger, I would not say you were like a man skilled
In contests of the many sorts that exist among men,   160
But are like one who is used to a ship with many oarlocks,
A leader of sailors who are also merchantmen
With his mind on a load, an overseer of cargoes
And of gain got by greed. You do not resemble an athlete."
Odysseus of many wiles answered, glowering at him: 165
"You have spoken not well, stranger; you are like a fool,
And so the gods do not grant delightful gifts
To all men, in shape or in mind or in speaking.
One man is rather insignificant in look;
But a god crowns his speech with grace, and men behold him   170
And are pleased. And he speaks without faltering,
With soothing deference, and he stands out in the gathering.
And they look upon him like a god as he goes through the city.
And another man will be like the immortals in look,
But there is no gracefulness to crown his speech;   175
And so you are striking in look, and not even a god
Could make you otherwise. But you are of futile mind.
You have aroused the spirit inside my own breast,
As you spoke unbecomingly. I am not unskilled in contests,
As you have said, but I think I was among the first   180
So long as I relied on my vigor and my hands.
But now I am held in pains and misfortune. I have suffered much,
Passing through the wars of men and the troublesome waves.
But even though I have felt many ills, I will try the contests,
For your speech gnaws my heart. What you say urges me on."   185
So he said. Springing up with cloak and all, he took a weight,
A broad one, not by a trifle larger and stouter
Than the ones the Phaeacians threw among themselves.
He whirled it around and shot it from his stout hand.
The stone whirred, and the Phaeacians, who have long oars,   190
Men famous for ships, crouched down upon the ground

At the stone's rush. It flew past the marks of all,
Speeding quickly from his hand. Athene set the distance,
Likened in body to a man; she spoke out directly:
"Even a blind man, stranger, could make out this mark   195
By feeling it, since it is not mingled at all with the throng,
But is first by far. Take heart, at least for this contest.
None of the Phaeacians will reach or exceed this mark."
So she said, and godly Odysseus, who had borne much, rejoiced,
Pleased to behold a helpful companion in the game.   200
Then he addressed the Phaeacians in a lighter spirit:
"Reach this mark now, young men. I believe someone else
May soon hereafter hurl an equal distance, or greater.
Of all the rest, come and try what your heart and spirit
Bid you to try—since you have got me highly angered—   205
In boxing or wrestling or running—I say nothing against it—
Any of the Phaeacians except Laodamas himself,
For he is my host. And who could contend with a friend?
That man would be indeed a senseless and worthless person
Who should bring competition in contests upon his host   210
In a foreign land. He would cut all short for himself.
But of the others I do not refuse or slight a one.
I should like to know them and try them out face to face.
I am not bad in any of the many kinds of games among men.
I know well how to handle a well-polished bow;   215
I would be first, shooting in a crowd, to hit my man
Among the enemy, even if many companions
Were standing close to me and shooting at people.
Philoctetes alone surpassed me with the bow
In the land of the Trojans when we Achaians were shooting.   220
But I say I am far more outstanding than any
Of the mortals who now eat bread upon the earth.
I should not want to contend with men of earlier times,
Either with Heracles or Oichalian Eurytos,[6]
Who contended even with immortals in archery.   225
For that, great Eurytos died quickly; old age did not
Come on him in his halls, for Apollo got angry
And killed him because he challenged him to shoot.
I shoot farther with a spear than anyone else with an arrow.
In running alone do I fear that some Phaeacians   230
Might surpass me. I was very disgracefully overcome
In the numerous waves, since there was no lasting
Provision on my ship. Therefore my knees are slackened."
So he said, and the others were silent in stillness.
Alcinoos alone addressed him in answer: 235

6. A legendary archer, slain by Apollo in a contest; Heracles was the most famous of Greek
legendary heroes, noted especially for his performance of twelve nigh-impossible labors.

"Stranger, you have said this to us not ungracefully,
But you would like to show the excellence that belongs to you,
Angry that this man has stood up to you in the games
And blamed you, as no man would reproach your excellence
Who knew in his mind how to speak sensibly.   240
But come now, give heed to my word, so you may tell it
To another hero when you are in your halls
Dining beside your wife and your own children,
And remember our excellence in such deeds as Zeus
Bestows on us steadily since the time of our fathers.   245
We are not blameless in boxing or in wrestling,
But we do run nimbly in races and are best in ships.
Feasting is dear to us always, the lyre, and dances,
Changes of clothes and hot baths, and the bed.
But you who are the best dancers of the Phaeacians, come   250
And frolic, so the stranger may report to his friends,
When he returns home, how much we surpass others
In seamanship and running and dancing and in song.
Let someone go at once and bring for Demodocos
The clear-toned lyre which is lying somewhere in our halls."   255
So said the godlike Alcinoos, and a herald rose
To bring the hollow lyre from the home of the king.
The umpires appointed for the district stood up,
Nine in all, who attended well to details of the games.
They smoothed a dancing place and broadened a lovely ring;   260
The herald came near, carrying the clear-toned lyre
For Demodocos. He went to the middle then. Young men
In their first youth stood round him, skillful in the dancing,
And beat the godly floor with their feet. Odysseus
Gazed at their flashing feet and wondered in his heart.   265
Then playing the lyre, the man struck up a beautiful song
Of the love of Ares and fine-crowned Aphrodite,[7]
How they first had lain together in the home of Hephaistos,
Secretly. He gave her many gifts and shamed the marriage bed
Of her lord Hephaistos. A messenger came at once to him,   270
Helios,[8] who perceived them lying together in love.
Hephaistos, when he heard the spirit-hurting story,
Went into his bronze works plotting evil in his mind
And put a great anvil on the anvil block, and hammered bonds
Unbreakable and indissoluble, that would hold them there fast. 275
And when in his anger he had fashioned a snare for Ares,
He went into his bedroom where his own precious bedstead stood
He spread bonds all around the bedposts in a circle
And he spread many out from the rafters up above,

7. Daughter of Zeus; the goddess of love.
8. The sun god.

Subtle as spider web, that no one would ever see,   280
Even of the blessed gods, so well for deceit did he make them.
And when he had put the whole snare around in the bedding,
He made as if to go to Lemnos, the well-built citadel
That is the dearest by far to him of all the lands.
Nor did Ares of the golden rein keep a blind watch   285
When he saw the famed craftsman Hephaistos going off.
He went to the home of the highly renowned Hephaistos,
Craving for the love of Cytherea [9] with the fine crown.
She had recently come from her father, the mighty son
Of Cronos, and had sat down. And he went into the house,   290
Took her hand, and spoke right out directly to her:
"Come, darling, let us enjoy the couch and the bed ourselves.
Hephaistos is no longer in the district. Already
He is gone off to Lemnos among the wild-speaking Sintians."
So he said. It struck her as delightful to go to bed.   295
The two of them went to sleep in the bed clothes. And the bonds
Fashioned by various-minded Hephaistos were spread about them,
So they could not move or raise their limbs at all.
And then they knew it when they could no longer escape.
The far-famed double cripple came up close to them;   300
He had turned back again before reaching the land of Lemnos,
As the Sun had kept watch for him and told him the story.
He went into his home, troubled in his own heart.
He stood in the doorway, and a wild anger seized him.   .
Terribly he shouted and cried out to the gods: 305
"Father Zeus and you other blessed ever-living gods,
Come see deeds to laugh at that are not to be endured,
How Aphrodite, the daughter of Zeus, dishonors me always,
Lame as I am, and loves the destructive Ares
Because he is handsome and nimble of foot, while I   310
Was born feeble. I know no other cause of that
Than my two parents; would that they had never had me!
But you shall see how the two of them have gone into my bed
And are making love there. It grieves me to see it.
But I suppose they would not like to be that way a moment more,   315
Though they love one another much. Nor will they soon
Want to sleep, but the snare and the bond will constrain them
To the point where our father gives me back all the bride gifts
I paid to him for the sake of the bitch-faced maiden,
Since his daughter is lovely, but does not restrain her heart."   320
So he said, and the gods gathered in the bronze-floored hall.
Poseidon came, who holds up the earth, and Hermes,
The helper; the far-darting Lord Apollo came.
Of the feminine goddesses each stayed home out of shame.

9. Another name for Aphrodite; from Cythera, an island where a shrine to her was located.

The gods, givers of good things, stood in the doorways.   325
Unquenchable laughter rose up among the blessed gods
To see the devices of many-minded Hephaistos.
This is what one of them would say as he looked to his neighbor:
"Evil deeds do not win. The slow man finds out the swift,
As even now Hephaistos, who is slow and a cripple,   330
With his devices caught Ares, swiftest of the gods
Who possess Olympos. He owes the adulterer's fine."
This was the sort of thing they said to one another.
The son of Zeus, Lord Apollo, addressed Hermes:
"Hermes, son of Zeus, runner and giver of good things,   335
How would you like to be constrained in strong bonds
And sleep in a bed alongside golden Aphrodite?"
Then the Runner, the slayer of Argos, answered him:
"Far-darting Lord Apollo, I wish that might come about!
Three times as many endless bonds might hold me fast   340
And all you gods and all the goddesses might look at me,
But I should be sleeping alongside golden Aphrodite."
So he said, and laughter arose among the immortal gods.
Laughter did not touch Poseidon; he kept imploring
Hephaistos, renowned for his works, to release Ares;   345
And he spoke out to him and uttered wingèd words:
"Release him, and I will promise for him what you ask:
He will pay all that is proper among the immortal gods."
Then the widely renowned double cripple addressed him:
"Poseidon, holder of earth, do not ask me to do this.   350
The pledges of the worthless are worthless to be kept as pledged.
How should I constrain you before the immortal gods
If Ares should go off, avoiding the debt with the bond?"
Then the earth-shaker Poseidon spoke to him:
"Hephaistos, even if Ares gets out from under the debt   355
And goes off in flight, I shall pay it to you myself."
Then the widely renowned double cripple answered him:
"It is not seemly or right to deny your request."
When he had said this, Hephaistos in his force undid the bond.
When the two were released from the bond, strong as it was,   360
They rushed off right at once. He went away to Thrace,
And Aphrodite of the lovely smile got to Cyprus,
To Paphos, where she had a sacred grove and fragrant altar.
There the Graces washed her and anointed her with immortal
Olive oil, such as is poured on the ever-living gods;   365
And they put her in charming clothes, a wonder to see.
This was what the widely renowned singer sang. Odysseus
Was delighted in mind as he listened, and so were the others,
The Phaeacians, who have long oars, men famous for ships.
Alcinoos bade Halios and Laodamas   370
To dance alone, since no one would contend with them.

And so when they had taken a lovely ball in their hands,
A purple one that skillful Polybos had made them,
One of them threw it up to the shadowy clouds,
Doubling himself backward. The other rose high off the earth   375
And easily caught it before touching ground with his feet.
And when they had tried their skill at throwing the ball straight up,
The two of them danced upon the much-nourishing earth,
Rapidly changing position. The other youths beat time,
Standing in a ring; and a great sound of stamping arose.   380
Then godly Odysseus spoke to Alcinoos:
"Lordly Alcinoos, illustrious among all peoples,
You did claim that these dancers were most excellent,
And it has been shown true. Awe holds me as I look."
So he said, and Alcinoos in his sacred strength rejoiced.   385
Right away he spoke to the Phaeacians, who are fond of rowing:
"Listen, leaders and counselors of the Phaeacians,
The stranger seems to me to be very prudent.
Come now, let us give him a guest's gift, as is seemly.
There are in the district twelve distinguished kings,   390
Rulers who hold sway, and I am myself the thirteenth.
Each of you give him a well-washed mantle and tunic
And bring him a talent of precious gold. Let us at once
Bring all these together so the stranger may hold them
In his hands and go to dinner rejoicing in his heart.   395
But let Euryalos propitiate him in person
With words and a gift, since he spoke an improper speech."
So he said, and they all assented and gave the order,
And each one sent off a herald to bring the gifts.
Then Euryalos answered him and addressed him: 400
"Lordly Alcinoos, illustrious among all peoples,
I will propitiate the stranger just as you bid me,
And I shall give him this sword all of bronze, whose hilt
Is silver, and a sheath of newly sawn ivory
Circles it about. It is worth a great deal for him."   405
When he had said this, he placed a silver-studded sword in his hands;
And he spoke out to him and uttered wingèd words.
"Greetings, father stranger: if any terrible word
Has come out, let storms at once snatch it and carry it off.
May the gods grant that you see your wife and reach your father-
      land,   410
Since you have long suffered troubles far from your dear ones."
Odysseus of many devices addressed him in answer:
"Kind greetings to you, friend. May the gods grant blessings to you,
And may there come to you henceforth no longing for this sword
Which you have given me, appeasing me with words."   415
So he said, and put the silver-studded sword over his shoulders.
The sun went down, and the glorious gifts for him were brought.

Noble heralds carried them to the home of Alcinoos.
The sons of excellent Alcinoos, when they had taken them,
Lay the beautiful gifts before their respected mother.   420
Alcinoos led the way for them in his sacred strength.
When they had entered, they sat down on the high armchairs,
And Alcinoos in his might spoke to Arete:
"My wife, bring a fine coffer here, the best there is,
And put a well-washed mantle and tunic in it yourself,   425
Warm the bronze cauldron round the fire for him and heat up water
So that when he has bathed, he may look at all the gifts,
Well arrayed, that the excellent Phaeacians have brought,
And enjoy dinner and listen to the strain of a song.
I shall present him myself with this beautiful cup   430
Of gold, so that he may remember me all his days
When he pours in his halls to Zeus and the other gods."
So he said, and Arete gave the word to her handmaids
To set a big cauldron over the fire as quickly as they could.
They stood a cauldron for bath water on a blazing fire,   435
Poured in water, took wood, and kindled it beneath.
The fire circled the cauldron's belly, and the water heated.
Meanwhile Arete brought the lovely coffer for the stranger
From the chamber, and put in it the splendid gifts,
The clothing and the gold that the Phaeacians had given.   440
She herself put in a mantle and a lovely tunic.
And she spoke out to him and uttered wingèd words:
"Look to the lid yourself, and quickly fasten the knot,
Lest someone rob you of it on your trip, at a time when
You are resting in sweet sleep as you go in the black ship."   445
When godly Odysseus, who had endured much, heard that,
He at once fitted the lid on and quickly fastened the knot,
The subtle one that queenly Circe[1] had once taught his mind.
At the same moment a housekeeper called him to go
To the bathtub to be washed. He saw the hot water   450
With gladdened heart, as he had received no such treatment
Since he had left the home of Calypso with the lovely locks.
The care he got all that while was as it would be for a god.
When the handmaids had washed him and anointed him with oil,
They threw a lovely mantle around him and a tunic,   455
And out of the bathtub he stepped, and he went amid the men
As they were drinking wine. Nausicaa, who had her beauty
From the gods, stood by the column of the stoutly made roof
And wondered at Odysseus as she took him in with her eyes.
She spoke out to him, and she uttered wingèd words: 460
"Farewell, stranger; and even when you are in your fatherland
May you remember me as the one you first owe the ransom of life."

1. An enchantress living in Aiaia; daughter of the sun.

Odysseus of many devices addressed her in answer:
"Nausicaa, daughter of great-hearted Alcinoos,
May Zeus, the thunderer, husband of Hera, now grant   465
That I go homeward and see the day of my return,
And that there, too, I may pray to you as to a god
Forever all my days. For you saved my life, maiden."
He spoke, and sat on an armchair beside King Alcinoos.
They were already passing out portions and mixing wine,   470
And a herald came near, leading the trusty singer
Demodocos, honored by the people. And he set him
In the midst of the diners, propped against a tall pillar.
Then Odysseus of many devices addressed the herald
When he had cut some off the back—but more was left on it—   475
Of a shining-tusked boar; and swelling fat was about it.
"Herald, take this portion over to Demodocos
So he may eat, and I will embrace him, grieved as I am,
For among all the men on the earth singers are sharers
In honor and respect, because the Muse has taught them   480
Poems, and she cherishes the tribe of singers."
So he said; the herald brought the meat and put it in the hands
Of the hero Demodocos. He took it and rejoiced in his heart.
They stretched forth their hands to the food that was spread out ready,
And when they had taken their fill of food and drink,   485
Odysseus of many devices addressed Demodocos:
"Demodocos, I give you praise above all mortal men,
Either a Muse, a child of Zeus, has taught you, or Apollo.
Very becomingly did you sing the fate of the Achaians,
All they acted and endured, all the Achaians suffered,   490
As though you had somehow been there yourself or heard one who was.
Come, change your subject and sing of the stratagem
Of the wooden horse Epeios made with Athene's help,
The trap that godly Odysseus once led to the citadel,
When he had filled it up with the men who sacked Ilion.   495
If you do tell me these matters in proper form,
Then at once I will proclaim among all men
How a propitious god endowed a divine singer."
So he said. Inspired by the god, he began and showed forth his song,
Starting from where some of the Argives on the well-timbered ships 500
Boarded and sailed off, when they had set fire to the huts,
And the others who were round the famous Odysseus already
Were seated in the assembly of the Trojans concealed within the horse,
For the Trojans themselves dragged it to their citadel.
So it stood, and they made many ill-considered speeches   505
Seated about it. Three plans there were that pleased them:
To strike through the hollow wood with the pitiless sword,
To drag it to the peak and throw it off the rocks,
Or to let the great ornament be a charm for the gods.

Even then it was destined to end in just this way.   510
Fate was, they should be destroyed, since the city enfolded
The great wooden horse, where all the best men of the Argives
Were seated, bringing death and destiny on the Trojans.
He sang how the sons of the Achaians sacked the city,
When they had poured from the horse and abandoned the hollow
    ambush;   515
He sang how one man ravaged one place and one another,
In the lofty city, and Odysseus like Ares went
To the halls of Deiphobos, with godlike Menelaos.
There he said the man dared fight his most dreadful battle
And won, that time too, through great-hearted Athene.   520
This did the renowned singer sing. And Odysseus
Melted, and a tear from under his eyelids wet his cheeks,
As a woman weeps embracing her beloved husband
Who has fallen before his own city and his own people,
Warding off from city and children the pitiless day,   525
And she sees the man dying and breathing heavily,
And falls down upon him and piercingly shrieks. The enemy
From behind strike her back and her shoulders with spears
And lead her off in bonds to have trouble and woe,
And her cheeks are wasted for her most wretched grief;   530
Just so did Odysseus shed a piteous tear under his eyebrows.
Then, as he shed tears, he escaped the notice of all the others
But Alcinoos alone took note of him and perceived him
While seated near him, and heard him as he deeply groaned.
At once he addressed the Phaeacians, who are fond of rowing.   535
"Hear me, leaders and counselors of the Phaeacians,
And let Demodocos hold off now from the sharp-toned lyre.
For he does not give everyone pleasure when he sings this.
Since we have been dining and the divine singer rose,
The stranger has not at all ceased his woeful lament,   540
For grief has very much compassed his mind about.
But come, let him hold off, so we may all alike take pleasure,
Hosts and the guest, since it is much more pleasant so.
All this has been done for the sake of our respected guest,
The convoy and the precious gifts we give him in friendship.   545
A guest and a suppliant is held equal to a brother
By a man who has even a little grasp with his wits.
And so in your cunning notions do not yourself now conceal
What I ask you about. It is better for you to speak.
Tell the name which your mother and father called you there,   550
And the others who dwell in that city and about it,
For no one among men is wholly without a name,
Neither a worthless man nor a noble, from the time he was born;
Parents when they have children bestow them on everyone.
Tell me your land and your district and your city,   555

So that the ships that are steered by thought may convey you there,
For there exist no pilots among the Phaeacians,
And there are no rudders at all such as other ships have,
But the ships themselves know the intentions and minds of men.
They know the cities and fertile fields of all men   560
And very swiftly, shrouded in mist and a cloud,
They traverse the gulf of the sea. There is no fear
At all for them that they suffer harm or be lost.
But once I heard my father Nausithoos
Say this: he asserted that Poseidon bore a grudge   565
Against us, because our convoys are safe for all men.
He said a well-made ship of the Phaeacian men
Coming back sometime from an escort on the murky ocean
Would be dashed, and a great mountain would hide our city round.
So the old man said. And the god will either fulfill it   570
Or it will be unfulfilled, as his spirit desires.
Come tell me this, and speak out truthfully.
Where have you wandered, and what places have you reached
Among men: tell of them and their well-inhabited cities,
Those that were difficult and savage and without justice,   575
And those who were friendly to strangers and have a godfearing mind.
Tell also why you lament and grieve in your heart
When you hear the fate of Ilion and the Danaan Argives.
That did the gods fashion, and they spun the thread of death
For men, so that it would be a song for those to come.   580
Did some kinsman of yours perish before Ilion,
A nobleman, son-in-law, or father-in-law,
Those who are dearest, next to one's blood and family,
Or perhaps some companion of sympathetic mind,
A noble one? Since not inferior to a brother   585
Is a companion who possesses a prudent mind."

IX

Odysseus of many devices addressed him in answer:
"Lordly Alcinoos, exalted among all your people,
Indeed it is pleasant to listen to such a singer
As this one is, who resembles the gods in his voice.
I would say myself there is no more delightful result   5
Than when happiness so prevails through a whole district
And when diners seated in order through the halls
Listen to a singer, and the tables nearby are full
Of bread and meat, and the wine pourer draws wine off
From the bowl, carries it around, and pours it in the cups.   10
To my mind this seems to be the loveliest thing.
But your heart turns toward me to ask of my woeful cares,

So that I may grieve still further as I lament.
What then shall I tell you first, what tell last,
Since the heavenly gods bestowed many cares upon me?   15
Well now, I shall tell you my name first, so that you too
May know it, and then, when I have escaped the pitiless day
I may be your guest friend, though I dwell far off in my halls.
I am Odysseus, son of Laertes, who for my wiles
Am of note among all men, and my fame reaches heaven.   20
I dwell in sunny Ithaca. A mountain is on it,
Neritos, with trembling leaves, conspicuous.
Many islands lie about it quite close to one another,
Dulichion and Samê and wooded Zakynthos;
She herself sits low-lying, farthest out to sea   25
Toward dusk, and they are apart toward dawn and the sun,
Rugged but good for bringing up young men. And I
Can look upon nothing sweeter than a man's own land.
Well, Calypso, the divine goddess, kept me in one place,
In a hollow cave, desiring that I be her husband.   30
The same way in her halls would the wily Aiaian
Circe have held me back, desiring that I be her husband.
But they never persuaded the heart within my breast.
So nothing grows sweeter than a man's own fatherland
And his parents, even if he dwell in a fertile home   35
Far off in a foreign land apart from his parents.
But come, let me tell you of the much-troubled return
That Zeus put upon me when I went away from Troy.
The wind bearing me from Ilion brought me near the Cicones,[1]
To Ismaros. There I sacked the city and killed its men.   40
From the city we took the wives and many possessions
And divided them so none for my sake would lack an equal share.
Then I gave the order for us to take rapid flight,
But the men, great fools as they were, did not obey;
They had drunk much wine there and slain many sheep   45
Along the strand, many shamble-footed, crumple-horned cattle.
Meanwhile the Cicones went and called other Cicones
Who were their neighbors, at once more numerous and brave,
Who dwelt on the mainland, skilled in fighting with men,
From horses, and, when necessary, on foot.   50
As thick as leaves and flowers grow in their season,
They came, in early morning. Then an evil fate of Zeus was with us
In our dread destinies, so we might suffer many pains.
They took their stand and fought a battle by the swift ships,
And they threw bronze-tipped spears at one another.   55
So long as it was morning and the sacred day increased,
We stayed and warded them off, many as there were.

1. Thracian allies of the Trojans raided by Odysseus.

But when the sun declined to the time of ox-loosing,
Then the Cicones turned back the Achaians and routed them.
Six from each ship of my well-greaved companions   60
Perished. The rest of us escaped death and destiny.
Then we sailed on further, grieving in our hearts,
Glad to escape death, having lost our dear companions.
My bobbing ships, however, did not proceed further
Till someone had thrice called for each of our wretched companions 65
Who had died on the plain, slaughtered by the Cicones.
Cloud-gathering Zeus raised a North Wind against the ships
In an immense storm, and covered land and ocean alike
Over with clouds. And night rose up out of heaven.
The ships were borne headlong, and the force of the wind   70
Ripped the sails up into three fragments and four.
We lowered them onto the ships, fearing destruction,
And rowed the ships forward to the mainland hastily.
There for two whole nights and two days continually
We lay, eating our hearts with pain and fatigue alike.   75
But when fair-braided Dawn had brought the third day to the full,
We set up our masts and hoisted the white sails
And took our seats. The wind and the pilots steered them,
And I would have arrived unscathed at my fatherland,
But as I rounded Malea a rushing wave   80
And a North Wind pushed me off and drove me past Cythera.
Thence for nine days I was borne by destructive winds
On the fish-laden ocean. But the tenth day I set foot
On the land of the Lotus-eaters, who eat a flowery food.
Then we went onto the dry land and drew off water,   85
And at once my companions took dinner beside the swift ships.
But when we had partaken of food and of drink,
I sent my companions forth to go and find out
Who these were of the men who eat bread on the earth.
I picked out two men and sent on a third as a herald.   90
They went off at once and mingled with the Lotus-eaters.
And the Lotus-eaters did not plot destruction
For our companions, but gave them the lotus to taste of.
Whoever among them ate the honey-sweet fruit of the lotus
Wished no longer to bring word back again or return,   95
But wanted to remain there with the Lotus-eaters
To devour the lotus and forget about a return.
Back weeping to the ships I led them, by compulsion,
Dragged them and bound them in the hollow ships under the benches,
And I called all my other trusty companions   100
To hasten and to get on board the rapid ships,
Lest someone perchance eat the lotus and forget a return.
They got in at once and took their seats at the oarlocks.
Seated in order, they beat the hoary sea with their oars.

Then we sailed further on, grieving in our hearts,   105
To the land of the Cyclopes, an overweening
And lawless people, who, trusting in the immortal gods,
Do not sow plants with their hands and do not plow
But everything grows for them unplowed and unsown,
Wheat and barley and vines that produce a wine grape   110
Of large clusters, and a rain from Zeus makes them grow.
They have neither assemblies for holding council nor laws,
But they inhabit the crests of the lofty mountains,
In hollow caves, and each one dispenses the laws
For his children and his wives and is not concerned for the others.   115
A fertile island stretches there from the harbor
Of the land of the Cyclopes, not near and not far away,
A wooded one. And on it numberless wild goats flourish,
For there is no beaten path of men to keep them away.
Nor do hunters land upon it, who in the woods   120
Undergo pains and chase them over the mountain peaks.
And it is not held, either, with flocks or with plowed lands,
But it lies unsown and unplowed day after day
Bereft of men, and it nourishes bleating goats.
There are no vermilion-prowed ships for the Cyclopes,   125
As there are no shipwrights among them who might work
At good-timbered ships to accomplish it all for them
So they may visit cities among men, as frequently
Men do cross the sea in ships toward one another;
And these would have worked to make the island well settled for
      them,   130
As it is not really bad, and would bear all things in season.
There are meadows in it along the banks of the hoary sea,
Soft, moist ones. And there would be fine, unwithering vines
And smooth plowing, and they would mow the deep-standing
Grain in season, as it is very rich beneath the surface.   135
There a sheltered harbor is, where there is no need of a rope
Or of throwing out anchor stones or fastening cables,
But they could put in and stay a time till the hearts
Of the sailors urged them on and breezes should be blowing.
And shining water flows down from the head of the harbor,   140
A spring under a cave. Poplars grow about it.
There we sailed on in. And some god guided us
Through the murky night. There was not light enough to see.
Dark air was deep about the ships, nor did the moon
Show forth from heaven, but it was contained in clouds.   145
There no one looked upon the island with his eyes,
And we did not behold the great waves rolling up
On the mainland, before we beached our well-timbered ships.
When the ships had been beached, we took down all the sails,
And got out ourselves beside the surf of the sea.   150

We fell asleep there and awaited the godly dawn.
And when the early-born, rosy-fingered dawn appeared,
We wondered at the island and traveled all around it.
The nymphs, daughters of aegis-bearing Zeus, roused up
Mountain goats, so that my companions might have dinner.   155
At once we took curved bows and long-socketed goat spears
Out of the ships. We divided into three groups
And went shooting. At once the god gave us satisfying game.
The men of twelve ships followed along with me. Nine goats
Fell the lot of each ship. They picked ten out just for me.   160
So then for the whole day till the setting of the sun
We sat dining on the endless meat and sweet wine,
For the red wine from the ships had not yet been exhausted,
But was still there. Each group had drawn off much in jars
When we sacked the holy citadel of the Cicones.   165
We were looking over to the land of the Cyclopes nearby,
To their smoke, to their sound and that of their sheep and goats.
But when the sun went down and the darkness came on,
We lay down to sleep beside the surf of the sea.
And when the early-born, rosy-fingered dawn appeared,   170
I called an assembly and spoke out to them all:
'Stay here now, the rest of you, my trusty companions;
But I will go myself with my ship and companions
To inquire about these men, whoever they may be,
Whether they are proud and savage and without justice   175
Or are friendly to strangers, and have a god-fearing mind.'
When I had said this, I went on the ship and called my companions
To go on board themselves and to undo the stern cables.
At once they got on and took their seats at the oarlocks;
Seated in order, they beat the hoary sea with their oars.   180
And when we had arrived at the place that was nearby,
There we saw a cave on the verge, close to the sea
High up, overhung with laurel. Many animals
Usually slept there, sheep and goats; a courtyard
Was built high around it out of deep-bedded stones   185
And tall pines and oak trees with lofty foliage.
There a monstrous man usually slept, who alone
And aloof tended the animals. He did not consort
With the others, but stayed apart and had a lawless mind.
And indeed he was formed as a monstrous wonder. He looked   190
Not like a grain-eating man but like a wooded crest
On lofty mountains that appears singled out from the others.
And then I ordered the rest of my trusty companions
To remain there beside the ship and to guard the ship.
But I myself picked out twelve of my best companions   195
To go on. Now I had a goatskin flask of black wine,
A sweet wine that Maron gave me, Euanthes' son—

The priest of Apollo, who watches over Ismaros—
Because we protected him along with his wife and son,
And reverenced him. He dwelt in the tree-filled grove   200
Of Phoebos Apollo. And he gave me glorious gifts:
He gave me seven talents of well-fashioned gold,
And he gave me a mixing bowl all of silver, and then
Into two-handled jars, twelve in all, he drew off wine
Sweet and unmixed, a godly drink, nor was any   205
Maidservant or serving man in the house aware of it,
But himself and his wife and one single housekeeper.
And whenever they drank that honey-sweet red wine,
He would fill one cup and pour it into twenty measures
Of water, and a sweet aroma came from the bowl   210
Of marvelous fragrance: to abstain then would not have been easy.
I filled a great skin with it and brought it, and also I put
Provisions in a bag. At once my bold spirit
Sensed that the man would approach, clad in his great strength,
The wild man who had clear in his mind neither justice nor laws.   215
Speedily we came to the cave and did not find him
Within. But he was tending rich flocks in a pasture.
We entered the cave and gazed at each separate thing.
Baskets were weighed down with cheeses, and the folds were thronged
With lambs and kids. All were divided in groups,   220
And confined; here the first born, there the middlers,
The dew-fleeced apart too. All the pails flowed with whey,
The vessels and the pans, well wrought, in which he milked them.
Then at first my companions besought me with speeches
To go back again, when we had picked some cheeses and then   225
When we had hastily driven the kids and lambs out of the pens
On board the swift ship, to set sail upon the salt water.
But I did not listen—that would have been far better—
So I might see the man and he give me the gifts of a guest.
But when he appeared, he was not to be joyful to my companions.   230
We kindled a fire there, sacrificed, and ourselves
Also picked out some cheeses and ate, and awaited him
Seated inside, till he did come driving sheep. He carried
A stout burden of dry wood to use for his supper.
Throwing it down inside the cave, he made a din;   235
And we drew back in fear into a nook of the cave.
But into the broad cavern he drove his fat flocks,
All those that he usually milked, and he left the males
By the entrance, rams and he-goats, in the deep yard outside.
Then he put a great doorstone on, raising it aloft,   240
A mighty one. And twenty-two excellent wagons
With four wheels could not pry it up from the ground,
So great was the towering rock he set on the entrance.
He sat down and milked the sheep and the bleating goats,

All in due order, and set each young one to his mother;   245
And at once when he had curdled half the white milk,
He skimmed it off and put it up in wicker baskets,
And half of it he stood in pails so he would have it
To drink when he reached for it, to have it for supper.
And when he had hurried at attending to all his tasks,   250
He kindled a fire, and looked at us, and spoke to us:
'Strangers, who are you? Whence have you sailed the watery ways?
For some sort of gain, or do you wander at hazard
The way pirates do who wander over the sea
Risking their lives, bearing evil to foreigners?'   255
So he said, and our own hearts were shattered within us,
In terror at his deep voice and the monster himself.
Yet even so I answered him with a speech and addressed him thus:
'We are Achaians coming from Troy, driven off course
By all kinds of winds over the great gulf of the sea;   260
Wanting to go homeward, we came by other passages,
By another way. So Zeus I suppose wished to devise it.
We declare we are the men of Agamemnon, son of Atreus,
The glory of whom is now the most under heaven,
So great a city did he sack, and he destroyed many   265
People. And so we have arrived here and come up to your knees
To see if you may provide some guest gift or otherwise
Give a present, such as is the custom among guest friends,
Mighty one, revere the gods. We are your suppliants.
Zeus is the protector of suppliants and guest friends,   270
The god of guests, who accompanies respectful guests.'
So I said, and he answered me at once in his pitiless spirit:
'You are a fool, stranger, or have come from afar,
To bid me to be afraid or to shrink from the gods.
Cyclopes have no regard for aegis-bearing Zeus,   275
Or the blessed gods since we are mightier by far.
Nor to shrink from the hatred of Zeus would I spare
You or your companions, unless the spirit moved me.
But tell me where you have come and put your well-made ships,
Whether on the mainland or nearby, so I may know.'   280
So he said, testing us; I who knew much was not deceived.
I addressed him in return with guileful words:
'The earth-shaker Poseidon has shattered my ship,
Throwing it on the rocks at the borders of your land,
Driving it on the cape, but a wind bore it from the ocean.   285
And I escaped with these men from sheer destruction.'
So I said; in his pitiless spirit he answered nothing,
But he leaped up, stretched his hands to my companions,
Snatched up two together, and dashed them like whelps to the earth.
Their brains flowed out onto the ground and wet the earth.   290
Then he tore them limb from limb and made them his meal.

He ate like a mountain-reared lion, and did not leave off
Their entrails and their flesh and their marrowed bones.
We wailed and held our hands out to Zeus when we
Had seen the cruel deeds. Helplessness held our hearts.   295
And when the Cyclops had filled up his great belly
By eating human flesh and then drinking unmixed milk,
He lay down in the cave, stretched full length through the sheep.
And in my great-hearted spirit I made a plan myself
To go closer to him, draw the sharp sword from my thigh   300
And wound him in the chest where the midriff holds the liver,
Striking with my hand. But another spirit restrained me;
For there we too would have perished in sheer destruction,
Since from the lofty entrance we could not push away
The mighty rock with our hands that he had set upon it.   305
And so we lamented then and awaited the godly dawn.
And when the early-born, rosy-fingered dawn appeared,
He kindled a fire and milked his glorious flocks,
All in due order, and set each young one to his mother.
And when he had hurried at tending to all his tasks,   310
He again snatched two men together and made them his meal.
When he had finished, he drove the rich flock from the cave,
Taking the great doorstone off easily. And then
He put it back, as one would put the lid on a quiver.
With a great whistling, the Cyclops turned his fat flock   315
To the mountain. I was left deeply devising evil,
If I might somehow avenge me and Athene give me glory.
And this seemed to me in my heart to be the best plan.
In the fold a great club of the Cyclops was lying,
A green one of olive wood. He had cut it to carry   320
When it was dry. As we beheld it, we thought it
To be as large as the mast of a black, twenty-oared ship,
A wide freighter that traverses the great gulf:
So great was its length, so great its breadth to behold.
I stood by and cut off a piece the size of a fathom   325
Gave it to my companions and told them to plane it;
They made it smooth, and I stood by and sharpened it to a point.
I took it at once and brought it to a glow in the blazing fire;
Then I hid it well, placing it under the dung
Which was strewn through the cave in great abundant heaps.   330
Then I ordered the others to cast lots for a choice
Of the one who would dare to raise the pole along with me
And bore it in his eye when sweet sleep had come upon him.
The lots fell to those I would have wished to choose myself,
Four men, and I picked myself as the fifth among them.   335
He came at evening driving the flocks with their lovely fleece.
At once he drove the fat flocks into the broad cave,
All, and did not leave any outside in the deep yard;

Either he suspected something or a god bade him so.
Then he put the great doorstone on, raising it aloft,   340
And he sat down and milked the sheep and the bleating goats,
All in due order, and set each young one to his mother.
And when he had hurried at attending to all his tasks,
He again snatched two men together and made them his meal.
Then I addressed the Cyclops, standing close to him,   345
Holding in my hands an ivy bowl of black wine:
'Here, Cyclops, drink wine, now you have eaten human flesh,
So you may see what sort of wine this is that our ship contained.
I brought it for libation to you that you might pity me
And send me home. Your rage may be borne no longer;   350
Cruel wretch, how could anyone else come to you later on
Of the number of mankind, since you have not acted properly.'
So I said. He took and drank it. He was fearfully pleased
As he drank the sweet wine, and he asked me for a second.
'Kindly grant me something more and tell me your name   355
At once now, so I may give you a guest gift to delight you.
Yes, indeed, for the Cyclopes the grain-giving land bears
Large-clustered wine grapes, and a rain of Zeus makes them grow,
But this is a runnel of nectar and ambrosia.'
So he said. And I gave him more of the sparkling wine.   360
Thrice I brought it and gave it, thrice he thoughtlessly drank.
And when the wine had overcome the mind of the Cyclops,
At that point I addressed him with soothing words:
'Cyclops, do you ask me my famous name? Well, I
Will tell you. Then give me the guest gift you promised.   365
Noman is my own name. Noman do they call me,
My mother and my father and all my companions.'
So I said, and he answered at once in his pitiless spirit:
'Noman I shall eat last among his companions
And the others first. This will be my guest gift to you.'   370
With that he leaned over and fell down on his back. And then
He lay with his massive neck twisted. All-subduing
Sleep seized him. Wine poured out of his gullet,
And chunks of human flesh. He belched out drunkenly.
And then I drove the pole up under a mass of ashes   375
Until it should heat. And I encouraged all my companions
With speeches, lest one of them should draw back from me in fear.
But just when the olive pole was ready to catch fire,
Green as it was, and was glowing dreadfully,
At that moment I came closer and took it out of the fire. My
    companions   380
Stood about. And some god breathed great courage into them.
They lifted the olive pole that was sharp at its tip
And thrust it in his eye; I myself, leaning on it from above,
Twirled it around as a man would drill the wood of a ship

With an auger, and others would keep spinning with a strap
    beneath,   385
Holding it at either end, and the auger keeps on going.
So we held the fire-sharpened pole in his eye
And twirled it. The blood flowed around it, hot as it was.
The fire singed his eyebrows and eyelids all around
From the burning eye. Its roots swelled in the fire to bursting,   390
As when a smith plunges a great ax or an adz
Into cold water and the tempering makes it hiss
Loudly, and just that gives the strength to the iron;
So did his eye sizzle around the olive pole.
He wailed a great terrible wail; the rock resounded,   395
And we were afraid and rushed back, while he drew
The pole out of his eye spattered with much blood;
Then he threw it from him with his hands, maddened by pain,
And let out a great roar for the Cyclopes, who dwelt
All around him in caves throughout the windy peaks.   400
When they heard the shout they trailed in from every side;
They stood around the cave and asked what bothered him:
'Polyphemos, how is it you are hurt so much as to shout so
Through the ambrosial night and to make us sleepless?
No mortal drives your flocks against your will, does he?   405
And no one is murdering you by craft or by force?'
Mighty Polyphemos addressed them from the cavern:
'Friends, Noman is murdering me by craft, not by force.'
And they answered him and addressed him with wingèd words:
'If no one is compelling you when you are alone,   410
There is no way to escape a sickness from great Zeus.
Come now and pray to our father Lord Poseidon.'
So they said and went away; and my own heart laughed
At how my name had deceived him, and my faultless device.
The Cyclops, though, was in pain as he groaned, and felt pangs.   415
Groping with his hands, he took the stone from the entrance
And sat in the entrance himself, stretching out his hands
To see if he could catch someone going outdoors with the sheep;
So foolish did he in his mind think me to be.
And I myself kept planning what way might be far the best   420
If I could find some release from death for my companions
And for myself. I wove all sorts of wiles and deceit
As for very life, since a great ill was near at hand.
This seemed to me in my heart to be the best plan:
The males of the sheep were well nourished and shaggy coated,   425
Handsome and large, with a fleece of dark violet.
These I joined fast in silence with easily twisted twigs
On which the monster Cyclops slept, lawless in his mind.
I bound them in threes, and the middle one would carry a man.

The other two went on either side, protecting my companions.   430
So three sheep bore each mortal man. As for myself,
There was a lead ram, by far the finest of all the sheep,
Whose back I grasped and lay under his shaggy belly
Curled up. And with my hand twisted in his marvelous wool
I held on relentlessly with an enduring heart.   435
So then, lamenting, we awaited the godly dawn.
And when the early-born, rosy-fingered dawn appeared,
At that moment he drove the male flocks to pasture,
And the females were bleating unmilked around the pens.
Their udders were swollen. And then the master, afflicted   440
By bad pains, felt over the backs of all the sheep
As they stood erect. And the fool did not perceive
How the men were bound under the breasts of the thick-fleeced sheep.
Last of all the lead ram of the flock went outdoors
Encumbered by his wool and by me with my rapid thoughts.   445
The mighty Polyphemos felt him over and addressed him:
'Friend ram, why of all the sheep do you move this way as the last
Out of the cave? You were not left behind by the sheep before;
You were much the first to pasture on the tender flowers of grass
With your long strides, and you came first to the rivers' streams,   450
And you were the first to desire to return to the fold
At evening. But now you are last of all. Ah, you long
For the eye of your master that an evil man put out
With woeful companions, overcoming his mind by wine,
Noman, who I say has not yet escaped destruction.   455
And if you could sympathize and become able to speak,
To say in what place that man is evading my rage,
Then once he were struck, his brains should be dashed through the cave
In all directions on the threshold. And then my heart
Should be relieved of the ills worthless Noman brought me.'   460
When he had said this, he sent the ram from him out the entrance.
When I had gone a short way away from the cave and the yard,
I first got loose from the ram and then freed my companions.
Speedily we drove the long-legged sheep, rich in fat,
Rounding the many of them up, until we came   465
To the ship. We were welcome to our dear companions,
We who escaped death. The others they would have lamented, wailing,
But I did not allow it and nodded with my eyebrows to each
Not to weep. I ordered them to put the many sheep
With lovely fleece quickly on the ship and sail the salt water.   470
They got on board at once and took their seats at the oarlocks;
Seated in order, they beat the hoary sea with their oars.
And when I was as far off as a man's shout would carry,
I addressed the Cyclops myself with taunting speeches:
'Cyclops, you were not destined to eat in your hollow cave,   475

For your powerful might, the companions of a strengthless man.
And truly it was destined for your evil deeds to find you out,
Cruel wretch, since you did not shrink from eating the guests
In your house. Zeus and the other gods have paid you for that.'
So I said. Then he got the more angry in his heart.   480
He broke off the crest of a great mountain and threw it,
And it fell down in front of the dark blue-prowed ship,
Just short, and it missed hitting the end of the rudder.
The sea was heaved up by the rock as it descended,
And a great back-washing wave bore the ship at once to land,   485
As it swelled from the ocean, and drove it to hit the mainland.
And I took hold of a very long pole in my hands
And pushed on out. I called to urge on my companions,
Nodding with my head, to throw themselves on the oars,
So we could flee misfortune. Falling to it, they rowed.   490
When we had crossed twice as much water and were far away,
Then I would have shouted to the Cyclops, but my companions around
    me
From all sides tried to restrain me with soothing speeches:
'You wretch, why did you want to provoke the wild man,
Who, even now, when he threw his missile into the ocean,   495
Has brought the ship back to land? And we really thought we would die
    there.
And if he had heard anyone speaking or shouting out
He would have broken our brains and our ship timbers
Casting a jagged piece of sparkling rock. So powerfully does he throw!'
So they said, but they did not sway my great-hearted spirit.   500
But in my angry spirit I answered him back:
'Cyclops, if someone among mortal men should inquire
Of you about the unseemly blindness in your eye,
Say that Odysseus, sacker of cities, blinded it,
The son of Laertes, whose home is in Ithaca.'   505
So I said. He moaned and answered me with a tale:
'Well then, the decrees uttered of old have come upon me.
Once there was a prophet here, a man fine and great,
Telemos, Eurymos' son, who excelled in prophecy,
And grew old prophesying among the Cyclopes,   510
Who said all these things in the future would come to pass,
That I would be deprived of my sight at Odysseus' hands.
But I always expected some mortal great and handsome
To arrive in this place decked out in great strength.
And now, a man small and worthless and feeble   515
Has blinded my eye when he overcame me with wine.
Come here now, Odysseus, so I may present you with gifts,
And urge the famed earth-shaker to give you an escort,
For I am his son, and he declares he is my father.
He himself, if he wishes, will heal me. No one else   520

Can do it, of the blessed gods or of mortal men.'
So he said, and I myself addressed him in answer:
'Would I might as surely be able to make you devoid
Of breath and life and send you to the hall of Hades,
As I am sure not even the earth-shaker will heal your eye.'   525
So I said, and then he prayed to Lord Poseidon,
Stretching his hand up to the heaven filled with stars:
'Hear me, earth-holding Poseidon of the dark-blue locks,
If truly I am yours, and you declare you are my father,
Grant that the city-sacker Odysseus not go homeward,   530
The son of Laertes whose home is in Ithaca.
But if it is his fate to see his dear ones and arrive
At his well-established home and his fatherland,
May he come late and ill, having lost all his companions,
On someone else's ship, and find troubles at home.'   535
So he said in prayer. The god with the dark-blue locks heard him.
And then once more he lifted up a far bigger stone.
Whirling it, he shot it and thrust it with boundless strength
And threw it down behind the dark blue-prowed ship,
Just short, and it missed hitting the end of the rudder.   540
The sea was heaved up by the rock as it descended.
A wave bore the ship forward and drove it to hit land.
And when we arrived at the island, where the other
Well-timbered ships were waiting, gathered, and our companions
Sat lamenting all around, forever awaiting us;   545
As we came there, we beached our ship upon the sand
And got out ourselves beside the surf of the sea.
Taking the flocks of Cyclops out of the hollow ship,
We divided them so none would lack an equal share for my sake.
But my well-greaved companions chose the ram especially   550
For me alone, when the flocks were divided. On the strand
We slew it and burned the thighs to black-clouded Zeus,
The son of Cronos, who rules all. But he received not the rites;
Instead he kept on plotting how all the well-timbered ships
And the companions faithful to me might be destroyed.   555
So then the whole day till the setting of the sun
We sat dining on endless meat and sweet wine.
But when the sun went down and darkness came on,
We lay down to sleep beside the surf of the sea.
And when the early-born, rosy-fingered dawn appeared,   560
I myself called to my companions and bade them
To go on board themselves and to undo the stern cables;
At once they got on and took their seats at the oarlocks.
Seated in order, they beat the hoary sea with their oars.
Then we sailed further on, grieving in our hearts,   565
Glad to escape death, having lost our dear companions.

X

"Then we came to the island of Aeolia, where dwelt
Aeolos,[1] Hippotas' son, who is dear to the immortal gods,
On a floating island. All about it there was
An unbreakable bronze wall, and up it the stone ran smooth.
And there are twelve children of his living in his halls;   5
Six of them are daughters and six are blooming sons.
So he gave the daughters to the sons to be their wives.
They always take their meals with their dear father
And devoted mother. Numberless dishes lie ready for them;
The redolent house resounds all round with the flute   10
In the day, and at night beside their respected wives
They sleep in blankets and upon their jointed bedsteads.
And so we came to their city and their lovely halls.
A whole month he befriended me and asked in detail
About Ilion, the Argives' ships, and the Achaians' return,   15
And I told him everything in its due order.
But when I inquired about the way and asked him
To send us, he did not refuse, and he made a conveyance.
He gave me the skin of a nine-year-old ox he had flayed,
And in it he had bound the courses of the blustering winds.   20
For the son of Cronos had made him steward of the winds,
So he could make the one he wished rise up or subside.
He bound it in the hollow ship with a shining cord
Of silver, so it would not blow at all, not a little.
Then he set a breeze of the West Wind blowing for me   25
That would carry the ship and the men onward. He was not
Destined to complete it. We were lost by our own foolishness.
Nine days we sailed alike by night and by day;
On the tenth the soil of our fatherland already appeared,
And we were close enough to see men tending the fire.   30
Then sweet sleep came upon me in my weariness,
For I always saw to the ship's sheet, and did not give it
To another companion, so we might reach the fatherland quicker.
But my companions addressed one another with speeches
And said that I was bringing gold and silver home   35
As gifts from Aeolos, the great-hearted son of Hippotas.
This is what one, looking at his closest neighbor, would say:
'Well now, how beloved and honored this man is
Among all those men at whose city and land he arrives.
He is bringing much fine treasure out of Troy   40
As booty. And we, who have accomplished the same journey,
Are going homeward, all of us, with empty hands.

1. Lord of the winds.

Now Aeolos has given him these things as a favor
In friendship. Come, let us see quickly what they are,
How much there is of gold and silver in the skin.'   45
So they said, and evil advice won my companions over.
They undid the skin, and the winds all rushed out.
At once a storm seized them and bore them onto the ocean,
Far away from our fatherland, weeping. And I,
As I awoke, wondered in my own blameless heart   50
Whether I should drop from the ship and perish in the ocean
Or endure silently and stay among the living still.
But I endured and waited, and lay with head covered   .
In my ship. The ships were borne in a bad storm of wind
Back to the island Aeolia, and my companions groaned.   55
Then we went onto the dry land and drew off water,
And at once my companions took dinner beside the swift ships.
But when we had partaken of food and of drink,
I took a herald and a companion along with me
To the famous halls of Aeolos. And I found him   60
Having a meal along with his wife and his children.
When we came to the hall we sat beside the columns
On the threshold. They wondered in their hearts, and asked right out:
'How have you come, Odysseus? What evil god has attacked you?
We did send you off kindly, so that you might reach   65
Fatherland and home and whatever is dear to you.'
So they said, and I spoke out, grieved in my heart:
'My evil companions ruined me; and besides them, a wretched
Sleep. But give relief, friends. You have the power.'
So I said, addressing them with gentle words.   70
But they grew silent. The father answered with a speech:
'Go quickly from the island, most shameful of living men.
It is not lawful for me to help or to send on his course
Any man who is despised by the blessed gods.
Go, since you came to this place despised by the gods.'   75
When he had said this, he sent me deeply groaning from his halls.
Then we sailed further on, grieving in our hearts.
The spirit of the men was worn down by the rowing, painful
Through our folly, since conveyance appeared no more.
Six days did we sail alike by night and by day.   80
And on the seventh we came to Lamos' sheer citadel,
Lestrygonian [2] Telepylos, where a shepherd driving in the flock
May call to a shepherd, and the one driving out answers.
And there a sleepless man could have earned double pay
For tending cattle and for pasturing bright sheep,   85
For the courses of the day and night are close together.
There, when we came to the famous harbor, about which a rock

2. The Lestrygonians were a tribe of savage giants whose king was Lamos.

Is set towering on both sides without a break,
And crags jutting out against one another
Are projecting at its mouth, and the entrance is slight, 90
There all the others brought their bobbing ships on inside.
The ships were tied up inside the hollow harbor
Close to one another, for no wave rose in it,
Either great or small, but there was a white calm all around.
But I myself alone brought my black ship outside 95
There on the verge and tied the cables to a rock.
I got up and stood on a rugged point of outlook.
There nothing that was done by oxen or man appeared,
But we saw a lone smoke column rising from the land.
Then I sent my companions to go and find out 100
Who these were of the men who eat bread on the earth.
I picked out two men and sent a third as a herald.
They went off, going by a smooth path where wagons
Brought wood down to the town from the high mountain.
And they happened on a girl getting water before the city, 105
The goodly daughter of Lestrygonian Antiphates.[3]
She was going down to Artacia, a spring with a lovely stream.
From there they carried water on to the city.
Standing beside her, they spoke out to her and asked
Who the king of these men was and over whom he ruled. 110
She at once pointed out the high-roofed house of her father.
When they entered the glorious hall, they found his wife
As big as the crest of a mountain, and they loathed her.
Right away she called renowned Antiphates from assembly,
Her husband, who planned a woeful destruction for the men. 115
Snatching one companion at once, he made a meal of him.
The other two rushed in flight and came to the ships.
But he sent a shout through the town. They heard it, the mighty
Lestrygonians, and ran out from all directions,
Thousands of them, like giants and not like men. 120
From the cliffs they threw boulders the size of a man's load.
And at once an evil din rose up among the ships
Of men being destroyed and ships being crushed together.
Spearing the men like fish, they bore off their gruesome meal.
While they were destroying the men in the very deep harbor, 125
I myself drew my sharp sword from along my thigh
And with it cut the cable of the dark blue-prowed ship.
At once I called and urged my companions on
To throw themselves on the oars so we could flee misfortune.
They all strained together, in fear of destruction. 130
To my joy my own ship escaped from the overhanging rocks
Onto the ocean. But the others were lost there all together.

---

3. A king of the Lestrygonians.

From there we sailed further on, grieving in our hearts,
Glad to escape death, having lost our dear companions.
We came to the island of Aiaia. There did dwell   135
Fair-braided Circe, dread god with a singing voice,
The blood sister of destructive-minded Aietes.[4]
They were both descended from the sun who gives light to mortals,
And from their mother Perse, whom Oceanos had for a child.
There we put in silently to land on the shore with the ship   140
Into a sheltered harbor, and some god guided us.
When we had got out there, for two days and two nights
We lay still, eating our hearts with pain and fatigue alike.
But when fair-braided Dawn had brought the third day to the full,
I myself took hold of my spear and my sharp sword   145
And went up speedily from the ship to a place of lookout,
To look for the works of mortals or to hear their sound.
I went up onto the rugged lookout and stood there,
And smoke appeared to me from the wide-traveled earth
In the halls of Circe through dense thickets and a wood.   150
Then I deliberated in my mind and my heart
About going and finding out, since I had seen the lurid smoke.
As I thought about it, it seemed to be better so:
First to go to the swift ship and the strand of the sea
To give my companions a meal, then send to inquire.   155
But when on my way I got close to the bobbing ship,
Some one of the gods pitied me, as I was alone,
And he sent me in my very path a great stag
With high horns who was going down from the wood grove
To the river to drink. For the strength of the sun gripped him.   160
As he was coming out, I hit him along the spine
In the middle of his back. The bronze spear went right through him.
He fell with a cry in the dust and his spirit flew off.
I put my foot on him and drew out the bronze spear
From his wound. Then I laid it there along the ground   165
And left it. Thereupon I pulled up brushwood and twigs;
I twined a rope of a fathom in length, well twisted
From both ends, and tied the feet of the vast creature,
Carried it across my back, and went to the black ship
Leaning on my spear, since I could not carry it on one shoulder   170
With my other hand, for the animal was very large.
I threw it down before the ship, roused my companions,
Stood by each man, and spoke to him with soothing words:
'My friends, though we are grieving, we shall not yet go down
To the halls of Hades before the fated day arrives.   175
Come now, while there is food and drink in the swift ship,
Let us take thought of food and not waste away in hunger.'

4. King of Colchis; father of Medea.

So I said, and they swiftly hearkened to my words.
Uncovering their heads by the strand of the barren sea,
They gazed at the stag, for the animal was very large.   180
And when they had taken their joy of looking with their eyes,
They washed their hands and prepared a glorious feast,
And so the whole day till the setting of the sun
We sat dining on endless meat and on sweet wine.
And when the sun went down and the darkness came on,   185
We lay down to sleep beside the surf of the sea.
And when the early-born, rosy-fingered dawn appeared,
I called an assembly and spoke out to them all:
'Hear my speech, my companions, though you have suffered ills;
My friends, we do not know where dusk is, or dawn,   190
Nor where the sun that gives light to mortals sets under earth
Nor where it rises. Let us consider quickly
If there is any plan left. I do not think there is.
When I went up to the rugged lookout I saw
An island that an endless sea girds all around.   195
The island itself is low lying. I saw with my own eyes
A smoke in the middle through dense thickets and woods.'
So I said, and the heart of each man was shattered
To remember the deeds of Lestrygonian Antiphates
And of Cyclops, great-hearted in strength, the eater of men.   200
So they wailed piercingly, and they shed swelling tears,
And yet no result came from their lamentation.
But I numbered all my well-greaved companions
Into two groups and appointed a leader for each.
I led one of them, godlike Eurylochos [5] the other.   205
Quickly we shook the lots in a bronze-fitted helmet.
The lot of great-hearted Eurylochos leaped out.
He went off, and along with him went twenty-two companions,
Lamenting. And they left us grieving behind them.
In the glen they found the hall of Circe, constructed   210
Out of polished stone in a place with a view all around.
About her were wolves of the mountains and also lions
That she had charmed herself when she gave them evil drugs.
Nor did these creatures rush upon the men, but instead
They reared up on them and fawned over them with their long tails.   215
As when dogs fawn about their master when he comes
From dinner, and he always brings blandishments for their temper,
So did the wolves with powerful claws and the lions
Fawn about them. They were afraid when they saw the dread creatures.
So they stood in the forecourt of the fair-braided goddess   220
And they heard Circe singing in a lovely voice within
As she went to and fro at a great immortal web, such as are

5. The chief companion of Odysseus.

The works of goddesses, fine woven, pleasing, and bright.
Then Polites, chief of the men, began speaking to them:
He was dearest to me of my companions, and the most devoted.   225
'My friends, some woman within, as she tends a great web,
Sings beautifully, and the whole ground echoes about;
A god or a woman; well, let us quickly call out.'
So he said to them, and they did call out, shouting.
At once she opened the shining doors and came out   230
And called. They all went with her in their ignorance.
Eurylochos hung back, thinking it to be a trick.
She led them in and sat them in seats and in armchairs.
She mixed for them cheese and barley and green honey
With Pramnian wine. And she stirred into the food   235
Woeful drugs that make one forget his fatherland wholly.
But when she had given it and they had drunk, she at once
Struck them with her wand and shut them up into sties.
They had the heads of swine and the voice and the hair
And the body, but the mind was steady as before.   240
So they were penned in, weeping, and to them Circe
Threw two kinds of acorns and the fruit of the cornel tree
To eat, such as swine who sleep on the ground always eat.
Eurylochos came back at once to the swift black ship
To tell the news of his companions and their harsh fate.   245
He was not able to speak a word, though he wanted to,
Struck in his heart with a great grief; and his eyes
Were filled with tears, and his heart brooded on weeping.
And when all had questioned him and were amazed,
He recounted the ruin of our other companions: 250
'We went, as you bid, through the thicket, noble Odysseus,
And in the glen we found lovely halls constructed
Of polished stones in a place with a view all around.
There a woman tending a great web sang clearly,
A god or a woman. They called out to her, shouting.   255
At once she opened the shining doors and came out
And called. They all went with her in their ignorance.
But I hung back myself, thinking it to be a trick.
They all vanished together. Nor did one of them
Appear. And I sat for a long time and kept watching.'   260
So he said. And I threw my silver-studded sword
On my shoulders, a big bronze one, and a bow about me.
I ordered him to lead me back by the same path.
But he clutched my knees with both of his hands and begged me;
And lamenting to me, he uttered wingèd words: 265
'You whom Zeus nourished, do not lead me there against my will;
Leave me here. I think you will not come back or lead back
Any of your companions. No, let us quickly flee
With these men, for we may still avoid the fatal day.'

So he said, and, answering him, I addressed him: 270
'All right, Eurylochos, you stay here in this place,
Eating and drinking by the hollow black ship.
But I will go myself; strong necessity is on me.'
When I had said this, I went up from the ship and the sea.
And when I was about to go through the sacred glen   275
To come to the great house of Circe of the many drugs,
Hermes of the golden wand came across my path
As I was going to the house, resembling a young man
With his first beard, at the most pleasing time of youth.
He took my hand and spoke right out directly to me: 280
'Where are you going, alone through the hills, hapless man,
Ignorant of the place? These companions of yours are confined
In Circe's house as swine, and keep to their dense lairs.
Are you going there to free them? I do not think
You will return yourself, but will stay where the others are.   285
Well, I will release you from evil and rescue you.
Here, take this excellent drug to the halls of Circe
And enter; so it may ward off from your head the evil day.
I shall tell you all of Circe's pernicious wiles.
She will make you a mixture and drop drugs into the food.   290
But she will not be able to charm you so. The excellent drug
I shall give you will not permit it. I will tell you the details.
At the moment when Circe hits you with her very long wand,
Draw your sharp sword at once from along your thigh
And rush upon Circe as if intending to kill her.   295
She will be afraid of you and ask you to go to bed.
And from that point on do not refuse the bed of the god,
So she may free your companions and guide you yourself.
But order her to swear a great oath by the blessed gods
That she plot no other bad trouble against your person,   300
Lest when you are naked she make you unmanly and a coward.'
When he had said this, the god, the slayer of Argos, gave me the drug
He had plucked out of the earth, and showed me its nature.
It was black at the root, but its flower was like milk.
The gods call it moly. It is difficult to dig   305
For mortal men. But gods are able to do all things.
Then Hermes went away toward tall Olympos
Along the wooded island. And to the halls of Circe
I proceeded. My heart was greatly disturbed as I went.
I stood in the courtyard of the goddess with the lovely hair.   310
As I stood there I shouted, and the goddess heard my voice.
She came out right away and opened the shining doors
And called. I followed her, grieving in my heart.
She led me in and seated me on a silver-studded chair,
Lovely and cleverly wrought. A footstool was beneath my feet.   315
She made me a mixture in a golden cup to drink

And put in a drug, devising evil in her heart.
When she gave it and I drank and it did not charm me,
She struck me with a wand and spoke right out directly:
'Come to the sty now. Lie down with the others, your companions.' 320
So she said, but I drew the sharp sword from along my thigh
And rushed on Circe as if intending to kill her,
She gave a great shout, ran up under and took my knees;
And lamenting to me, she uttered wingèd words:
'What men are you from? Where are your city and parents?   325
Wonder holds me that you drank this drug and were not charmed.
No other man at all has been able to bear this drug
Once he had drunk it and let it pass the bar of his teeth.
You have in your breast some mind that is not to be charmed.
Surely you are the Odysseus of many turns, who,   330
The gold-wanded slayer of Argos always told me
Would come on his way out of Troy in a swift black ship.
Well, come, put your sword in the sheath and let us now
Go up to our bed so that when we have lain together
In love and in bed we may rely on one another.'   335
So she said; and answering her, I addressed her:
'Circe, how can you request that I be mild to you,
Who in your halls have turned my companions to swine
And now with wiles on your mind you request me
To go into your bedroom and to enter your bed,   340
That when I am naked you may make me unmanly and a coward.
I myself do not want to enter your bed, goddess,
Unless you will put up with swearing me a great oath,
That you will not plot some other bad trouble against me.'
So I said, and she swore at once as I had asked her.   345
And when she had sworn the oath and completed it,
I went up to the bed of the beautiful Circe.
Serving maids busied themselves around her halls,
Four of them, who are servants for her in the house.
These women are born from the springs and from the groves,   350
And from the sacred rivers that flow down to the sea.
One of them threw lovely blankets upon the armchairs,
Purple ones about them, and underneath she put linen.
Another one out in front of the armchairs arranged tables
Of silver and set out golden baskets before them.   355
The third one mixed sweet mind-honeying wine
In a bowl of silver and set out golden goblets.
The fourth one carried water and lit up a large fire
Underneath a great cauldron. And the water was warmed.
And when the water was boiling in the gleaming bronze,   360
She set me in a bathtub and washed me, from the great cauldron
    pouring
Water mixed to a pleasing warmth on my head and shoulders

Till it took the spirit-destroying fatigue from my limbs.
And when she had washed and anointed me richly with oil
And had thrown a lovely mantle about me and a tunic,   365
She led me in and seated me on a silver-studded armchair,
Lovely and cleverly wrought. A footstool was beneath my feet.
A handmaid poured water from a pitcher she was carrying,
A lovely golden one over into a silver basin,
For washing the hands; she set up a polished table alongside.   370
A respected housekeeper served bread she was carrying,
Laying out many dishes, gracious with the provisions,
And bade me eat. But no pleasure was in my heart.
I sat thinking other thoughts. My heart foreboded ills.
Circe, when she perceived that I sat there and did not   375
Reach my hands to the food, and that powerful grief held me,
Came and stood nearby and uttered wingèd words:
'Why do you sit this way, Odysseus, as one with no voice,
Eating your heart out, and do not touch food or drink?
Perhaps you expect another trick. There is no need   380
To fear; I have already sworn you a powerful oath.'
So she said, and in answer to her, I addressed her:
'Circe, what man is there, if he be righteous,
Who could endure to be partaking of food and drink
Before he got his companions free and saw them with his eyes?   385
If really in good faith you bid me to eat and drink,
Free them, so my eyes may behold my trusty companions.'
So I said, and Circe walked on out through the halls
Holding a wand in her hand; she opened the gates of the sty
And drove out the men, who looked like swine nine years old.   390
They stood opposite us. She went in their midst
And with another drug she rubbed each one of them.
The hair fell off their limbs that the baleful drug
The queenly Circe gave them before had made grow there.
They became men again, younger than they were before   395
And far more handsome and larger to behold.
They recognized me, and each one grasped my hands.
The longed-for weeping came on them all. The house about
Terribly resounded, and the goddess herself felt pity.
The divine goddess stood close to me and addressed me: 400
'Zeus-born son of Laertes, much-contriving Odysseus,
Go on now to your swift ship and the strand of the sea,
And first of all, draw your ship up on the mainland,
Put your property and all your gear into caves.
Then come back yourself and bring your trusty companions.'   405
So she said. Then the bold heart was persuaded within me
And I went down to the swift ship and the beach of the sea.
There I found my trusty companions on the swift ship,
Lamenting piteously, shedding large tears.

As when calves of the fields all skip around together   410
In front of the drove of cows that are coming into the dung yard
When they are filled up on grass, and the pens no longer
Hold them, but they run in throngs around their mothers,
Lowing on and on, so did those men act when their eyes saw me:
They shed tears, weeping. And it seemed to their hearts   415
As though they had come to the fatherland and the very city
Of rugged Ithaca, where they were born and brought up.
And lamenting to me, they uttered wingèd words:
'At your return, Zeus-nourished one, we have rejoiced
As if we had come to Ithaca, our fatherland.   420
Come and tell about the ruin of our other companions.'
So they said. And I addressed them with soothing words:
'First of all, let us draw the ship up onto the mainland
And bring our possessions and all our gear into caves.
Then press on yourselves and follow me all together   425
So you may see our companions in Circe's sacred halls,
Eating and drinking; they have unfailing abundance.'
So I said, and they quickly hearkened to my words.
Eurylochos alone tried to hold back all my companions,
And addressing them, he uttered wingèd words: 430
'Ah, wretched men, where are we going? Why long for these ills,
And go down to the halls of Circe, who will make us all
Into swine or wolves or lions, so that we may guard
The great house for her, and by necessity,
The way the Cyclops acted when our companions came   435
To his middle yard, and bold Odysseus went with them,
And they were all destroyed because of his recklessness.'
So he said, and I pondered myself in my mind
About drawing my sharp-pointed sword from my stout thigh,
To cut his head off and to bring it to the ground,   440
Though he was very close kin to me. But my companions
Restrained me on every side with soothing words:
'You who were born of Zeus, let us leave this man here
Beside the ship, if you bid it, and guard the ship,
And you lead the way for us to Circe's sacred halls.'   445
When they said this they went up from the ship and the sea.
Nor was Eurylochos left beside the hollow ship,
But he followed, for he feared my striking rebuke.
Meanwhile Circe in her halls had kindly washed the rest
Of our companions and anointed them richly with oil.   450
She threw woolen mantles and tunics about them.
And we came upon them all dining well in the halls.
When they had seen and looked at each other face to face,
They wept, lamenting, and the halls rang around.
The divine goddess stood near me and addressed me: 455
'Zeus-born son of Laertes, Odysseus of many wiles,

Raise this swelling lament no longer. I myself know
How many pains you have suffered on the fish-laden ocean
And how many wrongs hostile men did to you on land.
So come now and eat victuals and drink wine   460
Until you have taken the spirit into your breast again
As it was when you first left your fatherland
Of rugged Ithaca. Now, wasted and without spirit,
You remember hard wandering always, and your spirit has never
Been in gladness, since you have suffered very much!'   465
So she said, and the bold spirit was persuaded in us.
There day by day till the year was brought to a close
We stayed, dining on endless meat and on sweet wine.
But when the year was up and the seasons turned round
As the moons were declining, and the long days came round to
    an end,   470
Then my trusty companions called me out and said to me:
'You fool, at this time now remember your fatherland,
If it is decreed that you be saved and arrive
At your well-established home and your fatherland.'
So they said, and the bold spirit was persuaded within me.   475
So then the entire day till the setting of the sun
We stayed, dining on endless meat and on sweet wine.
But when the sun went down and the darkness came on
They lay down to sleep through the shadowy halls,
And I went up to the beautiful bed of Circe   480
And took her knees in prayer. The goddess heard my voice.
Then I spoke out to her and uttered wingèd words:
'Circe, fulfill for me the promise you made,
To send me home; the spirit is eager in me already
And in my other companions, who consume my precious heart   485
In complaining around me whenever you are absent.'
So I said, and the divine goddess at once answered:
'Zeus-born son of Laertes, Odysseus of many devices,
Do not stay any longer in my home unwillingly.
Yet you must first achieve another journey and come   490
To the halls of Hades and dread Persephone,[6]
So you may consult the soul of Theban Tiresias,
The blind prophet in whom there is a steadfast mind.
To him alone, even when dead, did Persephone grant
A mind that could understand. The others flit, shadows.'   495
So she said, and my own heart was shattered within me.
Seated on the bed, I lamented, nor did my heart
Wish still to live and to see the light of the sun.
But when I was sated with lamenting and wallowing,   500
I answered her and addressed her with a speech:

6. Daughter of Zeus and Demeter; queen of the underworld.

'O Circe, who will be my guide on this journey?
No one ever got to the place of Hades in a black ship.
So I said, and at once the divine goddess answered:
'Zeus-born son of Laertes, Odysseus of many devices,
Give heed to no longing for a guide upon your ship,   505
But set up a mast and stretch out the white sails,
And then sit down. The blast of the North Wind will carry it for you.
And when in your ship you have traversed Oceanos,
Where the scrubby strand and groves of Persephone are,
Both tall poplars and willows that lose their fruit,   510
Beach your ship there by deep-whirling Oceanos;
But go on yourself to the moldy hall of Hades.
There into Acheron flow Puriphlegethon
And Cocytus, which is a branch of the Styx's[7] water,
And a rock and a concourse of the two resounding rivers.   515
Then go up near there, hero, as I bid you to;
Dig a pit the size of a cubit on all sides.
Pour a libation about it for all the dead,
First of honey mixture, and then of sweet wine,
And the third one of water; sprinkle white barley on it.   520
Beseech the feeble heads of the dead with many prayers,
Saying that when you go to Ithaca you will sacrifice
Your best barren cow in your halls, heap a pyre with goods,
And consecrate apart for Tiresias alone
A sheep all of black that stands out among your flocks.   525
And when you have besought the famed tribes of the dead with prayers,
Sacrifice a ram and also a black female,
Bending their heads to Erebos;[8] turn the other way yourself,
Setting on for the streams of the river. And there many
Souls will come of the corpses of those who have died.   530
And then urge your companions on and command them
To take sheep which lie slain with the pitiless sword,
To flay them and burn them and pray to the gods,
To mighty Hades and dread Persephone.
You yourself draw your sharp sword from beside your thigh.   535
Stay put, and do not let the feeble heads of the dead
Go near the blood till you learn from Tiresias.
At once, then, leader of the people, the prophet will come,
Who will tell you the course and measures of the way
And about a return, how you may go on the fish-laden ocean.'   540
So she said, and at once the golden-throned Dawn came.
She clothed me in garments, a mantle and a tunic,
And the nymph herself put on a great shining mantle
Finely made and pleasing, and a lovely gold sash

---

7. Rivers of the Underworld. Their names mean Distress, Fire-flaming, Lament, and Hate.
8. Outer darkness for the dead.

Around her waist, and she put a veil on her head.   545
I went through the halls and urged my companions on,
Standing by each man and speaking with soothing words:
'Slumber now no longer as you lie in sound, sweet sleep,
But let us go. Queenly Circe has already informed me.'
So I said, and the bold spirit in them was persuaded.   550
But I did not lead my companions from there unscathed.
There was one very young man, Elpenor, not overly
Courageous in battle and not steadfast in his mind,
Who apart from my companions in Circe's sacred halls,
Longing for coolness, lay down drunk with wine.   555
Hearing the noise and din of his companions moving,
He rose up suddenly and wholly forgot in his mind
To go back down again by way of the long ladder.
But he fell right down off the roof. And his neck
Was broken from the joint. His soul went down to Hades.   560
Then I addressed a speech to the men as they were going:
'You think, perhaps, you are going home to your dear
Fatherland. Circe has decreed another way for us,
To the halls of Hades and dread Persephone,
So that we may consult the soul of Theban Tiresias.'   565
So I said, and their own hearts were shattered within them;
They sat on the spot lamenting and tearing their hair.
And yet no result came from their lamentation.
And when we had gone grieving to the swift ship
And to the strand of the sea, shedding large tears,   570
Circe had meantime gone alongside the black ship
And bound down a ram and also a black female.
She passed by nimbly; for who could see with his eyes
A god who did not wish it, whether going this way or that?

XI

"And when we came down to the ship and to the sea,
First of all we dragged the ship to the godly water
And set up the mast and the sails upon the black ship.
We took sheep and brought them on board, and we ourselves
Went on, grieving and pouring down swelling tears.   5
Then a driving wind full in the sails, a fine companion,
Did the fair-braided Circe, dread god with a singing voice,
Send on for us from behind the dark blue-prowed ship.
And when we had tended to the gear through the ship, piece by piece,
We took our seats. The wind and a pilot steered her.   10
The sails were stretched all day long as she fared on the ocean.
The sun went down and all the ways were shadowed.
She arrived at the bounds of deep-flowing Oceanos.

There is the land and city of Cimmerian men,
Who are shrouded in mist and cloud. Never does the sun   15
Look down upon them, glittering with his rays—
Never when he climbs up into the starry heaven
Or when he turns back from the heaven to the earth,
But deadly night is stretched out for hapless mortals.
Arriving there, we beached the ship and took out the flocks.   20
Then we ourselves went along the stream of Oceanos
Until we arrived at the place that Circe had said.
There Perimedes and Eurylochos held the victims.
I myself drew my sharp sword from along my thigh,
Dug a pit the size of a cubit on all sides,   25
And poured a libation about it for all the dead,
First of honey mixture, and then of sweet wine,
And the third one of water; I sprinkled white barley on it.
I besought the feeble heads of the dead for many things,
Saying that when I went to Ithaca I would sacrifice   30
My best barren cow in my halls, heap a pyre with goods,
And consecrate apart for Tiresias alone
A sheep all of black that stands out among my flocks.
And when I had besought the tribes of the dead with prayers and vows,
Then I took the sheep and cut their throats into the pit.   35
And the black-clouded blood poured out. And out of Erebos
The souls gathered of the corpses of those who had died,
Brides and bachelors and old men who had suffered much,
And tender maidens whose hearts were fresh in sorrow,
And many who had been wounded by bronze-tipped spears,   40
Men slain in battle wearing gore-spattered armor,
Many of whom hovered round the pit on every side
With a tremendous shout. And sallow fear seized me.
Then I urged my companions on and commanded them
To take the sheep which lay slain with the pitiless sword,   45
To flay them and burn them and then pray to the gods,
To mighty Hades and to dread Persephone.
I myself drew my sharp sword from beside my thigh
And stayed put, and did not let the feeble heads of the dead
Go near the blood till I could learn from Tiresias.   50
First came the soul of our companion Elpenor,
For he had not yet been buried beneath the wide-traveled earth;
We ourselves had left his body in the hall of Circe,
Unwept and unburied, since another labor drove us on.
I wept when I saw him and pitied him in my heart.   55
So I spoke out to him, and uttered wingèd words:
'Elpenor, how did you get here under the murky dusk?
You went faster by foot than I did with the black ship.'
So I said, and he wailed and answered me with a speech:
'Zeus-born son of Laertes, Odysseus of many devices,   60

The ill fate of some god destroyed me, and abundant wine.
When I lay down in the hall of Circe I did not think
To go back down again upon the long ladder,
But I fell straight down off the roof. And my neck
Was broken from the joint and my soul came down to Hades.   65
Now I beseech you by those left behind who are not here,
By your wife and the father who reared you when you were small,
And by Telemachos, whom you left alone in your halls,
For I know on your way from here out of the hall of Hades
You will stop the well-made ship at the island of Aiaia.   70
There at that time, lord, I ask you to remember me.
Do not go and leave me henceforth unwept and unburied
And turn not from me, lest I bring on you the wrath of the gods,
But burn me with all the armor that belongs to me
And heap a tomb for me by the strand of the hoary sea,   75
Hapless man that I am, so that those to come may learn of me.
Do this for me, and set my oar fast on the mound
With which when alive I rowed among my companions.'
So he said, and then I addressed him in answer:
'Wretched man, I shall do this for you and carry it out.'   80
Exchanging grim words this way with one another,
We sat, and on one side I held my sword over the blood.
On the other side the phantom of my companion told me much.
Then there came the soul of my mother who had died,
Anticleia,[1] daughter of great-hearted Autolycos,   85
Whom I had left alive when I went to sacred Ilion.
I wept when I saw her and pitied her in my spirit,
But though I grieved heavily, I did not let her
Get near the blood first till I could learn from Tiresias.
Then the soul of Theban Tiresias came up,   90
Holding a gold scepter; he knew me and spoke to me:
'Zeus-born son of Laertes, Odysseus of many devices,
Why, hapless man, have you left the light of the sun
And come here to see the dead and a joyless place?
But draw back from the pit and hold back your sharp sword   95
So I may drink the blood and speak to you unerringly.'
So he said. I drew back and thrust the silver-studded sword
Into the sheath. And when he had drunk the black blood,
The excellent prophet addressed me with a speech:
'You seek a honey-sweet return, noble Odysseus;   100
A god will make it disastrous for you. I do not think
You will elude the earth-shaker; against you he has laid up a grudge,
In his heart, enraged that you blinded his beloved son.
You may get there yet, even so, though you suffer ills;
If you are willing to check your spirit and your companions',   105

1. Wife of Laertes and mother of Odysseus.

At the time when you first bring the well-made ship up close
To the isle of Thrinacria, fleeing the violet ocean,
And you find grazing there the cattle and goodly sheep
Of the Sun, who sees everything and hears everything.
If you let them go unmolested and think of your return   110
You may yet get to Ithaca, though you do suffer ills.
If you molest them, then I prophesy destruction
For your ship and companions. And even if you escape yourself
You will return late and ill, having lost all your companions,
On another's ship. You will find troubles in your house,   115
Presumptuous men who consume your livelihood
While wooing your godlike wife and giving her bridal gifts.
But when you get there, then you will avenge the violence of those men,
But when you have killed the suitors in your own halls,
Whether by guile or openly with the sharp sword,   120
Thereupon take a well-fitted oar and go on
Till you arrive at the place of men who do not know
The sea and eat a food that has not been mixed with salt,
And where they do not know about ships with purple cheeks,
Or about well-fitted oars that are the wings for ships.   125
I will tell you a very plain token; do not forget it:
When another wayfarer has confronted you
And says you have a winnowing fan[2] on your gleaming shoulder,
Then set your well-fitted oar fast in the earth
And carry out fine sacrifices to Lord Poseidon,   130
A ram, a bull, and a boar, the mounter of sows.
Then go back home and sacrifice sacred hecatombs
To the immortal gods who possess broad heaven,
To all of them in order. Far from the sea will death come,
Ever so gently to your person and slay you   135
When you are worn out with sleek old age. And the people about you
Will be happy. I tell you this unerringly.'
So he said, and then I addressed him in answer:
'Tiresias, the gods themselves have perhaps spun this thread,
But come tell me one thing, and speak out truthfully: 140
I see here the soul of my mother who has died.
She sits in silence close to the blood and does not dare
To look her son in the face or speak out to him.
Tell me, lord, how may she know me as who I am?'
So I said, and at once he addressed me in answer: 145
'Easily shall I say the word and put it in your mind.
Whomever you permit of the souls of the dead
To approach the blood closer will speak without error to you.
The one you begrudge it to will go back away.'
When he had said this, the soul of Lord Tiresias went   150

2. A tool for sifting grain.

Within the halls of Hades, after it spoke what was decreed.
I waited there steadily until my mother
Came up and drank the black-clouded blood. She knew me
At once, and, lamenting, she uttered wingèd words:
'My child, how have you come down under the murky dusk   155
While yet alive? This is dangerous for the living to see.
In between us there are great rivers and dread streams,
Oceanos first, that it is not possible to cross
On foot; one must possess a well-made ship.
Have you just got this far in wandering from Troy   160
A long time with ship and companions? Have you not yet come
To Ithaca and seen the wife within your halls?'
So she said, and then I addressed her in answer:
'Mother, need led me down to the place of Hades
To consult the soul of Theban Tiresias.   165
I have not yet come close to Achaia. I have not yet
Set foot on our land, but wander always, possessing woe,
From the very first time I followed godly Agamemnon
To Ilion with its fine horses to fight the Trojans.
But tell me one thing, and speak out truthfully: 170
What fate overcame you of long-sorrowful death?
A lengthy sickness, or did Artemis who shoots arrows
Visit you and slay you with her gentle shafts?
Tell me of the father and the son I left behind.
Is my honor still with them, or does some other man   175
Already have it, and they say I will return no more?
Tell me about the purpose and thought of my wedded wife;
Does she stay with my son and steadily guard all,
Or has the best man of the Achaians wed her already?'
So I said, and at once my queenly mother answered me: 180
'Too long that woman in her enduring spirit waits
Within your halls. And the miserable nights
And the days always waste away for her as she sheds tears.
No one else yet holds your fine honor, but Telemachos
Possesses the acres securely, and he dines   185
On well-shared feasts, whereof it befits a judge to partake.
All invite him. But your father remains in one place
In the country and does not visit the city. No bed
He has, no bedclothes and mantles and glistening blankets,
But he sleeps all winter where servants do in the house,   190
In the ashes by the fire, and he puts bad clothes on his flesh.
But when the summer comes and the blossoming autumn,
Everywhere along the knoll of the wine-bearing vineyard
His beds of fallen leaves have been strewn on the ground.
He lies there grieving; great sorrow grows in his mind   195
As he longs for your return. Hard old age has come upon him.
And so I myself have perished and have met my fate.

And the far-sighted one who shoots arrows did not
Visit me in the hall and slay me with her gentle shafts,
Nor did sickness come on me, such as especially   200
With grim wasting away takes the spirit from the limbs.
But longing for you and your counsels, noble Odysseus,
And your kindliness, reft my honey-sweet spirit away.'
So she spoke. And pondering in my mind, I wished
To take hold of the soul of my mother who had died.   205
Three times I tried and my spirit bade me to grasp her.
And three times like a shadow or a dream she flew
Out of my hands. Sharp grief grew ever greater in my heart.
So I spoke out to her and uttered wingèd words:
'Mother, why do you not wait as I strive to grasp you,   210
So that even in the place of Hades we might throw our dear hands
Round each other and take pleasure in cold lamentation?
Or is this some phantom that noble Persephone
Sends me, so that I may grieve and lament still more?'
So I said, and my queenly mother answered at once: 215
'Alas, my child, ill-fated beyond all mortals,
Persephone, daughter of Zeus, does not beguile you;
But this is the rule for mortals, whenever one dies.
No longer do the sinews hold the bones and the flesh,
But the mighty power of burning fire subdues them   220
When first the spirit has abandoned the white bones,
And the soul, flying off like a dream, flutters.
But be eager to go to the light as fast as you can,
And note all this to tell it to your wife hereafter.'
So we exchanged words with one another. Women   225
Came up, and noble Persephone sent them forth,
All of whom were the wives and daughters of excellent men.
They gathered in clusters around the black blood.
And I thought about how I might question each one.
This seemed to me in my heart to be the best plan: 230
To draw the long-pointed sword from beside my stout thigh
And not allow all to drink the black blood together.
They came on in succession, and each one
Announced her descent. I inquired of them all.
First I saw Tyro³ there, who had a fine father,   235
Who claimed to be descended from blameless Salmoneus.
She said she was the wife of Cretheus, son of Aeolos;
She had fallen in love with a river, the godly Enipeus,
Which flows loveliest by far of the rivers on earth,
And she frequented the lovely streams of the Enipeus.   240
Likened to him, the earth-shaker who holds up the earth
Lay beside her at the mouth of the eddying river.

3. Grandmother of Jason and Nestor.

The purple wave stood up around them like a mountain
Arching, and it hid the god and the mortal woman.
He loosened her virgin sash and shed sleep down upon her.   245
And when the god had completed the deed of love
He took her hand and spoke out to her directly:
'Rejoice in this love, woman, and when the year comes round
You will bear glorious children; not barren are the beds
Of the immortals. Take care of them and bring them up.   250
And now go to your home; stay quiet and do not mention it.
Behold, I am Poseidon, the shaker of the earth.'
When he had said this, he went down under the wave-breaking ocean.
She was pregnant and gave birth to Pelias and Neleus,[4]
Who became mighty servants of great Zeus, both of them.   255
Pelias in Iolcos of the broad dancing-place,
Dwelt rich with flocks, and the other in sandy Pylos.
And to Cretheus the queen of women bore other sons,
Aeson[5] and Pheres and Amythaon, whose delight was in horses.
After her I saw Antiope, Asopos' daughter,   260
Who declared she had lain in the embrace of Zeus
And gave birth to two sons, Amphion and Zethos,
Who first founded the seat of Thebes with the seven gates
And built its rampart, since without a rampart they could not,
Though mighty, inhabit Thebes of the broad dancing-place.   265
And after her I saw Alcmene, Amphitryon's wife,
Who bore Heracles of steadfast boldness and a lion's heart
After she had lain in the embrace of great Zeus;
And Megara, the daughter of haughty-spirited Creon,[6]
Whom Amphitryon's son, ever unwearied in his strength, had wed.   270
I saw the mother of Oedipos,[7] lovely Epicaste,
Who did an enormous deed in the ignorance of her mind
And married her son. He slew his own father
And married her. The gods soon made these things known to men.
But he suffered pains in his much-beloved Thebes,   275
And ruled the Cadmeians through the destructive plans of the gods;
And she went to the place of the mighty gatekeeper Hades.
She hung up a high noose from the lofty roofbeam,
Possessed by her grief. For him she left many pains
Behind her, the kind a mother's Furies bring to pass.   280
And I saw the Beautiful Chloris,[8] whom Neleus once
Married for her beauty, and gave numberless bridal gifts.
She was the youngest daughter of Amphion, son of Iasos,
Who once ruled by force in Minyan Orchomenos.

---

4. Pelias, Pheres, and Amythaon are uncles of Jason; Neleus, father of Nestor.
5. Father of Jason.
6. A king of Thebes.
7. A king of Thebes; son of Laios and Epicaste (in Homer).
8. Mother of Nestor.

She was queen over Pylos; she bore him glorious children,   285
Nestor, Chromios, and honored Periclymenos,
And she bore, besides, goodly Pero, a wonder to mortals,
Whom all her neighbors wooed. Nor would Neleus give her
To one who could not drive away from Phylace
The crumple-horned, broad-browed cattle of mighty Iphiclos,   290
Difficult as they were. An excellent prophet[9] alone
Undertook to drive them. The hard fate of the gods bound him,
And difficult bonds, and the cowherds of the fields.
But when the months and the days were finished out
Of the year coming back around, and the seasons came on,   295
Then mighty Iphiclos released him when he had told all
That was decreed. And a plan of Zeus was accomplished.
I saw Leda also, the wife of Tyndareus,[1]
Who bore to Tyndareus two sons of mighty mind,
Horse-taming Castor and Polydeuces, who is good at boxing,   300
Both of whom the grain-giving earth holds alive.
Even beneath the earth they have honor from Zeus.
One time they live, on alternate days, and another time
They are dead. Honor equal to the gods is allotted them.
And after her I saw Iphimedeia, the wife   305
Of Aloeus, who said she had lain with Poseidon,
And she had two sons that were born short-lived,
The godlike Otos and the far-famed Ephialtes,
Who were the tallest men nourished by the grain-giving earth,
And by far the handsomest, next to famous Orion,   310
For after nine seasons these men were nine cubits
In breadth, and they were also nine fathoms in height.
They made threats to the immortals upon Olympos
That they would start the combat of an impetuous war.
They strove to put Ossa on Olympos, and to put on Ossa,   315
Leaf-quivering Pelion, so that heaven might be scaled.
And they would have done it had they reached the measure of their
    prime;
But the son of Zeus,[2] whom fair-haired Leto bore, destroyed
Both of them, before the whiskers beneath their temples
Had flowered and their chins got thick with blossoming down.   320
I saw Phaedra and Procris and lovely Ariadne,[3]
Daughter of destruction-minded Minos, whom Theseus
Once was leading out of Crete to the knoll of sacred Athens

---

9. The seer Melampos, whom Iphiclos first captured and then released.
1. Father of Clytemnestra.
2. Apollo.
3. Phaedra: daughter of the Cretan king Minos and wife of the Athenian hero Theseus after he
   killed the Minotaur. Procris: daughter of Erechtheus, king of Athens, unfaithful to a husband
   who accidentally killed her. Ariadne: Phaedra's sister who, after helping Theseus out of the
   labyrinth and escaping with him, was abandoned by him on the island where Artemis killed
   her.

But did not enjoy her, for Artemis slew her beforehand
In flood-circled Dia for what Dionysos testified.   325
Maire and Clymene I saw and hateful Eriphyle,[4]
Who took precious gold in return for her own husband.
I cannot tell or mention all of the women
I saw in numbers there, wives and daughters of heroes.
Ambrosial night would wane first. Now it is time   330
For me to sleep, whether I go to my companions on the swift ship
Or stay here. The convoy shall be your concern, and the gods'."
So he said. And they all became silent in stillness.
They were held in rapture through the shadowy halls.
Then white-armed Arete began to speak among them: 335
"Phaeacians, how does this man appear to you to be,
In form and in size, and in his mind well-balanced within?
He is my guest, and yet each has a share in the honor.
Let us not hasten to send him off, and do not stint
Of gifts to a man so needy, since, by favor of the gods,   340
Many possessions lie stored for you in your halls."
And the old hero Echeneus spoke out among them,
Who was an elder among the Phaeacian men:
"My friends, our prudent queen has not spoken to us
Wide of the mark or of repute. Do as she says.   345
On Alcinoos here the word and the deed depend."
Then Alcinoos spoke to him and gave him an answer:
"So shall this word come about, if I be indeed
Alive and rule the Phaeacians, who are fond of rowing.
Let the stranger, though greatly desiring a return,   350
Still endure to wait till tomorrow until I complete
The entire gift. The convoy will concern all the men,
And me especially, as I have power in the land."
Odysseus of many wiles addressed him in answer:
"Lordly Alcinoos, exalted among all your people,   355
Even if you should bid me to stay here for a year
And urged on an convoy and gave glorious gifts,
I would want to do it, since it would be better by far
To reach one's dear fatherland with a fuller hand;
Then I would be more respected and loved by all   360
The men who might see me return to Ithaca."
Alcinoos gave him an answer and spoke to him:
"Odysseus, as we look on you we would not think you
To be a deceiver and cheat the way many men are
Whom the black earth nourishes, and are widely dispersed,   365
Fashioning falsehoods out of what no one could see;
There is grace in your words and your thoughts are noble.

4. Maire: a nymph of Artemis, killed for breaking her vow of chastity. Clymene: wife of a king of
   Minyan Orchemenos. Eriphyle: wife of Amphiaraos, whom she persuaded to join the siege of
   Thebes, where he knew he would be killed.

As a singer would, you have skillfully told the tale
Of all the Argives' sad troubles and of your own.
But come, tell me this and speak out truthfully: 370
Did you see any of the godlike companions that went
Along to Ilion with you and there met a fate?
This night is prodigiously long. It is not yet time
To sleep in the hall. Do tell me your wondrous deeds.
I would hold out until the godly dawn, so long   375
As you could endure to recount your cares in the hall."
Odysseus of many wiles addressed him in answer:
"Lordly Alcinoos, exalted among all your people,
There is a time for many tales and also a time for sleep.
But if you are still longing to listen, I would not myself   380
Refuse you in this, to tell other more piteous things,
The cares of my companions who perished afterward,
Who escaped from the grievous war cry of the Trojans
But died on returning at the will of an evil woman.
Moreover when holy Persephone had scattered the souls   385
Of the womanfolk off in all directions,
The soul came of Agamemnon, son of Atreus,
Grieving; and others gathered about who had died
And had met their fate with him in the house of Aigisthos.
He recognized me at once when he had drunk the black blood.   390
He wailed piercingly and shed a swelling tear,
Stretching his hands toward me in striving to reach me.
But his strength was not still steadfast and he had no force
Such as there used to be before in his supple limbs.
I wept to see him and pitied him in my heart.   395
And speaking out to him, I uttered wingèd words:
'Glorious son of Atreus, lord of men, Agamemnon,
What fate has overcome you of long-sorrowful death?
Was it that Poseidon overcame you in your ships,
Raising up a dreadful blast of disastrous winds?   400
Or did hostile men ravage you upon the mainland
As you were cutting off cattle and the fine fleece of sheep,
Or as you were fighting over their city and their women?'
So I said, and he at once addressed me in answer:
'Zeus-born son of Laertes, Odysseus of many devices,   405
Poseidon did not overcome me in my ships,
Raising up a dreadful blast of disastrous winds.
Nor did hostile men ravage me on the mainland.
But Aigisthos fashioned for me my death and my fate.
With my cursèd wife he killed me, inviting me to his house,   410
Feasting me, the way a man slaughters an ox in a crib.
So I died a most grievous death, and my other companions
They killed without blenching, as boars with shining tusks
Are killed in the house of a rich and very powerful man

At a marriage or a joint feast[5] or a fruitful banquet.   415
You have encountered already the slaughter of many men
Slain singly, and also in a mighty combat,
But you would most have grieved in your heart to see that,
How we lay in the hall about the mixing bowls
And the full tables, and the whole ground swam with blood.   420
Most pitiful of all, I heard the voice of Priam's daughter,
Cassandra, whom wily Clytemnestra murdered
Next to me. But I reached my hands to the earth,
Then threw them as I died around the blade. The bitch-faced woman
Turned away; as I went to Hades she could not bear   425
To shut my eyes with her hands and close up my mouth.
So there is nothing more dreadful and shameless than a woman
Who would set out within her mind such deeds at these,
The sort of disgraceful deed which that woman plotted,
Devising murder for her wedded husband. I thought   430
Indeed that I would come home welcome to my children
And my servants. But she, with utter evil on her mind,
Poured shame upon herself and upon womenkind to come
Hereafter, even on one who might do good deeds.'
So he said, and then I addressed him in answer: 435
'Alas, broad-seeing Zeus has terribly hated
The descent of Atreus from the outset because of the plans
Of women. Many men perished because of Helen;
Clytemnestra made a plot against you while you were far away,
So I said, and he at once addressed me in answer: 440
'So never be mild yourself, henceforth, even to your wife.
Reveal to her no entire story that you know well,
But tell a part of it and let the rest be concealed.
But your own death, Odysseus, will not at all be from your wife.
Highly trustworthy and of good care in her mind   445
Is Icarios' daughter, the prudent Penelope.
We left her as a young bride when we went off to war
And she had an infant child at her breast, who now
Is seated, I suppose, amid the number of the men;
Blessed, for his dear father will see him when he comes,   450
And the man will embrace his father, as is right.
My wife never allowed me to fill my eyes up
With my son. She killed me beforehand, my very self.
I will tell you another thing and put it in your mind:
Hold your ship on course secretly, not openly,   455
To your fatherland. There is no longer any trust in women.
But come, tell me this and speak out truthfully:
Or perhaps you men have heard of my son as still living
In Orchomenos or else in sandy Pylos

---

5. *Eranos*: a feast to which each guest brought an equal share.

Or perhaps with Menelaos in broad Sparta.   460
For godly Orestes is not yet dead on the earth.'
So he said, and I addressed him in answer:
'Son of Atreus, why do you ask me this? I know nothing
Whether he is dead or alive. It is bad to utter windy things.'
The two of us stood there exchanging dreadful speeches   465
In that way, grieving, and shedding our swelling tears.
The soul of Achilles, son of Peleus, came up;
The soul of Patroclos and of excellent Antilochos,
And of Ajax who was the finest in body and form
Of all the Danaans, after the excellent son of Peleus.   470
The soul of the swift-footed offspring of Aeacos[6] knew me,
And in lamentation he uttered wingèd words:
'Zeus-born son of Laertes, Odysseus of many devices,
Rash man, what still greater deed will you plot in your mind?
How have you dared to come down to Hades, where the dead   475
Dwell senseless, the phantoms of mortals who are worn out?'
So he said, and I addressed him in answer:
'Achilles, son of Peleus, bravest of the Achaians,
I came in need of Tiresias, if he might tell me
Some plan whereby I might come to craggy Ithaca;   480
For I have not yet come close to Achaia, I have not yet
Set foot on my land, but have ills always. Achilles,
No man in the past or hereafter is more blessed than you.
When you were alive before, the Argives honored you
Equal to the gods. Now you greatly rule over the dead,   485
Being here as you are. So do not grieve now you are dead, Achilles.'
Thus I spoke, and he at once addressed me in answer:
'Noble Odysseus, do not commend death to me.
I would rather serve on the land of another man
Who had no portion and not a great livelihood   490
Than to rule over all the shades of those who are dead.
Come now and tell me the story of my noble son,
Did he follow to battle and become a chief or not?
Tell me about blameless Peleus, if you have heard anything;
Does he have honor still with the many Myrmidons,   495
Or do they show him no honor through Hellas and Phthia
Because old age constrains him in his hands and feet?
For I am no protector under the rays of the sun
Of the kind I was at one time when in broad Troy
I slew their best men, defending for the Argives.   500
If I could come that way just a while to my father's house,
Then I would make my might and invincible hands hateful
To any of those who compel him and force him from honor.'
So he said, and I for my part addressed him in answer:

6. Grandfather of Achilles.

'No, I have not heard anything about blameless Peleus.   505
But about your beloved son Neoptolemos
I shall tell you the whole truth, as you request me.
I brought him myself on my hollow, balanced ship,
Out of Scyros after the well-greaved Achaians.
And when we declared our proposals about the city of Troy,   510
He always spoke first, and he did not err in his speech.
I believe godlike Nestor and I alone did surpass him.
And when on the plain of the Trojans we Achaians fought
He would never remain in the throng or the crowd of men.
He ran far out front, yielding in his strength to no one.   515
In the dreadful combat he slaughtered numerous men.
I shall not myself mention and tell of them all,
The great host he killed, blameless among the Argives.
Yes, how he slaughtered with the sword the son of Telephos,
The hero Eurypylos! Many companions about him   520
Of the Ceteians were killed for the gifts of a woman.
He was the handsomest man I saw next to godly Memnon.
And when we, the best of the Argives, went into the horse
That Epeios had made, the whole rule was laid on me
Of opening and closing the door of the stout decoy.   525
There the other leaders and counselors of the Danaans
Wiped their tears, and the limbs of each trembled beneath him.
But that man I never saw with my eyes at all
Go pallid on his fair flesh or wipe off the tears
From his cheeks. He besought me very frequently   530
To let him go out of the horse. He kept stroking his sword's hilt
And his bronze-heavy spear; and he planned ills for the Trojans.
And when we had sacked the lofty city of Priam,
He went on board the ship with a noble portion and prize,
Unscathed; he had not been hit by the sharp bronze spear   535
Or wounded in close combat, such as many times
Happens in war; Ares does rage helter-skelter.'
So I said; the soul of the swift-footed son of Aeacos
Moved on with great strides through the asphodel meadow
In joy that I said his son was illustrious.   540
The other souls of the shades of those who had died
Stood there grieving, and each one asked of his cares.
Alone did the soul of Ajax, son of Telamon,
Stand off apart, angered about the victory
That I had won over him when judgment was made by the ships   545
About the armor of Achilles. His queenly mother had set it.
The sons of the Trojans judged it, and Pallas Athene.
Would I had not won in a contest of that kind!
For the sake of those arms the earth closed over the great head
Of Ajax, who by his form and his deeds had surpassed   550

The other Danaans, after Peleus' blameless son.
I myself spoke out to him with soothing words:
'Ajax, son of blameless Telamon, are you destined
Not to forget, even in death, your anger at me
For the cursèd armor? The gods gave it as a trouble to the Argives,   555
Since you died, such a bulwark of them. The Achaians
Grieved constantly for you when you perished, just as much
As for Peleus' son Achilles. There was no one else
To blame but Zeus, who terribly hated the host
Of Danaan spearsmen, and set your fate upon you.   560
But come hither, lord, so that you may hear our speech
And our story. Subdue your strength and your bold heart.'
So I said, but he answered me nothing and went with the other
Souls of the shades of the dead to Erebos.
And he would have spoken in anger, just as I to him,   565
But the spirit within my own breast desired
To see the souls of the other men who had died.
There I saw Minos, the illustrious son of Zeus,
With a golden scepter dealing out justice to the dead,
Seated. And they kept asking that lord about laws,   570
While they sat and stood in the wide-gated house of Hades.
After him I caught sight of the enormous Orion,
Driving beasts together through the asphodel meadow
That he had slaughtered himself on the lovely mountains,
Holding in his hands an all-bronze club, ever unbroken.   575
And I saw Tityos, the renowned son of Gaia,
Lying on the ground. He lay more than nine measures long.
And two vultures, perched on both sides, rent at his liver,
Plunging into the caul. He could not ward them off with his hands,
For he had dragged off Leto, the glorious mistress of Zeus,   580
As she came to Pytho through fair-lawned Panopeus.
And I saw Tantalos, who had difficult pains,
Standing in a lake. He was plunged up to his chin,
And pressed on in his thirst, but he could not reach to take a drink.
As often as the old man bent over striving to drink   585
The water disappeared, swallowed, and at his feet
Black earth appeared; and some god kept drying it up.
Trees with lofty foliage from their tops shed fruit,
Pears, pomegranates, and apples with shining fruit,
And sweet figs and blossoming wild olives;   590
And when the old man straightened to stretch his hands for them,
The wind kept tossing them toward the shadowy clouds.
And then I saw Sisyphos, who had difficult pains
Pushing a monstrous stone up with both of his hands.
And indeed he made a leaning effort with hands and feet   595
To push the stone up the crest. But when it was about

To go over the top, then it turned back down with its force;
The shameless stone rolled on down again to the plain.
Then he pushed it back again, exerting himself, and the sweat
Flowed off his limbs and dust rose up around his head.   600
After him I caught sight of powerful Heracles,
A phantom. For he himself with the immortal gods
Enjoys abundance and has Hebe of the fair ankles,
Child of great Zeus and of Hera with the golden sandals.
There was a shrieking about him of the dead as of birds   605
Terrified on all sides. And he like the gloomy night
Held his bare bow with an arrow on the string,
Peering dreadfully like one who is ever about to shoot.
Terrible was the sword strap circling him round the chest,
A golden belt on which wonderful things were fashioned,   610
Bears and savage boars and lions with glaring eyes,
Battles and combats and slaughters and murders of men.
May he never make or never have made any other,
The man who conceived that belt in his own skill.
He knew me at once when he saw me with his eyes,   615
And lamenting to me, he uttered wingèd words:
'Zeus-born son of Laertes, Odysseus of many devices,
Wretched man, what an evil fate you too are carrying on,
Such as I bore myself beneath the rays of the sun!
I was a child of Zeus, son of Cronos, but I had   620
Boundless woe, for I was subdued to a mortal,
Inferior by far, who put difficult tasks on me.
He sent me here once to bring the dog. He did not think
Any task would be more difficult for me than this.
But I did take the dog and lead him out of the place of Hades.   625
Hermes escorted me, and bright-eyed Athene.'
When he had said this, he went back into the hall of Hades.
But I stayed there on the spot in case anyone came
Of the heroes, men who had perished in time before,
And I still would have seen men of old whom I wished to see,   630
Theseus and Perithous,[7] glorious children of the gods,
But first numberless bands of the dead came on
With a tremendous shout, and sallow fear seized me
Lest noble Persephone send the Gorgon[8] head
Of the dread monster from the hall of Hades against me.   635
At once I went on the ship and called my companions
To board it themselves and to untie the stern cables.
They boarded it at once and sat down at the oarlocks,
And a wave of the stream bore it to the river Oceanos;
First there was rowing, and after that a fair breeze.   640

7. Proverbial friend of Theseus.
8. The dead head of a fearful monster (possibly not the same as the later Gorgon).

XII

"And when the ship had left the stream of the river
Oceanos, and reached the wave of the wide-pathed sea
And the island Aiaia, where the home and the dancing floors
Of the early-born dawn are, and the risings of the sun;
When we arrived there, we beached the ship on the sands   5
And got out ourselves beside the surf of the sea.
We fell asleep there and awaited the godly dawn.
And when the early-born, rosy-fingered dawn appeared,
I sent my companions off to the halls of Circe
To bring the body of Elpenor, who had died.   10
At once we cut logs where the shore jutted highest out,
And we buried him, lamenting and shedding a swelling tear.
When his dead body had been burned, and the gear of his body,
We heaped up a mound, dragged a grave marker up on it,
And set up his well-shaped oar on top of the mound.   15
We talked out the details, nor did we escape the notice
Of Circe as we came from Hades, but very swiftly
She adorned herself and came. Servants with her carried
Bread, many pieces of meat, and sparkling red wine.
The divine goddess took her stand in our midst and spoke: 20
'Rash you are, who have gone alive into the hall of Hades,
Dying twice, when other men die a single time:
Well, come, eat of the provisions and drink wine
All day long in this place, and as soon as dawn appears
You shall set sail. I shall show you the way and point out   25
All the details, lest by some troublesome complication
You be hurt and suffer pain on land or on the sea.'
So she said, and the bold heart was persuaded within us.
So then for the entire day till the setting of the sun
We sat there dining on the endless meat and sweet wine.   30
But when the sun went down and the darkness came on
The men lay down by the stern cable of the ship.
She took me by the hand aside from my dear companions,
Sat me down, lay next to me, and asked me the details,
And I told everything to her in its due order.   35
Then the queenly Circe addressed a speech to me:
'So all this has been brought to an end. Now listen
To what I tell you; a god himself shall remind you.
First you will come to the Sirens, who enchant
All men, whenever anyone comes upon them.   40
Whoever in ignorance nears them and hears the voice
Of the Sirens—for that man, his wife and infant children
Do not stand by or rejoice at his homeward return,
But the Sirens enchant him with their clear-toned song,

Seated in a meadow. About is a large heap of bones,   45
Of men rotting, and the skin is shrinking around them.
But go on past; soften honey-sweet wax and smear it
In the ears of your companions lest any of the rest
Should listen. And if you yourself desire to listen,
Let them bind you upon the swift ship hand and foot   50
Erect at the mast; and let the rope ends be made fast from it,
So that you may hear and enjoy the Sirens' song.
If you implore your companions and call on them to free you,
Then have them bind you in further fastenings.
And when your companions have got on past those women,   55
At that point I shall no longer tell you in full detail
Which one of two ways will be yours, but you yourself
Must decide in your heart. I will tell you the alternatives:
In one place there are overhanging rocks; and against them
The great wave of dark blue-eyed Amphitrite roars.   60
Those, indeed, do the blessed gods call the Wandering Rocks,
Where nothing that flies can get by, not even the timid
Doves that carry ambrosia to father Zeus.
And the sheer rock always takes away one of them,
But the Father sends another to make up the number.   65
No ship of men that arrives there ever escapes,
But sea waves and storms of destructive fire carry off
The timbers of the ships and the bodies of the men alike.
One seafaring ship alone did sail past the place,
The Argo, known to all men, as it sailed from Aietes,[1]   70
And it would swiftly have been dashed there on the great rocks
But Hera sent it past, since Jason was dear to her.
The other way there are two crags; one reaches to broad heaven
With its sharp peak, and a dark blue cloud surrounds it
That never recedes, nor ever does a clear sky   75
Hold the peak of it, either in summer or in autumn.
No mortal man could ever climb it or get on top,
Not even if he had twenty hands and twenty feet,
For the rock is sheer, as though polished all around,
And in the middle of the crag is a murky cave   80
Turned facing to the dusk toward Erebos, and there,
Noble Odysseus, you should steer your hollow ship.
Nor could a vigorous man shooting with a bow
From the hollow ship reach to the open cave.
There within dwells Scylla, who barks dreadfully,   85
And her voice comes as loud as that of an unweaned puppy.
But she herself is an evil monster, nor would anyone
Take pleasure to see her, not if a god should confront her.
There are twelve feet on her, all dangling in air;

1. King of Colchis, father of Medea. The *Argo* was Jason's ship.

She has six very long necks, and on each one   90
A terrible head, and on it three rows of teeth
Thick-set and in a cluster, and full of black death.
She is withdrawn to her middle down in the hollow cave;
She holds her heads outside of the dreadful abyss,
And there she fishes and reaches all around the crag   95
For dolphins and dogfish and whatever larger sea creature
She may catch that roaring Amphitrite feeds by the thousands
There no sailors may ever claim to have escaped past
Unharmed with their ship. She carries off in each head
A mortal she has snatched up from a dark blue-prowed ship.   100
The second crag you will see lying lower, Odysseus,
Close to the other. And you could shoot an arrow across it.
Upon it is a large wild fig tree blooming with leaves;
There divine Charybdis sucks black water back under.
Three times daily she sends it up, three times sucks back   105
Terribly. Do not happen to be there when she sucks,
For not even the earth-shaker could save you from evil then,
But sail to the crag of Scylla very rapidly
And drive your ship on past, since it is better by far
To miss six companions on the ship than all at once.'   110
So she said, and I spoke out to her in answer:
'Come now, goddess, tell me this unerringly,
May I get away from destructive Charybdis somehow
And ward off the other, once she has despoiled my companions?'
So I said, and the divine goddess answered at once: 115
'You rash man, do the works of war concern you again
And toil? Will you not yield to the immortal gods?
She is not mortal for you, but an immortal evil,
Dreadful, oppressive, wild, and not to be fought.
And there is no defense. It is best to flee from her.   120
But if you linger and helm yourself beside the rock,
I fear that she may search and light on you again
And take away as many mortals as she has heads.
No, drive very strongly on, cry aloud for Cratais,
The mother of Scylla, who bore her as a bane for mortals.   125
Then she will stop her from reaching out a second time.
You will arrive at the isle of Thrinacria. There many
Oxen of the Sun and goodly sheep are pasturing,
Seven herds of cattle and as many lovely flocks of sheep,
Fifty in each. No offspring are born from them,   130
Nor do they ever wane. Goddesses and shepherds over them,
The fair-braided nymphs, Phaethusa and Lampetie,
Whom divine Neaira bore to Hyperion, the Sun.
When their queenly mother had borne them and raised them,
She sent them to the isle of Thrinacria to live far off,   135
To guard the sheep and crumple-horned cattle of their father.

If you let them go unmolested and think of your return,
You may get to Ithaca, though you do suffer ills.
But if you molest them, then I prophesy destruction
For your ship and companions. And even if you escape yourself   140
You will return late and ill, having lost all your companions.'
So she said, and at once the golden-throned Dawn came on.
The divine goddess herself returned then up the island,
But I went on to the ship and urged my companions
To go on board themselves and to undo the stern cables.   145
At once they got on and took their seats at the oarlocks.
Seated in order, they beat the hoary sea with their oars.
A driving wind full in the sails, a fine companion,
Did the fair-braided Circe, dread god with a singing voice,
Send on for us from behind the dark blue-prowed ship.   150
At once when we had tended to the gear through the ship piece by piece
We took our seats. The wind and a pilot steered her.
Then, grieving in my heart, I spoke to my companions:
'My friends, not one person or two alone need to know
The prophecies that the divine goddess Circe told me.   155
But I will tell them, so you may know whether we
Shall die or might avoid death and escape fate.
She ordered us first to avoid the voice of the marvelous
Sirens, and also their meadow full of flowers.
Me alone she ordered to hear their voice; but bind me   160
In hard bonds so that I may stay firm in my place
Erect at the mast. And let the rope-ends be fastened from it.
And if I implore you and call you to untie me
Then constrain me yourselves in further fastenings.'
So I declared, and made known the details to my companions.   165
Meanwhile the well-made ship arrived speedily
At the isle of the Sirens. A fair breeze drove it on.
Then at that point the wind died down, and there was
A windless calm, and some god put the waves to sleep.
My companions stood up and furled the sails on the ship.   170
They threw them in the hollow ship; then, seated at the oars,
They made the water white with the blades of smooth fir.
But I cut up a great disc of wax with the sharp sword
Into small pieces and kneaded it with my stout hands.
At once the wax softened when my great force had compelled it,   175
And the gleam of the Sun, Hyperion's lordly child.
I smeared it in all my companions' ears one by one,
And they bound me on the ship by my hands and feet
Erect on the mast and fastened rope ends from it.
Taking their seats, they beat the hoary sea with their oars.   180
But when it was as far off as a man's shout would carry,
While we pushed swiftly on, the fast-sailing ship did not get past
The Sirens—as it drew near, they struck up their clear-toned song:

'Come near, much-praised Odysseus, the Achaians' great glory;
Bring your ship in, so you may listen to our voice.   185
No one ever yet sped past this place in a black ship
Before he listened to the honey-toned voice from our mouths,
And then he went off delighted and knowing more things.
For we know all the many things that in broad Troy
The Argives and the Trojans suffered at the will of the gods.   190
We know all that comes to be on the much-nourishing earth.'
So they said, sending their lovely voice out. My heart
Desired to listen, and I told my companions to free me,
Signaling with my eyebrows. Falling to it, they rowed.
Standing up at once, Perimedes and Eurylochos   195
Bound me in further bonds and constrained me more,
And when we had got on past them and could no longer
Listen to the cry of the Sirens or their voice,
At once my trusty companions took out the wax
I had smeared in their ears and freed me from my bonds.   200
But when we had left the island, then at once
I saw smoke and a great wave and heard a noise.
As the men were afraid, the oars flew from their hands;
They all splashed down on the current. And the ship held
In place, since they could no longer drive the sharp-bladed oars with
    their hands.   205
But I went on through the ship, urging my companions
With soothing speeches, standing close to each man:
'Friends, so far we are not unacquainted with evils,
And this is really no greater evil upon us than when the Cyclops
Penned us in his hollow cave by his powerful force.   210
Yet even from there, through my prowess and my plan and thought,
We escaped, and I think perhaps we shall remember this too.
Come now, do as I tell you, let us all obey.
Beat the deep breakers of the sea with your oars,
Seated at the oarlocks, so that Zeus somehow   215
May grant that we escape and avoid this destruction.
To you, pilot, I give this command. And put it
In your heart as you tend the rudder of the hollow ship.
Keep the ship on the outside of this smoke and this wave,
And make for the crag lest the ship get away from you   220
As it rushes out there and you plunge us all into evil.'
So I said, and they obeyed my words right away.
I said no more of Scylla, the unavoidable danger,
Lest somehow in their fear over me my companions
Should cease from the rowing and crowd themselves within.   225
And then I forgot the hard injunction of Circe
When she ordered me in no way to arm myself.
I put on my famous armor, took two long spears
In my hands, and went up on the deck of the ship

At the prow, for from that place I expected rocky Scylla   230
First to be sighted, who bore me woe for my companions.
I could not discern her anywhere. My eyes were tired
As I peered everywhere out toward the murky rock.
And we sailed on through the narrow passage, lamenting.
There was Scylla, and on the other side godly Charybdis   235
Sucked back terribly the salt water of the sea.
Whenever she disgorged, like a basin in a large fire,
She seethed, all stirred up. And from overhead, foam
Fell down on both sides of the peaks of the crags,
And when she swallowed down the salt water of the sea   240
She appeared all stirred up within, and the rock roared
Terribly about, and the earth appeared underneath
In dark blue sand. Sallow fear seized the men.
We looked toward her in fear of our destruction.
Meanwhile Scylla snatched off of the hollow ship   245
Six of my companions, who were mightiest in strength.
But when I looked into the swift ship toward my companions
I saw already their hands and their feet from above
As they were lifted on high. They called to me with a cry,
Calling me then by name for the last time, grieving in heart.   250
As a fisher on a promontory with a very long rod
Throws down morsels as a lure for the little fish
And sends down into the ocean the horn of a field ox;
Then when he catches one writhing, throws it ashore;
So they, writhing, were raised up toward the rocks.   255
There at the entrance she ate them as they shrieked,
Reaching their hands toward me in their dread struggle.
That was the most piteous thing I saw with my eyes
Of all that I suffered as I sought out the paths of the sea.
But when we had fled the rocks and terrible Charybdis   260
And Scylla, we arrived at once at the blameless island
Of the god, where the beautiful broad-browed cattle were,
And the many goodly flocks of Hyperion, the Sun.
Then, while I was still on the ocean in the black ship,
I heard a lowing of cattle coming to the fold   265
And a bleating of sheep. Then there fell on my heart the speech
Of the blind prophet Theban Tiresias,
And of Aiaian Circe, who enjoined me many times
To avoid the isle of the Sun, who delights mortal men.
So then I addressed my companions, grieving in my heart: 270
'Hear my speech, though you have suffered ills, my companions,
So I may tell you the prophecies of Tiresias
And of Aiaian Circe, who enjoined me many times
To avoid the isle of the Sun, who delights mortal men.
They said a most dreadful evil would come on us there.   275
So let us drive the black ship on past that island.'

So I said, and their own hearts were shattered within them.
Eurylochos answered me at once with a hateful speech:
'You are tough, Odysseus, with your superior strength; your limbs
Do not get tired, but they are made all of iron for you   280
Who will not let your companions, worn out with fatigue
And sleepiness, set foot on land, where, moreover,
On the flood-circled island we might make a pleasant dinner,
But you bid us to wander as we are through the sudden night,
Carried away from the island upon the murky ocean.   285
And hard winds come up out of the night, the destroyers
Of ships. Where might one escape sheer destruction
If suddenly a storm of wind by chance came on,
Of the South Wind or the hard-blowing West Wind, that most
Tear ships to pieces beyond the will of the ruling gods?   290
No, but indeed, let us now give in to the black night.
Let us prepare dinner as we stay by the swift ship.
At dawn we shall get in and proceed on the broad ocean.'
So Eurylochos said, and my other companions agreed.
Then I knew that some god had devised evils,   295
And I spoke out to him, uttering wingèd words:
'Eurylochos, indeed you compel me, single as I am.
Come then, all of you, and swear me a mighty oath.
If we find some herd of cattle or a great flock
Of sheep, that no one in evil recklessness   300
Will slaughter any cow or sheep. But be secure
And eat the provisions that immortal Circe gave.'
So I said, and they at once swore an oath as I bid them.
And when they had sworn the oath and completed it,
They set the well-fashioned ship in a hollow harbor   305
Near sweet water. My companions got out and away
From the ship and then prepared dinner skillfully.
But when they had taken their fill of food and drink,
They then remembered and wept for our dear companions
Whom Scylla had snatched out of the hollow ship and eaten.   310
Balmy sleep came upon them as they were weeping.
When it was the third part of night and the stars had gone by
Cloud-gathering Zeus raised a wind to blow against them
In a tremendous storm, and he covered land and ocean alike
Over with clouds. And night rose up out of heaven.   315
And when the early-born, rosy-fingered dawn appeared,
We beached the ship, dragging her into a hollow cave
Where the fair dancing-floors and the haunts of the nymphs were.
And then I made an assembly and addressed them a speech.
'My friends, since there is food and drink in the swift ship,   320
Let us hold off from the cattle, lest we suffer something.
These are the cattle and goodly sheep of a dreadful god,
The Sun, who sees everything and hears everything.'

So I said, and the bold spirit was persuaded in them.
The South Wind blew steadily a whole month; no other   325
Wind came up then except the East Wind and the South.
So long as they possessed grain and red wine
They held off from the cattle in their desire for life.
But when all the provisions had been used up from the ship,
They went out on the hunt, roving from necessity   330
For fish and birds, with bent hooks, for whatever came
Into their own hands. Hunger wore down their bellies.
Then I went away, up into the island so that I might pray
To the gods, for one to show me the way to return.
When I had gone through the island and got clear of my com-
    panions,   335
I washed my hands where there was shelter from the wind,
And I prayed to all of the gods who possess Olympos.
But they poured sweet sleep on me over my eyelids.
And Eurylochos unfolded a bad plan to my companions:
'Hear my speech, companions, though you have suffered ills.   340
There are all kinds of hateful deaths for wretched mortals,
But most piteous is to die and meet one's fate by hunger.
Come then, let us drive the best of the cattle of the Sun
And sacrifice them to the immortals who hold broad heaven,
And if we ever get to Ithaca, our fatherland,   345
We shall at once build a rich temple to Hyperion,
The Sun, and put in it many noble ornaments.
But if he is at all enraged for his straight-horned cattle
And wishes to destroy the ship, and the other gods follow,
I would rather gasp once into a wave and lose my life   350
Then to be starved a long time on a desert island.'
So Eurylochos said, and the other companions agreed.
At once they drove the best of the cattle of the Sun
From nearby. For not far away from the dark blue-prowed ship
Did the fine crumple-horned, broad-browed cattle pasture.   355
They surrounded them and made prayers to the gods,
When they had plucked tender leaves from an oak with high foliage,
For they did not have white barley on the well-timbered ship.
But when they had prayed and had slaughtered and flayed them,
They cut out the thighs and covered them over with fat.   360
They made two folds and lay the raw flesh upon them,
Nor did they have wine to pour on the burning sacrifices,
But used water for libation and roasted all the entrails.
And when the thighs were burned and they had eaten the inward parts,
They cut the rest in pieces and pierced it on spits.   365
And then balmy sleep flew away from my eyelids.
I went down to the swift ship and the strand of the sea.
And when I got up close to the bobbing ship,
The sweet aroma of roasting came over to me.

Then I groaned and cried out to the immortal gods: 370
'Father Zeus, and you other blessed, ever-living gods,
To my ruin, indeed, have you lulled me in relentless sleep;
And my companions, while waiting, have devised an enormous deed.'
Then a messenger came swiftly to Hyperion the Sun,
Long-gowned Lampetie, to say we had killed his cattle.   375
At once he addressed the immortals, angered in his heart:
'Father Zeus, and you other blessed, ever-living gods,
Take vengeance on the companions of Laertes' son Odysseus,
Who have presumptuously killed my cattle, in which I
Took delight when I went into the starry heaven   380
And when I turned back again from heaven to earth.
If they do not pay fitting recompense for the cattle,
I will go down to the place of Hades and shine among the dead.'
Cloud-gathering Zeus spoke out to him in answer:
'O Sun, do indeed shine among the immortals   385
And among mortal men on the grain-giving earth.
I shall smite their swift ship soon with a gleaming bolt
Into small pieces, and burn it in the middle of the wine-faced ocean.'
I heard these things from Calypso of the fair hair,
Who said she had heard them herself from the runner Hermes.   390
And when I had got down to the ship and the sea,
I rebuked them one after another on the spot. Nor could we
Find any remedy. The cattle were already dead.
Then at once the gods showed forth portents to the men;
The skins were creeping, meat lowed upon the spits,   395
Both roast and raw, and there came up the voice as of cattle.
And so for six days did my trusty companions
Feast on the fine cattle of the Sun they had driven off.
But when Zeus, son of Cronos, had added the seventh day,
At that point the wind ceased raging in a tempest.   400
We boarded at once and set out upon the broad ocean,
When we had set the mast up and hoisted the white sails.
And when we had left the island behind, no other land
Appeared at all, but only heaven and the sea.
Then the son of Cronos halted a dark blue cloud   405
Over the hollow ship, and the ocean darkened beneath it.
She ran on not too long a time. For at once there came
The shrieking West Wind raging in a great tempest,
And a storm of wind broke the forestays of the mast,
Both of them, and the mast fell backward, and all the tackle   410
Was thrown into the hold. On the stern of the ship
It hit the pilot's head. And in an instant it crushed
All the bones of his head together. Like a diver
He dropped down from the deck, and the bold spirit left his bones.
Zeus at that instant thundered and threw a bolt on the ship.   415
It whirled all around, struck by Zeus's thunderbolt,

And was filled with brimstone. My companions fell from the ship,
And they resembled sea crows around the black ship
As they were borne on the waves; a god took away their return.
I wandered through my ship until the surge had loosed   420
The planks from the keel, and the wave carried it stripped.
It broke the mast off the keel, and then the backstay,
Which had been made out of oxhide, was flung up on it.
Then I bound both the keel and the mast together.
Seated on them, I was carried by the destructive winds.   425
And then the West Wind ceased raging in a tempest
And the South Wind came quickly, bearing pains for my heart,
That I should still remeasure my course to destructive Charybdis.
All night long I was carried, and with the rising sun
I came to the crag of Scylla and to dreadful Charybdis.   430
And she had sucked back the salty water of the sea,
But I raised myself high up against the tall wild fig tree
And held myself fastened to it like a bat. Nor anywhere
Could I plant my feet firmly or climb up on it,
For its roots held far off and its branches were high swaying,   435
Tall and great, and they shadowed Charybdis over.
I held there steadily, till she should disgorge back
The mast and keel again. I longed for them, but they came late.
At the time when a man gets up from the assembly for dinner,
One who judges many quarrels of youthful adversaries,   440
At that time did the timber appear out of Charybdis.
I let my hands and feet be brought down from above
And plunged right on in the midst of the lengthy timbers.
Seated upon them, I rowed on with my hands.
The father of men and gods no longer let Scylla   445
See me, or I would not have escaped sheer destruction.
Nine days I was borne thence, and on the tenth night
The gods brought me near the island of Ogygia, where lives
Fair-braided Calypso, dread god with a singing voice.
She befriended me and cared for me. Why tell this story?   450
Already I have told it in your house yesterday
To you and your goodly wife. It is hateful to me
To tell over again a story that has been clearly told."

XIII

So he said, and they all became hushed in silence.
They were held in rapture through the shadowy halls.
Then Alcinoos gave him an answer and spoke to him:
"Odysseus, since you have come to my bronze-based home
With its high roof, I think you will not be driven off course   5
In your return back, though you have suffered much.

And I say this in urging every man of you,
All those who in my halls are forever drinking
The sparkling wine of the elders and listening to the singer.
Clothes are laid up for the stranger in a polished chest,   10
And highly wrought gold and all sorts of other gifts
That the members of the Phaeacian council brought here.
Come now, let us give him a great cauldron and a basin,
Man by man. Then we shall collect among the people and get paid
   back.
It is hard for a single man to give freely for nothing."   15
So Alcinoos spoke, and his speech was pleasing to them.
They all went off, each to his house, to lie down to sleep.
And when the early-born, rosy-fingered dawn appeared,
They hastened to the ship and brought bronze that is a help for men.
Alcinoos in his sacred strength stored it well under the benches,   20
Going himself through the ship so it might not hamper
Any of the rowing crew as they sped with the oars.
They went to the home of Alcinoos and partook of dinner.
Alcinoos in his sacred strength sacrificed an ox for them
To black-clouded Zeus, son of Cronos, who rules all.   25
When they had burned the thighs, they dined on the illustrious feast
And enjoyed it. Among them the godly singer played,
Demodocos, who was honored by the people. But Odysseus
Turned his head many times to the resplendent sun,
Impatient for it to set. So eager was he to return;   30
As when a man longs for dinner whose wine-faced oxen
Have drawn the jointed plow on his fallow land all day:
He is glad when the light of the sun goes down on him
As he heads for dinner, and his knees fail as he goes;
So was Odysseus glad when the sun's light went down.   35
At once he addressed the Phaeacians, who are fond of rowing.
And to Alcinoos especially did he make known his speech:
"Lordly Alcinoos, exalted among all your people,
Pour a libation and send me home unharmed. Farewell to you!
What my own heart was wanting has now been brought to pass,   40
An escort and friendly gifts; and may the heavenly gods
Make them blessed for me! On my return may I find
My wife at home blameless, with my friends safe and sound.
You, though, stay here and give pleasure to your wedded wives
And to your children. May the gods grant excellence   45
Of all sorts to you, and no evil be among your people."
So he said, and they all assented and gave the order
To escort the stranger, since he had spoken properly.
Then Alcinoos in his might spoke out to a herald:
"Pontonoos, mix up a bowl and pass out wine   50
To all through the hall, so we may pray to Father Zeus,
And escort the stranger to his own fatherland."

So he said, and Pontonoos mixed the mind-honeying wine.
He passed it to all in turn. From the seats where they were
They poured libation to the blessed gods   55
Who possess broad heaven. Godly Odysseus stood up,
Placed a cup with two handles in Arete's hand,
And speaking out to her he uttered wingèd words:
"May you constantly fare well, my queen, till old age
And death come upon you, which do exist for men.   60
But I am going now. Enjoy yourself in this house,
With your children and your people and King Alcinoos."
When he had said this, godly Odysseus went over the threshold.
Alcinoos in his might sent a herald along with him
To lead him to the swift ship and the strand of the sea.   65
And Arete sent serving women along with him,
One of whom held a well-washed mantle and tunic,
Another she sent with her to bring the stout chest along,
And still another was carrying bread and red wine.
And when they had come down to the ship and the sea,   70
At once his noble escorts took those things and placed them
Inside the hollow ship, all of the food and drink.
They spread out a blanket and linen cloth for Odysseus
On the deck of the hollow ship, so he might sleep without waking,
Upon the stern. He himself boarded too and lay down   75
In silence. Each of them sat down at the oarlocks
In order. They loosed the cable from the pierced stone.
As soon as they leaned on the oars and flung up salt water with the blade,
For him there fell down upon his eyelids a balmy sleep,
Unwaking, most sweet, nearest in semblance to death.   80
As for the ship, the way four yoked stallions on a plain
All rush on together under the blows of a whip,
Leap up high, and pursue their journey rapidly;
So was her stern raised up, and behind her there surged
A great purple wave of the loud-roaring sea.   85
She ran safely and steadily, nor could the circling
Hawks, the nimblest of winged things, have kept up,
So rapidly did it run as it cut the waves of the sea
Carrying a man who had plans like those of the gods,
Who in time past had suffered very many pains in his heart,   90
Passing through the wars of men and the troublesome waves,
But at this time he slept without a tremor, forgetting what he had suf-
    fered.
When the brightest star rose up that most of all
Comes on to announce the light of early-born dawn,
At that time did the seafaring ship reach the island.   95
There is a certain harbor of Phorcys, the old man of the sea,
In the land of Ithaca; and there, jutting out on it,
Are two headlands broken off, sloping down to the harbor.

They give shelter against the great wave from hard-blowing winds
Outside. And inside of it well-timbered ships remain   100
Without a cable when they reach the measure of mooring.
At the head of the harbor is an olive with long leaves,
And close to that is a pleasant and shadowy cavern
Sacred to the nymphs who are called Naiades.
And in it there are mixing bowls and two-handled jars   105
Of stone. And the bees store up their honey in them.
There are very long stone looms in it, where the nymphs
Weave sea purple mantles, a wonder to behold,
And ever-flowing waters are there. It has two doors,
One toward the North Wind, accessible to men,   110
And the other one divine is toward the South Wind, nor may men
Approach by that one, but it is a path for immortals.
The men, who knew it beforehand, drove the ship in there;
And then she was beached on the mainland, half her whole length
As she ran in, so fast was she pushed on by the rowers' hands.   115
They got out of the well-benched ship onto dry land.
First they raised Odysseus out of the hollow ship,
The linen sheet and the glistening blanket and all;
They set him down on the sand overcome with sleep.
They lifted out the goods the noble Phaeacians had given   120
As he was going home through great-hearted Athene's help,
And then put them in a heap by the base of the olive tree,
Out of the path lest by chance some wayfaring man
Might find and despoil them before Odysseus woke up.
Then they started back homeward. Nor did the earth-shaker   125
Forget the curses he had made originally
Against godlike Odysseus. And he asked about Zeus's plan:
"Father Zeus, I myself shall no longer be honored
Among the immortal gods when mortals do not respect me,
The Phaeacians, who are of my very own descent.   130
For I just now said Odysseus would suffer many ills
Before he got home; I have never deprived him of a return
Entirely, since you promised this first and nodded agreement.
Yet these men have brought him asleep on the ocean in a swift ship,
Have set him down in Ithaca and given him prodigious gifts,   135
Bronze and gold and woven clothing aplenty,
Much more than Odysseus ever would have taken from Troy
If he had arrived unharmed with his share of booty."
Cloud-gathering Zeus addressed him in answer:
"Well now, wide-powered earth-shaker, what a speech you have
    made!   140
The gods do not at all insult you. It would be hard
To attack with insults the oldest and finest god—
And if some man, yielding to his strength and might,
Does not honor you, vengeance is yours forever after.

Do as you wish and as is pleasing to your own heart." 145
And then the earth-shaker Poseidon answered him:
"Black-clouded one, I would do at once as you say.
But always I respect and do deference to your heart.
And now I would like to dash the beautiful ship
Of the Phaeacians as it comes from escort on the murky sea, 150
So that henceforth they may hold back and refrain from escort
For men; and I would hide their city round with a great mountain."
Cloud-gathering Zeus addressed him in answer:
"Dear friend, in my heart this seems to me the best course:
When all the people are away from the city and catch sight 155
Of the ship coming on, make it into a stone near the land
Resembling the swift ship, so that all the men may be
Amazed; and hide the city round with a great mountain."
And when earth-shaker Poseidon had heard this speech,
He went on to Scheria where the Phaeacians dwell 160
And stayed there. The seafaring ship came very near,
Running on nimbly. The earth-shaker came near it,
And he turned it to stone and rooted it beneath,
Pressing it with the flat of his hand. Then he departed.
The Phaeacians with their long oars, men famous for ships, 165
For their part addressed wingèd words to one another.
This is what a man who saw it would say to his neighbor:
"Ah me, who has detained the swift ship in the ocean
As it was coming home? It has just appeared all in view."
So one man would say. They did not know how this was done. 170
Then Alcinoos spoke out to them and addressed them:
"Ah well, the prophecies have come upon me, spoken of old
By my father, who used to say Poseidon resented us
Because we are secure escorts for everyone.
He said a beautiful ship of the Phaeacian men 175
Coming back sometime from an escort on the murky ocean
Would be dashed, and a great mountain would hide our city round."
So the old man said. Now it has all come to pass.
But come now. Let us all observe what I shall say:
Give up escorting mortals when anyone comes 180
To our city, and let us sacrifice to Poseidon
Twelve chosen bulls so that he may take pity
And not hide our city round with a very tall mountain."
So he said; they were afraid, and prepared the bulls.
And so the leaders and counselors of the land 185
Of the Phaeacians were praying to Lord Poseidon,
Standing round the altar. But godly Odysseus woke up
From sleeping on his fatherland soil and did not recognize it,
For he had been gone a long time. A god shed a mist round him,
Pallas Athene, the daughter of Zeus, so she could make him 190
Unrecognizable, and tell him the details,

Lest his wife recognize him, and his townsmen and friends,
Before the suitors had paid for all their transgressions.
And so everything appeared of a changed form to its lord;
Continuous pathways and harbors with mooring all round,   195
Towering rocks and trees that were blossoming.
He sprang up, stood still, and looked on his fatherland soil,
And then he uttered a groan and struck both his thighs
With the flat of his hands. And he made a speech, lamenting:
"Woe is me, to the land of what mortals have I come this time?   200
Are the men proud and savage and without justice
Or are they friendly to strangers and have a god-fearing mind?
Where am I carrying these many goods? Where do I myself
Wander? Would that they had stayed with the Phaeacians
In that place. But I would have come on another of the exalted
    kings   205
Who would have befriended me and sent me on my return.
As it is I do not know where to put these things. Nor can I
Leave them here, lest they become a prey to others.
Well now, the leaders and counselors of the Phaeacians
Were not wholly prudent and just when they led me off   210
To another land. They did say they would lead me   .
To sunny Ithaca, and they did not bring it to pass.
May the Zeus of suppliants pay them back, who watches
Over all men and punishes whoever errs.
All right, I shall number the goods and look at them   215
Lest they have taken some from me and gone on the hollow ship."
When he had said this, he counted the beautiful cauldrons
And the basins and the gold and the lovely woven clothes.
He missed none of them. But he bemoaned his fatherland,
Dragging himself along the strand of the loud-roaring sea   220
And grieving much. And Athene came up close to him,
Likening her body to a young man's, a feeder of sheep,
All tender, the way the children of rulers are.
She wore a well-made double-folded mantle on her shoulders
And had sandals under her glistening feet, a javelin in her hand   225
Odysseus rejoiced to see her and came up facing her.
And speaking out to her, he uttered wingèd words:
"My friend, since you are the first one I find in this place,
Greetings. And may you not confront me with an evil mind.
But save these things and save me; I pray to you   230
As to a god, and I come up to your precious knees.
Tell me this one thing, truly, so I may know it well;
What land is this, what people? What men are native here?
Is it some sunny island, perhaps, or some shore
Of the rich-loamed mainland that lies sloping to the sea?"   235
Then the bright-eyed goddess Athene spoke to him:
"You are simple, stranger, or have come from far away

If you ask what this land is. To no great degree
Is it nameless. Very many men know which it is,
Both all those who are living toward dawn and the sun   240
And also all those who live back toward the murky dusk.
Indeed it is rough and not for driving horses,
Nor is it excessively poor, though not broad in shape.
In it is produced immense food and also wine.
Rain holds it perpetually and the fertile dew.   245
It is a good goat pasture and cow pasture. Woods
Are all over it, and it affords year-round watering places.
And so, stranger, the name Ithaca has reached even to Troy,
Which they say is far off from the Achaian land."
So she said, and godly Odysseus, who had endured much, rejoiced, 250
Glad at his fatherland soil, that Pallas Athene,
The daughter of aegis-bearing Zeus, told him of,
And speaking out to her, he uttered wingèd words.
He did not speak the truth, but he held back his story,
Forever managing the very shrewd thought in his breast: 255
"I have heard of Ithaca even in broad Crete,
Far over the ocean. And now I have come myself
With these goods; leaving as much again to my children,
I fled, since I had killed the dear son of Idomeneus,
Swift-footed Ortilochos, who in broad Crete   260
Surpassed all bread-earning men with his swift feet,
Because he wanted to deprive me of all my booty
From Troy, for which I had suffered pains in my heart,
Passing through the wars of men and the troublesome waves,
And because I was not graciously willing to serve his father 265
In the Trojans' land, but led other men as companions.
I hit him with the bronze-tipped spear as he was coming back
From a field, lying in ambush with a companion by the path.
A very dark night held the heavens, nor did any man
Perceive us, and I took away his life unnoticed.   270
But when I had killed the man with the sharp bronze spear
I went on a ship at once and pleaded with the noble
Phoenicians, and I gave them booty to their heart's desire.
I asked them to bring me to Pylos and put me to shore,
Or close to godly Elis, where the Epeians are ruling.   275
But then the force of the wind drove them away from there,
Much against their will, for they did not want to deal falsely,
Wandering from there we arrived at this place by night.
With haste we rowed into the harbor, nor did any of us
Have dinner in mind, though we wanted much to take it;   280
But getting off the ship, we all lay down as we were.
Then sweet sleep came on me, fatigued as I was,
And they took my goods out of the hollow ship
And set them down where I was lying on the sands.

Embarking for well-inhabited Sidonia,   285
They went off, and I was left grieving in my heart."
So he said, and the bright-eyed goddess Athene smiled.
She reached her hand to him and likened her body to a woman's,
Lovely and tall and skilled in glorious tasks;
And speaking to him, she uttered wingèd words: 290
"Cunning would he be and deceitful, who could overreach you
In various wiles, and even if a god should confront you.
Versatile-minded wretch, insatiate in wiles, you would not
Cease from deceits though you are in your own land,
Or from fraudulent stories that from the ground up are dear to you.   295
Come, let us say no more of this, as both of us are skilled
In shrewdness, since you are by far the best of mortals
In plans and in stories, and I among all the gods
Am famed for planning and shrewdness, and you did not know
Pallas Athene, daughter of Zeus, who always stands   300
Beside you and guards you in all sorts of troubles
And made you beloved by all of the Phaeacians.
And now I have come here so I may weave a plot with you
And hide all the goods the noble Phaeacians gave you
When you came homeward by my plan and my thought.   305
And I shall tell you how many cares it is your lot to put up with
In the well-made halls. But endure them, for you must,
And do not declare to any one of them all,
Men or women, that you came here wandering. But in silence
Suffer many pains, submitting to the violence of men."   310
Odysseus of many wiles addressed her in answer:
"It is hard, goddess, for a mortal who meets you to recognize you,
Even one who is knowing. You liken yourself to anything.
I know this well, that you were mild to me before,
While we sons of the Achaians were making war in Troy,   315
But when we had sacked the lofty city of Priam,
And went off in ships and a god scattered the Achaians,
I did not see you then, daughter of Zeus, or discern you
Boarding my ship to ward any pain off from me.
But having always a heart cut asunder in my breast   320
I wandered until the gods freed me from evil,
Till the time when in the rich land of the Phaeacians
You cheered me with words and led me yourself to the city.
Now I embrace your knees for your father—I do not think
I have come to sunny Ithaca, but turn on through   325
Some other land. And I think you ridicule me
By saying this, so that you may deceive my mind.
Tell me truly if I have reached my dear fatherland."
And then the bright-eyed goddess Athene answered him:
"You have an idea like this forever in your breast.   330
And so I cannot forsake you when you are wretched,

Because you are polite, ready-minded, and of steadfast thought.
Gladly another man who had come in his wandering
Would push on to see his wife and children in his halls.
But it is not dear to you to find out or inquire   335
Before you may yet try your wife out; and she sits
As ever in the halls. Woeful for her always
The days and the nights waste away as she sheds tears.
I never failed to believe it myself, but in my heart
Knew you would return, having lost all your companions.   340
And yet I did not want to quarrel with Poseidon,
My father's brother, who laid up a grudge against you in his heart,
Enraged at you for having blinded his dear son.
Come, I will show you Ithaca's site, to convince you.
This is the harbor of Phorcys, the old man of the sea;   345
This at the harbor's head the olive with long leaves,
And close to it the charming and shadowy cavern
Sacred to the nymphs who are called Naiades.
This is the broad, high-roofed cave where you used to offer
Many acceptable hecatombs to the nymphs.   350
And that is Neriton, the mountain clothed over with woods."
When she had said this, the goddess scattered the mist; ground showed.
Then godly Odysseus, who had suffered much, rejoiced,
Glad at his own land, and he kissed the grain-giving soil.
At once he prayed to the nymphs, holding up his hands: 355
"Nymphs, Naiades, daughters of Zeus, I never thought
I would see you myself. And now, do take pleasure
In my kindly prayers. I shall give gifts as before,
If Zeus's daughter, driver of the spoil, graciously allows
Me to live myself and makes my dear son grow up."   360
Then the bright-eyed goddess Athene spoke to him:
"Take cheer. Do not give heed to this in your mind,
But right away now we shall place the goods in a nook
Of the marvelous cavern, so they may stay there safe for you,
And let us ourselves discuss how it may be for the best."   365
When she had said this, the goddess entered the shadowy cave,
Searching out the recesses in the cave. And Odysseus
Brought everything nearer, the gold and unyielding bronze
And the well-made clothes that the Phaeacians gave him.
Pallas Athene, the daughter of aegis-bearing Zeus,   370
Put them in well and placed a stone at the entrance.
They both sat down at the base of the holy olive tree
And talked about destruction for the presumptuous suitors.
The bright-eyed goddess Athene was the first to speak:
"Zeus-born son of Laertes, Odysseus of many devices,   375
Take thought about how you may lay hands on the shameless suitors
Who for three years have held sway over your hall,
Wooing your godlike wife and giving her bridal gifts.

But she always grieves in her heart for your return.
She gives them all hope and makes promises to each man,   380
Sending out messages, but her mind plans other things."
Odysseus of many devices addressed her in answer:
"Well now, I might surely have perished in my halls
By the evil fate of Agamemnon, son of Atreus,
If you, goddess, had not duly told me the details.   385
Come, devise a plan, that I may do vengeance on them.
Stand beside me yourself, putting in me such courageous might
As we had when we undid Troy's shining diadems.
And if you stood as then pressing on so beside me, bright-eyed one,
I myself would do battle against three hundred men   390
With you, honored goddess, when you would earnestly help me."
Then the bright-eyed goddess Athene answered him:
"Yes, I shall surely stand strongly beside you, nor shall you miss me
When we are busy with these matters, and I think
Some of the suitors who devour your livelihood   395
Shall spatter the immense ground with their blood and brains.
Come, I shall make you unrecognizable to all mortals.
I shall shrivel the lovely flesh on your supple limbs,
Destroy the blond hair from your head, and cloak you about
In rags a man seeing you wear would loathe you for.   400
And I shall mar your eyes that were beautiful beforehand,
So that you may appear ill-favored to all the suitors,
And to your wife and your child that you left in the halls.
But first of all go on up yourself to the swineherd
Who is guardian of your swine, kindly disposed to you also,   405
And a friend to your son and the constant Penelope.
You will find him staying with the swine. They pasture
Beside the rock of the Raven and the spring Arethusa.
They eat the satisfying acorn and drink black water,
The things that nourish abundant fat on swine.   410
Stay there, remain beside him and ask him everything,
So that I may go to Sparta that is lovely in women
And summon Telemachos, your dear son, Odysseus,
Who went to Menelaos in Lacedemon of the broad dancing-place
To learn tidings about you, if you were still alive."   415
Odysseus of many wiles addressed her in answer:
"Why did you, who know all in your mind, not tell him?
So that he too might wander and undergo pains
On the barren sea and others eat his livelihood?"
Then the bright-eyed goddess Athene answered him: 420
"As for him, do not really take him too much to heart.
I escorted him myself so he might gain noble renown
When he went there. But he has no trouble; he sits secure
In the halls of Atreus' son, and he has endless bounty.
The young men do wait in ambush for him with a black ship,   425

Wanting to kill him before he reaches his fatherland.
But I do not think that will be; sooner shall the earth contain
Some one of the suitors who devour your livelihood."
When she had said this, Athene touched him with a wand.
She shriveled the lovely flesh on his supple limbs,   430
Destroyed the blond hair on his head, and put the skin
Of an aged old man around all of his limbs.
And she marred his eyes that were beautiful beforehand.
She threw other clothing about him; a foul rag and a tunic,
Dirty and full of holes, begrimed with foul smoke,   435
And she clothed about him the great skin of a swift deer,
Bare of hair, and she gave him a staff and a sorry wallet
Thick with holes; a rope shoulder strap was on it.
When they had this plan the two of them parted. And she
Went to godly Lacedemon after the child of Odysseus.   440

XIV

Then he went over the rugged path from the harbor.
Up wooded country through the heights, to where Athene
Had showed him the way to the godly swineherd, who, of all the servants
Godly Odysseus owned, best took care of his livelihoods.
He found him seated in the forecourt where the courtyard   5
Was built up lofty in a place with a view all around,
Lovely and large, circled round, that the swineherd himself
Had built for the swine when his master had gone away,
Secretly from his mistress and the old man Laertes,
Out of quarried stones; and he coped it with a prickly shrub.   10
Outside when he had hewn off the black part of an oak
He drove in stakes, stout and close set, right through on either side,
And inside of the courtyard he made twelve pig sties
Close to one another, beds for the swine. In each
Fifty swine that sleep on the ground were shut up,   15
The females for breeding. And the males slept on the outside,
Fewer by far. The godlike suitors diminished those
By eating them, since the swineherd always sent
The best one out of all the well-nourished hogs.
Three hundred and sixty there were of them in all.   20
And dogs that resembled wild beasts slept always beside them,
Four of them, that the swineherd, chief of the men, had reared.
He himself was fitting sandals about his feet,
And cutting oxhide of good color. The other men
Were gone off in different directions with the droves of swine,   25
Three of them. And he had sent the fourth one off to the city
To bring a pig to the presumptuous suitors, under constraint,
So they might sacrifice it and glut their hearts on meat.

The yelping dogs sighted Odysseus suddenly
And ran on after him barking, and Odysseus   30
Sat down in cunning, and the staff fell from his hand.
And then by his own pen he would have suffered a sorry pain,
But the swineherd came up quickly on nimble feet,
Rushed in the front gate, and the leather fell from his hand.
He shouted at the dogs and scattered them this way and that   35
With showers of stones. And he addressed his master:
"Old man, in a little while the dogs would suddenly
Have torn you to pieces, and you would have heaped reproach on me.
To me also have the gods given other pains and griefs.
As I groan and lament over my godlike master,   40
I sit here and keep fattening swine for other men
To eat. But that man, perhaps, longing for food,
Wanders to the city and the land of alien men,
If he is indeed still alive and sees the light of the sun.
But follow me, old man, let us go to the hut, so for yourself   45
When you are satisfied in your heart with food and wine,
You may tell where you come from and how many cares you have
    endured."
When he had said this, the godly swineherd led him into the hut.
He brought him in and sat him down; and heaped shaggy brushwood
And spread on it the hide of a hairy wild goat   50
Great and shaggy, which was his own bedding. Odysseus rejoiced
That he had received him so. He spoke out directly:
"Stranger, may Zeus and the other gods grant you whatever
You wish the most, since you have received me kindly."
And you addressed him in answer, swineherd Eumaeos: 55
"Stranger, it would not be right for me to dishonor
A stranger, not if one worse than you came. In Zeus's care
Are all strangers and beggars. And a gift that comes from us,
Even a small one, is friendly, because the rule for servants is always
To be afraid when young masters hold power over them.   60
And indeed, the gods have hindered the return of the man
Who kindly befriended me and gave me possessions,
A home and a portion and a wife wooed by many,
Such things as a good-hearted master gives his servant
Who toils much for him, and a god also fosters the work,   65
As he fosters for me too this work at which I abide.
And so my master would have given me much, had he aged here.
But he is dead. Would that the whole race of Helen had died
On their knees, since she undid the knees of many men.
But that man went off for the honor of Agamemnon   70
Toward Ilion that abounds in horses to fight with the Trojans."
When he had said this he quickly bound his tunic with his belt
And went to the sties where the herds of pigs were shut up.
Then he took two, bore them off, and sacrificed them both.

He singed them and cut them up and pierced them on spits.   75
When he had roasted it all he brought it over to Odysseus,
Hot on the very spits, and sprinkled white barley on it,
And in a bowl made of ivy he mixed up honey-sweet wine;
He sat across from him and spoke out, urging him on:
"Eat now, stranger, the food that is furnished to servants,   80
Plain pork. But the suitors eat the fatling swine
And in their minds do not think of divine surveillance or pity,
For the blessed gods are not fond of cruel deeds;
No, they reward justice and the righteous deeds of men.
And even the hostile and unfriendly men that approach   85
The country of others, and Zeus gives booty to them,
When they fill up the ships and go to return home—
Even on their minds does a strong fear of the surveillance fall.
But these men know—they have heard some voice of a god—
Of that man's woeful death, and so they do not wish to pay court   90
Justly, or to return to their own goods, but at their ease
They presumptuously devour his goods, and there is
No restraint. As many days and nights as there are from Zeus
I think they have never made one sacrifice, or two.
They presumptuously draw off the wine and waste it.   95
His living was unspeakably great. Not so much was there
For any of the heroes, not upon the black mainland
Or Ithaca itself. Not twenty mortals together
Have so much wealth. I shall tell you all about it myself.
There are twelve herds on the mainland, as many flocks of sheep,   100
As many of swine and as many extensive droves of goats
That strangers pasture, and also his own herdsmen.
There are eleven extensive droves of goats here in all
That pasture at the verge, and good men watch over them.
Each one always brings them an animal every day,   105
Whichever of the well-nourished goats seems to be best.
I watch over these swine and protect them myself
And I make a good choice and send them the best of the swine."
So he said. The other gratefully ate meat and drank wine,
Reaching for it in silence. And he was sowing ill for the suitors.   110
But when he had dined and satisfied his heart with eating
The other filled a cup from which he drank himself and gave it to him
Full of wine. He took it and rejoiced in his spirit.
And speaking out to the other, he uttered wingèd words:
"My friend, who was it that bought you with his resources,   115
And he so very rich and so mighty as you say?
You say he was destroyed for the honor of Agamemnon.
Tell me, if I might somehow know him for the man he is.
Zeus knows, perhaps, and the other immortal gods,
If I might give news of having seen him; I have wandered much."   120
Then the swineherd, the chief of the men, answered him:

"Old man, no wanderer who came here bringing news of him
Could ever convince his wife and his dear son.
Yet anyway, wanderers who need entertainment
Tell lies, and they are not willing to speak the truth.   125
Whoever in wandering reaches the land of Ithaca
Comes to my mistress and utters deceptive stories.
She receives him, befriends him, and asks for the details,
And as she laments, the tears fall from her eyelids,
As is right for a woman when her husband has perished abroad.   130
And you too, old man, would quickly fashion a story
If someone gave you a mantle and a tunic and clothes.
By now the dogs and swift birds have probably
Torn the skin from his bones and the soul has left him,
Or fish have eaten him in the ocean and his bones   135
Are lying on a mainland wrapped over with much sand.
So he has perished there, and afterward many cares
Have been made for all his friends, most for me; I shall not again
Find another master so mild anywhere I go,
Not if I should reach my mother's and father's home again,   140
Where I was first born and they themselves brought me up.
Nor should I yet mourn them so much, though I do want
To see them with my eyes in my own fatherland.
But longing takes hold of me for Odysseus who is gone away.
I am in awe to speak his name, stranger, though he is not here.   145
For he loved me exceedingly and cared for me in his heart.
But I call him 'honored sir' even when he is far away."
Godly Odysseus, who had endured much, spoke to him then:
"My friend, since you wholly deny it, you do not still think
That man will come, and your heart is ever unbelieving;   150
I shall still say it, not just that way, but with an oath:
Odysseus shall return. Let me have reward for good news
Right away when that man arrives at his own halls;
Clothe me in a mantle and a tunic, lovely clothes.
Before then, though I need them much, I will take nothing.   155
Hateful to me as the gates of Hades is that man
Who yields to poverty and tells deceitful stories.
May Zeus now be my witness, first of the gods, and this guest table,
And the hearth of the blameless Odysseus, to which I have come.
Truly, all these things shall come to pass as I say.   160
Within the light of this very month will Odysseus be coming here:
While one moon is waning and another is on the rise
He will return home and do vengeance on anyone
Who here dishonors his wife and his glorious son."
And you addressed him in answer, swineherd Eumaeos: 165
"Old man, I shall not reward you for this good news,
Nor will Odysseus still come home. But at your ease,
Drink. Let us think of quite other things. Do not

Remind me of these matters. The heart in my breast
Is grieved when anyone mentions my beloved master.   170
Well, we will let the oath go, but may Odysseus
Come, as I wish myself, and Penelope wishes,
And the old man Laertes, and godlike Telemachos.
I mourn ceaselessly now for the son Odysseus fathered,
Telemachos. When the gods had reared him like a young tree,   175
And I thought among men he too would be not inferior
To his own dear father, wondrous in body and form,
Then one of the immortals hurt his mind, balanced within,
Or else some man. He went after hearsay about his father
To sacred Pylos. And the noble suitors lie in ambush   180
For him as he comes home so that out of Ithaca
The race of godlike Arkesios [1] might perish nameless.
Well, let us forget that man, whether he is captured
Or escapes, and the son of Cronos holds his hand over him.
But come now, old man, tell me about your own cares,   185
And tell me this really so I may know it well.
What men are you from? Where are your city and parents?
On what sort of ship did you come? How did sailors
Bring you to Ithaca? What men did they claim to be?
For I do not think you could have got here at all on foot."   190
Odysseus of many wiles addressed him in answer:
"All right, I shall tell you this quite truthfully.
And now a long time for the two of us might there be
Both food and sweet wine while we stayed within the hut
To feast in quiet while others performed the work: 195
Easily in that case even for an entire year
I would not come to an end of telling the cares of my heart,
All the many things I have suffered at the will of the gods.
I declare I am of the race of those who live in broad Crete,
The son of a wealthy man. And many other sons   200
Were both born and nourished in his hall, legitimate,
From his wife. A bought mother bore me, a concubine.
But Castor, son of Hylax, of whose race I declare I am,
Honored me as he did the sons rightfully born.
Then among the Cretans he was honored as a god in the land   205
For his prosperity and his wealth and his glorious sons.
But the fates of death came and carried him off
To the halls of Hades. His haughty-spirited sons
Divided his living up and cast lots for it.
Yet they gave me a very poor part and assigned me a dwelling.   210
I took a wife among men who had a large portion,
Because of my excellence, since I was not a good-for-nothing
Or a coward in battle. And now it has all left me.

---

1. Grandfather of Odysseus.

Nevertheless I think if you look at the stubble
You can know what the grain was. For a great deal of distress holds
    me.   215
Ares and Athene gave me the courage and power
To break the ranks of men, whenever I picked for ambush
Excellent men, sowing evils for enemies;
Never did my bold spirit look forward to death
But I leapt forward by far the first and took with my sword   220
Any man of the enemy who yielded to me in running.
Such was I in war. Labor was not dear to me
Or household-tending, that raises glorious children.
No, ships with good oars were always dear to me
And battles, and well-made javelins and arrows,   225
Woeful things, that for others are to be shuddered at.
But to me things are precious, I think, that a god put in my mind,
For one man delights in one task, one man in another.
Before the sons of the Achaians arrived at Troy
Nine times I had been a leader of men on swift-faring ships   230
Against alien men, and many things fell in my hands.
Of them, some satisfying things I chose, but got many
Afterwards by lot. At once my house increased, and then
I became respected and feared among the Cretans.
But when broad-seeing Zeus devised that hateful journey   235
Which has undone the knees from under many man,
Then they kept urging me and renowned Idomeneus
To lead them in ships to Ilion. There was no means
For us to refuse; the stern talk of the people held.
There for nine years we sons of the Achaians waged war.   240
In the tenth we sacked the city of Priam and went
Home in our ships, and a god scattered the Achaians.
But Zeus, the counselor, planned evil for my poor self.
A single month I remained delighting in my children
And my wedded wife and possessions. But then my heart   245
Ordered me to equip the ships well and embark
On a voyage to Egypt with my godlike companions.
I equipped nine ships, and my crew collected quickly.
For six days then my trusty companions dined with me
And I presented as victims many animals   250
To offer the gods and to prepare as dinner for themselves,
And on the seventh day, as we set off from broad Crete,
We sailed on in a fair, steadily blowing North Wind
Easily, as if down a stream. Nor did anyone
Give trouble on my ships, but we sat there unharmed   255
And without disease, and the wind and pilots steered them.
On the fifth day we came to the fair-flowing river of Egypt.
I beached my bobbing ships by the Egyptian river
And then I called upon my trusty companions

To remain there beside the ships and to guard the ships,   260
And I ordered spies to go up on places of lookout.
But they gave in to excess; relying on their own strength,
They sacked the beautiful fields of the Egyptians
At once and carried their women and infant children off.
They killed the men. And soon the noise reached the city.   265
They perceived the shouting, and at the appearance of dawn
Came on. The whole plain was filled with foot soldiers and horses
And the flash of bronze. Zeus, who hurls the thunderbolt,
Threw evil panic among my companions, nor could any
Bear to stay face to face; ills surrounded us on all sides.   270
Then they slaughtered many of us with the sharp bronze
And led some off alive to work for them under constraint.
But Zeus himself put the following idea
In my mind: I wish I had died and met my fate
There in Egypt, for trouble was still to welcome me.   275
I at once took the well-made helmet off my head and the shield
From my shoulders and threw the spear out of my hand.
Then I came up in front of the horses of the king.
I took his knees and kissed them. He pitied me and spared me.
He put me on the chariot and led me weeping to his home.   280
Very many men rushed upon me with ashwood spears,
Wanting to kill me, for they were angered highly.
But he held them off and showed awe for the wrath of Zeus,
Who protects strangers and gets highly incensed at evil deeds.
Then I stayed seven years there, and I gathered many   285
Goods among the Egyptian men, for they all gave me some.
But when the eighth year in its course came round for me,
Then a Phoenician man came, skilled in deceits,
A sharp dealer who had worked many evils among men.
He led me and induced me by his cunning till we came   290
To Phoenicia, where his own home and possessions lay.
There I stayed with him till the completion of the year.
But when the months and the days had been filled out
Of the year coming round again, and the seasons came on,
He put me on a seafaring ship to Libya   295
On the false plan that I should bring cargo with him,
But so that he might sell me there and get an immense price.
Though suspicious, I followed him onto the ship, by constraint.
The ship ran under a fair, steadily blowing North Wind
On the main above Crete. Then Zeus planned their destruction.   300
And when we had left Crete, no other point
Of land appeared, but just the heaven and the sea.
Then the son of Cronos halted a dark blue cloud
Over the hollow ship, and the ocean darkened beneath it;
Zeus at that instant thundered and threw a bolt on the ship.   305
The whole ship quivered, struck by the bolt of Zeus,

And it was filled with brimstone. All fell from the ship.
The men like sea crows all about the black ship
Were borne in the waves. A god took away their return.
Though I had many pains in my heart, Zeus himself   310
Put the enormous mast of the dark blue-prowed ship
Into my hands so I might still escape from distress.
Embracing it, I was carried in the destructive winds.
I was carried nine days, and on the tenth black night
A great rolling wave brought me near the Thesprotians' land,   315
Where the hero Pheidon, king of the Thesprotians,
Saved me without reward. His dear son came on me,
Overcome by cold and fatigue, and led me to his home,
Taking me by the hand till we reached his father's halls.
He clothed me about in garments, a mantle and tunic.   320
There I heard of Odysseus. That man said he had entertained
And befriended him as he was going to his fatherland.
And he showed me all the possessions Odysseus had gathered
Of bronze and of gold and of heavily wrought iron.
They would support each man in turn to the tenth generation,   325
So many were the treasures that lay in the lord's halls.
He said the man had gone to Dodona[2] in order to hear
The plan of Zeus from the lofty-leaved oak of the god
As to how he might return to the rich land of Ithaca,
Openly or in secret, as already he had been long away.   330
He swore to me personally, pouring libation in his house,
That a ship had been drawn down and companions were ready
Who would conduct him to his beloved fatherland.
But he sent me off first. For a ship happened to come
Of Thesprotians headed for Dulichion, rich in wheat.   335
And thither he bade them to convey me attentively
To King Akastos. But an evil plan for me pleased their minds.
That I should still come wholly to the woe of grief.
And when the seafaring ship had sailed a great way from land,
At once they were contriving my day of slavery.   340
They took off my tunic, my mantle, and my clothes
And put another evil rag and tunic around me,
The torn one that you see yourself before your eyes.
At evening they reached the tilled fields of sunny Ithaca,
And there they tied me up on the well-timbered ship,   345
Tightly with a well-twisted cord. They themselves
Went off hastily to the strand of the sea and took dinner.
But the gods themselves bent the bonds back for me
Easily. I covered my head over with the rags,
Went down the smooth loading plank, and slid to my breast   350
Into the sea. Then I stroked through it with both hands,

2. A shrine of Zeus.

Swimming. Very quickly I got out and away from them.
Then I came up where there was a copse of much-flowering wood
And lay crouched down. They were groaning greatly
As they wandered around. But it did not seem any good to them   355
To search further, and so they went back again
On board the hollow ship. And the gods themselves concealed me
Easily. They led me and brought me to the homestead
Of a man with knowledge. For it is still my fortune to live."
And you addressed him in answer, swineherd Eumaeos: 360
"Ah, wretched stranger, you have stirred my heart very much
As you tell the details of how you suffered and wandered.
But this I think is not in order, nor will you convince me
When you speak about Odysseus. Why does a man like you need
To lie fruitlessly? Well do I myself also know   365
Of my master's return, that he has been very much hated
By all the gods, as they did not subdue him among the Trojans
Or in the arms of his friends, after he had wound up the war.
Then all the Achaians would have made him a funeral mound,
And he would have won great glory for his son, too, hereafter.   370
As it is, the storm winds have snatched him off without glory.
But I myself live apart among the swine. Nor do I
Go to the city unless prudent Penelope happens
To urge me to come when a message comes from somewhere,
But then the men sit there and ask for the details,   375
Both those who grieve for the master who is gone so long
And those who enjoy devouring a livelihood scot free.
But for myself, I do not like to ask or inquire
Since the time an Aetolian cheated me with a story—
One who had killed a man and wandered far on the earth.   380
He came to my home and I embraced him in friendship.
He said he saw him among the Cretans with Idomeneus
Repairing his ships that storms had broken to pieces.
And he said he would come toward summer or harvest time
Bringing many possessions, with his godlike companions.   385
And you, much-grieved old man, since some god led you to me,
Do not blandish me or charm me at all with lies,
As I shall not respect and befriend you for that, but in fear
Of Zeus, the god of strangers, and pity for your person."
Odysseus of many wiles addressed him in answer: 390
"Surely you have an unbelieving spirit in your breast,
When I do not bring a man like you round by oath, or persuade you.
But come, let us make an agreement. Let the gods
Who hold Olympos be henceforth witnesses for both.
If your master does return to this very home,   395
You will dress me in clothes a mantle and a tunic and send me
On a trip to Dulichion, where I would like in my heart to be.
But if your master does not come as I say he will,

You may urge the servants to throw me from a great rock,
So any other beggar may shrink from deceiving."   400
The godly swineherd spoke out to him in answer:
"Stranger, there would surely be much honor and excellence
For me among men both at present and in after time
If when I led you to the hut and gave you a guest's gifts
I then should kill you and take your dear life away!   405
Then I might zealously pray to Zeus, son of Cronos!
But now is the time for dinner. May my companions soon
Be here inside, so we may make a tasty dinner in the hut."
In this way they addressed such words to one another.
Then did the swine approach, and the men who were swineherds.   410
The men shut them up in their sties to go to sleep,
And an immense clamor arose from the pigs that were penned up.
Then the godly swineherd called to his companions:
"Bring the best swine, so I may slaughter it for the stranger
From far away. And we too may enjoy it, who have long   415
Had sorrow as we labored for the swine with shining tusks,
And other men do devour our hard work scot free."
When he had said this, he split wood with the pitiless bronze,
And they led in a very fat pig five years of age.
Then they stood it by the hearth, nor did the swineherd   420
Forget the immortals, for he had good understanding.
He began by cutting the hairs of the head off the shining-tusked boar,
Threw them into the fire, and prayed to all the gods
That many-minded Odysseus return to his own home.
He stood up and hit it with a chunk left from the oak he had split,   425
And the life left it. They cut its throat and singed it.
At once they divided it; the swineherd took a first part
From all the limbs and laid the raw pieces on the rich fat.
And he threw some in the fire, sprinkling on barley meal.
The rest of it they cut up small and pierced it on spits,   430
Roasted it carefully, and pulled it all off.
They put it in a mass on platters, and the swineherd
Stood up to carve it. He understood what was right.
Dividing it, he apportioned it all in seven parts.
One he gave with a prayer to the nymphs and to Hermes,   435
The son of Maia, and the others he distributed to each.
To Odysseus he did honor with the whole long back
Of the shining-tusked swine, and pleased his master's heart.
Odysseus of many wiles spoke out and addressed him:
"Eumaeos, would you might be as dear to Father Zeus   440
As you are to me, that you honor a man like me with good things!"
And you addressed him in answer, swineherd Eumaeos:
"Eat, marvelous stranger, and enjoy these things
That are here. A god gives one thing and lets another go
As he wishes in his heart. For he can do all things."   445

So he said, and offered the first parts to the ever-living gods.
He poured sparkling wine, put the cup in the hands of Odysseus,
The sacker of cities, and sat down with his own share.
Mesaulios passed bread to them, a man that the swineherd
Had got by himself alone while his master was gone,   450
Secretly from his mistress and the old man Laertes;
He bought him from the Taphians with his own resources.
They stretched forth their hands to the food that was spread out ready,
But when they had eaten their fill of food and drink
Mesaulios took the bread off, and they hurried   455
Away for sleep, satiated with bread and meat.
A bad night came on, dark of a moon. Zeus rained
All night, and a great watery West Wind steadily blew.
Odysseus spoke to them, testing the swineherd out,
If he would take off his mantle and give it to him, or urge   460
Another of his companions to, since he cared much for him.
"Listen now, Eumaeos, and all you other companions,
I have a boast, and will tell a story, for crazing wine
Bids it, that sets even a man of many thoughts on
To sing and to laugh gently, and it drives him to dance,   465
And he brings out a story that would be better untold.
But since I was the first to speak up, I shall not hide it:
Would that I were in my prime and my strength were steadfast
As when we prepared and led our ambush up under Troy!
Odysseus led, and Menelaos, son of Atreus.   470
I was third leader among them. They ordered it themselves.
But when we arrived before the city and the sheer wall,
We lay around the town in the thick brushwood
Among the reeds and the marsh, crouching under our armor,
And as the North Wind fell off, a bad night came,   475
A freezing one. And snow came from above like hoar frost,
Cold, and ice clustered all around on our shields.
Then the other men all had mantles and tunics.
They slept securely, covering their shoulders with their shields.
But I, when I went, left my mantle with my companions,   480
Foolishly, since I thought I would not freeze in any case.
I went along with only my shield and a shining apron.
When it was the third part of night and the stars had gone past,
I shouted out then to Odysseus, who was near at hand,
Nudging him with my elbow. He hearkened quickly: 485
'Zeus-born son of Laertes, Odysseus of many devices,
I shall not be long among the living, but the cold
Overcomes me. I have no mantle. Some god tricked me
To have just one tunic. And there is no way out any longer.'
So I said. And then he had this purpose in his heart,   490
Such a man was he for deliberation and fighting.
Speaking in a little voice, he addressed a speech to me:

'Silence now, lest someone else of the Achaians hear you.'
And he held his head on his elbow and said his speech:
'Listen, friends, a godly dream came to me in my sleep.   495
We have come too far from the ships. Would there were someone
To go tell Agamemnon, son of Atreus, shepherd of the people,
That he might urge on more of the men from beside the ships.'
So he said. Then Thoas rose up, son of Andraemon,
Hastily. And he took his purple mantle off   500
And ran off to the ships. In that man's clothing I
Lay gladly. Then Dawn of the golden throne appeared.
So would I were now in my prime and my strength steadfast!
Then might someone in the swineherds' lodge give me a mantle,
For two reasons: friendship and respect for a good man.   505
Now men dishonor me for the bad clothes I wear on my skin."
Then you addressed him in answer, swineherd Eumaeos:
"Old man, the story is excellent that you have told.
And no profitless word did you speak improperly.
So you shall not want for clothes or for anything else,   510
Of the things that befit a long suffering suppliant one meets—
For now. But at dawn you shall bundle your own rags on,
As there are not many mantles and changes of tunic
To put on here, just a single one for each mortal man.
But when the beloved son of Odysseus comes,   515
He himself will give you clothes, a mantle and tunic,
And will send you wherever your heart and spirit bid."
When he had said this, he rose up and made a bed for him
Near the fire. And on it he threw skins of sheep and goats.
There Odysseus lay down. He threw on him a mantle   520
Great and thick, which lay beside him as a change
To put on when any terrible storm arose.
So Odysseus slept. And beside him those young men
Were sleeping. But to lie there was not pleasing
To the swineherd, to be sleeping apart from the swine.   525
He went out to go and get ready. Odysseus was pleased
That the man took care of his livelihood when he was away.
First the man threw a sharp sword around his stout shoulders
And put on a very thick mantle that warded off wind.
Then he put on the fleece from a great well-nourished goat.   530
He grasped a sharp javelin, a defense against dogs and men,
And he went on to lie down where the shining-tusked swine slept
Beneath a hollow rock under shelter from the North Wind.

XV

Pallas Athene had gone to Lacedemon of the broad dancing-place
To remind the illustrious son of great-hearted Odysseus

About his return and to urge him to go back.
She found Telemachos and the noble son of Nestor
Lying in the forecourt of glorious Menelaos.   5
The son of Nestor was overcome with soft sleep,
But sweet sleep did not hold Telemachos. In his heart
Concern for his father kept him awake through the ambrosial night.
Bright-eyed Athene stood close to him and addressed him:
"Telemachos, it is no longer good to wander far from home,   10
And leave behind in your home the possessions and the men,
Presumptuous as they are, lest they divide and devour
All your possessions and you have gone on a fruitless journey.
But right away urge Menelaos who is good at the war cry,
To send you on, so you may still find your blameless mother at
    home.   15
For already her father and her kinsmen are calling on her
To marry Eurymachos. He outdoes all the other
Suitors with presents and greatly augments the bridal gifts.
Let her bear no goods from your home against your will.
You know what sort of heart there is in a woman's breast.   20
She wishes to increase the house of the man she weds;
She no longer remembers or inquires of her former
Children or of her dear wedded husband who is dead.
But you should go yourself, and turn each piece of property
Over to whichever of the maids appears best to you,   25
Till the gods reveal to you an illustrious wife.
I will say something else to you; store it in your mind.
The best of the suitors lie ready in ambush against you
In the strait between Ithaca and the rugged Samê,
Wanting to kill you before you reach your fatherland.   30
But I do not think that will be: sooner shall the earth contain
Some one of the suitors who devour your livelihood.
But keep your well-made ship far from the islands
And sail by night as well. Whoever of the immortals
Guards and protects you will sent a breeze behind you.   35
And when you arrive at the first shore of Ithaca
Send your ship on to the city, and all your companions,
But first of all go on up yourself to the swineherd
Who is guardian of your swine, and kindly disposed to you also.
Rest the night there. And send him on inside the city   40
To give the message to the prudent Penelope
That you are safe for her and have arrived from Pylos."
And when she had said this, she went off to tall Olympos.
Then he woke the son of Nestor out of his sweet sleep,
Nudging him with his foot, and addressed a speech to him: 45
"Wake, Peisistratos, son of Nestor! Lead the single-hooved horses,
And harness them to the chariot, so we may hurry away."
Then Peisistratos, son of Nestor, replied to him:

"Telemachos, though we press on our way, we cannot
Drive through the dusky night. Soon it will be dawn,   50
But wait till the hero, son of Atreus, spear-famed Menelaos
Has brought the gifts and put them on the chariot
And has addressed us with gentle words and sent us off.
For a guest remembers all of his days the man
Who has received him as a guest and shown friendliness."   55
So he said, and at once Dawn of the golden throne came.
Menelaos, good at the war cry, came up close to them
When he had got out of bed from beside the fair-haired Helen.
And when the beloved son of Odysseus noticed him,
The hero hurried and put the glistening tunic on   60
Over his skin and threw a great mantle on his stout shoulders.
Telemachos, beloved son of godly Odysseus,
Went outside, stood beside him, and addressed him:
"Zeus-nourished Menelaos, son of Atreus, chief of the people,
Send me off right away to my dear fatherland,   65
For already my heart is longing to return home."
Then Menelaos, good at the war cry, answered him:
"Telemachos, I shall not hold you back here a long time,
Wanting to return as you do. I would resent another
Who, receiving a guest, acted excessively friendly   70
Or excessively hostile. All things are better when in measure.
It is equally bad when a man urges a guest to go off
Unwillingly, and when he holds back one who strains to go.
One must welcome a guest who stays, send one off who wishes.
Well, wait till I have brought the lovely gifts and put them   75
On the chariot, till your eyes behold them, and I tell the women
To make dinner in the halls out of the abundance inside.
It is glory, splendor, and refreshment all together
For men, after dining, to go far on the unbounded earth.
If you would like to wind through Hellas and middle Argos,   80
So that I should go with you, I will yoke up horses for you;
And lead you to the cities of men. No one will send us off
The way we are, but will give us some one gift at least to carry,
Some sort of cauldron of good bronze or a basin
Or a pair of mules or a golden libation cup."   85
Sound-minded Telemachos addressed him in answer:
"Zeus-nourished Menelaos, son of Atreus, chief of the people,
I would rather go right now to our home. For I did not
Leave a guard behind for my possessions when I went.
I fear I may perish myself in seeking my godlike father   90
Or have some noble treasure perish from my halls."
And when Menelaos, good at the war cry, heard him
He at once called to his wife and his serving women
To make dinner in the halls out of the abundance inside.
Eteoneus, son of Boethoüs, came up close to him   95

When he got out of bed, as the man did not live far from him.
Menelaos, good at the war cry, told him to kindle a fire
And to roast some meat. The other heard and did not disobey.
And he himself went off to his fragrant chamber,
Not alone, but Helen went with him, and Megapenthes. 100
And when they had reached the place where the treasures lay,
The son of Atreus took out a two-handled cup
And ordered his son Megapenthes to carry a mixing bowl
Of silver. And Helen took her stand alongside the coffers,
Where there were all the embroidered robes she had made herself. 105
Helen, godlike among women, picked one up and brought it,
The one that was largest and loveliest in embroidery.
It shone like a star; it lay beneath all the rest.
They went on further through the house till they reached
Telemachos. And blond Menelaos addressed him: 110
"Telemachos, may Zeus, Hera's loud-thundering husband,
Fulfill for you the return you desire in your mind.
And of the gifts that lie stored as keepsakes in my house
I will give you the one that is loveliest and of highest worth.
I shall give you a well-fashioned mixing bowl. It is all 115
Of silver, and its rim is finished round with gold,
The work of Hephaistos; the hero Phaidimos gave it,
King of the Sidonians, when his house took me in
As I had returned that far. I would like to give it to you."
When he had said this, the hero, son of Atreus, put 120
The two-handled cup in his hands, and stout Megapenthes
Carried the shining mixing bowl out and set it before him,
The silver one. Helen of the fair cheeks stood alongside
With the robe in her hands; she said her speech right out:
"I, too, give you a gift, dear child, this remembrance 125
From the hands of Helen for your own wife to wear at the time
Of your lovely marriage. And until then, let it lie
In the hall with your dear mother. And may you come, I pray,
Rejoicing to your well-built home and your fatherland."
When she had said this, she put it in his hands. He took it and
rejoiced. 130
The hero Peisistratos took the things and put them
In the wagon box, and he marveled in his heart at them all.
Blond-headed Menelaos led them to his house.
And they took their places in seats and in armchairs.
A handmaid poured water from a pitcher she was carrying, 135
A lovely golden one, over into a silver basin,
For washing the hands; she set up a polished table alongside.
A respected housekeeper served bread she was carrying,
Laying out many dishes, gracious with the provisions.
Near her, the son of Boethoüs carved meat and served it in portions, 140
And the son of glorious Menelaos poured the wine.

They stretched forth their hands to the food that was laid out ready
But when they had taken their fill of food and drink,
Then Telemachos and the glorious son of Nestor
Hitched the horses up, mounted the inlaid chariot,   145
And drove out of the forecourt and resounding portico.
With them went blond Menelaos, the son of Atreus,
Holding in his right hand the mind-honeying wine
In a gold cup, so both might pour libation and go.
He stood before the horses and spoke with a pledging gesture: 150
"Farewell, young men. And to Nestor, shepherd of the people,
Give greetings. To me he was always mild as a father
While we sons of the Achaians waged war in Troy."
Then sound-minded Telemachos answered him:
"All this that you say, you who are nourished by Zeus,   155
We shall certainly tell that man when we arrive.
Would that thus, returning to Ithaca and finding
Odysseus at home, I might tell him how I come from you
As one who got all your friendship and also bear many noble treasures."
A bird flew to the right of him, as he was speaking,   160
An eagle bearing a huge, bright goose in his claws,
A tame one from the courtyard. The men and the women
Followed them shrieking. He came up close to them
And rushed off to the right before the horses. When they saw it,
They rejoiced, and the spirit was warmed in all their minds.   165
Peisistratos, son of Nestor, began speaking to them:
"Consider, Zeus-nourished Menelaos, chief of the people,
Whether a god has shown this portent to the two of us or to you."
So he said, and Menelaos, dear to Ares, pondered
So that he might give a proper judgment when he had thought.   170
Helen of the long gown began speaking before he could:
"Listen to me, and I shall prophesy the way the immortals
Have put it in my heart, and how I think it will end.
Just as this bird seized the goose reared in our home
When he came from the mountain where his descent and his
    birth are,   175
So Odysseus who has suffered many ills and wandered much
Will return homeward and do vengeance. Or else already
He is at home and breeds evil for all the suitors."
Then sound-minded Telemachos answered her:
"May Zeus, Hera's thundering husband, make it so.   180
And then, even there, I should pray to you as to a god."
He spoke and lashed the whip at the two horses. They swiftly
Rushed to the plain, pressing on through the city.
All day they shook the yoke, holding it up on either side.
The sun went down and all the ways were shadowed.   185
They arrived at Pherai to the home of Diocles,
Son of Ortilochos, whom Alpheus sired as his son.

There they rested at night, and he gave them the gifts of a guest.
And when the early-born, rosy-fingered dawn appeared,
They yoked up the horses and mounted the inlaid chariot   190
And drove out of the forecourt and resounding portico.
He whipped them to go, and both flew on, not unwilling.
Soon thereupon they reached the sheer citadel of Pylos.
Then Telemachos addressed the son of Nestor:
"Son of Nestor, will you promise me, if you can, to carry out   195
What I ask? We declare we are guest friends in unbroken line
Through our fathers' friendship. And we are the same age.
This trip will bring us to greater congeniality.
You who are nourished by Zeus, do not carry me on past the ship,
But leave me there, lest the old man keep me unwilling   200
In his house, wanting to befriend me. I must arrive quicker."
So he said, and the son of Nestor deliberated in his heart
How he might promise him this and duly carry it out.
And thus it seemed to him to be best as he thought about it.
He turned the horses to the swift ship and the strand of the sea   205
And unloaded the beautiful gifts on the ship's stern,
The clothing and the gold Menelaos had given him.
Then urging him on, he uttered wingèd words:
"Board quickly now and call all your companions,
Before I reach home and announce it to the old man.   210
For this I know well in my mind and in my heart,
How overbearing his heart is. He will not let you go,
But he would come here to invite you himself. I think
He would not go back empty handed, but still would be very angry."
When he had said this, he drove the fair-maned horses back   215
To the town of Pylos and rapidly reached his home.
But Telemachos urged his companions on and called them:
"Put the gear in order, my companions, on the black ship,
And let us get on board ourselves, so we may press on the journey."
So he said, and they listened to him and obeyed him.   220
At once they got on board and took their seats at the oarlocks.
So he busied himself, prayed, and sacrificed to Athene
At the stern of the ship. And a man came up close to him,
An alien who had killed a man and was fleeing from Argos,
A seer. He was descended from the race of Melampos   225
Who dwelt once long ago in Pylos, the mother of sheep,
A rich man who dwelt among the Pylians in a very large house.
But then he reached the country of others, fleeing from his fatherland
And from great-hearted Neleus, noblest man of the living,
Who held as many goods by force, till the completion   230
Of the year. The first one, meanwhile, in the halls of Phylacos
Was bound in a harsh bond, having suffered strong pains
For the daughter of Neleus and for the deep madness
That Fury, the hard-smiting goddess, had put in his mind.

Still, he fled from fate and he drove the lowing cattle   235
To Pylos from Phylace. He paid the godlike Neleus
With a wretched deed and brought the woman for his brother
To the halls. And then he went to the land of other men,
To horse-nourishing Argos. There it was fated for him
To dwell while ruling over many of the Argives.   240
Then he married a wife and set up a high-roofed house,
And had Antiphates and Mantios, mighty sons.
Antiphates fathered great-spirited Oikles;
Oikles had Amphiaraos, rouser of the people,
Whom aegis-bearing Zeus loved in his heart and Apollo   245
Loved with all affection. Still, he did not reach the threshold of age,
But perished in Thebes on account of gifts to a woman.
The sons born to him were Alcmaeon and Amphilochos.
And Mantios fathered Polypheides and Kleitos,
But Dawn of the golden throne seized Kleitos away   250
On account of his beauty, that he might be with the immortals,
And Apollo made high-spirited Polypheides a prophet,
By far the best of mortals, after Amphiaraos died.
He migrated to Hyperesia in anger at his father,
Where he dwelt and prophesied to all mortal men.   255
This man's son came up, whose name was Theoclymenos,
And stood close to Telemachos. He found him
Pouring a libation and praying by the swift black ship,
And speaking out to him, he uttered wingèd words:
"My friend, since I find you sacrificing in this place   260
I pray you by the burnt offerings, by the god, and then
By your own head and by the companions who follow you,
To tell me unerringly what I ask; do not hide it.
What men are you from? Where are your city and parents?"
Then sound-minded Telemachos answered him: 265
"Indeed I shall speak to you, friend, quite truthfully.
My descent is from Ithaca, my father is Odysseus,
If he ever was. He has already died by a woeful death.
So now I have taken companions and a black ship
And come to find out about my father who is gone so long."   270
And then the godly Theoclymenos spoke to him:
"I have gone from my fatherland too, having killed a man
Of my tribe. He has many kinsmen and relatives
In horse-nourishing Argos; they rule the Achaians mightily.
Escaping from them, I flee death and black fate,   275
Since it is now my lot to wander among men.
Do put me on your ship, since as a fugitive I beseech you,
So they may not kill me. I believe I am pursued."
Then sound-minded Telemachos answered him:
"Since you wish to be on the balanced ship, I shall not push you
    off.   280

Come, you shall be befriended there, with what we have."
When he had said this, he took his bronze spear from him
And put it along on the deck of the bobbing ship.
And the man himself got on board the seafaring ship.
Then he sat him down on the stern and at his side he sat   285
Theoclymenos. And they loosed the stern cables.
Telemachos called to his companions and urged them
To take hold of the gear. And they hastily obeyed.
They stood a fir-wood mast in the hollow mast block;
They raised it up, and with forestays they made it fast.   290
Then they hauled up the white sails with well-plaited oxhide ropes.
Bright-eyed Athene sent on a driving breeze for them,
Rushing rapidly through the air so the ship might soon
Arrive as it ran over the salt water of the sea.
They went past the Springs and the fair-flowing Chalcis.   295
The sun went down and all the ways were shadowed.
She came close to Pheai drawn on by the breeze of Zeus,
And passed godly Elis, where the Epeians rule.
And then he drove it on forward to the Sharp Islands,
Wondering whether he should flee death or be taken.   300
Meanwhile, both Odysseus and the godly swineherd
Were dining in the hut. The other men dined with them.
But when they had taken their fill of food and drink
Odysseus addressed them, trying the swineherd out,
Whether he would still kindly befriend him and ask him to stay   305
There in the fold, or would urge him on to the city:
"Listen now, Eumaeos, and all you other companions,
I am longing to go off to the town at dawn
To beg, so I may not wear down you and your companions.
But advise me well and send a good guide along with me   310
Who may lead me there. I myself from necessity
Shall stray to the city to try to get a cup and a loaf.
And when I come to the dwelling of godly Odysseus,
I would like to give a message to prudent Penelope
And mingle with the presumptuous suitors, to see   315
If they who have countless dishes give me a dinner.
Right away in their midst I could do whatever service they wished.
I shall speak out to you; put it in your mind and hear me:
Through the favor of the runner Hermes, who provides
Grace and glory for the actions of all men,   320
No other mortal could ever rival my service
At kindling a fire and splitting up dry wood,
At carving and roasting and pouring out wine,
The sort of service humble men do for noble ones."
Greatly disturbed, you spoke to him, swineheard Eumaeos: 325
"Alas, stranger, what is this thought that has come about
In your mind? You must surely long to die on the spot

If you wish to enter the company of the suitors,
Whose presumption and might reaches iron heaven.
Not men of your sort are the servants under them,   330
But young men, clothed well in mantles and in tunics,
Perpetually sleek on their heads and fair of face,
The ones who serve them. And their well-polished tables
Are loaded down with bread and with meats and with wine.
But stay, no one is troubled at your being here,   335
Not I or any other of the companions who are with me.
But when the beloved son of Odysseus comes,
He will clothe you in garments, a mantle and a tunic,
And he will send you wherever your heart and spirit bid."
Then godlike Odysseus, who had suffered much, answered him: 340
"Eumaeos, would that you might be as dear to father Zeus
As to me, that you stop me from straying and from dire woe.
There is nothing worse for mortal man than wandering.
But for the cursed belly's sake men have evil cares,
Anyone that straying and trouble and pain come upon—.   345
Now, since you hold me back and bid me, as I am, to stay,
Come, tell me about the mother of godly Odysseus,
And the father whom he left on the threshold of old age when he went.
Are they perchance still living under the rays of the sun,
Or are they already dead and in the halls of Hades?"   350
Then the swineherd addressed him, a chief of the men:
"All right, stranger, I shall tell you that quite truthfully:
Laertes is still alive; he forever prays to Zeus
That the spirit may waste from his limbs in his own halls.
He mourns terribly for his son who is gone away   355
And for his wise wedded wife who, when she perished,
Brought the greatest grief on him and put him in raw old age.
She did perish for grief over her renowned son
By a miserable death, and may no one who dwells here die
That way who is kind to me and acts in a kindly way.   360
And so as long as that woman lived, even though she grieved,
I always liked to ask and inquire about her,
Because she brought me up along with long-gowned Ktimene,
Her goodly daughter, whom she bore youngest of her children.
I was reared along with her; she honored me little less.   365
But when both of us arrived at youth that is full of love,
They married her off in Samê, and they took countless gifts,
But me she clothed in a mantle and a tunic, clothes
That were very lovely, gave me sandals for my feet
And sent me off to the fields. But she loved me much in her heart.   370
As it is, I am now deprived of these things. Yet for me
The blessed gods foster the work at which I abide.
From them have I eaten and drunk and given to respected men.
And of the mistress there is nothing pleasant to be heard,

Neither word nor deed, since an evil has fallen on the house,   375
These presumptuous men. The servants greatly miss
Speaking in their mistress' presence and hearing tidbits,
And eating and drinking, and then carrying something off
To the fields, the things that always warm servants' hearts."
Odysseus of many wiles addressed him in answer: 380
"Well, swineherd Eumaeos, what a little one you were
When you wandered far from your parents and your fatherland!
But come, tell me this, and speak quite truthfully:
Was the broad-streeted city of that people destroyed
In which your father and your queenly mother were dwelling,   385
Or while you were alone with cattle or with sheep
Did hostile men take you in ships and bring you for sale
To the home of this man, and he gave a worthy price?"
Then the swineherd addressed him, the chief of the men:
"Stranger, since you ask me and inquire of these matters,   390
Listen in silence now, and take pleasure; drink wine
While you are sitting. These nights are immense. One can sleep
And one can listen if he enjoys it. There is no need
To lie down before it is time. And much sleep is a weariness.
As for the others, let any man leave and go to sleep   395
By what the heart and the spirit bid, and when dawn appears
Let him eat and follow the swine that are the master's;
But let us two be in the hut drinking and dining,
And we shall take pleasure in one another's sad sorrows
As we recall them; for a man takes pleasure even in pains,   400
One who has suffered very much and wandered much.
And I will tell you this of which you ask and inquire.
There is a certain island called Syria, as you may have heard,
Above Ortygia where the turnings of the sun are.
It is not very populous, and yet it is good,   405
Rich in cattle and sheep, full of wine, with much grain.
Poverty never comes to the land, nor any other
Disease exists there that is sad for wretched mortals.
But when the tribes of men grow old in the city
Apollo of the silver bow comes with Artemis   410
And slays them by visiting them with his soothing shafts.
In that place are two cities. They are wholly divided asunder.
My father used to rule as the king over both of them,
Ktesios, son of Ormenos, who resembles the immortals.
There the Phoenicians came, men who are famous for ships,   415
Sharp dealers, who brought in a black ship countless trinkets.
There was a Phoenician woman in my father's house,
Lovely and tall and skilled at excellent tasks.
The very wily Phoenicians deceived her.
One lay with her first, as she was washing clothes by the hollow
  ship,   420

In the bed and in affection which deceives the minds
Of womankind, even one who is good in what she does.
Then he asked her who she was and where she was from,
And she at once pointed out my father's high-roofed house.
'I declare I am from Sidon that is full of bronze,   425
And I am the daughter of Arybas, a man of overflowing wealth.
But Taphian men, pirates, snatched me away
As I was coming from the fields. They brought me here and sold me
To the home of this man. And he gave a worthy price.'
Then the man who had secretly lain with her said to her: 430
'Well then, would you follow along with us back to your home.
So you may see the high-roofed house of your father and mother,
And themselves? For they still exist, and are called wealthy.'
Then the woman spoke to him and answered with a speech:
'This too, might come about, sailors, if you are willing   435
To pledge me an oath and take me back home safe and sound.'
So she said, and they all swore an oath as she asked.
But when they had sworn and had completed the oath,
The woman addressed them again and answered with a speech:
'Keep silence, now, and let none of your company   440
Speak out to me as he comes upon me in the street
Or at the well, perhaps; lest someone go to the house
And tell the old man, and when he learns he bind me
In a hard binding and devise destruction against you.
But keep my words in your mind; hurry your buying for the
    journey,   445
And when the ship gets filled up with the goods of life,
Let one quickly come with a message for me to the house.
For I shall bring gold, too, whatever comes to my hand.
And I would willingly give other things, too, as fare,
For I am rearing the son of this nobleman in his halls.   450
Such a clever one he is, who runs along when I go outdoors.
I might bring him into the ship, and he would gain for you
A boundless price if you brought him to alien men.'
When she had said this, she went off to the lovely home.
They remained there with us for an entire year   455
And traded to get many goods in the hollow ship.
When the hollow ship was loaded for them to go,
They sent a messenger to give the woman word.
He came, a very shrewd man, to the home of my father
Bearing a gold chain strung round with amber beads.   460
The serving maids in the hall and my queenly mother
Felt it with their hands and looked at it with their eyes
And offered his price. He nodded to the woman in silence.
When he had nodded, he went off to the hollow ship.
She took me by the hand and led me from the house outdoors.   465
In the forecourt she found the cups and the tables

Of the men who attended on my father, banqueting.
They were gone to the session and assembly of the district.
At once she concealed three tankards under her bosom
And bore them off. I followed in my thoughtlessness.   470
The sun went down and all the ways were shadowed.
We went swiftly and arrived at the famous harbor
Where there was a swift-sailing ship of the Phoenician men.
They boarded it then and sailed on the watery ways,
When they had boarded us both. And Zeus sent on a breeze.   475
For six days we sailed alike by night and by day.
But when Zeus, the son of Cronos, added the seventh day,
Artemis, who pours forth arrows, struck the woman,
And she crashed as she fell in the hold like a tern of the sea,
And they threw her out to become the prey of seals   480
And fishes. But I was left grieving in my heart.
The wind and the water carried and brought them near Ithaca,
Where Laertes bought me with his resources.
In that way did I see this country with my eyes."
Then Zeus-born Odysseus answered him with a speech: 485
"Eumaeos, you have stirred the heart very much in my breast
As you tell the details of the pain you suffered in your heart.
But Zeus has provided good for you along with evil
When, having suffered much, you reached the home of a man
Who was mild, and who furnished you with food and drink   490
Kindly. And you live a good life. But as for me,
I reach here after wandering to many cities of men."
And so they told such stories to one another.
And the two of them did not sleep much time, but a little.
For soon the fair-throned Dawn came on. Telemachos' companions   495
At the mainland, slacked their sails, and took the mast down
Speedily, and pulled the ship to the mooring with the oars.
They threw out the anchor stones and tied the stern cables.
They themselves got out at the surf of the sea,
And they prepared a dinner and mixed sparkling wine.   500
But when they had taken their fill of food and drink,
Sound-minded Telemachos began speaking to them:
"You men, bring the black ship over now toward the town,
And I myself shall hurry to the fields and the herdsmen.
I shall go to the town at evening when I have seen my own lands.   505
And at dawn I shall provide for you as the journey's pay
A good banquet of meat and of wine sweet to drink."
Then godlike Theoclymenos addressed him:
"But where shall I head, dear child? To what man's house
Shall I go, of those who rule over rocky Ithaca,   510
Or shall I go straight to your mother's house and yours?"
Then sound-minded Telemachos answered him:
"In another case I myself should advise you to go

To our house, for there is no lack of hospitality. Still,
It would be worse for you, since I am gone, and my mother   515
Will not see you. She does not appear often in the house
To the suitors, but apart from them weaves a web in her room.
But I shall tell you about another man you may go to:
Eurymachos, noble son of skillful Polybos,
Whom the Ithacans look upon as equal to a God.   520
He is far the most excellent man and is the most eager
To marry my mother and have the honor of Odysseus.
But in that, Olympian Zeus who dwells in the upper air, knows
If he will bring an evil day to pass for them before the marriage."
A bird flew to the right of him as he was speaking,   525
A hawk, swift messenger of Apollo. In his claws
He was plucking a dove he held and strewing its feathers on the ground
Between the ship and Telemachos himself.
Theoclymenos called him aside from their companions,
Took his hand, and spoke right out directly to him: 530
"Telemachos, not without a god did that bird fly to the right.
I knew when I saw it head on it was a bird of omen.
There is no other descent more royal than yours
In the land of Ithaca. You are the strongest always."
Then sound-minded Telemachos answered him: 535
"Would that this speech, stranger, might be fulfilled.
And then you would soon know friendship and many gifts
From me, so that someone who met you would call you blessed."
And then he shouted to Peiraeos, his trusty companion:
"Peiraeos, son of Klytos, in all else you hearken to me   540
Most of all the companions who followed me to Pylos.
And now bring this guest for me into your house.
Befriend him kindly and honor him until I come."
Then Peiraeos, renowned for his spear, answered him:
"Telemachos, even if you stay here for a long time   545
I will conduct this man, and he shall not lack hospitality."
When he had said this, he went on the ship and called his companions
To get on board themselves and untie the stern cables.
They got on board at once and took seats at the oars.
Telemachos bound the lovely sandals beneath his feet   550
And took a valiant spear pointed with sharp bronze
From the deck of the ship. They untied the stern cables
And pushed it off and sailed to the city, as Telemachos,
The beloved son of godly Odysseus, had commanded.
His feet bore him forward fast, as he strode, till he reached   555
The farmyard where the numberless swine were, beside which slept
The noble swineherd whose mind was mild to his masters.

XVI

Then both Odysseus and the godly swineherd in the hut
Were preparing breakfast at dawn when they had kindled a fire,
And had sent out shepherds along with the droves of swine.
The dogs, prone to bark, fawned around Telemachos
And did not bark as he approached. Godly Odysseus noticed   5
The fawning dogs, and the sound of footsteps carried to him.
Right away to Eumaeos he uttered wingèd words:
"Eumaeos, surely some companion is coming here
Or some other acquaintance, since the dogs do not bark
But fawn around him. And I hear the low noise of his feet."   10
The speech was not yet fully said when his dear son
Was standing in the doorway. The swineherd started, dumbstruck.
From his hands the bowls fell that he was tending to
As he mixed the sparkling wine. He went over to his master
And kissed him on the head and on both lovely eyes   15
And both of his hands. A swelling tear fell from him,
As a father receives lovingly the dear son he sees
Coming in the tenth year from a faraway land,
His precious only son, for whom he suffered many pains;
So then the godly swineherd embraced and kissed all over   20
The godlike Telemachos, as if he had escaped from death.
And while he was sobbing he uttered wingèd words:
"Telemachos, you have come as a sweet light. I myself thought
I would never see you again when you went by ship to Pylos.
But come in here now, dear child, so that in my heart   25
I may delight to see you here inside, come afresh from elsewhere.
You do not often visit the shepherds and the fields,
But remain in town. Indeed, it has pleased your heart
To look upon the destructive throng of the suitors."
Then sound-minded Telemachos answered him: 30
"So it shall be, father. I have come here on your account,
So that I may see you with my eyes and hear your story
As to whether my mother stays in the halls or already
Some other man has wed her and the bed of Odysseus
Lies with foul spider webs, perhaps, deprived of bedding.   35
Then the swineherd addressed him, the chief of the men:
"Yes, long now indeed does that woman in her enduring spirit wait
Within your halls. And the miserable nights
And the days always waste away for her as she sheds tears."
When he had said this, he took the bronze spear from him,   40
Then he himself went in and crossed the stone threshold.
His father Odysseus yielded him a seat as he entered.
But Telemachos, for his part, checked him and spoke out:
"Sit down, stranger. We will find a seat somewhere else

In our hut. Here is a man who will furnish one:"   45
So he said. The other went and sat down. Then the swineherd
Spread yellow-green brushwood beneath and fleeces on top.
And there the beloved son of Odysseus took a seat.
The swineherd offered platters of meat slices to them,
Of the roast meat that they had left from eating before.   50
And in baskets he hastily heaped up bread,
And he mixed honey-sweet wine in a bowl of ivy wood.
He himself sat down facing the godly Odysseus.
Then they stretched forth their hands to the food that was laid out ready,
But when they had taken their fill of food and drink,   55
Telemachos spoke out to the godly swineherd:
"Father, where did this stranger come from? How did sailors
Bring him to Ithaca? What men did they claim to be?
For I do not think he could have arrived here at all on foot."
Then you addressed him in answer, swineherd Eumaeos: 60
"Well then, my child, I shall tell you all of the truth.
He declares he is of the race of those who live in broad Crete,
And he says he has been to many cities of mortals
In his wandering, for that was the way the god spun his thread.
And now, having escaped from a ship of the Thesprotians,   65
He has come to my hut, and I hand him over to you.
Do as you wish. He declares he is a suppliant to you."
Then the sound-minded Telemachos answered him:
"Eumaeos, this speech you have spoken is distressing.
How indeed shall I receive the stranger in my home?   70
I myself am young and have not yet trusted my hands
To defend me against some man when he outrages me first.
As for my mother, the heart in her breast ponders two ways,
Either that she remain here with me and attend to the house,
Respecting the bed of her husband and the talk of the people,   75
Or that she already go at once with whichever of the Achaians
Is the best man that woos her in the halls and offers the most.
Yet, indeed, since this stranger has come to your house,
I shall clothe him in a mantle and a tunic, lovely garments.
I shall give him a two-edged sword and sandals for his feet,   80
And I shall send him wherever his heart and spirit bid.
But if you wish to, care for him and keep him in your hut.
I shall send the garments here myself and all the food
To eat, so that he will not strain you and your companions.
I for my part should not allow him to come there   85
Among the suitors, for they have too much reckless presumption,
Lest they mock him, and that be a dread grief to me.
It is difficult for a single man, even a mighty one,
To succeed at all against many, since they are far stronger."
Then godly Odysseus, who had suffered much, answered him: 90
"My friend, since surely it is proper for me to reply,

My own heart is torn to pieces when I hear
About the reckless deeds you say the suitors contrive
In your halls, against the will of a man as good as yourself.
Tell me, are you willingly subjected or do the people 95
Despise you in the district, yielding to the voice of a god?
Or do you blame your kinsmen, those on whom a man
Should rely for fighting, even if a great quarrel arises?
Would that, with this heart of mine, I were as young as you,
Or the child of excellent Odysseus, or that the man himself 100
Should come roaming; for there is still a share of hope.
And may an alien mortal at once cut off my head
If I did not become a curse to all of those men,
As I come into the hall of Odysseus, son of Laertes.
And if they should beat me, a single man, by their numbers, 105
I would rather be killed in my own halls and die
Than perpetually to look upon these sorry deeds:
Strangers being maltreated, and men disgracefully
Dragging the servant women through the lovely halls,
And wine being drawn off, and men eating bread 110
Rashly this way, and limitlessly, acts without end."
Then sound-minded Telemachos answered him:
"Very well, stranger, I shall speak to you truthfully.
The whole district is not hostile or enraged against me,
Nor do I blame any kinsmen, those on whom a man 115
Should rely for fighting, even if a great quarrel arises;
For thus did the son of Cronos make ours a single line.
Arkesios sired Laertes, a single son,
And his father sired Odysseus alone; Odysseus sired me
Alone, and left me in the halls, and got from me no joy. 120
So now there are countless enemies in the house.
All the noblemen who rule over the islands,
Dulichion and Samê and wooded Zacynthos,
And all those who are masters in craggy Ithaca,
Are paying court to my mother and wearing down my home, 125
She neither refuses the hateful wedding nor can she
Make an end of it. But they are wasting my home away
As they devour it. Soon they will tear me to pieces myself.
Well, all these matters lie in the laps of the gods.
Go quickly, father, to constant Penelope. 130
Tell her I am safe and have arrived from Pylos.
I myself shall remain here, but you come back here
When you have told just her. Let no one else of the Achaians
Find out about it, for many devise evils against me."
And you addressed him in answer, swineherd Eumaeos: 135
"I know, I see; you say this to an understanding man.
But come, tell me this, and speak out truthfully,
Should I go or not by the same path to tell Laertes,

That wretched man, who, while he grieved much for Odysseus,
Used to oversee the fields, and with the servants in his house   140
Ate and drank when the heart in his breast bade him to.
But now from the time you were gone in the ship to Pylos,
They say he no longer eats and drinks the way he did,
Nor looks over the fields, but with groaning and wailing
He sits and laments, and the flesh shrinks round his bones."   145
Then sound-minded Telemachos answered him:
"That is the more painful. Still, let us leave him, though we are grieved,
For if all things were somehow free for mortals to choose,
We should first choose the day of my father's return.
But you, when you have told the news, come back and do not   150
Wander in the fields after that man. But tell my mother
To send the housekeeper on as soon as possible,
Secretly. And she may announce it to the old man."
He spoke, and roused the swineherd. He took sandals in hand,
Bound them under his feet, and went to the city; nor did   155
The swineherd Eumaeos escape Athene as he went from the lodge,
But she came up close. She likened her body to a woman's,
Lovely and tall and skilled in excellent tasks.
She stood and appeared to Odysseus at the hut doorway,
Nor did Telemachos see her face to face or perceive her.   160
For in no way do the gods appear clearly to all men.
But Odysseus and the dogs saw her. They did not bark;
They slunk with a whimpering to the other side of the lodge.
She signaled with her eyebrows. Godly Odysseus perceived it
And went out of the room along the great farmyard wall   165
And stood in her presence. Athene addressed him:
"Zeus-born son of Laertes, Odysseus of many devices,
Now is the time, say the word to your son, and do not conceal it
So you may both work death and destruction on the suitors,
And come to the renowned city together. Nor shall I   170
Myself be long from you, as I desire to fight."
Athene spoke and touched him with a golden wand.
At first she placed a cloak and a well-washed tunic
About his shoulders, increased his body and his youth.
His skin became dark again, and his cheeks filled out,   175
And the beard around his chin turned into dark blue.
When she had done this, she went back again, and Odysseus
Went into the hut. His dear son marveled at him.
He cast his eyes the other way, alarmed lest it be a god.
And he spoke out to him and uttered wingèd words: 180
"You appear other to me, stranger, than a moment before.
You have other garments, and your skin is not as it was.
You must be some one of the gods who possess broad heaven.
Well, be gracious, so we may give pleasing sacrifices
And well-made golden gifts to you. Be sparing toward us."   185

Then godly Odysseus, who had suffered much, answered him:
"I am not any god. Why liken me to immortals?
But I am your father for whose sake you are grieving
And suffer many pains, receiving the assaults of men."
When he had said this, he kissed his son and sent a tear to the
    ground   190
Off his cheeks. Before, he had always held them back without
    blenching.
Telemachos—he did not yet believe him to be his father—
Answered him right away with words and addressed him:
"You surely are not my father Odysseus, but some god
Enchants me, so that I may grieve and lament still more;   195
For in no way would a mortal man in his own mind
Devise these things, unless a god came by in person
Who might easily if he wished make one young or old.
Just recently you were an old man and had on sorry clothes.
And now you resemble the gods who possess broad heaven."   200
Odysseus of many wiles addressed him in answer:
"Telemachos, it is not seemly when your father is within
To wonder exceedingly and to be amazed.
No other Odysseus, indeed, shall ever come to you here.
I am the very man; suffering evils, wandering much,   205
I have come in the twentieth year to my fatherland.
And now this is the work of the forager Athene,
Who has made of me what she wishes, for she can do that,
Sometimes in the semblance of a beggar and sometimes
That of a young man who has lovely clothes on his skin.   210
It is easy for the gods who possess broad heaven
To glorify a mortal man or to disfigure him."
When he had said this he sat down. Telemachos
Embraced his noble father and moaned, shedding tears.
In both of them there arose a longing for lamentation.   215
They wailed piercingly and more incessantly than birds,
Sea eagles or falcons with hooked claws whose children
Farmers have snatched off before they were fully fledged.
So they lamented and shed tears from under their eyelids,
And the light of the sun would have gone down on their moaning   220
If Telemachos had not at once spoken out to his father:
"In what kind of a ship, dear father, did sailors
Bring you to Ithaca? Who did they claim to be?
For I do not believe you reached here at all on foot."
Then godly Odysseus, who had suffered much, addressed him: 225
"Well then, my child, to you I shall speak out the truth.
The Phaeacians, famous for ships, brought me, who escort
Other men too, whenever anyone reaches their people.
They brought me sleeping in a swift ship on the ocean,
Put me down at Ithaca, and gave me glorious gifts,   230

Bronze and gold in abundance and woven clothing;
These things now lie in caverns, by the will of the gods.
Now I have come here at Athene's instigations,
So we may plan about slaughter for our enemies.
Come now, speak out, and number the suitors for me,   235
So I may know how many men they are, and what sort.
Then as I deliberate in my own blameless heart
I may consider whether we can oppose them ourselves,
Alone without others, or shall seek for others."
Then sound-minded Telemachos spoke to him in answer: 240
"Father, I have always heard of your great renown
For being a skillful fighter with your hands and prudent in counsel.
But you speak of something enormous. Awe holds me. It could not
Be that two men might fight against so many stout men.
Truly, there are not ten of the suitors or twenty only,   245
But far more. You shall soon know their number here:
Out of Dulichion there are fifty-two
Chosen young men, and six servants to follow them.
Out of Samê there are four and twenty mortal men;
Out of Zacynthos there are twenty young men of the Achaians;   250
Out of Ithaca herself, twelve, all of the best;
And Medon is with them as herald, and the godly singer,
And a pair of servants who are skilled at carving the meat.
If we opposed all of those who are within, I fear
In bitterness and dread would you avenge their violence   255
Now that you have come. But if you can, think of some defender;
Take thought for someone well disposed to defend us."
Then godly Odysseus, who had suffered much, addressed him:
"I shall tell you, then, mark it well and listen to me,
And consider whether Athene with Father Zeus   260
Will protect us, or I shall think up some other defender."
Then sound-minded Telemachos answered him:
"These are excellent defenders of whom you speak,
Both seated high upon the clouds, and the two of them
Rule over all others, both men and the immortal gods."   265
Then godly Odysseus, who had suffered much, addressed him:
"Those two, indeed, shall not be for a long time far
From the mighty combat, when the strength of Ares
Is put to the proof in my halls between us and the suitors.
Well now, you go on home at the appearance of dawn   270
And mingle in with the presumptuous suitors,
And the swineherd will bring me later to the town
In the semblance of a beggar, miserable and old.
And if they dishonor me in the house, let the heart
In your own breast endure it that I suffer evilly.   275
Even if they drag me by the feet through the house out the doors
Or throw at me with darts, look on and restrain yourself.

No, just order them to cease their foolishness,
Speaking to them with soothing words. And they will surely
Give no heed at all, because for them the fated day stands at hand.   280
I shall tell you another thing, and keep it in mind.
When Athene of many plans puts it in my mind,
I shall nod to you with my head, and then you yourself take note
How many weapons of war are lying in the halls;
Pick them up and put them in a nook of the lofty chamber,   285
All of them. And appease the suitors deceptively
With soft speeches when they miss them and ask you questions:
'I have put them out of the smoke, since they no longer look like those
That Odysseus once left behind when he went to Troy,
But they are befouled, so much has the smoke of the fire got to
    them.   290
And the son of Cronos, too, has put this greater thought in my mind:
That, perhaps, drunk with wine, you may set up a quarrel
Among you, wound one another, and disgrace the banquet
And your wooing. For iron of itself draws a man on.'
And for us alone leave two swords and two spears   295
And a pair of oxhide shields to grasp with our hands
So we may rush upon them and capture them. And then
Pallas Athene will charm them, and the counselor Zeus.
I shall tell you something else, and keep it in mind,
If you are indeed truly my own and of our blood: 300
Let no one at this time hear Odysseus is within;
Let Laertes not know it, and not the swineherd,
No one of the servants, not Penelope herself.
Let you and me alone find out the bent of the women,
And we shall further try out certain of the menservants,   305
To see where one honors us and respects us in his heart,
And who does not heed you and dishonors the man you are."
His illustrious son spoke out to him in answer:
"Father, you shall know my disposition, I think,
And soon, for no slackness of mind holds me at all.   310
But I for my part think this will not be an advantage
To the two of us. I ask you to consider it;
A long time in vain would you go and test each person
By visiting the fields. And they in our halls unharmed
Devour goods insolently; there is no restraint.   315
And I ask you to find out for yourself the women
Who dishonor you, and those who are innocent.
As for the men, I myself would not want us to go
To their lodgings to test them; but attend to these matters later
If you truly know some portent from aegis-bearing Zeus."   320
And so such things did they say to one another.
Then the well-made ship was brought up to Ithaca
That had borne Telemachos and all his companions from Pylos.

When they had arrived within the very deep harbor
They drew the black ship up upon the land themselves   325
While proud-spirited servants carried their gear off.
At once they brought beautiful gifts to Klytios' house,
And they sent on a herald to the home of Odysseus
With a message to tell the prudent Penelope
That Telemachos was in the fields and had ordered the ship   330
To sail off to the town, so that the goodly queen
Might not fear in her heart and shed a tender tear.
The herald and the godly swineherd met each other
On account of the very same message they were to tell the woman,
And when they reached the home of the divine queen   335
The herald spoke out in the midst of the serving maids:
"Your beloved son, my queen, has already come."
And the swineherd, standing near Penelope,
Told her all her beloved son bade him to say.
And when he had told her all he was to deliver,   340
He went on his way to the swine and left the enclosures and the hall.
The suitors were grieving and depressed in their hearts;
They went out of the hall along the great wall of the courtyard
And they sat down there out in front of the portals.
Eurymachos, son of Polybos, began speaking to them: 345
"Friends, a great task is arrogantly achieved
By Telemachos, this voyage. We thought he would not achieve it.
Come now, let us drag down a black ship, the one that is best,
And gather seamen as rowers, so they may quickly
Give a message to those men to go swiftly home."   350
He had not said all, when Amphinomos saw the ship,
As he turned in his place, inside the very deep harbor;
And men lowering the sails and holding oars in their hands.
He gave a sweet laugh and said to his companions:
"Never mind sending a message now. Here they are inside;   355
Either some god told them this, or else they themselves
Saw the ship coming in that they were not able to catch it."
So he said, and they stood up and went to the strand of the sea.
They dragged the black ship up at once on the dry land
And proud-spirited servants carried the gear off for them.   360
They themselves went off to the assembly together. Nor did they
Allow anyone else to sit with them, of young men or old.
Antinoos spoke to them, son of Eupeithes:
"Well now, the gods have delivered this man from harm!
Lookouts were sitting day by day on the windy heights,   365
In quick succession always, and at the setting sun
We never rested a night on land, but on the ocean,
Sailing in the swift ship we awaited godly dawn,
In ambush for Telemachos that we might capture him
And kill him. And meanwhile some god has brought him home.   370

But let us here think of a woeful destruction
For Telemachos, and let him not escape us. I think
These deeds will not be accomplished while he is alive.
He himself is skilled in deliberation and thought,
But the people no longer wholly bear favor toward us.   375
Well, come now, before he convenes the Achaians
Into assembly—for I think he will not let anything go,
But will be angry. He will stand up among all and tell
How we contrived sheer murder for him and did not catch him.
And they will not approve when they hear of the evil deeds.   380
I fear they will do some evil and drive us out
Of our own land, and we shall reach the country of others.
Let us forestall him and take him in fields far from the city
Or on the path. We should then have his living and property
To divide duly among us, and then we might give   385
The house for his mother and for the one who weds her to have.
But if this speech displeases you, and you wish
The man to live and have all his paternal goods,
Let us not then gather here and devour his goods
In their pleasing abundance, but let each from his own hall   390
Woo her and seek her with gifts. And she then may wed
Whoever gives the most and comes as the destined man."
So he said, and they all became hushed in silence.
Amphinomos then spoke out to them and addressed them.
The illustrious son of King Nisos, son of Aretias,   395
Who out of Dulichion, grassy and rich in grain,
Was leader of the suitors and pleased Penelope
The most with his speeches, for he practiced good sense.
With favorable intent he spoke out and addressed them:
"My friends, I would not myself at all want to kill   400
Telemachos. Dreadful it is to kill the race
Of kings. But let us first ask the gods for advice
If the decrees of great Zeus do agree with this,
I shall kill him myself and order all others to do so,
But if the gods turn aside, I give the order to cease."   405
So Amphinomos said, and his speech was pleasing to them.
They got up then at once and went to the home of Odysseus,
And when they got there, they took their seats in polished armchairs.
But the prudent Penelope had another thought:
To appear to the suitors with their presumptuous pride;   410
For she had heard death was to be in the halls for her son.
The herald Medon, who found out their plans, had told her.
She went on into the hall along with her serving women.
And when the godly woman arrived before the suitors,
She stood beside the pillar of the stoutly fashioned roof;   415
Holding the glistening headbands before her cheeks
She rebuked Antinoos and spoke right out directly:

"Antinoos, for all your pride and evil devices, they say
You are the best of your peers in the land of Ithaca
For advice and speeches. But you are not really so.   420
You madman, why do you devise murder and death
For Telemachos, and do not heed the suppliants
Who have Zeus for a witness? It is not holy to plot ills for one another.
Do you not know that your father came here in flight
And in fear of the people? And they were highly enraged   425
Because he had come along with Taphian pirates
And troubled the Thesprotians, who were our close friends.
They wished to destroy him and to tear out his own heart,
And to devour his great and satisfying livelihood.
But Odysseus held them back and restrained them, though they wanted
   that.   430
Now you devour his home without payment, and woo his wife,
And kill off his son, and you anger me very much.
Well, I tell you to stop and to order the others so.
Eurymachos, son of Polybos, answered her:
"Prudent Penelope, daughter of Icarios,   435
Take heart. Do not give heed to these matters in your mind.
The man does not exist, nor shall, nor come to be,
Who would lay hands on your son Telemachos
While I at least am alive and have sight on the earth.
I declare this to you, and it shall surely come to pass.   440
Right away his black blood shall run on my spear,
Since Odysseus, the sacker of cities, many times
Sat me upon his knees and placed a piece of roast meat
In my hands, and also held the red wine up to me.
And so Telemachos is by far the dearest to me   445
Of all men, and I bid him not to tremble for death,
From the suitors at least. But from the gods it is not to be escaped."
So he said, cheering her, and himself wrought destruction for him.
But she went on into the shining upper chamber
And wept there for Odysseus, her dear husband, until   450
Bright-eyed Athene cast sweet sleep on her eyelids.
At evening the godly swineherd came to Odysseus
And his son. They were preparing dinner attentively,
Sacrificing a year-old swine. And Athene
Stood close beside Odysseus, son of Laertes,   455
Struck him with a wand, and made him an old man again.
She clothed his skin in wretched garments, lest the swineherd
Look straight at him and know him and go announce it
To constant Penelope, and not keep it back in his mind.
Telemachos was the first to address a speech to him: 460
"You have come, godly Eumaeos. What is the news through the town?
Are the bold suitors already within and back
From their ambush, or do they still watch for me on my way home?"

And you addressed him in answer, swineherd Eumaeos:
"I did not bother to ask and inquire about these matters   465
As I went down through the town. My heart bade me at once.
After I had told the message, to come back here again.
The swift messenger from your companions joined me,
A herald, who first gave the word to your mother.
I know something else, for I saw it with my eyes.   470
Just now over the city where the hill of Hermes is,
I was going along when I saw a swift ship coming on
Into our harbor. There were upon her many men.
It was loaded down with shields and with two-edged spears.
And I thought it to be those men, but do not at all know them.   475
So he said, and Telemachos smiled in his sacred strength.
He looked with his eyes at his father and avoided the swineherd.
And when they had ceased from their toil and made dinner,
They dined, nor did their hearts want for a well-shared meal.
But when they had taken their fill of food and drink   480
They remembered rest, and they took the gift of sleep.

XVII

And when the early-born, rosy-fingered dawn appeared,
Telemachos, the dear son of godly Odysseus,
Bound the beautiful sandals underneath his feet,
And he took the stout spear that fitted in his hand,
Heading for the town, and he spoke out to his swineherd: 5
"Uncle, I am going to the city, so that my mother
May see me; I do not believe that she will cease
From hateful wailing and tearful lamentation
Until she sees me in person. I give you this order:
Lead this wretched stranger to the city, so that there   10
He may beg a dinner. Whoever wishes may give him
A loaf and a cup. It is not possible for me to endure
All sorts of men, with the pains in my heart that I have.
And if the stranger gets very angry, it will be the more painful
For himself. Yes, indeed, I like to speak the truth."   15
Odysseus of many wiles addressed him in answer:
"My friend, I do not wish to be held back myself.
It is better for a beggar to beg dinner in the city
Than in the fields. Whoever wishes will give it to me.
I am not yet of an age to remain at the folds,   20
So as to obey in everything a master who gives orders.
But come, this man that you are bidding will lead me
The moment I get warm from the fire and the sun's heat comes.
I have miserably poor clothes on, and I fear the frost

Of morning may overcome me. You say the town is far away."   25
So he spoke, and Telemachos went through the lodge
At a brisk pace; he was sowing the seeds of ill for the suitors.
And when he arrived at the well-situated house,
He stood the spear he carried against a tall pillar.
Then he went in himself and crossed the stone threshold.   30
The nurse Eurycleia was by far the first to see him.
She strewed fleeces upon the cleverly wrought armchairs,
And then she broke out in tears and came straight to him.
The other serving women of hardy-minded Odysseus gathered,
And they kissed him affectionately on his head and shoulders.   35
The prudent Penelope went on out of the chamber,
Resembling Artemis or golden Aphrodite.
Weeping, she threw her arms around her beloved son;
She kissed him on the head and on both lovely eyes.
And while she was sobbing she uttered wingèd words: 40
"You have come as a sweet light, Telemachos. I thought
I would see you no more when you went secretly in a ship
Against my will to Pylos for word of your dear father.
But come, tell me in what way you got sight of him."
And sound-minded Telemachos answered her: 45
"Mother, do not raise lamentation in me, nor arouse
The heart in my breast, since I did escape sheer destruction.
But bathe and put pure garments upon your skin
And go on into the upper chamber with the serving women.
Vow to all the gods you will sacrifice full hecatombs   50
If somehow Zeus may bring about deeds of retribution.
And I shall go on to the assembly, so that I may call
On a stranger who accompanied me hence as I came here.
I sent him on myself with my godlike companions,
And I ordered Peiraeos to lead him to the house,   55
To befriend him kindly and respect him till I should come."
So he said, and for her the speech was without a wing.
She washed herself and put pure garments upon her skin,
Vowed to all the gods she would sacrifice full hecatombs
If somehow Zeus might bring about deeds of retribution.   60
Telemachos then went on through the hall
Holding a spear, and two swift dogs accompanied him.
Moreover, Athene shed a marvelous grace about him.
All the people wondered about him as he came on.
The bold suitors gathered together around him,   65
Speaking fine words but plotting evils in their minds.
And then he avoided the entire group of them.
But where Mentor sat down, and Antiphos and Halitherses,
Who were his father's companions from the beginning,
He went and took a seat. They asked him for the details.   70
Peiraeos, renowned for the spear, came close to them,

Bringing the stranger through the city to the assembly. Not long
Did Telemachos turn aside from the stranger, but stood beside him.
First to him did Peiraeos address his speech:
"Telemachos, go urge the women at once on to my house   75
So that I may send the gifts that Menelaos gave you."
Then sound-minded Telemachos answered him:
"Peiraeos, we do not know how the present acts will come out.
If the bold suitors in the halls secretly
Kill me and divide up all the goods of my father,   80
I would rather you gained them yourself than any of those.
But if I myself breed death and destiny for these men,
Then carry them gladly to the house, and I shall be glad."
When he had said this, he led the long-suffering stranger to the house.
And when they reached the well-situated hall,   85
They put their mantles down over the seats and armchairs,
Got into well-polished bathtubs, and washed themselves.
When the serving maids had washed and anointed them with olive oil,
And thrown woolen mantles around them, and tunics
They got out of the bathtubs and sat on the seats.   90
A handmaid poured water from a pitcher she was carrying,
A lovely golden one, over into a silver basin,
For washing the hands; she set up a polished table alongside.
A respected housekeeper served bread she was carrying,
Laying out many dishes, gracious with the provisions.   95
His mother sat opposite him by the doorpost of the hall,
Leaning back in her seat, turning the fine threads on the distaff.
They stretched forth their hands to the food that was laid out ready,
But when they had taken their fill of food and drink,
The prudent Penelope began speaking to them: 100
"Telemachos, when I have gone up into the upper chamber
I shall lie down in my bed, which is made full of groans for me,
Ever sullied with my tears since the time Odysseus
Went to Troy with the sons of Atreus. Nor did you dare,
Before the bold suitors came into this house   105
To tell clearly of your father's return, if you did hear of it."
And sound-minded Telemachos answered her:
"All right, then, Mother, I shall speak the truth to you.
We went to Pylos and to Nestor, shepherd of the people.
The man received me and kindly befriended me   110
In his lofty home, as a father would his own son
Come afresh after a time from somewhere else. So the man
Kindly entertained me with his glorious sons.
But of hardy-hearted Odysseus, alive or dead,
He said he had never heard anything from anyone on earth.   115
He sent me on with horses and well-jointed chariots
To the son of Atreus, Menelaos, famed for the spear.
There I saw Argive Helen, on whose account

Trojans and Argives suffered much at the will of the gods.
Menelaos, good at the war cry, asked me at once   120
What I had come in search of to godly Lacedemon.
And I declared to him myself the entire truth.
Then he addressed me and answered me with a speech:
'Well now, they who are themselves without courage
Have wished to lie down in the bed of a stouthearted man!   125
As when a deer in the thicket of a mighty lion
Has put her newborn milk-sucking fawns to sleep,
And goes questing over the spurs and the grassy gorges
For grazing, and just then he comes to his own lair
And upon the two of them brings a wretched fate;   130
So upon these men will Odysseus bring a wretched fate.
By Father Zeus, Athene, and Apollo, I wish
He might be as he once was in well-established Lesbos
When he stood up and wrestled in a fight with Philomelides,
Threw him down mightily, and all the Achaians rejoiced;   135
As that sort of man might Odysseus contend with the suitors.
They would all be swift in their doom and bitter in marriage.
As for what you ask and beseech me about, I myself
Will say nothing at all off the point, nor will I deceive.
But what the unerring old man of the sea told me,   140
Not a word of that shall I hide from you or conceal.
He said he saw him on an island, that he had strong pains
In the halls of the nymph Calypso, who by compulsion
Is holding him back. And he cannot reach his fatherland,
For he has no ships there with oars, and no companions   145
Who might convey him over the broad back of the sea.'
So said Atreus' son, Menelaos, famed for the spear.
When I finished this, I went off. The immortals gave me
A breeze, and they brought me swiftly to my dear fatherland."
So he said, and he stirred up the heart in her breast.   150
And the godlike Theoclymenos spoke among them:
"Respected wife of Odysseus, son of Laertes,
Indeed this man has no clear knowledge, but mark my word;
For I shall prophesy to you truthfully and conceal nothing.
May Zeus now be my witness, first of the gods, and this guest table,   155
And the hearth of the blameless Odysseus, to which I have come,
That Odysseus is already on his fatherland soil.
He is here, sitting still or moving, and is finding out
These evil deeds, and he breeds evil for all the suitors.
Such was the meaning of the bird I observed as I sat   160
On the well-timbered ship, and declared it to Telemachos."
And then the prudent Penelope spoke to him:
"Would that this speech, stranger, might be fulfilled.
Then you would soon know friendship and many gifts
From me, so that one who met you would call you blessed."   165

And so they said such things to one another.
The suitors out in front of the hall of Odysseus
Were amusing themselves by throwing weights and javelins
On the leveled terrace as before, in their insolence.
And when it was time for dinner, and from everywhere   170
In the fields sheep came that the men drove as they did before,
Then Medon spoke to them, who was most pleasing to them
Of all the heralds, and he attended on them for the meal:
"Young men, now that you have all amused your minds with contests,
Come into the house so that we may partake of a meal.   175
It is not a bad thing to take dinner at the right time."
So he said. They stood up, went, and obeyed his word.
And when they had arrived at the well-situated house,
They put mantles down on the seats and on the armchairs;
And they sacrificed great sheep and goats rich with fat,   180
They sacrificed sleek hogs and a heifer of the herd,
Preparing the meal. But Odysseus and the godly swineherd
Were hastening on to go from the field to the city.
The swineherd, chief of the men, began speaking to them:
"Stranger, since you do desire to go to the city   185
Today, as my master commanded, I myself would like
To leave you here as a guardian of the folds,
But I hesitate and fear him, lest afterward
He reproach me for it. Harsh are the rebukes of masters.
Come now, let us go. The day is mostly past,   190
And soon it will be colder for you, toward the evening."
Odysseus of many wiles addressed him in answer:
"I know, I see. You say this to an understanding man.
Well, let us go. Lead us all the way on yourself,
And give me any staff that may have been cut for you   195
To support me, since they say the roads are slippery."
He spoke, and put the sorry wallet around his shoulders,
Full of rents. And there was a twisted strap on it;
Eumaeos then gave to him a staff that he liked.
The two of them then went on. The dogs and the herdsmen   200
Who stayed behind guarded the lodge. He led his master
To the city in the likeness of a beggar miserable and old,
Walking with a staff. Sorry clothes were on his skin.
And when, as they went on along the rugged path,
They got near the city, they arrived at a spring,   205
Paved and fair-flowing, whence the townswomen drew water,
Which Ithakos, Neritos, and Polyktor had made.
About it was a grove of poplars nourished by water
In a circle on all sides, and cold water flowed down
From the rock above. An altar had been built above   210
To the nymphs, where all travelers made offerings.
There Melanthios, son of Dolios, came upon them

While he was leading goats that were best among all the herds,
As dinner for the suitors. And two herdsmen followed along.
When he saw them he upbraided them and spoke directly,   215
A striking, disgraceful speech. He stirred Odysseus' heart.
"Now a man wholly foul leads a man who is foul;
So the god always brings a like to his own like.
Miserable swineherd, where are you leading this wild pig,
This tiresome beggar, desecrator of feasts,   220
Who stands by many door posts and rubs his shoulders on them,
Begging for morsels, but not for basins or swords?
If you give him to me to become a guard of the folds,
To be a stall sweeper and carry greens for the kids,
Then he could drink whey and put on a great thigh.   225
But since he has learned foul deeds, he will not wish
To approach work, but wants to beg through the district
And to ask food for his insatiable belly.
I tell you this straight out and it will be fulfilled:
If he ever comes to the home of godly Odysseus,   230
Many stools about his head thrown from the hands of men
Will his ribs wear out as he is tossed through the hall."
So he said, and in his foolishness rushed with a kick
On his flank. But he did not drive the man off the path;
Odysseus stood steadfast. And he deliberated   235
Whether to rush on the other with the staff and take his life
Or to lift him by the middle and dash his head to earth.
But he braced himself and checked his mind. The swineherd
Looked at the other and scolded him; he raised his hands and prayed
    aloud;
"Nymphs of the springs, Zeus's daughters, if ever Odysseus   240
Burned thighs to you, enclosing them in rich fat,
Of lambs or of kids, bring this wish of mine to pass:
May the man himself come, and may some god bring him.
Then he would scatter all these vainglories far and wide
That you bring now in your insolence, forever straying   245
To the town. And evil herdsmen are destroying the flock."
Then Melanthios, herdsman of the goats, spoke to him:
"Well now, what has this dog of pernicious mind said!
Someday I shall take him on a black, well-timbered ship
Far from Ithaca, where he might get me a large fortune.   250
Would that silver-bowed Apollo might shoot Telemachos
Today in the halls, or he be overcome by the suitors,
As Odysseus' day of return has been lost afar."
When he had said this, he left them there as they walked quietly on.
Then he went on and swiftly reached the master's house.   255
He went in at once and sat down among the suitors
Opposite Eurymachos, for the man liked him very much.
Those who were serving offered him a portion of the meat

And a respected housekeeper offered bread she was carrying,
To eat. Both Odysseus and the godly swineherd   260
Stood still as they got near. About them came the sound
Of the hollow lyre. For Phemios struck up a song among them.
The other took the swineherd by the hand and addressed him:
"Eumaeos, this is surely the lovely home of Odysseus,
Easy to recognize when seen, even among many.   265
One part is right next to another, and its court is finished off
With wall and copingstones. And there are doors well fenced
In a double gate. No man could look down upon them.
I know that many men are holding banquets
In the place, since meat smoke rises from it, and the lyre   270
Sounds there, which the gods make the companion of a banquet."
And you addressed him in answer, swineherd Eumaeos:
"You know it clearly, as you are not otherwise without sense.
So come now, and let us discuss how these acts shall be.
Either you first enter the well-situated house   275
And go among the suitors, and I shall be left behind here,
Or, if you wish, stay back, and I shall go forward myself.
Do not linger, lest someone perceive you outside
And hit you or drive you; I bid you to consider this."
Then godly Odysseus, who had suffered much, answered him: 280
"I know, I see. You say this to an understanding man.
Go forward now, and I shall remain here behind,
For I am not unacquainted with tosses or with blows.
My heart is enduring, since I have suffered many ills
On the waves and in war. Let this one be added to them.   285
There is no way of concealing an eager stomach,
The accursèd thing that gives many evils to men,
On whose account also well-rigged ships set out
Over the barren ocean, carrying evils for enemies."
And so such things did they say to one another,   290
And the dog held his head and his ears up where he lay,
Argos, stout-hearted Odysseus', that he himself
Had once reared and did not enjoy, but he went off beforehand
To holy Ilion. Some time back, young men used to take him out
After the wild goats and the rabbits and the deer.   295
But now he was lying unwanted while his master was gone,
In much dung from mules and oxen, which was heaped
In abundance before the gates, till Odysseus' servants
Should bring it when they had a great plot to fertilize.
There the dog Argos lay, full of the vermin of dogs;   300
And then, when he perceived that Odysseus was nearby,
He fawned over him with his tail and dropped both his ears.
But then he was no longer able to go closer
To his master. The man looked away and wiped off a tear.
He hid easily from Eumaeos, and he at once asked a question: 305

"Great wonder is it, Eumaeos, that this dog lies here in the dung;
He is handsome in body, but I do not clearly know
Whether along with this look he used also to be swift to run
Or was simply the sort of table dog that belongs to men
And that masters take care of on account of their graceful look." 310
And you addressed him in answer, swineherd Eumaeos:
"Ah yes, this is the dog of a man who died far away,
And if he were the same in body and in his actions
As when Odysseus left him behind on his way off to Troy,
You would wonder at once when you saw his speed and his force. 315
No wild beast that he chased could escape him at all
In the recesses of the deep woods. And tracks he knew well.
Now he is caught in misery, and his master is dead somewhere
Far from his fatherland. The careless women do not tend him.
And the servants, since the masters are holding sway no more, 320
Hence are no longer willing to perform proper tasks.
And broad-seeing Zeus takes away half the excellence
Of a man, from the time the day of slavery comes upon him."
When he had said this he entered the well-situated halls,
And he went straight through the hall to the noble suitors. 325
But the fortune of black death took Argos away
Once he had seen Odysseus in the twentieth year.
God-like Telemachos was by far the first to see
The swineherd coming to the house; and then he quickly
Nodded and called him. The man looked around and took a stool 330
That was lying where a server usually sat and carved
Many pieces of meat for the suitors as they dined in the hall.
He brought it to Telemachos' table on the other side,
Put it down, and sat on it himself. And a herald
Brought him a share, set it down, and lifted bread out of a basket. 335
Odysseus entered the halls close behind him
In the semblance of a beggar, miserable and old,
Walking with a staff. Sorry garments clothed his skin.
He sat at the ashwood threshold inside of the portals
Leaning on a cypress post that a workman once 340
Had skillfully planed and drawn straight to the line.
Telemachos called the swineherd to him and addressed him;
He took an entire loaf from the beautiful basket
And as much meat as his hands held around it could contain:
"Bring this and give it to the stranger and tell him 345
To go around to all the suitors and beg in turn,
For shame is not a good thing for a needy man."
So he spoke, and the swineherd went when he had heard what he said.
He stood close to the man, and uttered wingèd words:
"Telemachos gives this to you, stranger, and tells you 350
To go around to all the suitors and beg in turn,
Since shame, he says, is not good for a needy man."

Odysseus of many wiles addressed him in answer:
"Lord Zeus, grant me that Telemachos be blessed among men,
And all that he wants in his mind come about for him."   355
So he said, and received it with both hands, and set it down
In front of his feet there, upon the disgraceful wallet.
And he ate while the singer was singing in the halls.
When he had had dinner and the godly singer had ceased,
The suitors made a din through the halls. And Athene   360
Stood close beside Odysseus, son of Laertes,
And urged him on to gather loaves from the suitors,
So he might know who were righteous and who lawless;
And yet she did not intend any to escape from misfortune.
He went along begging of each man, from left to right,   365
Stretching his hand every way as though he had long been a beggar.
They pitied and they gave, and they marveled at him
And asked one another who he was and whence he came.
And then Melanthios, the goatherd, spoke out among them:
"Suitors of the famous queen, listen to what I say   370
About this stranger here. For I have seen him before.
And surely the swineherd guided him to this place.
But I do not know him clearly, or whence he declares his birth to be."
So he said, and Antinoos upbraided the swineherd with a speech:
"Notorious swineherd, why did you lead this man   375
To the city? Are there not enough vagrants for us,
Insatiable beggars, defilers of the banquet?
Do you treat it lightly that those who are gathered here
Devour your master's living, that you called this man here too?"
And you addressed him in answer, swineherd Eumaeos: 380
"Antinoos, though you are noble, you have said what is not good.
For who invites some other stranger when he comes himself
From elsewhere, unless he is one of the district craftsmen,
A prophet or a healer of ills or a worker of wood
Or a wonderful singer who gives delight as he sings?   385
These are invited among mortals throughout the boundless earth.
No one would invite a beggar to eat his substance away!
But always you are harsh beyond the other suitors
To the servants of Odysseus, and especially to me.
I do not care, though, while constant Penelope   390
And god-like Telemachos are alive for me in the halls."
Then sound-minded Telemachos answered him:
"Silence, and please do not answer this man so much with words.
Antinoos has the habit of always giving evil provocation
With harsh speeches, and he urges others also to do it."   395
So he said, and he uttered wingèd words to Antinoos:
"Antinoos, you care for me nicely as a father for his son
When you order me to drive the stranger from the halls
With a word of constraint. Let a god not bring this to pass.

Take and give to him; I begrudge it not. In fact, I command it.   400
And do not stand in awe of my mother, or of anyone else
Among the servants who are in the halls of godly Odysseus.
And yet you have no such intention in your breast.
You would rather eat yourself than give to another."
In answer to him, Antinoos addressed him: 405
"High-talking Telemachos, unchecked in your anger, what have you
     said?
If all the suitors should offer him as much as this,
The house would keep him at a distance for three months."
So he said, and out from under the table he brought a footstool
That lay there, on which he held his glossy feet while feasting.   410
All the others gave and filled his wallet with bread and meat.
And soon Odysseus was again ready to go back again
To the threshold and get a taste from the Achaians free.
He stood by Antinoos and addressed a word to him:
"Give, my friend; you do not seem to me to be the worst   415
Of the Achaians, but the best, since you look like a king.
And so you ought to give bread more liberally
Than the others. I shall speak your fame through the boundless earth.
For I myself was once blessed, and I inhabited
A rich house among men, and gave to a tramp like this   420
Many times, no matter who came, whatever he needed.
I had numberless servants and many other things
Men have who live well and are called prosperous.
But Zeus, son of Cronos, destroyed me, as he somehow wished;
He sent me along with pirates who wandered much,   425
To go to Egypt, a long journey, so I might die.
I beached my bobbing ships by the Egyptian river,
And then I called upon my trusty companions
To remain there beside the ships and to guard the ships.
And I ordered spies to go up on places of lookout,   430
But they gave in to excess, and, relying on their own strength,
They sacked the beautiful fields of the Egyptians
At once and carried their women and infant children off.
They killed the men. And soon the noise reached the city.
They perceived the shouting, and at the appearance of dawn   435
Came on. The whole plain was filled with foot soldiers and horses,
And the flash of bronze. Zeus who hurls the thunderbolt
Threw evil panic among my companions, nor could any
Bear to stay face to face. Ills surrounded us on all sides.
Then they slaughtered many of us with the sharp bronze   440
And led some off alive to work for them under constraint.
But they gave me to a stranger they met bound for Cyprus,
Dmetor, son of Iasos, who ruled over Cyprus by force.
From there have I now come here this way, suffering troubles."
Then Antinoos answered him and addressed him: 445

"What god has brought this trouble, this annoyance at the banquet?
Stand as you are in the middle, apart from my table,
Lest you soon arrive at a bitter Egypt and Cyprus,
Because you are some bold and shameless beggar.
You stand beside all in turn. And they give to you   450
Wantonly, since they have no restraint or remorse
At giving of others' goods freely, since each has much."
Odysseus of many wiles withdrew and addressed him:
"Well now, your mind is not a match for your appearance.
You would not give salt from your house to your own suppliant,   455
You who now sit among others' things and cannot bear
To take off a little bread and give it to me; yet much is there."
So he said, and Antinoos was very angry in his heart,
And glaring at him, he uttered wingèd words:
"I think you will no longer withdraw through the hall;   460
In peace, since you are even uttering reproaches."
So he said, and took the footstool and hit his right shoulder
At the very base of his back. He stood there just like a rock,
Steadfast. Nor did the throw of Antinoos make him fall,
But he moved his head in silence, plotting evils deep inside.   465
He went back to the threshold and sat down, and he put
His full wallet beside him and spoke to the suitors:
"Listen to me, suitors of the illustrious queen,
So that I may say what the heart in my breast bids me to.
There is no pain in a man's mind or any grief   470
When he battles over possessions of his own
And is wounded for the sake of his oxen or shining sheep.
But Antinoos hit me on account of my woeful belly,
A cursed thing that gives many evils to men.
But if perchance gods and Furies exist for beggars,   475
May the end of death find Antinoos sooner then marriage."
Then Antinoos, son of Eupeithes, addressed him:
"Sit and eat in peace, stranger, or go somewhere else,
Lest the young men drag you through the halls for what you say,
By the foot or by the hand, and tear you all to pieces."   480
So he said, and they all grew presumptuously angry.
And this is what one of those overbearing young men would say:
"Antinoos, you did not do well to hit a hapless wanderer.
You are cursed, if perchance he is some heavenly god.
Yes, the gods in the semblance of alien strangers   485
Do appear in all forms and go about among cities
Looking upon the excess and the good order of men."
So said the suitors, and he did not attend to their speech.
Telemachos was nursing a great grief in his heart
For the struck man, but he cast no tear on the ground from his
    eyelids;   490
But in silence moved his head, plotting evils deep inside.

When the prudent Penelope heard that the man
Was struck in the hall, she spoke out to her servants:
"Would that bow-famed Apollo might so strike the other himself."
Then Eurynome, the housekeeper, addressed her in a speech: 495
"Would that there might come a fulfillment for our prayers!
None of these men would get as far as the fair-throned Dawn."
Then the prudent Penelope spoke to her:
"Good mother, they are all foes, since they devise evils.
Antinoos most of all is like a black fate.   500
Some hapless stranger wanders into the house
Begging from the men. Lack of means calls him on.
Then all the others filled him up and gave to him there,
And this one hit him with a footstool at the base of the right shoulder."
And so did she speak among her serving women,   505
Seated in her chamber. And godly Odysseus was eating dinner.
She called out to the godly swineherd and addressed him:
"Come, godly Eumaeos, go order the stranger
To come, so that I may embrace him in some way and ask of him
If he has perchance heard news of stouthearted Odysseus,   510
Or seen him with his eyes. He looks like a man who has much roamed."
And you addressed her in answer, swineherd Eumaeos:
"Well then, my queen, let the Achaians be silent.
The man tells such tales as would enchant your own heart.
Three nights I had him, and I held him for three days   515
In my hut. He first came to me running away from a ship.
Nor did he ever make an end of telling his misfortune.
As when a man looks upon a singer who sings
The words pleasing to mortals that he has learned from the gods,
And they endlessly long to hear him whenever he sings: 520
So that man enchanted me as he sat in the halls.
He says he is a paternal guest-friend of Odysseus
And he dwells in Crete, where the race of Minos is.
And now he has come here this way, suffering pains,
Rolling on and on. He claims to have heard news of Odysseus   525
Near us, in the fertile land of the Thesprotians;
That he is alive and is bringing many treasures to his home."
Then the prudent Penelope spoke to him:
"Come, call him here, so he may speak himself, face to face.
And let these men sit sporting either at the doors   530
Or here through the halls, since their hearts are merry.
Their own possessions lie undisturbed at home.
Bread and sweet wine. These are what their house servants eat,
But they themselves cluster to our house day after day
Slaughtering oxen and sheep and fat goats.   535
They carry on their revel and drink the sparkling wine
Wantonly. Many things are wasted. And there is no man
Of the kind Odysseus was, to ward off harm from the house.

But if Odysseus were to come and reach his fatherland,
With his son he would at once avenge the men's violence."   540
So she said, and Telemachos sneezed loud. About the house
It resounded terribly. And Penelope laughed.
At once to Eumaeos she uttered wingèd words:
"Come to me, and summon the stranger so, face to face.
Did you not see that my son sneezed at all the words?   545
So death will come not unfulfilled for the suitors,
All of them, nor will any ward off death and destiny.
I shall tell you something else; keep it well in mind.
If I acknowledge that he says everything truthfully,
I shall clothe him in a mantle and a tunic, lovely clothes."   550
So she said; the swineherd went when he heard the speech,
Stood close beside him, and uttered wingèd words:
"Father stranger, the prudent Penelope calls to you,
The mother of Telemachos. Her heart bids her to ask
Something about her husband, though she has suffered cares.   555
If she acknowledges that you say everything truthfully,
She will clothe you in a mantle and a tunic, the things that you need
The most. And then, begging bread through the district,
You will feed your belly; whoever wishes will give to you."
Then godly Odysseus, who had suffered much, spoke to him: 560
"Eumaeos, straight off I would tell all truthfully
To the prudent Penelope, daughter of Icarios.
For I know well about that man; we have got the same woe.
But I fear the throng of the difficult suitors
Whose insolence and force reach iron heaven.   565
Why, just now, when this man, as I was going to the house
Doing no evil, struck me and presented me with pains,
Telemachos could not at all prevent it, or anyone else.
So now go bid Penelope to remain in the halls,
Though she is eager, till the setting of the sun.   570
Then let her ask me about the day of her husband's return,
Seating me closer to the fire. For the clothes I have
Are woeful. You yourself know it too, since I besought you first."
So he said. And the swineherd went when he heard the speech.
Penelope spoke to him as he went over the threshold: 575
"Do you not bring him, Eumaeos? What does the wanderer mean by
    this?
Does he fear someone excessively, perhaps, or otherwise
Feel ashamed in the house? A tramp who feels shame is a bad one."
Then you addressed her in answer, swineherd Eumaeos:
"He speaks in measure, as anyone else would think   580
Who would avoid the insolence of presumptuous men.
But he bids you to wait until the setting of the sun;
And this way, queen, it will be far better for yourself
To speak alone to the stranger and to hear his speech."

Then the prudent Penelope addressed him: 585
"The stranger is not senseless; he thinks the way it may be.
For never, in this way, surely, did any among mortal men
So devise reckless deeds in their insolence."
So the woman spoke, and the godly swineherd went off
To the conclave of suitors, when he had told her everything.   590
And at once he uttered wingèd words to Telemachos,
Holding his head close, so the others could not hear:
"My friend, I am going off to guard the swine and the other things there,
Your living and mine. Let everything here be your affair;
Protect yourself first and give heed in your heart   595
Lest you suffer something. Many Achaians plot evils.
May Zeus destroy them before trouble comes upon us."
And then sound-minded Telemachos answered him:
"So it will be, father. Go when you have had supper.
Come at dawn and bring fine victims for sacrifice.   600
But all these things will be my affair, and the immortals'."
So he said, and the man at once sat on the polished stool,
When he had filled his heart with eating and with drinking.
He went after the swine, and left the enclosures and the hall
Full of banqueters. They were enjoying themselves with dancing   605
And with song, for the evening of the day was already coming.

XVIII

Then up came the beggar of the whole district, who begged
Through the town of Ithaca; he was outstanding for his greedy belly,
For incessantly eating and drinking. Nor did he have
Strength or force, but his form was very large to behold.
Arnaios was his name. His queenly mother gave it   5
At the time of his birth. But all the young men called him Iros,[1]
Because he went with a message when anyone asked him.
He came up and tried to drive Odysseus from his own home,
And, upbraiding him, he uttered wingèd words:
"Leave the doorway, old man, lest you soon be dragged off by the
    foot.   10
Don't you understand that they are all winking at me
And call on me to drag you? Still, I am ashamed to.
But get up, lest our quarrel soon come even to fists."
Odysseus of many wiles glowered at him and addressed him:
"My fine friend, I do not do or speak any wrong to you.   15
Nor do I begrudge anyone's giving, even if much is taken.
This threshold can contain us both. There is no need
To begrudge what others have. You seem to me to be

1. The messenger of the gods.

A tramp, like me; and the gods are supposed to bestow wealth.
But do not challenge with your fists too much, lest you anger me;   20
Lest, old man though I am, I stain your chest and your lips
With blood. And then there would be still greater peace for me
Tomorrow. And indeed I think you will not return at all
A second time to the house of Odysseus, son of Laertes."
Getting angry at him, the tramp Iros spoke to him: 25
"Well now, how fluently does the wild pig talk,
Like an oven woman; I should devise evils for him,
And beat him with both hands, and knock all his teeth
Out of his jaw to the ground like a crop-devouring sow's.
Gird yourself now so all these men may look upon us   30
As we fight. How would you contend with a younger man?"
And so outside in front of the lofty portals,
On the polished threshold, they grew fierce in full wrath.
Antinoos noticed them in his sacred might,
Laughed out sweetly, and spoke before the suitors: 35
"My friends, nothing like this has ever happened before.
Such a delight has the god brought to this house!
The stranger and Iros are quarreling with one another
To battle with their fists. Let us quickly set them together."
So he said, and all of them sprang up in laughter   40
And clustered about the beggars in their foul clothes.
Antinoos, son of Eupeithes, spoke out to them:
"Listen to me, bold suitors, so I may say something.
These stomachs of goats are lying in the fire that we
Have stuffed with fat for dinner and filled up with blood.   45
Whoever wins and turns out to be the better man,
Let him stand up and take whichever one of them he wishes.
And he may always dine with us, nor shall we allow
Any other beggar inside to mingle and make requests."
So Antinoos spoke, and his speech was pleasing to them.   50
Odysseus of many wiles spoke to them with a plan in his mind:
"My friends, there is no way for an old man worn out with grief
To fight against a younger. Still, my criminal belly
Urges me on, that I be overcome with blows.
But come, all of you, and swear a mighty oath,   55
That no one favoring Iros will recklessly
Strike me with heavy hand and overpower me for him."
So he said, and all of them swore as he had asked.
But when they had sworn and had completed the oath,
Telemachos again addressed them in his sacred might: 60
"Stranger, if your heart and bold spirit urge you on
To ward this man off, do not fear any of the other
Achaians, since he who smites you shall fight with many.
I am myself the host, and the two kings agree,
Antinoos and Eurymachos, both sound-minded men."   65

So he said, and they all assented. Then Odysseus
Girded his rags round his private parts and displayed his thighs,
Handsome and large; and his broad shoulders appeared,
And his chest and his powerful arms. Then Athene
Stood near and filled out the limbs of the shepherd of the people,   70
And all the suitors were exceedingly amazed.
So one of them would look at his neighbor and say:
"Soon Iros, un-Irosed, shall have an ill he brought on himself,
So great a thigh muscle does the old man show from his rags."
So they said, and the heart in Iros was sorely stirred.   75
And so the servants, when they had girded him, led him by force
In his fright. And the flesh trembled all over his limbs.
Antinoos rebuked him and spoke out to him directly:
"You ought not to exist now, ox-braggart, or have been born,
If you tremble before this man and dreadfully fear him,   80
An old man overwhelmed with the grief that has come upon him.
But I shall tell you this, and it shall be brought to pass;
If this man overcomes you and turns out the better man,
I shall throw you on a black ship and send you to the mainland,
To King Echetos, destroyer of all mortal men,   85
Who will cut off your nostrils and ears with a sharp bronze sword;
He will tear off your private parts and give them to dogs to eat raw."
So he said, and still greater trembling seized the other's limbs.
They led him out to the middle; both men held out their hands.
And then godly Odysseus, who had endured much, considered   90
Whether to strike him so his soul whould would leave him as he fell
Or to strike him softly and stretch him out on the ground;
And as he thought, it seemed to him to be better this way:
To strike softly so the Achaians would not take note of him.
Then they both drew themselves up. On the right shoulder   95
Iros hit him. But the other struck his neck under the ear and crushed
The bone inside. At once gory blood came out of his mouth.
He fell bellowing in the dust. He knocked his teeth together,
As he kicked the ground with his feet. Then the noble suitors
Held their hands up and died with laughter. And Odysseus   100
Took him by the foot and dragged him through the door till he reached
The courtyard and the doors of the porch. He leaned him up
Against the fence of the courtyard, put his staff in his hands,
And speaking to him, he uttered wingèd words:
"Sit there from now on and keep off the swine and the dogs,   105
And do not be a lord over strangers and beggars,
Woeful as you are, lest you incur a greater evil."
He spoke, and put his sorry wallet around his shoulders,
Full of rents. And there was a twisted strap on it.
Then he went back to the threshold and sat down. But they went
    inside,   110
Sweetly laughing, and they welcomed him with speeches.

And this is what one of the overbearing young men would say:
"Stranger, may Zeus and the other immortal gods
Grant you what you wish and is most dear to your heart,
Since you have stopped this insatiable man from wandering   115
In the district. And soon we will bring him to the mainland,
To King Echetos, destroyer of all mortal men."
So he said, and godly Odysseus rejoiced at the omen he heard.
Antinoos put a large stomach before him
Full of fat and blood. And Amphinomos   120
Lifted two loaves out of the basket and gave them to him.
He toasted him with a golden cup and spoke forth:
"Hail, father stranger, henceforth may prosperity
Be yours in the future. But you are held now in many ills."
Odysseus of many wiles addressed him in answer: 125
"Amphinomos, you seem to me to be quite sound minded,
For such was your father, because I heard of his noble renown,
That Nisos of Dulichion was prosperous and good.
They say you are his son; you seem like a discreet man.
So I shall speak to you; pay attention and listen to me.   130
Earth nourishes nothing of slighter account then man
Of all the things that breathe and move on the earth.
For he thinks he will not suffer any evil in the future
As long as the gods provide excellence and his limbs stir.
But whenever the blessed gods bring woeful things to pass,   135
He bears them, too, against his will, in his enduring heart.
The disposition of men who dwell on earth is the same
As the kind of day the father of men and gods may bring.
And I myself was accustomed to be happy among men;
But I did much recklessly, yielding to my strength and might,   140
Relying on my father and on my relatives.
And so let no man ever be lawless by any means.
He should keep the gods' gifts in silence, whatever they give.
So I see the suitors devising such reckless deeds,
Consuming the property and dishonoring the wife   145
Of a man who I think will not be away much longer
From his dear ones and his fatherland. He is very near. May some god
Lead you back safely, and may you not encounter that man
At the time he returns to his dear fatherland.
I think when that man enters his hall, the suitors   150
And he shall not be pulled apart without bloodshed."
So he said; he poured libation, and drank honey-sweet wine.
Then he put the cup back in the hands of the chief of the people.
The other went through the house, grieving in his own heart,
Nodding his head. For indeed in his spirit he apprehended evil.   155
Yet not even so did he flee fate. Him too had Athene bound
To be overcome in power by the hands and spear of Telemachos.
Then he sat down again in the chair from which he had stood up.

The bright-eyed goddess Athene put it in the mind
Of Icarios' daughter, the prudent Penelope,   160
To appear to the suitors so she might the most expand
The hearts of the suitors, and might get more honor
From her husband and her son than she had before.
She laughed inanely and spoke quite directly out:
"Eurynome, my spirit longs, as it did not before,   165
To appear to the suitors, though they are detestable;
And I shall say something to my son, that it would be better
Not always to associate with the presumptuous suitors,
Who speak nicely but are thinking of evil for the future."
Then the housekeeper Eurynome addressed a speech to her: 170
"Yes, indeed, child, you have spoken all this properly;
But go, say the word to your son and do not conceal it,
When you have wiped off your skin and anointed your cheeks.
Do not go with your countenance befouled this way
By tears, since it is very wrong to mourn endlessly.   175
Already your son is of the age that you have most
Prayed to the gods to see him at, growing a beard."
And then the prudent Penelope addressed her:
"Eurynome, do not say this, though you care for me,
That I should wipe off my skin, and anoint me with oil.   180
The gods who possess Olympos have destroyed in me
My charm, from the time he went off in the hollow ships.
But give the order for Autonoe and Hippodameia
To come to me, so they may stand by me in the halls.
I shall not go alone among the men. I am ashamed."   185
So she said, and the old woman went out through the hall
To give the word to the women and urge them to come.
But the bright-eyed goddess Athene had another thought.
She shed sweet sleep over the daughter of Icarios.
And she sank back in sleep, and all her joints relaxed   190
There in her armchair, while the divine goddess gave her
Ambrosial gifts, so the Achaians might wonder at her.
First she purified her lovely face with ambrosial beauty
Like that with which the well-crowned Cytherea anoints herself
When she goes to the delightful dancing of the Graces;   195
And then she made her taller and fuller to look upon
And made her to be whiter than sawn ivory.
When she had done that, the divine goddess went off,
And the white-armed servants came out of the hall,
Coming up with their voices. Sweet sleep let go of her.   200
And she wiped her cheeks off with her hands and spoke out:
"In my dread suffering a soft slumber covered me round.
Would that chaste Artemis might bring soft death upon me
At once now, so that I should no longer waste my life away
Mourning in my heart and longing for my dear husband,   205

Who had excellence of all kinds, since he was foremost of the Achai-
ans!"
When she had said this, she went down from the glistening upper cham-
bers,
Not alone, but two servants followed along with her.
And when the godly woman had come to the suitors,
She stood by the pillar of the stoutly fashioned roof,   210
Holding the glistening headbands before her cheeks.
A devoted servant maid stood near her on either side.
The men's knees were loosened on the spot and their hearts were charmed
with desire,
And they all voiced the prayer of lying beside her in bed.
Then she addressed Telemachos, her beloved son: 215
"Telemachos, your mind and intent are steadfast no longer.
While you were still a child you managed plans in your mind better.
But now that you are big and have reached the measure of youth,
And one would say you were the offspring of a prosperous man:
For so an alien mortal would say who saw your beauty and stature,   220
Yet your mind and intent are no longer correct,
Since a deed of this sort has been performed in the halls,
In that you have allowed the stranger to be outraged this way.
What now, if the stranger seated in our halls as he is
Should suffer some harm from the miserable maltreatment?   225
Shame and disgrace would come about for you among men."
Then sound-minded Telemachos answered her:
"Mother, I do not hold it against you for being angry.
But I perceive in my heart and know about every matter,
The good and the worse. Until now I was a child.   230
Still, I cannot always have ideas that are sound,
For they dismay me, seated on one side and the other,
Those men who plot evils. And there is no one to help me.
The struggle between the stranger and Iros did not come out
To the suitors' liking—but he was the stronger in might.   235
By Father Zeus, Athene, and Apollo, I wish
The suitors that are now in our house in the same way
Might nod their heads, overcome: both those in the courtyard
And those within the house, and the limbs of each might be loosed,
The way that man Iros at the door of the courtyard now   240
Sits nodding with his head like a drunken man,
And cannot stand up straight on his feet or return home,
Wherever that may be, since his precious limbs are loosed."
And so such things did they say to one another.
But Eurymachos addressed a speech to Penelope: 245
"Daughter of Icarios, prudent Penelope,
If all the Achaians through Iasian Argos should see you,
More suitors still would be dining in your halls
From the morning on, since you excel among women

For form and stature, and for a mind well balanced within." 250
Then the prudent Penelope addressed him in answer:
"Eurymachos, the immortals destroyed my excellence
Of form and body at the time the Argives went aboard ship
Toward Ilion, and with them went my husband Odysseus.
If that man should come and minister to my life, 255
My renown would be greater that way, and lovelier,
But now I am grieved. So many ills some god has sent me!
Yes indeed, at the time when he went to leave his fatherland
He took me by the right hand at the wrist and said to me:
'My wife, I do not believe the well-greaved Achaians 260
Will all get back safely uninjured out of Troy,
For they say that the Trojans are men who are fighters,
Both as throwers of javelins and as drawers of arrows,
And mounters of swift horse chariots, such as most quickly
Decide the great contention of impartial war. 265
So I know not if the god will restore me, or I shall be taken
There in Troy. But do look after everything here.
Remember my father and my mother in the halls
As you do now, or even more, when I am gone away.
And when you see that my son is growing a beard, 270
Marry whom you may wish to and leave your own home.'
So the man said. Now all these things are brought to pass.
And there will be a night when hateful marriage shall come
Upon my cursèd self, whose bliss Zeus has taken away.
And the dreadful grief reaches my heart and spirit. 275
This is not the just way established in the past for suitors
Who wish to rival one another and pay court
To a good woman and the daughter of prosperous man.
Such men as those are bring oxen and goodly sheep,
A banquet for the lady's friends, and give glorious gifts, 280
But they do not consume another's livelihood scot free."
So she said; godly Odysseus, who had endured much, rejoiced
That she extracted their gifts from them and charmed their hearts
With soothing speeches, but her mind devised other things.
Then Antinoos, the son of Eupeithes, addressed her: 285
"Daughter of Icarios, prudent Penelope,
Let whoever of the Achaians wishes bring gifts here,
And you receive them. For it is not good to refuse a gift.
And we shall not go to our fields or anywhere else
Until you have married the noblest of the Achaians." 290
So Antinoos said, and his speech was pleasing to them.
Each one sent for a herald to bring his gifts.
For Antinoos one brought a great, beautiful tunic,
Embroidered. And twelve brooches were on it in all,
Made of gold, fitted with well-fastening clasps. 295
One brought for Eurymachos a necklace cunningly wrought

Of gold, strung with amber beads, and it was like the sun.
For Eurydamos two servants brought in earrings
With three droplets, clustering. Much grace shone from them.
And from the lord Peisander, son of Polyktor,   300
A servant brought a necklace, a beautiful ornament.
Each of the Achaians brought some other lovely gift.
Then the godly woman went up to the upper chambers,
Where servants followed her bearing the beautiful gifts.
The men turned then to dancing and delightful song   305
And took their pleasure, and waited for evening to come.
As they took their pleasure black evening came upon them.
Right away they stood three braziers up in the halls
To give light: they put seasoned pieces of wood around,
Dried a long time, very parched, newly split with the ax.   310
And they mixed torches between. The maids of stouthearted Odysseus
Kept their light up high, taking turns. But he himself,
Zeus-born Odysseus of many wiles, spoke out to them:
"You maids of Odysseus, the master who is gone so long,
Do come to the halls where the respected queen is;   315
Twist up her distaff wool for her and do her pleasure,
Seated in the hall, or else card the wool with your hands,
And I myself shall furnish light to all these people.
Even if they wish to await the fair-throned dawn,
They will not overcome me; I can hold out very well."   320
So he said, and they laughed and looked at one another.
But fair-cheeked Melantho upbraided him shamefully;
Dolios fathered her, and Penelope cared for her,
And reared her as her own child, and gave her toys to her liking;
Yet even with that, she did not keep Penelope's grief in mind;   325
But she had lain with Eurymachos, and loved him.
And with reproachful speeches she rebuked Odysseus:
"Wretched stranger, you are a man knocked out of his mind,
As you do not wish to go and sleep in the bronzesmith's house,
Or, say in the public court; but you speak very much here   330
Boldly among many men, nor are you at all frightened
In your heart. Wine possesses your mind, or your mind is always
The way it is now, so that you utter vanity.
Are you beside yourself for beating the tramp Iros?
Take heed lest a better man than Iros soon stand up against you 335
Who would beat you around the head with his stout hands
And send you from the house, defiling you with much blood.'
Odysseus of many wiles glowered at her and spoke:
"Soon I shall tell Telemachos what you say, bitch,
When he comes here, so he may cut you up limb from limb."   340
When he had said this he terrified the women with his words.
They went through the hall, and the limbs of each one went slack
In alarm. For they thought that he had spoken the truth.

And he himself stood by the flaming braziers keeping the light up
And looked at all the men. The heart in his breast planned   345
Other matters, and those were not to be unachieved.
Athene by no means allowed the bold suitors
To keep from grievous outrage, so that still more pain
Might enter the heart of Odysseus, son of Laertes.
Eurymachos, son of Polybos, began speaking to them,   350
Abusing Odysseus, and he caused laughter in his companions.
"Listen to me, suitors of the illustrious queen,
So I may tell you what the heart in my breast bids me to.
Not without the gods has this man reached the house of Odysseus;
Indeed, the light of the torches seems to me to be his own,   355
From his head, since there are no hairs on it in the least."
He spoke, and addressed Odysseus, sacker of cities:
"Stranger, would you like to labor, if I should take you on,
At the field's very verge—the pay will be enough for you—
Gathering stones for the walls and planting tall trees?   360
There I myself shall furnish unfailing bread,
Clothe you in garments, and give you sandals for your feet.
But since you have learned foul deeds, you do not wish
To approach work, but want to beg through the district
So that you may have food for your insatiable belly."   365
Then Odysseus of many wiles addressed him in answer:
"Eurymachos, I wish a contest of work might come between us
In the spring season, when the long days come around,
In the grass, and I held a well-bent sickle myself
And you held the same kind, so we might test us at the work,   370
Fasting right up until dusk, and the grass should still be there;
And if there were oxen to drive, the best there are,
Great tawny ones, the pair of them filled up on grass,
The same age, equal at plowing, their strength not slight,
And the field were four lengths and the clod should yield to the
   plow;   375
Then you should see if I cut ahead an unbroken furrow.
And if the son of Cronos should raise up a battle somewhere
On this day, and I should have a shield and two spears
And a helmet all of bronze and fitted to the temple;
Then you should see me mingling in the forefront of combat,   380
Nor would you address me in reproach of my belly.
But you are quite insolent and your mind is unbending.
Perhaps you think yourself a great and mighty man
Because you associate with small men of no worth.
But if Odysseus should come and reach his fatherland,   385
Right away the portals, although they are very broad,
Would be narrow for you as you fled through the entrance outdoors."
So he said, and Eurymachos got still angrier in his heart.
Glowering at him, he uttered wingèd words:

"Wretch, I soon shall bring evil to pass for you, since you   390
Speak boldly among many men. Nor are you at all frightened
In your heart. Wine posesses your mind, or your mind is always
The way it is now, so that you utter vanity.
Are you beside yourself for beating the tramp Iros?"
So he said, and he took hold of a footstool. Odysseus   395
Sat down at the knees of Dulichian Amphinomos
In fear of Eurymachos. But that one struck the wine server
On his right hand; the pitcher clattered as it fell on the ground.
The man himself groaned and fell on his back in the dust.
The suitors made a din through the shadowy halls.   400
And this is what one of them, looking at his neighbor, would say:
"I wish that the stranger had strayed elsewhere and perished
Before coming. So he would not have set such a noise among us.
And now we are contending over beggars, and no delight
Shall be in the noble banquet, but worse matters win out."   405
And Telemachos spoke to them in his sacred might:
"You fools, you are enraged and no longer hide in your hearts
Your eating and drinking. One of the gods stirs you up.
But since you have dined well, go on home and lie down,
Whenever the spirit bids. I shall not pursue anyone."   410
So he said, and they all bit their lips with their teeth
And wondered at Telemachos, that he spoke boldly.
Then Amphinomos spoke to them and addressed them,
The illustrious son of lord Nisos, the son of Aretias:
"My friends, surely no one should become enraged   415
At a just saying, and rebuke someone with hostile words.
Do not maltreat the stranger at all, or any one
Of the servants who are in the halls of godly Odysseus.
Come now, let a wine server pour the first drops in the cups,
So we may pour libation and go on home to sleep.   420
And let the stranger go into the halls of Odysseus,
In the care of Telemachos; for he has reached his dear home."
So he said, and spoke a speech pleasing to all of them.
The hero Moulios, the herald from Dulichion, mixed
A bowl up for them. He was a servant of Amphinomos.   425
He gave it in order to all. They poured libation
To the blessed gods and drank the honey-sweet wine;
But when they had poured libation and drunk all they wished
They went off, each one to his own home to sleep.

XIX

So godly Odysseus was left behind in the hall
Devising slaughter for the suitors, with Athene's aid.
At once he uttered wingèd words to Telemachos:

"Telemachos, we must put the weapons of war inside,
All of them, and beguile the suitors deceptively   5
With soft speeches, when they miss them and ask you questions:
'I put them out of the smoke since they no longer look like those
That Odysseus once left behind when he went to Troy.
But they are befouled, so much has the smoke of the fire got to them.
And some god has put this other, greater thought in my mind: 10
That besides, drunk with wine, you might set up a quarrel
Among you, wound one another, and disgrace the banquet,
And your wooing too. For iron of itself draws a man on.' "
So he said. And Telemachos obeyed his dear father.
He called the nurse Eurycleia and spoke to her: 15
"Good mother, come hold the women back in the halls,
So that we may put away the weapons of my father up into the chamber,
The fine ones that smoke tarnishes uncared for in the house
Since my father went off, and I was still a foolish child.
Now I wish to put them away where the fire's smoke will not get to
     them."   20
Then his dear nurse Eurycleia spoke to him:
"My child, would that some time you might get hold of prudence
To take care of your house and watch over all your goods.
But come, who will go get a light and carry it for you?
You do not let the maids, who might have given light, go ahead."   25
Then sound-minded Telemachos answered her:
"This stranger. I shall not let any man go idle
Who has touched my rations, though he has come from far away."
So he said, and for her the speech was without a wing.
She shut the doors of the well-situated halls.   30
Odysseus and his illustrious son both leaped up
And carried the helmet plumes and the bossed shields in,
And the pointed spears. Pallas Athene in front of them
Held a golden lantern and made a beautiful light.
Then Telemachos at once spoke to his father: 35
"Father, this is a great wonder I see before my eyes.
Indeed, the walls of the halls and the lovely pedestals,
The fir-wood beams and the pillars holding them high,
Appear bright to my eyes as if from a glittering fire.
Some god must be inside, one of those who possess broad heaven."   40
Then Odysseus of many wiles addressed him in answer:
"Silence. Keep this in your mind and ask no question.
This is the rule of the gods who possess Olympos.
You go lie down, and I shall stay behind here,
So I may stir up still more your mother and the serving maids.   45
And she, as she laments, will ask me for details."
So he said, and Telemachos went out through the hall
Under the shining torches to lie down, to the chamber
Where he went to bed before whenever sweet sleep came upon him.

He lay down there then also and awaited the godly dawn.   50
But godly Odysseus was left behind in the hall
Devising slaughter for the suitors with Athene's aid.
And the prudent Penelope went out of her chamber
In the semblance of Artemis or golden Aphrodite.
They put a chair by the fire for her where she used to sit,   55
A chair whorled with ivory and silver that Ikmalios
The craftsman had once fashioned; to it he had attached
A footstool under the feet; and over it a large fleece was thrown.
Then the prudent Penelope sat down on it.
White-armed serving women came out of the hall   60
And were taking away a great amount of bread, and the tables,
And the cups from which the insolent men had drunk.
They threw the fire from the braziers to the ground and heaped
Much fresh wood upon them for light and for warming.
Melantho upbraided Odysseus again a second time;   65
"Stranger, will you still bother us here even now through the night,
Prowling through the house; and will you be ogling the women?
Well, go on outdoors, you wretch, and enjoy your meal,
Or soon you will be struck with a firebrand and go outdoors."
Odysseus of many wiles glowered at her and spoke: 70
"You terror, why do you hold at me so in rancorous spirit?
Is it because I am dirty and wear foul garments on my skin
And beg through the district? Necessity drives me on.
This is the way that beggars and wandering men are.
I myself was once blessed, and I inhabited   75
A rich house among men, and gave to such a wanderer
Many times, no matter who came, whatever he needed.
I had numberless servants and many other things
Men have who live well and are called prosperous,
But Zeus, son of Cronos, destroyed me, as he somehow wished.   80
So take heed, woman, lest soon you, too, lose all the grace
In which for the present you excel among the serving maids,
Lest perhaps your mistress get angry and bear hard on you,
Or lest Odysseus come. For there is still a share of hope.
And if he has died, as you think, and is no more to return,   85
Yet already, thanks to Apollo, he has a son like himself,
Telemachos. And no women in the halls who acts recklessly
Escapes his notice, because he is no longer so young."
So he said, and the prudent Penelope heard him.
She rebuked her servant and spoke out to her directly: 90
"Bold woman, fearless bitch, you indeed do not escape my notice
When you do this enormous deed, that you shall wipe off on your head.
And you know this full well, as you heard me say it myself,
That I intended to ask the stranger in my halls
About my husband, since my griefs come thick and fast."   95
She spoke, and said a speech to the housekeeper Eurynome:

"Eurynome, bring a chair and a fleece upon it here
So that the stranger may sit down and speak with me,
And listen; I should like to ply him with questions."
So she said, and the woman very quickly brought a well-planed chair   100
And set it up, and upon it she threw a fleece.
Then godly Odysseus, who had endured much, sat down there.
And the prudent Penelope began speaking between them:
"Stranger, I myself shall ask you this question first:
What men are you from? Where are your city and parents?"   105
Odysseus of many wiles addressed her in answer:
"My good woman, no one among mortals on the boundless earth
Would find fault with you. Your renown reaches broad heaven,
As though of some blameless king who in a god-fearing way
Holds sway over numerous and valiant men,   110
Who upholds good laws, and his black earth produces
Wheat and barley, and his trees are laden with fruit.
His sheep bear young without fail, and the sea provides fish
From his good leadership, and the people excel under him.
And so ask me anything else now in your house,   115
But do not inquire of my race and my fatherland,
So that you may not fill my heart up further with pains
While I remember. I am a man of much grief. There is no need
For me to sit wailing and moaning in another's home,
Since it is always worse to grieve endlessly,   120
Lest one of the maids resent it, or you yourself,
And say my tears flow because my mind is heavy with wine."
And then the prudent Penelope answered him:
"Stranger, truly the immortals destroyed my excellence
Of form and body at the time the Argives went aboard ship   125
Toward Ilion, and with them went my husband Odysseus.
If that man should come and minister to my life,
My renown would be greater that way, and lovelier.
But now I am grieved, so many ills has some god sent me!
All the noblemen who rule over the islands   130
Of Dulichion and Samê and wooded Zacynthos,
And who dwell round about sunny Ithaca itself,
Woo me against my will and are consuming my house.
And so I have no regard for strangers or suppliants,
Nor for heralds at all, who are craftsmen of the district;   135
But, longing for Odysseus, I pine away in my heart.
They are eager for marriage, and I weave deceits.
First some god inspired my mind with the thought of a robe;
I should set up a great loom in the halls and weave on it
A large and delicate fabric. I told them at once: 140
'Young men, my suitors, since godly Odysseus is dead,
Wait, though you are eager for this marriage of mine, till I finish

This robe, so that the yarn may not waste in vain,
This burial sheet of hero Laertes for the time
When the ruinous fate of long-sorrowful death seizes him,   145
Lest one of the Achaian women in the district blame me
If he who had won so much lie without covering.'
So I said, and the bold spirit was persuaded in them.
Every day I kept weaving there on the great loom,
And the nights I undid it when I had the torches set up.   150
So for three years I fooled the Achaians and persuaded them.
But when the fourth year came and the seasons came on
As the months waned, and many days came to an end,
Then indeed through my maid servants, uncaring bitches,
They came and caught me, and all shouted at me together.   155
And so I finished it, though unwilling and under duress.
And now I can neither escape marriage nor find
Any further plan. My parents urge me on very much
To marry, and my son chafes at those who devour his living,
And he notices it; for he is already a man quite able   160
To care for the sort of house to which Zeus gives renown.
But tell me of your descent, wherever you are from,
For you are not from the oak of ancient tale or from rock."
Odysseus of many wiles addressed her in answer:
"Respected wife of Odysseus, son of Laertes,   165
Will you never leave off inquiring of my descent?
Well, I shall speak out to you, and you will give me to more woes
Than those I am held in. For this is the rule, when a man
Has been away from his fatherland as long as I now have,
Wandering to many cities of mortals, suffering pains.   170
Yet even so I shall tell you what you ask and inquire about:
There is a certain land, Crete, in the midst of the wine-faced ocean,
Lovely and fertile, circled by the sea. Many men
Are in it, innumerable, and ninety cities are there;
One tongue is mingled with others. There are Achaians,   175
Great-hearted true Cretans and Cydonians,
Dorians, of three settlements, and godly Pelasgians.
And among those is Cnossos, a great city, where Minos,
The intimate of great Zeus, ruled nine years as king.
The father of my father, great-hearted Deucalion.   180
Deucalion begat me and the lord Idomeneus.
And that man went off up to Ilion in the curved ships
With the sons of Atreus. Aithon is my well-known name.
I was the younger by birth; he was older and more valiant.
And there I myself saw Odysseus and gave him guest gifts.   185
For in fact, the force of the wind had brought him over toward Crete
When he was eager for Troy, driving him off course past Malea.
He anchored at Amnisos, where the cave of Eileithyia is,
A difficult harbor, and he barely escaped the storms.

He went up to the city at once and asked for Idomeneus   190
And said he was his guest friend, a dear and respected one.
But the tenth or eleventh dawn had already come for the man
Since he had been gone in the curved ships to Ilion.
I led him to my house and entertained him well,
Befriending him kindly, as there was much in my home.   195
To him and to the others, his companions who followed him
I gave barley gathered from the region and sparkling wine
And oxen for sacrifice so their hearts might be satisfied.
There the godly Achaians remained for twelve days.
A great North Wind held them back, and did not allow them   200
To ride at anchor near land; some harsh god raised it up.
The thirteenth day the wind fell, and they put to sea."
He spoke many falsehoods and made them seem like the truth.
Tears flowed from her as she listened and her flesh melted.
Just as snow melts down upon the peaks of the mountains   205
Which the East Wind melts when the West Wind pours it down,
And when the snow melts the flowing rivers are full;
So her lovely cheeks melted as she poured down her tears,
Weeping for her husband who was sitting by. Odysseus
Felt pity in his heart for his wife as she lamented,   210
But his eyes stood fast, as though they were horn or iron
Untrembling in his eyelids. And by guile he hid his tears.
But when she had her fill of tearful lamentation,
She once more answered him and addressed him, saying:
"And now, stranger, I think I shall test you out,   215
If truly in that place with his godlike companions
You entertained my husband in your halls, as you say.
Tell me what sort of clothes he had on over his skin,
What sort of man he was, and what companions went with him."
Odysseus of many wiles addressed her in answer: 220
"My good woman, it is hard to say, for a man who has been so long
Parted, since already it is the twentieth year
From the time he went thence and left my fatherland.
But I shall tell you the way my heart pictures it for me:
Godly Odysseus had on a purple mantle of wool,   225
A double one. And the brooch upon it was made of gold,
With twin sockets. And on its face it was skillfully wrought:
In his front paws a dog was holding a dappled fawn
And gazed at it while it writhed. All men marveled to see
How the one, being of gold, gazed at the fawn he throttled,   230
And the other strove to get away as he writhed with his feet.
I noticed the tunic over his flesh glistening
The way the husk does on an onion that is dried,
So soft it was, and it was shining like the sun.
Many women indeed looked with wonder upon him.   235
I shall tell you something else, and keep it well in mind:

I do not know if Odysseus had these clothes on his skin from home,
Or if some companion gave them as he went on the swift ship,
Or perhaps some guest friend, since Odysseus was dear
To many men. For few of the Achaians were equal to him.   240
And I myself gave him a bronze sword and a lovely double-folded
Cloak of purple and a tunic with a fringe on it,
And I sent him off with honor on his well-timbered ship,
And a herald a little older than he was himself
Followed him. I will tell you the sort of man he was, too: 245
He was bent in the shoulders, black-skinned, with a wooly crown;
Eurybates was his name. Odysseus honored him foremost
Among his companions, because he had a mind that matched his own."
So he said, and roused in her still more desire for weeping
When she recognized as sure ones the signs Odysseus gave her.   250
And when she had her fill of tearful lamentation,
She replied to him with a speech and addressed him:
"And now, stranger, though you were pitied by me before,
You shall now be beloved and respected in my halls.
I myself gave him those garments that you speak about   255
From my chamber, after folding them; and I put on the shining brooch
To be an ornament for him. But I shall not welcome him again
On his return home to his dear fatherland.
So did Odysseus go off by an evil fate on a hollow ship
On his way to see evil Ilion, the unspeakable."   260
Odysseus of many wiles addressed her in answer:
"Respected wife of Odysseus, son of Laertes,
No longer mar your lovely skin, nor waste your heart
Lamenting for your husband. I do not blame you at all.
For indeed one would mourn a wedded husband she had lost,   265
To whom she had coupled in love and borne children, even
Another sort than Odysseus, who they say is like the gods.
But cease from lamentation and hearken to my speech.
I shall tell you unerringly and shall not conceal
That I have already heard about the return of Odysseus;   270
He is nearby in the rich land of the Thesprotians,
Alive. And he is bringing many excellent treasures,
Begging them through the land. But his trusty companions
And his hollow ship he lost on the wine-faced ocean.
Going from the island Thrinacria. At him did Zeus   275
And the Sun get angry, for the companions killed his cattle.
All of them perished in the much-surging sea.
But a wave threw him on the ship's keel upon the mainland,
The country of the Phaeacians, who are close kin to the gods.
They honored him heartily as they would a god,   280
And gave him many things, and wished themselves to send him
Homeward unharmed. And long ago would Odysseus have been here,
But this course seemed to him in his heart to be better:

To get together goods while going to many lands,
Because Odysseus knows beyond all mortal men   285
About great gains, and no other person might contend with him.
So Pheidon the king of the Thesprotians told me.
He swore to me personally, pouring a libation in his house,
That a ship had been drawn down and companions were ready
Who would conduct him to his beloved fatherland.   290
But he sent me off first. For a ship happened to come
Of Thesprotians headed for Dulichion, rich in wheat,
And he showed me all the possessions Odysseus had gathered.
They would support each man in turn to the tenth generation,
So many were the treasures that lay in the lord's halls.   295
He said that man had gone to Dodona in order to hear
The plan of Zeus from the lofty-leaved oak of the god
As to how he might return to his beloved fatherland,
Openly or in secret, as already he had been long away.
And so he is safe and very near, and he will come   300
Soon, nor will he be absent much longer, far
From his friends and fatherland. Indeed, I shall give you an oath:
Zeus now be my first witness, the highest and best of the gods,
And the hearth of blameless Odysseus to which I have come:
That all these things shall come to pass as I say.   305
Within the light of this very month will Odysseus be coming here
While one moon is waning and another is on the rise."
Then the prudent Penelope answered him:
"Would that this saying, stranger, might be brought to pass,
And then you would soon know friendship and many gifts   310
From me, so that a man who met you might call you blessed.
And yet it seems to me in my heart it will be this way:
Odysseus will not come home again, nor shall you be granted
An escort, since there are no masters in the house of the sort
That Odysseus was among men, if he ever existed,   315
To send respectable strangers off and receive them.
Well now, servants, wash him off and lay him down a bed
Of bedclothes and of mantles and of glistening blankets
So that he may reach, well-warmed, Dawn of the golden throne.
And very early in the dawn wash him and anoint him,   320
So he may think of a meal seated in the hall within
Beside Telemachos. And it will be very painful
For whoever of these grievous men annoys him. He shall not
Gain anything here any more, though he be dreadfully angry.
How shall you learn about me, stranger, that I at all excel   325
Among other women for purpose and a thoughtful plan,
If, squalid and clothed in evil garments, you dine
In the halls? Men come to their growth just a tiny while.
On whoever is himself harsh and versed in what is harsh
Do all mortal men invoke the curse of future pains   330

While he is alive, and all jeer at him when he dies.
Whoever is himself blameless and versed in what is blameless,
For him do strangers carry renown far and wide
Among all men, and many speak of him as noble."
Then Odysseus of many wiles addressed her in answer: 335
"Respected wife of Odysseus, son of Laertes,
Mantles and glistening blankets have in fact been hateful to me
From the time when I first left behind the snowy mountains
Of Crete, going upon the ship with its long oars.
I shall lie down, as indeed I spent slumberless nights before.   340
Yes, for many nights in an ill-favored bed
I have rested and waited for the fair-throned Dawn.
No water for washing my feet is at all pleasing
To my heart. Nor shall any woman touch our feet
Among those who are active for you in your house,   345
Unless there is some aged woman with a sense of devotion,
Someone who has suffered in mind as much as I have myself:
I shall not hold it against her if she touches my feet."
And then the prudent Penelope spoke to him:
"Dear stranger, never yet has a man so sound in mind   350
Of strangers from far away come more welcome to my house,
Because you so thoughtfully speak of all that is sound.
I have an old woman whose mind is packed with thoughts,
Who nourished that hapless man well and brought him up,
Taking him in her own hands when his mother first bore him.   355
She shall wash your feet, though indeed her strength is slight.
Come and stand up now, prudent Eurycleia;
Wash a man the same age as your master. Perhaps Odysseus
By this time is just like him in his hands and feet,
For quickly in misfortune do mortals become old."   360
So she said, and the old woman covered her face with her hands,
Shed hot tears, and uttered a speech of lamentation:
"Alas, for you, my child, I am helpless. Zeus hates you
Beyond other men, though you have a god-fearing heart.
No mortal ever yet burned so many fat thighs or sacrificed   365
Such choice hecatombs to Zeus, who hurls the thunderbolt,
As you bestowed on him, praying that you might come
To a sleek old age and rear your illustrious son.
For you alone is the day of return now all taken away.
And so perhaps the women jeered at him also   370
Among far-off strangers when he reached someone's home,
As these bitches, all of them here, are jeering at you.
And now, to avoid their reproach and their many insults,
You do not allow them to wash you. But me did Icarios' daughter,
The prudent Penelope, ask, and not against my will.   375
So I will wash your feet on Penelope's own account,
And on your own, since the heart is aroused within me

By sorrow. And now understand the speech that I speak:
Many long-suffering strangers have reached this place:
I think I have never yet seen one who resembles him   380
'As you resemble Odysseus, in voice, body, and feet."
Odysseus of many wiles addressed her in answer:
"Old woman, that is what all men say who have seen us both
With their eyes , that we are very similar to one another,
As, indeed, you yourself have discerned and said."   385
So he spoke, and the old woman took a glittering basin
That she used for washing feet; she poured in much water,
The cold; then she transferred in the hot. Odysseus
Was sitting by the hearth, and suddenly turned toward the darkness.
For at once he was apprehensive in heart lest when she touched
   him   390
She notice his scar and the facts become apparent.
She went near and was washing her master, and right away knew
The scar which once a boar dealt him with its shining tusk
When he had come to Parnassos to see Autolycos and his sons,
His mother's noble father who excelled among men   395
In trickery and oath making. The god Hermes himself
Endowed him, for he burned the thighs of lambs and kids
Pleasing to the god, who zealously attended the man.
Autolycos had gone to the rich land of Ithaca
And found a son newly born to his own daughter.   400
Eurycleia placed him upon the man's own knees
As he finished dinner, and spoke out to him directly:
"Autolycos, now find yourself a name you may give
To the dear son of your child; he has been much prayed for."
Then Autolycos answered her and addressed her: 405
"My son-in-law and daughter, give him the name I say.
I myself come here as one who has been enraged at many,
At men and at women, throughout the much-nourishing earth,
And let him be named Man of Wrath: Odysseus. For my part,
When he reaches his prime, and comes to the great house   410
Of his mother, to Parnassos where I have my possessions,
I shall give him some from them and send him back in joy."
Odysseus went for them, so the man might give him glorious gifts.
Autolycos and the sons of Autolycos greeted him
With handclasps and welcomed him with soothing speeches.   415
The mother of his mother, Amphithea, embraced Odysseus
And kissed him on the head and on both lovely eyes.
Autolycos called to his illustrious sons
To get dinner ready. They heeded as he urged them on
And at once they drove in a male ox five years old.   420
They flayed it and worked round it and dismembered it all
And cut it up skillfully and pierced it on spits,
Roasted it carefully, and distributed the portions.

So then for the whole day till the setting of the sun
They dined, nor did their hearts want for a well-shared meal.   425
And when the sun went down and the darkness came on,
They lay down to sleep and took the gift of slumber.
And when the early-born, rosy-fingered dawn appeared,
They went on the hunt, both the dogs and themselves,
The sons of Autolycos. With them godly Odysseus   430
Went along. They approached the sheer mountain covered with woods
Of Parnassos, and soon they reached the windy ravines.
At that moment the Sun was freshly striking the fields
Up from the deep stream of gently flowing Oceanos,
And the beaters reached the glen. In front of them   435
Dogs moved on, tracking the footprints, and behind them
Came the sons of Autolycos. With them godly Odysseus
Moved close to the dogs, brandishing a long-shadowed spear.
And there in a thick-copse was lying a great boar.
The blowing winds' watery force did not blow through to it,   440
Nor did the Sun strike it with the beams of his rays,
Nor did the rain get all the way through, so thick
It was, and a plentiful deposit of leaves was there.
The beating of the feet of men and dogs came round to him
As they came rushing on. Facing them out of the thicket   445
He bristled his back well, glanced fire with his eyes,
And stood very close to them. Odysseus first of all
Rushed on, holding the long spear up in his stout hand,
Eager to hit him. The boar got the start and struck him
Above the knee, and gashed his flesh deep with a tusk,   450
Charging at him slantwise, but did not get to the man's bone.
Odysseus wounded him, hitting him on the right shoulder.
And the point of his shining spear went straight on through him.
He fell in the dust, squealing, and his spirit flew off.
The beloved sons of Autolycos attended to the boar   455
And bound up the wound of excellent, godlike Odysseus
Skillfully. And with an incantation they held back
The black blood. At once they reached their dear father's home.
Autolycos and the sons of Autolycos healed him
Well, and they provided him with glorious gifts,   460
And sent him in joy speedily to his dear fatherland,
To Ithaca. His father and queenly mother welcomed him
On his return, and they inquired about the details
Of how he had suffered the scar. He told them about it fully.
How the boar had struck him with his shining tusk while he was
     hunting   465
When he had gone to Parnassos with the sons of Autolycos.
The old woman took the scar in the palms of her hands and knew it
As she touched it; she let the foot drop that she held,
And his shin fell into the basin and the bronze clattered.

It tipped back to one side and the water spilled out onto the ground. 470
Both delight and pain gripped her mind, and her two eyes
Filled with tears, and her resonant voice was held back.
She touched Odysseus' chin and spoke to him:
"Indeed you are Odysseus, dear child; not even I
Knew you at first, till I had touched my master all over."   475
She spoke, and then glanced at Penelope with her eyes,
Wishing to tell her that her dear husband was within.
But the other could not sight her face to face or perceive her,
For Athene had turned her mind. Odysseus groped for her
With his hands and took her by the throat with his right hand,   480
And with the other he drew her closer to himself and spoke:
"Good mother, why do you wish to destroy me? You brought me up
At your breast yourself. Now, having suffered many pains,
I have come in the twentieth year to my fatherland.
Since you have recognized me, and a god put it in your heart,   485
Be quiet, lest someone else in the halls find out.
For I shall speak out as follows, and it shall be fulfilled;
If a god does subdue the noble suitors underneath me,
I shall not hold off from you for being my nurse
When I kill the other serving women in the halls."   490
And then the prudent Eurycleia addressed him:
"My child, what sort of a speech has got past the bar of your teeth?
You know how much my strength is steadfast and unyielding.
I shall hold out like iron or some rigid stone.
I shall tell you another thing, and keep it well in mind.   495
If a god does subdue the noble suitors underneath you,
Then I shall tell you about the women in the halls,
Those that dishonor you and those that are innocent."
Odysseus of many wiles addressed her in answer:
"Good mother, why tell me of them? There is no need.   500
I myself shall observe and know each one quite well.
But keep your story in silence and turn it over to the gods."
So he said, and the old woman went on through the halls
To bring water for the feet, since the first had all been spilled.
And when she had washed him and anointed him richly with oil,   505
Then Odysseus drew the chair up closer to the fire
To warm himself. And he hid the scar in his rags.
Then the prudent Penelope began speaking between them:
"Stranger, I myself shall ask just this little thing;
For indeed it shall soon be the hour for pleasant slumber.   510
Sleep is sweet, whomever it seizes, though he has cares.
However, to me some god has given unmeasured grief.
For I enjoy my days in lamentation, mourning
And looking after my tasks and those of the servants in the house.
But whenever night comes and slumber seizes them all   515
I lie in my bed, and thronging about my throbbing heart,

The sharp anxieties plague me as I lament.
As when the daughter of Pandareus, the nightingale of the green,[1]
Sings beautifully when spring has freshly risen,
Seated amid the thick foliage of the trees,   520
And, often modulating, pours out her loud-sounding song,
Lamenting her dear son Itylos, child of lord Zethos,
Whom one day she killed with a sword unwittingly;
So my heart is aroused, divided this way and that,
Whether I should wait with my son and steadfastly guard   525
All my property, the maids and the high-roofed house,
Respecting the bed of my husband and the talk of the people,
Or by this time should follow the best of the Achaians
Who woos me in the halls and offers endless bridal gifts.
My son while he was yet childish and weak of mind   530
Would not let me marry and leave my husband's home;
But now that he is big and has reached the measure of youth
He implores me to go home again out of the hall,
Chafing at the property that the Achaians consume.
But come, listen to this dream and interpret it for me: 535
Twenty geese are eating the wheat in my house,
Out of the water, and I am warmed to look on them.
Then a great crooked-beaked eagle came off a mountain,
Broke all their necks and killed them. They were heaped
Together through the halls, and soared to the divine air.   540
But I wept and lamented in the very dream,
And the fair-haired Achaian women gathered about me,
As I piteously grieved that the eagle killed my geese;
But he came back and perched on a projecting rafter,
And he checked me and spoke out with a mortal voice: 545
"Take courage, daughter of widely renowned Icarios,
Not a dream it is, but a good vision, that will come to pass:
The geese are the suitors, and I who previously
Was the eagle have come back now as your own husband,
Who shall inflict on all the suitors a sorry destiny.'   550
So he said, and then honey-sweet sleep let me go.
And looking over the geese in the halls, I perceived
That they were pecking up wheat at the trough where they did before."
Then Odysseus of many wiles addressed her in answer:
"My good woman, there is no way to interpret this dream   555
By twisting it off another way, since Odysseus himself
Has shown how he will achieve it. Destruction is plain for the suitors,
All of them; and not one shall ward off destiny and death."
And then the prudent Penelope spoke to him:
"Stranger, hard to handle and confused in their stories do dreams   560
Come, and not all in them is brought to pass for men.

1. Aedon ("nightingale, singer") killed her son Itylos by mistake and was turned into a bird.

For double are the portals of flickering dreams.
One set is made of horn, the other of ivory.
And as for those that come through the sawn ivory,
They deceive, carrying words that will not be fulfilled;   565
But those that pass on outside through the polished horn
Do fulfill the truth whenever any mortal sees them.
But I do not think my awesome dream has come
From these gates. That would truly be welcome to me and to my son.
I shall tell you something else, and keep it well in mind: 570
This dawn of evil name shall come that will make me leave
The home of Odysseus, for now I will set up a contest
Of axes, which the man used to stand up in a row
In his halls, as trestles, all twelve of them.
He would stand at a great distance and shoot an arrow through.   575
And now I will set up this contest for the suitors:
The one who most nimbly strings the bow in his hands
And shoots an arrow through all twelve of the axes,
Him will I follow, leaving this very lovely
Home of my marriage, full of the goods of life,   580
Which I think I shall ever remember even in dreams."
Odysseus of many wiles addressed her in answer:
"Respected wife of Odysseus, son of Laertes,
Do not delay this contest any longer in the house.
Odysseus of many wiles shall come to you in this place   585
Long before these men who handle this well-made bow
Have stretched the bowstring and shot an arrow through the iron."
And then the prudent Penelope spoke out to him:
"Stranger, if you should like to sit by me in the halls
And delight me, sleep would never be shed on my eyelids.   590
But it is not possible for men to be without sleep
Forever. The immortals have set down a limit
For everything among mortals on the grain-giving earth.
Well, I shall go up myself into the upper chamber
And lie down in my bed, which is made full of groans for me,   595
Ever sullied with my tears since the time Odysseus
Went off to see evil Ilion, the unspeakable.
There I shall lie down. You lie down in this house,
Spreading a bed on the ground; or let them put bedding down for you."
When she had said this, she went up to the glistening upper
    chambers,   600
Not alone, but with her went the others, her serving women.
She entered the upper chamber with her serving women
And then wept for Odysseus, her dear husband, until
Bright-eyed Athene cast sweet sleep upon her eyelids.

XX

But godly Odysseus went to bed in the portico.
Under him he spread an undressed hide, and above
Many fleeces of the sheep the Achaians had been sacrificing.
Eurynome threw a mantle on him when he lay down.
Then Odysseus lay awake devising evils in his heart   5
For the suitors. And the women who up to then
Used to lie with the suitors went out of the hall,
Entertaining one another with laughter and with mirth.
As for him, the heart was aroused in his own breast.
He deliberated much in his mind and in his heart,   10
Whether to rush among them and bring death on each one
Or else allow them to lie with the bold suitors
A last and final time. The heart within him growled;
As when a bitch standing over her feeble puppies,
Not recognizing a man, growls and is eager to fight,   15
So his heart growled within him, indignant at their evil deeds.
But he struck his breast and rebuked his heart in a speech:
"Stand it, my heart. You stood something still more shameful
On the day the Cyclops with irresistible force devoured
My mighty companions. And you endured, until a plan   20
Led you out of the cave when you thought you were to die."
So he said, and upbraided the heart in his own breast,
And so his heart kept enduring steadfastly
In submission. But he himself turned this way and that,
As when a man shifts an intestine full of fat and blood   25
On a great blazing fire quickly this way and that
And longs for it to be roasted very rapidly;
So this way and that did he toss about, pondering
How he might lay his hands upon the shameless suitors,
Being one man against many. Athene came close to him,   30
Descending from the sky; she likened her body to a woman's.
She stood above his head and addressed a speech to him:
"Why are you awake, ill-fated beyond all mortal men?
This is your house, and this is your wife in the house,
And your child, the kind anyone would long to have for a son."   35
Odysseus of many wiles addressed her in answer:
"Yes, in all this, goddess, you have spoken properly.
But this is what the heart in my breast worries somewhat about:
How I might lay my hands upon the shameless suitors,
Being a single man, but they are always within, in a body,   40
And I also think over this greater point in my mind:
If I were to slay them with your help and that of Zeus,
Where would I get away? I ask you to think of that."
Then the bright-eyed goddess Athene addressed him:

"Stubborn man, some will trust an inferior companion   45
Who is a mortal and does not know such wisdom as mine.
But I myself am a god, who constantly protects you
In all your trials. I shall speak to you openly.
If fifty troops of articulate men in ambush
Were to stand around us, striving to kill us in war,   50
Yet should you drive off their cattle and goodly sheep.
But let sleep take you. It is also a trouble to keep watch
And lie awake all night. You shall soon rise up from your ills."
So she said. And she shed sleep over his eyelids;
Then the divine goddess herself went back to Olympos.   55
While sleep, the looser of the limbs, seized him, loosing
The troubles of his heart, his wife, who had a sense of devotion,
Woke up and wept while sitting up in her soft bed.
And when she was sated in her own heart with weeping,
The divine woman prayed to Artemis first of all: 60
"Artemis, queenly goddess, daughter of Zeus, would that now
You might strike my chest with an arrow and take my life away
At this very time, or that a storm would now snatch me up
And depart carrying me forth upon the murky ways,
And throw me in the streams of backward-flowing Oceanos;   65
As when storms snatched up the daughters of Pandareus,
Whose parents the gods destroyed, and they were left themselves
Orphaned in the halls. Divine Aphrodite tended them
With cheese and with sweet honey and with pleasant wine.
Hera endowed them beyond all other women   70
With form and wisdom. Chaste Artemis gave them stature,
And Athene taught them how to do illustrious tasks.
When divine Aphrodite proceeded to tall Olympos,
To Zeus who hurls the thunderbolt, to ask for an outcome
Of lusty marriage for the maidens, as he knows all things well—   75
What is fated and what not fated for mortal men—
At that time did whirlwinds snatch the maidens away
And give them to the hateful Erinyes to take care of.
So may those who hold Olympos's hall annihilate me,
Or may fair-braided Artemis strike me, so that   80
With Odysseus in my mind's eye, I may go beneath the hateful earth,
Lest perchance I gladden the thought of a lesser man.
But it is an unendurable evil when anyone
Weeps by day, when his heart is abundantly grieved,
And sleep holds his nights: it brings forgetting of all   85
Things good and evil when it closes about his eyelids,
But even the dreams that some god sent me were evil.
For this night again there slept beside me one like the man himself,
As he was when he went off with the host. And my heart
Rejoiced, since I thought it not a dream, but a waking fact."   90
So she said. And at once the golden-throned Dawn came.

Godly Odysseus heard her voice as she was weeping,
And then he thought it over; she seemed to him in his heart
Already to know him and be standing at his head.
He gathered up the mantle and the fleeces in which he slept   95
And put them on a chair in the hall; he carried the hide out,
Set it outside, and raised his hands in prayer to Zeus:
"Father Zeus, if you gods have brought me willingly,
Over dry ground and wet sea, to my land, when you had hurt me much;
Let someone inside wake up and tell me an omen,   100
And outside let another portent appear from Zeus."
So he said in his prayer, and the counselor Zeus heard him,
And he thundered at once from glittering Olympos
High up out of the clouds. Godly Odysseus rejoiced,
And a woman grinding sent an omen out of the house nearby   105
Where the mills were set for the shepherd of the people,
And at them twelve women in all usually plied the work,
Producing barley grain and wheat flour, marrow of men.
The others were sleeping, since they had ground up the wheat.
But one had not yet ceased, the weakest; she was still working.   110
She stopped the mill and said a word, a sign to her master:
"Father Zeus, you who rule over the gods and men,
Greatly have you thundered out of the starry heaven,
Nor is there a cloud anywhere. You show this as a portent to someone.
Fulfill now, even for my poor self, what I say: 115
May the suitors this day for the last and final time
Partake of a delightful banquet in the halls of Odysseus,
Those who have undone my knees in heart-hurting toil
To make barley flour. May they dine now for the last time."
So, she said, and godly Odysseus rejoiced at the omen and thunder   120
Of Zeus. For he expected him to take vengeance on the guilty.
The other serving women in the lovely house of Odysseus
Woke up and kindled an unwearying fire on the hearth.
Telemachos, a man like a god, rose up from his bed
And put on his clothes. He put his sharp sword round his shoulder   125
And bound the lovely sandals beneath his shining feet.
Then he took his stout spear pointed with sharp bronze,
Went to stand on the threshold, and spoke to Eurycleia:
"Good mother dear, how have you honored the stranger in the house?
With bed and food? Or does he lie uncared for entirely?   130
For that is the way my mother is, though she be discreet;
Indeed, among articulate men she honors the worse one
Impulsively, and the better man she sends off with no honor."
And then the prudent Eurycleia addressed him:
"Child, please do not now blame one who should not be blamed.   135
He sat and drank wine, in fact, as long as he wished to.
He said he was not hungry for food, for she asked him.
But when he would think about going to bed and sleep,

She ordered the servants to spread the bedding down.
Then, like a man wholly woeful and lacking his fate,   140
He did not wish to lie down to sleep on a bed and in blankets,
But on an undressed oxhide and the fleeces of sheep
He lay down in the portico. We put a mantle on him ourselves."
So she said, and Telemachos went out through the hall
Holding his spear. And two swift dogs followed with him.   145
He went on to the assembly to join the well-greaved Achaians.
Then to the serving maids the godly woman called,
Eurycleia, daughter of Ops, the son of Peisenor:
"Come here. Some of you get busy and sweep the house,
Sprinkle it, and throw down purple coverlets   150
On the well-fashioned chairs; others wipe off with sponges
All of the tables, and clean the mixing bowls out,
And the well-wrought two-handled cups. Others of you go
To the spring for water, and come bringing it quickly.
For the suitors will not be long absent from the hall: 155
They will come very early, since it is a feast day for one and all.
So she said. They listened closely to her and obeyed her.
Twenty of them went on to the dark-watered spring,
And the rest busied themselves skillfully through the house.
Then the lordly menservants came in. And these   160
Split pieces of wood up skillfully and well. The women
Came back from the spring. The swineherd came after them,
Leading on three porkers who were the best of all.
And he let them out to feed in the lovely enclosures.
Then he himself spoke to Odysseus with soothing words: 165
"Stranger, do the Achaians look on you in any way better?
Or do they dishonor you in the halls as they did before?"
Odysseus of many wiles addressed him in answer:
"Eumaeos, may the gods avenge the injury
That those insolent men have recklessly devised   170
In another's home, and they have no share of shame."
And so they said such things to one another;
But Melanthios the goatherd came up close to them,
Leading goats that were outstanding in all the flocks
As a meal for the suitors. Two herdsmen followed with him,   175
And they tied the goats up inside the resounding portico;
And then he himself spoke out to Odysseus with taunts:
"Stranger, will you now still give trouble in the house,
Begging of the men, and you will not go on outdoors?
I think the two of us will not be separated wholly   180
Till we have tasted fists, since indeed you do not beg
Decently. And there are other banquets of the Achaians, too."
So he said, and Odysseus of many wiles said nothing,
But moved his head in silence, deliberating evils.
Philoitios, a chief of men, came up as a third among them,   185

Driving a sterile heifer for the suitors, and fat goats.
Ferrymen had brought them over, who also conduct
Other men, whoever may come up to them.
And he tied the beasts up well under the resounding portico.
He himself stood close by and questioned the swineherd: 190
"Who is this stranger, swineherd, who is newly arrived
At our house? Out of what men does he declare he is?
Where indeed are his race and his fatherland soil?
He is ill-fated, yet he looks in form like a lordly king.
But the gods do afflict much-wandering men 195
Whenever they weave a fate of sorrow, even for kings."
So he said, stood close, and pledged him with his right hand,
And speaking out to him he uttered winged words:
"Hail, father stranger; may bliss come to pass for you
Hereafter. But, now at least, you are held in many ills. 200
Father Zeus, none of the gods is more destructive than you.
You do not pity men when once you yourself give them birth,
Getting them involved in misfortune and wretched woes.
I sweated when I thought, and my eyes were filled with tears
To remember Odysseus, since I believe he too 205
Wanders among men wearing such tatters as these,
If he is yet alive and sees the light of the sun.
But if he is already dead and in the halls of Hades,
Alas then for blameless Odysseus who put me as a small boy
In charge of oxen in the land of the Cephallenians. 210
Now they have grown numberless, nor did any race
Of broad-browed cattle give better increase for any man.
Others order me to drive them in for themselves to eat,
Nor do they care in any way for the son in the halls,
Or tremble at the surveillance of the gods. They strive even now 215
To divide the goods of the master who is gone so long.
But this thing the heart inside my own breast turns over
Many times: it is very bad while the son is alive
To go off to the land of others with the oxen and all
Among alien men. But it is more dreadful to remain here 220
And undergo pains while abiding by the oxen of others.
Indeed, I would have fled long ago and come to another
Proud king, since matters are no longer to be borne.
But still I think of that hapless man, if from somewhere
He may come and make the suitors scatter through the halls." 225
Then Odysseus of many wiles addressed him in answer:
"Herdsman, you do not seem like a bad or senseless man,
And I know for myself that prudence attains your mind.
So I shall speak out to you and swear a great oath on it:
May Zeus now be my witness first of the gods, and this guest table, 230
And the hearth of blameless Odysseus, to which I have come;
While you are in this place Odysseus shall come home

And you shall see with your own eyes, if you desire,
The suitors being slaughtered who are lording it here."
Then the man who was a herdsman of the oxen spoke to him: 235
"Stranger, would that the son of Cronos might bring this to pass!
You should learn what my strength is and how my hands go with it."
And so Eumaeos prayed the same way to all the gods
That many-minded Odysseus should return to his own home.
Such matters did they speak of to one another.   240
Meanwhile the suitors were contriving death and destiny
For Telemachos; still a bird came to him on the left,
A lofty-flying eagle and he held a trembling dove.
Amphinomos spoke out to them and addressed them:
"My friends, this plan shall not concur with our wish,   245
The murder of Telemachos. Let us take thought for a banquet."
So Amphinomos said, and his speech was pleasing to them.
They went into the house of godlike Odysseus,
And they put mantles down on the seats and on the armchairs.
Then they sacrificed great sheep and goats rich with fat,   250
They sacrificed sleek hogs and a heifer of the herd.
Then they roasted the entrails and distributed them
And mixed wine up in bowls. And the swineherd passed the cups.
Philoitios, a chief of men, passed out bread to them
In lovely baskets, and Melanthios poured the wine.   255
Then they stretched forth their hands to the food that was laid out ready.
Telemachos, managing for advantage, sat Odysseus down
Inside the well-built hall next to the stone threshold,
Setting down an insignificant stool and small table.
Beside him he put portions of entrails and poured wine   260
In a golden cup, and addressed a speech to him:
"Sit in this place now and drink your wine among the men.
I myself shall personally hold off the jibes and the fists
Of all the suitors, since this house is not public
But belongs to Odysseus, and he gained it for me.   265
As for you, suitors, keep your hearts in check from taunting
And from using your fists, so no strife or quarrel may arise."
So he said, and they all bit their lips with their teeth
And wondered at Telemachos that he spoke boldly.
Then Antinoos, the son of Eupeithes, addressed them: 270
"Achaians, let us accept the speech of Telemachos,
Though it is a harsh one. He speaks with great threat to us.
For Zeus, son of Cronos, did not allow it, or by now
We would have stopped him in the halls, clear speaker though he be."
So Antinoos said. But the man gave no heed to his speech.   275
Meanwhile, heralds were leading a sacred hecatomb to the gods
Through the town. And the long-haired Achaians gathered
Under the shadowy grove of far-darting Apollo.
When they had roasted the top parts of meat and drawn it off,

They divided up the portions and shared in the glorious feast.   280
Those who were serving placed beside Odysseus a portion
Equal to what they got themselves, as Telemachos,
The beloved son of godly Odysseus, had ordered.
And Athene by no means allowed the bold suitors
To refrain from grievous outrage, so that still more pain   285
Might enter the heart of Odysseus, son of Laertes.
There was a man among the suitors who had a lawless mind.
Ktesippos was his name, and in Samê he made his home.
Relying on his own prodigious property,
He wooed the wife of Odysseus who was gone so long.   290
He then spoke out before the insolent suitors:
"Listen to me, bold suitors, so I may say something.
This stranger has long had, as is seemly, a share
Which is equal. It is not good or just to slight
The guests of Telemachos, whoever comes to this house.   295
Come then, I too shall give him a gift, so that he also
May give a prize to the water pourer or someone else
Of the servants who are in the home of godly Odysseus."
When he said this he threw an ox's foot from his stout hand,
Picking it up from the basket where it lay. And Odysseus   300
Dodged it by quickly ducking his head, and smiled in his heart
A very scornful smile. It struck the well-built wall.
Telemachos rebuked Ktesippos in a speech:
"Ktesippos, this was much better for you in your heart
That you did not hit the stranger. He dodged the missile himself.   305
For I would have struck you through the middle with my sharp spear,
And your father would be arranging a tomb for you, not a wedding,
Right here. So let no one show any unseemly deeds
In my house. For I am now aware and know the facts,
The good ones, and the worse. I was a foolish child before,   310
And still we endure these things as we look on them,
While sheep are being slaughtered, wine is being drunk, and bread
Being eaten. It is hard for one man to check many men.
Come then, do me no more evil in your hostility.
If you are already eager to kill me with the bronze,   315
I should prefer that; it would be better by far to die
Than perpetually to look upon these sorry deeds,
Strangers being maltreated and men disgracefully
Dragging the servant women through the lovely halls."
So he said, and all of them grew hushed in silence.   320
Finally Agelaos, son of Damastor, spoke out:
"My friends, surely no one should become enraged
At a just saying and rebuke someone with hostile words.
Do not maltreat the stranger at all, or any one
Of the servants who are in the halls of godly Odysseus.   325
I myself would say to Telemachos and his mother

A mild speech that should please the hearts of both of them.
So long as the spirits in your breasts were expecting
That many-minded Odysseus would return to his own home,
There was no resentment that you waited and kept the suitors   330
In check within the house, since that was preferable
If Odysseus had returned and did get back to his house.
But now it is clear already he is to return no more.
Come then, sit beside your mother and tell her this:
To marry him who is the best man and provides the most,   335
So you may possess all your paternal goods in joy,
Eating and drinking, and she may tend to the house of another."
Then sound-minded Telemachos answered him:
"Agelaos, by Zeus and the pains of my father, who may
Have perished or have wandered far from Ithaca,   340
I shall not delay my mother's wedding at all. I bid her
To marry whom she wishes, and I shall add on endless gifts.
But I am ashamed to drive her out of the hall against her will
By a word of constraint. May a god not bring this to pass."
So Telemachos said. But Pallas Athene aroused   345
Quenchless laughter in the suitors and set their wits astray.
They were already laughing with the jaws of other men,
And they were eating meat spattered with blood. Their eyes
Filled up with tears and their hearts sensed an anguish coming.
Godlike Theoclymenos also spoke out among them: 350
"Wretched men! What evil is this you suffer? Your heads
And faces are shrouded in night, and your knees beneath;
Wailing blazes up, and your cheeks are covered with tears,
The walls and the lovely pedestals are sprinkled with blood.
The porch is full of phantoms; the courtyard is also full   355
Of those eager for Erebos under the dusk. The sun
Has perished out of heaven, and an evil mist has rushed in."
So he said, and all of them laughed sweetly at him.
Eurymachos, son of Polybos, began speaking to them:
"This stranger newly come from elsewhere is out of his mind.   360
So send him at once, young men, out of the house outdoors
To go to the place of assembly, since it seems like night to him here."
Then godlike Theoclymenos addressed him:
"Eurymachos, I do not ask you to furnish guides for me.
I have my eyes and my ears and both of my feet,   365
And the thought in my breast is not at all shabbily formed.
With their help I shall go on outdoors, since I perceive
An evil coming on you, that no one of you suitors
Who outrage men in the home of godlike Odysseus
And devise reckless deeds shall escape from or avoid."   370
When he said this he went out of the well-situated house
And came to Peiraeos, who kindly welcomed him.
Then all the suitors, looking at one another,

Provoked Telemachos, laughing about his guests.
And this is what one of those overbearing young men would say: 375
"Telemachos, no one is worse off with guests than you;
Insofar as you have for one of them this filthy tramp
Who requires bread and wine and is not at all skilled
At tasks or in strength, but is just a burden on the land.
Moreover, this other man has stood up to prophesy.   380
But if you listen a little to me it would be far better.
Let us throw the guests into a ship with many oarlocks.
And send them to Sicily, where you would get a worthwhile price."
So the suitors said. But he did not heed their speeches.
No, he glanced at his father in silence, ever on watch   385
For the time when he might lay hands on the shameless suitors.
The daughter of Icarios, prudent Penelope,
Put down a beautiful stool opposite
In the halls where the men were and listened to the words of each.
For the men themselves while they laughed and prepared a dinner,   390
Sweet and satisfying since they had sacrificed many animals.
No other more joyless supper might ever come to be
Than the one the goddess and the mighty man were soon
To set out. For the others were first to contrive sorry deeds.

XXI

Now the bright-eyed goddess Athene put it into the mind
Of Icarios' daughter, the prudent Penelope,
To set the bow before the suitors and the gray iron
In Odysseus' halls as a contest and a start for slaughter.
She stepped up on the high stairway of her quarters   5
And in her stout hand took hold of the well-curved key,
A lovely one of bronze. And an ivory handle was on it.
And she went on with her serving women into a chamber,
The last room, where the treasures of her lord were lying,
Bronze and gold and iron that was highly wrought.   10
There a springy bow was lying, and also a quiver
For arrows, and in it were many arrows that bring grief;
These gifts a friend had given him who met him in Lacedemon,
Iphitos, son of Eurytos, who was like the immortals.
The two of them came upon each other in Messene,   15
In the house of skillful Ortilochos. Odysseus
Had gone there after a debt that the whole people owed him.
Messenian men had taken up three hundred sheep
And their shepherds out of Ithaca in many-oared ships.
For their sake Odysseus had gone a long way on his errand   20
While a boy. His father and the other elders had sent him forth.
And Iphitos came after horses, twelve females of his

That he had lost, along with unweaned, work-enduring mules.
Then these, indeed, brought upon him murder and destiny
When he went in the presence of the stout-hearted son of Zeus,   25
The mortal Heracles, who was experienced in huge deeds
And slaughtered the man as a guest in his own house,
A cruel wretch, as he did not respect the gods' wrath or the table
That he had set before him. And then he killed the man himself.
He himself kept the mares with the powerful hooves in his halls.   30
Seeking these, the man met Odysseus and gave him the bow,
Which great Eurytos had carried before, and then
Had left when he died to his son in the lofty house.
Odysseus gave him a sharp sword and a mighty spear,
The start of a close-binding friendship; but they did not know   35
One another at the table, since before that Zeus's son slew
Iphitos, son of Eurytos, a man like the immortals,
Who gave him the bow. And never would godly Odysseus
Take it when he went off on the black ships to war.
But he left it lying there in the halls as a reminder   40
Of his dear friend. And he did carry it in his own land.
And when the divine woman had arrived at her chamber
And had gone over the oak threshold that a craftsman once
Skillfully planed for her and straightened with a line—
He fitted doorposts up and set shining doors on them—   45
Right away she quickly took the thong from the hook,
Inserted the key, and shot back the bolts of the door,
Aiming them straight; and they groaned like a bull
Feeding in a meadow, so loud did the lovely door sound
As it was struck by the key and was quickly opened wide.   50
She stepped up on the lofty planking. And there chests
Were standing, inside of which fragrant clothing was stored.
From there she stretched herself up and reached the bow from its peg,
Along with the bow case that surrounded it handsomely.
She sat down right there, putting it on her own knees,   55
And wept aloud as she took down her husband's bow.
And when she had her fill of tearful lamentation,
She went on into the hall among the noble suitors,
Holding in her hand the springy bow and the quiver
For arrows. In it were many arrows that bring grief.   60
Her servants brought her a case in which iron lay
In plenty, and so did bronze, the prizes of her lord.
And when the godly woman had come to the suitors,
She stood beside the pillar of the stoutly fashioned roof,
Holding the glistening headbands before her cheeks.   65
A devoted servant maid stood near her on either side.
At once she spoke out to the suitors and addressed a speech to them:
"Listen to me now, bold suitors, you who have always
Beset this house, perpetually eating and drinking

While my husband has been gone away for a long time.   70
You could make up no other story as an excuse
Than that you wanted to marry me and make me your wife.
Well, come now, suitors, since this appears as your prize.
I will set up the great bow of godly Odysseus.
The one who most nimbly strings the bow in his hands.   75
And shoots an arrow through all twelve of the axes,
Him will I follow, departing from this very lovely
Home of my marriage that is full of the goods of life,
Which I think I shall ever remember, even in dreams."
So she said, and she called to Eumaeos, the godly swineherd,   80
To set up for the suitors the bow and the gray iron.
Eumaeos took them, weeping, and he set them out.
The herdsman for his part wailed when he saw his master's bow.
Then Antinoos rebuked them and spoke out to them directly:
"Foolish yokels, who consider only the things of the day.   85
You wretches, why are you dripping tears? Why arouse
The heart in the breast of a woman whose heart lies in pain
In any case, since she has lost her dear husband?
But sit down and eat in silence, or else go on
And wail outdoors, leaving the bow behind right here,   90
An inviolable contest for the suitors. So I think
This polished bow is not to be strung easily,
And there is no man present among all of you
Of the kind Odysseus was. I saw him my own self,
And I do remember him though I was still a foolish child."   95
So he said, but even so the heart in his breast hoped
To string the bowstring and shoot an arrow through the iron.
Yet he was destined to be the first to taste an arrow
From the hands of blameless Odysseus, whom he was flouting just then
As he sat in the halls, and he was rousing all his companions.   100
Telemachos spoke out to them in his sacred might:
"Well, Zeus, son of Cronos, has made me lacking in sense.
My dear mother says, even though she is prudent,
That she will follow another and leave this house behind.
Yet I am laughing and am pleased in my senseless heart.   105
Come now, you suitors, since this appears as the prize,
A woman whose like now exists not in the Achaian land,
Not in sacred Pylos or in Argos or Mycenae,
Or in Ithaca herself, or upon the black mainland.
You know it yourselves. Why need I praise my mother?   110
Come, do not put it off with excuses or turn away
From stringing the bow any more, so we may see.
And I my very own self might make a try at the bow.
If I were to string it and shoot an arrow through the iron,
My queenly mother would not leave me in any grief   115
If she went off with another, since I should be left behind

As already one able to take up my father's fine weapons."
He spoke, and put the purple tunic off his shoulders,
Sprang upright, and off his shoulders took the sharp sword.
First he stood up the axes, digging one long trench through   120
For all of them, and he straightened it with a line,
And stamped earth down about them. Wonder seized all who saw
How neatly he stood them, but he had never viewed them before.
He went and stood on the threshold and tested the bow.
Three times he made it quiver, striving to draw it,   125
And three times he slackened his strength, hoping in his heart
To string the bowstring and shoot an arrow through the iron.
And he would have drawn it the fourth time, bending it with his strength.
But Odysseus nodded and checked him, impelled as he was.
Then Telemachos spoke out to them in his sacred might: 130
"Well, how weak and cowardly I shall be even in the future,
Or else I am too young and cannot yet rely on my hands
For warding some man off if he gets angry first.
Come now, you who are superior to me in strength,
Try the bow out and let us conclude the contest."   135
So he said, and put the bow away from him on the ground,
Leaning it against the tight-fitted, well-made doors.
And then he leaned a swift dart against its fine tip.
Then he sat back down on the chair from which he had stood.
Antinoos, the son of Eupeithes, spoke out to them: 140
"Rise, all my companions, in order, from left to right,
Beginning at the place from which the wine is poured."
So Antinoos said, and his speech was pleasing to them.
Leodes, son of Oinops, was the first to stand up.
He was their soothsayer, and he always sat   145
Furthest in by the lovely mixing bowl. To him alone
Was recklessness hateful; he resented all the suitors.
He was the first then to take the bow and the swift dart.
He went and stood on the threshold and tried out the bow.
He did not string it. Before that, drawing it up,   150
He tired his soft, unworn hands. And he spoke to the suitors:
"My friends, I cannot string it. Let another take it.
Many excellent men shall this bow have bereaved
Of life and spirit, since it is better by far
To die than to live and miss what perpetually   155
We are gathered for here, expectant day after day,
And even now someone hopes in his mind and desires
To marry Penelope, the wife of Odysseus.
But when he has seen the bow and tested it out,
Let him then woo some other of the well-gowned Achaian women   160
And seek her in marriage with gifts. She then may wed
Whoever gives the most and comes as the destined man."
When he had said this he put the bow away from him,

Leaning it against the tight-fitted, well-made doors.
And then he leaned the swift dart against its fine tip.   165
Then he sat back down on the chair from which he had stood.
But Antinoos rebuked him and spoke out to him directly:
"Leodes, what sort of speech has got past the bar of your teeth?
A wretched and grievous one. I am angered as I hear it,
If this bow indeed shall deprive excellent men   170
Of spirit and life, when you cannot string it yourself.
Your queenly mother did not bear you as the sort of man
Who would be capable of drawing a bow and arrows;
But other noble suitors shall quickly string it."
So he said, and he called to Melanthios, the goatherd.   175
"Come, Melanthios, and kindle a fire in the halls.
Put a large stool down alongside and a fleece upon it,
And bring in a great round piece of the fat from inside,
So we young men, when we have warmed it and rubbed it with grease,
May try the bow out and may conclude the contest."   180
So he said. Melanthios at once kindled a quenchless fire,
Brought in a stool, put it down, and set a fleece upon it.
Then he carried in a great round piece of the fat from inside.
This the young men tried, when they had warmed it. But they were not
Able to string it: they were far too lacking in strength.   185
Antinoos and godlike Eurymachos, chief of the suitors,
Still held back. They were by far the best in excellence.
Accompanying each other, the oxherd and the swineherd
Of godly Odysseus had both gone out of the house.
Divine Odysseus came after them from the house himself.   190
And when they were outside of the doors and the courtyard
He raised his voice and addressed them with soothing speeches:
"Oxherd, and you, swineherd, shall I tell you something
Or keep it to myself? My heart bids me to speak.
How would you fend for Odysseus if he came from somewhere   195
Very suddenly this way and some god had brought him in?
Would you fend for the suitors or fend for Odysseus?
Speak the way your heart and your spirit command you to."
Then the man who was in charge of the oxen addressed him:
"Father Zeus, would that you might fulfill this wish,   200
That the man himself might come, and some god might bring him.
You would learn what my strength is and how my hands go with it."
And so Eumaeos prayed the same way to all the gods
For many-minded Odysseus to return to his own home.
And when he had recognized their unerring intent,   205
He answered them right away and addressed them with a speech:
"Here I am, home, myself, having suffered many pains;
I have come in the twentieth year to my fatherland.
I realize that you alone of the servants I come to
Are longing for me. I have heard none of the others   210

Praying for me to reach home again on my return,
And I shall speak the truth to you both as it shall be.
If a god indeed subdues the noble suitors beneath me,
I shall give you both wives and provide you with property
And houses built close to my own. Then you shall be 215
Companions and kinsmen of Telemachos and myself.
Come now, I shall show you another manifest sign
So you may know me well and trust me in your hearts:
A scar a boar once inflicted on me with his shining tusk
When I went to Parnassos with the sons of Autolycos." 220
When he had said this he drew his rags away from the great scar.
Both of them, when they had seen and well noted the details,
Wept and threw their arms around the skillful Odysseus,
And they kept kissing him, embracing his head and shoulders.
Odysseus kept kissing their heads and hands the same way. 225
The light of the sun would have gone down on them as they moaned
If Odysseus himself had not checked them and spoken out:
"Stop wailing and lamenting, lest someone come out
Of the hall, see us, and then tell it within too;
But go inside, each in turn and not all together, 230
I first, and you afterward. And let this be made the sign.
When all the others, the whole number of noble suitors,
Will not allow the bow and quiver to be given to me,
Then you, godly Eumaeos, carry the bow through the house,
Place it in my hands, and then tell the women 235
To lock up the closely fitted portals of the hall,
And if anyone inside hears in our enclosures
A groaning and beating of men, let her not go forth
Out the door at all, but be there in silence at the task.
And you, godly Philoitios, I order to bolt the gates 240
Of the courtyard with a bolt, and quickly lash on the cord."
When he had said this he entered the well-situated halls.
Then he went and sat down on the stool from which he had stood,
And the two servants of godly Odysseus also went in.
Eurymachos was already turning the bow in his hands, 245
Warming it here and there in the fire's flame. But he could not
String it that way; his mighty heart swelled heavily.
Angered, he uttered a speech and spoke out directly:
"Well now, there is grief in me for myself and for all.
Not for the marriage, though distressed, do I moan so greatly. 250
There are many other Achaian women, some in this very
Sea-circled Ithaca; and some in other cities.
But if we are to such a degree lacking in the force
Of godlike Odysseus that we cannot string his bow,
It is a disgrace even for men in the future to hear of." 255
Then Antinoos, son of Eupeithes, spoke to him:
"Eurymachos, it will not be so. And you know it yourself.

234 THE ODYSSEY

For now through the district is a feast day of that god,
A holy one. And who would bend the bows? Put them down
Quietly. But as for the axes, suppose we let them   260
All stand. For I think no one will come into the hall
Of Odysseus, son of Laertes, and carry them off.
Come now, let the wine-pourer begin the rite with the cups,
So we may pour libation and lay down the curved bows.
And at dawn summon Melanthios, the goatherd,   265
To bring the goats that are far outstanding in all the herds,
So that, setting out thighs to Apollo, famed for the bow,
We may try the bow out and conclude the contest."
So Antinoos said, and his speech was pleasing to them.
Heralds poured out water for them over their hands.   270
Young men were filling bowls up to the brim with drink.
And served round to all, putting the first drops in the cups.
When they had poured libation and drunk what their hearts wished,
Odysseus of many wiles spoke to them with a trick in mind:
"Listen to me, suitors of the illustrious queen,   275
So I may tell you what the heart in my breast bids me to.
Eurymachos especially and godly Antinoos
Do I beseech, since he spoke properly when he said:
We should let the bow go now, and leave the matter to the gods,
And at dawn the god will give the strength to the one he wishes.   280
Come then, give me the polished bow, so that among you
I may test out my strength and hands, whether the force
Is in me still that once was in my supple limbs,
Or whether wandering and lack of care have ruined me already."
So he said, and they all grew insolently angry,   285
Fearing that he might put the string on the polished bow.
Antinoos rebuked him and spoke out to him directly:
"Wretched stranger, you have no sense, none in the least.
Are you not content to dine among us exalted men,
Secure, not to be deprived of food at all, and to hear   290
Our speeches and our discourse? Nor does anyone else,
Whether stranger or beggar listen to our speeches.
Honey-sweet wine besets you, that harms other men, too,
Whoever takes it down in gulps and drinks to excess.
Wine blinded the Centaur too, illustrious Eurytion,   295
In the hall of great-spirited Perithöus,
When he came to the Lapiths. After his mind was blinded with wine
He went mad and did evils in the house of Perithöus.
Distress seized the heroes. They leaped and dragged him outdoors
Through the forecourt and sheared his ears and nostrils off   300
With the pitiless bronze. Then he grew reckless in his mind
And went on, bearing madness in his impetuous heart.
From that came the quarrel between Centaurs and men.
But first for himself he found evil, being heavy with wine,

And so I declare great trouble for you if you should string   305
This bow. You would not encounter any gentle use
In our district. We should send you speedily
To King Echetos, the destroyer of all mortal men,
In a black ship. And you would not be saved there. But drink
Quietly, and do not wrangle with men younger than you."   310
And then the prudent Penelope answered him:
"Antinoos, it is not good or just to slight
The guests of Telemachos, whoever comes to this house.
Do you think, if this stranger does string the great bow
Of Odysseus, relying on his hands and his mighty force,   315
That he will lead me to his home and make me his wife?
He himself has never yet thought this in his breast.
Let no one of you dine here grieving in his heart
On that account, since it is not seemly at all."
Eurymachos, son of Polybos, answered her: 320
"Daughter of Icarios, prudent Penelope,
We do not think this man will lead you home. It is not seemly,
But we are ashamed at the rumor among men and women,
Lest sometime some other foul person of the Achaeans may say:
'Yes, far inferior men are wooing the wife   325
Of an excellent man and cannot string his polished bow.
But someone else, a beggar, who came on his wanderings,
Easily strung the bow and shot through the iron.'
So they would say, and this would be a reproach to us."
Then the prudent Penelope spoke to him: 330
"Eurymachos, there is no way that good reports may exist
In the district for those who dishonor and devour
A noble man's home. And why make a reproach of this?
The stranger here is very large and of a well-knit frame.
He declares he is by descent a good father's son.   335
Come now, give him the polished bow, so we may see.
For this do I proclaim, and it shall be brought to pass.
If he does string it and Apollo gives him the praise,
I shall clothe him in a mantle and a tunic, lovely clothes.
I shall give him a sharp javelin, a defense against dogs and men,   340
And a two-edged sword. I shall give him sandals for his feet
And send him wherever his heart and spirit bid."
Then sound-minded Telemachos addressed her in answer:
"My mother, as for the bow, none of the Achaians has more power
Then I have to give or refuse it to whomever I wish.   345
Not any of those who rule in craggy Ithaca
Or who rule over the islands towards horse-pasturing Elis.
None of them will compel me against my will even from giving
This bow once for all to the stranger to take off, if I wish.
But go into the house and attend to your own tasks,   350
The loom and the distaff, and give orders to your servants

To set at the work. The bow shall concern all the men
But me especially. For the power in the house is mine."
She was amazed at him, and back into the house she went.
The sound-minded speech of her son she took to heart.   355
She went into the upper chamber with her serving women,
And then wept for Odysseus, her dear husband, until
Bright-eyed Athene cast sweet sleep upon her eyelids.
Then the divine swineherd took the curved bow, and was carrying it,
And all the suitors made an outcry in the halls.   360
This is what one of those overbearing young men would say:
"Where are you carrying the curved bow, miserable swineherd,
You vagabond? Soon the swift dogs you reared yourself
Shall eat you amid the swine, apart from men, alone,
If Apollo is gracious to us, and the other immortal gods."   365
So they said; but he carried it and put it right where he was,
Afraid because many made an outcry in the halls.
But Telemachos from the other side shouted a threat:
"Uncle, bring the bow out. You will soon not do well to heed all,
Lest, though younger than you, I drive you to the fields   370
And throw stones at you. I am mightier than you in strength.
Would I were that much mightier in strength and with my hands
Than all of the suitors who are inside the halls.
Then I should soon send one of them grimly on his way
Out of our house, since they are devising evils."   375
So he said, and all of the suitors sweetly laughed
At him, and they relaxed their oppressive anger
Toward Telemachos. The swineherd carried the bow through the house,
Stood beside skillful Odysseus, and put it in his hands.
Then he called forth the nurse Eurycleia and addressed her: 380
"Prudent Eurycleia, Telemachos orders you
To lock up the closely fitted portals of the hall.
And if anyone inside hears in our enclosures
A groaning and a beating of men, let her not go forth
Out the door at all, but be there in silence at the task."   385
So he said, and for her the speech was without a wing.
She locked up the doors of the well-situated halls.
Philoitios hastened in silence out of the house,
Outdoors, and locked up the gates of the well-fenced court.
Under the portico lay the papyrus-fiber cable   390
Of a bobbing ship. With it he tied the gates, entered,
And then went and sat down on the stool from which he had stood
And looked at Odysseus. He was already handling the bow,
Turning it in all directions, testing it this way and that,
For fear worms had eaten the horns while the master was away.   395
And this is what one of them, looking at his neighbor would say:
"This is some fancier and an expert with bows,
And perhaps such as these are lying in his home too,

Or else he wants to make one, he handles it so
This way and that in his hands, the beggar skilled in evils." 400
And another of the overbearing young men would say:
"Would that he might encounter profit only to the degree
That he shall ever be able to string this bow himself."
So the suitors said. But Odysseus of many wiles,
At once when he raised the great bow and viewed it on all sides— 405
As when a man skilled at the lyre and at singing
Easily stretches a string over a new peg,
Tying at both ends the flexible gut of the sheep—
So without effort did Odysseus string the great bow.
He took it in his right hand and tested the cord. 410
It sang sweetly beneath like a swallow in its sound.
Great distress came upon the suitors, and the skin of all
Turned color. Zeus thundered greatly, showing signs.
Then godly Odysseus, who had endured much, rejoiced
That the son of crooked-counseling Cronos sent him a portent. 415
He took a swift arrow that lay by him on the table,
Bare. The others were lying within the hollow quiver,
The ones the Achaians were soon to experience.
He put it to the bridge, drew the string and the notches,
And shot the arrow right from there, sitting on the stool, 420
Aiming it straight, and he did not miss one handle tip
Of all of the axes. The arrow heavy with bronze
Went straight on out the end. He spoke to Telemachos:
"Telemachos, the stranger seated in the halls
Does not discredit you. I did not miss my aim, 425
Nor did I toil long to string the bow. My strength is steadfast still
And is not such as the suitors scorn, despising me.
And now it is time for the Achaians to have a meal prepared
In the light, and then to make sport in other ways
With singing and the lyre; they are the ornaments of a feast." 430
So he said, and signaled with his eyebrows. Telemachos,
The dear son of godlike Odysseus, girded on his sharp sword,
Put his own hand round his spear, and stood close to him
Beside his armchair, equipped with the glittering bronze.

XXII

Then Odysseus of many wiles bared himself from his rags
And sprang upon the great threshold, holding the bow
And the quiver full of arrows. He poured the swift shafts out
There before his feet. And he spoke out among the suitors:
"This inviolable contest has been brought to an end. 5
And now I shall know another mark that no man has ever hit,
If I happen to hit it, and Apollo grant me glory."

So he said, and aimed a bitter arrow at Antinoos.
The man was about to lift up the lovely libation cup,
A gold double-eared one, and he held it up in his hands   10
So that he might drink wine. There was no thought of slaughter
In his heart. Who would think a single man among so many
As the banqueters were, though he was very powerful,
Would bring upon him an evil death and black fate?
Odysseus took aim and shot him with an arrow in the throat;   15
The point of it went straight on through his tender neck.
He leaned to one side and the cup fell from his hand
As he was hit; at once a thick spurt of human blood
Came through his nostrils. He quickly pushed the table from him,
Striking it with his foot. He spilled the food on the ground,   20
And the bread and roast meat were defiled. The suitors made
A din through the halls when they saw the man fall.
They rose up from their chairs, panicking through the house,
Peering on all sides along the well-constructed walls.
And nowhere was there a shield or stout spear to be grasped.   25
They upbraided Odysseus with words full of rage:
"Stranger, to your ill do you shoot at men. You shall no longer
Enter other contests; now your sheer destruction is certain.
Now you have slain the mortal who was the greatest by far
Of the young men in Ithaca. So vultures shall eat you here."   30
Each man guessed so, since they thought he had killed the man
Without wanting to. And the fools did not perceive
That already the bonds of destruction were fastened on them all.
Odysseus of many wiles glared at them and spoke:
"Dogs, you thought I would no longer come home in return   35
From the land of the Trojans; and so you wore my house away
And slept alongside my serving women by force
And underhandedly courted my wife while I was myself alive,
And you did not fear the gods who possess broad heaven,
Or that there would be any vengeance of men in time to come.   40
Now the bonds of destruction are fastened on you all."
So he said, and sallow fear got a grip on all of them.
Each one peered for where he might flee sheer destruction.
Eurymachos alone spoke to him in answer:
"If indeed you are Ithacan Odysseus, who have come,   45
You have rightfully told all this that the Achaians have done:
Many wicked things in the halls, and many in the fields.
And here he lies already who was guilty of them all,
Antinoos. He it was who instigated these deeds,
Not so much wanting or desiring the wedding at all,   50
But plotting other acts which the son of Cronos did not bring about
For him: that over the well-tilled land of Ithaca
He might himself be king, and might kill your son in ambush.
Now he is slain, as was his due. Spare your people

And we shall give satisfaction in the land hereafter   55
For all that has been drunk up and eaten in the halls,
Each one bringing separately a recompense worth twenty oxen,
And we shall give bronze and gold in return till your own heart
Is softened. Till then no one would blame you for getting angry."
Odysseus of many wiles glared at him and spoke: 60
"Eurymachos, not if you gave me all the paternal goods
That you possess, and any others you added from somewhere,
Not even then should I yet stay my hands from slaughter
Until the suitors had paid for all their insolence.
And now it lies with you either to fight face to face   65
Or to flee, whoever would avoid death and destiny.
But I think that no one shall escape sheer destruction."
So he said; and their knees and their own hearts went slack
On the spot. And Eurymachos addressed them yet again:
"My friends, this man will not check his invincible hands,   70
But once he has taken the polished bow and quiver
He will shoot from the smooth threshold until he has killed
All of us. But let us remember the ardor of battle;
Draw your swords out and hold the tables up in the way
Of the swift-fated arrows. And let us all go at him   75
In a body, hoping we may force him from the threshold and the door-
    way.
And may come to the town, and an alarm quickly be raised.
And soon then this man would have shot for the last time."
When he had spoken so, he drew out his keen sword
Of bronze, sharpened on both sides; and sprang on the man   80
With a terrible cry. At the same time godly Odysseus
Shot off an arrow, and he hit his chest by the nipple;
He drove the swift shaft into his liver. And from his hand
He let the sword drop to the ground. He fell down sprawling
Doubled up on the table. He spilled the food on the ground,   85
And the two-handled cups. He beat the earth with his forehead,
Agonized in his heart. He kicked the armchair with both feet.
And made it shake. A mist was shed over his eyes.
Amphinomos charged upon the mighty Odysseus
Rushing up against him, and he drew his sharp sword   90
That the man might somehow yield the door to him. Telemachos
Was too fast for him, and hit him from behind with a bronze spear
In the middle of the shoulders, and drove it through his chest.
He made a noise falling and struck the ground flat with his forehead.
Telemachos sprang away, leaving his long-shadowy spear   95
There in Amphinomos. For he greatly feared that, as he drew out
The long-shadowy spear, some Achaian might thrust him through
By rushing on with a sword, or hit him as he stooped forward.
He ran on and very quickly reached his dear father.
He stood close beside him and uttered wingèd words: 100

"Father, I shall now bring you a shield and two spears,
And a helmet all of bronze, fitted to the temples.
I shall put it on me when I come, and I shall give other arms
To the swineherd and the oxherd. It is better to be armed."
Odysseus of many wiles addressed him in answer: 105
"Bring them on the run, while the arrows may defend me,
Lest they force me out the doors, single man that I am."
So he said, and Telemachos obeyed his dear father.
He went on into the chamber where lay the glorious arms.
And from that place he took away four shields, eight spears,   110
And four bronze-fitted helmets with shaggy horsehair plumes;
He came carrying them and very soon reached his dear father.
He himself put the bronze on over his flesh first of all.
The two servants put their fine armor on the same way.
They flanked the skillful and subtle-minded Odysseus.   115
He himself, so long as there were arrows to defend him,
Kept aiming at the suitors in his house one by one
And always hit his mark. They fell one after another.
But when the arrows had all left the master as he shot,
He leaned the bow to stand it up against the doorpost   120
Of the well-built hall, against the resplendent walls.
He himself put the four-layered shield round his shoulders
And placed on his mighty head the well-fashioned helmet
With a horsehair crest; terribly the plume nodded on top of it.
And he took two valiant spears fitted out with bronze.   125
There was a certain side door in the well-built wall
Along the highest point of the well-based hall's threshold.
It was a way to the passage, and well-fitted doors held it.
Odysseus ordered the godly swineherd to stand close to it
And watch over it. It was the one single way of approach.   130
Then Agelaos spoke to them, declaring his speech to all:
"My friends, will not someone go up through the side door
And tell the people, so an alarm may quickly be raised,
And then this man would soon have shot now for the last time."
Then Melanthios, herdsman of the goats, spoke to him: 135
"There is no way, Zeus-bred Agelaos. The court's fine doors
Are dreadfully close, and the mouth of the passage is hard,
And a single man who was valiant could hold back all.
But come, I shall bring you arms to gird yourselves with
From the chamber. Within, I think, and nowhere else   140
Have Odysseus and his glorious son put their armor up."
When he had said this, Melanthios, the goatherd, went up
To Odysseus' chambers through the slits of the hall.
There he took out twelve shields and as many spears
And as many bronze-fitted helmets with shaggy horsehair plumes. 145
He came out and brought them quickly and gave them to the suitors
Then Odysseus' knees and his heart went slack

When he saw them putting on the armor and brandishing
The long spears in their hands. It seemed to him a great task.
Right away he uttered wingèd words to Telemachos: 150
"Telemachos, some one of the women in the halls.
Stirs up an evil battle against us, or Melanthios does."
Sound-minded Telemachos addressed him in answer:
"Father, I myself made this mistake, and no one else
Is guilty. I left the closely fitted door of the chamber   155
Hanging open. One of them spied it better than I.
But go, godly Eumaeos, and close the door
And observe whether one of the women is doing this,
Or Melanthios, son of Dolios, the one I think."
And so they said such things to one another.   160
Then Melanthios, the goatherd, went again to the chamber
To bring the fine armor. The godly swineherd perceived him
And at once he addressed Odysseus, who was near:
"Zeus-born son of Laertes, Odysseus of many devices,
That destructive man who we ourselves think is the one   165
Is going to the chamber. And tell me unerringly
Whether I should kill him if I am more powerful,
Or bring him here to you to pay for the many
Insolences this man has plotted in your house."
Odysseus of many wiles addressed him in answer: 170
"Indeed, Telemachos and I shall hold the noble suitors
Inside of the halls, though they may struggle very much.
But both of you twist his feet behind him and his hands above,
Throw him into the chamber, and bind planks behind him,
And then fasten a plaited rope to the man himself.   175
Drag him up the lofty pillar and bring him near the beams
So he may long be alive and suffer oppressive pains."
So he said. They hearkened closely to him and obeyed him.
They went on into the chamber unseen by the man inside;
He in fact was searching a corner of the chamber for the arms.   180
The two remained standing on either side of the posts.
When Melanthios, the goatherd, was going over the threshold
Carrying a fine-horned helmet in one of his hands
And in the other a broad, old shield spattered with mold
Of the hero Laertes, which he used to bear as a young man—   185
But at this time it was laid by, and the seams of its thongs were loose—
The two rushed upon him, seized him, and dragged him inside
By the hair; they threw him, grieved at heart, on the ground.
They bound his hands and his feet with a spirit-hurting bond,
Turning it around very thoroughly and well, as the son   190
Of Laertes had ordered, godly Odysseus, who had endured much.
They fastened a plaited rope to the man himself,
Dragged him up the lofty pillar, and brought him near the beams.
Then you spoke and taunted him, swineherd Eumaeos:

"Now, indeed, Melanthios, you will keep watch the whole night,   195
Lying down in a gentle bed, as is fitting for you.
Nor shall the early-born, golden-throned one as she comes
From the streams of Oceanos escape your view at the time
You drive goats for the suitors to prepare a feast in the house."
And so he was left there, stretched in the ruinous bond.   200
The two put on armor, closed the shining door,
And went to the skillful crafty-minded Odysseus.
There did they stand, breathing force, the four of them
On the threshold, but there were many noblemen within the house.
Athene, daughter of Zeus, came to close quarters with them,   205
Likening herself to Mentor in form and in voice.
Odysseus rejoiced to see her, and spoke to her:
"Mentor, fend off harm; remember the dear companion
Who used to do you good. You are the same age as I."
So he said, thinking it was Athene, rouser of the people.   210
The suitors on the other side made a din in the halls.
Agelaos, son of Damastor, reproached her first:
"Mentor, let Odysseus not win you over with speeches
To fight against the suitors and to defend himself,
For I think our own purpose shall be carried out this way;   215
When we have killed these men, the father and the son,
Then you yourself shall be slain with them for what you plan
To do in the halls. You will pay it here with your own head,
And when we have deprived you of your power with the sword,
All the possessions you have, both indoors and out   220
We shall mix with those of Odysseus, and we shall not
Allow your sons to live in the halls or your daughters
Or your devoted wife to move round in the city of Ithaca."
So he said, and Athene grew very angry in her heart,
And she upbraided Odysseus with angry words: 225
"No longer, Odysseus, have you a steadfast mind or strength
As when, over white-armed Helen, who had a noble father,
You fought the Trojans, always relentlessly, for nine years
And in the dreadful combat slaughtered many men,
And Priam's broad-streeted city was taken by your plan.   230
How is it that now, when you have reached your home and possessions,
You wail about being valiant against the suitors?
Come now, old friend, stand by me and see the deed,
So you may see what sort Mentor, son of Alkimos, is
To repay well-doing in the midst of hostile men."   235
So she said, and did not yet wholly give him victory
With decisive strength, but still tested the power and strength
Both of Odysseus and of his glorious son.
Then she herself rushed up and sat upon the roof
Of the smoky hall facing them, in the form of a swallow.   240
Agelaos, the son of Damastor, urged on the suitors,

And so did Eurynomos, Amphimedon, Demoptolemos,
Peisander, the son of Polyktor, and skillful Polybos,
Who were by far the best of the suitors for excellence—
Of those who were still living and fighting for their lives.   245
The bow and frequent arrows had already overcome the others.
Agelaos spoke to them, declaring his speech to all:
"My friends, this man shall soon hold back his invincible hands.
Mentor has gone from him, uttering empty boasts,
And they are left alone out in front of the gates.   250
Do not all of you let your long spears fly together.
Come now, you six hurl your javelins first, so that Zeus
May perchance grant that Odysseus be hit and we gain glory.
For the rest there will be no trouble when this man has fallen."
So he said, and they all threw their javelins as he bade,   255
Eagerly. But Athene made them all of no effect.
One of them hit against the pillar of the well-based hall,
Another one hit against the closely fitted door
And another's bronze-heavy ash spear fell on the wall.
And then, when they had avoided the spears of the suitors,   260
Godly Odysseus, who had endured much, began speaking to them:
"My friends, let me say myself that we, too, right now
Should shoot into the throng of suitors who are striving to kill us
And strip our armor, adding this to their former evils."
So he said, and all of them hurled their sharp spears,   265
Aiming them straight. Odysseus slew Demoptolemos;
Telemachos, Eurypades; and the swineherd, Elatos;
The man who was in charge of the oxen slew Peisander.
All these together bit the broad floor with their teeth,
And the suitors drew away into the corner of the hall.   270
But the others rushed on them and drew spears out of the dead.
Then the suitors hurled their sharp spears right away,
Eagerly. But Athene made their number of no effect.
One of them hit against a pillar of the well-based hall,
Another one hit against the closely fitted door,   275
And another's bronze-heavy ash spear fell on the wall.
Yet Amphimedon hit Telemachos' hand at the wrist
With a glancing blow, and the bronze wounded his outer skin.
Ktesippos grazed Eumaeos with a long spear on the shoulder
Above his shield. It leaped off and fell to the ground.   280
Then those round the skillful and subtle-minded Odysseus
Hurled their sharp spears into the throng of the suitors.
Then Odysseus, sacker of cities, hit Eurydamas.
Telemachos hit Amphimedon, and the swineherd hit Polybos;
And then the man in charge of the oxen hit Ktesippos   285
Upon the chest, and he spoke right out with a boast:
"Son of Polytherses, you lover of jeers, never again
Yield wholly to folly and talk big; but turn the tale over

To the gods, since they are more powerful by far.
This is a guest gift in return for the foot you once gave   290
To godlike Odysseus as he went begging in the house."
So said the driver of the crumple-horned cattle. Odysseus
Wounded the son of Damastor at close hand with a long spear.
Telemachos wounded Leocritos, son of Euenor,
In the middle of the flank with a spear; he drove the bronze through
    him.   295
The man fell on his face and struck the ground flat with his forehead.
Then Athene held up the aegis deadly to mortals,
On high from the roof. The minds of the men were dismayed.
They fled through the hall like cattle in a drove
That a darting gadfly, when it is stirred up, stampedes   300
In the season of spring, when the days are getting long.
And then, as falcons with bent claws and hooked beaks
Come down from the mountains and dash upon the birds—
These are driven over the plain cowering from the clouds,
But the others pounce on them and kill them; and no help   305
Comes, and no escape, and men rejoice at the chase—
So they rushed on through the house upon the suitors
And struck them one after another. Their wretched groaning
Rose as their heads were struck. The whole ground ran with blood.
Leiodes rushed on and seized Odysseus by the knees,   310
And imploring him, he uttered wingèd words:
"I pray to you, Odysseus, respect me and pity me.
Never yet, I say, have I spoken or done anything reckless
To any woman in the halls. But I kept stopping
The other suitors when anyone did such things.   315
But they did not heed me and keep their hands from evil,
And so in their recklessness they have come to a wretched fate.
Yet I who as a soothsayer among them did nothing evil
Shall be laid low, since there is no future grace for good deeds."
Odysseus of many wiles glared at him and spoke: 320
"If you indeed declare you are a soothsayer among them,
You are likely to have prayed many times in the halls
That the end of a sweet return be kept far from me;
That my beloved wife follow you and bear you children.
And so you may not escape death that brings bitter pain."   325
When he had said this, he seized in his stout hand a sword lying there
That Agelaos had let fall to the ground when he was killed.
With it he drove through the middle of the man's neck.
His head as he spoke was mingled with the dust.
And the son of Terpes, the singer, still tried to avoid black death, 330
Phemios, who sang for the suitors under constraint.
He stood holding the clear-toned lyre in his hands
Close to the side door, and he was thinking two ways in his mind,
Whether to abandon the hall and take a seat

At the well-made altar of the great Zeus of the Court,   335
Where Laertes and Odysseus had burned many thighs of oxen,
Or to rush up and implore Odysseus at his knees.
And so, as he thought, it seemed to him to be better
To take hold of the knees of Odysseus, son of Laertes.
He put his hollow lyre down upon the ground   340
Between the mixing bowl and the silver-studded chair
And rushed up himself and took Odysseus by the knees,
And imploring him, he uttered wingèd words:
"I pray to you, Odysseus; respect me and pity me.
There will be grief for yourself hereafter if you slay   345
A singer like me who sings for gods and for men.
I am self-taught, and a god has planted all kinds
Of lays in my mind. I am fit to sing before you
As before a god. And so do not be eager to cut my throat.
And Telemachos, your beloved son, may tell you this: 350
That not at all by my wish or need did I frequent
The suitors in your house to sing for them at their feasts.
But, being far more, and stronger, they brought me by constraint."
So he said, and Telemachos in his sacred might heard him.
At once he addressed his father, who was close beside him: 355
"Hold off, do not wound this guiltless man with the sword.
Let us also spare the herald Medon, who always
Looked after me in our house when I was a child,
Unless indeed Philoitios or the swineherd has slain him
Or he came on you as you were stirred up in the house."   360
So he said, and Medon, who was sound of mind, heard him.
He lay crouching underneath an armchair and had covered himself
With the new-flayed skin of an ox, to avoid black fate.
He rose at once from beneath the chair, took the oxhide off,
Then rushed up and grasped Telemachos by the knees,   365
And imploring him, he uttered wingèd words:
"My friend, here I am, myself. Hold! Tell your father;
Lest in his greater strength he kill me with the sharp sword,
From his anger at the suitors who have devoured his goods
In the halls, and the fools did not honor you at all."   370
Odysseus of many wiles smiled at him and spoke:
"Take courage, as indeed this man has rescued you and saved you,
So that you may know in your heart and even tell someone else
How doing good deeds is much better than doing bad.
But come out of the hall and sit down outdoors in the court   375
Away from slaughter, you and the singer full of stories,
Till in the house I have myself taken care of what I must."
So he said, and the two of them went out of the hall.
They both sat down before the altar of great Zeus
And peered round on all sides, ever expecting slaughter.   380
Odysseus peered round his house lest some one of the men

Might still be concealed alive, avoiding black fate.
But he saw they had all fallen, in great numbers,
In blood and dust, like fish that the fishermen
Have drawn up on the curved beach out of the hoary sea   385
In a net that has many meshes; and all of them
Are heaped up on the sands longing for the waves of the sea;
But the sun in his shining is taking away their life;
So then the suitors were heaped up on one another.
Then Odysseus of many wiles addressed Telemachos: 390
"Telemachos, go and call the nurse Eurycleia for me,
So that I may tell her what it is my desire to tell."
So he said, and Telemachos obeyed his beloved father.
He shook the door and spoke to the nurse Eurycleia:
"Rise and come here, old woman, you who were born long ago,   395
And who watch over our serving women in the house.
Come, my father calls you, so he may tell you something."
So he said, and for her the speech was without a wing.
But she opened up the doors of the well-situated halls
And came on out. Telemachos went on ahead to lead.   400
Then she found Odysseus among the bodies of the slain,
Bespattered over with blood and with gore like a lion
Who goes along when he has eaten from an ox of the field,
And all his breast and also his cheeks on either side
Are bloody, and his face is terrible to look upon;   405
So was Odysseus bespattered, on his feet and his hands above.
Now when she saw the corpses and the unspeakable blood,
She made ready to exult, since she beheld a huge deed.
But Odysseus checked her and held her, eager as she was,
And speaking out to her, he uttered wingèd words: 410
"Old woman, rejoice in your heart; hold back and do not exult.
It is not holy to boast over men who have been slain.
The gods' fate has worsted these men, and their cruel deeds,
For they honored no one of the men upon the earth,
Either evil or noble, whoever encountered them.   415
And so in their recklessness they met a sorry fate.
Come now, and tell me about the women in the house,
Which ones dishonor me and which ones are innocent."
Then his beloved nurse Eurycleia spoke to him:
"All right, then, my child, I shall tell you the whole truth: 420
There are fifty women of yours inside the halls,
Serving women whom we have taught how to do their tasks,
How to card wool and how to endure servitude;
Of these, twelve in all have gone the way of shamelessness
And do not honor me or Penelope herself.   425
Telemachos grew up recently, and his mother has not
Allowed him to give orders to the serving women.
Well, now, let me go up to the glistening upper chamber

And tell your wife, in whom some god has induced sleep."
Odysseus of many wiles addressed her in answer: 430
"Do not wake her up yet. Go in and tell the women
To come, the ones who devised sorry deeds in the past."
So he said, and the old woman went on through the hall
To announce this to the women and to hasten their coming.
But he himself called Telemachos and the oxherd   435
And the swineherd to him and uttered wingèd words:
"Begin now to carry the corpses, and command the women;
And then have the tables and the beautiful armchairs
Cleaned off with water and with the porous sponges.
And when you have set in order the entire house,   440
Bring the serving women on out of the well-based hall
Between the round-room and the excellent fence of the courtyard,
And strike them with the long-edged swords until you have taken
The lives of all away, and they have forgotten the love
They had under the suitors, when they lay with them secretly."   445
So he said, and the women all came in a body together,
Lamenting dreadfully and shedding a swelling tear.
Then they first carried away the bodies of those who were dead
And they set them down under the portico of the well-fenced court,
Propping them on one another. Odysseus gave the orders,   450
Urging them on himself. They bore them out by constraint.
And then the tables and the beautiful armchairs
They cleaned off, with water and the porous sponges.
Then Telemachos, the oxherd, and the swineherd
Scraped down the floor of the stoutly built house with shovels.   455
Those servants kept carrying the scrapings and put them outdoors.
And when they had set in order the entire hall
They led the serving women out of the well-based hall
Between the round-room and the excellent fence of the court.
They cooped them in a narrow place, from which was no way to
    escape.   460
And sound-minded Telemachos began speaking to them:
"I would not take away with a clean death the lives
Of these women who have heaped reproaches on my head
And upon my mother, and have slept with the suitors."
So he said, and a cable from a dark blue-prowed ship   465
He threw round a pillar of the great round-room and tied it on,
Tightening it high up, so none could reach the ground with her feet.
As when either thrushes with their long wings or doves
Rush into a net that has been set in a thicket,
As they come in to roost, and a dreadful bed takes them in;   470
So they held their heads in a row, and about the necks
Of all there were nooses, that they might die most piteously.
They struggled a little with their feet, but not very long.
They brought Melanthios through the forecourt and the yard,

Cut off his nose and ears with the pitiless bronze,   475
And tore off his private parts for the dogs to eat raw,
And chopped off his hands and feet in their furious spirit.
Then, when they had washed off their hands and their feet,
They went into the house of Odysseus, and the work was done.
And he addressed Eurycleia, his beloved nurse: 480
"Bring brimstone, old woman, the cure of ills; bring me fire
So that I may purge the hall. You yourself go tell
Penelope to come here with her attendant women
And urge all the serving women in the house to come."
Then the dear nurse Eurycleia spoke to him: 485
"Yes, my child, you have said these things properly.
Come now, I shall bring you a tunic, a mantle and clothes
So your broad shoulders may not be covered with rags this way
As you stand in the halls. It would be a cause of blame."
Odysseus of many wiles addressed her in answer: 490
"First of all now let a fire be made for me in the halls."
So he said, and his dear nurse Eurycleia did not disobey.
Then she brought in fire and brimstone, and Odysseus
Thoroughly purged house and courtyard and hall.
The old woman went off through the fine halls of Odysseus   495
To announce this to the women and hasten their coming.
They came out of the hall bearing torches in their hands.
They gathered round Odysseus and greeted him in welcome;
They kissed him and embraced his shoulders and his head
And his hands. And a sweet longing took hold of him   500
For moaning and wailing; in his mind he recognized them all.

XXIII

The old woman went chuckling on into the upper chamber
To tell her dear mistress that her husband was inside.
Her knees moved quickly and her feet stumbled along.
She stood above her head and addressed a speech to her:
"Wake up, Penelope, dear child, so you may see   5
With your own eyes what you desire all your days.
Odysseus has come and reached home, though arriving late.
He has killed the bold suitors who disturbed his house
And devoured his property and oppressed his son."
And the prudent Penelope spoke to her: 10
"Dear mother, the gods have made you mad, who have the power
To make a man senseless, even one who is quite sensible;
And also they put the slack-minded on the way of prudence.
They have injured you, you were balanced in mind before.
Why do you mock me who have a heart full of grief,   15
To tell me these wild things and wake me out of the sweet

Sleep, which has bound me and shrouded my own eyelids?
Never have I had such a sleep from the time Odysseus
Went off to see evil Ilion, the unspeakable.
But come now, depart and go back into the hall.   20
For if anyone else of the women who belong to me
Had come to tell me this and waked me from sleep,
I myself should soon have sent her off hatefully
To go back again to the hall. In this, old age shall help you."
The beloved nurse Eurycleia then spoke to her: 25
"I am not mocking you, dear child, but it is true;
Odysseus has come and reached his home, as I say;
He is that stranger whom they all dishonored in the halls.
Telemachos has known for a long time he was within
But concealed out of prudence the purpose of his father   30
Till he might take revenge on the insolent men for their presumption."
So she said. The woman rejoiced, leaped out of her bed,
Embraced the old woman, and shed a tear from her eyelids.
Speaking out to her, she uttered wingèd words:
"Come now, dear mother, and tell me unerringly,   35
If he has truly arrived at his home, as you say,
How did he set his hands upon the shameless suitors,
A lone man, when they always stayed in a body inside?"
Then the beloved nurse Eurycleia spoke to her:
"I did not see or learn it, but I heard only the noise   40
Of men being killed. In a corner of the well-built chambers
We sat terrified, and the well-fitted doors held us
Until the time when your son Telemachos called me
From the hall. His father sent him out to call me.
Then I found Odysseus standing among the bodies   45
Of the slain. They surrounded him on the hard-stamped ground
Lying one upon the other. Your heart would have warmed to see him
Bespattered over with blood and with gore like a lion.
And now all of them are at the gates of the courtyard
In a heap, and he is purging the beautiful house,   50
Having kindled a great fire. He sent me to call you.
But come with me so you may both enter into gladness
In your own hearts, since you have suffered many ills.
And now this long desire is already fulfilled;
He has himself come alive to his hearth and found in the halls   55
Both you and his son. Though the suitors acted to him
Evilly, he has punished them all in his own house."
And then the prudent Penelope spoke to her:
"Dear mother, do not chuckle yet and make a great boast,
For you know how welcome in the halls he would appear to all,   60
And especially to me and the son that we both had.
But this story is not really so, the way that you tell it.
Some one of the immortals has killed the bold suitors,

Offended at their heart-hurting insolence and evil deeds,
For they honored no one of the men upon the earth, 65
Either evil or noble, whoever encountered them.
So they suffered evil through their recklessness. And Odysseus,
Far from Achaia lost his return, and is lost himself."
Then the beloved nurse Eurycleia answered her:
"My child, what sort of word has got past the bar of your teeth, 70
To say that your husband who is within at the hearth
Would never come home? Your heart is ever untrusting.
Well, then, I shall tell you another manifest token:
The scar a boar once dealt on him with a shining tusk
I noticed as I washed it. And I wanted to tell it 75
To you yourself. But he seized my mouth with his hands
And did not let me speak, in his resourcefulness of mind.
Come along, then, and I shall myself stake my own person.
If I deceive you, kill me with a most piteous death."
And then the prudent Penelope answered her: 80
"Dear mother, the counsels of the ever-living gods
Are hard for you to comprehend, though you are very shrewd.
In any case let us go to my son, so I may see
The suitors dead and also the man who has killed them."
When she had said this she went down from the upper chamber. Her heart
85
Pondered much whether to question her dear husband at a distance
Or to stand beside him and clasp and kiss his hands and head.
When she had gone on in and crossed the threshold of stone,
She sat across from Odysseus, in the gleam of the fire
By the other wall. And he sat against a tall pillar 90
Looking down, waiting to see if his goodly wife
Would say something to him when she saw him with her eyes.
But she sat a long time in silence, and stupor came over her heart.
With her gaze sometimes she looked him full in the face,
And sometimes did not know him for the vile clothes he had on his skin.
95
Telemachos rebuked her and spoke out to her directly:
"My mother, cruel mother, you have a heart that is harsh!
Why do you turn from my father so and do not sit
Beside him and ply him with speeches and question him?
No other woman, indeed, with a resisting heart 100
Would so stand off from the husband who had suffered many ills
And come back for her in the twentieth year to his fatherland.
Always the heart in you is harder than a stone."
And then the prudent Penelope spoke to him:
"My child, the heart within my breast is amazed, 105
And I am not at all able to speak a word or to ask
Or to look him in the face directly. If really
He is Odysseus and he has arrived home, we two

Shall know one another, and more fully. There are signs
For us that the two of us know, hidden from others."   110
So she said, and godly Odysseus, who had endured much, smiled.
At once he uttered wingèd words to Telemachos:
"Telemachos, permit your mother to test me out
Within the halls. She shall quickly discern even better.
Now, because I am dirty and have bad clothes on my skin,   115
She does not respect me and does not yet say I am he.
But let us consider how it shall come out for the best.
For whosoever kills a single man in the district,
Though there be not many advocates for man thereafter,
He flees, abandoning his kinsmen and fatherland.   120
And we have killed the mainstay of the city, the very best
Of the youth in Ithaca. I bid you to consider this."
Then sound-minded Telemachos answered him:
"Look to these matters yourself, dear father. They say
Your counsel is the best among men, nor could any   125
Other man among mortal men contend with you.
We shall follow along with you eagerly; I do not think
We should lack any courage so far as we do have power."
Odysseus of many wiles addressed him in answer:
"Well then, I shall tell you what seems to me to be best,   130
First of all wash yourselves and put tunics on,
And order the serving women in the halls to take their clothes.
Then let the godly singer, holding his clear-toned lyre,
Be the leader for us in a reveling dance,
So a listener outside would think this was a wedding,   135
One who walked on the road, or one of those who dwell round about;
So that a wide report about the slaughter of the suitors
Shall not first get through the town, before we have gone outside
To our own well-wooded land. And then afterward
We may think of any advantage the Olympian may bestow."   140
So he said, and they listened closely and did not disobey.
And first they washed themselves off and put on tunics,
And the women adorned themselves, and the godly singer took
The hollow lyre and aroused the desire among them
For sweet melody and also for excellent dancing.   145
The great house about them resounded at the feet
Of men frolicking and of women with lovely gowns.
And this is what a man who heard them outside the house would say:
"Someone indeed must have married the much-wooed queen.
The cruel woman, she did not hold out for her wedded husband   150
And tend the great house steadfastly till he arrived."
So a man would say: they did not know what had been done.
But the housekeeper Eurynome washed great-hearted Odysseus
Inside his own house and anointed him with olive oil.
She put a lovely mantle and a tunic over him.   155

Then Athene poured much beauty upon his head,
Made him bigger to look at and stouter, and made his hair
Flow in curls upon his head like the hyacinth flower.
As when some man overlays gold upon silver,
A skilled man whom Hephaistos and Pallas Athene have taught   160
Art of all kinds, and he turns out graceful handiwork;
So she poured grace upon his head and his shoulders.
He stepped from the bathtub in form like the immortal gods,
And he sat back down on the chair from which he had risen,
Across from his wife, and he addressed a speech to her: 165
"Strange woman, those who have their home on Olympos put in you
A heart implacable beyond that of womankind.
No other woman, indeed, with a resisting heart
Would so stand off from the husband who had suffered many ills
And come back for her in the twentieth year to his fatherland.   170
Come now, old mother, spread me a bed, so that I
May lie down alone, for the heart in this woman's breast is iron."
And then the prudent Penelope answered him:
"Strange man, I do not at all exalt myself or slight you,
Nor am I too much amazed. I know well the sort of man you were   175
When you went off from Ithaca on the long-oared ship.
Come now, Eurycleia, spread for him the thick bed
Outside the well-based bedroom which the man made himself.
Put the thick bed out for him there and throw bedding on,
Blankets and mantles and the glistening coverlets."   180
So she said, testing her husband. But Odysseus
Grew angry and spoke to his wife, who had a sense of devotion:
"My wife, this is a heart-hurting speech you have made.
Who has put my bed elsewhere? That would be hard
Even for one very skilled, unless a god came in person,   185
And easily, if he wished, might put it in another place.
No mortal man alive, not even one in his vigor,
Could dislodge it easily, since a great token was made
In the well-wrought bed. I worked on it, and nobody else.
The long-leaved bush of a wild olive grew inside the yard   190
Flourishing in bloom. It was thick as a pillar is.
So I built the bedroom round it till I finished it
With close-fitted stones and roofed it well up above.
And I put portals on it, jointed and closely fitted.
Then I cut off the crown of the long-leaved wild olive;   195
Chopping the stump from the root up, I hewed it with the bronze ax
Well and skillfully, and straightened it with a line.
When I had fashioned the bedpost, I bored it all with an auger.
Starting with that, I hewed out a bed till I finished it,
Adorning it with gold and silver and ivory.   200
And I stretched over it an oxhide thong shining with purple.
So I declare this token to you. I do not know at all

Whether the bed is still steadfast, wife, or already
Some man has put it elsewhere, cutting the olive base beneath."
So he said, and her knees and her own heart went slack   205
As she recognized the steadfast tokens Odysseus had shown to her.
Then she wept, ran straight over, and threw her arms
About the neck of Odysseus, kissed his head and spoke:
"Do not scowl at me, Odysseus, since in everything else
You have been the wisest of men. The gods have given us woe   210
Who begrudged it to us that, staying with one another,
We should enjoy our vigor and reach the threshold of age.
But be not angry at me now for this, and do not resent
That I did not embrace you this way when I saw you first,
For always the spirit in my precious heart went cold   215
Lest someone among mortals come and deceive me
With speeches. Many men think up evil devices.
Nor would Argive Helen, who was a child of Zeus,
Have lain in love and in bed with an alien man
If she had known that the warlike sons of the Achaians   220
Were to bring her back home to her dear fatherland.
Yes, a god stirred her up to do a sorry deed.
She did not lay up in her heart beforehand that woeful
Madness, out of which, from the first, sorrow reached us too.
But now, since already you have declared very plain tokens   225
About our bed, which no other mortal has seen,
But you and I alone, and one single handmaiden,
Aktoris, whom my father gave me when I came here,
She who tended for us the doors of the stout bedchamber;
Now you have convinced my heart, harsh indeed though it be."   230
So she said. In him rose a still greater desire for wailing.
He wept, holding his pleasing wife, who had a sense of devotion.
As when land appears welcome to men who are swimming,
Whose well-made ship Poseidon has dashed in the ocean
As it was driven on by wind and a solid wave,   235
And few have escaped from the hoary sea onto the mainland
By swimming, and much brine has caked upon their skin,
And they walk up on land glad, having fled misfortune,
So welcome was her husband to her as she looked upon him.
In no way could she quite let her white arms go from his neck,   240
And rosy-fingered Dawn would have appeared while they wept
If the bright-eyed goddess Athene had not had another thought.
She held the night long on its course, and then kept
The golden-throned Dawn upon Oceanos, and did not allow her
To yoke her swift-footed horses that bear light to men,   245
Lampos and Phaethon, who are the colts that bring the dawn.
Then Odysseus of many wiles spoke to his wife:
"My wife, we have not yet come to the end of all
Our trials, but a measureless labor yet remains,

A long and a hard one that I must wholly carry out.					250
So did the soul of Tiresias prophesy to me
On the day when I went down into the house of Hades
Seeking a return for my companions and myself.
But come, let us go to bed, my wife, so that now
We may lie down and take pleasure beneath sweet sleep."					255
And then the prudent Penelope addressed him:
"The bed shall be for you indeed whenever you wish
In your heart, since the gods have made you to arrive
At your well-established home and your fatherland.
But since you have thought of it and a god has put it in your heart,					260
Come tell me of the trial, since hereafter I think,
I too shall hear of it; and it is no worse for me to learn of it at once."
Then Odysseus of many wiles addressed her in answer:
"Strange woman, why do you strongly urge me and bid me to speak?
Well, I will tell it myself and shall not conceal it.					265
But your heart shall not rejoice, nor do I myself
Rejoice, since he ordered me to visit many towns
Of mortals, holding in my hands a well-fitted oar,
Till the time I come unto those who do not know
The sea and do not eat a food that has been mixed with salt,					270
And where they do not know about ships with purple cheeks
Or about well-fitted oars that are the wings for ships.
He told me a very clear token; I shall not conceal it:
When another wayfarer has confronted me
And said I had a winnowing fan on my gleaming shoulder,					275
He bade me to fix my oar then into the earth
And offer fine sacrifices to lord Poseidon,
A ram, a bull, and a boar, the mounter of sows,
Then to go back home and sacrifice sacred hecatombs
To the immortal gods who possess broad heaven,					280
To all of them in order. Far from the sea will death come
Ever so gently, to my person, and slay me
Worn out with sleek old age. And the people about me
Will be happy. He told me all this would come to pass."
And then the prudent Penelope spoke to him:					285
"If the gods do bring a better old age to pass,
Then there is hope for you there will be an escape from evils."
And so they said such things to one another.
Meanwhile Eurynome and the nurse prepared the bed
With soft bedclothing, underneath shining torches.					290
And when they had made haste and strewn the thick bed,
The old woman went back into the house to lie down
And Eurynome, servant of the chamber, conducted them
With a torch in her hand as they went on to bed.
She led to the bedroom and went away again. They then					295
Arrived happily at the site of their old bed.

But Telemachos, the oxherd, and the swineherd
Stopped the men's feet from dancing and stopped the women too,
And went to bed themselves through the shadowy halls.
The two, when they had taken their pleasure of delightful love,   300
Enjoyed themselves with stories, talking to one another:
She, the godly woman, told how much she endured in the halls
To look upon the destructive throng of the suitors
Who on her account had slaughtered oxen and goodly sheep
In numbers, and much wine had been drawn off from the jars.   305
And Zeus-born Odysseus told of the many cares he had brought
Upon men, and the many he had suffered himself in his woe.
He told them all, and she enjoyed hearing, nor did sleep
Fall upon her eyelids before he had told it all.
He began how first he had conquered the Cicones and then   310
Had gone to the fertile land of the Lotus-eating men,
And all the Cyclops did, and how he made him pay the penalty
For the valiant companions he ate and did not pity.
And how he got to Aeolos who at first kindly received him
And sent him on. But it was not yet his lot to reach   315
His dear fatherland; but a storm snatched him up again
And bore him heavily groaning on the fish-laden ocean.
And he told how he reached Lestrygonian Telepylos,
Whose men destroyed his ships and all his well-greaved companions.
Odysseus alone got away from them with his black ship.   320
And he told about Circe's wiles and resourcefulness,
And how he went down to the dank dwelling of Hades
So he might consult the soul of Theban Tiresias
In a ship with many oarlocks and saw all his companions
And the mother who bore him and reared him when he was small,   325
And how he listened to the voice of the chanting Sirens,
And how he reached the Wandering Rocks and dread Charybdis
And Scylla, which men have never yet escaped unharmed.
And how his companions slew the oxen of the Sun,
And how high-thundering Zeus struck the swift ship   330
With a smoldering thunderbolt, and his noble companions died
All together, but he himself escaped the evil fates.
And how he reached the island Ogygia and the nymph Calypso.
She held him back, longing for him to be her husband
In the hollow caves, and she nourished him and said   335
She would make him immortal and ageless all his days,
But she never persuaded the heart within his breast.
And he told how, having suffered much, he came to the Phaeacians
Who honored him heartily the way they would a god
And conducted him in a ship to his dear fatherland,   340
Giving him bronze and gold and clothing in abundance.
This was the last tale he told, when sweet, limb-loosing sleep
Came upon him, releasing the cares of his heart.

Then the bright-eyed goddess Athene had another thought.
When she had supposed in her heart that Odysseus   345
Had taken pleasure with his wife of the bed and of sleep,
At once from Oceanos she roused the early born one
Of the golden throne to bring light to men. Odysseus
Rose from his soft bed and laid a charge on his wife:
"My wife, we are already glutted, the two of us,   350
With many trials. Here you wept for my troublesome return,
But, while I was wanting to go, Zeus and the other gods
Held me back in pains from my own fatherland.
Now since we have arrived at the bed of much desire,
Give heed to the goods which are mine in the halls.   355
As for the sheep of mine the presumptuous suitors pillaged,
Many others I shall myself plunder back; still others the Achaians
Shall give me until they have filled up all the folds.
And then I shall go on myself to the well-wooded land
To see my noble father, who is heavily grieved for me.   360
And, my wife, I charge you this, prudent as you are:
At once at the rising of the sun the report will travel
About the suitors whom I slaughtered in the halls.
Go into the upper chamber with your serving women
And sit, and do not look at anyone or ask any question."   365
He spoke, and put the lovely armor about his shoulders.
He roused Telemachos, the oxherd, and the swineherd
And ordered them all to take the war gear in their hands.
They did not disobey, but armed themselves in bronze.
They opened the doors and went out. Odysseus led.   370
Light was on the earth already, and Athene hid them
In night and led them rapidly out of the city.

XXIV

And Hermes of Cyllene summoned forth the souls
Of the suitors, and he held in his hand the lovely gold wand
With which he enchants the eyes of those men he wishes,
And others he wakens even when they are asleep.
He stirred them with it and drove them. They followed squeaking,   5
As when bats in the corner of a prodigious cave
Squeak as they fly when one of them falls away
From the cluster on the rock where they cling to one another;
So they squeaked as they went together. And Hermes,
The deliverer, led them on along the dank ways.   10
They went past the streams of Oceanos, past the White Rock;
Past the gates of the Sun also, and the district of dreams
Did they go. And at once they reached the asphodel meadow
Where the souls dwell, phantoms of those who are worn out.

They came upon the soul of Achilles, son of Peleus,   15
The soul of Patroclos and of excellent Antilochos,
And of Ajax, who was the finest in body and form
Of all the Danaans, after the excellent son of Peleus.
So they thronged around that man, and right close to them
The soul of Agamemnon came on, the son of Atreus,   20
Grieving. And the others drew in together, all those
Who had died with him and met their fate in Aigisthos' house.
The soul of the son of Peleus spoke out to him first:
"Son of Atreus, we thought you were dear beyond other heroes
To Zeus who hurls the thunderbolt, for all your days,   25
Because you were lord over many valiant men
In the land of the Trojans where we Achaians suffered pains.
And yet the destructive fate that no one who is born
Can avoid was destined to come early upon you as well.
Would that when you were enjoying the honor of which you were
          master   30
In the land of the Trojans, you had met death and destiny!
Then all the Achaians would have made you a funeral mound
And you would have won great glory for your son hereafter.
As it is, you were fated to be caught in a grievous death."
Then the soul of the son of Atreus spoke to him: 35
"Blessed are you, son of Peleus, godlike Achilles,
You who died in Troy far from Argos. Around you, others,
The best sons of the Achaians and of the Trojans were killed
Contending over you. You in a whirling cloud of dust
Lay great and greatly fallen, having forgotten horsemanship.   40
And we contended the whole day. Nor would we at all
Have stopped the battle if Zeus had not stopped it with a storm.
But when we had brought you up on the ships out of battle,
We set you down upon a bier and cleaned off your lovely skin
With warm water and oil, and the Danaans shed   45
Many hot tears over you and sheared off their hair.
Your mother came from the sea with the deathless girls of the sea
When she heard the report. A prodigious cry arose
Over the ocean, and a trembling seized all the Achaians,
And they would have sprung up and gone to the hollow ships   50
If a man had not restrained them who knew many ancient matters,
Nestor, whose advice had also before seemed best.
With good intent he spoke out to them and addressed them:
"Hold back, Argives; do not flee, young Achaians. His mother
This is, here from the sea with the deathless girls of the sea;   55
She has come to be beside her son who has died."
So he said, and the great-hearted Achaians were held back from flight.
About you stood the daughters of the old man of the sea,
Wailing piteously; they clothed you in ambrosial garments.
All the nine Muses, changing off with lovely voice,   60

Sang a dirge. There you would have seen none of the Argives
Who did not weep, so stirring was the clear Muses' song.
Seventeen days for you, and also the nights alike,
Did we lament, both immortal gods and mortal men.
On the eighteenth we gave you to the fire and about you   65
Killed many fat sheep and cattle with crumpled horns.
You were burned in the clothes of the gods and with much oil
And with sweet honey. Many of the Achaian warriors
Marched around the fire in armor while you were being burned,
Foot soldiers and horsemen, and a great din arose.   70
But when the flame of Hephaistos had made an end of you,
At the dawn, Achilles, we gathered your white bones
In unmixed wine and in oil. And your mother gave
A golden two-handled jar. She said it was a gift
Of Dionysos, the work of highly renowned Hephaistos.   75
So in it, glorious Achilles, your white bones lie,
Mingled with those of dead Patroklos, Menoitios' son;
Apart are those of Antilochos, whom you honored
Above all your other companions after the dead Patroklos.
And then we, the sacred army of Argive spearmen, heaped   80
A great and excellent funeral mound up over them
On a strand jutting forward on the broad Hellespont,
So that it might be seen far over the ocean by men,
Both those who are born now and those who shall be hereafter.
And your mother asked the gods for beautiful prizes   85
And set them up for a contest amid the best of the Achaians.
Already you have been present at the burial of many men,
Of warriors; when, because a king has passed away,
The young men gird themselves and prepare for the prizes.
But you would have marveled in your heart most to see those,   90
The beautiful prizes that the goddess set up for you,
Thetis [1] of the silver foot. You were very dear to the gods.
So you did not lose your name even when you died, Achilles.
There shall be noble renown for you always among all men.
But what pleasure did I have, when I had wound up the war?   95
For Zeus planned woeful destruction for me on my return
At the hands of Aigisthos and my accursèd wife."
And so they said such things to one another.
The Runner, the slayer of Argos, came up close to them,
Leading the souls of the suitors subdued by Odysseus.   100
The two, marveling, went straight up when they saw them.
The soul of Agamemnon, son of Atreus, recognized
The dear son of Melaneos, renowned Amphimedon,
For he was a guest friend of his who dwelt in Ithaca.
The soul of the son of Atreus spoke out to him first: 105

---

1. A sea nymph and mother of Achilles.

"Amphimedon, what did you suffer to go under the gloomy earth,
All you chosen men of the same age? Not otherwise
Would someone pick out and gather the best men in a city.
Was it that Poseidon overcame you in your ships
By raising up oppressive winds and giant waves,   110
Or did hostile men ravage you upon the mainland
As you were cutting off their cattle and fine flocks of sheep,
Or as they were fighting on behalf of their city and women?
Tell me what I ask—I declare I am your guest friend.
Do you not remember when I came there to your house,   115
Urging Odysseus on to come along to Ilion
With godlike Menelaos upon the well-timbered ships?
An entire month we spent crossing the whole broad ocean
Since we could scarcely persuade Odysseus, the sacker of cities."
And then the soul of Amphimedon addressed him: 120
"Glorious son of Atreus, Zeus-nourished Agamemnon,
Lord of men, I do remember all the things you say,
And I shall tell you everything truthfully and well,
The evil end of our death, the way it came about.
We wooed the wife of Odysseus, who was gone so long;   125
She neither refused the hateful wedding nor carried it out,
Contriving for us death and black destiny;
And she devised in her mind this other deceit:
She set a great loom in the halls, and on it she wove
A large and delicate fabric. She told us at once: 130
'Young men, my suitors, since godlike Odysseus is dead,
Wait, though you are eager for this marriage of mine, till I finish
This robe, so that the yarn will not waste in vain,
The burial sheet of hero Laertes for the time
When the ruinous fate of long-sorrowful death seizes him,   135
Lest one of the Achaian women in the district blame me
If he who had won so much lay without covering.'
So she said, and the bold heart was persuaded within us.
Then every day she kept weaving there on the great loom,
And in the nights she undid it when she had the torches set up.   140
So three years she fooled the Achaians and persuaded them.
But when the fourth year came and the seasons came on
Of the waning months and many days came to an end,
Right then one of the women who perceived it clearly told it.
And we happened upon her undoing the shining fabric.   145
Then she finished it, though unwilling and under duress.
And when, having woven the great fabric and washed it,
She showed forth the robe that resembled the sun or the moon,
Just then some evil god led Odysseus from someplace
To the verge of the field where the swineherd had his home.   150
There, too, the beloved son of Odysseus had come
When he went from sandy Pylos in his black ship.

The two of them, contriving an evil death for the suitors,
Had arrived at the city of great renown. Odysseus
Was last, and Telemachos led the way ahead of them. 155
The swineherd brought the man, who wore vile clothes on his skin
And resembled a wretched beggar who was an old man
Walking with a staff. He had sorry clothes on his skin.
None of us could recognize that it was he
When he appeared suddenly, not even those who were older, 160
But we rebuked him with missiles and evil speeches.
Still, he held out all the while with enduring heart
When he was being beaten and rebuked in his own halls.
But when the purpose of aegis-bearing Zeus aroused him
He took up the beautiful weapons with Telemachos 165
And placed them in the chamber and locked the fastenings,
And resourcefully he gave the order to his wife
To set before the suitors the bow and the gray iron,
A contest and start of slaughter for us in our dread fate.
No one of us was able to stretch out the string 170
Of the mighty bow, for we were too weak by far.
But when the great bow came into Odysseus' hands,
Then all of us made a common outcry with speeches,
Not to give him the bow, however much he might say.
Telemachos alone urged him on and gave him the order. 175
Then godly Odysseus, who had endured much, took it in his hand,
Easily strung the bow and shot through the iron.
He went and stood on the threshold, poured the swift arrows out,
Peering round terribly, and hit King Antinoos.
And then on the others he let the groan-carrying darts fly, 180
Taking aim straight across. And they fell thick and fast.
It was known then that one of the gods was their helper for them.
For at once they went on through the house in their rage
And killed them one after another. A sad groaning
Rose as their heads were struck. The whole ground ran with blood. 185
Agamemnon, this is the way we perished, we whose bodies
Are still lying uncared for now in the halls of Odysseus.
For the dear ones in the home of each man do not know it yet,
Those who, when they have washed the black gore from the wounds,
May lay us out weeping. For that is the prize of the dead." 190
Then the soul of the son of Atreus spoke out to him:
"Blessed son of Laertes, Odysseus of many wiles,
Truly you have won a wife of great excellence.
How good was the mind of blameless Penelope,
Daughter of Icarios, who remembered Odysseus well, 195
Her wedded husband! And so the fame of her excellence
Shall never die. The immortals shall make for men on the earth
A delightful song about constant Penelope.

Not so did the daughter of Tyndareus[2] devise her evil deeds,
Who killed her wedded husband; and a hateful song shall there be   200
Among men, and she will bestow a harsh reputation
On womankind, even on one who is good in what she does."
And so they said such things to one another,
Standing in the halls of Hades under the depths of the earth.
The others, when they had gone out of the city, quickly reached   205
The fine, well-worked field of Laertes that Laertes had once
Acquired for himself when he had toiled very hard.
There his home was. And all around it a shed ran
In which the bondservants who did the tasks at his pleasure,
Took their meals and sat down and went to sleep.   210
In it there was an old Sicilian woman, who carefully
Attended to the old man in the field far from the city.
There Odysseus addressed a speech to his servants and his son:
"Come on inside of the well-built house now, and at once
Make a sacrifice of the best of the swine for dinner   215
And I shall test my own father out for myself,
Whether he recognizes me and perceives me with his eyes,
Or does not know me since I have been away for a long time."
When he had said this, he gave the arms of war to the servants.
They went then swiftly into the house. But Odysseus   220
Went close to the fruitful vineyard to try him out.
As he entered the large orchard he did not find Dolios
Or any of the servants or their sons. They were gone off
Gathering wall-stones that would serve as a fence
For the vineyard. And the old man led the way for them.   225
He found his father alone in the well-laid vineyard,
Digging around a plant. He had a dirty tunic on,
A sorry patched one. And greaves of oxhide were bound
In patches on his calves to keep him from getting scratched.
He had gloves on his hands on account of brambles. On his head   230
He was wearing a goatskin cap, cherishing his grief.
When godly Odysseus, who had endured much, perceived the man
Worn down by age and with a great grief in his mind,
He stood under a stately pear tree and shed a tear,
And then he turned over in his mind and in his heart   235
Whether to kiss and embrace his father and tell the details
Of how he had come and arrived at his fatherland
Or should first ask him for details and test him out.
To him as he thought about it this seemed to be better:
To test him out at first with words of bantering.   240
With this in mind, Odysseus went directly to him.
The man was holding his head down and digging around the plant.

2. Clytemnestra.

Standing beside him, his illustrious son spoke out:
"Old man, no lack of skill is yours as you tend
The orchard, but good care is yours. Nothing at all,   245
No plant, no fig tree, no vine, no wild olive tree,
No pear tree, no leek bed in the garden is without your care.
I shall tell you something else, and do not feel rage in your heart;
Your person is not well cared for, but along with woeful old age
You have a foul squalor and are wearing sorry clothes.   250
Not for idleness, surely, does your master not take care of you;
And nothing about your appearance conforms to the slave
In form or in stature. You look like a man who is king.
You look like such a man, who, when he has washed and eaten,
Should sleep softly. For this is the just way of old men.   255
Come, tell me this, and speak out truthfully:
Of whom among men are you slave? Whose orchard do you tend?
Tell me this really, so I may know it well,
If this place we reach is truly Ithaca, as this man
Has told me who met me just now when I was coming here.   260
He is not very clever, for he did not venture to tell
The details or to listen to my speech when I inquired
About my guest friend, whether he still lives and exists
Or is already dead and in the halls of Hades.
I shall speak out to you; understand and hear me well.   265
I once entertained a man in my dear fatherland
When he came to our place, and no other mortal yet
Among alien strangers came dearer to my house.
He declared his descent was from Ithaca, and he said
His father was Laertes, son of Arkesios.   270
I led him into my house and entertained him well,
Befriending him kindly, as there was much in my home,
And I provided him with the gifts of a guest, fitting ones;
First I gave him seven talents of well-wrought gold,
And I gave him a mixing bowl all of silver decked with flowers,   275
Twelve mantles of single fold, and as many coverlets,
And as many lovely robes, and as many tunics besides,
And in addition four shapely women who were versed
In excellent tasks, the ones he wished to pick out himself."
Then his father answered him, shedding a tear: 280
"Stranger, you have indeed come to the land you ask about;
But insolent and reckless are the men who possess her.
In vain you bestowed these gifts, if you gave countless ones.
But if you had found him alive in the land of Ithaca
He would have requited you well with gifts before sending you back,   285
With good hospitality, which is right toward the man who begins it.
But come now, tell me this, and speak out truthfully:
How many years ago is it you entertained that man,
Your hapless guest, my son, if he ever existed,

That ill-fated man? Perhaps far from his friends and his fatherland   290
The fish in the ocean have devoured him, or on the mainland
He has become the prey of wild beasts and birds. His mother
And father, we who had him, did not lay him out and mourn,
Nor did his richly dowered wife, the constant Penelope,
Wail for her husband on his bier and close his eyes,   295
As it is seemly to do. For that is the prize of the dead.
And tell me this really, so I may know it well:
What men are you from? Where are your city and parents?
Where indeed does the swift ship stand that brought you here
And your godlike companions? Or did you come as a passenger   300
On the ship of others who put you ashore and went away?"
Odysseus of many wiles addressed him in answer:
"All right, I shall tell you everything truthfully:
I am from Alybas, where I live in my famous halls.
I am the son of Lord Apheidas, the son of Polypemon.   305
My own name is Eperitos. But some god drove me astray
To come here from Sicania against my will.
My ship is moored yonder by the fields apart from the city,
But with regard to Odysseus, this is the fifth year
From the time he went away and left my fatherland,   310
That ill-fated man. Still, as he went, he had birds of good omen
On the right, in which I rejoiced as I sent him off.
And he rejoiced as he went. The hearts in us hoped yet
To exchange hospitality and give glorious gifts."
So he said, and a black cloud of grief covered the other.   315
He picked up the ashen dust in both of his hands
And heavily moaning poured it over his gray head.
The other's heart was aroused, and a piercing throb had already
Struck through his nostrils when he saw his dear father.
He leaped up, kissed, and embraced him, and spoke to him: 320
"Here I am, father, the very man you ask about;
I have come in the twentieth year to my fatherland.
But hold off from weeping and tearful lamentation.
I shall tell you right out; nevertheless, we must hurry.
I have slain the suitors within our own halls,   325
Punishing their heart-hurting injury and evil deeds."
And then Laertes answered and spoke out to him:
"If you are my son Odysseus who have arrived here,
Tell me now some very plain sign, so I may be convinced."
Odysseus of many wiles spoke to him in answer: 330
"First of all, take notice with your eyes of this scar
That a boar inflicted on me with shining tusk on Parnassos
When I had gone there. You and my queenly mother sent me
To my mother's dear father Autolycos, so I might get
Gifts that when he came here he promised me with a nod.   335
Come now, and in the well-laid vineyard I shall also tell you

The trees that you gave me once, and I asked you for each,
Myself as a child, following you through the yard. We went on
Through these very ones, and you named them and told me of each.
You gave me thirteen pear trees and ten apple trees   340
And forty fig trees. You named the vine rows the same way
To give me fifty of them. And throughout the grape season
Each was fruitful in turn. And there all sorts of clusters are on them
Whenever the seasons of Zeus weigh them down from above."
So he said. The man's knees and his own heart went slack   345
When he recognized the sure tokens Odysseus had shown him.
He threw his arms round his dear son and went faint for breath
As godly Odysseus, who had endured much, grasped him.
But when he caught his breath and the spirit was brought to his mind,
He answered him right away and addressed him with a speech: 350
"Father Zeus, you gods are still on tall Olympos, if truly
The suitors have paid for their reckless insolence.
But now I dreadfully fear in my mind that the Ithacans
Will soon all come against us here and send messengers
Everywhere to the cities of the Cephallenians."   355
Odysseus of many wiles answered him and spoke:
"Take courage, and do not give heed to this in your mind.
But let us go to the house that lies close to the orchard.
For there did I send Telemachos forth, and the oxherd
And the swineherd, to prepare a meal as soon as they could."   360
As they said this the two went on to the lovely house.
There, when they had reached the well-situated home,
They found Telemachos, the oxherd, and the swineherd
Carving abundant meat and mixing the sparkling wine.
Meanwhile the Sicilian servant woman in his house   365
Washed Laertes and anointed him with olive oil,
And she put a lovely mantle round him. Then Athene stood near
And filled out the limbs of the shepherd of the people.
She made him taller than before and stouter to look upon.
He stepped out of the bathtub. His dear son was amazed at him;   370
As he saw him, the man looked like the immortal gods.
Then addressing him, he uttered wingèd words:
"My father, surely one of the ever-living gods
Has made you better to look on in form and stature."
Then sound-minded Laertes said to him in reply: 375
"Father Zeus and Athene and Apollo, would that I were just the way
As I was when I took Nerikos, the well-built citadel,
A headland on the shore, when I ruled the Cephallenians;
That way I might have been yesterday in our own halls,
Bearing armor on my shoulders, to stand by and ward off   380
The suitors. So in the halls I would have loosed the knees
Of many of them. In your mind you would have rejoiced."
And so such things did they say to one another.

But when the others had ceased from work and prepared dinner
They sat down one after another in seats and in armchairs,   385
Then they laid their hands on the meal. The old man Dolios
Came near, and with him were the sons of the old man,
Wearied from their tasks, since their mother had gone and called them,
The old Sicilian woman who fed them and carefully
Tended to that old man, since old age had taken hold of him.   390
And then, when they had seen Odysseus and noticed him
In their hearts, they stood in the halls amazed. And Odysseus
Addressed them with soothing speeches and spoke to them:
"Old man, sit down to eat; fully forget your wonder,
For we have waited a long time in the halls in desire   395
Of laying our hands on the bread, always expecting you."
So he said, and Dolios came straight to him, stretching forth
Both his hands. He took Odysseus' hand and kissed his wrist.
And speaking out to him, he uttered wingèd words:
"My friend, since you have returned to us who longed for that   400
But never thought to see it—the very gods themselves brought you—
Good health and great welcome! May the gods grant you wealth!
And tell me this truly, so I may know it well:
Does the prudent Penelope already clearly know
You have returned here, or shall we send her a messenger?"   405
Odysseus of many wiles addressed him in answer:
"Old man, she knows already. Why need you bother about this?"
So he said, and the other sat down again on the polished stool
And the sons of Dolios around glorious Odysseus
Greeted him with speeches the same way and clasped his hands.   410
They sat down one after another beside their father Dolios.
And so they busied themselves with a meal in the halls.
Now the messenger Rumor went everywhere fast through the town
Declaring the suitors' hateful death and destiny.
When all had heard it, they strayed in from every side   415
With murmur and groaning in front of Odysseus' halls.
They carried their corpses, each from his house and buried them.
They sent those from other cities, each one to his home,
Putting them upon swift ships for the fishermen to bring them.
Then they went in a body to the places of assembly, grieving in
   heart.   420
And when they were gathered and had come together,
Eupeithes stood up among them and spoke to them,
As unforgettable grief lay on his mind for his son
Antinoos, the first one whom godly Odysseus had slain.
Shedding tears for him, he spoke out and made a speech: 425
"Friends, this man has planned a huge deed against the Achaians.
Some men he led away in ships, many noblemen,
And he lost the hollow ships, and he lost the men.
Others he killed when he came, the best Cephallenians by far.

Come now, before this man may get quickly to Pylos   430
Or to godly Elis where the Epeians rule;
Let us go. Or else hereafter we shall always be disgraced.
These deeds are a shame to learn about, even for future men;
Unless we avenge us on the murderers of our kinsmen and sons.
To my mind at least it would not then be sweet to live,   435
But I would die as soon as I could and be among the dead.
Come then, lest those men get a start on us crossing the sea."
So he said, shedding a tear. Pity seized all the Achaians.
Medon and the divine singer came up close to them
Out of the halls of Odysseus, since sleep had let them go.   440
They stood in their midst. Amazement seized every man.
Then Medon, who was sound in knowledge, spoke out to them:
"Listen to me now, Ithacans. Odysseus has not
Planned these deeds against the will of the deathless gods.
I myself saw an immortal god who stood close beside   445
Odysseus and resembled Mentor in every way.
Now the deathless god appeared in front of Odysseus
Encouraging him, and now he aroused the suitors
And rushed on through the hall. They fell down one upon the other."
So he said, and sallow fear got hold of all of them.   450
Then the old hero Halitherses spoke to them,
The son of Mastor; he alone saw both before and after.
With good intent he spoke out and addressed them:
"Hear me now, Ithacans, in what I am to say:
My friends, these deeds have come about through your wickedness.   455
You did not obey me or Mentor, shepherd of the people,
To make your sons cease from their stupidities.
They did a huge deed in their evil recklessness,
Wasting away the goods and dishonoring the wife
Of an excellent man. They thought he would come no more.   460
And now, so be it. Obey me in what I say,
And let us not go, so no one may find self-inflicted pain."
So he said, but they rushed on with a great war cry,
More than half of them, while the others stayed in a body there,
For his speech did not please their minds, but they were persuaded 465
By Eupeithes.[3] And then at once they ran on for their armor.
When they had put the glittering bronze round their skin
They gathered in a body before the town with a broad dancing-place.
Eupeithes was the leader for their foolishness.
He thought he would avenge his son's murder, but he was not   470
Destined to get back; there he was to meet his fate.
Then Athene spoke out to Zeus, the son of Cronos:
"Our father, son of Cronos, highest of all rulers,
Tell me when I ask, what plan of yours is concealed here?

---

3. The name means "good persuader."

Will you fashion further an evil war and dread battle,   475
Or will you establish friendship between both sides?"
And cloud-gathering Zeus addressed her in answer:
"My child, why do you ask me and question me about this?"
Why did you not think out this idea by yourself,
That Odysseus might indeed take vengeance on them when he
  came?   480
Do as you wish, but I will tell you what seems fitting.
Since godly Odysseus has done vengeance on the suitors,
Let them solemnize an oath, that he may always reign.
And let us bring about oblivion for the murder
Of their sons and kinsmen. Let them love one another   485
As before, and let there be abundant wealth and peace."
When he said this, he aroused Athene, who was eager before.
She went down in a rush from the summits of Olympos.
And when the men had taken their fill of mind-honeying food,
Godly Odysseus, who had suffered much, began speaking to them: 490
"Let someone go out and see lest they are coming close."
So he said, and the son of Dolios went out as he bid.
He went and stood on the threshold and saw them all close.
Right away he addressed wingèd words to Odysseus:
"Here they are nearby. Let us quickly arm ourselves!"   495
So he said. They rose up and got their armor on,
Four including Odysseus, and the six sons of Dolios,
And among them Laertes and Dolios put armor on,
Gray though they were, warriors by necessity.
And when they had put the glittering bronze round their skin,   500
They opened the doors and went out; Odysseus led.
Athene, daughter of Zeus, came up close to them,
Likening herself to Mentor in form and in voice.
Godly Odysseus, who had endured much, rejoiced to see her;
At once he spoke out to his dear son Telemachos: 505
"Telemachos, you will soon learn, now you have come yourself
To where men are fighting and the best ones are judged,
Not to disgrace the family of your fathers, who before
Were distinguished for strength and prowess on the whole earth."
Then sound-minded Telemachos said to him in answer: 510
"In my present spirit, dear father, you will see, if you wish,
That, as you say, I shall not at all disgrace your family."
So he said, and Laertes rejoiced and spoke a word:
"What a day is this for me, dear gods! I greatly rejoice
That my son and my grandson contend over excellence."   515
Bright-eyed Athene stood beside him and addressed him:
"Son of Arkesios, dearest by far of all my companions,
When you have prayed to the bright-eyed maid and to Father Zeus,
Brandish your long-shadowy spear at once and hurl it forth."
So she said, and Pallas Athene breathed great strength into him.   520

Then he prayed to the daughter of the mighty Zeus
And brandished his long-shadowy spear at once and shot it forth.
He hit Eupeithes through the bronze cheek piece of his helmet.
This did not keep the spear back; the bronze went right through.
He made a crash as he fell, and his armor clattered upon him.   525
Odysseus and his glorious son fell upon the fighters in the front
And struck at them with their swords and their two-edged spears.
Now they would have destroyed all and made them without return,
If Athene, the daughter of aegis-bearing Zeus, had not
Shouted with her voice and restrained the whole host: 530
"Ithacans, hold off from war, which is disastrous,
So you may separate without bloodshed as soon as you can."
So did Athene say. And sallow fear got hold of them.
As they were afraid, all their arms flew out of their hands
And fell on the ground, as the goddess uttered her voice.   535
They turned back toward the city, longing for life.
Godly Odysseus, who had endured much, shouted dreadfully.
He bunched himself up and swooped down like a high-flying eagle.
Then the son of Cronos shot a smoldering thunderbolt.
It fell before the bright-eyed daughter of the mighty father.   540
Then bright-eyed Athene spoke out to Odysseus:
"Zeus-born son of Laertes, Odysseus of many wiles,
Hold off and cease from the strife of impartial war,
Lest Zeus, the broad-seeing son of Cronos, in some way get angry."
So Athene said. He obeyed, and rejoiced in his heart.   545
Then Pallas Athene, daughter of aegis-bearing Zeus,
Established oaths for the future between both sides,
Likening herself to Mentor in form and in voice.

Glossary

Achaians a collective appellation of the Greeks besieging Troy

Achilles the captain of the Myrmidons and the greatest hero of the Greeks at Troy

Aeolos lord of the winds

Agamemnon the leader of the Greeks at Troy; killed by Clytemnestra on his return home

Agelaos son of Damastor and a suitor of Penelope

Aiaia the legendary island home of Circe

Aietes the king of Colchis; father of Medea and brother of Circe

Aigisthos the cousin of Agamemnon and lover of Clytemnestra; after Agamemnon's murder, he became king of Mycenae

Ajax (1) son of Telamon; second to Achilles in prowess among the Greeks at Troy

(2) son of Oileus

Alcinoos grandson of Poseidon; king of the Phaeacians at Scherie

Alcmene the wife of Amphitryon and mother of Heracles

Amphimedon a suitor of Penelope killed by Telemachos

Amphinomos a suitor of Penelope killed by Telemachos

Anticleia the daughter of Autolycos, wife of Laertes, and mother of Odysseus

Antilochos a son of Nestor killed at Troy

Antinoos son of Eupeithes; the ringleader and most insolent of Penelope's suitors

Antiphates king of the Lestrygonians

Antiphos one of Odysseus' crew eaten by the Cyclops

Aphrodite daughter of Zeus; the goddess of love

Apollo son of Zeus and brother of Artemis; the god of sun and light

Ares son of Zeus; the god of war

Arete the queen of the Phaeacians; wife of Alcinoos and mother of Nausicaa

Argos the general name for Agamemnon's kingdom

Artemis daughter of Zeus and sister of Apollo

Athene the goddess of the arts and special patron of Odysseus

Atlas the father of Calypso and the supporter of the pillars of heaven

Autolycos the grandfather of Odysseus

Cadmos founder of Thebes

Calypso a goddess living on Ogygia; daughter of Atlas; Odysseus stays with her for seven years

269

Charybdis   a legendary whirlpool opposite Scylla
Cicones   Thracian allies of the Trojans raided by Odysseus
Circe   an enchantress living in Aiaia; daughter of the sun
Clytemnestra   wife and murderer of Agamemnon
Creon   a king of Thebes
Cronos   one of the older gods, the father of Zeus, Poseidon, Hera, Hades
Cyclopes   a lawless race of giants met by Odysseus

Danaans   like "Achaians," a general designation for the Greeks at Troy
Delos   an Aegean island sacred as the birthplace of Apollo and Artemis
Demodocos   the blind bard of the Phaeacians
Diocles   the son of Ortilochos, living at Pherai
Diomede   the ruler of Argos, a major Greek hero at Troy
Dodona   site of an ancient oracle of Zeus

Elpenor   one of Odysseus' crew; he falls off Circe's roof
Erebos   outer darkness for the dead
Erinyes   goddesses who fulfill curses and avenge crimes
Eumaeos   the faithful swineherd of Odysseus
Eupeithes   the father of Antinoos; killed by Laertes
Euryalos   a Phaeacian youth who taunts Odysseus
Eurycleia   the nurse of Odysseus and housekeeper in his palace
Eurylochos   the chief companion of Odysseus
Eurymachos   a suitor of Penelope's killed by Odysseus
Eurynome   a servant of Penelope's
Eurynomos   an Ithacan suitor of Penelope's

Hades   the god of the underworld
Halitherses   an Ithacan; son of Nestor and friend of Odysseus
Helen   wife of Menelaos; carried off by Paris to Troy
Hephaistos   son of Zeus and husband of Aphrodite; god of fire and the forge
Hera   queen of the gods; wife and sister of Zeus
Hermes   son of Zeus; messenger of the gods and guide of the dead
Hyperion   cognomen of the sun god

Ktesippos   from Samê; one of the suitors of Penelope

Icarios   the father of Penelope
Idomeneus   the grandson of Minos and king in Crete
Ilion   another name for Troy
Iros   nickname of Arnaios, the beggar at Ithaca

Laertes   the father of Odysseus and former king at Ithaca
Laodames   a Phaeacian; son of Alcinoos
Lestrygonians   a tribe of savage giants whose king was Lamos
Leto   the mother of Apollo and Artemis

Megapenthes   an illegitimate son of Menelaos

Melanthios son of Dolios; the faithless goatherd of Odysseus
Menelaos brother of Agamemnon and husband of Helen; co-commander of the Greeks at Troy
Mentes king of the Taphians, in whose guise Athene visits Telemachos
Mentor an Ithacan friend of Odysseus, in whose guise Athene guides Telemachos to Pylos
Minos legendary king of Crete and a ruler in the underworld
Mycenae the chief city of Homeric Greece and residence of Agamemnon
Myrmidons the followers of Achilles at Troy

Nausicaa Phaeacian princess, the daughter of Alcinoos and Arete
Nausithoos the colonizer of Scherie; son of Poseidon and father of Alcinoos
Neleus the founder of Pylos; son of Poseidon and father of Nestor
Nestor the aged king of Pylos and chief adviser for the Greeks at Troy
Nisos father of Amphinomos

Ogygia the legendary island home of Calypso
Oedipos a king of Thebes; son of Laios and Epicaste (in Homer)
Orestes son of Agamemnon; kills Clytemnestra and Aigisthos in avenging his father's murder
Orion mighty hunter slain by Artemis; he appears as a constellation
Ortilochos a nobleman living at Pherai

Pallas an epithet of Athene
Patroclos the alter ego of Achilles at Troy; his death inspires Achilles to return to battle
Peiraios son of Klytios and companion of Telemachos
Peisander a suitor of Penelope's
Peisistratos Nestor's youngest son; Telemachos' companion on his journey to Sparta
Perimedes one of Odysseus' crew
Persephone the daughter of Zeus and Demeter; queen of the underworld
Pheidon king of the Thesprotians
Phemios son of Terpis ("Pleasure") and bard at Odysseus' palace
Philoitios the faithful herdsman of Odysseus
Phorcys a lesser sea divinity; the grandfather of the Cyclops
Polybos an Ithacan, the father of Eurymachos; also the name of a Phaeacian
Polyphemos a Cyclops; son of Poseidon
Poseidon son of Cronos and brother of Zeus; god of the sea; especially hostile toward Odysseus
Priam the aged king of Troy killed by the Greeks

Scylla a monster inhabiting a sea cave opposite Charybdis
Sirens two enchantresses luring sailors to destruction by their songs
Styx "Hateful" river of the underworld

Tiresias   the blind seer of Thebes summoned by Odysseus on his visit to
  Hades
Theoclymenos   a seer at Ithaca, friend of Telemachos
Theseus   the great legendary hero and king of Athens
Thetis   a sea nymph and mother of Achilles
Tyndareus   from Sparta; father of Clytemnestra

Zeus   son of Cronos; king of the gods and specifically the god of the sky
  and of weather

The Greek World WITH PLACES MENTIONED IN The Odyssey

A map of probable locations for legendary places mentioned in *The Odyssey*

BACKGROUNDS

The *Odyssey*
in Antiquity

For a millennium and a half, Homer occupied a central position in Greek culture, as a sacred text and then as a schoolbook. His very centrality, from the poet Pindar in the sixth century on, meant that comment on him would be imbedded in a much larger context, or used as a point of reference, as Aristotle uses him when writing about Greek tragedy in the excerpts quoted below.

The "Homer" of Aristotle, of course, existed as the most eminent of a group of ancient epic poets whose texts are lost to us, though descriptions of them are given in the anthology-handbook *(Chrestomathy)* of Proclus, who probably wrote in the second century A.D. His account of the *Telegony*, a sort of sequel to the *Odyssey*, given below, was meant to provide information about an important part of the tradition studied in the rhetorical schools of the Roman Empire. Nero's tutor, the philosopher Seneca, in the first century A.D. used the *Odyssey* as a basis for moralizing. Longinus, a critic who wrote perhaps a shade earlier, was using Homer and other writers to make distinctions for a similar audience.

Something of the ancient notion that Homer was a sacred text may have led the neo-Platonic philosopher Porphyry (232–305) to base what others have taken as a whole mystic system on one passage of the *Odyssey*. His *On the Cave of the Nymphs*, key extracts of which appear below, allegorizes Homer powerfully enough to have impressed Renaissance and Romantic hermeticists, right down to Blake.

All this time, and later, the text of Homer was receiving commentary in the schools. Large portions of the vast annotation, the *scholia*, have come down to us, and we also have the thousands of pages of such notes gathered by Eustathius, a late twelfth-century Greek Orthodox bishop, who compiled from various sources his own compendious commentary on the poem. Brief extracts of both are given below.

PINDAR: *Nemean* VII †

> If one has luck in his deeds, he comes on a honeyed cause
> In the Muses' flowings. Mighty feats

† Translated by Albert Cook.

Hold much darkness when they are lacking hymns.
But for fair deeds we know a mirror with one way,
If for Memory of the shining diadem
A reward of efforts is found in the glorious songs of verse.
Wise men know a wind when it is coming
Two days off, nor are injured for gain.
Rich and poor past the bound of death
Go together. I think the tale
Of Odysseus has got greater than the suffering,
Through sweet-voiced Homer,
Since for lies there stands in him with suasive means
The lofty, yes. Skill cheats, leading
Along with myths. A blind heart
Does the main throng of men possess. If it had been
His to see the truth, powerful Ajax
Would not have driven the clear sword
Through his chest in anger.

                                                    Lines 14–27

PROCLUS: The *Telegony* †

After the *Returns* comes the *Odyssey* of Homer, and then the *Telegony* in two books by Eugammon of Cyrene, which contain the following matters. The suitors of Penelope are buried by their kinsmen, and Odysseus, after sacrificing to the Nymphs, sails to Elis to inspect his herds. He is entertained there by Polyxenus and receives a mixing bowl as a gift; the story of Trophonius and Agamedes and Augeas then follows. He next sails back to Ithaca and performs the sacrifices ordered by Teiresias, and then goes to Thesprotis where he marries Callidice, queen of the Thesprotians. A war then breaks out between the Thesprotians, led by Odysseus, and the Brygi. Ares routs the army of Odysseus and Athena engages with Ares, until Apollo separates them. After the death of Callidice Polypoetes, the son of Odysseus, succeeds to the kingdom, while Odysseus himself returns to Ithaca. In the meantime Telegonus, while travelling in search of his father, lands on Ithaca and ravages the island: Odysseus comes out to defend his country, but is killed by his son unwittingly. Telegonus, on learning his mistake, transports his father's body with Penelope and Telemachus to his mother's island, where Circe makes them immortal, and Telegonus marries Penelope, and Telemachus Circe.

---

† From Proclus, *Chrestomathy*, in *Hesiod*, translated by H. G. Evelyn-White (Cambridge, MA: Harvard UP, Loeb Classical Library edition, 1964).

PORPHYRY: *De Antro Nympharum* in *Opuscula Selecta* †

Because he has not made mention of the matters transmitted in accordance with fact *(historia)*—the geographers writing about the island have clearly mentioned no such cave on the island as Kronios says—and because he would be poetically unconvincing if he had expected to be believed when he had imagined a place of such circumstances that some men in Ithaca had fashioned passages for both men and gods, * * * so it is quite clear not only to the wise, but also to ordinary people, that in these details the poet speaks through allegory and through enigma.

Sections II–III, pp. 55–56

The naiad nymphs are souls going toward their birth. * * * And what is holy to them on earth would be a pleasant and shadowy cavern according to the image of the universe, in which as in the holy of holies the souls linger. * * * "Sea-purple veils".—Well, on the bones and about the bones is flesh; the former in living animals are stone or like stone, whence these bones are made of no other material, but are spoken of as being of stone. The "sea-purple veils" would be the flesh interwoven with blood. * * * [As for the bees and their honey] the theologians use honey for many and varied symbols because of its composition from many powers, and since it has the power to heal and preserve.

Sections XII–XV, p. 65

* * * And so the cave has not one gate but two * * * one that is proper for gods and those who are good, the other for mortals and those who are inferior.

Section XXXI, p. 77

And the olive tree is not "at the head of the harbor"—by any chance, but it sustains itself the middle of the cave, planted, in addition to the cave-image of the universe as a symbol of the thought of god. For it is a plant of Athena, and Athena is thought.

Section XXXII, p. 78

ARISTOTLE: From *Poetics* ‡

The *Iliad* is at once simple and "pathetic" and the *Odyssey* complex (for "recognition" scenes run through it), and at the same time "ethical."

1459^{b}14

---

† Edited by Nauck (Leipzig, 1886).
‡ From S. H. Butcher, *Aristotle's Theory of Poetry and Fine Art* (London: Macmillan & Co., Ltd., 1911). Translated by S. H. Butcher.

Other poets appear themselves upon the scene throughout, and imitate but little and rarely. Homer, after a few prefatory words, at once brings in a man, or woman, or other personage; none of them wanting in characteristic qualities, but each with a character of his own.

1460ª8

* * * But Homer, as in all else he is of surpassing merit, here too—whether from art or natural genius—seems to have happily discerned the truth. In composing the *Odyssey* he did not include all the adventures of Odysseus—such as his wound on Parnassus, or his feigned madness at the mustering of the host—incidents between which there was no necessary or probable connection; but he made the *Odyssey*, and likewise the *Iliad*, to center around an action that in our sense of the word is one.

1451ª22

* * * But once the irrational has been introduced and an air of likelihood imparted to it, we must accept it in spite of the absurdity. Take even the irrational incidents in the *Odyssey*, where Odysseus is left upon the shore of Ithaca. How intolerable even these might have been would be apparent if an inferior poet were to treat the subject. As it is, the absurdity is veiled by the poetic charm with which the poet invests it.

1460ª35

SENECA: From *Epistles* †

You ask where Ulysses will have wandered instead of acting so as to keep us from always wandering? There is no time to listen for whether he was tossed between Italy and Sicily or outside the world known to us—nor could he have wandered so long in a space so narrow. The storms of the soul toss us daily, and inquity drives us into all the ills of Ulysses. The beauty is not lacking to assail our eyes, nor is an enemy lacking. Here wild monsters delighting in human gore; there the subtle blandishments of gold, shipwreck, and every kind of evil. Teach me how to love my fatherland, my wife, my father; how, even shipwrecked, I may steer towards honor. Why do you ask if Penelope was immodest or caused scandal to her age? If she suspected before she knew for sure that the man she saw was Ulysses? Teach me what modesty is, and the amount of good there is in it, and whether it be located in the body or the soul.

LXXXVIII. 7–8

† Translated by Albert Cook.

LONGINUS: *On the Sublime*

Yet throughout the *Odyssey*, which for many reasons we must not exclude from our consideration, Homer shows that, as genius ebbs, it is the love of myth that characterizes old age. There are indeed many indications that he composed this after the *Iliad* beside the fact that throughout the *Odyssey* he introduces as episodes remnants of the adventures at Ilium; yes, and does he not in this poem render to his heroes their meed of lamentation as if it were a debt long due? In fact the *Odyssey* may be called an epilogue to the *Iliad:*

> There then Ajax lies, great warrior; there lies Achilles;
> There, too, Patroclus lies, the peer of the gods in counsel;
> There, too, mine own dear son.

It was, I imagine, for the same reason that, writing the *Iliad* in the heyday of his genius he made the whole piece lively with dramatic action, whereas in the *Odyssey* narrative predominates, the characteristic of old age. So in the *Odyssey* one may liken Homer to the setting sun; the grandeur remains without the intensity. For no longer does he preserve the sustained tension of the great *Iliad* lays, the consistent sublimity which never sinks into flatness, the flood of moving incidents in quick succession, the versatile rapidity and actuality, brimful of images drawn from real life. It is rather as though the Ocean had shrunk into its lair and lay becalmed within its own confines. Henceforth we see the ebbing tide of Homer's greatness, as he wanders in the incredible regions of romance. In saying this I have not forgotten the storms in the *Odyssey* and such incidents as that of the Cyclops—I am describing old age, but the old age of a Homer—yet the fact is that in every one of these passages the mythic dominates the actual. * * *

There is another justification for our considering the *Odyssey* as well as the *Iliad*. I wanted you to realize how with the decline of their emotional power great writers and poets give way to character-study. For instance, his character-sketches of the daily life in Odysseus's household are in the style of some comedy of character.

10. Well, then, let us see further whether we could find anything else that can make style sublime. Since with all things there are associated certain elements, essentially inherent in their substance, it follows that we shall find one factor of sublimity in a consistently happy choice of these constituent elements, and in the power of combining them together as it were into an organic whole. One writer for instance attracts the reader by the selection of ideas, another by the soldering of these selected. Sappho, for instance, never fails to take the emotions incident to the passion of love from the symptoms which accompany it in real life. And wherein does she show her excellence? In the skill with which

she selects and combines the most striking and intense of those symptoms.

DEMETRIUS: *On Style*

Homer uses such means sometimes in order also to make a scene more intense and telling. When he is jesting he is all the more fearful, and he seems to have been the first to devise fearful pleasantries, as in the passage describing that most unpleasant personage the Cyclops: "Noman will I eat last, but the rest before him"—that "guest-gift" of the Cyclops. No other detail reveals so clearly the grimness of the monster—not his supper made from two of the comrades of Odysseus, nor his crag-door, nor his club—as this show of urbanity.

SCHOLIA: *Graeca in Homeri Odysseam* †

They say in the myth that Poseidon went to the Ethiopians at a certain season and was honored by them. But in the allegory, Poseidon is a term for water. Since water, that is, the ocean, circles the whole earth, and because the Nile at a certain season waters the land of the Ethiopians and makes the trees grow, on this account they say Poseidon, or water, is honored by them as the cause of many good things for them.

I, 15, on *Odyssey* I.22

[*Drugs of such devices*]—or those discovered by the intelligence ["devices"] and proposed by the [drugs] theoretical skill—both the theory of medicine and that which leads through general discourse and method to a knowledge of the parts. And the parts of this are the semiotic, the etiological, and the practical. And of the one, that which proceeds through its effects. And the parts of this, in turn, are the dietetic, the chirurgical, and the pharmaceutic.

I, 194, on *Odyssey* IV.227

If the gods do not drink anything but nectar, how did Calypso "mix" it with water? Simply before pouring in by the old custom. For they poured into a horn [*keras*] and drank. So "mixing" [*kerase*], as Aristotle and Porphyry say, meant not adding water as another ingredient, but simply pouring in.

I, 251, on *Odyssey* V.93

† *Scholia, Graeca in Homeri Odysseam*, edited by W. Dindorf (London: Oxford UP, 1895). Translated by Albert Cook.

[*And if he has come down as one of the immortals*] If a god comes in human form, the gods plan something strange. For the gods have never yet appeared to us in altered form, but manifestly. And he says they appear to us manifestly not only in sacrifice, but in person.

I, 342, on *Odyssey* VII.199

[*And the Lotus-Eaters did not plot destruction*] Being just men, they do not gain over by force, but by persuasion. And the "oud . . . medont' " ["they did not intend"] shows it was not by their will that the destruction came about.

II, 414, on *Odyssey* IX.92

The Cyclops in Homer was not one-eyed by nature, but he had lost his other eye through some misfortune. For he had two eyebrows. For he says in [line 389] "eyebrows and eyelids."

II, 434, on *Odyssey* IX.383

The Gods call it "moly." He does not say what men call it. Indeed, he introduced it as unknown to men.

II, 467, on *Odyssey* X.305

Why did Circe fear the sword of Odysseus, since she was a goddess? We say that daimons who live a long time, but are nevertheless subject to death, the poet habitually calls "gods." Or else Circe fears the sword from her nature as certain daimons also fear certain other materials. So too did Dionysius say in his "Treatise on Stones," "By nature is crystal and holy jasper repugnant to Bogeys and other phantoms."

II, 469, on *Odyssey* X.323

And how did trees stand in water? We say by imagination, for the punishment of Tantalus.

I, 523, on *Odyssey* XI.588

Allegorically [holy cave of the nymphs] designates the cave as the universe, the nymphs as the souls, the bees the same too, and men as bodies. And the two doors of the bodies are the exit, or birth, and the entrance for souls, in which nothing of the bodies comes in, but only souls. For they are immortal.

I, 562, on *Odyssey* XIII.103

EUSTATHIUS: *Commentarii ad Homeri Odysseam*

"As a steward of the winds Aeolus is spoken of not only allegorically, but according to the truth of history. A man is shown to be wise and honored for predicting the blowing of the wind.

On *Odyssey* X.21–23, p. 364

"It is fitting that Circe has four servants as the myth has fashioned it, and they are clearly nymphs, the ones that, as poetry tells, are born from springs and groves and rivers and such, showing them to be certain powers of nature; and more, the ones who serve luxuries for Circe, through the birth of animals and seasonal fruits, and elemental causes of other things. * * * And some of the old interpreters say—discordantly and confusedly, though they were on the right track—that Circe is the year and her four servants the four seasons.

On *Odyssey* X.248, p. 384

"Eratosthenes [the great Alexandrian geographer] said jokingly, in reference to the mythical and incredible nature of Odysseus' wandering, that the locations of his travels would be established by anyone who found the cobbler who sewed the bag the winds were kept in."[1]

On *Odyssey* X.19, p. 365

G. S. KIRK†

Heroic Age and Heroic Poetry

The narrative oral poet sings of the deeds of heroes, usually heroes of the past, and sometimes too of gods, giants or folk-tale figures. This heroic poetry is nearly always sung in lines with a uniform metrical pattern, a rapid and flowing rhythm like that of the Homeric hexameter or the looser decasyllable of Serbo-Croat verse. Metrical regularity is essential for learning and composing long oral poems; though in some traditions, especially those affected by Latin, quite complex factors like rhyme, alliteration or division into stanzas may be added. Even with the help of an easy and regular rhythmical framework, a restricted and standardized poetical vocabulary, and the great powers of memory of the non-literate, the oral heroic poet must almost invariably be a professional or semi-professional, one who begins his training as a boy and thereafter has constant practice.

Songs sung from memory need not only be narrative ones, though there is often little or no surviving evidence of other categories. Work-songs, dance-songs and dirges must always have had a place in the kind of culture that gave rise to the oral narrative poet, and in some societies gnomic and didactic oral poetry flourished too. Yet songs of these other genres were in most ways less important than the heroic songs: they were shorter, often less formally arranged, and less closely associated with the

1. Translated by Bernard Knox.
†From G. S. Kirk, *The Songs of Homer* (Cambridge: Cambridge UP, 1962) 56–61, 63–69, and 280–81. Reprinted by permission of the publisher.

nobility. Two common features of nearly all kinds of oral poem, however, are that they were composed and remembered without the aid of
writing and that they were sung or chanted, usually to a musical accompaniment. Poems are songs, and the Homeric word for a poet is ἀοιδός
(aoidos) or singer, one who accompanies himself on the lyre-like instrument known in Homer as the *kitharis* or *phorminx*.

It is strange that great heroic narrative poems of comparable structure
and ideology should have grown up in different periods and parts of
Europe: the Homeric poems in early Iron Age Greece, the Teutonic
poems, including *Beowulf* and the *Nibelungenlied*, in the 4th to the 8th
centuries A.D., the Celtic narratives in Ireland and Wales (in which,
however, prose saga was mixed with poetry), especially down to the 13th
or 14th century, the great Norse poems and sagas which flourished from
the 9th to the 13th century, and the Russian and South Slavic heroic
epics which have developed from the 14th century to the present day—
not to speak of Finnish heroic songs, or the *Chanson de Roland*, or the
Byzantine epic of Digenes Akritas, or the much earlier and rather different Near Eastern tradition exemplified in the stories of Gilgamesh and
Keret or in the Babylonian creation hymn. In some of these, especially
the Scandinavian and Near Eastern poems, the element of magic,
demonology or folk-tale is much stronger than in Homer. In others, like
the *Chanson de Roland*, writing has played some part. Yet the heroic
quality and the oral quality remain predominant. The reason for the
similarity of these products is that they arose from basically similar cultures; each of them derives from a Heroic Age or its immediate succes-
sor. The main components of such an age, which tends to occur in the
development of many different nations, seem to be a *penchant* for war-
fare and adventure, a powerful nobility, and a simple but temporarily
adequate material culture devoid of much aesthetic refinement. In such
conditions the heroic virtues of honour and martial courage dominate
all others, ultimately with depressive effects on the stability and prosperity of the society. It is usually during the consequent period of decline
that the poetical elaboration of glorious deeds, deeds that now lie in the
past, reaches its climax; though narrative songs are a favourite recreation
of the tired warrior throughout the whole heroic period.

The Homeric epic, developed in its monumental form by about 700
B.C., is an outcome of the in most ways typical Heroic Age of the late
Mycenaean period, an age which had ended, historically speaking, as
far back as 1100. That a tradition of oral heroic song maintained itself
for so long, and grew to so late and stupendous a culmination, is surprising enough. But fortunately the final collapse of the Mycenaean system, drastic as it was, had not produced a total dispersal of population;
many survivors were able to cultivate and transmit the memory of the
heroic past. Another event which fortified the Greek heroic tradition
throughout a post-heroic age was the submergence of writing for a period

of several centuries; and this in its turn had been helped by the laborious and imprecise nature of the Mycenaean script. During the period of total illiteracy of the 11th and 10th century oral poetry would be as much a necessity of life as it ever had been before—perhaps more so. Other heroic ages in other lands tended to be followed much more rapidly by the spread of writing, and their oral traditions may have been relatively less pure; though in parts of Europe an oral tradition has continued for even longer than four hundred years, because until recently writing never touched more than a small minority of the population. Even in Mycenaean Greece only a small minority seems to have been literate; from the 7th century onwards, on the other hand, the impact of writing on the Greeks was rapid and pervasive.

In spite of these and other differences between one nation and another the concept of the Heroic Age as a recurrent phenomenon in the development of cultures, especially in Europe, is valid and useful; its isolation is largely the work of H. M. and N. K. Chadwick. It allows us to understand the picture of the *aoidos* or professional singer as given in the Odyssey, and to envisage the way in which Homer himself—the first 'monumental' poet, that is—may have grown out of such a figure. It allows us, too, to credit the successors of singers like Demodocus with songs longer and more complex than those mentioned in the Odyssey, songs of the scale of *Beowulf* or the earlier Icelandic sagas. Yet the concept of the court poet of the Heroic Age must be diversified by the study of the popular or market-place poet. This is the kind that survives most tenaciously when a Heroic Age is ended and when the noblemen's houses are divided or abandoned. The court minstrel is the typical poet in the Heroic Age, but we must be careful not to regard the composers of the Iliad and Odyssey as necessarily resembling that kind of singer in every respect. These poems were brought to perfection long after the Achaean Heroic Age had ended. Their audience must have included comparatively rich patrons and noblemen, but also, probably, the general populace in various kinds of gathering. . . . Heroic poetry appeals to the people as well as to heroes and their descendants; and the oral poets that can be studied best, those of modern Yugoslavia, have for long been popular poets who sing in coffee-houses, not court poets. Yet their subjects are mainly heroic and aristocratic.

The Languages of Formulas in Homer

The case for describing Homer as an oral poet would be incomplete if it depended solely on the importance of the minstrel in other heroic or post-heroic societies, together perhaps with the description of Phemius and Demodocus in the Odyssey and the absence of writing from Greece during much of the interval between the downfall of Mycenae and the probable date of the Iliad. Some or all of these factors, however, interpreted with varying degrees of accuracy, had led many critics, even before Milman Parry, to conclude that Homer composed in a very different manner from Apollonius of Rhodes, Virgil or Milton. Furthermore the language of the poems had for long been closely scrutinized, and by the early 1920's Witte, Meister, Meillet and others had made a strong case for its classification as a formalized and traditional development, in which alternative dialect forms, for example, were chosen mainly to suit the requirements of metre. Of Parry himself, whose importance was generally overlooked until some time after his premature death in 1935, much has now been written. His contributions to Homeric scholarship are twofold: he saw the relevance of the modern oral poetry of Yugoslavia and succeeded in recording a great deal of it; and he demonstrated beyond doubt that Homer was an oral poet, depending on a gradually evolved traditional store of fixed phrases which covered most common ideas and situations—a store that was neither unnecessarily luxurious nor restrictively parsimonious.

These essential qualities of the oral poet's treasury of verbal formulas were termed by Parry *economy* and *scope*. Düntzer and a few others had already recognized that the many recurrent phrases in Homer, most obviously the name-epithet formulas like 'divine Odysseus' and 'gleaming-helmeted Hector', were used in a way that was not just haphazard or unimaginative, but on the contrary was somehow essential to the poet. Parry first showed that such fixed phrases in Homer composed a system so tight and logical that it could only be the outcome of many generations of refinement. This process of refinement consisted in the rejection of the otiose—the merely decorative alternative—and the consolidation and expansion of whatever was functional and organic. Now the Homeric hexameter verse tends to be more or less self-contained in meaning; its ending usually coincides with a major or minor pause, the end of a sentence or clause or at least the point at which a predicate is divided from its subject. This means that there is plenty of opportunity for the repetition of whole lines, the verse being treated as a formula; and in fact about one-third of the verses in the Iliad and Odyssey recur at least once. It is more important, however, that the verse itself is divided into smaller sections by word-breaks which are part of its structure; and into these sections are fitted recurrent phrases or sense-units. The most important internal divisions, which must coincide with a gap between words, are the compulsory main caesura in the third foot, either male or female (i.e. after the first syllable of that foot, the 'strong' position, or after its first trochee, $- \cup$, the commoner 'weak' position); the extremely common 'bucolic' diaeresis before the fifth foot; and the word-break after the first measure of the fourth foot in many lines which contain a female, or trochaic, main caesura. The intervals between the beginning of the verse and the male caesura, or between the male, female, fourth-foot or bucolic caesuras and the end of the verse, are the main places in which standard phrases or fixed formulas are employed. Since the verse-end is marked by the fixed rhythm $-\cup\cup-\cup$ (as opposed to all other parts of the line, where the spondee can be substituted for the basic dactyl at will) the poet must first be sure of filling the latter part of the line. Thus the majority of fixed phrases are designed to fill out portions of the verse-end. At the beginning of the verse the commonest formula-lengths are the whole portion down to the main caesura, or less often the first one-and-a-half feet. * * *

There is, in fact, amazingly little unnecessary reduplication of formulas in Homer. To take the large number of name-epithet phrases in the nominative case: the table on pp. 50f. of Parry's classic study, *L'Épithète traditionnelle chez Homère* (Paris, 1928), shows that for eleven prominent gods and heroes there are no less than 824 uses of 55 different formulas in the Iliad and Odyssey as a whole. These formulas, some of which are of course very frequent (πολύμητις 'Οδυσσεύς comes 81 times) are those which fill out the four commonest metrical segments of the verse. * * * Out of the 824 uses only 15, involving only three different formulas, are reduplicative in the sense of being exact metrical equivalents of other commoner ones. * * *Thus in the extensive name-epithet nominative system there is an astounding *economy* of phrases, not more than 5 per cent of reduplication. At the same time the coverage or *scope* is almost equally striking. The four main parts of the verse to be filled, in the case of these eleven prominent characters, make a possibility of 44 name-epithet groups. Two of these positions cannot in any case be filled by particular names because of their metrical value, but out of the 42 remaining we find formulas for no less than 37, making roughly 88 per cent perfect coverage.

This degree of scope and economy cannot be accidental; nor can it be the creation of a single poet. No one singer could construct a system so rich in metrical alternatives and at the same time so closely shorn of unfunctional variation. Even a pen and paper composer would be hard pressed to achieve such a system, and to do so he would have to behave not like a poet but like a cryptographer—or a classical scholar; and his effort would be quite pointless, since the only reasonable purpose of such a construction is to enable the oral, non-literate poet both to assimilate and to increase a great stock of traditional heroic song. The system is so extensive because for generation after generation individual singers had added a fresh phrase here and another there, as the necessity of their particular contexts demanded; it is so economical, spare and thrifty because needless alternatives—a mere encumbrance to the singer—were systematically if gradually discarded. Human skills being fallible, and the creative urge not always responding to systems, a new and unfunctional alternative would naturally be added from time to time, so that the economy at any one period would never be quite complete.

Closer examination of the details of the formular system shows how it helps the poet to remember traditional verses; for if a line is divided into three familiar phrase-units, say, rather than ten or a dozen word-units, it is obviously easier to remember and reproduce. It also helps him to compose his own fresh lines with the minimum of effort. Epithets are standardized not only for people but also for many familiar objects, and once again they vary according to the portion of verse that it is desired to fill. If the idea 'of a ship' has to be expressed in the latter part of a verse, the ship will be described as 'equal', 'curved around' or 'dark-prowed' simply according as the final 2, 2½ or 3¼ feet have to be filled—in other words, according as the phrase has to succeed the bucolic, hephthemimeral or trochaic caesura. The formulas are νηὸς ἐίσης, νεὸς ἀμφιελαίσσης and νεὸς κυανοπρώροιο: note that the form of the word 'ship' itself is varied solely for metrical convenience. If the case is changed, and a dative, for example, is needed after the bucolic cae-sura—because the other concepts to be expressed use the whole of the verse up to that point—then the epithet may have to be changed too, and νηὸς ἐίσης becomes νηί μελαίνη. That is not because ships in the dative are any blacker and less equal than those in the genitive, nor is it because a ship in a particular context is envisaged as black rather than equal: it is black simply and solely because after the word νηί, and to fill the measure ∪ — ∪, we require an epithet of that value begin-ning with a consonant—since νηί ends in a vowel. ἐίση will not do and μελαίνη will. Prepositions, too, can be incorporated in these noun-epithet groups, and may require fresh epithets with new metrical values: thus 'on a ship', if it is to fill the last 2½ feet, for instance, entails replac-ing the standard epithet of the simple noun-epithet group in that place, namely 'curved around', by the shorter word 'hollow'—κοίλης ἐπὶ νηός in place of νεὸς ἀμφιελίσσης.

Other common types of formula express the verb, or the verb and its object, and so on, and are designed to fill either the first or the second part of the verse and often to be mated with an appropriate subject-formula in the other part. Thus αὐτὰρ ὁ μερμήριξε, or τὸν δ᾽ αὖτε προσέειπε, or αὐτὰρ ἐπεί τό γ᾽ ἄκουσέ, for instance, may be fol-lowed by an 3¼-foot noun-epithet group beginning with a consonant. Such formulas are themselves often built up from shorter fixed compo-nents—thus there are many different phrases beginning with αὐτάρ: αὐτὰρ ὁ with different verbs, αὐτάρ ἐπεί or ἐπειδή, αὐτὰρ ἔβη and so on. * * *

The singers of the Ionian oral tradition sometimes adapted a phrase to a new position or a new use without much conscious thought, by ear and by instinct. The formula in its standard use and form had a familiar metrical value, and it seems to have been assumed, sometimes wrongly, that this value persisted even after the standard form had been slightly altered; or perhaps it would be truer to say that there was no conscious assumption of any kind, that this problem is one that often does not occur to the oral singer. Thus μερόπων ἀνθρώπων, for example, is a well-known formula, evidently developed for use in a genitive case, which occurs at the verse-end seven times in the Iliad and twice in the Odyssey. Once in the Iliad it is successfully adapted to the dative, μερόπεσσι βροτοῖσιν, but at XVIII. 288 we see that at some stage some not very careful singer required a *nominative* phrase meaning 'men' for the same part of the line, and so transposed the familiar formula into μέροπες ἄνθρωποι, thus producing a technical fault of metre. In performance the singer would presumably disguise this fault by artificially prolonging the -ες, and the audience would probably not notice the difference. Similarly many Homeric instances of hiatus—that is, of irregularly leaving a final vowel unaffected before a succeeding initial vowel—are the result of the minor adaptation of fixed phrases; though Parry exaggerated when he made this the primary cause of metrical anomalies, since many cases of hiatus are caused by the loss of digamma or other initial semi-vowels, or by the assumption of such a loss, or by a feeling that hiatus sometimes did not matter at the major divisions of the verse. An analogous result of the careless placing of formulas is inappropriateness not of metre but of sense. Thus the basic idea 'with the hand' is often expressed by the formula χειρὶ παχείῃ, in which the epithet 'thick' helps to fill up the part of the verse following the bucolic caesura. When this epithet is applied not to the powerful fist of a warrior, which must have been its usual and so 'proper' function, but to the ladylike hand of the refined (sometimes over-refined) Penelope, the result, if it is noticed at all, is ludicrous. The same is the case with 'blameless Aegisthus' *(1.29)* and perhaps with the revolting Irus's 'lady mother' *(18.5)*—I am not sure that in the last case any contradiction would be felt. These are obvious and familiar cases, but there are others in which the redeployment of a formula reveals itself in more subtle ways; thus one of a pair of repeated passages may reveal itself as adapted from the other—or from the type of which the other is a fair representative—because of the forced adjustment of a component formula.

What is the minimum length of a formula? The maximum may be several complete lines, composing a passage which is repeated whenever a typical scene, like the preparation of a meal or sacrifice or the launching or beaching of a ship, is to be described. The minimum may be two words like ὣς φάτο or Τρώεσσι δέ, if we insist on the formula as a phrase-unit. But even single words have definite formular tendencies, since they gravitate strongly to certain positions in the verse according to their metrical value; and there are fewer exact metrical alternatives of single words having a similar meaning than one would find in written poetry—though more than in the case of most formular phrases. The fixity of position of individual words within the line is indeed remarkable, though it quite escapes the notice of most readers or hearers. The longer the word the less remarkable this fixity becomes; there are only two positions which a word like φιλοπτολέμοισι, for example, can occupy without disturbing the natural articulations of the hexameter line. Yet even disyllables like ἦτορ or δῶμα show a strong preference for one or perhaps two positions in the verse, whereas there are theoretically several in which they could occur * * *; and παιδός, παιδί regularly avoid the line-end (only once in 61 uses), while παῖδα and the plural forms do not. Sometimes this preference is due to the fact that the word in question occurs predominantly in a particular formula, itself restricted in position. Where this is not the case the tendency toward fixity arises in part out of the pure mechanics of the hexameter verse, a subject which we do not yet fully understand; but at least a perusal of Eugene O'Neill Jr.'s article on metrical word-types in the Greek hexameter shows that the tendency had reached a considerable degree of formalization or stylization in the Homeric poems. Thus metrical word-values, rather than particular single words, are formular in Homer, and this apparent restriction, like that imposed by fixed phrases, was of a kind to help rapid composition rather than to hinder it. The singer begins to crystallize a thought of which the pivotal concept is 'house': he assigns δῶμα, for instance, to its preferred position, and can then confidently fit verbal and other nominal formulas round it. His verse is made with the minimum of conscious effort.

The Oral Tradition and the Advent of Writing

I hope to have outlined the broad principles of formular composition and to have shown by a small number of examples that Homer manifests the scope and economy of a developed oral tradition. To illustrate all the complexities and potentialities of this type of composition would need a complete book; not even Parry produced such a comprehensive explanation, nor is one necessary. What is necessary is to grasp the principle. One consequence of Parry's demonstration is that every single line of the great poems must be assessed in terms of a traditional and formalized language and a traditional subject-matter. Fulsome lipservice has been paid to Parry's conclusions, and some scholars have even been tempted to make the one-sided claim that the only way in which Homeric scholarship can progress is by closer examination of the formular system. In spite of this, relatively little has been achieved since Parry died.

Even less attention has been given to post-Homeric hexameter poetry from this viewpoint. Hesiod's *Theogony* and the fairly copious fragments of his Catalogue poetry are composed in a distinctly Homeric style, somewhat debased but traditional in essence. There are many new phrases, some of them repeated several times and tending to become fully formular; these are confined primarily to fresh subject-matter. Where the subject is traditional—as for example in many of the Catalogue fragments—the traditional language is used, though often with drastic adaptations. The subject of *Works and Days*, on the other hand, is so different from those of the regular heroic narrative that hundreds of new words and phrases are needed. Native Boeotian poets may have developed a tradition which included didactic and gnomic poetry, so that even the non-Homeric language of *Works and Days* may still be oral and formular in character. Unfortunately there is no contemporary material for comparison, nor have the economy and scope of the new phrases been evaluated in detail; but Hesiod could well have used the aid of writing, in some way or other, in the genuine parts of this later poem. The earlier 'Homeric' Hymns, particularly those to Demeter, Apollo, and Aphrodite, are probably entirely oral. They depart from Homeric vocabulary often enough, and have many new phrases; but these, especially the decorative and lyrical ones, are in the style of certain relatively late elements in Homer, like the Beguilement of Zeus in Iliad XIV and XV, which there is no reason to associate with writing and which indeed preserve a scope and economy which preclude it. As for the few surviving fragments of the poems of the Homeric Cycle, they are for the most part easily distinguishable in style from Homer. The later Cyclic poems, like the *Telegony* of Eugammon, almost certainly belong to written literature. The earlier, like the *Aithiopis* and the *Iliou Persis* of Arctinus, may have been composed not long after 700 in the decadent oral manner of certain later expansions of Homer. * * *

Nevertheless by the probable time of composition of the *Theogony*, the *Aithiopis*, and the *Hymn to Demeter*, none of which is likely to be very much later than 650, writing was reaching the point at which it could be used for literary purposes. Archilochus, who was certainly a literate composer, refers to an eclipse of the sun which must be that of 648. Moreover *graffito* inscriptions on certain unambitious pots show that writing was used in different parts of the Greek world, and sometimes for casual and inessential purposes, as early as the last decades of the 8th century. The Dipylon prize jug with a hexameter couplet to the effect that the best of the dancers (? shall receive this prize) is datable from its shape and decoration seen that these special occasions are not particularly likely to have provided the conditions to elicit an exceptionally large-scale poem, and I think it quite possible that the humbler and more frequent occasions would have been no worse, and perhaps better, in this respect. *Weddings* in Yugoslavia, Hungary, Greece and many other traditionally peasant communities sometimes still last for as long as a week, and are most commonly arranged for the slack times of a farmer's year. Eating, drinking, telling stories, singing and listening to songs are the main occupations. In Muslim Yugoslavia the month of Ramadan, with its nights devoted to eating and drinking, is the chief occasion for a singer to deploy his repertoire to the full, and best provides a continuous audience. No such comparable festival existed in ancient Greece, but weddings and perhaps funerals—humble no less than aristocratic—and small horse-fairs and the like would in some cases have lasted long enough for the development and singing even of a song as vast as the Iliad. It could have been in such circumstances as these that Homer first strung together elements of his Trojan repertoire—much of it acquired from older singers—so as to form a coherent poem with one or two strong central themes.

The truth remains that none of these possible occasions—feast or festival, fair or wedding or funeral or informal gathering in market-place or tavern—seems to possess any special quality that could easily and naturally have actually *elicited* a large-scale epic. The concept of the oral poem as functional is a useful one—but it is not going to help us much with the monumental poem, simply because by the normal canons of heroic song this kind of poem is an aberration. Rather I believe we should accept that the chief factor in the making of the new literary form was not function or occasion, but—and this is horribly obvious once one comes to say it, though it has been avoided like the plague by most Homeric critics in the last sixty years—the special ability, aims, imagination and reputation of a particular singer; the singer in fact who compounded the first large-scale Iliad and who was known as Homer. An outstandingly accomplished singer may be seen to acquire a tremendous reputation in any oral society, first in his own district and then further afield; often he may acquire a prestige equalling that claimed by Demodocus in the Odyssey. I am driven towards the provisional conclusion that it was this prestige that enabled Homer to outstrip normal performances, normal audiences and normal occasions—that enabled him to *impose* his own will and his own vast conception on his environment, so as eventually to produce an Iliad. Admittedly if circumstances were such that no one would listen to a poem of this length, or more or less take in its whole span, the Iliad would hardly have survived in the tradition—unless it could be recorded in writing without delay, which* * *I regard as an improbable and unnecessary hypothesis. But there is no reason to suspect that circumstances *were* such—weddings and fairs, to look no further, could have provided audiences consistent enough to encourage the great singer, if only his own powers and reputation were high enough to hold them. The crucial factor was the creative imagination, the singer of outstanding brilliance and an exceptionally large Trojan repertoire who suddenly saw that many of its songs could be interlocked to make a complete and universal Trojan song. This was not like the evolution of tragedy, for example, each stage of which may have seemed a logical development from the last; it was more like the evolution of the monumental Geometric amphora or crater. The evidence of archaeology does not suggest that pots become systematically larger and larger until eventually one was made that was seven feet tall, but rather that there was a leap from the largeish pot to the perfectly colossal one, a leap which must have been made for the first time by a particular potter who suddenly had a flash of ambition and the inspiration of sheer size, and at the same time realized that he possessed the necessary materials and technique. This kind of leap, incidentally, is far easier to understand in one man than in a group or a corporation—though others will inevitably follow the example of magnitude once it has been given.

MARTIN P. NILSSON

[Homeric Anthropomorphism and Rationalism] †

* * *The words of Andromache after Hektor's death are significant of the total disappearance of the old understanding of the meaning of funeral gifts:

O yea, no profit to thee—they shall not swathe thee on the pyre;
But to be for thine honour in Troy-town's sons' and daughters' eyes.

The continued cult of the dead man, the offerings upon the tomb, are not mentioned and seem no longer to exist. With the cessation of these the power of the dead over the living is broken.

In connexion with this change is associated a revision and a weakening of the ideas about that part of man which lives on after death, and about its existence. That which survives man is *psyche*, the soul, the shade: it is nothing more. It is true that the most important descriptions of the souls are contained in the two Nekyiae, which are later additions to the *Odyssey*. With a faint squeak as of bats—here the old idea of the birdlike appearance of the soul is seen—the souls of the murdered suitors follow Hermes, their guide, into the underworld. Odysseus three times seeks in vain to embrace his mother's shade; she yields before his grasp. The 'impotent heads' of the souls have neither flesh nor bone; they flit away like dreams. Like a phantom the still unburied Patroklos shows himself to Achilles, in all things, even in size, resembling the dead man; the vision draws from Achilles the significant cry:

O strange! then even in Hades' homes—and I knew not this—
They have spirit and shape (ψυχὴ καὶ ἐίδωλον), albeit in these
no life there is.

As in the Nekyia, the shade of Patroklos vanishes 'like smoke with a rustling sound.' In the Nekyia the prevailing idea, although it is not consistently carried out, is that the souls have no consciousness and can acquire this only by drinking the blood of the sacrificial animal, an idea

†From Martin P. Nilsson, A *History of Greek Religion*, translated by F. J. Fielden (London: Oxford UP, 1949) 137–40, 159–63, and 170–72. Reprinted by permission of the publisher.

which originates in the blood-offerings poured out upon the grave. The souls are shades possessing neither strength nor consciousness, and such figures there is no need to propitiate and worship. A continued existence of this kind is of no value to man.

Rather would I be a hireling to drudge in the fields all day
With a landless master, who sparely would feed me and niggardly pay,
Than over the hosts of the dead which have perished a sceptre to sway,

Achilles replies to Odysseus. The life after death becomes so pale and empty that it is not far from non-existent. The man who makes Death and Sleep twin-brothers and calls death 'a brazen sleep' does not really believe in any future life.

The kingdom of the dead is modelled upon these ideas. There the detested Hades rules, the most odious of all gods to men, and his consort, the dreaded Persephone. His kingdom is dark and noisome. Its terror chiefly lies in the fact that the way back is closed to any who have once passed within its portals. Hades is the strong custodian of the gates; his dog is mentioned in connexion with the Herakles myth. Pylos, where Herakles strove with Hades, is originally nothing else than the gate of the realm of the dead. The idea of a common kingdom of the dead is naturally much older than Homer and recurs among most other peoples. It arises of itself as soon as man, in order to depict the life hereafter, makes use of the ever-present analogy with human life. It generally exists without difficulty side by side with the idea that the dead man lives and is active in his grave, but in Homer it has completely prevailed and may be said to be a kind of anthropomorphism. The life after death has been brought closer to the life on earth but has also lost its power and intensity. Instead of a copy it has become a pale shadow.

The kingdom of the dead lies beneath the earth, for there the dead are buried. During the battle of the gods Hades springs up in terror from his throne, for he is afraid that the roof over his head will fall in. Where are its gates? In later times grottoes and deep lakes were thought to be entrances to Hades. The idea is certainly old, but for a seafaring people, who naïvely imagined the earth to be a flat disk surrounded by the Ocean, the world had an extreme edge, and over this men passed into the realms below. On this idea is based the famous description of Hades in the journey of Odysseus to the underworld, but it exists also in the *Iliad*. Patroklos exhorts Achilles to bury his body as soon as possible, for the shades will not permit him to pass the river which bounds the kingdom of the dead. This is a transposition to the Homeric world of ideas belonging to the old belief that a man who has not been buried can find no peace; if his body does not rest in the ground he must wander about unceasingly like a lost spirit. Accordingly Odysseus on his visit to the lower regions meets the shipwrecked Elpenor before any other shades; for he has not yet been buried.

The bond between the two worlds of the living and of the dead has been weakened but by no means severed, and the doctrine that this bond was broken by the burning of the corpse overstates the case. The poet certainly makes the shade of Patroklos declare that after his burial he will never come back, but this is merely an expression adapted to the particular occasion and must not be erected into a general theory. Homeric ideas are not without mutual contradictions. Passages have already been adduced to show that burial was regarded as necessary, since without it the dead man would not be admitted into the kingdom of the dead; but not withstanding this it is declared in numerous instances that the slain go down to the dwellings of Hades, and Achilles himself says of the shade of the unburied Patroklos that it dwells there. Cremation by no means originated in a desire to be liberated from the troublesome claims of the dead; it is an old funeral custom alongside of which the notion of the continued life and activity of the dead in the grave can still exist and does exist in later times. In the expression 'appease in the fire' ($\pi\upsilon\rho\grave{o}\varsigma$ $\mu\epsilon\iota\lambda\iota\sigma\sigma\acute{\epsilon}\mu\epsilon\nu$) lies neither more nor less than the old idea of burial as the undisputed right of the dead, the same feeling that forbids the Homeric warrior to refuse burial even to a dead foe. * * *

* * *The man of the people sees from below what the nobility views from above. The nobility in its turn views from below the class of highest rank, that of the gods. And it is precisely of their relationship to man that the above two words are used. The thirst for fame and an unlimited self-esteem urge the man of the nobility forwards, and when misfortune overtakes him it is described as the envy of the gods; the gods regard his success as beyond what human powers should achieve. The explanation is constantly present: it is used when a bowstring breaks in the fight, so that the foe escapes the shot; Calypso thinks that the gods grudge a goddess life with a mortal man. The expression finally becomes stereotyped; Penelope says that the jealousy of the gods had prevented her and Odysseus from living together. Thus anthropomorphism found in the settled order of society the ultimate barrier between gods and men. The Greeks never lost sight of the idea and the problem involved in it. Insolence towards the gods must be regarded by any genuine religious feeling as the most deadly ethical and religious sin. That it was not so regarded by the Greeks was due to their anthropomorphism, which made the gods resemble men and then measured them by the same moral standards as mankind.

Actually, no living person has ever seen a god, and Homer makes the gods associate personally only with favoured fabulous peoples such as the Ethiopians and the Phaeacians. But he is not consistent; on rare occasions a god does reveal himself to certain heroes in an untransformed shape. Rationalism overcame the difficulty that the gods were so frequently supposed to intervene in human affairs and were yet nowhere to be seen by supposing that they assumed human shape. This device is characteristic of Homer's divine apparatus, and popular belief assisted it. There was thought to be something mysterious about the stranger, and it was upon occasion believed that a god was concealed under his form.

Religious experience had still less to say about the activities of the gods than about their epiphany. Many had doubtless experienced the intervention and influence of a god, but simple religious feeling does not ask how or by what agency this comes about. It sees something which it must ascribe to divine power, it knows its prayer to be answered; with this it is satisfied and inquires no further. Rationalism succumbed to the temptation of representing the influence and intervention of the gods in a visible form credible to ordinary reason. Anthropomorphism by investing the gods with human shape had shown the way. What best accorded with reality was to make a god intervene in the disguise of a human being.

This became the normal fashion in which the gods are made to intervene, but there are certain distinctions. Zeus directs the battle from afar by means of his will and the messages he sends. He intervenes personally but once, when he hurls the lightning before the horses of Diomedes. Apollo strikes Patroklos with his powerful hand, and the armour falls from the hero's body. He goes before Hektor with the aegis and smoothes out with his feet the ditch around the Greek ships as easily as a child at play fills up a hole in the sand. But he never condescends to the office of a squire or to pure deception as Athena does. The intervention of the other gods displays still less of the divine power, is still more strongly humanized. Athena in the *Odyssey* becomes a familiar spirit, except that she is not invoked and compelled to appear but comes freely and spontaneously.

Another rationalistic explanation of the presence of the gods and of certain of their actions is the cloud or darkness which is always at hand when a god wishes to appear among men or to help and save one of his favourites. The gods sit upon the wall of Troy and descend to the fight hidden in a cloud. They withdraw heroes from the contest by wrapping them in a mist; Athena covers Odysseus in the same way when he walks into the town of the Phaeacians, and also when he returns to Ithaca. Apollo protects Hektor's body with a mist. When a cloud lies spread over Olympus and when Zeus on Ida sits enthroned upon a cloud we have a reminiscence of visible Nature. At a later stage the cloud becomes a means of making invisible, resembling the helmet of Hades, the magic hat of our popular belief, and it is probably a rationalistic adaptation of this old popular idea. It is significant of the desire to visualize things that the cloud finally becomes a garment which the gods cast over their shoulders. The outstanding instance is that of Ares turning aside from the fight and sitting in a cloud against which he has leaned his spear. The converse notion of a cloud or darkness covering a person's eyes and preventing him from seeing seldom occurs.

At every point of human life Homer recognizes the influence of a divine power. The gods are the donors of physical and mental advantages, skill, and wealth. The prophetic eye of Calchas, Skamandrios' skill in hunting, Phereklos' art of ship-building, the house-wife's art of weaving, the sceptre of the Pelopides, the armour of Achilles, Pandaros' bow—all are the gifts of the gods. They are lords of the fates of men. They grant the fall of Troy, a safe home-coming, bride and children. The issue of the contest between Hektor and Achilles, the kingship in Troy, Penelope's hand, all these lie in the lap of the gods. They exalt and they cast down, they send prosperity and misfortune. Above all they are lords of life and death. The idea of an all-powerful conscious government of the universe has arisen, a government not according to a uniform plan but in accordance with a single will. It has been much disputed what is the relationship of the individual god's own will to this general idea. The question cannot be decided in the dogmatic fashion usually adopted in the discussion. We must appeal to religious experience, remembering that this finds no insuperable difficulty in allowing contradictory ideas to persist-alongside of one another, and does so all the more easily the older and simpler they are.

Hitherto we have been principally concerned with the poet's own presentation, in particular with his divine apparatus. We have every reason to suppose that this form is adopted by the poet for the purpose of describing the relationships of the gods among themselves and to men, a description which is part of his poetic scheme, but that it does not accord with the Homeric man's real beliefs and expectations in regard to his gods. A means of distinguishing between the poetic presentation and the religious experience and belief has been furnished us in the observation that the gods are treated quite differently in the poet's own presentation and in the speeches which he puts into the mouths of men. The divine apparatus belongs to the former, the speech of men does not make use of it. Where the poet can tell exactly which god it was that intervened, the human character, in reference to the same events, will speak quite vaguely about a *daimon* or some god or the highest god of all, Zeus. There is no mention of Athena in Odysseus' own story of his adventures; in the poet's account she is the ever-present protectress. Exceptions occur, but they belong, characteristically enough, to the special spheres of activity of certain gods, originating in ancient cult and belief: a sudden death is ascribed to the arrows of Apollo and Artemis, the turmoil of the sea to Poseidon, the gift of artistic skill to Athena, the scourge of famine to Demeter's wrath. The king is under the protection of Zeus, but the personal protecting goddess belongs to the myth and therefore to the divine apparatus. With certain definite and easily determined exceptions, therefore, the people of Homer do not make individual gods responsible for all the experiences which they attribute to divine intervention. And these form a large element in their life. * * *

Here, however, we find once again the idea of the universal 'power', even though in a disguised form, developed by the increasing tendency to reflection upon the destinies of human life. For the different events in life have not each a separate *moira* as they have a separate *daimon*. Just as the word is one, so also are events manifestations of one *moira*. The word is nowhere found in the plural except in one late passage, in which personification has already taken place.

This circle of ideas moreover was exposed to the influence of mythological conceptions, which in part contributed to anthropomorphize *moira* and in part to develop fatalism. Just as the *moira* of death is assigned upon the day of birth, so the idea arises that the whole course of life is predetermined at birth. We see it in the well-known image of the destinies that the gods or the powers spin and wind for men, as the spun thread is wound upon the distaff, destinies, that is to say, which the gods allow to come upon them. This predetermination arises from the folk-tale motif of the gifts which the gods bring men on their birthdays or wedding-days, gifts which are to serve them in life. The myths of Meleager and Herakles are examples of this motif. The developing idea of the portion, *moira*, laid hold upon it, and thus arose the notion that fate, the course of life, is determined at birth.

Moira and the *daimones* upon one side, and the gods upon the other represent two stages in religious evolution. The one is earlier and less definite, but has developed in a later and peculiar manner; the other is younger and is characterized by individual and highly specialized anthropomorphic figures. The latter are therefore incapable of appearing as the causes of all the emotions, all the events in which man feels the working of a higher power. The Homeric gods were obliged on account of their special character to leave one sphere of activity to 'power' and 'the powers'. As they themselves were to a great extent Nature-gods, this sphere became first and foremost the life of man in so far as it is not determined by Nature. The limits are neither fixed nor clearly drawn. The word *daimon* also includes 'god', and 'god' can also be used indefinitely or collectively to denote 'power'. As soon as 'power' has gained substantival denomination, for instance, as *moira*, the tendency to personification makes itself felt, and anthropomorphism follows in the train of personification. One god, Zeus, is of so universal and all-embracing a nature that his influence can be traced everywhere. He rules destinies as Moira does, because he, like her, is an expression for the all-embracing 'power'.

The two systems, that of the gods and of 'power', stand upon different foundations: the powers remain behind upon the old foundation which the gods have abandoned. The dispute as to the relationship between the gods and Fate is from the point of view of the history of religion a dispute about words. Simple faith has no difficulty in acquiescing in such contradictions. But the two systems may come into conflict with each other. Homer has left *naïveté* behind and is a rationalist. Logic has, therefore, imposed a problem upon religion. Sometimes, with the simplicity of an earlier time, the gods and *moira* are unconcernedly placed side by side: sometimes *moira* is conceived as determined by the gods and Zeus. Zeus feels himself able to correct *moira*, and refrains from doing so not from lack of power but upon the exhortation of Hera. One system is here subordinated to the other. *Moira* is not taken seriously; we have merely one of the customary conflicts between two gods. But as soon as the underlying sense of order, and therefore of something determined by Fate, was taken seriously, the conflict was brought to a head. The problem was momentous, for the very existence of religion was ultimately involved in it. Religion in the proper sense was not strong in Homer, and this fact is in great measure due to the powerful rivalry of the other system.

It sometimes happened that 'power' received a name adapted to its particular expression. Ate (Blind Folly) is one, but there are several: Strife (Eris), Fear (Deimos, Phobos), Uproar (Kydoimos), in fact perhaps even Ares (the Destroyer) himself, all belong to the same company. These powers are written with capital letters and are called gods, but they are without personality and individuality because they are each nothing but a power of a certain kind. They are personifications. Personification is not an abstraction belonging to a late and far advanced period, as is often said; it is the bastard descendant of 'power' and the god. In its train followed allegory, and of this too there are elaborate examples in Homer. In regard to religious problems, he left a rich and fatal inheritance to later ages, both positively and negatively.

CRITICISM

JEAN RACINE

[Homer Begins Modestly] †

Horace praises the beginning of this poem in his *Art of Poetry* and says that Homer is very far from the practice of those poets who make big promises at the start of a work and fall afterwards to the ground. Homer, instead, begins modestly and then shows big things.

Homer leaves Ulysses on Calypso's island during the first four books and does not have him appear till the fifth. .

JOHANN WOLFGANG VON GOETHE

From *Letters* ‡

I sought to subsume the law of [narrative] retardation under a higher law, and it appeared to belong under this: one could know—yea must know—the outcome of a good poem. The pure and simple "How" should really make for the interest. * * *

The *Odyssey* delays, so to speak, in its smallest parts, and thereby it is affirmed and assured perhaps fifty-fold that the matter will have a happy outcome. So many foreshadowings and predictions that anticipate the end give a counterbalance, I think, to the perpetual delay.

No. 303 (22 April 1797), Vol. I, p. 350

Besides, one would have to struggle against the *Odyssey*, which has already taken away [from a tale of voyage] the most interesting motifs. The arousal of a woman's feeling through the arrival of a stranger,—the loveliest motif—is not to be undertaken any more, given Nausikaa. * * *

For us inhabitants of the mainland it is only the mores in the poem that charm us really. Our imagination rises to the descriptions in it only in an imperfect and sorry way. In what a lustre, though, did this poem appear to me when I read its Cantos in Naples and Sicily! It is as when one puts varnish on a painting whose colors have sunk in; the work appears at once clear and in harmony. I confess it no longer seems a poem but Nature itself, something the more necessary with those ancients when their works were read in the presence of nature. How many of our poems would stand up if read in the market place or under the open sky!

No. 424 (16 February 1798), Vol. II, pp. 48–49

† Jean Racine, *Oeuvres* (Paris: Pléiade, 1966) 2.725. Translated by Albert Cook.
‡ H. S. Chamberlain, ed., *Briefwechsel zwischen Schiller und Goethe* (Jena, 1905). Translated by Albert Cook.

EZRA POUND

[The Homeric World] †

The Homeric world, very human. The *Odyssey* high water mark for the adventure story, as for example Odysseus on the spar after shipwreck. Sam Smiles never got any further in preaching self-reliance. A world of irresponsible gods, a very high society without recognizable morals, the individual responsible to himself.

GABRIEL GERMAIN

Polyphemus and African Initiation Rites ‡

We are now ready to advance the following conclusions:

1. The theme of the Cyclops constitutes a special case in the vast group of tales about ogres. This theme is well defined by its characteristic traits: the single eye of the monster, the puncturing of that eye, flight under the cover of a ram. The outline and the atmosphere remain identical.

2. In treating the theme the way it does, the *Odyssey* distinguishes itself fundamentally from parallel tales (even from the ones closest to it, those of the Caucasus and Berber Morocco) by the contamination which it effects with another theme from folklore: that of deception by means of a name. Moreover, it enriches the folklore with all its borrowing from an already developed dramatic and poetic imagination; but, by interesting contrast, it nevertheless remains very close to the particular logic which governs popular narratives. It receives—it does not *invent*—the historical base. The master of the *Odyssey*, whose much more modern intellectual qualities are affirmed by the general construction and detail of the poem, would not have known how to imitate folklore on this point, even if he had thought of it. If some tales of Hackman's collection are suspected of literary influence, the relative ease with which this is disclosed makes the authenticity of the other tales still more convincing; for them it does not pose a serious question. Besides, if literature often finds its source in the popular tradition, has not the popular tradition sometimes been known to grant its riches to a purely literary theme?

† Ezra Pound, *Guide to Kulchur* (New York, New Directions Publishing Corporation, n.d.) 38. Copyright © 1970 by Ezra Pound. All rights reserved. Reprinted by permission of New Directions Publishing Corporation.

‡ From Gabriel Germain, *Genèse de l'Odyssée* (Paris: Presses Universitaires de France, 1954) 76–81. Translated by A. C. Goodson. Reprinted by permission of the publisher.

3. It is fitting, then, that one seek in this tradition the explanation of the Odyssean narrative, looking as much at its general spirit as at certain details whose original foundation that narrative has obscured.

Under these conditions, the interpretation of stories about ogres from primitive sources is to be taken into serious consideration. P. Saintyves has connected the stories of the "Petit Poucet" (Tom Thumb) series with initiation ceremonies for young men, and the result seems interesting enough for us to try the same method here, *mutandis mutandi*.

The scene, we have said, is almost always in a deserted place. It seems unusual for the heroes to meet a whole population of ogres. The *Odyssey* furnishes Polyphemus with companions, but it leaves us ignorant—we insist on this point—of whether they have the same tastes as him. He remains nothing less than the monster who lives alone ((οἶος), far away from and in front of the others ($\dot{\alpha}\pi\acute{o}\pi\rho o\theta\varepsilon\nu$), always apart ($\dot{\alpha}\pi\acute{\alpha}\nu\varepsilon-\nu\theta\varepsilon\nu$). His kith live within calling distance, but Ulysses is able both to arrive and to escape without passing under their eyes.

It is true that solitude is propitious to the crime without being an inevitable condition for it. It would therefore be possible to seek no more distant explanation for it if what followed did not call for it. Now isolation is obligatory in those tribal initiations in which the secret of the initiation must be absolute. That is why "houses of initiation" are, most frequently, huts built apart from the villages, in the forests. But caves are used as well when they can be found. The facts are too well known to need insistence.

One of the essential characteristics of initiation is its representation of a first death of the novice, which permits him to be reborn again as a transformed being. This is not the place to enumerate all the ways known which simulate that death; only one is of interest here, because it shows in what direction we must look for the origin of the type of the ogre. This is the practice of certain tribes of New Guinea who lend the cabin of initiation a vaguely human form, with a mouth through which the adolescent is passed: He is then considered devoured. But the monster relents through the gift of a boar and consents to reject his prey, who retains the traces of a bite: circumcision. In these and similar rites we may see the explanation for which we are looking.

It is necessary to pick up here, with particular attention, a small but, for the interpretation of our Berber tales, very important fact: in the Magoussaoua of the Sahara, already cited, in the course of initiation, "at the culminating point of ecstasy," the young men are wounded sexually by a leopard—that is, by an initiatory instructor with a leopard mask—from whom it is thought that they suffer a bite. The same mask is used by certain of Adamaoua (Negroes of the western Cameroons), by the man who practices circumcision. Now, we recall that it is a leopard which plays the role of ogre in Text B of these tales. The ritual attachment of this detail appears, from this point on, quite probable.

Let us now go into the house of initiation, ready to consume whatever presents itself, for a moment or for several years. We always find there one, or several, terrifying personages. With the Australians, it is a mythical being called Thuremlin, or Daramulun, or Thrumalun, or Tavanyaika, or Katajalina, or Tumana, or Eruba, or Witurna, or Tundun. The *tubuan* of the Solomon Islands; the magician of the lower Congo; and the celestial, masked visitor of the Fuegians assume, in their dress, frightening aspects as well. The mask is conspicuous among many "primitives," in all ceremonies which have to do with both scaring the uninitiated and "severing the initiating official from his usual surroundings" until he is identified more or less with the being which he represents; as such, his design always answers to "an anti-realistic effort." Failing the mask, the initiator is at least covered with feathers and daubed with color.

It is not so astonishing, then, that ogres easily grow to the height of a house or are distinguished by a deformed face. The ones we are concerned with here conform to the common rule. The form of Polyphemus is like a mountain rather than a man. The Berber monsters, badly disengaged from animality, find their real prototype at the southern edge of the Sahara or with the Sudanese. There, where the "leopard" does not bite the circumcised initiate, he at least steps in to test his courage. "A leopard mask frightens the young initiate in the passage of a subterranean cavern."

We begin to understand the deformity which appears to our voyagers: the single eye. But it is possible to be even more precise. For the primitive mentality, which is extremely conformist, any individual who is not "like everyone else" is disquieting and malevolent. This is carried so far that certain African peoples kill or abandon children whose teeth do not come in in the usual order. Even today, in the popular or infantile environments of Europe, deformities sometimes activate a kind of unconscious hostility, the legacy of ancestral fears. It is easy to see why the masks of the initiators seek grimacing expressions: they really terrify those for whom they are meant; it is only to more evolved spirits that they appear grotesque.

It is quite certain that even today, in North Africa, the person with one eye is considered charged with a baneful power. The same is true among certain black peoples.

In Irish legends, numerous malevolent personages, possessors of supernatural powers, have only one foot, one hand, one eye. Others, who are not at all misformed by nature, have paid for the acquisition of their magic powers by a mutilation of this kind. Similarly, in Germanic traditions, Odhinn had to lose an eye in order to understand the runes.

The invention of the one-eyed ogre is, on the basis of these diverse sources then, quite easy to explain. We have indicated examples of it outside our group of narratives. We also find at least one case of an ogre with three eyes.

T. W. ADORNO

Odysseus, or Mythos and Enlightenment †

Just as the story of the Sirens affirms the interlocking relation between mythos and rational labor, so does the *Odyssey* bear complete witness to the dialectic of enlightenment. The epic appears, in its oldest layer at least, to be tied up with mythos: its adventures derive from folkloristic transmission. But while the Homeric spirit takes possession of myths— organizes them, so to say—it comes also to contradict them. The familiar equation of epic and mythos; which has in any case been discarded by recent classical philology, has been shown by philosophical criticism to be deceiving. The two concepts diverge. They mark two phases of an historical process which can be recognized at the seams of Homeric narrative itself. Homeric diction creates a universality of language if it does not already presuppose this; it dissolves the hieratic social order through the esoteric shape of its presentation, even where it glorifies that same order; to sing of the wrath of Achilles and the wanderings of Odysseus is already a nostalgic stylization of that which no longer can be sung, and the hero of the adventure proves to be the very prototype of bourgeois individuality, whose conception derives from that central self-assertion whose preconceptual model the wandering hero furnishes. In the epic—this opposite of the novel in its philosophy of history—we still find novelistic strains, and the venerable cosmos of the Homeric world, filled as it is with significations, is revealed as the achievement of orderly reason, which destroys mythos by means of rational order, in which this same reason mirrors mythos. * * *

In Homer, epic and mythos, form and content do not so much separate as come to settlement. This aesthetic dualism testifies to a tendency regarding a philosophy of history. "The Apollonian Homer is just the transmitter of that universal human artistic process to which we owe the concept of Individuation."[1]

The myths themselves have been suppressed in the layers of content in Homer; but the report of them, the unity which has been forced onto

† From Max Horkheimer and Theodor W. Adorno, *Dialektik der Aufklärung: Philosophische Fragmente* (Amsterdam: Querido Verlag N. V. 1947). Excursus I, "Odysseus oder Mythos und Aufklärung," pp. 58–83. Translated by A. C. Goodson. Reprinted by permission of the publisher.
1. Friedrich Nietzsche, *Works*, vol. 9, p. 289.

diffuse tales, is nonetheless the description of the path of flight of the subject in the face of mythical powers. This is true in a deeper sense in the *Iliad*. The wrath of a Mycenean son of a goddess against the rational leader-king and organizer, the undisciplined inactivity of that hero, and finally an understanding of this victorious victim of death by way of the Greek national need—no longer just a tribal one—achieved through mythical loyalty to dead companions: these are strands which hold fast this twisting mixture of prehistory and history. This is as much more valid for the *Odyssey* in its contiguity to the form of the novel of adventure. In the exposure of a single surviving ego to a manifold fate, it stamps enlightenment onto mythos. The course of wandering from Troy to Ithaca is the course of the infinitely weak subject's engagement of the power of nature: the path of the self, coming for the first time into self-consciousness, through the world of myth. The preconceptual world is secularized in the space through which the hero travels; old demons people its distant edge and the islands of the civilized Mediterranean Sea, driven back to rock and cave from which, once—in the horror of prehistory—they came into being. The adventures provide each place with its name; and from them a rational view of space is derived. The shivering shipwreck victim anticipates the work of the compass. The very physical weakness of this man to whom no part of the sea is unknown aims at disarming these mythical forces. But the simple failure of truth in the myths (the fact that sea and earth are not actually inhabited by demons—a fantasy and diffusion accountable to the received folk-religion) comes to be seen by the matured hero as "error" in the face of his resolute goal of self-preservation, of his return to home and possessions. The adventures which Odysseus endures are all of them dangerous enticements which draw the self away from the track of its logic. He gives himself up time and again to new experience, tests it as an uninitiated but eager learner, even sometimes as a foolish curiosity-seeker, in the same way that a mime-actor probes insatiably around in his role. "But where there is danger, there grows/ Too the force that saves":[2] knowledge, in which his identity is constituted and which enables him to live through his wanderings, has its substance in the experience of the manifold, the distracting, the dissolving; and the knowledgeable, enduring hero is the same one who, at his boldest, gives himself up to the threat of death and by this becomes durable and strong in life. This is the secret object of contest between epic and mythos: the self does not make adventure out of obstinate opposition, rather it comes to create its own obstinacy by means of this opposition, a stark unity in a world of multiplicity which negates that unity. Odysseus, like the heroes of all real novels after him, gives himself away in order that he may come to win himself; the distancing from nature which he effects is realized in

2. Friedrich Hölderlin, "Patmos," in *Collected Works*, Leipzig, p. 230.

the abandonment to nature which in every episode he eschews; and, ironically, the relentless force which he commands triumphs—he comes home a relentless hero, as judge and avenger of the heritage of the forces he escaped. The identity of self in Homer is so much a function of the realm of the unidentified, of dissociated, inarticulate myths, that it is compelled to borrow itself from these. The internal, organizational form of individuality—time—is still so weak that the unity of adventure, externally—its succession of spatial changes of stage—remains the geographical centers of local deities toward which the storm diverts him. Whenever, historically, the self has again experienced such a weakening, or the artistic representation presumes such weakness in the reader, the story of life again slides off in a succession of adventures. Laboriously and revocably, historical time is discharged in a portrait of journey through space, from the irrevocable scheme of all mythic time.

Cunning is the agent of the self: it enables the hero to withstand adventure, throw himself away, maintain himself. The sailor Odysseus cheats the natural deities as a civilized traveler cheats the savage, offering him colored glass beads in exchange for ivory. It is only occasionally that Odysseus appears in the role of trader. At these times gifts of guest-friendship are given and taken. The Homeric gift of guest-friendship stands somewhere between barter and sacrifice. As a sacrifice it exists to satisfy blood lost, whether that of a foreigner or that of a resident besieged by pirates, and to obtain a vow of peace. At the same time, though, the principle of equivalency is enunciated in the gift of guest-friendship: the host obtains, actually or symbolically, the equivalent value of his gesture while the guest gets provision for his journey, enabling him in some important way to reach home. If the host obtains no negotiable ware for his troubles, he can still figure that he or one of his relations has at some time been similarly received: as a sacrifice to the gods of the elements, the gift of guest-friendship is also a rudimentary kind of insurance in the face of their power. The extensive and dangerous sea travel of early Greece offers an empirical condition for this expedient. Poseidon, Odysseus's elemental enemy, himself thinks in concepts of equivalence, even as he continues to wreak hardship: Odysseus obtains at the stations of his wanderings more in gifts than his portion of the booty at Troy would have been, had he been able to convey it to Ithaca without Poseidon's interference. * * *

The moment of deception in the victim is the prototype of Odyssean cunning just as many of Odysseus's tricks are introduced as a kind of offering to the nature deities. These deities are outwitted by the solar deities as well as by the hero. The Olympic friends of Odysseus use the visit of Poseidon to the Ethiopians, backwoodsmen who worship and offer huge sacrificial victims to him, to lead their ward out of danger. Deception is involved even in the sacrifice which Poseidon gratefully accepts: the enclosure of the amorphous god of the sea at a fixed locality, his holy precinct, contains his power as well, and he is forced to forego his huge meal of Ethiopian oxen in order to vent his rage on Odysseus. All sacrifices by men, systematically carried out, deceive the god for whom they are intended: they subordinate him to the primacy of human purpose, dissolve his power, and his deception is perfectly achieved by the unbelieving priest who carries it out in the believing community. The quality of cunning arises from the cult. Odysseus himself functions as both victim and priest. By the calculation of his own activity he effects the negation of power toward which that activity contrives. So it is that he wins his declining life by bargaining. But deception, trick, and rationality by no means stand in simple opposition to the archaic principle of sacrifice. Through Odysseus, the moment of deception in the victim, perhaps the most profound base of the character of appearance in mythos, is raised to self-consciousness. The realization that symbolic communication with the deity by means of sacrifice is not real must be a primal experience. The sacrificial substitute, glorified by recent irrationalists, cannot be separated from the deification of the sacrificed, from the deception worked by the priest: rationalization of death through the apotheosis of the chosen. Something of this sort of deception, which elevates the weak human being to the role of bearer of the divine substance, has been noticeable ever since in the ego, which owes the sacrifice of the present to the fact of the future. Its substance is appearance, like the immortality of victims of battle. Not without cause was Odysseus mistaken by many as a deity. * * *

It is formulaic for the cunning of Odysseus that the detached, instrumental spirit—yielding to Nature in resignation—gives Nature some of her own and deceives her in the process. The mythical monsters into whose realm of power he falls present fossilized agreements and demands from prehistory. The older folk-religion presented itself thus to the developed patriarchal time in its scattered relics: beneath the Olympian heaven they became figures of abstract Fate and obscure Necessity. That it would have been impossible to choose some other route than the one between Scylla and Charybdis, one may rationalistically come to understand as the mythic transformation of the superiority of the ocean current to the small ships of antiquity. But in the mythically objectified translation, the natural condition of might and powerlessness has already assumed the character of the just condition. Scylla and Charybdis have a right to whatever comes between their teeth, just as Circe has a right to change the shape of the unprotected and Polyphemus the right to the bodies of his guests. Every one of the mythical figures is obliged always to do the same thing. Each exists in repetition: their failure would be their end. All bear strands of that which is grounded by Olympian decree in the punishment myths of the underworld—Tantalos, Sisyphus, the Danaids. They are figures of compulsion: the horrors which they com-mit are the curse that weighs upon them. Mythic inevitability is defined by the equivalence between that curse, the misdeed that atones for it, and the guilt which grows out of it, which guilt reproduces the curse. All justice in hitherto existing history bears the trace of this schema. In mythos, every moment of this circular track satisfies the previous one and helps to install the guilt-connection as law. This is what Odysseus comes up against. The self represents rational universality against the inevitability of fate. But because the self discovers the universal and the inevitable to be interlocked, his understanding assumes a necessarily confined form—that of the exception. He must extract himself from the enclosing and threatening conditions of justice which are to some extent prescribed for every mythical figure. He satisfies the imperative of justice in such a way that it loses its power over him—he confines this power. It is impossible to hear the Sirens and not fall to them: he does not try to defy them. Defiance and infatuation are one, and he who defies them loses with that the mythos to which he stands in relation. The quality of cunning is a kind of rational defiance. Odysseus does not try to travel any other route than the one past the island of the Sirens. He also does not try to presume on the superiority of his knowledge and freely listen to the temptresses, imagining his freedom to suffice as protection. He makes himself insignificant, the ship assumes its predestined, fatal course, and he realizes that he, as listener, is still subject to them, though consciously distanced from nature. He keeps the covenant of his bondage to himself and he still struggles at the mast, trying to throw himself into the arms of the seductresses. But he has found a hole in the covenant through which he escapes the fulfillment of the decree. The prehistoric covenant does not specify whether the victim, passing through Scylla and Charybdis and listening to the song, must be bound or unbound. Bondage first belongs to a stage in cultural development at which prisoners are not immediately killed. Odysseus recognizes the archaic superiority of the song and, being technologically enlightened, he has himself bound. He is aroused by the song of desire and frustrates it as he does death. The bound listener wants to go to the Sirens as much as anyone else. Only he has struck upon an arrangement by which he, though subject to them, is not in fact subjugated. He cannot with all the force of his desire (which reflects the force of the demi-goddesses themselves) go to them, because his rowing companions are deaf not only to the demi-goddesses but also to the desperate cry of their commander. The Sirens have what is theirs, but it already has been neutralized in bourgeois prehistory and become a longing for that which has passed. The epic is silent about what happens to the seductive singers after the ship has disappeared. But in tragedy it must have been their last hour, as it was for the Sphinx when Oedipus solved the riddle, fulfilling her command and overturning her in the process. Since the fortunate (or unfortunate) encounter of Odysseus with the Sirens, all songs have been upset, and the whole of Western music suffers from the absurdity of song in civilization—with which absurdity, however, the moving power of all art music dispenses.

With the breaking of agreement by the verbal observation of it, the historical position of speech is altered: it starts to become designation. The mythic fate *(Fatum)* was one with the spoken word. The circle of performance, to which the maxims of the unalterably executed about fate belong, still does not recognize the difference between word and fact. The word is destined to have immediate power over the object; expression and intention run together. The quality of cunning consists in taking advantage of the distinction. One fastens on the word in order to change the object. In this way the consciousness of intention emerges: Odysseus, in his need, becomes aware of dualism as he discovers that the same word may mean various things. Because the hero, as well as no-man, is referenced by the name *outis*, he is able to break the name taboo. * * * Self-preservational cunning lives on that ruling process of refinement between word and object. The two contradictory acts of Odysseus in his encounter with Polyphemus, his obedience to the name and his dissociation from it, are in fact the same. He knows himself even as he renounces himself as "no man," he saves his life even as he makes it disappear. * * *

One of the first adventures of the actual return to Ithaca reaches very far indeed back in time, even farther back than the barbaric age of grimaced demons and magical gods. It deals with the tale of the Lotus-eaters. He who partakes of their food is subjugated just like anyone who hears the Sirens or is touched by the staff of Circe. But nothing unpleasant awaits the man who thus succumbs: "But from the Lotus-eaters no evil befell the men / Of our crew" (IX.92). Forgetfulness and the dissolution of his will threaten him. The curse damns him to nothing more than the primitive state without work and struggle in the "fruitful field" (XXIII.311). "He who tasted of the lotus plant, sweeter than honey / Thought no more of pronouncement nor of the future;/But tried out the industry of the Lotus-eaters / Remaining to pick lotus and renounce his home" (IX.94). Such an idyl, which is reminiscent of the happiness of a narcotic drug—with the help of which, in hardened social orders, underprivileged classes are made capable of bearing the unbearable—cannot be permitted, for reasons of self-preservation, by their social order. * * *

The next shape to which Odysseus is driven in his wanderings—to be driven out of one's course and to be crafty are equivalents for Homer—is that of the Cyclops Polyphemus, who bears his single eye, large as a wheel, as a mark of this same preconceptual world: the one eye recalls the nose and the mouth, more primitive than the symmetry of the eyes and ears, which—in the unity of two convergent perceptions—first provides identification, depth, and objectivity. He nevertheless represents a later development than the Lotus-eaters, the actual barbaric age of hunters and shepherds. The definition of barbarism coincides, for Homer, with the stipulation that no systematic agriculture be practiced and therefore still no systematic, gradually arranged organization of work and society be achieved. He calls the Cyclopes the "unlawed arrogant" (IX.106) because (and herein lies something like a secret admission of guilt by civilization itself) they "depend on the deathless gods / Nor plant with their hands nor cultivate plants, / But these grow unsown and unploughed / Wheat, barley and vine, which bears / The wine of fine grape-clusters and the rain of Zeus makes them grow" (IX.107–11). This plentitude needs no law, and the civilized accusation of anarchy sounds almost like a denunciation of plenitude itself. "For them there are no council meetings and no laws / But they inhabit the crowns of high-lying mountains / In hollow caves, each proclaiming the law / For his own children and wives, nor do they care about the others" (IX.112–15). This is already a patriarchal, tribal society based on the repression of the physically weak, but not yet organized on the principle of private property and its hierarchy, and it is the disconnectedness of those who dwell in the cave that accounts for the lack of objective law and with it the Homeric reproach of reciprocal indifference, of their wild condition. In this the pragmatic fidelity of the narrator contradicts at a later place his own civilized judgment: at the desperate cry of the blinded Cyclops his tribe comes out to help him in spite of that "indifference," and only Odysseus's name-trick keeps these foolish creatures away, standing beside their own kind. Stupidity and lawlessness appear as the same attribute: if Homer calls the Cyclops that "monster knowing the state of lawlessness" (IX.428), this means not just that his thought does not respect the laws of civilization, but also that his thought itself is lawless, unsystematic, and rhapsodic; just as he is unable to deal with a lesson in bourgeois thought—the way in which his uninvited guests are able to escape the cave by fastening themselves to the sheep's undersides instead of riding upon them—so the sophistical double sense of Odysseus's false name does not occur to him.* * *

CEDRIC H. WHITMAN

The *Odyssey* and Change †

The *Odyssey* is the work of a master, though perhaps of a master whose zenith, as Longinus suggests, has gone by.

Whether or not it was the same master who wrote the *Iliad* is a question which must probably remain unanswered, except in the personal convictions of individuals. Suffice it to say here that, for all the real and even extreme contrast between the two poems, there has yet to be produced a single cogent argument to the effect that they must belong to different hands, or different eras. Arguments drawn from minor points of subject matter, such as Phoenicians, the knowledge of riding astride of horses, familiarity with Egypt, and all such, provide intolerable examples of argument from silence, at best, and at worst betray convictions about Homer more positivistic than well-informed. Attempts on linguistic grounds to prove the *Odyssey* later fail utterly; the epic language, save for what differences must exist because of the differences in the setting and the story, is the same for both poems, and in the *Odyssey* no neologisms exist of such a convincing sort that we must put the poem very much later than the *Iliad*. Also, on the grounds of oral theory, the *Odyssey* cannot be pushed very far into the period when literacy and a changing society were popularizing the various forms of lyric poetry, and relegating oral composition to the obscure corners of the Greek world. If the *Odyssey* belonged in any real sense to the seventh century, it must have been composed in some such obscure corner by a poet with old-fashioned tastes, bent on following in the wake of the *Iliad*, and essentially unmoved by the world around him. If such a poet existed—and many may have—it is hard to see how his work ever became known as Homer's. In the seventh century, the least of poets signed his work, and even the poems of the *Cycle* have names other than Homer's (and sometimes several) attached to them. To say the least, it is an uneconomical hypothesis to put the *Odyssey* so late. Both great epics belong to the most mature period of oral composition; both reflect the synthetic and formalized vision of the heroic Bronze Age in essentially the same way; both have ecumenical breadth, and tend to draw into their schemes large sections of the myth of Troy not immediately involved in the plot; both are complex, monumental, and retrospective; and both show much in common with the Athenian artistic approach, at once vivid, lucid, and subtle.

Such basic similarities point to similar poetic concerns and a similar

† From Cedric H. Whitman, *Homer and The Homeric Tradition* (Cambridge: Harvard UP, 1958) 286–89. Reprinted by permission of the publisher. Copyright 1958, by the President and Fellows of Harvard College.

period of composition. But if one looks at certain differences of compositional approach, one may be able to guess the relation between the two poems a little more accurately. That the *Odyssey* is later than the *Iliad* most will agree, albeit the agreement is often based on the groundless assumption that the *Odyssey* is more "civilized," because more concerned with civilization as such, and the *Iliad* more primitive. The reverse could be asserted with equal truth, and, in any event, the *Iliad* penetrates further into the frontier mysteries of human psychology. But the relative outlooks upon character and experience cannot be decisive in such a matter. More significant is the relative structure of the two poems. The *Iliad*, as already shown, follows a strict Geometric design comparable to nothing except the sepulchral vases of the Dipylon. Very little of the sort occurs in the *Odyssey*, and where it does occur, asymmetrical elements are more frequent, the responsions less careful and less significant. The antithetical polarities of the hysteron-proteron technique enhance meaning in the *Iliad*; insofar as they exist in the *Odyssey*, they are somewhat perfunctory, and the sense of form which one derives from the poem comes far less from repeated or inverted themes and episodes than from the substance of the narrative itself, its progress through time, and its achievement of a long-awaited end. The *Iliad* is tightly designed in every instant; the *Odyssey* sings itself, proceeding with a natural, leisurely pace, entirely suited to the prevailing mood of a large landscape with figures. For this reason, perhaps, the *Odyssey* has far fewer similes than the *Iliad*: the latter concentrates on one *mise en scène*, one major action, one monolithic idea of the heroic; visions of the rest of the world therefore knot themselves into hard images which cluster luminously around the rush of action. The *Odyssey* has a wider lens; it peers less deeply, but takes time to describe. Its object, like that of its hero, is often simply to see:

> Standing there, divine long-suffering Odysseus gazed.

And there is very little which Odysseus will not take time to look at. The same objective scrutiny falls on Cyclops, Circe, the suitors, Eumaeus' steading, the gardens of Alcinous, the faithless maidservants, and weeping Penelope—"eyes like horn or iron." The *Odyssey* keeps building scenic episodes, typical and often static, and in these lie its chief symbols, not, as in the *Iliad*, in continuous and ever-shifting motifs.

This is not to say, however, that no evidences of Geometric design are to be found in the *Odyssey*. Certain parts, especially the *Adventures* and the Phaeacian episode, show conscious scenic antithesis and framing patterns. The *Adventures* are particularly elegant, grouped as they are around the supreme adventure, the Journey to the Dead. This central episode, with its retrospect upon the whole heroic tradition in the ghosts of Ajax, Achilles, Agamemnon, and Heracles, and its mysterious prospect of peace at last and "death from the sea" in the prophecy of

316 CEDRIC H. WHITMAN

Teiresias, is carefully framed, first by the two Elpenor episodes, and then by the two scenes with Circe. For the rest, the poet summarizes two out of every three adventures rather briefly, and dramatizes one at greater length, so that the pattern of Odysseus' narrative is as follows:

Odyssey 9–12

{ Ciconians
{ Lotophagi
   CYCLOPS
{ Aeolus
{ Laestrygonians
┌CIRCE
│┌Elpenor
││ NEKYIA
│└Elpenor
└CIRCE
{ Sirens
{ Scylla—Charybdis
   THRINACIA
{ Scylla—Charybdis
{ Calypso

Calypso, of course, is dramatized in her own right in Book 5, but not in the narrative of the hero. Book 8 offers, perhaps, a more interesting Geometric structure. Here Odysseus is deliberately contrasted with his Phaeacian hosts, who grow more and more impressed and mystified by him until finally nothing will satisfy save the full narrative of his adventures. The whole book turns on the two principles of music and gymnastic, keynotes of civilization to the Greek mind, and both highly developed by the peace-loving and somewhat soft Phaeacians. Odysseus proves the supremacy in bodily arts of the lonely and experienced hero over those who dwell in the ivory tower on the edge of the world. As for music, he is not a singer, but he emerges as the living substance of the heroic lays of Demodocus, which are mere amusement to the Phaeacians. Of Demodocus' three songs, the middle one of Ares and Aphrodite, with its ring of Olympian laughter, is a lighthearted romance appropriate to the people who love warm baths and bed; the first and the last are Trojan songs appropriate to Odysseus, deeply involved with his identity, and prompting those tears which in turn lead to the full revelation of his experience. Few episodes in Homer are more skillfully handled than the Eighth Odyssey; form and purpose are truly one:

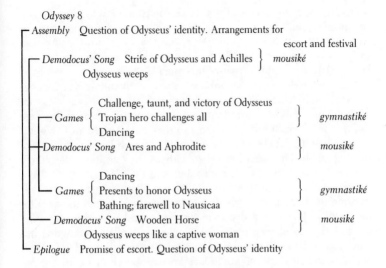

Odyssey 8

Assembly Question of Odysseus' identity. Arrangements for escort and festival

Demodocus' Song Strife of Odysseus and Achilles } *mousiké*
 Odysseus weeps

Games { Challenge, taunt, and victory of Odysseus
 Trojan hero challenges all } *gymnastiké*
 Dancing

Demodocus' Song Ares and Aphrodite } *mousiké*

Games { Dancing
 Presents to honor Odysseus } *gymnastiké*
 Bathing; farewell to Nausicaa

Demodocus' Song Wooden Horse } *mousiké*
 Odysseus weeps like a captive woman

Epilogue Promise of escort. Question of Odysseus' identity

ANNE AMORY

The Reunion of Odysseus and Penelope †

At this point, the poet cannot pause for a detailed explanation of Penelope's state of mind and reasons for deciding to set the contest now. He simply states that Athene inspired her to go and get the bow (21.1–2). For those who misunderstand the role of the gods in Homer, Penelope's decision here inevitably seems abrupt and unmotivated, and Athene's intervention appears an arbitrary resort to a *dea ex machina*. But Homer habitually objectifies internal mental processes in the figures of gods, and always with due regard for the psychological reality of his characters. Here Athene's intervention is a kind of shorthand for a psychological process at a moment when the narrative is too crowded to permit fuller presentation, but it also symbolizes the fact that Penelope, acting only on intuition, without a full knowledge of the situation, does just the right thing at the right time.

There are several other indications in what follows that Penelope is acting without full conscious knowledge either of the situation or of her own emotions. When she takes down Odysseus' bow she weeps for a while, but no explanation of her tears is given, as it is on the other occasions when she weeps. It is not hard to furnish reasons. She weeps, in part, simply because the bow reminds her of Odysseus, just as Eumaeus and Philoetius weep when they see it (21.82–83). Sheer nervous ten-

† From Charles H. Taylor, Jr., *Essays on the Odyssey* (Bloomington, Ind: U of Indiana P, 1963) 113–17. Reprinted by permission of Charles H. Taylor, Jr.

sion, too, accounts for her tears, since she is committing herself to a course of action which is irrevocable, and about whose outcome she feels the utmost anxiety. Nonetheless, the absence of any stated reason suggests that Penelope herself does not entirely know why she weeps, because she does not really know how she feels.

Next, when she makes her announcement to the suitors, she does not give the reason which the suitors might expect—that she has at last given up hope of Odysseus' return. Instead she speaks rather as if she were calling the suitors' bluff. First she says they have feasted in Odysseus' house while he was absent and could not put forward any pretext except that they wished to marry her. Then without any transition, she simply goes on—"Come now, since the contest is ready" (21.73).

She watches silently while the suitors one after another try, and fail, to string the bow. Leodes, the first to try, speaks a word of ill omen for the suitors: "This bow will strip many good men of their life and soul" (21.153–154). Antinous replies angrily that he is talking nonsense, but Odysseus, Telemachus, and Penelope, who have understood the import of Theoclymenus' vision, would take Leodes' speech as a confirmatory *klēdōn*.

Eventually Odysseus, who has in the meantime disclosed himself to Eumaeus and Philoetius, comes forward and asks to try the bow so that he can see if any of his old strength remains. The suitors are afraid he may succeed (having seen him at work on Irus) and Antinous violently denies his request. But Penelope intervenes and tells Antinous not to insult Telemachus' guests. "Do you suppose," she goes on, "that the stranger will expect to marry me if he succeeds in stringing Odysseus' great bow? I am sure such a thought hasn't entered his mind" (21.312–317). Eurymachus replies that, of course, they do not expect the beggar to marry Penelope. But they are concerned about what the common people will say—that they have been unable to measure up to the man whose wife they are courting, while some poor beggar was easily able to string the bow (21.321–329).

Penelope retorts that they need not be so careful of their reputations, which have suffered already because of their disgraceful behavior. Even if the stranger should succeed, it would be no reflection on them, for he is big and well-built and claims to come of a noble family. She promises that if the stranger strings the bow she will give him clothes and arms and send him wherever he wishes to go.

Penelope's speeches are most delicately done and show to the best advantage on the assumption that her recognition of Odysseus is still mostly unconscious. If she has definitely recognized him, as Harsh thinks, her words seem a little bland; we expect a sharper edge of double meaning. If she has no suspicions of his real identity, as many scholars assume, they are too apropos. Even the pressing claims of Greek hospitality do not demand her lavish promises. And why should she champion the beggar's request at all, or why should the idea that he might marry her need disclaiming? He has only asked to string the bow, not to enter the contest. As it is, she hovers charmingly between saying almost too much and not quite enough.

What she says is the literal truth, as far as the action which will result from the contest is concerned. The beggar will not marry her, for he has done that already. She will furnish him with new clothes and arms, but they will be his own. She will send him where he wants to go, but he will not want to go anywhere, except to her—at least for the moment. At the same time, her words are almost startlingly removed from the truth of what she will feel when she knows the result of the contest. This is a very curious state of affairs, appropriate only to the particular way in which the story is told in our *Odyssey*.

There is one other consideration that is often overlooked in assessing Penelope's reasons for setting the contest of the bow at this moment. The contest itself is a means of divination. One modern critic complains that Penelope might "just as well have invoked the chances of the lot." [1] Indeed she might, and with good reason, according to ancient belief. For subjecting an important choice to an apparently chance process, including that of drawing lots, was a regular means of ascertaining the will of the gods and insuring the right choice. Hence Penelope, since her feelings are too complex and contradictory to guide her clearly, is doing the only safe thing in resorting to the contest. For if the omens are right, if the stranger had good reason for his advice, then she is doing exactly what Odysseus wants her to do. If, on the other hand, the omens are wrong and her trust in the stranger a result of self-deception, so that one of the suitors may win the contest, then she will at least be marrying a man who is the least inferior to Odysseus. If, that is, any one of the suitors succeeds; there is after all a good chance that none will, so that if Odysseus is neither present nor coming, the contest will prove merely another delaying device, as her web was in the original version of the story.

In the revenge theme, the stringing of the bow is itself an omen of success for Odysseus, for it assures him that his old prowess is still intact. This decisive moment is preceded by a *klēdōn*, marked by similes, and followed by an omen. The suitors make scornful remarks when Odysseus first picks up the bow; one wishes that the bow may be as likely to give him profit or delight *(onesios)* as he is likely to succeed in stringing it (21.402–403). But Odysseus fits the string to the bow as easily as a bard strings his lyre, and the first arrow sings like a swallow. The suitors,

1. W. J. Woodhouse, *The Composition of Homer's Odyssey* (London: Oxford University Press, 1930), pp. 82–83.

at last realizing that their doom is at hand, turn pale, while Zeus thunders giving signs *(sēmata)*, and Odysseus rejoices at the omen *(teras)*.

When the battle begins, the long sequence of omens in the *Odyssey* is almost complete. There is only one more real omen, at the very end of the poem. Zeus hurls a thunderbolt to convince Odysseus that he must not continue the fight with the Ithacans (24.539–540). Zeus is the special protector of kings in Homer, and it is possible to interpret this omen as a symbol which marks the final supremacy of the true king returned. On the other hand, the action of the end of the *Odyssey* is only sketched in rapidly, because the major significant themes have been completed. Zeus' thunderbolt accomplishes something that the poet wants in the action—which is the simplest function of omens in the narrative of Homer—and the symbolic overtones are only lightly sounded.

Meanwhile there remains Athene's appearance during the slaying of the suitors. The incident is a perfect illustration and summary of the principles which govern the action of the gods in the Homeric poems. At a critical point in the battle Athene appears in the guise of Mentor, an old friend of Odysseus. Odysseus greets her joyfully, just as if he thought it was Mentor himself, but he knows, or suspects, that it is really Athene (22.210). The suitors also address Athene as if she were Mentor, but without any suspicion of her real identity. She then turns to Odysseus and accuses him of being less brave now than he was at Troy fighting for Helen's sake, although he should be braver when fighting for his own possessions (22.226–235). The goddess does not bring immediate victory; she flies up to the roof, leaving Odysseus on his own. At this the suitors rally and attack. But Athene makes their spears miscarry, while helping Odysseus' party to hit their targets. Only at the very end does she raise her aegis and spread panic among the remaining suitors.

In this scene, Athene's speech represents Odysseus' own momentary fear of failure when his arrows are gone (21.147–149) and the way in which he regains his courage by reminding himself that he survived Troy and is now fighting for something more important to him personally. Athene's appearance as Mentor represents the suitors' feeling that they will not be able to defeat Odysseus; her disappearance indicates their surge of confidence as they remind themselves of their far superior numbers and realize the weakness of Odysseus' position. Their confidence is overconfidence, however, and they miss their aim. The raising of the aegis is a sign of the decisive moment in any battle where one side breaks completely. The whole scene is a fine blending of the miraculous and the natural, and a good example of the economy of narrative and impressiveness of dramatic effect which epic gained by using the gods as it did.

ALBERT COOK

The Man of Many Turns †

The epic poem is all-embracing; it is comprehensive, rather than encyclopedic, in character. It is their focus, more even than their lack of verse form, which deprives *Finnegans Wake* or *La Comédie Humaine* of an epic aura, and which almost gives one to *War and Peace*. The distinction, while elusive, is nicely illustrated by the contrast between the encyclopedic *Tesoro* of Dante's master Brunetto Latini and the comprehensiveness of the *Divina Commedia* itself.

The code that is to press the mortality of the hero, the verse style that is to sound the depths of his objectified feeling, though they must derive from tradition, cannot simply be received from it, even if the tradition be that of the man's earlier work.

An epic poem must find its embodiment in a wholly adequate fable. The test of adequacy is not to be found in some generality such as War, the subject of many long poems, or Wandering, the subject of many others. An epic adequacy, moreover, cannot be said to be guaranteed by the resonance of an archetypal plot. Poems with stories, short and long, in all conventions, draw as heavily on the archetypal situation as they do on the rhythmic emphasis of a meter—that is to say all but universally—and perhaps for related reasons. It may be said, in brief, that epic adequacy resides in some myth that can unify all the incidents of a given poem into a view of experience large enough to pose completeness for the life of the protagonist. The poet's great task of invention is finding the myth for his particular poem, a problem that Homer had to solve by centering on Achilles no less than Milton did by centering on Adam. Such adequacy may not be gained by merely choosing a subject which superficially resembles some other adequate myth. Each epic, to possess its own universality, must fully articulate the view it envisions on ground it wins for itself. It is the poet of *Beowulf* who makes his myth superior to that of the *Waltharius*. Looking at epic poems after the fact, we can remark on the aptness of the invention: if such aptness were completely bound up with generic laws, we would have more epic poems than we do. Getting the right myth and a "classic line" together at full pitch is one of the rarest of literary acts.

So Homer—if we may conceive of the same man moving on with the same traditional equipment from *Iliad* to *Odyssey*—did not repeat himself by selecting some similar myth. He did not go on to the Seven Against Thebes or some other war, as Apollonius superficially chose Jason because Odysseus had been done, as Statius and so many others

† From Albert Cook, *The Classic Line* (Bloomington, Ind.: Indiana UP, 1966) 120–37. Reprinted by permission of the publisher.

opted for their own or another national myth of war, aping the *Iliad*. Nor did he handle his verse in quite the same way.

Homer managed the complexity of the *Iliad* by coordinating an entire society at war. This achievement was unique, and since it was, it could not serve him for a poem which presents a like complexity in the sequential experience of a single hero.

Achilles stands at the center of the *Iliad*, but his world measures him. Odysseus, however, measures his world as he moves through it. And it does not alter him; he remains the same from first to last, not only in the actual time span of the poem, but also, essentially, over the twenty years of his wanderings.

In his dominance of the action he resembles Beowulf, Roland, and the Cid. But their experience is also single, while Odysseus goes through varieties of experiences that intimately mirror his complexity while testing his mind and emotions. In its characteristically light and subtle way, the *Odyssey* exhibits a hero whose experience is internalized; whose psyche is plumbed. So the heroes of the best epic poems after Homer— Aeneas, Dante, Adam—resemble Odysseus more closely than they do Achilles. And Pound has taken Odysseus in *The Cantos* for the persona most fit to mirror his varieties of experience.

The actual fable *(logos)* of the *Odyssey* is short, as Aristotle points out. And yet the poem is complexly interwoven *(peplegmenon)*. This is because we have recognition *(anagnorisis)* throughout, he says, and this simple term serves as well as any other to describe Homer's mediation between his single hero and the hero's manifold experience.

The poem insists on this singleness, and this complexity, in its very first line:

Ἄνδρα μοι ἔννεπε Μοῦσα, πολύτροπον, ὃς μάλα πολλὰ
Tell me, Muse, about the man of many turns, who many . . .

Man, the first word. Complexity is named twice, in *polutropon*, "of many turns," and also in *polla*, "many."

Odysseus' situation deepens in time, and the situation of the poem deepens as it progresses; yet Odysseus' adequacy remains everywhere the same in all its aspects *(polutropos)*. Only by a kind of alteration of the substance of the poem can we accept Cedric Whitman's reading of a developing self for Odysseus. His wholeness appears from the beginning in the memory of friends and comrades about him, in the persistence of his return, in his adroitness at meeting the enigmas of societies so variable that beside them the forms of Proteus which Menelaus must master seem simple indeed.

Through all the "change" of the poem—the term is Whitman's— Odysseus, by intelligence and striving (as the opening tells us) copes consistently with minds and peoples:

> Tell me, Muse, about the man of many turns, who many
> Ways wandered when he had sacked Troy's holy citadel;
> He saw the cities of many men and he knew their thought.

The variations of scene in the Odyssey involve a progression from the young to the mature (Telemachus to Odysseus), from the old to the new (Ithaca to a Phaeacian present), from the single to the complex (Nestor to Menelaus; Calypso to and through Circe), from the hostile to the hospitable (Ciconians to Phaeacians), from the natural to the fantastic (Ciconians to Hades, to the Oxen of the Sun groaning on the roasting spits), from the known Troy far from home to the remote Phaeacia whence Odysseus may soon sail for Ithaca.

Underlying these progressions is the psyche of the hero, broad because we have narrow ones (Nestor, Telemachus) for comparison. And since everyone's experience is appropriate for his character, the experience becomes a figure of the extent and complexity and subtlety of his inner life.

Applying this principle of congruence between a man's self and his destiny to the smaller characters, to the other peoples, we may apply it *a fortiori* to Odysseus. In this principle lies the canon of unity for the whole poem. Character in the *Iliad* is a given affirmation of a man's stable situation. In the *Odyssey* the situation is in flux, which means not that character changes, but that the flux of situation itself is seen to rest obscurely on the predisposition of the person or persons involved, character as fate.

The heroes return from war on voyages that are revelatory to us of their very selves. The simple Nestor had a straight return, the proud Agamemnon a disastrous one. The subtle and elegant Menelaus, a slighter of the gods, finds a return which tests his subtlety. Prompted by a nymph, he must first grapple with Proteus' sleepy noon disguises on lonely Pharos; then sacrifice in Egypt to the gods. Far more various are the wanderings of Odysseus, and consequently far more famous is Odysseus himself. He is outstanding in all virtues (IV, 815: *pantoies aretesi*[1] *kekasmenon*). And the fullness of his humanity is mirrored in his wanderings.

Telemachus, too, voyages to learn to become like his father, to overcome his excessive respect (*aidos*, III, 24). He already has too much of what Achilles had too little. As the disguised goddess of wisdom says to him:

> Few are the sons who are equal to their fathers;
> Most are worse, but few are better than their fathers.
> If you would not be a coward hereafter, and senseless,
> If the counsel of Odysseus has not forsaken you wholly.
> Your hope in that case is to bring these deeds to pass.
>
> (II, 276–280)

1. The plural here forbids our reading *aretesi* in anything like a Platonic sense.

Telemachus passes over into his manhood; it is through him, as he moves into the present of the poem, that the narrative begins, evoking both memory and futurity in the longing for Odysseus, and also the dim sense that the father who has been gone so long may have come to his mortal end.

Telemachus, risking a voyage to learn the facts about his father, learns that no simple facts are forthcoming, because facts undergo the alteration of memory; the glorious Trojan war that Nestor tells about, in which he and Odysseus were equal counsellors, does not seem the exploit that subtle Helen and Menelaus remember, focusing as it does on the deceptions of the wooden horse.

How a man sees things depends on who he is; Intelligence is the presiding goddess. These gods are not objective, standing for the unknown-and-visible, as in the *Iliad*. They are clear in the *Odyssey*, and yet they too vary according to the observer, who is then himself objectively presented in the foreground of the poem. To Menelaus they are beings who must be propitiated. Nestor sees them as stubborn (III, 147), Helen as capable of great favor (IV, 220–222), the Phaeacians as always benign. At the same time this particular people takes the gods with sophisticated familiarity and humor, laughing at Demodocus' tale about Ares and Aphrodite; adultery occasions mirth for them—the very evil that Penelope has been avoiding for twenty years.

Character is fate: who a man is also determines how far he goes, how widely he is tested, what sort of a home he has made his own. In this sense men get exactly what they deserve, a moral transparently presented at the very outset in Zeus' speech to Athene and the other gods:

> Well now, how mortal men do accuse the gods!
> They say evils come from us, yet they themselves
> By their own recklessness get pains beyond their lot.

The Phaeacians are near to the gods (V, 35); they dwell far away from other mortals, having been close to the challenging Cyclops. Their location and their way of life are taken altogether for a total character that compasses Odysseus at this stage, but does not absorb him.

Each man is closed in the world of his own perceptions, and so is each people. Each place visited is an episode for the variable Odysseus, as in a lesser way for his searching son. Nestor lives a simple life, his boys doing his work for him. It is a comfortable life, too; there are smooth stones before his palace. Beyond his imagination, overland from his territory, lies the elegant court of Menelaus, come upon characteristically in the midst of a wedding celebration. In that court there is a dominance of ceremoniousness all but total. But neither of Telemachus' hosts exhibits any trait so surprising as the near-supernaturalism of the Phaeacians, who also marry their cousins; or the out-and-out incest of the forever dining children of Aeolus.

Pain [2] befalls man, but the gods have taken pain away from the Phaeacians. With pain, the gods have taken away the sort of wholeness exemplified, as always, by Odysseus, who lands naked and hungry on *their*
shore just before finally going home. Nestor can face pain in nostalgia,
but Menelaus can stand little pain. His "heart breaks," he tells us, when
he learns from Proteus that he must sail the relatively little distance from
Pharos to Egypt. And he has small patience for combat, as his words
imply:

> quick is the glut of cold lamentation
> (IV, 103)

Helen passes to her guests a drink with a nepenthe in it, to make the
drinker so forget all his pain that:

> He would not shed a tear down his cheeks the whole day long,
> Not if his mother and his father were both to die,
> Not if right in front of him his brother or his dear son
> Were slaughtered with bronze, and he saw it with his own eyes.
> (IV, 224–7)

Through the formality of Helen and Menelaus there is felt a certain
coldness. And to Odysseus the Phaeacians display a childish eagerness,
for all their own elegance. Menelaus has the servants bathe Telemachus, a task Nestor assigned to his own daughter. Anxious about their
cleanliness, Menelaus orders the bath as soon as they arrive; Nestor has
had it done as a send-off. Such coldness, in this poem of heartfelt pain
and joy, may evidence cruelty. Menelaus mentions casually that if
Odysseus should care to settle nearby, he would gladly sack and depo-
pulate a city for his old friend.

Each character, of place and society, becomes objectified in the comparing eye of the visitor; Telemachus, like his father, can compass the
varieties by encountering them. Home is the norm, and Ithaca—unlike
Aegea or Ogygia or Phaeacia or Pylos or Argos—has no special features
other than the chaos into which it has fallen.

Odysseus discovers himself on his way home. The wideness of the
way, the wideness of the character destined for so much turning, becomes
apparent by comparison with the briefer ways of others, and by the more
circumscribed societies, each of which objectifies a whole moral attitude
and destiny: a character *(ethos)* of the sort Aristotle asserted this poem to
be woven from *(peplegmenon)*.

Ithaca lacks the heightened felicity of Lacedaemon and Phaeacia, their
ordered painlessness and easy delight. Subject to pain and chaos, it is
the more rooted in the human variety known and sought by its absent

2. George Dimock finds pain the pervasive theme of the *Odyssey*, deriving Odysseus' name from
the verb for suffering.

overlord, and it stands waiting in memory, changing in reality, for his rearrival. When he does arrive, his reinstitution must be so deliberate as to take nearly half the poem. While Odysseus wanders, Ithaca stands in unseen relation to him, though from the beginning it is portrayed in its changed reality. Perpetually the poem holds his biased and unswaying nostalgia in a comparison, often unexpressed, between home and the place of sojourn. Explicitly he declares that Calypso surpasses Penelope in appearance and form, but such ideal excellence pales before the real rootedness of his mortality. Telemachus, in refusing Menelaus' gift of horses, admits that Ithaca affords poor pasturage; but he persists in his superlative praise of the island:

> In Ithaca there are no broad courses or any meadow;
> It has pasture for goats and is pleasanter than a horse pasture.
> But none of the islands that lie by the sea has good meadows
> Or a place for driving horses, and Ithaca surpasses them all.
>
> (IV, 605–8)

So he feels; and so does his father, enough to strain his ingenuity to return there.

This epic hero substitutes supple intelligence for the courage and prowess of the Cid, Beowulf, and Achilles. He follows not a code but the course of his own longing, an inner canon the poem sets out as equally to be trusted. Consistently, then, he does not gather all he knows in order to face the unknown. He acts on hunches (Lestrygonians) or social canniness (Phaeacia) or a surfaced feeling (Calypso) or luck (Circe) or improvised plan (Cyclops). In a sense there is nothing he can rely on as known, because he always copes with a wholly new situation in utter ignorance:

> For I have arrived here as a long suffering stranger
> From afar, from a distant land; so I know no one
> Of the men who conduct this city and its fields.
>
> (VII, 22–25)

He faces not the unknown but the new, not death but transience. Transience, itself a consequence of mortality and a kind of figure for it, replaces death in the imaginative vision of this epic. Longing for permanence drives the resourceful Odysseus round the changing seas and years.

Home itself changes, in the relentless metamorphosis of a third of a life-time. Permanence and change, satisfaction and longing, joy and pain, foresight and happenstance—these never get fixed in hard opposition because Odysseus moves too fast and copes too variously. His fable allows him to embody all these complexities without setting one stiffly against another; without overembroiling himself in any, and also without slighting the real difficulty or allure of a single one.

It is not death he must face. From the present time of the poem on, that risk is slight. In this epic, a life rounds itself out by return to an original mature circumstance that the very course of life has altered.

Change brings pain, and yet the joy of changelessness among the lotus eaters or the Phaeacians lacks the fullness of changeful life. Death may be taken as a fearful circumstance and at the same time as bland fact. The death of his mother Anticleia is spoken of matter-of-factly (XIII, 59) in a salutation wishing joy.

In the seeming universality of transience, arrival seems forever debarred, and Odysseus comes back a second time to Aeolus, who will not help him; to Circe, who greets him with a warning. Back again he comes, also, to Scylla and Charybdis. Death lies as a test in the future. Though the hero's own death is vague and remote, he must risk it and pass its country in order to return. Odysseus can get back only by visiting the dead, all the way past the eternally shrouded Cimmerians. Even then it takes the escort of the Phaeacians, who are near to gods, to get him back. The Phaeacian vessel, moving like a star, unerringly and effortlessly swift, bears Odysseus in a sleep "most like to death" (XIII, 879–92) to the home he has not been able to sight for twenty years.

Odysseus has changed so much himself, and Ithaca has become so remote to him, that he does not know where he is when he wakes up there. Of the disguised Athene he asks a question at once obvious and profound: are the inhabitants hospitable or wild?

All is old, and all is new. If Odysseus did not recognize old elements in any new situation, he could not exercise his many wiles. If he did not have to confront the new, there would be less need for any wiles at all.

The need dwindles at the end, but it has not disappeared. At the end of his life he must undertake another journey across the sea and set up a sacrifice to Poseidon among men who do not know the sea (XI, 12 ff).

Odysseus stands midway between the easier returners, achievers of a simpler permanence, Menelaus and Nestor, and those who have died on the return, the victims to change, Agamemnon and Ajax, not to mention all his own followers.

Permanence brings joy, transience, pain. The living sustain a subtle balance between permanence and transience, and so between joy and pain. The sea is sparkling but treacherous; to the solitary Odysseus Ogygia is joyful for its unearthly beauty but painful for its not being home. Pain coalesces with joy, or else a life is shown to lack the epic wholeness: if pain becomes total, one is to die; if joy fully dominates, one enters the lifeless permanence of the Lotus Eaters and the Phaeacians, whom Odysseus' long tale of suffering fills not with tears like his own but with a feeling of charm, the poem twice says (*kelethmos:* XI, 334; XIII, 2).

To return brings joy but causes pain. It is of the joy of return that

Agamemnon speaks (IV, 522)—he who least of all would have cause to remember that joy. Yet the pain of becoming reinstated in a changed home offsets, precedes, and intensifies, the joy of restitution.

In his coping, Odysseus works his way through contrarieties; pain and suffering he names at once when he is asked what his wanderings have brought. Joy can be as much a trial as pain; heartbroken with longing on Calypso's isle, he refuses her blissful immortality but enjoys her in the cave. He lives a year with Circe. The Lotus Eaters, and Phaeacians, and the Sirens all promise—the first could even fulfill—a painless existence wherein the pain might be obviated and even the longing be gone. But the fullness of life demands the wholeness of longing; and Odysseus, delighted and also pained, pushes on to his return. All sufferings of wandering are told, after the tears of a delightful song, to the banqueting, hedonistic court of an Alcinoos who has already promised escort home. The habit of Ithaca counters the novelty of the strange delights, and yet habit too is the enemy of the remembered home: Odysseus stays seven years on Calypso's island.

Within its scheme of variety, this broad poem can vary the key of an alternation between joy and pain without changing its tone. Each episode has a different flavor of joy or pain. As Odysseus sails away from Cyclops, he gets exulting delight in exchange for teeth-gnashing despair. Aeolus occasions first impulsive gladness and then a resigned, fearful despondency. An ocean of moods for the longing hero is held in the single vision of the poem.

2

The poem sustains a sense of the hero's fine equanimity in transience and permanence, in sorrow and joy, by having placed him in a flexible situation where he transcends every person and every people he meets. The equanimity of the hero also enters the verse, for example in its descriptions of the visible world through which Odysseus moves.

A fine veil of poetry, simple and delectating, limns the changing landscapes, none so fully described as Ithaca, and all consequently more immediately redolent of an almost lyric singleness, a seemingly mythic signification. But the significance merely impresses in passing, and does not construct allegories. What are the Cimmerians at the bounds of the deep-flowing ocean, shrouded in darkness and cloud, who never see the beams of the sun or the starry heavens? They are far (Ithaca is nearness) and shrouded (the mists part often in the clarity of the Adriatic sun; Ithaca sees sun and starry heavens). They stand before the underworld, sharing some of its obscurity.

As Stella points out, the fruits and trees of this landscape are described more realistically than the fabulous vegetation found not only in the

jewelled forests of Gilgamesh, but in such Greek legends as the Golden
Apples of Hesperides. Yet as Max Treu says, we cannot distinguish
between fairytale and real in the landscape descriptions of the *Odyssey*.
Its epithets are at once evocative and descriptive, far looser than those in
the *Iliad*:

> The sun arose, leaving the *lovely* lake,
> Into the *much-bronze* heaven, where for immortals it shone,
> And for mortal men upon the *life-giving* earth.
>
> (III, 1–3)

All the grandeur of the *Iliad*, as Longinus says, but less intensity.
Polychalchon,[3] much-bronze, sets off no contrasts between "lovely" and
"life-giving." The attributions are not faceted situationally, as they are
in the *Iliad*. They merely rise to their seemingly haphazard descriptive-
ness, and their rightness seems to reside somewhat in a mythic resonance. The real and the fairy-tale are mingled in the memory of the
recounting Odysseus and the perceptions of the poem's hearer. Against
the joy of a given place stands the hero's own pain; against the beauty of
life the hard risk of death, and the difficult, losing battle against time.
At the end of all the easy hospitalities of Phaeacia, of the checked Circe,
of Calypso, lies the difficult restitution in Ithaca. The transience of an
arriver's longing, of the guest's contingency, clings to the poetry, for
Odysseus' longing son as for himself:

> And they came to hollow Lacedaemon full of ravines.
>
> (IV, 1)

This is a new sight to Telemachus, a temporary one; his enjoyment
of the visual loveliness, the presence of this poetic line in the narrative,
is tinged with his fearful search for light about his father. Helen's nepenthe
does not last for him, though it may for the Lacedaemonian court.

> They when they saw it
> Wondered at the house of the king nourished by Zeus;
> Like the beam of the sun it was or like the moon.
>
> (IV, 43–5)

But the sun goes down, the moon rises, and by day or night there is toil.
Lacedaemon for the son, like Phaeacia or Ogygia for the father, is a
delightful interlude, something unreal in the reality of life. A man who
has a full life on his hands can see the loveliness, along with some of
the unreality. His eyes enjoy the glitter, but his heart is in his mouth;
the words catch the glitter, the rhythm moves wave on nostalgic wave in
the feeling of the poem.

3. Even if this word carries a memory of an Aegean primitive concept of a bronze heaven, as
Stella asserts, we must decide what the epithet denotes in the poem.

The hexameter—lightly!—bears the burden of sadness, reiterating in its "disappointed" last foot the sorrow of the total fable. Poetry makes people weep in the *Odyssey*, even finally in the Phaeacian court. Odysseus himself weeps to hear of Troy, though he weeps behind his veil.

"The accents of the Homeric hexameter are the soft rustle of a leaf in the midday sun, the rhythm of *matter*"—Spengler's fine ear has picked up the characteristic rhythm of the *Odyssey*. Not, I feel, of the *Iliad*. In both poems, of course, quantity determines the main rhythm, and not accent. Where Vergil patterns the subordinate accents, Homer lets them fall where they may. This randomness in the *Iliad* produces a surging afflatus, rather the way the free meter of the ballad does. In the *Odyssey*, I do not hear these free syllables as surging. The unaccounted accents play, as it were, over the surface of the statement, as the words themselves seem to do. In the *Iliad* the unaccounted accents do a more strenuous work, and yet are closer to prose in their lack of emphasis; in the *Odyssey* they twitch the veil of the poetry, rhythmically carrying a sense of the variety of life.

The poetry reveals its lightness in the very particularity of its designations; it touches lightly on literalness, and quite haphazardly (*pace* Auerbach). All is known, but the known is a mystery. Home remains the same, but time changes it. Take the line about the constellation Bear, "which they also call by the name Wagon":

οἴη δ ἄμμορός ἐστι λοετρῶν Ὠκεανοίο.
And it alone has no share in the washings of Ocean.
(v, 275)

The statement conveys a literal piece of astronomical fact, but with a light resonance that lies in each word. "*Oie*," alone, echoes the aloneness of Odysseus. "Has no share," or "unfated" (*ammoros*): in the very negation lies a whole sense of fate, at once specific and general. The "washings" (*loetroi*) are carrying Odysseus too; he is caught in the wash of the ocean stream above which gleams the Bear. In its suggesting of analogy, though, the line is not metaphoric. It merely speaks of the natural world, the stars and the sea, in words that usually apply to man, and so it hints at a participation in a total situation which is not patterned but merely moves ahead in its predictable but incalculable alterations. This hint is absent from the line when it occurs in the *Iliad* merely to describe a point of Achilles' shield.

And the tone of the poem, the fine veil of what, for lack of a more delicate term, we may call irony—that tone veils all the actions and the landscapes. The hexameter carries that tone, forbidding, as it were, even the most dire incident from carrying a tragic cast. The elegiac becomes a delectated likeness. At the height of the grisly Cyclops episode, a joke: Odysseus is "no man." Homer may have got this joke from a folk-tale or

not; it has the same effect in the poem, the consonant presentation of an
exultant joy within a crushing sadness.

Through its tone of equanimity, the verse conveys pain and joy without setting one paradoxically off against the other, as the *Iliad* somewhat
schematically sets the actuality of pain against the memory of joy. The
veil of mystery covers everything in the *Odyssey*; yet everything also shows
through the tonal veil. Deception comes up again and again, the host
of disguises and feints and subtle unmentioned calculations and adjust-
ments which every character makes, and preeminently the resourceful
Odysseus. Even gods deceive; right at the start in Book I they quickly
hold their committee meeting about Odysseus, while his enemy Poseidon, the opposition, is conveniently far away among the Ethiopians.

For all the deceptions, clarity. For all the caprice, justice. For all the
wanderings, return. Here the world is utterly clear and whole, and utterly
mysterious. Its clarity is its mystery, the poetry is declaring. The same
blue Aegean washes real and miraculous shores, and the real and the
miraculous differ only in incidental, equally perceptible details, which
the poetry proffers:

> On the hearth a big fire was burning, and the smell from afar
> Of cedar and easy-split pulp was exhaled to the island
> As it blazed. She within, singing in a lovely voice,
> Going to and fro at the loom, wove with a golden distaff.
> Wood was growing around the cave in abundance,
> Alder and black poplar and well-scented cypress,
> Where the birds with their long wings went to sleep,
> Horned owls and hawks and, with their long tongues,
> Salt water crows, who are busy with the things of the sea.
>   (v, 59–67)

A superlative place, but with a quality finely perceptible as of itself;
distinct from the superlative of Lacedaemon or Phaeacia or Aeaea. The
cave, the trees, the birds, and later the springs and meadows, characterize the physical world of Calypso, which is at the same time her world
of spirit, just as the deepness of Ithaca resides for the poetry, as for the
naming Telemachus, in the very physical homeliness and roughness of
the place.

Often we are given designations for the sea, wine-faced or grey, Pro-
tean as the numberless lands are different. Yet each is clear and whole
unto itself, each capable of receiving at times the enumerative detail
Auerbach claims is typical of the *Odyssey* generally.

Homer, however, is not so enumerative in his verse as Auerbach claims.
The poet does tend to linger over detail of the narrative, as Auerbach
follows Schiller in asserting; but not utterly for the sake of the detail. If

we cannot read some other significance into the detail—the ritual use of
Calypso's trees, for example—we cannot obliterate significance either.
Certainly to assert that Homer tells "everything" would be to make him
inarticulate. He must select, though more abundantly than the inspired
authors of *Genesis*.

Nor can it be said, with Auerbach, that the *Odyssey* has no "background," no hidden depths of motive. It is all foreground, to be sure,
but a light irony holds all the detail. That light irony constitutes the
background, the delicate and profound sense of success in transience, of
unfinality in any terror, which renders the epic sense of life to the *Odyssey*, lightening the poetry and unifying the fable; so that the poem stands
as something at once close to what we expect from a novel in its incident, and yet utterly different from a novel in its final bearing.

3

In all the alterings of circumstance, in all the pains, the hero's self
remains wholly adequate in its adaptability *(polutropos)*—and without
being defined. To take Odysseus' wanderings as deepening him, the way
Cedric Whitman does, involves reading the significance of the places he
visits as allegory or symbol. They do have the ring of archetype, and
they do figure a total spiritual condition, each of them, mysteriously.
Yet to read their significance as symbol or allegory is to pierce the veil
of mystery. The depth is all on the surface, a sunlit mystery. No totality
glides like a Moby Dick in the darkness beneath these waters. To interpret the surface of this poem metaphorically is to translate the surface as
gaining significance from some depth; but the significances are all there
on the surface, embodied simply in landscape and lightness of gesture.

Achilles develops and realizes his manhood. Odysseus moves ahead
with his into time, changing only as he ages, while events at once tax
and fortify him. He simply exists. No coordinated social world can deepen
him; there is only the series of unpredictable surfaces, each complete
and partial in itself, which he shows himself capable by meeting, and
whole by transcending. Intelligence attends him from first to last, and
the manifestation of Athene at his landing on Ithaca attests no special
consideration, no final success, but only a momentary embodiment, as
the world of his striving has actualized itself under his feet without his
being aware of it.

When Odysseus speaks to himself, as he does after having set out from
Ogygia (V, 299ff), the soliloquy explores no motive but merely develops
and estimates the incidence of misfortune. Once again, it is all on the
surface: the depth inheres in the irony with which it is presented, an
irony so slight as to seem transparent, vanishing at a breath.

The irony may at numerous moments emerge into event. Odysseus
slights Calypso in his account to Arete, falsifies his contact with Nausi-

caa, and delicately implies a refusal of Alcinous' marriage offer by men-
tioning in the course of his narrative how he has often refused such offers
elsewhere. Menelaus, who had to wander years because he had slighted
the gods, gives Telemachus a libation bowl! So, the poem hints, he has
learned his lesson. Athene sacrifices to her enemy Poseidon. But the
events need not be ironic; they may be deadly serious, and irony is still
conveyed in the uniform tone of the verse.

Without the *poetry*, the flexible Odyssean hexameter, the humor would
be episodic, and so would the nostalgia. The variety of incident would
then merely add up to a superficial romance of the picaresque with some
fine detail and occasional lyric moments, rather like the *Lusiads*. But in
the *Odyssey* nostalgia comments on humor. Humor and nostalgia blend
but do not fuse in the epic unity of this poem, lighter than the *Iliad*, but
no less profound.

Suffering, even the dark terror of Cyclops or Odysseus' wholesale
slaughter of the suitors, is kept serenely in vision, as it is not in even so
equanimous a comedy as the *Tempest*. Only loosely can the *Odyssey* be
called a comedy, or even a comic epic. It is an epic whose lightness
compasses comic events, and also tragic; that allows of both tragic and
comic events without inventing a whole philosophic relation for them
(or a Dantesque justification) beyond the unitary tonal feeling of myth
and verse.

ALBERT COOK

Visual Aspects of the Homeric Simile
in Indo-European Context †

Language conditions thought. Deep presuppositions are built into the
diction and syntax of the Indo-European languages. These are also built
into their public uses, including the poetic ones. As Émile Benveniste
has shown,[1] the presuppositions from people to Indo-European people,
and specifically from Indian to Greek, exhibit similarities in social institutions as well as in language—similarities in economic organization,
kinship and social structures, authority, law, and religion. Georges
Dumézil has expounded still further aspects of these assumptions common to Indo-European cultures. However, the visual practice within a
single culture goes so deep that I shall argue a marked difference between
the Greek and the Indic modes with respect to this deep integral procedure, however far ranging the Indo-European similarities among them

† From *Quadernt Urbinati di Cultura Classica* n.s. 17:39–59. Reprinted in *Figural Choice in
  Poetry and Art* (Hanover, N.H.: The UP of New England, 1985) 203–23, 247–50.
1. Émile Benveniste, *Le Vocabulaire des institutions indo-européennes* (Paris: Minuit, 1969).

may be. The sharpness, what may be called the dialectic of vision from Mycenean engravers of gems down through Pompeian painters, and in poets from Homer on, differs markedly from the early Indic tradition. The Greek and Roman acuity conditions the heritage that all the poets I have been discussing have effectually drawn on. And in looking at Homer's use of images in his similes, I shall try to bring this whole integral procedure into relief by comparing it to the other chief early Indo-European use, the Rig Veda, matching each tradition with its visual art.

Most early epics are sparing indeed of image and metaphor, even the elaborate Gilgamesh in the long time—more than a millennium—of the various recensions we have. Moreover, putting images into words in the first place for some function other than mere inventory constitutes an advanced mode of expression. Turning to the high art of Homer, we will notice that there is often an intricate visual or explanatory impetus discernible in the Homeric simile, especially when it is somewhat expanded.

As I have pointed out before in discussing the looseness for Homer of subsidiary elements in a comparison,[2] no special similarity exists between arrows and beans or chickpeas in the following simile:

> As when from a broad blade along a great threshing floor
> Beans with black skins or chickpeas are bouncing high
> Under the shrill blast and sweep of the winnower,
>   So from the breastplate of glorious Menelaus
>   The bitter arrow often rebounding away flew afar.
>   (*Iliad* 13.588–92)

A particular kind of motion is discerned, in a way that a modern painter might admire, a "found" motion underlying the bounce of peas on a winnowing fan and the rebound of an arrow from a breastplate. The visual impulse is not so different, I mean, from that of modern "found" sculpture, when Picasso calls a bicycle seat and handlebars a goat's head. The motion Homer describes requires a strain of attention for the auditor, since *beans* is plural but *arrow* is seen singly—it is in the singular—many times *(pollon)*.

Along with this visual acuteness the focus dwells on the scene. It constitutes a kind of framing. Details are got into language that poetry does not pick up until it is quite advanced. In English poetry, for example, one would have to wait till the seventeenth century for so concrete an epithet as *black-skinned*. That this is not merely a classificatory term for beans may be deduced from its other use in the Homeric poems, *Odyssey* 19.246, where it is used to heighten the visual appearance, and so the credibility, of a fictional Eurybates whom Odysseus in his wiles is inventing.

The visualization, pushed to this point, amounts to an extreme pre-

2. Albert Cook, *The Classic Line* (Bloomington: Indiana University Press, 1966), 98–106.

cision, demarcating a scene where we have the shape of the blade, the extent of the threshing floor, and the color of the beans, as well as the alternate chickpeas whose motion would be the same—a particularized sound and motion for the winnower himself. All this in addition to the firmly named four constituents of the scene: floor, blade, beans, and winnower.

The oddness of a comparison, this or another, may be resolved if its visual base is fully allowed. Both Lee and Fränkel find inappropriate the simile that compares Hector to a boar or a lion pressed by a pack of dogs and huntsman (*Il.* 12.41–49).[3] They are bothered by the fact that Hector is not at bay but mounting an attack. The difficulty is minimized, and really resolved, if we see the comparison as mainly a visual one—a single valiant figure surrounded by hosts of enemies, without regard to the success or failure of the outcome. Or again Edward M. Bradley points out in the comparison of Hector to a snowy mountain (*Il.* 13.754–55), "the quality of snow deemed most relevant is that of incessant movement," where an attention to visual cues, as indicated by other mentions of snow in Homer, solves an even more puzzling simile.[4]

Yet the implied contrast between such windows on a world of peace and the world of war that preoccupies the poem is already present in the difference between this attention to subsidiary visual elements and the contrasting attention to psychological effects in the military action.[5] The

3. D. J. N. Lee, *The Similes of the Iliad and the Odyssey Compared* (Melbourne: Melbourne University Press, 1964), 7–8. Lee alleges a type 4 of comparisons that do not hold. This class is smaller than he claims, and very likely empty of examples from Homer. Hermann Fränkel, *Die Homerischen Gleichnisse* (1921; reprint, Göttingen: Vandenhoeck and Ruprecht, 1977), 67.

4. Edward M. Bradley, "Hector and the Simile of the Snowy Mountain," *TAPA* 98 (1967): 37–42.

5. The point has been made often before. See C. M. Bowra, "The Simile," in *Tradition and Design in the Iliad* (Oxford: Clarendon Press, 1930), 114–28. Tilman Krischer (*Formale Konventionen der Homerischen Epik* [Munich: C. H. Beck, 1971], 13–90) elaborately classifies the many similes that occur in the narratives of combat. Hermann Fränkel (*Die Homerischen Gleichnisse*) discusses much about the variety and implication of the world of Homeric similes, expanding his remarks in a later study, *Dichtung und Philosophie der frühen Griechentum* (Munich, 1969, 45–49). K. Riezler ("Das Homerische Gleichnis und der Anfang der Philosophie," *Die Antike* 12 [1936]: 253–71), along with many sensitive comments on the contrastive aspects of the similes, extrapolates this function into the more formalized contrasts proposed by the pre-Socratic philosophers. G. P. Shipp (*Studies in the Language of Homer* [Cambridge: Cambridge University Press, 1953], 18–103), finds many evidences of special poetic freedom in the similes (as against the body of the narrative, which he adduces as evidence for the "lateness" of the similes), comparing them to Mycenean art, with citations. Paolo Vivante ("On Poetry and Language in Homer," *Ramus* 2 [1973]: 143–62) states that "Homer's similes mark the high points of what he sympathetically perceives—human actions, above all, whose manifestations seem to converge and blend into one with those of nature" (165). Michael Coffey ("The Function of the Homeric Simile," *Classical Journal*, 1957, 113–32) finds movement, appearance, sound, measurement of space and time, delineation of "situation," and finally "psychology" in the similes. David H. Porter ("Violent Juxtaposition in the Similes of the Iliad," *Classical Journal* 68 [1972]: 11–21) draws compositional conclusions from the remoteness of the domain in the tenor to that of the vehicle, as does D. F. Rauber ("Some Metaphysical Aspects of the Homeric Simile," *Classical Journal* 65 [1969]: 97–103). A whole world scheme hinges on the similes in Olga Freidenberg's conception (Elliott Mossman, ed., *The Correspondence of Boris Pasternak and Olga Freidenberg, 1910–1954* [New York: Harcourt Brace Jovanovich, 1982], 260, October 30, 1946):

two epithets in the tenor of the chickpea simile are *glorious (kudalimos)* and *bitter (pikros)*, these words belonging for us, if less definitely for Homer, to a more inward realm than *broad, great, black-skinned,* and *shrill.*

Further, there is the question as to why we are given the simile at this particular time in the narrative, and we notice that the battle at hand engages this important warrior for the next sixty lines. This simile is more expanded than the two that precede it, the comparison of Adamas' spear stuck in a shield to a "fire-burned stake" (13.564), and the reaction to his death wound, "he gasped as an ox does that oxherd men in the mountains / Have by force bound with ropes unwillingly and drag along" (571–72). What slows the narrative indicates its importance, and we tend to get similes at points of gathering action, as many commentators have pointed out.

These warriors have no time to harvest chickpeas or drag oxen. The Homeric simile, for its very looseness of subsidiary details in the comparison—by drawing on activities unrelated to the main narrative line of the poem—coordinates peace and war in a vast, balanced perspective. Thus war itself gets a still more profound connection, and the image gets by such contrast an anchorage in a coordinated view of life.

The simile is an important vehicle for this whole perceptual process. Thereby it expands as well as interrupts the narrative.

2

The civilized subtlety, and the particular global character, of figurative language in the Homeric poems falls into relief—and raises questions beyond those of rhetorical organization—if we compare metaphor and simile in Homer to the use of these figures in the other great body of early Indo-European poetry that we possess, the Rig Veda. While Greece, as Indo-Europeanists tell us, strangely scants the full repertoire

---

An analysis of similes from the *Iliad* shows that the second element of a simile (the plant, animal, cosmic, or everyday-life image, to which the first element is compared) is the one that is extended, independent, and realistic.

Animal comparisons are used to express rage, belligerence, and violence; cosmic comparisons express darkness, death, and destruction. Similes from the *Iliad* do not present images of sunlight, only of storm and tempest.

Moreover, in every extended simile the mythological plane provides the basis for that which is being compared, and the realistic plane provides the basis for that to which it is being compared.

The mythological concept of a simile is based on the idea of a struggle taking place between a totem's two phases: action and nonaction. Both phases are presented concretely and in images as the usual mythological opposites: when the evil force triumphs, it is represented as merely a likeness of the true totem, as its aggressive twin; when the good force triumphs, the false chthonian totem is vanquished and is temporarily silenced (as was the good force in the other instance).

Mythological thinking knows no similes because a simile requires purely conceptual processes of abstraction. Mythological thinking has recourse only to personification, animated by the idea of struggle.

See also her *Mif i literatura drevnosti* (Moscow: Nauka, 1978).

of Indo-European mythology, there are common gods—Zeus and Indra, the Dioscuri and the Ashvins. There are also common folkways and common staples of image—the cow, the horse, the sun, the eye, the chariot.[6] Yet, as Hirzel says, in the very assertion of similarity between the two Indo-European domains: "Direkte Parallelen aus unseren griechischen Dichtern lassen sich natürlich nicht geben" (Direct parallels from our Greek poets naturally do not occur) (18).

Similes are very common in the Rig Veda, and in one sense metaphors are too, if one allows as a metaphor an identification so fused as to permit no real separation between tenor and vehicle. Yet these similes are never as expanded as those of Homer, and they rarely contain a visual element. When they are visual, they do not focus in anything like the Homeric precision: on the contrary they offer a vagueness of flash and blur, as in these lines from a hymn to the Usas, the Dawns:

> ásthur u citrà Ushásaḥ purástan
> mitá iva sváravo adhvaréshu
> (4.51–52)
> In the East the brilliant dawns have stood
> Like posts set up at sacrifices

The point of comparison is the flash or shining, probably, since the word for sacrificial posts, as Macdonnell notes, may derive from the root *svar*, to shine. Yet these visual effects of brightness, *citra* and *svar*, are only potentially assimilable to one another. And the play of light across an ointment spread on a post has no other visual similarity than brightness to the more diffuse and more encompassing light of dawn in the sky. The subsidiary details of the comparison, in this light, cannot be ruled out: a general religious aura—these are hymns—takes in worshipped dawns and sacrificial acts of worship.

We are far from the sharp outlines of Homer, far enough to distrust any assimilation of his narrative epic to some tradition of common origin with the hymns of the Rig Veda. Moreover, the difference between Homer and the Rig Veda cannot be ascribed to some even progression that would place the Rig Veda at an earlier stage because of its earlier date. Homer has no general term for color; *chroma* is first used by Herodotus and Gorgias. The Vedas, however, easy in the interfusion of visual elements

---

6. Arnold Hirzel, *Gleichnisse und Metaphern im Rig Veda in kulturhistorischer Hinsicht zusammengestellt und verglichen mit den Bildern bei Homer, Hesiod, Aeschylos, Sophokles und Euripides* (Leipzig: Wilhelm Friedrich, 1890). Hirzel asserts, pretty much against his own evidence both positive and negative, that there is a congruence between the figures in the Rig Veda and those in Homer and his followers. In line with my point here, it is apposite to note that Edwin D. Floyd ("Kleos aphthiton: An Indo-European Perspective on Early Greek Poetry," *Glotta* 58, nos. 3–4 [1980]: 133–57) severely qualifies the parallel between *kleos aphthiton* in Homer and *śrávas akṣitam* in the Veda, pointing out that the phrases are differently used in each tradition. This difference in turn raises questions about metrical inferences drawn from the supposed identity of the two expressions, as in Gregory Nagy, *Comparative Studies in Greek and Indic Meter* (Cambridge: Harvard University Press, 1974).

under comparison, are comparably easy in abstracting the term. Indra "gives color to the colorless," as Geldner renders *peca*, "ornament, form" in 1.6.2.[7] And a more complex combination of color with form is offered in the more regular word, *varna*, as it occurs in a hymn to the Son of Waters: "He, the Son of Waters, of unfaded color" [*anabhimlátavarno*] / Works here with a body as of another" (2.35.13). Here we perceive the un-Homeric interfusion of the Vedas among the abstractions, and the casual equivocation of the regular comparative, *iva* (like, as), when the identification with some abstract "other" is made. Still another term, *rupa*, in the sense of "shape, form, beautiful color" is used in a dialogue hymn of the late tenth book. "The seer with his seership fastens color on heaven" (10.24.7). The term *varna* is often applied, with some qualification, as a superlative to the ritual beverage Soma.

The tendency away from visual representation, and concurrently also away from the sharp distinctness of categories, may be seen in a typical run from a hymn to the Maruts, gods of the thunderstorm:

> Who as great warriors shine forth with their spears
> Overthrowing even what has not been overthrown
> with their might
> When, Maruts, you thought-swift, to the cars,
> Have yoked the spotted mares, strong in hosts,
> When to the cars you have yoked the spotted mares,
> Speeding, O Maruts, the stone in the conflict,
> They discharge the streams of the ruddy steed
> And moisten the earth like a skin with waters . . .
> Self-strong they grew by their greatness;
> They have mounted to the vault, have made them
> a wide seat.
> When Vishnu helped the bull reeling with intoxication
> Like birds they sat down on their dear sacrificial grass.
> Like heroes, speeding like warriors, like fame-seekers,
> They have arrayed themselves in battles.
> All creatures fear the Maruts.
> Like kings of terrible aspect are the men.
>   (1.85.4–8; Macdonnell, somewhat revised)

The comparisons here are as momentary as the reminiscence of related stories about Vishnu and others. In the last line both a metaphor and a simile subvert what we would expect to be a firm distinction between men and gods; the Maruts are "men [*narah*] kings" (though *narah* = *aner*, in the sense "hero," does suggest a godlike superlative). *Thought-swift* is either a live metaphor or a dead one functioning as a conventional superlative. We can hardly disentangle animist elements from metaphors in the ruddy steed who pours forth the waters of the storm in

7. Karl Friedrich Geldner, *Der Rig Veda* (Cambridge: Harvard University Press, 1951).

Vedic mythology—nor is the color meant for sharp visualization; rather it is meant as another superlative. *Adrim* can mean a stone, a pressing stone, a mountain, or a cloud. All these senses are relevant here, almost blurring together. *Adrim* further suggests lightning, according to Macdonnell,[8] and for that reason it would assimilate easily to Indra, who is often associated with the Maruts as the bearer of the thunderbolt *(vajra)*.

In this culture, actually, the gods easily assimilate to each other in ways that would seem to contradict the extrapolability of underlying rules for myth systems, when distinctions are carefully maintained among the gods in the cultures studied by Lévi-Strauss. He characterizes the myths of South and North America as dominated by a fundamental conflict between fire and water. And yet Agni, the omnipresent fire god associated with the sun and given the major rituals of this culture, is said to be born of water (1.23.20–23). In this tradition the gods sometimes slide into one another, and into natural phenomena. In a later phase they "descend" into disguised shapes or *avatars*,—likeness can be casual or obscure but never extended on a base of firm logical distinction. As Gonda points out, metaphor in the Veda tends towards riddle.[9] Brhaspati is identified with Indra and with Agni, who in turn is declared to be Varuna, Mitra, and Vivasvat, all these gods having their seemingly distinct spheres. And instead of being associated with a single totemic animal, the Greek practice, Agni is compared to an eagle, a buffalo, a bull, a cow, a horse, a steer, a swan, a serpent, and a bird.[1] The lightning of the Maruts is compared to a mooing cow and their rain to a mother with a calf (1.38.8). In another hymn they are compared in swift succession to a buffalo, to mountains, to elephants, to lions, to a deer, and to serpents (1.64.7–8).

The cow, in fact, functions here as a further gathering of attributes and source of mythical associations. The Maruts are said to be born of cows, and their clouds or mountains are also conceived of as cows whose udders will burst with waters, as the "steed" also does. *Cows* without explanation in a hymn to Vishnu (1.154.6) means simply rays of sunshine, though the rapt language of the hymn forbids our taking this simply as a metaphor, "We desire to go to those abodes of you two / Where there are the many-horned nimble-cattle." Agni himself, in a seeming contradiction of his existence as fire, is "like the udders of a cow" (1.69.5–6). Indra is compared to a milk-cow at least six times. Narrative elements, even when they are the center of a hymn, are referred to only resumptively and glancingly. Homer, too, assumes his auditors know something of his story, but he achieves a discreteness of presentation that can be at once interrelated and linear.

8. Arthur Macdonnell, *A Vedic Reader for Students* (Oxford: Oxford University Press, 1913), 25.
9. Jan Gonda, *Vedic Literature* (Wiesbaden: Otto Harrassowitz, 1975), 132.
1. Geldner, *Der Rig Veda*, index.

With all this, the Rig Veda verges on an abstractness about the gods that the Greeks had to subvert Homer to achieve:

> The other Agnis are only branches of you, Agni.
> All the immortals feast with you, universal one [*vaísvānara:*
>   "belonging to all men"]
> You are the navel of the lands, you uphold
> The peoples like a supporting pillar.

(1.59.1)

We move quickly through these moments, so much so that the metaphors are not mixed. The navel and the pillar are both echoed in Greek mythology, but never together, never as nonce terms. And do not try to visualize the architecture!

3

Being often firm in the visual base of items brought into comparison, and always so in the implied clarity of visible elements it names, the Homeric simile can proceed assuredly and expansively towards enriching its complications.

Sometimes the visual base is odd, as in the above comparison of deflected spears to bouncing chickpeas (*Il.* 13.588–92) or of old men to grasshoppers (*Il.* 3.166), Odysseus to a ram (*Il.* 3.195), horses to birds (*Il.* 2.764), a helmet-weighted head to a garden poppy leaning under spring rains (*Il.* 8.306–8), a wave scattering timber to wind scattering husks (*Od.* 5.368–70), persistent fighters to bees or wasps in the hive (*Il.* 12.167–72), a speared warrior Patroclos drags to a hooked fish pulled out of water (*Il.* 16.406–10), bloodstains on Menelaus' thighs to coloring on an ivory check piece (*Il.* 4.141–47), the fight over Sarpedon's corpse to flies in the spring (*Il.* 16.640), Menelaus circling Hector to a cow tending a calf (*Il.* 17.4), the river pursuing Achilles to a spring runnel guided by a man with a mattock (*Il.* 21.257–63), snakes of dark-blue enamel to rainbows (*Il.* 11.24), bonds to spiderwebs (*Od.* 8.279), Odysseus and Ajax grasping each other to the rafters of a building (*Il.* 23.712–13), the curing of Ares' wound to milk curdling under added fig sap (*Il.* 11.902–4). Once we have verified the likeness visually, we are left, surely, with something like a sense of discovery—as the original audience may have been to the comparison of waves to mountains (*Od.* 3.290), a comparison by now conventional for our poetry. Still, the oddness seems unanalyzable beyond our noting that domains at some distance from one another have been linked through an underlying visual similarity.

Similes that are preponderantly visual can be very rich, as some of these are.

As when an octopus is pulled out of its den,
Numerous pebbles are caught in its suckers,
So against the rocks the skin from his stout hands
Was stripped off.

(*Od.* 5.432–35)

The octopus figures prominently in Minoan and Mycenean decoration, and it is here seen so sharply that a sort of close-up effect has been achieved. The hand is magnified so as to seem an octopus. For the pebbles against the suckers of the octopus, and also for the tears along the joined fingers of the hand, a random pattern—of pebbles or tears—has been superimposed on an ordered pattern, of tentacles with suckers or fingers. Moreover, the *polypus* is seen as having many tentacles rather than a specific number, which brings it more easily into line with the gripping and then flailing hand. That motion prior to the tearing must also be precisely in view, the gripping and then flailing of both hand and octopus. Odysseus like the octopus has been immersed in water, but water is short of being his native element. Moreover, his whole person is not compared to the octopus; just his hand. In the complications of this simile the visual element is predominant, as it is in this one from the *Iliad* (21.12–16):

As at the blast of a fire locusts flutter
Fleeing to a river, and the untiring fire flames,
Having started up suddenly, and they huddle at the water;
So at Achilles for the deep-whirling Xanthus
Was the sounding stream filled pell-mell with horses and men.

Achilles is not exactly compared to a fire here, as he is elsewhere and quite recently in the narrative (*Il.* 20.490–94). Nor is he compared to the swollen river that responds to him, though Hector is compared to a wave (17.262) and Ajax is compared to a rainswollen river uprooting trees in its course down a mountain (11 492–96).

Yet in light of these other comparisons we cannot wholly dissociate Achilles from either the fire of the vehicle or the river of the tenor. The visual element is reinforced by the fact that the river appears in both the tenor and the vehicle (though *potamon* suggests body of water and *roos* a rushing stream). Once again, too, the visual sharpness permits a shift of scale: the overall visual effect of locusts huddling against water, and men and horses whirled pell-mell in water, focuses in each case without regard for the fact that the men and the horses are considerably bigger than the locusts. The horses are also slightly bigger than the men, but in the swirl of the river their whole bodies would not show for the difference in size to figure in the visualization.

For these particular similes the visual richness keeps the details of both tenor and vehicle in some relation with the comparison. This would also be the case with similes that draw on some other sense than sight, as the comparison of an army's uproar to the noise of the sea (*Il.* 2.208–10), of Poseidon's shout to that of ten thousand men in battle (*Il.* 14.148–49), of a shout to the sound of a trumpet (*Il.* 18.219–21), of a wound's pain to birth pangs (*Il.* 11.269–72), of the squeaking of the suitors' souls to the squeaking of bats in a cave (*Od.* 24.5–9), of Penelope's melting flesh and ensuing tears to the melting and running of snow on a mountain (*Od.* 19.204–9).

For the last comparison the physiological effect begins to involve psychological attributes as well—and for that reason the comparison may seem less odd. The poet's command of his world, so apparent in other ways, permits the similes often to enlist a psychological situation, anchored as it may be in the physical. Take this simile, another moment in the rich play of Penelope's responses:

> The sharp anxieties plague me as I lament.
> As when the daughter of Pandareus, the nightingale of the green,
> Sings beautifully when spring has freshly risen
> Seated amid the thick foliage of the trees,
> And often modulating pours out her loud-sounding song,
> Lamenting her dear son Itylos, child of lord Zethos,
> Whom one day she killed with a sword unwittingly;
> So my heart is aroused, divided this way and that,
> Whether I should wait with my son and steadfastly guard . . .
> Or by this time should follow the best of the Achaeans
>
> (*Od.* 19.518–28)

The comparison is of a song to a feeling, but the song is in three aspects, each having a psychological correlative—(1) *sings (aeidesin)*, (2) *often modulating (thama troposa)*, and (3) *pours out (cheei)*. The feeling is designated as an "arousal" *(ororetai)*. Given the visual or other sensual base to the Homeric simile generally, what goes on internally may be seen to resemble what the ear takes in—or what a singer produces. There is a steady issue within (1), which is aroused to a pitch (3), and is involved in being "divided this way and that" *(dicha entha kai entha)*, something that may be coordinated with *often modulating* (2).

The details of the story in the vehicle cannot be brought into this complex physical-psychological comparison, but they may compare well with other features of Penelope's situation even if we do not allow this earliest version of the Procne story to suggest the marital infidelity of Tereus (or Zethos) to a Penelope who is, as she says, on the brink of entertaining what she considers might be infidelity. The family in the vehicle's myth has the same constituents as the one in the main tenor of the story itself: a father, a mother, and an only son. As with the speaker, the mother is the center of the story. Penelope is certainly concerned about Telemachus; she is concerned about him for himself and for the fact that he is Odysseus' son. Moreover the prosperity of the scene in which Penelope finds herself perplexed might be likened to the freshness of the foliage which she "unrelatedly" mentions. The details of the comparison play tantalizingly between the gratuitous and the analogous.[2]

Psychological as well as visual effects may come into the picture when the rise and motion of a ship's stern is compared to four yoked stallions on a plain (*Od.* 13.81–85), or when Agamemnon's weeping is compared to a dark-watered spring (*Il.* 9.13–15), or when Paris is said to move like a horse fresh from the crib (*Il.* 6.506), or when Agamemnon is said to be killed like an ox in a crib and his men like boars (*Od.* 11.411–14), or when Diomede is compared to an autumn star or to a full river (*Il.* 4.5; 4.85), or when the proceeding army is likened to fire or to large flocks of geese, cranes, and swans (*Il.* 2.455–65), or even when a warrior is felled like a poplar (*Il.* 4.482–88), and the suddenness and over-whelming totality of the action are suggested as well as the plunge of a vertical dead weight to horizontal position.

So the white dust that covers the Achaians under the stir of their horses, as it is compared to the white chaff that piles up under Demeter's winnowing (*Il.* 5.499–503), in addition to the likeness of two powdery substances, may associate this late, decisive moment in the war with a moment of harvest, as well as contrasting the world of peace with the world of war. There is confidence in the ranks like the mowing of the prosperous, as well as movement that looks like that of mowers (*Il.* 11.67–69). A simile striking in its psychological reach is the comparison of the abatement of Antilochus' anger to the softening of ears of grain by dew "in a shuddering field." And the visual sharpness remains, though the psychology is explicit (*Il.* 23.597–98).

The multiplicity of items in a simile allows for this play of association over possible analogies, without at the same time ruling out contrasts. The comparison of the interior of a house to the gleam of the sun or the moon (*Od.* 4.45; 7.84) offers alternative visual intensities but a common superlative of reference to the very cosmos itself, suggesting not only a physical look—a play of light from moony softness to solar dazzle—but also the assuredness and delight of an extraordinary prosperity crowned by *architectural* achievement: the source is a visual creation in addition to enlisting a visual effect. An exultation, heightened feeling as well as a visual expanse, may be felt to accompany the driving of the deep clouds into the sky of the simile quoted below, or similar ones as in *Il.* 5.770–72:

2. Anthony Podlecki calls the similes in the *Odyssey*, this one and others, "similes . . . by which the poet reminds us of an important theme in the poem but with a slight difference of focus or point of view" ("Some Odyssean Similes," *Greece and Rome* 18 [1971]: 81–90, 82). He makes the point that in one simile (21.406–11), Odysseus' stringing the bow is compared to a musician's stringing his instrument (again a predominantly visual simile) and then soon Odysseus spares the rhapsode Phemius from the general slaughter of the suitors (22.330ff.).

As far into the murk as a man may see with his eyes
Seated on a cliff gazing onto the wine-faced sea,
So far did the high-sounding horses of the gods spring on.

While we cannot assign exact proportions to physical and psychological elements, the psychological can predominate, as in the comparison
of Ajax's withdrawal to a lion whom dogs and men stay up all night to
fend off, so that at daylight he slinks away (*Il.* 11.548–56). This offers
the usual complex of elements, and its psychological angle is reversed
in the immediately ensuing simile: Ajax's withdrawal is alternately compared to that of a donkey persistently beaten in a field with sticks but not
leaving until he is sated (11.556–64). Elements of dissatisfaction dominate the first simile, of satisfaction the second. Yet both center on the
long difficulty of dislodging the hero, and on the psychological set of
both attacker and defenders. In this simile from the *Odyssey*, an almost
wholly psychological one, a connection cannot be excluded between his
weak but growing force and the "feeble puppies":

As when a bitch standing over her feeble puppies,
Not recognizing a man, growls and is eager to fight,
So his heart growled within him, indignant at their evil deeds.

(20.14–16)

Nestor's steadiness amid perplexities is compared to the steadiness of
an agitated sea (*Il.* 14.16–22), thereby characterizing two levels of the
mind, a surface one and something deeper. Finally the verbal resources
of the Homeric simile, even when it does not depart from some visual
reference, and with or without a visual comparison, is powerful enough
to accede directly to a large conceptual act, as when the turmoil of battle
is compared to the whole earth being on fire (*Il.* 2.780), words are said
to be like snowflakes (*Il.* 2.222, men to be like generations of leaves, (*Il.*
6.146–49), ideas tossed about like intestines tossed over a fire (*Od.* 19.25).
It is a concept of military order, not a view of marshaling troops (though
that may be residually present) when the arming is compared to a mason's
fitting stones into a wall (*Il.* 16.212–14). So when Nausikaa is compared
to Artemis dancing (*Od.* 6.102), or Apollo's havoc in war to a boy's
kicking down the structure he has built in the sand (*Il.* 15.362–66), or
Achilles looking at Priam as thick Ate at a murderer, and wonder strikes
the onlookers (*Il.* 24.480–83), or when the grace shed on a man is likened to a craftsman's work in gold or silver (*Od.* 6.232; 23.159). Odysseus' psychological reactions also enter a conceptual frame through the
simile, when he is glad to see land as a father is glad to see his children
(*Od.* 5.394), or when he weeps like a woman who has lost her husband
(8.525), or when he is glad to see the setting sun as a ploughman is
(13.31), or when he is glad to see his wife as a swimmer is to see the
shore (*Od.* 23.233–39). He has himself been such a swimmer, but the
displacing verbal form of the simile at once suggests the closing of the

circle and keeps it from being closed. The visual, the psychological, and the conceptual are provided with a firm tissue of connection without having to undergo full coordination.

4

Homer's special emphasis on the visual in his more expanded similes allows him a firmness that can afford complexity, for all the looseness of the fit in details of the comparison. It also allows him a perspectival wholeness, for all the sketchiness of the vocabulary at his disposal, as Snell and others have pointed out, where one word, *chros*, stands for both the skin and the flesh under it, and where general words tend to be lacking. It is not simply, as Auerbach shows, that Homer offers details;[3] he could have done so pell-mell or blurringly.

The famous simile of the watch fires across the plain compares them to the stars in the heaven (8.554–65), and the simile does not have to say that the stars will be shining above the fires for us to round them together in an imagined cosmic depth from hills to sky. A visual description of clouds adds physical depth to the ordinary momentousness of Zeus' action in starting a storm:

> As when a cloud goes inside the sky from Olympus
> From the bright upper air when Zeus stretches a tempest,
> So from the ships arose the shout and the panic.
>
> (16.364–66)

Lattimore spells out the three-dimensionality by rendering *eiso* (inside, within) as "deep into." The dimension of extent is also present in the word *teino*, to stretch. Both dimensions are present in the resulting quasi-aerial view of the panic among the ships, where the word I have rendered "panic," *phobos*, is both physical and psychological, the former getting an emphasis by being paired with the word for shout, *iache*.

A comparable visual expanse is evoked to explain the movement of Hera's horses "between earth and starry heaven" (*Il.* 5.770–72):

> As far as into hazing distance a man can see with his eyes
> Who sits gazing on the wine-faced ocean on a headland
> So leap forward the gods' high-sounding horses.[4]
>
> (Lattimore, revised)

As for complexity, we see it in the long description (18.483–607) of that imagined visual artifact that has no parallel in the visual arts of

3. Erich Auerbach, *Mimesis* (1946; reprint, New York: Anchor, 1957), 1–20.
4. Compare *Il.* 16.297–301:

> As when from the lofty crest of a great mountain
> Lightning-gatherer Zeus moves a thick cloud
> And all the crags show clear and the high headlands
> And valleys, and immense bright air breaks from the heavens,
> So the Danaans, thrusting the blazing fire from the ships.

Greece until a much later time, the shield of Achilles.[5] This elaborate image is neither simile nor metaphor, though its description does serve, like the similes, to displace, delay, and emphasize the narrative at a key point. It offers nothing less than a view of the whole world on an ordered plane, with everything in place while everything is visually distinct: the cosmos with the girdling river Oceanus, earth, sun, moon, sky, sea, and constellations; two cities of men, one at peace and the other at war; ploughing, harvesting, herding, dancing. The traditional Near Eastern icon of a lion attacking a domestic animal, frequent in the Homeric similes, is here coordinated with all the other scenes (18.587–89).

In this large image the visual distinctness of details permits the structural anchorage that holds the complexity in place. Even when Homer describes a motion of dancing on the actually stationary object, the contradiction does not obtrude, because of a kind of analogy to the sharpness of the other images, the sharpness of his images generally.

Or take the short simile adduced when Athene brushes Pandaros' arrows away from Menelaos:

> She kept it from his skin the same way as when a mother
> Keeps a fly from her child when he is bound in sweet sleep.
>
> (4.130–31)

The comparison is of a physical motion that results in constraint, *eergo*, the verb in both instances meaning "check, press in," though to our eye the arrow or the fly is being brushed away. "The same way," *toson*, might also be translated "to the same degree." No more force is needed from Athene to deflect an arrow than is needed from a mother to brush away a fly. Two kinds of motion, a heavenly and an earthly, are placed into equivalence—and something of the imperturbability of the gods, residual as it may be when they quarrel among themselves, rubs off on the warrior Menelaus. He is wronged by Helen, and he is also destined in the legend to survive the war. This plot that holds him may be said to be embodied in Athene, and to take precise visual form in the gesture of restraining the arrow. But, again, he is not compared to the infant, any more than there is anything other than a precise, panoramic view of the many tribes of Achaeans when their marshaling against the Trojans is compared to the swarming of flies around milk pails in the spring (2.469–73).

This extensibility of the visual in Homer's practice amounts to an act of steady affirmation, and Stanford contrasts Homer's "use of metaphor, in its always positive thrust," with the occasionally privative use in the Rig Veda, "the torrent is roaring but not like a bull," "fire eats up the

---

5. Kenneth John Atchity, *Homer's Iliad: The Shield of Memory* (Carbondale: Southern Illinois University Press, 1978), 148–87.

forest but not like a lion," etc.[6] When "the soul flew away like a dream" in one of the Odyssey's short similes (11.222), an act of perception that still retains a visual element has been extended to the night life and the afterlife all at once. Homer recurrently compares man to the gods, in the epithets *dios* and *isotheos* and in the simile-phrase *theo eikelos*, all meaning "godlike." The affirmation allows a transition onto such an exalted plane. The Rig Veda, by contrast, never does this,[7] though it does call gods men in the metaphor cited above, as easily as it calls them bulls or lions or even cows.[8]

The similes, as Vivante has penetratingly noticed of the epithets,[9] work at once to expand the narrative at very serious points and to delay it when it is not at a point of quick linear movement ahead. And all Vivante says of the epithets may be applied to the similes in their relation to the action: "The epithets generally belong to a [representational moment]; they tend to be dropped out when [a relational one] prevails." "The poetic quality of this verse mainly consists in the fact that the epithets have no connection with the narrative context." "They are used most often in dialogue when speaking of distant things." "What prompts their recurrence is a sense of recurrence in life itself."

5

The wonder surrounding the similes derives from a comparable sense of recurrence that takes form as it takes linguistic expression. In this sense the mere fact that the similes exist on such an elaborate plan at all is of more moment than the particular logical structure connecting their component parts. A possible measure for the power of visualization at a moment in the history of a culture is to be sought in the visual arts obtaining at that particular moment. This would not be in the aim of comparing poetry to painting and other arts, *ut pictura poesis*, as Horace's phrase has been falsely applied in modern discourse.[1] Rather, the aim would be to supplement the independent achievement of expression, as it issues in visualization, separately in the verbal and the visual modes. It cannot be an accident, surely, that almost no visual artifacts have survived from the culture of the Rig Veda, when we have figurines and seals and pottery and even a mirror from the Harapa and the Kulli cultures immediately preceding it and in a geographical area adjacent or overlapping. All we have of these early Aryans who produced the Rig Veda are some copper hoards of weapons, and a copper figure that may

6. W. Bedell Stanford, *Greek Metaphor* (1936; reprint, New York and London: Blackwell's, 1972), 135.
7. Hirzel, *Gleichnisse und Metaphern*, 12.
8. Ibid., 17.
9. Paolo Vivante, *The Epithet in Homer* (New Haven: Yale University Press, 1982).
1. See Cook, *Figural Choice in Poetry and Art*, 227.

or may not be the outline of a cult figure, and also some examples of simple gray pottery ware.

The visual resources become more complex in India, of course, well after the time of the Rig Veda, and especially after contact with the Greeks on Alexander's invasion, not to speak of persistent contact with the Near Eastern cultures that had already interacted with the Greeks. We may say—tentatively to be sure—that the culture of the Veda invested whatever visual perceptions it had in the great array of hymns, and yet the failure to expand those perceptions into visual artifacts has its counterpart in the facile blurrings and confusions of figurative language in the hymns, a blurring and confusion that is not merely visual but may be taken to characterize, not just negatively, a whole style of thinking and feeling.

Now Homer wrote about a time before his own, and the chronology in his poems involves more than just a present and a past. So if we are uncertain as to how we might locate the lion gate at Mycenae, or the Vaphio cups, or Mycenaean reliefs—to mention just a few signal objects— with respect to the Homeric poems, there are two arts that certainly flourished at the time we now believe the poems to have been composed (about 740 B.C.). Both of these arts suggestively incorporate features of the visual elements in the similes. The elaborately ordered funerary urns of "geometric" pottery certainly do parallel the persistent ordering in the poems, even if we do not go as far as Cedric Whitman does in pressing the parallel.[2] And if we look for sharp visual precision in an artifact, we find it strikingly in the miniature art of the seals which had flourished in Minoan and Mycenean times and again in Homer's own. If we take Homer's separate words, as Snell has done, the terms for body (*guia*, *melea*, etc.) accord well with the stick figures found on geometric vases and Archaic gems.[3] But if we move from diction to syntax, into the elaborate world of the simile itself, the visual analogues are strikingly not to pottery but to the sort of fuller art we find in Mycenean gems—an art that may not have died out wholly, from the evidence of island gems of the tenth century, as well as the fairly speedy resumption of full sculptural representation in later archaic gems.[4] Artifacts like the shield of Achilles or the gold and silver inlay work of a simile that refers to the body of Odysseus (*Od.* 6.232–33), or the gold and silver dogs and the gold lampadophore—*kouroi* of Alcinoos' palace (*Od.* 7.91–102), also suggest a fuller sense of the body, a richer visual sense, than the stick figures of eighth-century vases can represent.

---

2. Cedric Whitman, *Homer and the Heroic Tradition* (Cambridge: Harvard University Press, 1958).

3. Bruno Snell, *The Discovery of the Mind*, trans. T. G. Rosenmeyer (New York: Harper, 1960), 5–8.

4. John Boardman, *Archaic Greek Gems* (New York: Thames and Hudson, 1968).

The art work of the eighth century, taken in itself, does not offer a visual world full enough to parallel the visual fullness and acuteness of the Homeric similes, though certain parallels of iconographic subject can be drawn, as Roland Hampe has shown of shipwreck scenes on vases, myths in eighth-century friezes, the two lions attacking a deer in an eighth-century bracelet, and others.[5] The simile of a statue or a grave stele is used for motionlessness in *Il.* 13.437 and 17.434, as Bernard Fenik points out by way of indicating the typicality of the similes generally, especially where battles and journeys of the gods are in question.[6] But allowing for the fairly free distribution of works, and especially durable ones like gems, in the space and time of the early Mediterranean,[7] we may confidently look to Mycenean gems, where we do indeed find visualizations that correspond to the fullness and precision of the Homeric similes.

Several seals from Pylos, indeed, a site that Telemachus is said to have visited and that the legendary Nestor ruled, though they come from Mycenean times, have a visual sharpness scarcely inferior to that of the classical period. Further, they occasionally incorporate iconographic motifs that much later found their way into those poems about their Mycenean civilization, the *Iliad* and the *Odyssey*. One such seal shows a man in a conical hat spearing a wild boar at which his large dog is barking (294),[8] recalling the scene of Odysseus' boar hunt (*Od.* 19.437–49). Boldly utilizing the round form of the seal, the early but not primitive jeweler has bent each of his figures into a form that arranges the three of them in a running circle, a way that may be taken as analogous to the "ring composition" of passages in Homer. At the same time there are slight differences of scale and angle that reinforce the distinctnesses of dog, boar, and man from each other; and the most prominent visual binder is the crucial instrument of action, the man's spear. An agate of a lion killing a calf (278) recalls the numerous descriptions, usually in similes, of the beast-of-prey slaughter to be found in seals and other artifacts throughout the Near East. This agate from Pylos may also be said to recall, in its subject matter as well as in its vividly precise execution, the description of the brooch Odysseus owned:

> And the brooch upon it was made of gold,
> With twin sockets. And on its face it was skillfully wrought:

5. Roland Hampe, *Die Gleichnisse Homers und die Bildkunst seiner Zeit* (Tübingen: Niemeyer, 1952).
6. Bernard Fenik, *Typical Battle Scenes in the Iliad* (Wiesbaden: Steiner, 1968).
7. Scarabs were used as the models for Archaic gems. Emily Vermeule (*Greece in the Bronze Age* [Chicago: University of Chicago Press, 1972], 244), lists the find of thirty Near Eastern cylinder seals at Thebes as one among many examples of transfer across space. Transfer through time is more difficult to establish but quite plausible.
8. The seals, and their corresponding numbers, are reproduced in Friedrich Matz and Hagen Biesanz, *Corpus der Minoischen und Mykeneischen Siegel* (Berlin: Mann, 1964).

In his front paws a dog was holding a dappled fawn
And gazed at it while it writhed. All men marvelled to see
How the one, being of gold, gazed at the fawn he throttled,
And the other strove to get away as he writhed with his feet.

(19.226–31)

Other seals from Pylos show a feminine cult figure of Circe-like sinuos-
ity (279), and large steers much like the cattle of the sun lying down
beside a tree. (275).

To visualize, to express one's visualizations, to think, and to feel, are
all activities whose interrelations we have only begun to explore. The
similes in the Homeric poems, somewhat fortified by their analogues in
corresponding visual objects, testify to a precious level of achievement
in the mysterious human enterprise of self-awareness through correlat-
ing word or thought and image.

The sort of doubling capacity in art and in literature equally, which I
have argued for the Homeric poems, might be considered the normal
case, one that obtains in the Western world right to the present day. It
is not the only possibility, however. The intense images of the Hebrew
prophets, and the very differently structured, elaborately ornamented
edifice of Solomon's temple, are more countered than paralleled in the
stern biblical injunction against images. The Egyptians would seem to
have expended their imaginative energies almost wholly upon the plastic
arts, which then spill over into the act of writing but not into a literature
to parallel the friezes and statues and coffin lids through that long culture. The early Chinese, on the other hand, have an impressive but
limited group of artifacts, to be set beside lyric poems in the Confucian
Anthology, poems so sharp and full in their capacity for visual image
that similes, in translation at least, seem wholly to disappear. For Homer
the simile does by no means disappear; it is a window on the capacity
for perception and coordination that is still widening.

JOHN H. FINLEY, JR.

The Heroic Mind †

In the seventeenth book of the *Odyssey* when Odysseus, still in the
guise of a beggar, at last first approaches his house and the dog Argus,
left behind twenty years before and now old and neglected, sees his mas-

† Reprinted from *Four Stages of Greek Thought* by John J. Finley, Jr., with the permission of the
publishers, Stanford University Press. © 1966 by the Board of Trustees of the Leland Stanford
Junior University.

ter, lowers his ears, wags his tail, but lacks strength to move, does Odysseus commiserate with him or pat him? On the contrary, after secretly wiping away a tear, he says to his companion the swineherd, "What a handsome dog there on the dung-heap! But was he fast in the chase or simply a table-dog?" And the swineherd gives the expected answer, "That is the dog that Odysseus left behind when he went to Troy, and none was faster or braver to track down beasts in the depths of the thick woods." Odysseus enters the house, and the dog dies, the first to have recognized him at home. He had for a dog the virtue that Hector's helmet had for a helmet. Each, like all the other people and objects in the poems, keeps its inherent nature, and a chief marvel of the poems might be said to be the ineffable act of concentration whereby men and women, great people, small people, towns, fields, animals, seas, rivers, earth, sky, and the lucent gods themselves, remain each distinct while jointly comprising the brilliant world.

How conceive the working of such a mind? Theoretical answers, though hardly complete, go a certain distance, and chief among them, it scarcely needs be said, is the work of the Californian Milman Parry, who died at thirty-three in 1935 after revolutionizing Homeric studies. Apparently as early as when he first read Homer in college, he thought him so unlike other poets that he must have composed in some unusual way. This different way, Parry came to think, was the so-called oral method of composition which he spent his short life elaborating, partly by theory, partly by learning Serbian and coming to know at first hand the oral poetry of Jugoslavia. Briefly put, this theory of oral composition postulates two main conditions: first, a body of legend about bygone heroes whose feats gathered about a few famous enterprises; second, and more crucial, a body of language passed from generation to generation but freshly used and slightly changed by each age and singer that enabled singers to compose complete verses as they went along. The familiar Homeric line introducing a speech may illustrate in small the complex process: "Him answering addressed swift-footed Achilles." The line falls into halves: Achilles at the end, how he spoke at the start. Now Parry noted that any other character, if provided with a suitable epithet, might metrically replace Achilles at the end of the line, a character with a long name like Agamemnon being joined with a short epithet, a character with a short name like Zeus with a long epithet. Similarly at the start of the line "answering" was not the only stance in which a character might speak; he might do so "standing up," "with a scowl," "with good intent," "fainting," or in a number of other ways that—and this is the important point—are metrically equivalent to "answering." Taken together, the options at the end and at the start of the line give the singer a set of choices by which he may introduce any character speaking in some fitting way. One may not call such a line memorized in the usual sense of the word; rather, it is composed from memorized elements, proves metrical because these elements were so intended, suits all the characters and many kinds of situations because its terms had been perfected for that purpose—in short, lets the singer simultaneously advance his story and compose a verse.

Needless to say, this simple example does small justice to the subtle tradition that supplied a singer with fit and metrical words in the quick moment when he needed them, supplied him too with procedures and motifs for describing battles and banquets and messages and a thousand such recurrent events, supplied him even with the tone and cast of a gallery of characters. The extraordinary fact that oné must keep recalling is that through the centuries when the art was elaborated no one ever read a poem or had in fact learned anything by reading; in everyone's mind, singer and listener alike, lay the words of the poetic tradition that he had known since childhood and that alone lifted above the small present its arc of completer relevance and meaning. If everyone in a part of his being thought in this greater language and even Achilles in the *Iliad* is pictured as solacing himself by singing, some people by special gifts lived themselves more fully into it, each necessarily in his own way, since, though the language was traditional, it was not fixed in books but had to be recreated by each man, inevitably with the changes that time and temperament dictated. How the Homeric poems came to be written down when the very nature of the art implies the lack of writing is another kind of question, fixed in circumstance and doubtless lost beyond recall. Homer lived in Ionia—so much ancient tradition and his language make clear—in the late eighth century, it is thought, when writing was first emerging beside the oral art. Was he recognized as so great that professional singers, perhaps of his own family, wanted his songs as heirloom of their guild, and did some clever young man—a grandson, one would like to think—see how writing could serve the purpose? If one can only guess in such matters, the oral character of the poems is beyond guess, and it is this that brings us back to the crystalline Homeric world of Hector's helmet and the dog Argus. The helmet shines and the dog was swift, partly because Homer's epithets, that functional element of his oral style, declared them such. Similarly all the other characters and objects of the poems keep identities that the very nature of oral verse-making compelled them to keep. Had Homer conceived the thought of substituting new words and epithets for the received, he would in that act have become a literary poet, and the clear world of his recurrent shapes would have vanished.

Yet that world stayed fixed and clear not only by reason of the oral style, but because Homer and presumably his audience as well thought and wanted it such. The legendary figures of Troy and Mycenae, Ithaca and Pylos, lived on untouched by the thought that they were only thoughts. Hence we return to more elusive questions: what is implied by this unfaltering confidence in outer reality, and why has it so deep a grip on us? It may be said of literary styles that the more elaborate their structures, the more these reflect a man's conscious and ordering thought, and, by the same token, the less they reflect external objects. Thought proceeds by scheme and sequence; it manipulates, puts things where it wants them, makes different designs from any that the eyes see, and, what is more, knows that it is doing so. Conscious art selects from nature and by selecting adds. In the process the forms of nature inevitably take second place; their edges are blunted to fit the ruling design, and the complex final effect, being composed of many parts, diminishes the being of any one part. Yet the price of this triumph is violation of our senses. We evidently see at any moment a sequence of sharp particulars—light at a window, a tree trunk, the gray of a rock—single, peremptory impressions, moving in endless specificity across our vision. A part of our life belongs to them; we know the world and feel at home in it not least through these sure reminders. Happiness, one sometimes thinks, is clarity of vision, moments when things stand clear in sharpest outline, undimmed by familiarity as if revealed for the first time. Such moments bring back, so to speak, the memory of Eden sparkling on the first day of creation, the tree of life soaring in the middle, and if Eden be related to our childhood, they bring back childhood too. In this spirit Gladstone entitled his book on Homer *Juventus Mundi*, the world's youth—evidently not because the *Iliad* is comforting but because it is clear. Literary history abounds in reactions against elaborate and mental styles—for example, in recent times that of Hemingway against, say, Henry James. I remember from an otherwise forgotten story of Hemingway a sentence about a bare light bulb glaring in a diner; the sentence was complete; one saw just that. No more than Hector's shining helmet did the light bulb announce a happy ending, yet it was to this extent happy and confident: it signified impressions that one could trust. However intoxicating the attractions of intellect and however essential to the structures by which we live, something in us wants also the clear signals of the senses by which alone the world is made fresh and definite.

Now, needless to say, words and thoughts, being products of our minds, cannot capture reality, which remains beyond us, an object of faith, not of knowledge. Presumably no leaf or blade of grass or person or object exactly resembles another, but being unable to comprehend a world of unutterable and endless differences, we, as Aristotle said, put things into classes, and keep our sanity by speaking of oak tree or maple tree, man or woman, Frenchman or Englishman—just as if one of these quite resembled another. * * * Agamemnon concludes, "Thus not even in death did you lose celebrity; forever among all men will your great fame endure, Achilles. But where for me is this regard, after I wound the skein of war? At my return Zeus devised grim ruin for me at the hands of Aegisthus and my baleful wife." After this interchange they notice the ghosts of the suitors; and when Agamemnon asks them who they are and is told, he breaks into passionate praise of Odysseus: felicitous man, he got in Penelope a prudent and faithful wife, report of whose merit will never die but will be fashioned by immortals into song for earthly men. Here at the end of the poem Penelope shares the honor that Odysseus has had throughout it, and husband and wife emerge together as the fit and joint theme of poetry.

Now two of the most gifted recent writers on Homer, Schadewaldt and Whitman, emphasize in ways that may be omitted here the degree to which both the *Iliad* and the *Odyssey* are composed with a sense of the whole Trojan tradition; they illuminate it, sum it up, complete it. If so, this nearly final scene of the *Odyssey* gives something like the ultimate judgment. Of the three greatest figures, one, Agamemnon, though a king on earth and the most powerful of known men, is effectively eliminated; he died miserably, and if his death did not fit his life, it bears on and relates to it. The two remaining figures, Achilles and Odysseus— or in the latter case, the paired figures of Odysseus and Penelope—contain the sum and meaning. Of Odysseus, more in a moment by way of conclusion; of Achilles, he is in the keeping of the Muses. So Pindar later thought in a noble poem on the mingled ruin and grandeur of the Persian war; Achilles remained to him the example of those who had died, and then as formerly the Muses alone give comment. His fame approached him, so to speak, not from the front with foreseen and calculable invitation, but unexpectedly, out of disillusion, anger, and self-reproach. Yet he remains described by the first brightness of expectation that took him to the unknown of Troy, and by his affinity with the measureless sea that shines beyond the fixed and bounded present. The *Iliad*, like all tragedies but seemingly more clearly than any other, is at one and the same time paradoxically very dark and very bright: dark in the actual unfulfillment of what might have been expected and seemed possible, bright in the ardor of that expectation and its persistence over change. Hector's shining helmet and all the other clear and beautiful objects that comprise the visible flash of the world fit and solicit the ardor of this response.

Finally, to turn to Odysseus, the sea that partly describes Achilles obviously describes him too—it is his teacher and he its aptest pupil— but in a somewhat different way. Hector in the *Iliad* is a figure of the land, and the water that identifies him is the benign flow of streams and springs; in his last flight from Achilles, he runs beside the hot and cold springs where the wives and daughters of the Trojans had washed their shining clothes "in peacetime before the sons of the Achaeans came." Land and springs comprise an idyl of peace. Achilles in the *Iliad* is associated also with fire—the fire both of glory and of ruin—and his destruction of Hector and by implication of Troy suggests the lightning stroke that destroys the benign but impermanent house. The house is human; the lightning half-divine. These elements recur with changed suggestion in the *Odyssey*. One never quite knows whether Odysseus likes or dislikes his travels; we first see him on a headland of Calypso's island willing to die if he may only see the smoke upleaping from his rooftop at home; wrecked later at sea, he wishes that he might have died at Troy. Yet his insatiable curiosity keeps him in the Cyclops's cave when his companions want to leave, and he has to be reminded that he has stayed a year with Circe. He is marked by the sea, which makes him the great man that he is, yet in his humanity he renounces it for home. Two episodes describe his choice and its result. The first is when Calypso, justly claiming to be more beautiful than Penelope, offers him ageless-ness and immortality if he will stay with her; though aware of her divine beauty, he refuses. A famous description had recounted the island's rav-ishing freshness; in renouncing it, he gives up the eternity of nature—as it were, of untracked beaches and blue water forever flowing in and out of caves—in favor of his mortal identity at home. The second episode is the prophecy of the seer Teiresias in the underworld. Odysseus will indeed reach home, says the seer, but then must take an oar on his shoulder and seek a land where men are ignorant of salt and where a passerby, spying the oar, will call it a winnowing fan; he must then build an altar and sacrifice to Poseidon; returning home, he will rule in peace over a happy people and reach a shining old age, and a gentle death will come to him from the sea. Odysseus is like a runner who cannot stop at once on finishing a race; he must exorcise and placate some restlessness of the sea that survives in him; even when he does so and has pacified Posei-don, something of the sea will return in his death. This wonderful prophecy declares him the reconciler of two worlds; he does achieve home and is profoundly grateful to have done so, yet he would know its virtues less fully than he does—would miss its wonder—if travel had not taught him. He ends, if one may put it so, by crossing to the other side of the measureless sea of Achilles' youth, and the land that he finds is different from Hector's land, because return is different from never hav-ing gone away, and attainment different from keeping. In like spirit, the former destructive fire now becomes purifying. A sulphurous thunder-bolt destroys Odysseus's companions when they have sinfully eaten the cattle of the sun, and he purifies his house with sulphur after killing the suitors. The fire of the *Odyssey* is that of the hearth and of life itself. On finishing his last battle with the sea and reaching much-spent the land of the Phaeacians, he finds shelter in a fall of olive leaves beneath thick intertwined boughs, as a man on a remote farm shelters a brand beneath the black ash, saving the seed of fire.

CHARLES SEGAL

Bard and Audience in Homer †

The attempt to make Homer know everything, from farming to fighting, is like trying to make the sacred olive bough known as the *eiresione*
hold apples and pears and other things too heavy for it. Such is the
comparison of Hipparchus, quoted by Strabo in defending Homer against
Eratosthenes' attacks on his poems as merely frivolous, fanciful entertainment (ψυχαγωγία, Strabo 1.2.3). One sort of knowledge, however,
the ancient readers almost unanimously grant Homer: knowledge about
words and song, the arts of speech and persuasion, or what Strabo calls
ρητορικὴ φρόνησις, "rhetorical skill," best exemplified by Odysseus
in the *Iliad* (especially books 2, 3, and 9: see Strabo 1.2.5, ad init.).
Homer shows the same knowledge of the other side of making songs and
speeches, not just their creation, but also their reception. This essay is a
study, then, not of "Homer's Readers" but of "Homer's Hearers"—of
what he thinks, or might think, of his audiences, actual and possible.

The Homeric poems repeatedly depict ancient audiences listening to
singers. The gods banqueting on Olympus are entertained by Apollo and
the Muses (*Iliad* 1.602f.); grapepickers lighten their toil by joining the
young boy who sings the "Linus song" in the vineyard (*Iliad* 18.561–
72). In the former passage "banquet," Apollo's "lovely lyre," and "Muses"
with their "beautiful voice" are joined together in a coordinate construction as simultaneous attributes of divine happiness (1.601–4):

> ὣς τότε μὲν πρόπαν ἦμαρ ἐς ἠέλιον καταδύντα
> δαίνυντ᾽, οὐδέ τι θυμὸς ἐδεύετο δαιτὸς ἐίσης,
> οὐ μὲν φόρμιγγος παρικαλλέος, ἣν ἔχ᾽ Ἀπόλλων,
> Μουσάων θ᾽, αἳ ἄειδον ἀμειβόμεναι ὀπὶ καλῇ.

Thus they feasted the entire day to the setting of the sun, nor did
their spirit lack the equal *feasting*, nor the very lovely *lyre* which
Apollo held, nor the *Muses*, who sang in responsion with their
beautiful voice.

Like the Muses who inspire him, the poet of early Greece is a singer.
His aim is to produce songs performed at more or less public occasions,
ranging from a large panhellenic festival, such as those at Delos or Mycale,
to an affair of state such as Hieron's inauguration of his newly founded
city of Aetnaea with Pindar's First *Pythian Ode*, to local family gather-
ings, feasts, and symposia in the houses of the rich. While the Hellen-
istic Callimachus holds his writing tablet on his knees and doubtless a

† From R. L. Lamberton, and John J. Keaney, eds., *Homer's Ancient Readers: The Hermeneutics
of Greek Epic's Earliest Exegetes* (Princeton: Princeton UP, 1992) 3–29. Reprinted by permission
of Princeton University Press.

pen (or stylus) in his hand (Callimachus *Aetia* 1.21f., Pfeiffer), the
Homeric poet holds a lyre.

Our first detailed account of song in Homer, and therefore in Western
literature, depicts a scene of group festivity in the open air. On the shield
of Achilles girls and boys dance together, a lad plays a clear-sounding
lyre in their midst, and the dancers sing as they follow the tune and
"skip with their feet" (*Iliad* 18.567–72). There is also dancing accompanied by flute and lyre at a wedding feast, doubtless also outdoors as
women are watching from the forecourt. Later a large crowd watches a
dance "like that at broad Cnossus" (18.603), and two whirling acrobats
"lead off the singing" (18.604f.).

As such passages indicate, poetry is envisaged as part of a performance, as the living voice of song (what John Herington calls "the song
culture").[1] Whether secular or ritual, whether public or private, poetry
belongs to a social occasion. The spectators who "stand about" admiring
or enjoying on the Shield of Achilles are an inconspicuous but essential
element of the scene (18.496, 603).

* * *

Alcinous' palace in *Odyssey* 8 is the setting for Homer's fullest account
of bardic performance; and the scene has the richness, ease, and splendor that one would expect in this happy, comfort-loving land of the
Phaeacians. The palace and court gradually fill with the king's followers,
young and old (8.57f.). Alcinous makes an elaborate sacrifice for the
coming feast: twelve sheep, eight boars, two oxen. The meet is prepared,
and "they fashioned the lovely banquet" (τετύκοντό τε δαῖτ᾽ ἐρα-
τεινήν, 8.61). As the crowning touch, the herald leads in the bard, the
blind Demodocus. A silver-studded stool is set for him in the midst of
the banqueters; his lyre is carefully hung within reach, above his head;
and bread, meat and wine are placed before him (8.65–70). This bard,
like Phemius on Ithaca, is no wandering minstrel, to be classed with the
"craftsmen" (δημιοεργοί) who come and go from the palace (17.383–
85).[2] He is a permanent fixture in the royal establishment and has a
respected place and regular duties there.

Later, in book 13, Odysseus has finished his long tale in the palace of
Alcinous, and a charmed silence descends over the hall. The king, who
has already congratulated the speaker on his grace as a raconteur (11.367f.),
urges his guests to add more gifts (13.7–9): "To each one of you I speak
enjoining this, you who always drink the aged bright wine in my halls
and hear the bard" (αἴθοπα οἶνον / αἰεὶ πίνετ᾽ ἐμοῖσιν, ἀκουάζεσθε
δ᾽ ἀοιδοῦ). The implication is that the bard is a prized accoutrement of

1. C. J. Herington, *Poetry into Drama*, Sather Classical Lectures 49 (Berkeley and Los Angeles
1985) part 1, passim.
2. On this passage see George Walsh, *The Varieties of Enchantment: Early Greek Views of the
Nature and Function of Poetry* (Chapel Hill, NC, 1984) 15f.

a rich and generous house. Hearing him is like drinking the good wine of his patron, a privilege that puts the guests under an obligation.

The Demodocus scene probably reflects the ideal rather than the actual, and the wish-fulfilment may be as much for the poet as for his audience. Nevertheless, the basic situation may not be beyond the possibilities of an eighth-century aristocrat. As the princes of the Italian Renaissance collected sculptures or paintings to display their culture, affluence, and power and adorned their palaces with memorials of great men of the past in the form of busts, frescoes, and statues, so the nobles of the Greek renaissance, twenty-two hundred years earlier, may well have adorned their houses with poets who could monumentalize in song the great deeds of the past and thereby provide models of heroic excellence and grandeur. At this period material culture in Greece is still relatively modest; and a resident bard, for long or short term, probably represents an inexpensive investment.

The luxuries of the time are social and (fortunately for posterity) artistic. A good bard enhances a good feast. It is tempting, of course, to think that Homer actually sang at or after banquets (though perhaps not "for small earnings and good cheer," in Richard Bentley's notorious formulation); and bards like him may well have sung at the courts of nobles and princes. If, as Anthony Snodgrass argues, great scarcity and poverty lay in the not-so-distant past, his audience would appreciate images of a time when there was always an extra ox or hog to be sacrificed and the wine flowed endlessly.[3] Through such regal settings as those of Demodocus' songs Homer can transport his eighth-century audience into the wealth and abundance of the heroic age.

One of the Odyssey's most insistent messages is that eating properly and listening properly go closely together.[4] Only the rude, cannibalistic Cyclops asks his guest for a story before feeding him. The hospitable Eumaeus, who admiringly compares his disguised guest's narrative ability to that of a professional bard (17.518–21), feeds him two dinners (14.80–120 and 414–45). The best audience in the poem, the Phaeacians, permits the afterdinner tale to go on for the length of four books (9–12) as Odysseus tells his story with the skill of a bard (cf. 11.363–69).[5] When Eumaeus describes to Penelope the disguised beggar's "charm" with words, he begins with a wish that the suitors would be quiet so that Penelope too might feel the spell of his guest's tales, which he enjoyed for three nights and three days on his farm (17.513–21). Those noisy

---

3. On the economic duress of tenth and ninth century B.C. Greece, see Anthony Snodgrass, *Archaic Greece: The Age of Experiment* (Berkeley and Los Angeles 1980) 15ff. See also his *The Dark Age of Greece* (Edinburgh 1971) 413f.

4. See, for instance, Douglas Stewart, *The Disguised Guest* (Lewisburg, Pa. 1976) 68f; William G. Thalmann, *Conventions of Form and Thought in Early Greek Epic Poetry* (Baltimore 1984) 158ff.

5. The relevance of this scene to Homeric conceptions of bardic performative aspects of this scene have often been noted: see Walsh (above, p. 357, n. 2) 7ff.; Stewart (above, n. 4) 157.

suitors, however, are the most disrespectful audience we see, and they eventually get arrows from the bowstring instead of music from the lyre, as Athena/Mentor had hinted and as Telemachus had warned at the first feast of the poem (1.225–29, 253–59).

The close relation between song and feasting is crystallized into the formulaic phrase, ἀναθήματα δαιτός, song as "the accompaniment of the feasting." With intentional irony, the formula's first occurrence in the *Odyssey* describes an occasion when that "accompaniment" is reluctant: Phemius sings "by necessity" to Telemachus' unwelcome guests, the suitors who arrogantly appropriate the good things of the palace, bard included (see *Od.* 1.154). The only other occurrence of the phrase in the Homeric corpus comes after Odysseus has accomplished the trial of the bow and is about to make the singing of the bowstring into an "accompaniment of the feasting"—a feast that is the suitors' last meal (21.430).[6]

But, to return from the bow to the lyre, even "good" audiences do not sit in the rapt silence of the Phaeacian nobles around Odysseus (11.333f.). Menelaus, for example, whose tastes incline slightly toward the grosser side, has acrobats to entertain his guests. This detail may be as much a commentary on Menelaus as a reflection on the taste of Homeric audiences. Despite the importance of music and singing, there is good reason to think that when an *aoidos* sings people are expected to listen to what he says and not just enjoy a catchy tune. Thus when Demodocus performs among the Phaeacians, he plays to accompany choral dancing only once, whereas in his three other appearances his words are obviously the primary focus of interest.

But things in Homer, and especially in the *Odyssey*, are always a little more complicated than they seem. Consider the most frivolous and risqué story in the epic corpus, Demodocus' song of the adultery of Ares and Aphrodite, the beautiful gods who are caught in bed by the cunning net of Hephaestus. This song offers the delight or *terpsis* that is ideally suited to the rather brittle hedonism of the Phaeacians. Such was essentially the judgment of Plutarch, some two millennia ago, in his delightful essay on "How a Young Man Should Listen to Poetry." But this piece of apparently frothy entertainment proves, in fact, to be the model for Odysseus' own story: the grimy, hard-working little man of soot and sweat defeats the big, gorgeous hunk—a prefiguration of Odysseus combatting the Cyclops but also perhaps a hint of that anti-aristocratic sentiment that seems to creep in here and there.[7] But there is contrast as

6. In 8.99 Homer uses the similar expression ἢ δαιτὶ συνήορός ἐστι θαλείη, of the lyre *(phorminx)*, which he does not repeat elsewhere.

7. For the thematic relevance of the song of Ares and Aphrodite to the poem, see most recently S. Douglas Olson, *"Odyssey* 8: Guile, Force and the Subversive Poetics of Desire," *Arethusa* 22 (1989) 135–45, especially 137, 141, with further bibliography; also Rick M. Newton, "Odysseus and Hephaestus in the *Odyssey*," *Classical Journal* 83 (1987) 12–20, especially 14–

well as parallelism. The woman whom Odysseus will win back is not
the goddess of love or the embodiment of sex-appeal like Helen, but the
soul of domestic virtue, patience, and prudence. And Homer gives us a
further surprise: the trickery practiced around the bed will be not the
husband's but the wife's (the test of the living olive-tree). This singing,
then, exemplifies the multiple functions of the poet in his society: pure
entertainment at one level, concern with the central values and conflicts
in the world of the poem at another.

This is a revealing scene for differences in audience response.[8] Both
Odysseus and the Phaeacians "took pleasure in hearing" the song of
Aphrodite's adultery (8.367–69). Yet it is not this tale of the gods but
rather the song about the sufferings of the Achaeans that wins from
Odysseus the most extravagant praise that a bard receives in Homer (8.474–
83). Odysseus not only honors Demodocus with a choice cut of meat
but also suggests that he has been taught by the Muse and even by Apollo
himself (8.487; contrast 8.44 and 63, where Demodocus' skill derives
only from "a god" or "the Muse"). What Odysseus prizes is the ability
to evoke not the carefree realm of the remote Olympians but the human
woe that stirs the heart, told, he says, "as if you were present yourself or
heard from someone else" (8.491). So the Muses themselves, in the
poet's invocation to the Catalogue of Ships in the *Iliad*, "are present and
know everything," whereas we mortals have only hearsay (*Il.* 2.485f.).

The differences in response between the Greek warrior and the
hedonistic Phaeacians are already encoded into Demodocus' tale itself
in the contrasts among the divine spectators of the narrated events. The
female divinities stay away (8.324), while Hermes makes a locker-room
joke to Apollo. This releases the tension among the other (male) gods in
"laughter unquenchable," like Hephaestus' clumsy wine-service in the
Iliad that breaks the tension of this first feast on Olympus (*Il.* 1.597–
600). But even this male response is divided: Poseidon is not amused
and remains concerned, serious, and legalistic (8.344–58). This narrative of Olympian frivolity becomes itself a spectacle of audience response
within a performance, like the wedding song on the Shield of Achilles
(cf. 8.321 and 325 and *Il.* 18.495–97), with a major division in the
mood of the spectators.

Odysseus goes on to request a third song of Demodocus, the story of
the wooden horse and the capture of Troy. Again he weeps, and again
Alcinous observes him. This time, however, Alcinous does not hold his
peace (as he had in the case of the first song, 8.93ff.), but delivers a long
speech that ends with some generalizations on mortal suffering and the

---

16. For the question of anti-aristocratic sentiment in the poem see, e.g., S. G. Farron, "The
Odyssey as Anti-Aristocratic Statement," *Studies in Antiquity* 1 (1979–80) 59–101.

8. For some of these differences see Walsh (above p. 357, n. 2) 4ff., 6ff; also Thalmann (above,
p. 358, n. 4) 160ff.

request for Odysseus' identity. The gods, he says, "have spun out doom for men so that there may be song for those to come" (ἵνα ἦσι καὶ ἐσσομένοισιν ἀοιδη, 8.580). Helen makes a very similar reflection in her scene with Paris, but the differences are important. She speaks in the first person, and her concern is about men, Alcinous' is about song. The gods have set upon *us* an evil doom, she says, "so that *we* may be a subject of song for men to come" (ὡς καὶ ὀπίσσω / ἀνθρώποισι πελώμεθ' ἀοίδιμοι ἐσσομένοισι, Il. 6.357f.). The distance that Alcinous thus implies between the pleasurable effect *(terpsis)* of song on its hearers and the pain of its subject matter becomes even clearer as he goes on to ask if Odysseus has lost a kinsman or dear companion in the war (8.581–86). He thus acknowledges that an audience could feel a personal involvement in the subject of song, but he still does not envisage the possibility that the specific involvement of Odysseus' response lay in exactly the opposite direction, effacing the distance between the subject and its audience. Such is the effect of the simile that compares Odysseus' weeping at the fall of Troy in Demodocus' song to that of a woman in a captured city as she is led off to slavery—a city very much like the Troy of Demodocus' song (8.523ff.).

Everything about this scene, then, articulates two very different modes of response: the aesthetic distance of Alcinous that can treat poetry (fiction) as a source of pure pleasure *(terpsis)* and the intense, painful involvement of Odysseus as he participates, through memory, in the sufferings that are the subject matter of the song. The simile of the weeping captive woman further suggests the possibility that this identification with the subject matter of the song applies not just to the memory of an actual participant but also to vicarious, imaginary participation by one who has had nothing to do with the events. With the exception of the extraordinary scene between Priam and Achilles in *Iliad* 24, there is little in the heroic code that would encourage Odysseus to identify with his conquered enemy, especially one of the opposite sex.

Through these contrasting responses Homer reveals the paradox (of which Hesiod too is aware) between the pleasure that mimetic art affords its audience and the pain of its contents. For the hedonistic Phaeacians war itself is absorbed into *aoide,* song (8.580); for Odysseus the sufferings of war, even in song, are still sufferings and bring tears. The simile that compares him to a captive woman, however, creates a deliberate slippage between the two positions and at least raises the possibility that the division may not always be so sharp. Menelaus, like Alcinous, regards weeping as an undesirable response to an afterdinner song, the reverse of the *terpsis* (pleasure) that song should bring or enhance (4.193–95 and cf. 220–26; 8.538–43). Menelaus' court, however, having been touched directly by the sufferings of the narrator as Alcinous' has not, joins in the weeping (4.183–88).

A further detail complicates the contrast between Odysseus and the Phaeacians. In the long speech in which Alcinous makes his formal request for Odysseus' identity and asks the reasons for his weeping, he tells of a prophecy that Poseidon will one day destroy one of his ships as it returns from escorting a passenger to his homeland (8.564–69). Characteristically, he dismisses the prophecy as something that the god may or may not accomplish (8.570f.). Alcinous' lack of concern, as we learn later, is mistaken, for the angry god does fulfill the prophecy (13.170–83). In fact we see the Phaeacians for the last time gathering in fear about Poseidon's altar as they attempt to appease his wrath (13.183–87). These events have some bearing on poet and audience, for in Demodocus' second song, about Ares and Aphrodite, it was Poseidon who resolved the embarrassment. His solemn pledge assuages Hephaestus' anger and secures Ares' release (8.344–58). This is a Poseidon suited to Phaeacian aestheticism. He intervenes to keep the violation of marriage in the realm of play, without the consequences, for example, that it has on Ithaca. Odysseus' Poseidon, however, is not a god who soothes anger or intervenes in the name of peace. This wrathful, dangerous Poseidon, beyond the frame of Phaeacian song, is the god that Alcinous now begins to know, if only as a remote possibility (8.570f.; cf. 13.125–64).

From the point of view of "real" life, of course, the tales of Odysseus at Troy and of Ares and Aphrodite on Olympus are equally "mythical," and so are both Poseidons too. But for a moment Homer allows the two modes of "mythical" narration to cross over into one another. The Phaeacian king relates a kind of story (albeit in the future rather than the past) that thematically resembles Odysseus' life-story in its divine blocking-figure as the central antagonist. This story, moreover, will be fulfilled as "fact" in book 13. Homer thus brings together story as pleasurable entertainment (Demodocus' Poseidon) and story as emotionally involving exemplar of human suffering (the Poseidon who punishes the Phaeacians in book 13) that could also apply to "us" the listener. Such too is the involvement of Odysseus conveyed through the simile of the weeping captive woman.

This kind of narrative self-consciousness, typical of the *Odyssey*, forces the hearer to become aware of the work's construction of its fictionality or mythicality and thus of the disjunction between different levels of "reality." It is analogous to the self-consciousness about plot-construction that emerges in the retrospective narrative of the Second Nekyia. There the slain suitor Amphimedon tells a version of Odysseus' success that includes the conscious collusion of Odysseus and Penelope in setting up the contest of the bow. "Odysseus in his multifaced craftiness (πολυκερδείῃσιν)," Amphimedon says, "*ordered* his wife to set up for the suitors the bow and the hoary iron (of the axes)"; and this event, he adds, proved to be "the beginning of the slaughter" (24.167–69). Odysseus, of course, gave no such orders; but Homer thus shows his audience

an alternative dénouement, a version that he might have used but chose
not to. The "multifaceted craftiness" is in this case as much the poet's
as his hero's.[9] This bard has the same kind of flexibility to reshape his
tale as his chief character has to reshape his life-narrative.

Homer shows his control of the narrative in another way at one of the
poem's major transitions, the shift from Telemachus back to Odysseus
at the beginning of book 5. In book 1, when Athena formally introduces
Odysseus by winning Zeus's sympathy for his sufferings, Zeus replies,
"My child, what is this saying that has escaped the barrier of your teeth?
How then would I forget ($\lambda\alpha\theta o\acute{\iota}\mu\eta\nu$) divine Odysseus, who surpasses
mortals in intelligence . . .?" (1.64–66). In the corresponding scene in
book 5, Zeus repeats his formulaic first line (5.22 = 1.64), but omits the
second line about "forgetting Odysseus." Instead, Athena, as in book 1,
initiates the mention of Odysseus, absent from the narrative now for four
books, by "making mention" of him and his many sufferings ($\lambda\acute{\epsilon}\gamma\epsilon$ $\kappa\acute{\eta}\delta\epsilon\alpha$
$\pi\acute{o}\lambda\lambda$ ' $\mathrm{'O}\delta\upsilon\sigma\sigma\tilde{\eta}o\varsigma$ / $\mu\nu\eta\sigma\alpha\mu\acute{\epsilon}\nu\eta$, 5.5.f.). She then continues with the
complaint that "no one remembers divine Odysseus among the people
over whom he ruled" ($\dot{\omega}\varsigma$ $o\ddot{\upsilon}$ $\tau\iota\varsigma$ $\mu\acute{\epsilon}\mu\nu\eta\tau\alpha\iota$ $\mathrm{'O}\delta\upsilon\sigma\sigma\tilde{\eta}o\varsigma$ $\theta\epsilon\acute{\iota}o\iota o$ / $\lambda\alpha\tilde{\omega}\nu$
$o\tilde{\iota}\sigma\iota\nu$ $\ddot{\alpha}\nu\alpha\sigma\sigma\epsilon$, 5.11f.). She is here recalling Zeus's verse about "for-
getting divine Odysseus" in book 1 (1.65), but has put "memory" in
place of "forgetting" ($\mu\acute{\epsilon}\mu\nu\eta\tau\alpha\iota$, 5.11; $\lambda\alpha\theta o\acute{\iota}\mu\eta\nu$, 1.65). This change
comes just at the point when many of the people ($\lambda\alpha o\acute{\iota}$) in the audience
may well be asking themselves whether their bard has "forgotten divine
Odysseus"; and he reassures them by "reminding/relating" and "remembering" that he has forgotten neither the main hero nor his own plot-
line. Indeed, he brings back the "memory" of his hero with a foretaste
of his most spectacular and also almost most disastrous triumph in the
repeated $\mu\acute{\eta}$ $\tau\iota\varsigma$ . . . $o\ddot{\upsilon}$ $\tau\iota\varsigma$ of 5.8 and 11, a reference to Odysseus'
"guile" ($\mu\tilde{\eta}\tau\iota\varsigma$) of giving his name as Nobody ($o\ddot{\upsilon}$ $\tau\iota\varsigma$) to deceive the
Cyclops in book 9. As both "relating" and "remembering" are charac-
teristic activities of the oral bard, Homer is here delicately signalling to
his audience that he anticipates their possible malaise at the postpone-
ment of the main narrative concern and also asserting his own overall
command of the story's direction that should alleviate that concern.

*   *   *

In the *Odyssey*, to be sure, the contrast between aesthetic distance and
emotional involvement is not displaced from poetry into weaving or into
the kind of contrast that exists between Helen and Andromache in the
Iliad, but is developed with much stronger and more explicit focus on
poetry *per se*. Or, to put it differently, the *Odyssey* has a language of
overt poetic reflexivity that the *Iliad* lacks. It even takes a playful delight

---

9. On this episode see most recently Simon Goldhill, "Reading Differences: The *Odyssey* and
Juxtaposition," *Ramus* 17 (1988): 6f., who stresses how Homer here plays with his audience's
expectations.

in making a display of its own inventiveness. It is not perhaps accidental that the *Odyssey* is the first poem of Western literature to tell the myth of Proteus. Teiresias' prophecy that Odysseus must take off again after his return to Ithaca, and the effort with which Zeus and Athena have to hold him back from further fighting are the hallmark of a poet who can keep his many-turning hero and his own many-turning story going interminably, with ever new adventures and ever-continuing battles.

In contrast to the fluency and eagerness of this song, the first mention of song or singing in the *Odyssey* depicts a bard who sings "by necessity" (ἀνάγκη, 1.154). On this occasion—our introduction to the palace on Ithaca, Telemachus confides to the stranger (Athena in disguise) that the suitors think only of "the lyre and singing, since they are eating another man's substance without payment" (1.159f.; cf. 151f.). The sequence of ideas suggests that the suitors may like poetry well enough, but they like it particularly when it accompanies a good meal, that is, as Telemachus says in line 152, when it is ἀναθήματα δαιτός, an accompaniment of the feasting. We soon learn the title of Phemius' song: "The Grim Return of the Greeks"; but this is the only song in the palace whose actual subject is specified (1.325f.). Otherwise, very little is said of what the bard sings on Ithaca, nor are the suitors ever shown as reacting to or caring about the quality or the material of the songs they hear.

Characteristically, this first song brings a "pleasure" or *terpsis* that sharply divides its hearers. As in the case of Demodocus' song of "Odysseus and the Wooden Horse," one member of the audience weeps while the rest "take pleasure." The teenager, rather careless of mother's feelings, approves of the bard's recital of what is newest in fashion. Penelope, looking back to the past and the losses of which this song reminds her, withdraws after her ineffectual protest and weeps with her maids upstairs (1.360–64).

Despite her departure, her appearance has created a disturbance that Telemachus, in his first assertion of budding manly authority, has to quiet (1.368–71): "Suitors of my mother, you who practice insult most violent (ὑπέρβιον ὕβριν ἔχοντες), now let us take joy in the feasting, and let there be no shouting, since it is a lovely thing (καλόν) to listen to a bard such as is this one, godlike in his voice." The strange collocations reveal how anomalous singing is in this setting: insult and feasting, violence and pleasure, shouting and a godlike voice. In fact, this scene shows the suitors at their best; they never again behave even this well. After Telemachus' call for orderly listening, the first of the suitors to speak is the most shameless, Antinous, and he complains of Telemachus' "lofty address and bold speaking" (ὑψαγόρην τ' ἔμεναι καὶ θαρσαλέως ἀγορεύειν, 385), while the others bite their lips. At the suitors' last feast, he meets his end in silence, with Odysseus' first arrow in his throat, kicking away the table and scattering the food on the ground (22.15–21).

Phemius' song of the "Grim Return of the Achaeans" is the only song to which the suitors listen "in silence." Otherwise, song is for them only "the accompaniment to the feasting," a kind of Mycenaean muzak, to deaden the clatter of the cups. The bard is merely the physical background to their eating and drinking, as Telemachus perhaps implies when he describes the suitors to his father in book 16 and lists the bard along with the herald and the two carvers of meat (16.252ff.). The suitors would just as soon throw the javelin, the discus, or for that matter the odd ox-hoof or footstool. Their idea of real fun is to see the two beggars slug it out. At their last banquet there is no mention of song or bard at all. But instead of a bard, they have the prophet Theoclymenus, with his ominous vision of darkness and bloody meats (20.345–57). The suitors' last song is performed by Odysseus himself as he finally throws off his rags, handles the great bow as a bard handles the lyre, makes it sing like a swallow, and then with triumphant irony shouts that it is time "for singing and the lyre, accompaniments of the feasting"—with the irony in the formula that I mentioned above.

The *Odyssey*'s first scene of bardic performance gets special prominence from the suspense created by postponing the song of Phemius for nearly two hundred lines after his introduction. He enters with his lovely lyre and beautiful song in 1.153–55; but we have to wait until the end of the interview between Telemachus and Athena/Mentor (1.158–324) for the song (1.325, τοῖσι δ᾽ ἀοιδὸς ἄειδε, takes up ἦ τοι ὁ φορμίζων ἀνεβάλλετο καλὸν ἀείδειν, 1.155). And, as we have observed, this song then becomes the focus of a three-way conflict between Telemachus, Penelope, and the suitors (1.336ff.).

Demodocus' entrance receives an even fuller description than Phemius'. Homer tells us no less than six times that this bard's skill has a divine origin,[1] with the culminating praise that it comes from "either the Muse or Zeus's son Apollo" (8.488). Here too there is a steady progression of honors for the poet, from the initial epithet "divine bard" (8.43, repeated at the end by Alcinous, 8.539) to Odysseus' honorific speech and gift of meat when he asks for the Song of the Wooden Horse (8.474–91). Homer even suggests an etymological play on Demodocus' name as "honored among the people" (Δημόδοκον λαοῖσι τετιμένον, 8.472). And he also introduces a number of unique personal details: the Muses' gift of song in compensation for blindness (8.63f., the reverse of their punishment of Thamyris in *Iliad* 2.594–600), the combination of singing tales of gods and heroes and serving as an accompanist for the dance (8.256ff.); Odysseus' reflection that bards receive honor and reverence from all men because of the Muse's love and teaching (8.479–81); and Alcinous' generalization that "the gods weave doom for mortals so that there may be song for men of the future" (8.579f.).

1. *Od.* 8.44f., 63f., 73, 480f., 488, 498.

The Phaeacians fully appreciate their bard, but their score in audience attentiveness may even be a little too high, for when Arete and
then Alcinous compliment Odysseus on his bard-like skill, they urge
him to delay his return and thus present him with a delicate problem
out of which he tactfully maneuvers (11.335–61).[2] He finds a better
balance in audience response among the eager, attentive listeners who
constitute his true friends on Ithaca, especially Eumaeus and Penelope.
The trusty swineherd Eumaeus would gladly while away the long night
with the tales of his guest, listening to the woes that he has endured
(14.191–98). Later Eumaeus praises this guest to Penelope, telling how
he "enchanted" him with his tales, like a bard (17.513–22), unknow-
ingly repeating the terms of the Phaeacian praise of Odysseus in book
11: silence, "enchantment," and bard-like skill. But the respectful silence
that is reality on Scheria is only a wish among the noisy suitors on Ithaca
(cf. 17.513 and 11.333). "Wine is the mirror of a man," the lyric poet
Alcaeus wrote some hundred years after Homer. But in the *Odyssey*
song, or how one listens to song, is also such a mirror.

These scenes of telling one's life-story show us another appeal of bardic
song, and one that runs throughout all of archaic and classical Greek
culture. For Eumaeus the telling of tales—and, by implication, the singing
of songs—is a sharing of the woes of life that bind together all men as
"miserable mortals," δειλοῖσι βροτοῖσι. Hence the two men, Odysseus the beggar and the swineherd Eumaeus, exchange their experiences
of κήδεα, griefs, with sympathy on both sides (cf. 14.185). Eumaeus'
comment is characteristic (14.361f.): "Wretched among strangers, much
did you stir my heart telling each of these things that you suffered and
all your wanderings." Alcinous' reflection on seeing Odysseus weep over
Demodocus' song of Troy is the complement to this affective view of
song (8.579f.): "The gods have spun out doom for men so that there
may be song for those of the future." But the Phaeacian king, characteristically, looks at the song (ἀοιδή) from the outside, as an aesthetic object,
rather than at the sufferings that make up its contents. In the next book
Odysseus, hearing Eumaeus' tale, echoes Eumaeus' sympathy: "Alas,
how, small as you were, swineherd Eumaeus, were you tossed far from
your native land and your parents" (15.381f.). This is the kind of
involvement that a good story creates. Men weep over such tales, as
Odysseus did over Demodocus' song of Troy; and this emotional response
of tears, though concealed out of politeness to the host, is not regarded
as remarkable or shameful.

There is a direct line between this function of song as a celebration of
human solidarity in the face of suffering and the development of Attic
drama, that in so many other respects owes much to Homer. Drama,

---

2. For an interesting analysis of this tension from the point of view of the oral performer, see
William F. Wyatt, Jr., "The Intermezzo of *Odyssey* 11 and the Poets Homer and Odysseus,"
Studi Micenei ed Egeo-Anatolici 27 (1989) 235–53, especially 240–47.

among other things, creates the community of the theater as a community of shared grief and compassion. We may think of plays like Euripides' *Andromache, Suppliants, Hecuba,* or *Trojan Women.* Here, for
example, is the chorus' closing song in the *Hippolytus* (1462–66):

> This woe came without expectation
> as common to all the citizens.
> There will be an oar-beat of many tears;
> for the tales of the great that are worthy of grieving
> do more prevail.

Through the experience of this "common woe" in the tragic spectacle,
the individual spectator participates in the "community" of suffering
mortality and thereby experiences the brotherhood and the solace of
grief contained in the poetic tradition.[3] The epic equivalent is the ever-
present generality of the δειλοὶ βροτοί in the background of the poems,
the suffering, ephemeral mortals whose "wretchedness" of all times and
places is reflected in the innumerable victims, named and unnamed, of
war and its aftermath. If we leap ahead about a thousand years, we see
this community of shared suffering established as a regular topos of consolation literature. Plutarch, writing, not speaking, to a friend who has
lost a son, begins his *Consolatio ad Apollonium* thus: "I had long since
been sharing in your pain and your grief, Apollonius, when I heard of
your dearest son's departure from life . . . (1.102 E). And he concludes:

> Resume, therefore, the spirit of a brave-
> hearted and high-minded man and set free
> from all this wretchedness both yourself and
> the mother of the youth, and your relatives
> and friends, as you may do by pursuing a more
> tranquil form of life, which will be most grat-
> ifying both to your son and to all of us who
> are concerned for you, as rightly we should
> be (καὶ πᾶσιν ἡμῖν τοῖ κηδομένοις σου
> κατὰ τὸ προσῆκον, 36.122 A).

It is as if the letter effects the consolation itself by including Apollonius
within the community of "all" the kin and friends who share in his
suffering.

In terms of audience response, the most sympathetic and attentive
audience that we see in Homer is the longed-for wife to whom Odysseus
tells the tale of his wandering in book 23 (248–341). Even more than
the Phaeacians' response, Penelope's fascinated and involved hearing
provides a clue to what might be the bard's ideal audience: there is a
quiet, attentive, personally engaged, and patient listening, with "joy in

---

3. On this feature of tragedy see my "Theater, Ritual, and Commemoration in Euripides' *Hippolytus,*" *Ramus* 17 (1988):52–74, especially 62ff.

the hearing." There is no post-prandial or post-coital dozing; she stays awake "until he had related everything" (23.306–9). Here, as in the meeting of (disguised) husband and wife in book 19, we may also catch a glimpse of the privileged circumstances in which a bard might try out new songs or improve old ones: a quiet setting; a single, well disposed auditor; all the time he needs; and the opportunity to sing of something he loves. If Homer did in fact at some point dictate the "monumental composition" he finally achieved, might he have done it in an atmosphere of friendly calm analogous to that between Odysseus and Eumaeus or Odysseus and Penelope?

Making songs and telling tales, however, are always integral parts of the plot of the poem; and so is this scene between husband and wife. Their joy in listening and telling recreates and exemplifies that mutual trust and concern which belong to the ideal of ὁμοφροσύνη that Odysseus singles out as the greatest happiness in marriage at the point when he has overcome the biggest obstacles to his return (23.301–9; cf. 6.181–85).[4] Indeed, Penelope enacts this special involvement in the teller's story when she insists that, before they bed down for the full account of his wanderings (23.306ff.), Odysseus recount the prophecy of Teiresias, even though this is a tale that will definitely not give "joy to the heart" (23.256–67).

This telling gives a momentary flash of an anti-*Odyssey*: a tale received without the "pleasure" that aesthetic distance makes possible. It is a narrative of a long voyage to the "towns" of strange men (ἐπεὶ μάλα πολλὰ βροτῶν ἐπὶ ἄστε᾽ ἄνωγεν / ἐλθεῖν, 23.267f.; cf. 1.1–4). Like Odysseus hearing Demodocus' song of the Troy, it is also a tale that its audience (i.e. Penelope) hears with intimate personal concern and therefore without "joy" or "pleasure" in the woes about to be rehearsed (23.265–68):

> αὐτὰρ ἐγὼ μυθήσομαι οὐδ᾽ ἐπικεύσω.
> οὐ μέν τοι θυμὸς κεχαρήσεται οὐδὲ γὰρ αὐτὸς
> χαίρω, ἐπεὶ μάλα πολλὰ βροτῶν ἐπὶ ἄστε᾽ ἄνωγεν
> ἐλθεῖν . . .

Well, I will tell you the tale and not conceal it. Yet your spirit will take no joy in it; for I myself have no joy, since (Teiresias) ordered me to go to very many towns of men . . .

This reluctant exchange of personal fortunes between husband and wife also recreates a somewhat analogous situation between a differently reunited couple, Helen and Menelaus in book 4. But their exchange of life-stories contains implicit accusation, distrust, and guilt; and their talk

---

4. For a good discussion of ὁμοφροσύνη in the poem see Norman Austin, *Archery at the Dark of the Moon: Poetic Problems in Homer's Odyssey* (Berkeley and Los Angeles 1975) 181, 188f., 203f.

of the past brings them no delight or forgetfulness of woes (4.235–89).[5]
To resolve their conflict and bring them peace in their household, they
need the Circe-like drug that Helen puts in the wine (4.220–32), something external to the tales themselves. Odysseus' telling, by contrast, has
a magic spell of its own, its κηληθμός or θέλξις (cf. 11.334, 17.514,
521).

* * *

Giving pleasure, τέρψις, to his audience is obviously the Homeric
bard's first concern, but it is not his only one. By the very fact of creating
a tearful response of sadness, as we have seen, the *Odyssey*-poet also
calls attention to the paradoxical pleasure that its tales of woe create.[6] In
a culture where knowledge of the past is preserved largely through oral
transmission, the bard also preserves the memory of earlier generations
and the names of those who would otherwise be "invisible" in Hades,
ἄφαντοι or ἄϊστοι. What is alive is what is heard on the lips of men,
i.e. what the bards preserve in song.[7] Hence Homer can count on his
audience's interest in the catalogue of the Achaean princes and the cities
they rule (*Iliad* 2.494–759). The generations of men are as fleeting as
the seasonal growth of leaves, but Homer can give the generations of the
Lycian Glaucus a more than seasonal life by incorporating them into
his song (*Il.* 6.145–211).

In the *Odyssey* the first threat to the hero's return is the destruction of
memory: the Lotos-Eaters, the first people to be encountered beyond the
familiar limits of Troy and the heroic world, would keep Odysseus and
his men stranded in never-never land through the amnesiac drug that
would make them "forget their return" (νόστου λαθέσθαι, *Od.* 9.97).
The loss of the memory of his homeland in Circe's bed will deprive him
of his humanness just as surely as her drugs deprive his comrades of
their human form. The other side of that loss of human identity is to be
forgotten in the homeland that waits for him, to be carried off to some
unknown place "without fame, ακλειως, unseen, unknown," leaving
no trace in the "hearing" of men (*Od.* 1.241f.; cf. 4.727f.).

The Sirens' song holds a subtle form of this self-obliteration. It is a
deadly alternative to being remembered among the living generations
who define and continue one's human identity. Although their song of
Troy promises both "knowledge" and "pleasure" (12.188), these effects
are entirely detached from a human community. Sitting in the watery

---

5. See Thalmann (above, p. 358, n. 4) 166; also Anne Bergren, "Helen's 'Good Drug': *Odyssey*
IV 1–305," in S. Kresic, ed., *Contemporary Literary Hermeneutics and Interpretation of Classical Texts* (Ottawa 1981) 200–14, especially 205ff.; Goldhill (above, p. 363, n. 9) 21–24.
6. See *Od.* 1.340–55, 4.183–95, 8.536–43 and 572–78; also above, p. 360, n. 8.
7. See Eric A. Havelock, *Preface to Plato* (Cambridge, MA, 1963) passim, especially chap. 4;
also his *The Literate Revolution in Greece and Its Consequences* (Princeton 1982) 122ff. This
"presentness" of what oral communication keeps alive in the "hearing" of men in a pre-literate
society produces what anthropologists refer to as the homoeostasis of oral cultures: see Walter
J. Ong, *Orality and Literacy* (London and New York 1982) 46ff.

waste somewhere between Circe's island and the Clashing Rocks, these singers are surrounded not by a living, eager audience of men and women in a palace or a place of assembly but by the skin and bones of rotting corpses (12.45f.), the horrid truth behind the "flowery meadow" of their island (12.159) and the sweet seduction of their voice (12.44). This decay and putrefaction are the complete antithesis of the "non-perishable glory" (κλέος ἄφθιτον) conferred by song, just as the remoteness of their voice from any human society and the solitariness of Odysseus' listening are the negation of the communal context where life-giving memory has a place.

By keeping alive the memory of noble deeds, the bard also preserves and promulgates the values embodied in heroic action. Tyrtaeus' use of Homeric battle scenes to celebrate the rather unHomeric solidarity of the Spartan hoplite-formation will be a familiar example.[8] The bard's function as the vocal embodiment of the communal values exemplified in his songs is perhaps what leads Agamemnon to the step of putting his bard in charge of watching over Clytemnestra during his long absence at Troy.[9] The task in fact proves to be beyond the abilities of this anonymous singer, who clearly should have stuck to what he knew best (cf. *Od.* 3.267–71). Is this bard's anonymity in fact a mark of his failure?

Because the Greeks, at least to the end of the fifth century B.C., envisage poetry as part of a performance and as the living voice of song, they pay special attention to its vocal dimension. Its physical qualities recur again and again in metaphors of sweetness, flowing, abundance, or strength. Invoking the Muse in the poem to the Catalogue of Ships, Homer speaks enviously of a "voice unbroken" and "a heart of bronze"— reminders of the physical effort that sustained recitation demands of the oral poet.

*   *   *

This attention to the materiality and tangibility, almost the visibility, of the voice, extends to other features of the performance. The poet fills his scenes describing bards with concrete things, much as the painter of ripe geometric vases fills his surface with ornaments, animals, or designs. The moment of the song's beginning is adorned with rich objects that hold good cheer, comfort, and beauty (*Odyssey* 8.65–70):

> In the midst of the feasters Pontonoos placed
> for him (Demodocus) a silver-studded seat,
> and set it against a tall pillar. And the herald
> took down from its peg the clear-singing lyre
> above his head, and showed him how to take
> it into his hands.

8. See, for example, Tyrtaeus 8.31–33 and *Il.* 13.130–33.
9. See Stephen Scully, "The Bard as Custodian of Homeric Society: *Odyssey* 3.263–72," *Quaderni Urbinati di Cultura Classica* 8 (1981): 74ff.

> And beside him he set a basket of food and a
> lovely table and a cup of wine to drink, as his
> heart bade him.

When the song is done, the herald again "hung the clear-singing lyre from its peg and took the hand of Demodocus and led him forth from the hall" (8.105–7). This handing back and forth of the lyre is repeated three times in Demodocus' second song (8.254f., 257, 261f.).

The pattern had already been established, although far more briefly, at the first appearance of a bard, Phemius' song among the suitors on Ithaca (1.153). The details are omitted from Demodocus' third and last song, perhaps because Homer wants to give special emphasis to Odysseus' response, which takes the form of a signal mark of honor, having the herald put a cut of meat into the singer's hands (8.471–83). Close repetition of the formulas introducing Demodocus early in the book helps show both the continuity with the previous honor and the new, even more distinctive token of respect. In terms of the formulaic structure of the theme "respect for the bard," the chine of roast pork (whatever its effects on Demodocus' digestion and clarity of voice) replaces the lyre. Even here, however, the lyre is not forgotten, for at the end, when King Alcinous notices Odysseus weeping, he orders, "Let Demodocus stay his clear-singing lyre" (8.537).

*   *   *

Another scene of the *Odyssey* may contain an authentic kernel of physical detail about the performance, in this case the performer's attachment to his instrument as an especially precious possession. In book 22, after Odysseus has despatched the suitors, the bard Phemius makes his appearance. He crawls out of his hiding place and takes refuge at the altar of Zeus in order to ask for mercy (22.330ff). He enters the narrative here in the characteristically bardic pose of his first appearance, "holding in his hands the clear-singing lyre."[1] When he decides to approach Odysseus and clasp his knees in supplication, he "first places the smooth lyre on the ground, in between the mixing bowl and the silver-studded stool" (22.340f.). These details are gratuitous. Are they perhaps an indirect reflection of the singer's professionalism? The singer would protect his instrument as a modern violinist might his Stradivarius. We may recall too Achilles' lyre, precious booty from Eetion's city (*Il.* 9.188).

Homer chooses this setting of bloody corpses and overturned tables for what is probably his fullest account of poetic inspiration. You will feel grief if you kill a poet, Phemius tells Odysseus, for I am a poet who "sings for gods and men. I am *autodidaktos*, and a god breathed into my breast songs of every sort . . ." (22.345–48).

1. *Od.* 22.332; cf. 1.153; note too that 22.331 = 1.154; cf. also 8.67f. and 105f., of Demodocus.

372 CHARLES SEGAL

For all of the abject situation in which he finds himself, the bard manages to assert his privileged position. His songs are "for gods and men," and his inspiration comes from a god. When he calls himself *autodidaktos* he may mean that he "has learned the songs from himself," i.e. that he is not just repeating what he has acquired from a specific human teacher or model. Yet the word does not exclude divine aid. In fact, his next sentence makes it clear that the poet regards the sources of his inspiration as mysterious and therefore divine. In that contact with divinity lies his claim to a special value for himself. Inspired by "a god," he also sings "for men and gods"—*hominum divumque voluptas*, one might say, with Lucretius. By choosing this unlikely occasion to reflect on the poet's divine inspiration, Homer sets his special value into even higher relief.

When Phemius combines his point about self-learning, *autodidaktos*, with the inspiration of a god, he defines his ability to make songs as not just a personal quality or a mark of genius. The ancient poet views his art as coming *both* from his own power *and* from a god. He may sing, like Phemius among the suitors, "by necessity," ἀνάγκη (1.154 = 22.331); but he also sings, as does Demodocus, "in whatever way his *thymos*, his impulse, bids him" (8.45, ὅππῃ θυμὸς ἐποτρύνῃσιν ἀείδειν). In a variation on this expression, he sings "when the Muse has impelled him to sing the famed deeds of heroes" (8.73, also of Demodocus: Μοῦσ' ἄρ' ἀνῆκεν ἀειδέμεναι κλέα ανδρῶν). The bard needs the Muse, or the god, to keep him in touch with the memory of remote events, to provide inspiration, or to complete his limited knowledge (as in the invocation of the Muses in the Catalogue of Ships, *Iliad* 2.485f.). But at the same time he feels the surge of his *thymos*, an intensification of his own energies. At such moments, he is like the warrior into whom the god breathes *menos* at the height of battle. Homer uses the same term, ἐνέπνευσε, "breathed into," for both. At such times of full concentration, then, the bard, like the warrior, has access to all the strength and power of which he is capable. Conversely, the Muses, like the gods of the *Iliad*, can deprive their favorite of his special strength. Thus they deprive Thamyris of his bardic memory, that most necessary of all the singer's capacities (*Iliad* 2.600: ἐκλέλαθον κιθαριστύν).

The Homeric bard is a singer rather than a maker (*aoidos* rather than *poietes*) because he is the voice and the vehicle of an ancient wisdom. But if the poet's powers are divine, they are not irrational. There is no trace here of the ideas of the divine madness or Dionysiac frenzy that Plato connects with poetry, or certain kinds of poetry, in the *Ion* or *Phaedrus*. Though the poet's art bears the sign of its divine origin, it is none the less still a social art: he sings "for men" as well as for gods: θεοῖσι και ἀνθρώποισιν ἀείδω (*Od.* 22.346).

* * *

The Homeric bard presents himself as more attuned to his audience than to the situation of composition or creation. His chief concern, one could say, is pragmatics, not poetics (which is not to say that he lacks a poetics). His Muses are the repositories of social memory rather than principles of creativity *per se*. He identifies with his audience rather than claiming (as Pindar, for example, will do) that he is different from or superior to his audience and thus has a right to speak with a special moral authority on his own account. Homer and even Hesiod, though inspired by Muses, do not call themselves their "prophet" or "spokes-man," as Pindar does. Nor do they call attention to their own moralizing revisions of the tales that they tell, as Pindar does with the story of the gods' cannibalistic feasting on Pelops in *Olympian* 1 (48ff.). Neither Homer nor Hesiod ever sets himself apart from a large segment of his audience in the way that Pindar does when he labels "the crowd of men, in the largest part," as "blind in heart" and "unable to see the truth" (*Nem.* 7.23f.).

The Homeric bard certainly does convey moral judgments and ethical insights (one need only think of the proem of the *Odyssey* 1.32–43); but he does not define himself in terms of such tasks. This more critical spirit develops only with the more individualizing, independent, and self-assertive poetics of late archaic lyric (especially Simonides and Pin-dar); and of course it culminates in the dialogic presentation of myth and the conflictual situations dramatized in tragedy. However much tragedy owes to epic and lyric song, it also represents a radical break with the archaic view of the poet.

The Homeric bard remains, above all, a "singer of tales" (to use Albert Lord's phrase), a purveyor of pleasure (τέρψις), and a preserver of tra-ditions. But in that role he is indispensable to his memory-hungry and pleasure-loving audience, and he is valued and honored accordingly. The Phaeacians, idealized for many of their political and technological skills, are also idealized for their skills as an audience. They are the most eager for song and story, both about the gods and about men, take the most pleasure in hearing the bard, and accord him more honor than we see anywhere else in the poet. Telling his story in this privileged setting (whatever the risks and dangers in the background), even the habitually lying Odysseus exercizes the magical spell of an inspired singer (11.333f.); and for all we know he may even be telling them the truth.

PAOLO VIVANTE

Time and Life in Homer †

This indefinite sense of human time cannot come gratuitously, like
an idle dream. As everything in Homer, it must be occasioned by material conditions, it must be prompted by a vital need. What is required is
a distance between the characters. There must be a man that is cherished or feared, alive but absent, whose destiny is not known. Friends
or enemies visualize him far away. Only then can thoughts focus anx-
iously upon a given object, and yet be free to wander unencumbered by
its immediate presence. In such a way the life of an absent character can
be mentally realized. His distant experiences are questioned, imagined,
tentatively followed in their possible course, and not represented as
objective data. The momentary occasion of a day or of a night must be
left out of account. Time is here an indeterminate lapse of life, subjec-
tively felt and yet posited in the world at large.

The *Odyssey* fosters this sensibility. We are made aware of it right at
the beginning. For Odysseus emerges, as it were, out of nowhere. As he
is first presented, his feet do not rest on any ground, he does not stand
out in a particular stance, as Achilles and Agamemnon do at the beginning of the *Iliad*. He is unmistakably himself, but only by being strongly
entrenched in our imagination. His prominence is due to a certain aura
rather than to a single action. Where is he? When will he come? His
image is in everyone's mind, remembered, expected, fixed in no given
time or place, helplessly out of range.

The first book of the *Odyssey* gathers very quickly various threads of
time around absent Odysseus. Telemachus sees him in his mind's eye,
imagining the storms that might have killed him. Phemius sings the
return of the Achaeans, recalling the destinies of the expedition which
carried him away. Penelope hears and bids the minstrel stop, protesting
her life-long grief for his absence. The suitors pursue their quest, scarcely
concealing how they fear his return. All these characters survey the life
of Odysseus in their persistent thoughts; and Odysseus is, in turn, a
theme which keeps in unison their moods and their actions. A lapse of
indefinite years is thus covered in brief outline.

Such a rendering of time would have been impossible, if Odysseus
had been pictured in Ithaca, furthering his cause. His encompassing
presence could leave no room for vague expectation or regret. But, as it
is, his distance opens up the prospect of things to come and memory fills

---

† From Paolo Vivante, *The Homeric Imagination: Homer's Poetic Perception of Reality* (Bloomington, Ind.: Indiana UP, 1970). Reprinted by permission of the publisher. Copyright © 1970
by Indiana University Press.

his vacant place with images from the past. It is as if the poet had no other means to suggest such an extension in time. For it was not his genius to depict changing situations in the manner of a novelist or a historian; and now the radiance of a distant image afforded him an effective medium: here was a man whose spell could reverberate into a whole age.

The distance of Odysseus is essential to the sense of time in the *Odyssey*. Existence thereby recedes more and more from what is immediately visual. It becomes a course of life to be endured or struggled for—a destiny summing up all the days in its own terms. It is so throughout the poem. See how, under the approaching shadow of Odysseus, the quality of each character grows into what it is. Telemachus becomes resolute. The suitors are obstinate. Penelope is faithful. It could not be otherwise: they are weathered by fear or hope, and their feelings have matured into a habit of mind. Everyday business here becomes perfunctory. In Penelope's case, for instance: the daily tasks—which elsewhere in Homer are so self-sufficient—become for her an excuse, a device to keep alive, like the weaving of the famous web which seems to allegorize her long resistance.

Odysseus, on the other hand, thinks of Ithaca. This thought is a driving force, turning his scattered exploits into phases of a long effort. His endurance has a counterpart in that of Penelope: at a different pole of the earth there is a longing which is parallel to his own, affecting his own; and deeply related feelings converge from different angles, gathering all accidental happenings into one great protracted strain.

It is remarkable how this encompassing effect of time ultimately rests, once again, on the spell of the Homeric image—just as in the quick exchanges of the *Iliad*, but much more extensively. For that same spell works now on a larger range, over the distance that separates the characters; and it is the same character that exerts it throughout the poem. Odysseus is πολύτλας, "much suffering" by definition; and his very name evokes his destiny. But it is as if the burden of his epithet overflowed into his words, into his very features. For his sufferings are his great theme whenever he gives a condensed account of himself (cf. *Od.* 5. 222; 7. 24, 147, 152, etc.). Similarly, they are ever borne in mind whenever he is seen, remembered, imagined by others (cf. *Od.* 14. 42; 1. 161, 195, 235, etc.). As these instances accumulate, they haunt the mind of the reader. It is as if, each time, we saw Odysseus against a deepening background. Insofar as his suffering is expressed in a mere epithet, it is crystallized into his image; and we have no more than a heroic attribute. But, as the poem develops, this suffering is seen in a different light. We become aware of a capacity to suffer, to endure, to strive year after year. The heroic image is transformed into a complex character. Another Odysseus arises before us. Grief and hope have sob-

ered him. His experiences advance in time; and all the dangers or wonders of isolated moments take their allotted place in the large vital
movement of his life.

It is, of course, Odysseus himself who gives the full account of his
experiences, speaking directly to the Phaeacians. But he arrives from far
away. The distance which separated him heretofore from his listeners
still isolates him. He is there in their midst; but removed into a world of
his own by the legend that has gathered around him, by a past which is
all one with the spell of his presence. Here at last a direct contact takes
place—not suddenly, fleetingly, as in the scenes of the *Iliad*, but after a
long suspense, the intervening distances at last cut short. As the long-
suggested image strikes the beholder, the history of a whole lifetime is
prefigured even before it is told.

The way in which Odysseus gradually reveals himself to the Phaeacians in the eighth book of the *Odyssey* is visual rather than verbal. He
is not simply a stranger saying who he is and recounting his past. His
identity seems to transpire, hinted by the wonder of his first appearance,
by the wisdom of his words, by the power of his weatherworn limbs.
Then the minstrel sings about Troy, and he weeps. His tears offer a
glimpse of the actual truth, so that when he finally says his name, it
hardly comes as a surprise. It is as if the image of Odysseus hovered in
the consciousness of the audience right from the beginning. But what
was just divined or known by hearsay is now made flesh and bones, and
the timeless suggestion of a distant glory is transposed into the record of
a man, legend is turned to self-confession, fame to subjective acknowledgement. The whole Trojan cycle becomes just a phase in a man's life.
In that Phaeacian land where gods often consort with men Odysseus
insists upon his human character: not only is he a mortal, but the most
wretched of mortals. Only with this premise could his story be told in
terms of human experience. But, at the same time, he has to rise to the
full measure of his own prefigured image, in response to the expectation
of those who are there before him questioning and wondering. His past
must be elicited from his present spell, and not only from his tales. This
is why he does not proceed to give an orderly account of his adventures
from first to last. He begins, rather, with the last one—with the journey
which brought him there from Calypso's island, as a wanderer, a suppliant. It is his presence there and then which matters most—a wonder
for all to witness and account for. And later, when he actually recounts
his return from Troy, it is as if his story were a means of self-realization.
His past actions are each a parcel of the life which is gathered within
him; and time is like the shadow of his image, indefinitely prolonged.
He is not only surveying things gone by, he is giving a proof of himself.
His relation with the audience is here essential. The listeners progres-
sively contemplate, admire, learn, know; and their knowledge is in turn
a new feeling for what they apprehended at first sight. What amazes

them is not so much the narrative itself as the narrator who grows upon them as he speaks. His personality, surmised at first, is now recomposed more clearly in its human terms; and we have no chronological sequence of mythical ventures, but the progressive revelation of a man's life—a living process rather than a cycle artificially contrived.

The way in which Odysseus makes himself known in Ithaca is worked out in the same spirit. Again we have the penetrating spell of his image; again the questioning gaze of those who see him, and the distances finally cut short, an interval of absence which must be filled, words which recompose the lapse of time.

Only the circumstances are different than they were in the land of the Phaeacians. Odysseus is now transformed into an old beggar by Athena; and, when the occasion calls for it, again into a young man. These transformations, of course, are required by the plot. But we may also see them in a different light. His appearance as an old man can be justified in an ideal sense. It is an alteration, a disguise worked by the years of absence, a screen which gives way at an even pace with the process of recognition which exhumes the past.

Odysseus seems to emerge more and more clearly out of his rags. He becomes a power in Ithaca even before it is known who he actually is. For his relation with the island becomes more meaningful from hour to hour. He is moving into the circuit of old affections. His bodily presence gradually absorbs them all; and he advances dramatically to take his rightful place, filling the gap of separation and estrangement, retrieving an identity which seemed out of reach. Finally he is made one with the image which had haunted for so long the mind of his people.

His progress in Ithaca is at once a recovery of the past. As he advances, his background is enlarged. For, almost unintentionally, he attracts or challenges whomsoever he happens to meet; and long-standing attitudes are immediately brought into play. Thus Eumaeus is stirred to instant sympathy and impassioned recollection, while Odysseus, standing before him in his rags, participates in the drama of Ithaca with increasing intensity, as if he were drawing new blood from his ancient roots. Now a mysterious familiarity draws them closer to one another. He appears enhanced by an unexpected prestige, so keenly does he realize the true state of the island, so strongly does he judge and forecast the course of events. Who might this stranger be? Even before this is known, he is made to bear the mark of his true character, just as the makeshift story which he composes about himself comes as a preface to the true one, almost an allegory of his life, an intimation of his identity.

His broadening role also means an enrichment of his personality. Here again the element of time is important. For now a more intimate side of his life is opening up, a side of him which had remained concealed so far. Its values come upon him as a distinct awareness of facts and of people in their long careers. Penelope, Telemachus, Laertes, Anticleia

now take their pertinent part in his introspection, and a whole portion
of his past becomes intrinsic to his being. At a certain point, it is as if
the burden of this past could no longer be contained within him, as if
recognition were inevitably imminent through some force of its own.

It is extraordinary how his increasing awareness is matched by an
increasing transparency of his image to the eyes of others. More and
more does the beggar appear like Odysseus, as he meets the taunts of the
suitors and of the handmaids, as he endears himself to Penelope; more
and more, accordingly, does his life unfold. The climax comes, of course,
when Eurycleia, washing him, recognizes the famous scar. But a pre-
monition haunts her beforehand. At that moment her feelings for Odysseus are singularly stirred; and, as in a vision, she says to him: "Woe is
me, o son, for your sake; how helpless I am. Zeus has especially spurned
you in spite of your goodness" (*Od*. 19. 363 ff.). Then, turning to the
beggar: "Even so, I think, the attendants of far-off strangers have scoffed
at him, as now these shameless ones were scoffing at you" (Ibid. 370
ff.). Finally a sympathetic insight flashes upon her: "My heart is all astir
with your woes. But listen . . . of all the many wretched wanderers that
have come in the past to this house, none have I seen so resembling
Odysseus as you" (Ibid. 377 ff.).

The feeling of recognition becomes contagious. The sight of the beggar unmistakenly evokes the destiny of Odysseus. A little later Philoitios
echoes the words of Eurycleia: "O father Zeus, none of the gods brings
more woe than you. You do not take pity upon men though yourself
you bring them to birth, and you plunge them in misery and grief" (*Od*.
20. 201 ff.). Then turning to the beggar: "I perspire as I see you, tears
rise up in my eyes, remembering Odysseus; for he too, I think, is clothed
in such rags a wanderer among men" (Ibid. 204 ff.).

Recognition is the key word here. It implies a recovery of wasted times,
values made good again, features retraced to their ancient integrity. To
see, to know, to rediscover are now all one. The eyes of the characters
are endowed with a particular insight which seems to penetrate beyond
the surface. Odysseus, on his part, stands transfigured by the impact of
attentive looks. The past blends with the present, shimmering through
his outlines. The work of memory is wonderfully quickened. Unwittingly he bears in himself his story.

After a long time people are altered, and yet essentially the same.
Their lives might be suggested by their features. It is so with Odysseus:
his long suffering is witnessed by the wrinkles that disfigure him, while
the power of his limbs still betrays his native prowess. All this is quite
natural; but the plot seems so designed as to isolate and stress these effects
of time. More and more do we realize that Odysseus' transformations at
the hand of Athena acquire in this context a meaning which goes beyond
that of a mere stratagem. If he appears now young now old as befits the
occasion, is not this a way of rendering visually the suggestions of mem-

ory and of present awareness? Penelope, at the end (*Od*. 23. 93 ff.), sits
wondering. It is of no help that Odysseus should be made to assume
again the splendor of his youth (Ibid. 156 ff.). Her silence conceals the
effort to realize the unity of these varied appearances, to make the real
coincide with its idealization. She must reconcile her long-matured
restraint with her present longing. What are these transformations to her
eyes? Who is Odysseus? The husband she remembers, the begger she
has just been talking to, the bright metamorphosis now displayed before
her? All these are like illusions which time has played upon her baffled
consciousness—the dreams and visions which kept her waiting for so
long, shreds of her brooding experience which must now be made into
one coherent whole. Here is a heart-searching task which Homer does
not, cannot retrace in its subjective, passionate phases, but, again, through
the glimmer of shifting appearances.

Penelope cannot resist for long. She must reply to Odysseus' entreaty.
When she does so, it as if his transformation into a young man awaked
in her the feelings of her earlier life. "I am not proud, I am not disdain-
ful, I am now coming back to myself; I remember how you looked when
you sailed away in the long-oared ship," she says (*Od*. 23. 174 ff.). We
are reminded of the scene in which Helen is carried back to a past experience by a far different transformation.

Returning or welcoming back after twenty years is an engrossing experience, especially when those who meet again are an Odysseus and a
Penelope. In long regret they have idealized one another; and now they
stand out for what they are, weathered by the years. Here is a dissonance
between the mental image and the real one. Pent-up feelings suddenly
concur to fill up the gap, to restore the harmony. Now more than ever
can a long lapse of time be mentally realized. The initial shock clears
the way. It was characteristic of Homer to concentrate upon such a
moment, to work it up with all the wonder it naturally implies. A miraculous coincidence seemed to occur—destiny joining in with a sponta-
neous movement of human sympathy. Euripides must have had
something like it in mind in his *Helen* when he wrote "to recognize a
friend is a god" (*Hel*. 560). Homer could not be so abstract. He brought
into play Athena's spell, the transformation of Odysseus.

A long-awaited moment, when it comes, puts everything else in the
shade. Our feelings magnify it, gathering into it all that in the past was
missed or vaguely anticipated. But Homer could not render it as pure
inner experience. He conceived it visually, dramatically. Hence Odysseus' changing image, hence the devious ways of his return to Penelope.
There is no passionate celebration, no tender recollection. We have,
instead, overtures, approaches, meetings that become more and more
pressing, shifting appearances that become more and more significant.
All this is carried out as by a divine spell; but the element of wonder is
made convincing and forcible insofar as it stresses the human tensions

implied in each scene. Thus Odysseus' transfiguration, as we have seen, reflects Penelope's feeling of duration and change, of expectation and fulfillment. It is as if time had discharged upon a visual form the burden of persistent longings.

As in the *Iliad*, the images are suddenly brought before one another and reveal themselves. But here the meeting comes after a long climax; and the crowning moment must be made relevant to a previous story, broad vicissitudes of life compressed into the imagery and action of single scenes. The extent to which this could be done is no small proof of artistic power—of how the bulky epic material could be made to suggest, if not to express directly, the delicate complexities of human time.

Memories are stirred up almost unwittingly when people meet again at length. Time gathers spontaneously from many sides: what strikes a common chord comes to the fore, no matter when or where it happened. This is human time, this is life. And yet a survey of one's life is something different. It requires that an individual be followed in the course of his existence. What matters is not so much the significance of single occasions as a sense of continuity, of development, of growth. The idea of time must thus be gleaned from the signs of a vital spark that perseveres in its activity. We shall have to look for it in the notion of existence itself, and not in the self-revelation of characters that meet in dramatic moments.

In fifth century Greek, just as in English, the word "life" means both the fact of being alive and its duration. We easily abstract the sense of time from that of a vital organic principle and, by doing so, we make the word "life" synonymous with experience, history, biography (as when we say "a happy life" or "the life of Shakespeare"). It is not so in Homer. The temporal meaning is only implied. There are no such abstractions as time and life. These are ideal values, submerged as yet in the material which is their source. We find, instead, a stress on those organs or things which make life possible—what nourishes, what breathes, heart, spirit. Herein lies a vital function. By its very nature it yields a sense of time—a common capacity to be, to live, to resist, to endure.

The language of Homer will give us a cue. There are many words which might be translated as "life"; but not one which normally carries with it a sense of duration. What prevails is everywhere the idea of a vital force or sustenance whose extension in time may be indirectly conveyed by the context, as if the animate vigor were all there waiting to be drawn out. What we mean by "life span," "lifetime" is not something taken for granted; it is a value which is inferred from observing the ways of nature.

ELIZABETH STORZ

The Beginning of the *Odyssey* †

In the very beginning of the *Odyssey*, the singer sets forth the terms of his narrative:

> Tell me, Muse, about the man of many turns, who many
> Ways wandered when he had sacked Troy's holy citadel;
> He saw the cities of many men, and he knew their thought;
> On the ocean he suffered many pains within his heart,
> Striving for his life and his companions' return.
> But he did not save his companions, though he wanted to:
> They lost their own lives because of their recklessness.
> The fools, they devoured the cattle of Hyperion,
> The Sun, and he took away the day of their return.
> Begin the tale somewhere for us also, goddess, daughter of Zeus.
> (I 1–10)

At once, before the story properly begins, Homer reveals and constructs the scene of telling. First, in line 1, the twofold source of speech is given. The Muse, the figure who is conceived of as the ultimate source for the possibility of narrative, functions as motivator, for the phrase "tell me" *(moi ennepe)* generates the clause which introduces, in the next seven lines, the main subject of the story. Indeed, this whole passage, bracketed as it is by "Muse" and "goddess, daughter of Zeus," is dependent upon the transcendent presence and creative force embodied in the mythic muse. She stands on one side of the singer as a sort of poetic agent, however stylized such an epic invocation may be. The second source of speech is, of course, the singer himself, the oblique counterpart to the Muse, who cannot begin to narrate unless he identifies where his language is coming from.

In Book VIII a similar scene appears wherein the singer Demodokos does not begin his story about Odysseus' and Achilleus' quarrel until the source of his knowledge is twice named:

> Then a herald came near, leading the trusty singer
> Whom the Muse loved dearly and gave both good and ill.
> (VIII 62–63)

> The Muse bade the singer to sing famous deeds of men
> From the lay whose fame had by then reached broad heaven . . .
> (VIII 73–74)

In all these cases, Homer must account for his own narrative authority (either directly, as in the opening passage, or indirectly, as in the above

† Published here for the first time by permission of the author.

examples) as well as provide a reason for his ability to sing. In doing so, he sets up a series of terms, whose relations, though not strictly causal, definitely situate the singer between a poetic source and poetic material. In the course of the narrative itself, the singer only exists in relation to these two terms, the muse and his song.

Aside from these metapoetic concerns, the opening of the *Odyssey* also contains a number of words which acquire a thoroughgoing thematic treatment throughout the narrative. In line 3, for example, after a one-line, beautifully rendered encapsulation of the historical dimension, Homer in effect characterizes the as-yet unnamed Odysseus. The two verbs, "saw" *(iden)* and "heard" *(egno)*, describe someone who is primarily involved in perceiving and discerning, but the progression of the clause "he saw the cities of many men, and he knew their thought" *(iden astea kai noon egno)* maintains an equal emphasis on the objects of perception and knowledge. "Cities" and "thought" (or "purpose," "mind," "design," "intent") are literally held by the verbs "he saw" and "he knew" in such a way that the clause acts as a single syntactic unit. This is all to make the simple but important point that seeing and knowing are, from the beginning, intimately linked. Moreover, the notions of city and mind, of concrete and abstract, are appropriate to one another, and taken together with the rest of the line, are in a kind of appositional relationship to Odysseus: "Odysseus, the one who saw cities and knew the thought . . ."

Lines 4 and 5 broaden the description of the protagonist while they also implicitly broaden the narrative geography of the epic as a whole. Already we anticipate encountering cities and ways of thinking. Now we anticipate the sea, the sufferings of Odysseus, and his attempts at saving his own life. Once again Homer constructs a most economical phrase from which all these specific circumstances emanate. This time, the two words "life" *(psuchen)* and "return" *(noston)*, framed by their possessive words, are grammatically inclusive of one another. The phrase is read as one unit, as, in fact, it comprises a most fundamental thematic "argument" of the *Odyssey*. The various manifestations of "life" ("soul," "life," and "spirit" all translate *psyche*) are often conjoined in some way with the idea of return or homecoming *(nostos)*.

EDWIN DOLIN

Odysseus in Phaeacia †

The poet of the Odyssey was bold, and nowhere in the poem more so than in the Phaeacian episode,[1] where his artistic ambition required that he take on the many problems involved in placing his epic hero, the proud conqueror of Troy, in the condition of what we today would call a picaro. For this seems to be the correct name for the role seemingly awaiting Odysseus at his arrival, almost dead, on the beach of Scheria. He is a wanderer, alone in a foreign land, with no resources except his brain and tongue, and with a compelling reason to conceal his real identity. A condition as precarious and exposed as this would seem to demand that the hero play the picaro part to the full by devising for the occasion a new, safe and useful identity. The great surprise of the Phaeacian episode of the *Odyssey*, as well as the motive that binds it together from beginning to end, is that Odysseus does not, finally, choose to play the picaro part. Past master of deception and false personae, he nevertheless renounces these weapons and tells the truth about his name and, even more unpicaresque, about the reason why that name is so perilous for himself and for others.

But the decision for truth, a dangerous truth, is not made immediately. Between his arrival at the palace of Alcinous and the banquet the following evening there intervenes a time during which he carefully avoids any form of self-identification, either true or false. Why? What prevents this quick-witted extemporizer from taking the appropriate decision,

† From *Grazer Beitraege* 1 (1973). Reprinted by permission of Editions Rodopi and Edwin Dolin.
1. For discussion of the Phaeacian episode, see C. R. Beye, *The Iliad, the Odyssey and the Epic Tradition* (New York, 1966), pp. 194–199; S. Besslich, *Schweigen-Verschweigen-Uebergehen* (Heidelberg, 1966), pp. 42–47, 143–147; F. Bliss, "The Structural Unity of *Odyssey* 8," *Bucknell Review* XVI.3 (1968), pp. 57–73; W. Burkert, "Das Lied von Ares und Aphrodite," *Rheinisches Museum* CIII (1960), pp. 130–144; H. W. Clarke, *The Art of the Odyssey* (Englewood Cliffs, N.J., 1967), pp. 45–56; A. S. Cook, *The Classic Line* (Bloomington, Ind., 1966), pp. 120–137; G. E. Dimock, Jr., "The Name of Odysseus," in *Essays on the Odyssey*, ed. C. H. Taylor, Jr. (Bloomington, Ind., 1963), also in *Homer: Twentieth Century Views*, ed. by G. Steiner and R. Fagles; F. Eichhorn, *Homers Odyssee* (Goettingen, 1965), pp. 16–21, 54–56, 60–63; U. Hoelscher "Das Schweigen der Arete," *Hermes* LXXXVIII (1960), pp. 257–265; W. Mattes, *Odysseus bei den Phaeaken* (Wuerzburg, 1958); K. Reinhardt, *Tradition und Geist* (Goettingen, 1960), pp. 112–124; G. P. Rose, "The Unfriendly Phaeacians," *Transactions and Proceedings of the American Philological Association* 100 (1969), pp. 387–406; W. Schadewaldt, "Kleiderdinge," *Hermes* LXXXVII (1959), pp. 13–26; C. P. Segal, "The Phaeacians and the Symbolism of Odysseus' Return," *Arion* I, No. 4 (Winter 1962), pp. 17–64; W. B. Stanford, *The Ulysses Theme* (Oxford, 1954); C. H. Taylor, Jr., "The Obstacles to Odysseus' Return," in *Essays on the Odyssey*, ed. C. H. Taylor, Jr. (Bloomington, Ind., 1963); C. H. Whitman, *Homer and the Heroic Tradition* (Cambridge, Mass., 1958), pp. 285–309. On the picaresque, see C. Guillén, *Literature as System* (Princeton, N.J., 1971), pp. 71–106. On the Odysseus-Polyphemus episode, see E. M. Bradley, "The Hybris of Odysseus," *Soundings* LI (1968), pp. 33–44; C. S. Brown, "Odysseus and Polyphemus," *Comparative Literature* XVIII (1966), pp. 193–202; A. J. Podlecki, "Guest-gifts and Nobodies," *Phoenix* XV (1961), pp. 125–133.

whichever it is, almost immediately? Among the various possible answers to this question, the most generally adequate would seem to be that Odysseus is, during this time, *uncertain* about which course to take, the safe lie or the dangerous truth.

The facts which make a choice between these alternatives necessary were disclosed to Odysseus when he met a young girl, who is Athena in disguise, while walking from the beach to the city of the Phaeacians on the evening of his first day. The girl's information is of fundamental importance to Odysseus, whom we know as Poseidon's hated enemy (5.282 f., 6.324–331). First the girl mentions that the Phaeacians' skill with ships had come as a gift from Poseidon (7.34). Then she explains that the Phaeacian royal family is directly descended from this god (7.56–66). Earlier Odysseus had already heard from Nausicaa that the Phaeacian agora is centered on Poseidon's shrine (6.266).

Even a less prudent man than Odysseus would be compelled to pause at this news and wonder how ready Alcinous and the Phaeacians would be to help him if they knew the ominous nature of his connection with the god who dominates their nation and life. Under these circumstances it is only to be expected that Odysseus should give Alcinous, Arete and the Phaeacian nobles even less information about himself than he had previously given Nausicaa on the beach. There his account of himself included mention of having stopped once at Delos while leading a large army, and of having just now come from Ogygia. But in the palace before the royal family and court he has not a word to say about any aspect of his past except the immediate trip from Ogygia. In fact, he lets pass two opportunities to make a self-identification, one indirect, the other direct.[2] Then, on the following day, during an assembly in the agora, he again rejects an opportunity to give his name. Later this same day, challenged and insulted during the athletic contests, he slips to the extent of revealing that he has been a prominent warrior at Troy, but his self-control reasserts itself before a specific name or identifying detail is disclosed.

One artistic purpose of the outburst at the athletic contests is to emphasize for us the strain that prolonged reticence is causing the hero. A decision one way or another must be made soon, because the ship which will carry Odysseus to safety cannot sail without a destination, and the name of the destination would, if not inevitably, at least normally, be accompanied by the name of the traveller. After having been

---

2. Alcinous' reference to the possibility that Odysseus is a god (7.199) as an indirect invitation to Odysseus to identify himself is supported by *Iliad* 6.128. Odysseus' reference to Poseidon at 7.271 does not constitute a change from his policy of delay, or an anticipation of his self-revelation in Book 9. In saying to Alcinous and Arete that "Poseidon the earth shaker raised up a great trouble against me" he assumed they would understand him as merely using common language to refer to trouble at sea, not as suggesting any special reason for Poseidon to be angry with him as an individual.

the recipient of so much courtesy, merely to say "take me to such-and-such a port," with nothing more, would imply an attitude perilously close to coldness and ingratitude, or even contempt. The strain of reticence is made all the more burdensome by the obvious readiness of Alcinous to accept the stranger on any terms he gives. Almost any story would do, apparently, and Odysseus is the man to produce just the right one for the circumstances. Thus there is a stranger with a compelling reason to deceive and a host who is beyond any expectation susceptible to deception. What is restraining Odysseus? Only, it would seem, this same phenomenal trustfulness, generosity and nobility of the Phaeacian king. With any one else there would have been no grounds for hesitation. The most impressive and utilitarian lies would have been forthcoming with no delay. But with Alcinous—! If any man could be trusted to keep his promise, no matter what the consequences, it was he. Odysseus is faced with the surprising prospect that to tell the truth is for once a real and valid option.

By the evening of his second day in Scheria, Odysseus has apparently reached a decision on which option to take. He suggests to the court bard that he sing the episode of the Trojan horse,[3] because he foresees the effect that this theme will have on himself, tears, just as he foresees the effect his tears will have on Alcinous, another appeal to the stranger for his name and that of his city.[4] This time, since Odysseus has himself arranged for the question to be asked, we know that he is going to respond affirmatively to his host's appeal. But we do not know the content of his answer, only that there will be one. He could choose to lie, along the lines of his later story to Eumaeus, with a statement that he is so-and-so from Crete and would like passage to Ithaca in order to collect a debt. Brought that far by the Phaeacians, he would manage the rest of the way to Crete by himself. A feasible solution, but any tendency towards adopting it is destroyed for Odysseus by the language which Alcinous uses to him at this decisive moment:

3. In Book 8 Demodokos sings first of the Trojan War as something in the future, a foretold success (8.73–82) and the phrase used to describe the song is *klea andron*, the same phrase, invoking the glamor of saga, that was used to describe Achilles' song at *Iliad* 9.189. Finally, Demodokos, at Odysseus' suggestion, sings of the last victorious event of the Trojan War, Odysseus' mixture of deceit and violence, the wooden horse filled with soldiers. But Odysseus' reaction to this victory is a flood of tears like those of a woman being dragged away from her husband dying in front of his captured city. In other words, the thought of his victory brings to Odysseus, ten years and much suffering later, not a sense of satisfaction and self-congratulation, but a feeling of desolate, hopeless grief. The conqueror now knows what it is to be conquered. This is a fundamental perspective of the *Odyssey*, a view of the self-glorifying, warrior world of saga from a critical angle. It seems unlikely to be an accident that the epithet *ptoliporthios*, "sacker of cities," is chosen by Odysseus to proclaim himself to the Cyclops and is then repeated by the Cyclops when he curses Odysseus. The concept expressed by this epithet is the subject of Demodokos' song of the Trojan horse, which is followed immediately by the simile of the captured woman forced away from her dying husband. The man who ten years before was proud of having sacked cities now cries like a woman whose city has been sacked.

4. See Eichhorn, *op. cit.*, p. 9.

A guest and suppliant is held equal to a *brother*
By a man who has even a little grasp with his wits.
So, in your cunning notions, do not yourself conceal
What I ask you about. . . . (8.546–549, italics mine)[5]

The message is clear, Alcinous is as committed to the stranger as he
would be to his blood brother. Furthermore, Alcinous makes a pointed
contrast between himself and his guest. The stranger has "cunning notions"
(noemasi kerdaleoisin). In fact, *kerdaleos* implies the stranger is not only
secretive, but self-seeking, in sharp contrast to Alcinous himself. But
there is more than reproach in this speech. Alcinous also produces new
information, which dramatically involves not merely his own well-being
but that of the whole Phaeacian people in the decision about to be made
by the foreigner whom no one knows:

. . . once I heard my father Nausithous
Say this: he asserted that Poseidon bore ('would bear' alternate read-
ing) a grudge
Against us, because our convoys are safe for all men.
He said a well-made ship of the Phaeacian men
Coming back some time from an escort on the murky sea
Would be dashed and a great mountain would hide our city round.
So the old man said. And the god will either fulfill it
Or it will be unfulfilled, as his spirit desires.
Come, tell me this and speak out truthfully,
Where have you wandered. . . .(8.564–673)

The introduction of this ominous prophecy is Alcinous' proof that he is
willing to incur a serious risk to himself and his own in return for an
expression of trust from his "brother." Why should his "brother" refuse
to incur a risk comparable to his host's, if he is truly the man he has
been taken for? The lines constitute an appeal for a relationship on a
high ethical level, that of two courageous men who are willing to face
danger for the sake of their friendship, two brothers or two *hetairoi*,
"comrades," on the epic scale of Achilles and Patroclus.

Confronted by an appeal as direct, total and challenging as this, the
stranger at last gives a commensurate response:

I am Odysseus, son of Laertes, who for my wiles *(doloisin)*
Am of note among all men, and my fame reaches heaven.
(9.19f.)

What is implied by Odysseus' use of the word *doloisin*, "deceit," is that
Alcinous was perceptive in attributing to his guest "cunning notions"
(noemasi kerdaleoisin). He *is* a cunning man, ever seeking his own

5. The idea of the comrade-brother recurs at the end of this speech, 584–586. The translations
are from Albert Cook, *The Odyssey* (New York, 1993) (this Norton Critical Edition–*Editor*).

advantage, openly or secretly. He *could* have deceived Alcinous before, if he had wished, and might deceive him yet. All this is admitted by Odysseus' word *doloisin* in response to Alcinous' words *noemasi kerdaleoisin*. But the prospect of future deception is countered and rebutted by the content of the story Odysseus tells in reply to Alcinous' appeal. If Alcinous will risk an act of anger from Poseidon for friendship's sake, Odysseus in turn will risk a test of that friendship by disclosing why Alcinous' apprehensions about Poseidon are even better founded than he could have imagined. Alcinous had assured Odysseus of his truthworthiness. What Odysseus tells him now will put that assurance to a severe test. The confessional narrative of Odysseus' crime against Poseidon is Odysseus' gift to Alcinous, and is given on the terms Alcinous proposed, the confrontation of danger. The stranger begging for the Phaeacians' help is the enemy of the Phaeacians' stern god, on whose good will they depend absolutely.

This is the opposite of what a picaro could be expected to say. It is unnecessary, excessive frankness. Even if Odysseus had wished to make some gesture of friendship, he could have stopped with his name and some innocuous adventures. The name would have been risk enough, for how was Odysseus to know whether or not there was some prophecy known to Alcinous specifically naming Odysseus, as had been the case with Circe and Polyphemus? But Odysseus does not choose to make merely a partial gesture. He tells everything, not only the fact of Poseidon's hatred, but why Poseidon hates him. To tell this is to go beyond anecdote and externals. It is to confess a personal guilt which lays bare the whole ambiguous nature of the heroic life, the very life that is now providing the tone for Alcinous' and Odysseus' mutual understanding.

Contrary to the warnings of his crew, so Odysseus declares to Alcinous and the Phaeacians in the course of his narrative of the most crucial and pivotal episode of the whole *Odyssey*, he went into the cave of the Cyclops. Trapped but not outwitted, Odysseus gives a false name and then succeeds in blinding Polyphemus and escaping to sea. But once there, contrary again to the warnings of his crew, he proudly shouts out his true name to the enraged monster, curses him and at that moment hears the Cyclops' curse on him in return. From that point Odysseus is "hated by the blessed gods" (10.74) and wanders onwards leading his comrades from disaster to ruin.[6]

Thus Odysseus' story is a boldly candid response to Alcinous' challenge, since it places the enmity of Poseidon and the risks it occasions in central focus. But it is also a self-accusation, the confession of a fatal destructive act of egotism. That heroic, gloating, taunting self-advertisement of so many years before—

6. For the curse of Polyphemus and Odysseus' sense of responsibility for its consequences, see Reinhardt, *op. cit.*, pp. 47–112.

Cyclops, if some one among mortal men should inquire
Of you about the unseemly blindness in your eye,
Say that Odysseus, sacker of cities, blinded it,
The son of Laertes, whose home is in Ithaca. (9.502–505)

—that proclamation had originally been an act of pride and hate. But
now, repeated in the context of his helplessness in Scheria, it is an act
of humility. The contrast between the arrogant conqueror represented
in the narrative and the lonely wanderer who speaks the narrative is
total. The man who made that boast ten years ago had let his success in
the violence of the Trojan War confuse his sense of reality. The consequences are still being unfolded at the very moment he recreates the
distant event to his audience. Odysseus is, in effect, explaining to the
innocent what it means to be a bloody-handed, cunning man of war. It
means being precisely what *he* is, right there in front of them, defeated
by the very values of courage and vengeance-seeking that had made him
victorious in the first place. Through Alcinous the Phaeacians had asked
to be taught this lesson and had offered in exchange what they had to
give, the risk of final severance from the world of men. As Odysseus
speaks and the weight of his long punishment at the hands of Poseidon
grows ever more clear, they cannot help but be aware of the reality of
their own risk and of the mysterious mesh of all these destinies. Once
the Phaeacians had lived close to the Cyclopes, and had been injured
by them. But Alcinous' father, Nausithoos, had settled them far from
both Cyclopes and humans (6.2–8). Yet now this wanderer is here bearing the mark of the Cyclopes in his misery and asking the Phaeacians to
incur danger so that he can be safe. It is as though his presence were a
reminder that their kinship with the Cyclopes through their ruler could
not be evaded. Both Polyphemus and Alcinous are descendants of Poseidon. No matter how drastic the distance in space and custom that the
Phaeacians have put between themselves and the Cyclopes—scorn of
the gods vs. piety, murder of guests vs. hospitality, unorganized social
structure vs. highly organized social structure, no technology vs. developed technology—they have not escaped their old enemies.

 Odysseus has now restored the contact that Nausithoos had broken.
Odysseus has been harmed by the Cyclopes, as had the Phaeacians. He
has escaped, and so had they. But there is this difference between them.
The curse is over for Odysseus. He has come full circle, from one kind
of self-proclamation involving cursing and being cursed, to another kind
of self-proclamation involving prayers for blessing on others and for an
end of the curse on himself. The remainder of Poseidon's anger will fall
on the Phaeacians instead of on him: a returning Phaeacian ship will be
stricken and the threat of enclosure by a mountain will hang menacingly
over the city (13.125–187).

 Such is the price Alcinous will have to pay for having received Odys-

seus as a brother. That he is conscious of the complexity of the situation
enclosing him while Odysseus tells his story is made clear by what he
says during the pause in the narrative in Book 11:

> Odysseus, as we look on you, we would not think you
> To be a deceiver and cheat the way many men are
> Whom the black earth nourishes, and are widely dispersed,
> Fashioning falsehoods. . . . (11.363–366)

These words, at first view surprisingly blunt, are an acknowledgement
of Alcinous' understanding that Odysseus *could* have deceived him and
had reason to do so, but evidently has not. Taken with Alcinous' renewed
assurance of help and additional gifts, the lines constitute a reaffirmation
of the basis of the relationship between the two men, mutual trust. They
understand each other. Odysseus wants desperately to go home and would
do it honestly, without lies, if possible. Alcinous longs to participate in
the heroic world from which his Phaeacian destiny has separated him,
and to so participate he is willing to risk final severance from the human
world, and perhaps worse, for who knows exactly what Poseidon will do?

Alcinous' dangerous longing is comprehensible in view of his lineage
and family history. Did not his father give heroic names to him and to
his dead brother, Courageous and Man-Breaker (Alcinous, Rhexenor)?
His father's name, Swift-with-Ships (Nausithoos), was different, not
comparable to the warrior names of the *Iliad*. True to this name, Swift-
with-Ships had fled far from war with the violent Cyclopes, but he had
furnished his two sons with the same kind of name as their grandfather,
the king of the violent, powerful giants, Eurymedon, Wide-ruling, an
epic, heroic name. Alcinous' dead brother, Rhexenor, is gone now, no
breaker of men. But Odysseus, who has broken many, is there and knows
so well the cost of such a life. He is a man such as his brother, Rhexenor, might have been, if he had lived; this is what Alcinous sees in
Odysseus, a brother restored.[7]

The subtle relationship of appeal and hesitant response between Alcinous and Odysseus is the principle of composition in the Phaeacian
episode. But it might have been otherwise. There are other ways, other
atmospheres and other moods in which the poet could have brought his
hero home. For example, the tone could have been wholly heroic. The
Phaeacians would, in such a version, have no connection with Poseidon; Odysseus would meet the king's only *son*, not his only daughter;
would identify himself immediately, instead of delaying, and then show
his mettle in a military campaign important to his host, who would, in

---

7. If Odysseus, as the restored Rhexenor, married Nausicaa, as Alcinous had suggested (7.313),
   each brother would have married the other's daughter, so the family, in this ideal eventuality,
   would have had something of the symmetrical exclusiveness of the family of Aeolus, king of
   the winds, another entity immune in the vastness of the sea.

gratitude, have sent him home in a ship, not magical, but effective in the ordinary epic fashion.

Or the tone of the episode could have been entirely picaresque. The Phaeacians would be dependent on Poseidon, suspicious of the stranger and hostile to him. Odysseus would in self-defense seduce the princess, deceive the royal parents and win his passage home by cleverness.[8]

It should not be decided too quickly that the existing Phaeacis is obviously and inevitably what the poet had to do, whereas alternative versions are impossible. What a poet is going to do is never obvious until he does it. What we can see from posing the hypothetical heroic and picaresque versions is that neither permits the existing Alcinous-Odysseus relationship with its mutual commitment to danger, nor do they permit the drama of the meeting of a man who has challenged the Cyclopes and is the enemy of Poseidon with another man who has been protected from the Cyclopes, is a friend of Poseidon, and yet finds himself committed to the other. The Phaeacian episode acquires its peculiar atmosphere from the mingling, although in unequal measure, of two tones, the heroic and the picaresque, like a musical composition in which two rhythms are used at once, or rather like one in which an alternative to the dominant rhythm is constantly suggested.

It would seem evident that the poet who composed the Phaeacis as it stands in the present *Odyssey* (Books 6–8, 13) also refashioned the traditional material used in Odysseus' adventure-narrative (Books 9–12) so as to integrate the two sections. What the adventure-narrative of Books 9–12 was like before its refashioning by the *Odyssey* poet is open to many suggestions. However, a few details may seem more probable than others. For example, the hero of earlier versions probably coolly maintained his clever pseudonym, Noman, with the Cyclops, instead of proudly identifying himself, and so escaped the disaster of the curse of Polyphemus, who in that version ridiculously and uselessly implored the god to punish "nobody." As a consequence the troubles which befell the hero's comrades in those earlier versions were not his fault at all, but their own, as indeed the proem of the *Odyssey* asserts.

In those earlier versions the comrades were destroyed by their own foolishness. Odysseus never lost his cool self-possession, was never overcome by pride and vain self-glorification. What the poet gained from reshaping the older versions is a hero not simply defeated, but also profoundly guilty; and, among other things, an episode, the Phaeacis, in which that defeated, guilty hero is permitted to be true, instead of false, both to his dark past and to the human beings who enable him, finally, to escape from it.

---

8. For suggestions in the present text of what the heroic alternative might have been like, cf. 14.316–319, 13.223; for the picaresque alternative, cf. 13.254–255, 13.291–299.

NORMAN AUSTIN

Intimations of Order †

The *Odyssey* is structured in the form of a travelogue, but this is no Baedeker of some private traveller recording random curiosities in the world of men and nature. Rather, it is a collection of systems that function as paradigms of social and natural order, through which Odysseus and his imitative son pass on their way to the final re-creation of order in Ithaka. The cities and minds of men that the proem advertises as the content of Odysseus' journey prefigure, some directly and others as faint overtones, the possibilities for action in Ithaka. They are Odysseus' preparatory education, as Sparta and Pylos are the schools for Telemachos. The *Odyssey* reveals, through the progressive stages of Odysseus' journey, a hierarchy of order ranging from simple to complex and encompassing both society and nature. The *Odyssey*'s hierarchy is not the Aristotelian set of categories, much less Dante's perfectly calibrated realization of the distance separating utter chaos from absolute order, but comparisons are nevertheless viable. No less than the *Divine Comedy*, the *Odyssey* sets itself the task of realizing experience through a rational system of categories distinguishable from each other by their increasing complexity.

The simplest systems in the poem are those representations of purely natural phenomena. The tidal monster, Charybdis, scarcely anthropomorphized, is distinguished by her permanent and regular schedule. Three times daily she vomits up the sea, and three times swallows it again (12.104–105). By his knowledge of her recurrent and predictable schedule, Odysseus is able to escape past her threat to safety. In the description of the doves that fly past the Clashing Rocks we perceive a similar regularly recurring schedule (12.62–65). Whenever the doves fly between the rocks bearing ambrosia to Zeus, one falls victim to the rocks, but Zeus always sends in another to make up the full complement again. It is inviting to accept the later identification of Homer's *peleiai* with the Pleiades, which are traditionally seven in number although only six are visible to most observers. Homer hints nowhere at such an identification, and other possibilities have been conjectured. An argument in favor is that some feature that reveals a permanent cyclical nature is the defining characteristic of natural phenomena in the *Odyssey*. As Charybdis maintains a permanent cycle of operation, so the doves of Zeus maintain their permanent cycle, although theirs is an oscillation between loss and renewal. Whether the *peleiai* are the Pleiades or not, the regularity in

† From *Archery at the Dark of the Moon: Poetic Problems in Homer's Odyssey*, pp. 132–48. Copyright © 1975 The Regents of the University of California. Reprinted by permission.

their pattern is their claim to be some form observable in the seasonal and natural world.

We reach a higher level of complexity in the representations of natural phenomena that are endowed with anthropomorphic form. The winds are realized in an intricate system on the island of Aiole, where every aspect—the location and movement of the island, the behavior of the king, his family organization, and their form of entertainment—conjures up a particular aspect of the winds. Sociologists who have argued for the divine world as the replica of human social organization have failed to see how frequently humans erect divine societies that, although mirroring human society in many aspects, will yet contain certain features that mark them off as specifically nonhuman. King Aiolos may behave as any bad-tempered human king, but his island behaves as no known island does. Its special behavior is an ad hoc creation, a mythic principle to embody something in the special nature of the winds. But more important than that floating island, there is once again the cyclical pattern which marks the world of Aiolos as part of nature; here the feature is incorporated into the marriage arrangement. Aiolos has six sons and six daughters who live always with him, and the six sons are married to the six daughters (10.5–9). What can this permanent incestuous union, from which there issues no offspring, be but the representation of twelve winds, which never increase in number, but always pass back and forth? The north wind blows south, the south north; the east wind blows west, the west east. Homer depicts that perpetual reciprocity as six marriages, with each male offspring in an inviolable bond with his female counterpart. Into the fabric of a human society are thus woven the clues that reveal the nonhuman nature of the phenomena described.

Thrinakia is similar to Aiole in being a representation of natural phenomena expressed in a mythic system. Again we begin with the human disguise. Helios is the cattle owner on the island, with seven herds of cattle, fifty head to a herd, and seven flocks of sheep, fifty head to a flock (12.127ff.). His daughters Phaethousa and Lampetie (the shepherdesses Brilliance and Radiance) keep perpetual guard over his property. Aristotle and others in antiquity understood the 350 cattle and the 350 sheep as Homer's image of the days and nights of the year, in fact of the lunar year. To some his interpretation might seem anachronistic allegory, and yet others with a good memory for numbers may interrupt at this point to ask the significance of the 360 male porkers that Eumaios guards for Odysseus. To this we can reply that if the image of the winds translates into visual form so many aspects of the winds' behavior, is it anachronistic to expect as much in Homer's description of the sun? When Phaethousa and Lampetie are so clearly hypostases of aspects of the sun, should not his cattle, which are protected by the direst tabus, embody as much significance? The property of the sun, in mythic terms, surely can be nothing but the days of the year (though we need not press, perhaps, for a hidden lunar-solar equation here). Helios' cattle are, moreover, unlike any herds owned by man. They are always fixed in size, neither producing any increase *(gonos)* nor suffering any diminution (vv. 130–131). We are not told explicitly, but are left to assume that the herds replenished themselves to their full complement after the destruction inflicted on them by Odysseus' sailors. Once again the cyclical pattern appears, of loss and renewal, and once again we see the feature that reveals beneath the human trappings the specifically nonhuman forms of behavior found in nature.

There are, then, a series of mythic representations for the elements or elemental forces: Skylla, Charybdis, Proteus, Aiolos, and Helios' cattle. They have their laws which must be learned if Odysseus is to survive. Some, like Skylla, cannot be outwitted at all. Others can be outwitted by a prior knowledge of their cyclical pattern, as Odysseus turns Charybdis' schedule to his eventual advantage, as Menelaos does likewise with Proteus, whose polymorphous transformations he anticipates. Others have laws that are expressed as tabus. But even the tabu is not mere superstitious prohibition. Aiolos' bag of winds, which Odysseus must not open, is a perfectly lucid pictograph of the skill with which the mariner binds the winds to his control. It is a metaphoric representation for a rational process of experience and skill, for holding on course with a favorable wind and blocking out contrary winds—or else, says Homer, you'll find yourself right back where you started. We can be sure that the Homeric sailor had knowledge of weather and sea of a thoroughly practical sort, with the bag of winds and magical tabus replaced by entirely realistic technical advice on tacking to the wind. Homer chooses not to supply that kind of information; instead he presents the story of Aiolos' winds.

From the thirteenth century A.D. comes an excellent document to illustrate the mentality that operates simultaneously on both mythical and technical levels. The Old Norse work, *Konnungs Skuggsjá (The King's Mirror)* is unwittingly a rich commentary on the *Odyssey*. It purports to give, in its first part, practical advice for navigation, and in fact gives a wealth of information of great precision on the length of lunar cycles, the influence of the moon on tides, and the periods between solstices. Then it gives a long description of the action of the winds, in which the author abandons the technical entirely for the mythical. According to his description, the winds go through a perpetual cycle, again a representation of loss and renewal, forming a covenant, breaking it, and then forming a new covenant. No sailor could derive much practical benefit from this picture of the winds, yet it is clearly as much part of the seaman's lore as the table of tides. Similar in its use of imagery, the *Odyssey* adopts the mythical to represent that most practical sailor, Odysseus, losing control of his craft in a storm. There is, besides, another storm in the *Odyssey* which parallels even more closely the *Mirror's* conception. Poseidon, seeing Odysseus sailing for home, raises a violent storm in which the winds, Euros and Notos, Zephyros and Boreas, fall simultaneously on the sea (5.291–296). This storm, as we shall see later, marks the end of the sailing season, and at that moment the winds, hitherto accommodating, fall into disharmony, behaving exactly as *Konnungs Skuggsjá* predicts they will at the onset of winter.

Before Odysseus the sailor can discover the minds and cities of men he must conquer the natural perils at sea, by discovering and turning to his advantage the systems by which they maintain themselves. He must make his way through storms and past whirlpools. What part can Helios play in this drama of man against the elements? Odysseus' primary duel is with Poseidon, but his duel with Helios occupies a prominent second place. The Thrinakian catastrophe reverberates through the poem. A reference to it appears first in the proem when Homer reminds us that Odysseus' comrades brought about their own destruction by eating the cattle of Helios. It is the only incident that happens after repeated protreptic warnings. First Teiresias and then Kirke warn Odysseus against putting ashore on Thrinakia. Odysseus warns his men too against landing there; when Eurylochos insists on doing so, Odysseus makes them swear a solemn oath to leave the cattle intact. Their slaughter of the cattle is thus sacrilege of the most deliberate sort, and it has devastating results. Zeus, threatened by Helios with a sunless heaven and a sunless earth, causes the death of Odysseus' comrades, and accomplishes almost as much for Odysseus. Odysseus is bereft of ship and crew, is forced into a near fatal encounter with Charybdis, and is banished from sight for seven years. Helios vies with Poseidon as Odysseus' personal fury.

To resort to a theory of the conflation of two sagas, one in which Helios was Odysseus' enemy and the other in which Poseidon played that part, is in reality no explanation, since we are still left pondering on that original Helios myth. Why should there have been such a myth in which the sun pursued a sailor with relentless fury? More than that, why should that myth have seemed so appropriate to the story of Poseidon's fury against Odysseus that it could be joined to the Poseidon story and treated, in fact, not merely as another adventure but one fully as important in Odysseus' travels as Odysseus' blinding of the Kyklops? If conflation is at work here, we must assume that during the centuries of the poem's transmission the poem's audience was content to see any adventure at all inserted into a sailor's yarn, whereas Aristotle, who saw the plot of the *Odyssey* as a structural unity, was expressing a purely idiosyncratic view. If, like Aristotle, we admire the poem's discretion in narrating only the significant events in a man's life, we shall have to search for the connection between Helios and Poseidon elsewhere than in the faults of transmission.

The surface meaning of the myth of the attack on the cattle of the sun—reverence for the sun—is readily apparent. But Ikaros fell to his doom in striving to emulate the sun. Odysseus' comrades' sacrilege is of a different sort. They desecrate the property of the sun or, as Aristotle noted, the days and nights of the year. Theirs is in some way an attack on, a negation of, time. To see the connection of this attack with the poem's themes we must retrace our steps back to the opening lines where we discover that time plays a prominent part in this poem as it does not in the *Iliad*. This is the judicious moment for Odysseus' return, says the proem; the circling seasons have brought around the year that the gods in their spinning have marked for his return (1.16–18). Poseidon is absent from Olympos, feasting with the Aithiopians who live at the boundaries of the world, which is to say he is nowhere in sight (vv. 22–25). Zeus, musing on Orestes' vengeance on Aigisthos, is in a receptive mood for Athena's request for the man whom she considers to have sufficiently expiated any wrongdoing he may be guilty of. All things conspire to make this the right moment.

As the poem progresses we find that the proem's words on the judicious moment are not idly said. This is not simply the optimum moment, but the necessary moment. Odysseus has, though he does not know it, a precise timetable to adhere to, which will lead him to his revenge in Ithaka on the most important day of the year. His timing will be crucial to his success. Odysseus, exiled for seven years by his comrades' assault on Helios' property, is ready when the poem opens to make his reentry into the cycle of time.

Just as he is about to make that reentry, Kalypso makes one final attempt to seduce Odysseus. She offers him, quite literally, timelessness. Her temptation, "the euphoria of eternity," far from being unique, is one of the besetting trials of Odysseus' wanderings. In one way or another many other figures offer him a similar release from time. The Sirens promise memory total and intact, mind liberated from the barriers of past and future, mind thus transcending time. Only Odysseus is privileged to endure this transcendent temptation and he survives it only by being bound to the ship's mast. His comrades, on the other hand, fall easily to the temptation of the Lotos-eaters, which is mind delivered from memory altogether. Whoever ate of the lotos wished to forget his return (9.97). Saved from the lotos they then fall victim to Kirke's baneful drug which makes men forget their homes and turns them into swine— perhaps Homer's picture of the amnesiac's lot (10.236ff.). Saved from Kirke, Odysseus' sailors choose oblivion by incurring Helios' anger. Their suicidal wishes are finally granted: "they contrived their own destruction, the fools" (1.7). The lotos, Kirke's drug, Helios' cattle, each is different, but there is a clear sequence in which Odysseus' comrades attempt to forget their return, and finally succeed.

Thus there is a series of psychological threats encountered in Odysseus' travels, forms of psychic destruction, culminating in the incident on Thrinakia, where psychological and physical destruction coincide.

Modern psychology is well aware of the relation of memory to time. "In its first stages," writes Paul Fraisse, a contemporary psychologist, "the temporal horizon is simply a manifestation of memory, and it develops with the latter" (*The Psychology of Time*, p. 153). Memory is not merely the repository of experience but the constructive activity that creates our sense of time as a sequence of events and forms our sense of order. Clinical experiments that relate perception and memory only document one of the first axioms of Homeric psychology, that memory is survival and order. To remember is to be, as in the phrases "remember your *arete*," "remember your strength but not your panic" (*Il.* 13.48), or "they saw the bird sent from Zeus and remembered their warcraft" (*Il.* 8.252). Alkinoos says (7.192–194): "Tomorrow we shall remember our escort, how the stranger may reach his home safely under our escort." Here remembering comes close to making a plan for the future. Since memory is so much part of what a man is for Homer, the properties of the lotos and Kirke's drug, which cause forgetfulness of home or of the return home, are really statements on the dissolution of identity.

Odysseus himself makes clear how dependent survival is on memory. Odysseus, though he was not turned into a pig, succumbed to Kirke's spell anyway and suffered amnesia for a year until his sailors roused him (10.472–474): "Now remember your paternal soil if indeed it is the gods' will for you to be saved and to reach your home and your ancestral soil." That is Odysseus' only lapse. Thenceforth he clings tenaciously to the memory of his soil. Our first sight of him in the poem is as he sits on the shore of Kalypso's island wearing his spirit away in weeping for his return (5.151–153). To Kalypso's final offer of immortality Odysseus replies (5.219–220): "Even so, I wish and yearn every day to go home and to look on my day of return." At the Phaiakian court Odysseus expressly attributes his survival to his desire for home. He begins the tale of his adventures with a fulsome proem on the beauties of one's own land. "For my part, I cannot look upon anything sweeter than ancestral soil," so Odysseus concludes his description of his rugged island (9.27–28). He continues by describing Kalypso's and Kirke's attempts to detain him, and explaining their failure (vv. 33–36): "But that did not at all persuade the *thymos* in my chest since there is nothing sweeter than ancestral soil and parents, not even if a man dwells in a prosperous home in a foreign land far from his own parents." Only after this preamble on the choice he has made between eternity in Kalypso's prosperous house and that miniscule point in time and space of his own island home is Odysseus ready to begin the tale.

Against the background of these incidents concerned with the attrition or preservation of memory, the cattle of the sun will assume their full significance. The sea is chaos. That chaos is represented in a variety of ways through the poem. Those who would locate precisely in the Mediterranean all the sites Odysseus visits overlook that passage where Odysseus himself records the moment when he sailed out of known geography into the primeval disorder of the sea. There at the Cape of Maleia "we would have reached our homes," says Odysseus, had not the north wind come up and thrust him into *terrae incognitae* (9.79–81). This is not to be the simple mariner's yarn of expeditions to Egypt, but the poetic statement of the experience of the sea. That experience becomes at one point the picture of the winds unloosed from a bag, at another point a storm of winds that Poseidon arouses to hurl Odysseus to an island far even from the gods. It appears also in Odysseus' description of reaching an unknown island during a moonless night. These are all forms of disorientation. The disorientation can be simple spatial disorientation, as when Odysseus tells his comrades (10.190–192): "We know not where *zophos* is nor *eos*, neither where Helios goes beneath the earth nor where he rises." But it can be other forms of disorientation, as in Proteus' manifold transformations or in the strange forms of life the sea engenders, like Skylla and Charybdis and Poseidon's son Polyphemos. One simile, in which the sea is the epitome of chaos, links both Penelope and Odysseus in a single fate, she suffering on land the same threat of disintegration he had suffered at sea (23.233–240): "As the sight of land brings joy to men swimming, whose ship Poseidon has smashed into the sea . . . in joy they touch land, escaping evil, so the sight of her husband was joy for her and she would not release him from the embrace of her fair arms." The full simile is a capsule description of Odysseus' landing on Scheria, but now the brine-laden, ship-wrecked mariner touching soil is Penelope. Both sailors are at last home from the sea.

When Odysseus first sights Scheria there is another simile descriptive of disintegration at sea (5.392–399). Odysseus lifted high by a great wave saw land: "as when to children the life of a father appears most welcome, when he lies suffering and wasting away in sickness . . . but the gods free him from the illness and bring joy, so to Odysseus it was a joy when land and woods appeared." Odysseus himself will credit his survival to his desire to see his fatherland. It is appropriate here that the land is his father, and he at sea becomes the child disoriented by his father's withdrawal into sickness but suddenly joyful and oriented again when he discerns his father returning to life. Out of sight of land is to be reduced to the child's destitution when bereft of parents.

If Odysseus' voyage is one of disorientation, spatial disorientation is matched in the psychological sphere by amnesia, and not only the amnesia of the mariner. A watery death is a particularly vile fate because the lack of funeral rites and a monument to mark the burial threatens even that vestigial existence which survives in others' memory. "We would not grieve so much," says Telemachos, "if Odysseus had died at Troy and received full burial rites. But now the harpies have carried him away without glory, and he is gone unseen and unheard" (1.236–242). The psychological disorientation of amnesia is translated into the temporal sphere as an attack on Helios' days and nights. Melville's Ishmael suffers vertigo at the seductive prospect of the infinite expanse of ocean. What is the killing of Helios' cattle but the mythic representation of Ishmael's vertigo, transferred from the spatial dimension to the temporal? A more vivid description of vertigo at sea could hardly be found than Odysseus' sailors' refusal to heed the direct warnings and their slaughter of the sun's property, which is to say their slaughter of themselves, since for Homer life and sun are so closely associated as to be virtually synonymous. Odysseus' sailors negate time and are banished from time altogether; Odysseus disappears from time, exiled to Kalypso's hiding place for seven years of inactivity. Odysseus almost succumbs, but the memory of home is the one stable and enduring landmark in that maze of time and space that is the uncharted sea.

If we are dubious about applying symbolic interpretations to Helios' role, many indications later in the poem make the interpretation both permissible and necessary. When Odysseus is cast ashore on Ogygia he disappears temporally and spatially, from geography and time. When he starts his homeward journey from the island we get a whole constellation of signs and images which determines the time of his return. He sails from Ogygia following the stars, which are the navigator's compass (5.272–277). But stars are also the main determinants of the seasons, chronometers as well as compasses. The constellations listed contrast with Odysseus' earlier admission of disorientation—"we know not where *zophos* is nor *eos.*" Now with sleepless eyes he guides himself by the Pleiades, Boötes, and the Bear in their circling paths. He is oriented again, but we know from those constellations not only his spatial direction but the time of year. Or rather, those constellations hint at a certain time of year, and then subsequent similes and descriptions of weather corroborate their evidence. Those constellations are proof that Odysseus has aligned himself once more in harmony with time.

In Homer's portrayal of order and disorder there are, then, certain representations, like whirlpools and storms, that are of purely natural phenomena. There are others, like Helios, in which psychological and natural elements begin to blend. Helios provides a transitional mythos taking us from raw elements to elements that are represented as anthropomorphic cultures. In these cultures the connection with the natural elements remains, and in all there is clear evidence of superhuman powers. Kirke is the daughter of Sun and Ocean and has the power to transform men into animals. The Kyklopes are the sons of Poseidon and have almost invincible brute strength. Alkinoos is Arete's uncle (an incestuous marriage which in itself suggests a nonhuman society), both are descended from Poseidon, and their people have superhuman navigational skill. They seem in many respects to be a variant of the Aiolos myth, being the calm of the sea when all the winds are in harmony. Kalypso is the daughter of baleful Atlas and inhabits the island that is the navel of the sea. In all these there are features, in genealogy and powers, that proclaim them as representatives of the natural world, in particular of the sea, but they become vehicles principally for the study of anthropological systems.

Again there is a hierarchy from simple to complex, and the range of systems gives us something of Homer's idea of culture as measurable by the increasing complexity of social structures and by the degree of interaction between society and nature. At the lowest level are brutes like the Laistrygonians, but they need hardly detain us since in the Kyklopes, their next of kin in the evolutionary family, Homer has given a full portrait of the primitive. Polyphemos is by no means destitute of order. In his solitary world he is in fact addicted to system, though his system is, to be sure, no wondrous creation. A courtyard surrounds his cave, built up with stones, pine trees, and oaks (9.184–185). The organization within his cave would pass the most meticulous inspection. There are folds for the two kinds of young animals, lambs and goats, and each species is carefully subdivided into three groups according to age, the spring-born, the "middlings," and the newborn (9.219ff.). Two kinds of containers, pails and bowls, hold the whey. Polyphemos, when he returns at evening from the pasture, carries out his duties in a methodical way. He leaves the male goats and rams in the courtyard outside, drives the females inside and barricades his door with a stone (vv. 237ff.). He milks the sheep and goats, all in order (*panta kata moiran*, v. 245), then gives the young to their mothers. He then curdles the fresh milk, scoops the curds into wicker baskets, and puts the rest into pails to sit ready for him to drink. With his chores taken care of he turns his attention to his own comfort and lights a fire. This is a regular daily schedule from which he makes one significant deviation the following evening when he brings all his flock, male and female, into the cave with him (v. 338).

Gigantic oaf he may be, but Polyphemos has his *techne* and within the sphere of that *techne* he loses his clumsiness. He has the skills essential to his *techne*: he can build a wall and pen for his flocks, he can fashion pails for the whey, crates for the cheese, and plait wicker baskets for the curds. His *techne* is, of course, dairy farming; the whole dairy farm has been transported into his cave. Polyphemos' proficiency, whether in fashioning the necessary utensils or in performing his chores, is impeccable. Within the sphere of his craft he is an artist, as devoted to formal symmetries as any Geometric painter.

What Polyphemos lacks is not technical proficiency but the intelligence to go beyond his subsistence economy. Homer's portrait of Polyphemos is a vivid documentary on life without reason. Polyphemos suffers from two intellectual defects which prove to be his undoing: he has a total lack of curiosity and, as the corollary, a total lack of converse with other intelligent beings. The paradigmatic tale is woven around these two essential attributes of the Kyklopean character.

The Kyklopes, Homer says, had no shipbuilders, but this cannot be because of their lack of technical skill. Rather, they lacked shipbuilders because they had never thought of going to sea. Polyphemos shows himself, in his questions to Odysseus, acquainted with ships and marauding pirates, but to construct some conveyance which could carry his folk across to the island at the entrance of their harbor is an idea that has never occurred to Polyphemos or any of his clan. If the Kyklopes are indifferent about the possibilities on that island, they are positively obtuse about the possibilities of even their own land. They live in an agricultural paradise where everything grows in profusion without need for seeding, ploughing, or artificial irrigation. While fertile fields lie around him, laden with perpetual crops—wheat, barley, and grapes are specifically mentioned—Polyphemos blithely cultivates a dairy farm instead. Across the bay is the island that would be more suitable for men who eschew agriculture. Its soil is fertile but still uncultivated; it is the home of goats which, as we know, Polyphemos prefers to grain. Everything conspires to encourage the exploring instinct: the island is only a short distance off, it is unclaimed territory, it has besides its abundance of goats a good water supply, and, final irony, it has the absolutely ideal harbor where stern cables are never necessary and sailors can rest at their ease until their spirits prompt them to move on. The nautical technology necessary for crossing from the mainland to the island would be the very minimal. Even Kyklopes could have negotiated that placid bay if any possible motive for doing so had crossed their minds. But the paradise across the bay is not even a mystery for them; they have never noticed it any more than they have noticed the luxuriant crops on which their own flocks graze. Through this lack of curiosity about cereal agriculture Polyphemos falls victim to the potent wine Odysseus serves him. Though he claims that the Kyklopes are familiar with wine (9.357–358), we suspect he is merely boasting; he seems to be strictly a milk-drinker. Again, his lack of curiosity leads him to assume that he would be deprived of his eye by someone as large as himself. He had never given the prophecy much thought, there being little of the reflective in his temperament.

The limitation of intelligence extends to their social life. The *themis* of the Kyklopes is as limited as their technical skill. What they have is idiorhythmic; each Kyklopes lays down the *themis* for his own wife and children but there is no common code that binds the individual families into a larger community (9.114–115). Polyphemos as a bachelor has not even the nucleus of a community. There is no other person to receive or share his *themis* and that is why he in particular knows neither *dikas* nor *themistas* (v. 215). The lack of a community restricts the Kyklopes forever to a low level of proficiency. Homer spells out the advantages of community in verse 112: there are among the Kyklopes no decision-making assemblies (ἀγοραὶ βουληφόροι). Decision-making assemblies are among the most important features of Homeric life. Without them no Kyklops will urge another Kyklops to action, none will collaborate with another in planning or executing some action, there will be none to prevent another's rash mistake, to propose a better plan, to offer professional expertise or the lessons learned with greater experience. There is, simply, no tradition; each Kyklops starts afresh, truly a *tabula rasa*. In Homer, where so much motivation is external, issuing as much from a man's comrades as from his gods, where, even when a man develops a plan on his own initiative, he generally lays it before someone else before putting it into action, the Kyklopes' abhorrence of each other's company assumes ominous significance. Their isolation from each other and, apparently, from the gods means in effect a perpetual lack of motivation. Homeric men rarely suggest things to themselves when in isolation, but merely repeat old habits. Achilleus has no initiative once he retires from the Greek army, he can merely sing lays of ancient heroes. It is in the community that proposals are made and new actions taken. Polyphemos' cry of pain stirs some faint interest in the other Kyklopes, but they are quickly satisfied with his reply that Noman is killing him. Men with greater experience of communal life would have remained puzzled by Polyphemos' answer, would have found it as nonsensical as it was. Anyone with the slightest communal sense would have investigated further to discover the true cause of Polyphemos' pain.

Polyphemos' intelligence, adequate when he ranged along the pastures, becomes vastly deficient when he is confronted with another intelligence. He is an easy prey to Odysseus' cunning because he has never had to develop his wits in competition with another. To use men for food is a gory mistake, but only one of his several elementary mistakes. To preface his question on the whereabouts of Odysseus' ship by a boast that he pays no reverence to Zeus himself (how then expect him to reverence mere mortal strangers?), to promise Odysseus a guest-gift after he has already devoured six of Odysseus' men, to block up his doorway against trespassers from without before checking for possible trespassers already within, all these are most telling proofs of the hazards of life lived in isolation. The so flagrant pun in the name *Outis* escapes Polyphemos because he has never had the opportunity to learn what *tis* was. To a person with no acquaintance with names one name is as good as another. It takes only a rudimentary social converse to distinguish names from jokes, but that rudimentary level lies above Polyphemos' range of experience. Polyphemos' pathetic attempt at a pun on *xeinion*, his guest-gift to Odysseus, is but his gross admission that he has no knowledge of the social relationships that *xeinia* symbolize.

The story of the one-eyed giant is one to delight a child's sense of the absurd, though its too obvious gusto brings an occasional frown to the adult scholar's brow. What Homer has done is to transform the tale into a moral for adults, while retaining all the elements of the traditional tale. The pun on the false name undoubtedly is part of the tradition. In

Homer, the pun still induces its childlike glee—Odysseus prides himself
almost excessively on its wit—but it becomes only one particle in a more
sophisticated exposition. Since we are given several preliminary indications of the character of Polyphemos before the pun occurs, his failure
to see through the pun is not only consistent with his mental acumen
elsewhere but is also the culmination of the portrait the poet had been
carefully painting stroke by stroke. Absurd as the pun on *Outis* is as
Name-No Name, Homer's success is to make it plausible. Homer's
description of the Kyklopean character, their indifference to the utilitarian potential of the crops at their feet or of the island that fairly begs
them to cross the bay and their lack of social converse, becomes the
background for the pun and for the Kyklopes' reaction to Polyphemos'
cry. How could a person who never associated with other men, whose
life was a Sisyphean round of shepherding flocks in isolation, of milking
goats and making cheeses, how could he know anything of those other
categories of experience that names, true or false, represent? For names
presuppose communities and social relationships—only Jehovah has no
name. How could he know that every question he asked Odysseus deci-
sively betrayed his ignorance of social forms, betrayed, in short, his lack
of *experience*, and therefore made the trap that was to ensnare him that
much easier to set? The other Kyklopes' failure to make sense of Polyphemos' nonsensical cry is as absurd as his original mistake, but Homer
makes it plausible by his earlier references to their indifference to communal responsibilities. They too are caught in the same trap as Polyphemos, although he mistranslates *Outis* as a real name while they translate
it correctly back into the negative pronoun. It is a nicely double-edged
pun, a trap whether interpreted correctly or incorrectly.

JOHN PERADOTTO

Man in the Middle Voice: Name and Narration in the *Odyssey* †

Events in a narrative are determined by its end. That should be qualified. There are certainly determinants operating on narrative that come
from outside of it altogether—"cultural constraints of credibility" (Ricoeur),
if you will, varying in restrictiveness, governing the choice and shape of
situations and imposing rules of development conforming to accepted or
acceptable notions of truth, probability, necessity, propriety, logic, beauty,
nature, etc. This whole category we can call *motivation*, and the canon

† From *Man in the Middle Voice: Name and Narration in the Odyssey* (Princeton: Princeton UP,
1990) 44—48, 82—86. Reprinted by permission of Princeton University Press.

that restricts it *verisimilitude*.[1] What we are mainly concerned with, however, is that set of determinants *within* the narrative, relationships of logical implication, exclusion, compatibility by which an event B both presupposes an event A, which is prior to it, and makes possible an event C, which is subsequent to it. This category we can call *function*, defined, if we follow Propp, as the significance an event has in the development of the plot, or more precisely if we follow Bremond, the significance an event has in relation to some finality, whether it is some proximate, short-term finality or the ultimate finality, the end of the narrative (see Bremond, *Logique Du Récit*, Paris, 1973: 131).

This distinction between the function and the motivation of a narrative event is crucial. If its function is the purpose it serves in advancing the narrative towards its conclusion, its motivation is that which it finds necessary in dissimulating its function. Motivation is the domination of convention and tradition restricting the way a story may go; function is the internal play transcending or at least circumventing conventionally understood "reality." To use a metaphor derived from economics by Gerard Genette, function is a *profit*, motivation a *cost* (Genette 1968: 20). The most economical and, as an instrument of ideology, the most persuasive narrative units would therefore be those which require no explicit motivation—those, in other words, which offer no obstacle to credibility. In terms of motivation, then, narratives can be classified as follows:[2]

1. *Implicitly motivated narrative*: That which follows the canons of *verisimilitude* closely enough to require no explanation. It appears "right" or "proper" or "natural" to its audience, or, as Aristotle would·say, "necessary or probable." Example: *The queen asked for her carriage and went for a ride.*

2. *Explicitly motivated narrative*: (a) Attribution of motive to an *individual*. Example: *The queen asked for her carriage and then went to bed, for she was very capricious.* (b) Attribution of motive to a *class*. Example: *The queen asked for her carriage and then went to bed, for, like all women, she was capricious.*

3. *"Arbitrary" narrative*: that which puzzles its audience or taxes their credibility, requiring but not supplying motivation. Example: *The queen asked for her carriage and then went to bed.*

Formally, nothing separates type 1 from type 3. The difference depends on a judgment that is culturally variable and wholly extrinsic to the text. Depending on time and place, a class 1 narrative could become a class 3 narrative, and vice versa.

Consider briefly three examples from the *Odyssey*, two of them sub-

1. On verisimilitude, see *Communications* 11 (1968). This entire issue is devoted to verisimilitude, but see especially Gerard Genette, "Vraisemblance et motivation," 5–21.
2. This classification and the example are derived from Genette 1968: 21.

jects of more detailed discussion later in this book. The first is the point where, in the cave of the Cyclops, Odysseus is first asked his identity. He does something unusual from the point of view of a verisimilitude inferable from the *Iliad:* instead of naming himself and referring to his own *kleos* or reputation, he lists himself among the anonymous *laoi,* the "troop" or host of Agamemnon. To be sure, on the level of motivation this is a thinly veiled threat to warn the Cyclops that Odysseus has powerful allies. But even in such a context, the suppression of one's own name is unusual. Later on, when Odysseus is pressed to be more specific, he gives a fictitious name, calling himself anonymity itself, "Outis," or "Noman," and thus sets up the famous misunderstanding in which blinded Polyphemus, from within the cave, cries out to his neighboring Cyclopes that Noman is doing him harm. Now in neither case has Odysseus been able to foresee or to manage the precise set of circumstances that allows the pun on Outis to work. In retrospect, we see that his anonymity and the choice of that precise name, Outis, is functionally necessary to the pun that saves Odysseus's life, but its motivation in the progress of performance is extremely arbitrary. The effect achieved by the choice of the name Outis is not, as Odysseus claims (9.414), the product of his own cunning *mētis,* but of the poet's. No Odysseus can know his own future, as the poet knows it, and if he cannot, then neither should he be able to pull off the ingenious stunt here achieved. Beyond the intuitive power, the imaginative anticipation of probabilities that is *mētis,* the deed would require a knowledge of the indeterminate and coincidental. It is a remarkable narrative moment where the poet and his hero merge, but so clever is the motivational cover and the witty distraction of its climax that the casual reader or listener will miss the subterfuge. Odysseus's manipulation of Polyphemus is rudimentary compared to the poet's manipulation of his audience here, for their pleasure in the outcome is founded on a substantial deception. It is *mētis* at its best: a story about *mētis,* achieved by *mētis.*

The same goes for an action of Polyphemus. The first time he returns to his cave with his flocks, he acts presumably as any herdsman would and segregates the females and their young from the males, which are left in the yard outside the cave. The second time, however, he does something unusual: he brings the males inside the cave, because, we are told, "he suspected something or else because some god had so directed him" (9.339):

$$\mathring{\eta} \ \tau\iota \ \mathring{o}\ddot{\imath}\sigma\acute{a}\mu\epsilon\nu o\varsigma, \ \mathring{\eta} \ \kappa\alpha\grave{\iota} \ \theta\epsilon\grave{o}\varsigma \ \mathring{\omega}\varsigma \ \mathring{\epsilon}\kappa\acute{\epsilon}\lambda\epsilon\nu\sigma\epsilon\nu.$$

In retrospect, we see that the presence of the males is functionally necessary to the escape of Odysseus and his men under their bellies, but its motivation is patently hurried and comparatively weak. And verisimilitude is circumvented or suspended, as so often in the *Odyssey*, by the poet's activity posing as divine activity.

The third example is drawn from book 23, where Penelope's misgivings about Odysseus's identity are finally laid aside as he recounts the "unapparent signs" (σήματα κεκευμμένα, 23.110), the unique secret of their bed's construction. The incident functions to permit Penelope cleverly to test Odysseus as he had tested her and to resolve any lingering uncertainty about who and what kind of man has returned. This is why the poet makes Odysseus construct so singular and strange a bed, one of its posts an ancient olive trunk rooted in the earth. But Odysseus's own reason for constructing it is a motivation gap to be filled in by audience/ readers, if they are not in fact charmed away from it by the rich overlay of detail in the artificer's description.

As we have said, then, the function of every event in the narrative is ultimately determined by the end. But the end itself is determined from outside the narrative.[3] One formulation of this external determination of the end are the terms "tragic" and "comic." A more abstract formulation, sticking ever close to Bremond's universal model, would be to speak of the nonachievement (or frustration) of desire or its achievement. Although these two types do not differ essentially as narrative structures, the one tends to stress the mortality and relative impotence of the human subject in the face of what might be termed most generally *consistent external resistance*—the will of the gods, "fate," "the way things are," laws of nature inferred from experience, the incommensurability of the world, the inevitability of death. The other represents an optimistic, wish-fulfilling emancipation from this external resistance, born of human desire. In short, one is a story in which mainly things happen to the human subject; the other is a story in which mainly that subject acts.

*   *   *

Our general thesis is that many of the narrative idiosyncrasies of the *Odyssey*—idiosyncrasies by the norms of conventional classical philology—can be explained as the collision of, and attempted mediation between, two kinds of narrative ideology: one a "myth" of nature's recalcitrance to culture, of the kind we see perhaps most vividly in the cattle of the sun episode, and the other what Aristotle might have characterized as a philosophically irresponsible *Märchen*, of the kind that surfaces

3. This should be qualified. The relationship of influence between what happens in narrative and what happens in extranarrative "reality" is not simple, and is better characterized as dialectical or reciprocal, rather than as unidirectional. What I mean to suggest here is that the end of a *particular narrative* is determined from outside *that narrative*, even though that "outside" influence may be another or other narratives, or something itself conditioned by narrative. Furthermore, I would not wish to give the impression that the desperate problematic of what is "inside" a text and what is "outside" of it is being ignored. (On this last point, see Simon Goldhill, Exegesis: Oedipus (R)ex," *Arethusa* 17 (1984): 177–200.

in its purest form in the Menelaus episode of book 4, with its prophecy of Elysion and a more or less fortuitously gained immortality for the hero. The large inheritance of *Märchen* in the *Odyssey* has, of course, been long recognized. But my thesis is that the *Märchen* plot development suffers derailment again and again at precisely those points where it would be expected to make an unembarrassed leap into the world of wish-fulfillment or resort to the improbable or accidental, were it free to follow its own dynamics. On the other hand, its obstacle, a tragically oriented myth, is itself hindered by the contradictory claims of the *Märchen* from reaching its expected conclusion. The two passages I have discussed are stratagems of silence to avoid saying "yes" to one system of organizing experience and "no" to another, in a higher and more complicated system, the poem, that only precariously maintains them both. Reflection on the alternatives for concluding the narrative becomes itself an integral component of the narrative, a device in fact for evading conclusion to achieve, however tenuously, a union of its oppositions, a "dialogic" text.

Aristotle's description of the *logos* or "argument" of the *Odyssey* (in *Poetics* 1455b16) is curiously reticent about what I am calling the tragic or "mythic" system, treating it as if the wrath of Poseidon were only a prelude to the presumed substance of the poem, the return of Odysseus and the vengeance on the suitors. It is almost as if he were reluctant to suggest that a narrative of such long-standing prestige as the *Odyssey* has indeed a beginning and a middle, but no end, at least not the kind defined by him. Or else, perhaps more likely, like the suitors, he was duped by the syntactic tactic of a poet who, like Penelope, wanted it both ways.

This analogy between the poet's strategy and Penelope's is not mere whimsy. We have already seen how she uses the same kind of εἰς ὅ κε ("until") clause in book 2 to gain more time. Penelope wants it both ways (1.249–50):

ἡ δ' οὔτ' ἀρνεῖται στυγερὸν γάμον οὔτε τελευτὴν
ποιῆσαι δύναται.

(She neither refused marriage as hateful to her nor is she able to bring the matter to conclusion.)

When in book 2 Telemachus publicly charges the suitors with misconduct, Antinous with good cause blames Penelope for having "profiteering guile on her mind" (ἥ τοι περὶ κέρδεα οἶδεν, 88). For almost four years now, he explains, she has broken the hearts of the suitors, given them all cause for hope, dispatching promising missives to each. George Devereux, in a short but cogent piece,[1] points out what should have

1. George Devereux, "Penelope's Character," *Psychoanalytic Quarterly* 26 (1957): 378–86.

been obvious to readers of the poem all along: that her tears of grief in her dream of geese slaughtered by an eagle—interpreted right within the dream itself as the slaughter of the suitors by Odysseus—represent not what psychologists call "inversion of affect," as Dodds saw it, but "real affect." "It is hard to understand," Devereux says (382),

> how literary critics could have overlooked the obvious fact that a rapidly aging woman, denied for some twenty years the pleasures of sex and the company and support of a husband, would inevitably be unconsciously flattered by the attentions of young and highly eligible suitors, which is precisely what the chief suitor accuses her of in public. We therefore believe that Penelope cried over her geese for the simple reason that unconsciously she enjoyed being courted.

As Penelope herself confesses to disguised Odysseus, her mind is divided whether to hold out or go off with whichever of the suitors proves his superiority by offering her the biggest brideprice. And her behavior before the suitors in book 18 is a paradigm of what we might call the lucrative tease. To gain still more time, to maintain yet a little longer both the dream of Odysseus's return and the pleasure of the suitors' flattery, she uses another semantic ambiguity, closely approximating, if not syntactically identical to, the *until* clause employed earlier: "I am inclined," she says, "to go off with whoever most readily strings the bow and shoots through all twelve axes" (21.75–76):

ὃς δέ κε ῥηίτατ᾽ ἐντανύσῃ βιὸν ἐν παλάμῃσι
καὶ διοϊστεύσῃ πελέκεων δυοκαίδεκα πάντων.

* * * The suitors appear to take her statement as indicative of something sure to be accomplished, that is, *as a way of distinguishing one bridegroom among many suitors*, now that she has, they think, acquiesced to the marriage. But in fact her ος κε ("whoever") clause is not only relative but conditional. If in fact, as she may suspect and as it turns out, none of them can perform the task, it can be considered yet another way of gaining more time. That and/or a way of testing the suspicion some critics see in her that the beggar may be Odysseus, or, what I find more likely, that the beggar's prophecy about Odysseus's imminent return may be true, coinciding as it does with Theoclymenus's prophecy (17.155–59) and with Halitherses,' pronounced two decades earlier.

Penelope accomplishes her purpose. Her desire is fulfilled, but only momentarily. For her fate and the outcome of the inland journey are intimately linked. The *Odyssey* does not end with the dream of desire fulfilled, where the folktale would have ended, where both Aristophanes and Aristarchus—at this point at least, bad critics but good lovers—would have it end, in the nuptial embrace of Odysseus and Penelope (23.296).

A. C. GOODSON

Homer and *Ouranos* †

The name trick of Odysseus, his deception of the Cyclops Polyphemus by the word *outis* (no-man), has been described as a paradigm for the human discovery of the fundamental deceit of all language. Truncating the word from its usual referent, Odysseus alters the ground of the Cyclops's relation to language, his unthinking equation of words and things:

> Odysseus discovers in words what developing bourgeois society calls formalism . . . out of the formalism of mythical names and rules which, like nature, would rule indifferently over men and history, nominalism, the prototype of bourgeois thought, emerges.[1]

Polyphemus's name is a product of this formalism: his fellow Cyclopes address him thus (the word means "much-speaking") in response to his agonized cries. And though he attempts to communicate the substance of Odysseus' trick to his own kind, his words fail him; he cannot signify the linguistic act itself, cannot articulate the workings of a trick whose logic escapes him even as he suffers its dire consequences.

The name trick signals Odysseus's seminal reformulation of the world he traverses; his experience forges in him a sense of the permeability of that world, its access of penetration by the powerful instrumentality of human consciousness. The larger homeric consciousness partakes of this revelation: to render the tale thus is to have internalized its logos, to have realized a cultural sophistication that permits this sort of joke to have the force of myth. The homeric act finds its center in the fitting of the roots and rhythms of a received tongue to a genuinely visionary grasp of human experience strung together from the mythemes, the story-units of myth, which the poet receives by the same cultural process that gives him language. What the cunning Odysseus works on the powers that inhibit his return, Homer may be thought to work on the raw mythical materials of his song.

The homeric world, the space his characters traverse, is the product of an habitually fabricating consciousness. Homer's creation of world is heuristic—ever shifting, probing, and remaking. He creates the field of human experience as Odysseus tests the limits of human experience, and his own search is a preliminary exploration of its axes. It is a mistake to attribute to him a finished model of natural space, much less the geographical: for him the formulation of space can have only a tentative

---

† Published here by permission of the author.
1. Max Horkheimer and Theodor W. Adorno, *Dialektik der Aufklärung* (Amsterdam, 1947), p. 77.

solution. Received critical opinion holds that Homer conceives the elements of the natural world as a coherent and stable physical system. Succinctly, this system is reconstituted as follows:

> The surface of the earth would, as the dome above and the circle of the horizon suggest, naturally be conceived as circular, the Roman *Orbis terrarum*, and was apparently so conceived by the early Greeks—as a disk or cylinder. Above this was the dome of ouranos, conceived apparently as a hard shell, arching down to the surface of the earth at the rim, round which okeanos flows so that the stars are washed by the water of the latter.[2]

If this rigidly conceptual vision of space existed at all, it existed outside of the homeric epics. While there is sound evidence that, for instance, the shape of a war shield and its outer rim are conceived by Homer as structurally related to the earth and the river *okeanos* which surrounds it,[3] there is no evidence that this is a fixed conception, a spatial absolute to which he conforms and systematically refers. There is, further, no evidence that he thought of *ouranos*, "sky," as a "solid hemisphere like a bowl."[4] His use of the word suggests something very different.[5] He uses it in connection with two distinct referents—a solid, shining ceiling above the earth; and the space inhabited and charged by the gods, especially Zeus. These significations cannot be rigorously separated in context; residue of each may be presumed to remain in every act of signification. There is, further, a set of contexts relating to the heavenly bodies which breaks importantly with the conceptual implications of both of these referents. It reveals in this the nominal ground of the homeric imagination and the unsettled nature which it envisions.

He uses the word *ouranos* first to mean the solid ceiling of the sky. Atlas is said by Athena (*Od.* I, 53–4) to hold the great pillars that keep *ouranos* and *gaia* (generally, the ground of the earth) "apart." The relation of *ouranos* to *gaia* is thus an architectural one; it is that of a ceiling raised from a floor by columns, as in a megaron, and implies in this their separation. This architectural metaphor is anticipated a few lines earlier in the description of the gathering of the gods "in the palace-chambers of Zeus at Olympos." (*Od.* I, 27). The logic of this metaphor probably does not lie in imaginative description of natural features of a

2. Richard B. Onians, *The Origins of European Thought* (Cambridge, 1954), p. 249. Onians speculates interestingly about the relation of the elements of the world to the structure of an egg and it seems clear that Epicurus, for instance, rather systematically developed this conception, with the Orphic cosmogoners following him in this. But it would be a mistake to suggest that Homer shares this view. It seems, rather, a later development.

3. Homer, *Iliad* XVIII, 606–7: "On it he placed the great might of Okeanos River / Among the outer rim of the wisely made shield." See also G. S. Kirk and J. E. Raven, *The Presocratic Philosophers* (Cambridge, 1966), pp. 11–19. Translations from Homer are based on Cook and Lattimore.

4. Kirk and Raven, p. 10.

5. Cf. M. L. West, Hesiod. *Theogony* (Oxford, 1966), p. 127. West notes in passing that the space of *ouranos* has been misconstrued.

mountain. Zeus in his aspect of mediator among the gods and agent of justice for gods and men alike is understood as inhabiting internal, architectural space. We may think here of Minos, a son of Zeus, seated in "the wide-gated house of Hades," "dealing out justice to the dead." (Od. XI, 569–71).

The force of these metaphors is, clearly, to anthropomorphize and thus lend logic and credence to the difficult-to-conceive processes of divine principle: how it is, specifically, that the ceiling of the sky does not fall down, and how a man's fate is constituted. Zeus talks in this scene first of the fate of Aigisthos, and Athena follows him, calling Odysseus's misfortunes to the attention of the gathering. The evocation of the divine palace here suggests that the familiarity and cultural significance of Mycenaean royal architecture made it a sound base for the description of other systems. In the first instance, the balance of natural elements is involved; in the second, in a different way, divine balance in the disposition of fate. Palace architecture embodies a complex sense of social order, and the Mycenaean palaces in issue here were certainly emblems of the power of their royal inhabitants.[6]

Although this is the only instance in which Homer chooses to make the connection so explicitly, the architectural conception is implicit in his attribution of metallic solidity to *ouranos*. He calls it *chalkēon* (brazen) and *poluchalkon* (great-brazen);[7] he also calls it *sidēreon* (made of iron).[8] The variance here suggests that it is, in the first instance, its solidity that makes it like metal. This variety of metallic epithet corresponds to his variety of use in sea epithets: the gray sea and wine-dark sea, especially. Variety of naturalistic condition may be the impulse here—a brazen *ouranos* for the brightness of sunshine and *ouranos* made of iron for an overcast sky—though this is impossible to determine from context.

Another instance of the implied solidity of *ouranos* occurs in the description of a burning sacrifice to Apollo in the first book of the *Iliad*:

And they sacrificed to Apollo, performing hecatombs
Of bulls and goats along the barren sea's beach.
The smell of the burning, curling round the smoke, reached ouranos.

(*Il.* I, 315–317)

The verb here indicates *ouranos* as a concrete destination.[9] A similar usage occurs at a feast in the *Iliad*. Hector commands the preparations:

---

6. Jean-Pierre Vernant, *Les origines de la pensée grecque* (Paris, 1969), p. 30.
7. *Iliad* XVII, 425; and *Iliad* V, 504 and *Odyssey* III, 2.
8. *Odyssey* XV, 329 and XVII, 565.
9. It is noteworthy in this connection that Aristotle gives *horon einai tōn anō*, "the boundary of those things above," as the etymology of *ouranos*. This is uniformly rejected by philologists. See *De Mundo* in *Aristotelis Opera* (Berlin, 1960), v. I, p. 400 A7. Also Hjalmar Frisk, *Griechisches Etymologisches Wörterbuch*, Lieferung 15 (Heidelberg, 1965), pp. 446–7.

. . . and pile up much cut wood,
So that all night and until early-born dawn
We may burn many fires, and the brightness reach to ouranos.

(*Il.* VIII, 507–9).

On other occasions the "reach to ouranos" expression is used more col-
loquially.[1] The disguised Odysseus, replying to Penelope's initial questions about his home and parents, replies, ". . . your renown reaches
broad ouranos" (*Od.* XIX, 108)—involving its sense as the divine location but making it, in this same attribution, concrete as well. Circe,
relating to Odysseus the way of his return, describes the crag of Scylla
which "reaches to broad ouranos" (*Od.* XII, 73). This is similarly col-
loquial though far more concrete; it defines Scylla as supernatural in
spatial proportion and involves the sense in which *ouranos* is associated
with the divine mountain Olympos—a sense discussed below. By invoking the space of divinity it strikes Scylla out of nature and the realm of
ordinary experience.[2]

A further use of *ouranos* in this concrete sense occurs three times in
the *Iliad*.[3] This is illustrated by a homeric simile describing the marching Achaeans:

As destructive fire lights up a huge forest
On the peak of a mountain, and the flare appears far away,
So from the godly bronze of the marching men
The gleam, shining all through the aither, reached to ouranos.

(*Il.* II, 455–8)

Again, *ouranos* is understood as an actual, physical boundary, like the
roof of a house to an observer inside. Elsewhere Athena is seen to leap
from this boundary, suggesting how very literally its solidity is imagined:

Speaking this he roused Athena who was already eager,
And she in the shape of a broad-winged, thin-crying hawk
Leaped down from ouranos through the aither.

(*Il.* XIX, 349–51)

This use also invokes the association of *ouranos* with divine space, though
its usual abstraction—as if that space were not continuous with the space
inhabited by mortal men—is here breached by the unusually concrete
image.

Finally, there are two identical passages in the *Iliad* describing Athena's descent to battle from the "threshold" of Zeus:

1. See *Odyssey* XV, 329 and XVII, 565 for similar uses.
2. There is an especially interesting use of *ouranos* as a spatial quantifier in the *Iliad*: ". . . as far
   below Hades as *ouranos* stands from earth" (*Il.* VIII, 16).
3. The undiscussed use occurs at *Iliad* XVII, 425.

Hera then swiftly felt for the horses with a whip;
And moving by themselves the gates of ouranos, guarded by the Hours,
bellowed—
Those Hours to whom vast ouranos and Olympos is entrusted,
Both to open up thick darkness and also to close it.
                              (*Il.* V, 748–51; and VIII, 392–5)[4]

Commentators have tried to make this conform to a naturalistic conception of the sky by explaining these gates as a thick cloud which the Hours
open and shut like a trap door.[5] But they clearly refer to this same solid
ceiling. As in Athena's descent as a hawk, the space of *ouranos* is divine
as well as architectural in conception. Here it is imagined as having
gates, an attribution thoroughly incongruous to a ceiling. The poet would
seem here to continue invoking the architectural model while abandoning representational consistency within the confines of the model: gates
are architectural elements, even if they are not found in ceilings. Homer's
imagination does not ask a greater consistency. It does uniformly ask the
reduction of divine space to human terms and to one set of terms; within
these, however, it is generally free to operate. This is an indication of
the real latitude of the poet's spatial imagination. Space remains equiv-
ocal for him and in process of definition.

   The use of the word *ouranos* to signify the space of the gods is illustrated in the same gathering scene in the first book of the *Odyssey*. Replying
to Athena's charge that he is angry at Odysseus, Zeus states,

> How could I ever forget godlike Odysseus
> Who excels in thought among mortals, and for the sacrifices
> He has given the immortal gods who possess broad ouranos.
>   (*Od.* I, 65–7)

In the *Iliad*, Poseidon describes the division of the natural elements
among himself and his brothers:

> Everything was divided three ways, each of us receiving his due,
> And when the lots were shaken I drew the gray sea to live in always;
> Hades drew the misty darkness below,
> And Zeus drew broad ouranos, in the aither and the clouds.
> But earth and high Olympos are common to the three of us.
>   (*Il.* XV, 189–93)

In the first of these passages the sense of *ouranos* as a solid ceiling is
submerged; the eminent attribute of the sky is divine presence, rather
like the English word "heaven." The word is used emblematically rather
than descriptively, in an almost transspatial sense. The second passage

---

4. The somewhat irregular instance of the singular verb used with "ouranos and Olympos" may
   be related to an understanding of the two nouns as a single spatial unit. This accords with a
   possible earlier sense of *olympos* as "mountain," generically.
5. See thus H. G. Liddell and R. Scott, *A Greek-English Lexicon*, 9th edition, rev. H. S. Jones
   (Oxford, 1966), p. 1273.

includes naturalistic description and certainly involves the concept of a solid ceiling, suffused by clouds and the fiery upper air. It clarifies the relation between the two referents of *ouranos*.

There are several passages in Homer which attest a connection between the word *ouranos* and the word *olympos*. Nilsson[6] points out that *olympos*—evidently a pre-Greek word that may have meant "mountain," generically, before it came to signify a specific one—is actually one with *ouranos* in its sense of the rather abstract space of the gods which exists outside the vault of the sky and of which Zeus is lord in dominion. So in the *Iliad* Thetis, a sea-nymph,

> . . . arose from the waves of the sea
> Early in the morning and went up to vast ouranos and olympos.
> (*Il.* I, 496–7)

And Zeus, tricked by Hera,

> . . . swore a strong oath
> Lest ever again to olympos and starry ouranos
> Mischief, who misleads everyone, return.
> (*Il.* XIX, 127–9)

The space of *ouranos* remains abstract in these passages; the adjective *megan* (vast) is, in the one, too vague to be helpful visually. And in neither does the connection with the divine mountain modify the word spatially (in the exclusively physical sense) except perhaps to reiterate its size; rather, as a loose spatial synonym, it blocks out the cosmographically specific signification. The word remains, in its uses here, a formulaic attribution of divinity with little or no reference to the structure of the physical universe.

There is, finally, an interesting deviation from the normative senses of *ouranos*. A single example should illustrate the force of this usage. Homer on two occasions refers to an *ouranos* "crowned"—once (*Od.* V, 303) with clouds, by Zeus, and once (*Il.* XVIII, 485) with heavenly bodies.[7] This is a peculiarly flat metaphor for a description of the relation of such elemental forces; it is strictly one-dimensional, stating only the fact of the relation. If we were to extend its implications *ouranos* would become, perhaps, a head. But the metaphor defies, in fact, elaboration. It is eminently unconceptual. The deviance from the terms of the usual sense of *ouranos* (especially its architectural sense) suggests recourse to a nominal *ouranos*, however it is conceptually integrated to the spatial field of the natural world. These passages revert to this pre-

---

6. Martin Nilsson, *Geschichte der Griechischen Religion* (München, 1941), v. I, p. 354.

7. Several other passages describe the heavenly bodies' relation to *ouranos* in a similar way. Among these is the simple *ouranos asteroeis*, starry sky (*Il.* VI, 108; V, 769, and elsewhere). Hesperus, the evening star, is said to "stand" in *ouranos* (*Il.* XXII, 318); and the sun is said to perish completely from *ouranos* (*Od.* XX, 356–57), evidently a reference to an eclipse. These uses are all acceptable phenomenologically but fail to relate conceptually to *ouranos* conceived as a solid ceiling.

conceptual base in their lack of final definition: they are phenomenologically residual and do not submit to the analytical process that characterizes
Homer's refabrication of the natural world. Homer may understand *ouranos* as a ceiling or an abstract attribute of divinity (or both at once), but
he is in any case reliant on its nominal existence. *Ouranos* is—as the
word is, so is its referent.

This is a characteristic nominalism that Homer cannot escape without
evading the responsibility of the very mythos that is the unformed matter
of his creation. If his conception of cosmic space demands a reduction
of its physical axes to a single terminal field, these contexts of *ouranos*—
the only ones in which he truly deviates from the interlocking terminal
field that has been described—would seem to bypass that condition by
ignoring the spatiality of the objects they treat. If the clouds and heavenly bodies cannot be structurally related to an *ouranos* conceived as
architectural, they are returned to their ground state as words. They
revert in this to the nominalism of myth and to the implicit unity that
homeric epic imposes on material that resists integration to its constructs.

The referents of *ouranos* remain diverse after Homer and extend the
spatial configuration to which he assimilates it. Hesiod elevates *ouranos*
to an inhabited deity as the son of Erebos and Gaia,[8] and Orphic cosmogoners pick up this strain.[9] The abstract space of divinity is elevated
in this conception to proto-divinity. Aeschylus and Plato both use the
phrase "those from ouranos"[1] to signify the gods, continuing Homer's
sense of its divine habitation. Empedocles, inheriting the architectural
metaphor, describes *ouranos* as "solid";[2] and it was described by Zeno
as the "outer limit of the aither."[3] There are late instances of its use to
describe a vaulted roof, the palate of the mouth, and a tent.[4]

8. Hesiod, *Theogony*, 127 ff.
9. See Kirk and Raven, pp. 38–43.
1. Aeschylus, *Prometheus*, 897: Plato, *Republic*, 508a.
2. The word he uses is *steremnion*. Empedokles, in H. Diels, *Die Fragmente der Vorsokratiker*
   (Berlin, 1903), v. I, p. 209.
3. Zeno the Stoic, I.33.
4. Liddell and Scott, p. 1273.

Selected Bibliography

This bibliography includes works in English about the *Odyssey*; it does not include books or articles excerpted for this volume.

Adkins, A. W. H. *Merit and Responsibility: A Study in Greek Values*. Oxford, 1960.

Arnold, Matthew. "On Translating Homer." London, 1861; and "On Translating Homer; Last Words," London, 1862. Often reprinted. The best normative description of Homer's style.

Bernal, Martin. *Black Athena*. New Brunswick, 1987. A challenging and controversial study of "the Afro-Asiatic roots of classical civilization."

Burkert, Walter. *Greek Religion*. Cambridge, MA, 1985. A vast and pointedly detailed study of Greek religion that intersects with the *Odyssey* at many points.

Carpenter, Rhys. *Folk Tale, Fiction, and Saga in the Homeric Epics*. Berkeley, 1958. An engaging discussion of the interweaving of anthropological and archeological factors relating to Homer.

Clay, Jenny. *The Wrath of Athena: Gods and Men in the* Odyssey. Princeton, 1983.

Cook, Albert. *Myth and Language*. Bloomington, 1980. An inquiry into the interaction of two fundamental human activities, with much emphasis on how these derive in Greek culture from Homer.

Dimock, George. *The Unity of the* Odyssey. Amherst, 1989.

Finley, John. *Homer's* Odyssey. Cambridge, MA, 1978.

Finley, M. I. *The World of Odysseus*, New York, 1954.

Graves, Robert. *The Greek Myths*. London, 1955. Based on authoritative German sources, this is the most engaging handbook on myth available in English.

Griffin, Jasper. *The Odyssey*. Cambridge, 1987.

Havelock, Eric. *Preface to Plato*. Cambridge, MA, 1963. An inquiry into the intellectual implications of the use of Homer in classical Athens, notably by Plato.

Heubeck, Alfred, Stephanie West, and J. B. Hainsworth. *A Commentary on the* Odyssey. Oxford, 1988.

Katz, Marilyn A. *Penelope's Renown: Meaning and Indeterminacy in the* Odyssey. Princeton, 1991. An attempt to read the arguable inconsistencies in Penelope's behavior as an indeterminacy in the poem beyond the reach of characterological analysis.

Lorimer, H. L. *Homer and the Monuments*. London, 1950. An exhaustive survey of archeological evidence bearing on Homer.

Murnaghan, Sheila. *Disguise and Recognition in the* Odyssey. Princeton, 1987.

Onians, R. B. *The Origins of European Thought*. London, 1950. A study of the philosophical implications underlying the exact meanings of certain words in Homer.

Parry, Milman. *The Making of Homeric Verse: Collected Papers of Milman Parry*. Ed. Adam Parry. Oxford, 1971. The classic statements of the great discoverer of oral composition practices in early poetry.

Powell, Barry B. *Composition by Theme in the* Odyssey. Meisenheim am Glan, 1977.

Pucci, Piero. *Odysseus Polutropos: Intertextual Readings in the* Odyssey *and the* Iliad. Ithaca, 1987.

Snell, Bruno. *The Discovery of Mind*. Trans. Thomas Rosenmeyer. 1953. New York, 1960. A study of Homer's method of perception, on the evidence of his vocabulary, and the development of that method in later Greek thought.

Thalmann, William G. *Conventions of Form and Thought in Early Greek Epic Poetry*. Baltimore, 1984.

Thornton, Agathe. *People and Themes in Homer's* Odyssey. London, 1970.

Vermeule, Emily. *Greece in the Bronze Age*. Chicago, 1972. A survey of the world that preceded Homer.

Vernant, Jean-Pierre. *Myth and Thought among the Greeks*. London, 1983. Anthropologically informed essays about the play of ideas in early Greek culture.

Wace, A. J. B., and Stubbings. F. H. *A Companion to Homer*. London, 1962. A compendious collection of essays by specialists on nearly all phases of Homer.